ALL IN CHARISMA BOOK 1

ALL IN CHARISMA

KYLE WEST

*For my incredible wife and two sons, who inspire every word I write and fill
my life with endless adventure and joy.*

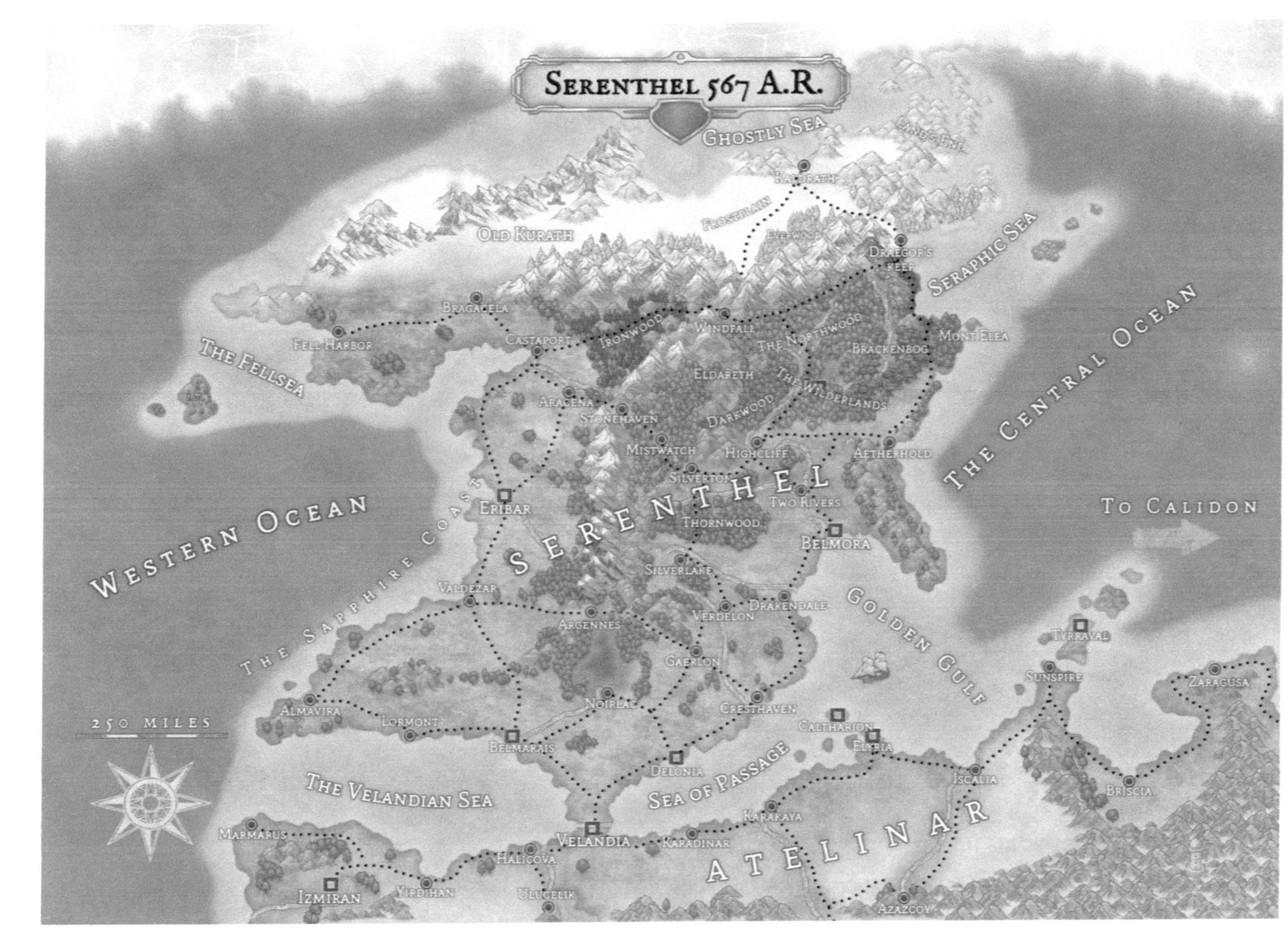

SERENTHEL 567 A.R.
250 MILES
GHOSTLY SEA
LAND'S END
SERAPHIC SEA
THE FELLSEA
WESTERN OCEAN
THE CENTRAL OCEAN
TO CALIDON
THE SAPPHIRE COAST
THE VELANDIAN SEA
SEA OF PASSAGE
GOLDEN GULF
SERENTHEL
ATELINAR
OLD KURATH
FROSTPLAIN
EVERWOOD
RALDRATH
DRAEGOR'S REEF
BRAGACELA
FELL HARBOR
CASTAPORT
IRONWOOD
WINDFALL
THE NORTHWOOD
BRACKENBOG
MONT ELEA
ELDARETH
THE WILDERLANDS
ARACENA
STONEHAVEN
DARKWOOD
MISTWATCH
HIGHCLIFF
AETHERHOLD
SILVERTON
ERIBAR
TWO RIVERS
THORNWOOD
BELMORA
SILVERLAKE
VALDEZAR
ARGENNES
VERDELON
DRAKENDALE
GAERLON
NOIRLAC
CRESTHAVEN
TYRRAVAL
SUNSPIRE
ZARAGUSA
ALMAVIRA
LORMONT
BELMARAIS
CALTHARION
ELYRIA
DELONIA
ISCALIA
BRISCIA
MARMARUS
VELANDIA
KARADINAR
KARAKAYA
HALICOVA
IZMIRAN
YIRDIHAN
ULUGELIK
AZAZCOY

PROLOGUE

Justin unleashed a mighty belch, scattering a fine orange dust of Cheetos and a misty cloud of spit. He took a quick whiff of the cheesy exhaust before it could waft too far from his nostrils, then smacked his thin pink lips set below a wispy mustache.

"Disgusting, Justin," Trina said over Discord Voice Chat.

Damn it. He thought he had muted himself.

He tried to cover the slip with a nervous laugh. "Heh, sorry. One too many Monsters."

On the upper walls of the basement, the windows rattled with a peal of thunder. One of the said Monster empties on his desk vibrated and tumbled to the floor.

Justin only had eyes for the raid. His mom had said something about storms earlier, but he didn't care too much at the moment.

He had bigger fish to fry.

"Stay focused," Jorbo said. "He's almost enraged."

Eyes bloodshot and fingers locked on the WASD keys, Justin's focus shifted entirely to the battle at hand. In the digital void of his Nightmare Realm server—a permadeath realm of Aether Quest, his game and drug of choice—his level 60 Barbarian, Kragthar the Unbroken, towered amid the swirling chaos.

Three relentless months of grinding, sleepless nights bleeding into dawn, and a life lived with more intensity in pixels than in the real world had all led to this final stand.

If they could finally take down the boss, Nyxion, Harbinger of Unmaking, bragging rights for life would be theirs. Even with the boss teetering at 1% health, one perfectly timed combo—one chain of devastating blows—could end this nightmare once and for all. Just the thought of the loot that would drop made him salivate.

His character lagged a bit, followed by a notification:

[Server connection is weak.]

"The fuck, Justin," Jorbo said. "Don't tell me you're about to drop."

"A bit rainy here in Oklahoma," he said. "Nothing to worry about."

A boom of thunder cut through the noise-cancelling of his headphones. He knew it wasn't safe to be anywhere near electronics.

But he had come too far to back out now.

"If your connection messes up the raid..."

Jorbo's warning trailed off as thunder once again rattled the windows in the upper part of the basement.

Justin's first real Nightmare Realm raid with the Celestial Vanguards, the server's best guild, was not going according to plan.

But at least here, he knew the rules. He knew how to play the game, how to measure success and failure in numbers and stats.

Social interactions, though? He never knew what people wanted from him in real life. Online, he could just play his role and not have to see anyone face-to-face.

"All right, we got him," Jorbo said. "Burn him! Burn him now!" A pause. "Justin, pop Overpower!"

"I'm on it!" Justin snapped, his in-game avatar already mid-animation for Overpower as he lined up a Titanic Cleave. Every muscle tensed, every finger danced over the keyboard with grace.

Victory shimmered just a keystroke away.

"Tank swap!" Rick screamed, his voice cracking under pressure.

"No cooldowns left!" Trina's voice blared over VC. "I told you—I'm OOM! I'M OUT OF MANA!"

"JUST AUTO ATTACK!" another voice hollered from the chatter.

A heavy, sinking feeling settled in Justin's stomach as the voice chat became a chaos of panicked voices. It was amazing how fast things could go to shit. Thunder rattled the windows again.

Then, from the inky void, the boss let out a guttural, distorted roar. The entire raid froze as the screen flashed a warning red—

[Nyxion casts Final Requiem.]

"*Oh fuck!*" Jorbo shouted.

In an instant, the boss vanished, plunging the arena into darkness. Justin's stomach dropped. A heartbeat later, a booming, mechanical voice resonated across the battlefield:

[ALL WILL BE UNMADE...]

"PHASE FIVE? WHAT THE ACTUAL—" someone screeched.

"This wasn't in the guide!" Jorbo howled.

"It must be something new with the Nightmare Realms," Trina said. "Did you grab the right guide?"

Her question went unanswered when, out of the blackness, dozens of ghostly apparitions surged forth, chaining each raid member in place. With a cruel flourish, Nyxion reappeared—its health bar reset to 25%.

[DoomBringer has fallen. His journey has ended.]

"NOOOOOOOOOOOOOO!" Rick howled. "Fucking A!"

[Dawnlight78 has fallen. Her light has been extinguished.]

"Kill adds! Kill the damn adds!" someone pleaded.

"I CAN'T MOVE! I'M ROOTED!" Blitzfang, the rogue, cried out in a panic.

[Blitzfang has fallen. His soul has ascended.]

"Justin, *INTERRUPT*, damn it!" Jorbo barked.

[Elder_of_Darkness has fallen. His journey ends.]

Desperation surged as Justin slammed his interruption move—but he was lagging again.

One by one, his party crumbled. Soon, only Justin and a couple of stragglers remained standing.

"Jorbo, this is my main," Justin said weakly. "I can't lose him."

"Retreat!" Jorbo shouted. "Just run! Just freaking run! Abort! The portal should still be open."

Kragthar the Unbroken sprinted toward the exit portal. Justin's heart pounded like a drum. One ally tumbled down beside him, then another, their death notifications flashing across his screen. They kept coming until, in the chaos, he found himself alone.

Could he really escape? Could he emerge as the sole survivor of this digital carnage?

A sinister laugh echoed in his headphones.

[HAHAHAHAHA. You cannot escape!]

[Nyxion casts Unmaking Pulse.]

A shockwave blasted through the arena, sending debris and despair flying. Justin wove desperately between the hazards. But there was no escaping the rock about to fall right on top of him.

Then, thanks to the lag, he blipped past the obstacle unscathed.

"HOLY CRAP, HE'S GONNA MAKE IT!" Trina screamed. "Go, Justin, go!"

The exit portal loomed ahead. With only 1% of his health remaining, every second throbbed with the weight of destiny.

If he could pull this off, he would be a legend in the guild, his standing secure.

Then, from the edge of the screen, a tiny, nearly invisible Void Tick mob scuttled up to Kragthar's ankle. Justin tried to swerve, but his avatar wouldn't obey him. Damn lag.

"No!" Justin screamed. "Please, God, no! NOOOOOO!"

It nibbled at Kragthar's ankle.

There was a moment's pause as his connection dropped, then resumed.

[You have died. Your journey has ended...]

Justin blinked at the notification, unbelieving, before rage welled up within him.

And then, from deep within his soul, he screamed—a raw, guttural sound that transcended mere inconvenience, channeling every failure, frustration, and disappointment of his twenty-five years on Earth into a single, unholy:

"REEEEEEEEEEEE!"

He got up and kicked over his stained computer chair and was about to give his monitor the same treatment before he saw in its black reflection his acne-ridden, pale, and pudgy countenance. The image of his greasy auburn hair and acne-ridden face was so offensive and alarming that instead of making him want to rage, it only made him want to cry.

The voices of his guildmates snapped him back to reality.

"Bruh," Rick said.

Jorbo's laughter crackled through VC. "Justin, did you just die to a trash mob?!"

"Dude," Blitz whispered. "You got *ticked* to death."

The channel erupted into a mix of wheezing laughter and teasing jabs, but Justin barely heard them. His ragged breaths filled the silence between their jokes. His hands hovered over the keyboard, fingers twitching.

One month of grinding, every sleepless night, every job he should have been applying for—all funneled into Kragthar the Unbroken.

And now...

Gone. As were his chances of proving himself to his new guild. That he had gotten this far in one month, not dying even once, proved he could grind harder than anyone.

Jorbo cleared his throat. "Well, uh...that sucked. But hey, that's what alts are for, right? Heh. We'll give it another go tomorrow. Justin, you've got a backup, right?"

Justin swallowed. "This was my only maxed Nightmare character. My main. I have a Level 15 alt."

"Oh."

A pause.

"So, uh...I guess that means you're out for the next run. You'll have to roll a new toon, but—uh—you know the guild rules. No mains under 60 in here. You'll have to grind back up in the Celestial Aspirants before you can apply to join the Celestial Vanguard again."

Justin said nothing, coldness washing over his skin. "You let Trina stay when her main died last time."

"Uh...she told you that?"

"Guess constantly flirting with the raid leader has its perks, huh?" When no one reacted, Justin laughed weakly. "Am I right, guys? Just spitting facts here."

The silence that followed curdled in his stomach. He'd crossed a line—again.

"Come on, man," Jorbo said. "If you'd just be...I don't know, *bearable* for once, people might be willing to give you a shot. You've gotta learn to win friends and influence people, bro."

Justin felt a flash of anger. "By dating the guild higher-ups? Thanks for the advice, *bro.* I'm sure that one will come in really handy."

Jorbo cleared his throat awkwardly. "That's not the same. Trina's a healer, and the guild is short on healers. She gets special treatment."

"Yeah, but it proves the rules can be bent a bit. I'll do better next time. I can have my new toon up to speed in a couple of weeks. Promise."

It was a tall order, but Justin was sure he could do it.

The silence stretched awkwardly as Jorbo sighed. "Sorry, man. I guess this is me telling you you're off the team. Maybe...maybe it's best if you find another guild." Another pause. "And take this as a learning opportunity. This isn't the first time you've stuck your foot in it. And you should have told us about your connection issues. It cost a lot of people their characters tonight."

"For real," Rick said.

Justin wanted to protest. He had been the only one who had almost escaped. The only one who had even *seen* the portal. If not for the storm, they might have even beaten the boss.

But even he knew it was pointless to say all that. He'd made Jorbo look stupid, and even Justin was socially aware enough to know that was unforgivable.

[You have been removed from the Celestial Vanguard.]

"Good luck out there, Justin." Jorbo's voice was insincere, already moving on. "Now, does anyone know another DPS? Shouldn't be hard, right? They're a dime a dozen—"

His voice was cut off as Justin received a private message from the guild's Discord server:

[You have been banned from the server. Reason: Violation of community conduct.]

His hands shook. The Discord icon winked out, leaving his screen barren.

Just like his résumé. Just like his life.

Justin scoffed. "I'm done with this shit."

He reached down to turn off the computer when it winked off of its own accord.

Justin frowned. Huh. That was weird.

Then the lights went completely out.

Justin removed his headphones, only to hear thunder and pouring rain. Damn, that was way louder than he expected. Even in the basement, he could hear the wind howling outside the basement's upper windows.

He should *probably* check on his mom. Where was she, anyway? It was a rare thing for her to intrude on his underground sanctuary, except to deposit the odd meal, but this storm had him worried.

"Mom? Mom!"

The wood floor above him vibrated ominously. That *definitely* wasn't normal.

"Hell, just what I need."

Decision made, Justin headed for the stairs. Though it was nearly pitch black in the basement, he knew his way by heart. He ascended as fast as his heft would allow.

He entered the dining room, where outside the window the sky was terribly dark. The scene was positively apocalyptic, with a sepia sky filled with boiling clouds and violently swaying trees.

And a strange, high whine.

Tornado siren.

He rushed to the television, but of course, there was no power.

"This is what I get for leaving the basement. Mom? Where are you?"

Had she been out at the time the storm rolled through? There could be no other explanation.

Before he could think to check his phone, the wind started pounding the wall something fierce. He realized that the best spot for him was right back where he had come from.

Justin fled, or at least *tried* to flee, but he tripped over his own feet, taking a tumble on the floor. Before he could get up, at that very moment, the ceiling was pulled out from over him as lightning slashed above.

But the ceiling did not fall, as expected; instead, it went *up*.

Up, into the funnel of a tornado.

"FUUUUU—"

The din was so loud that he couldn't even hear his own voice. Everything in the room moved, including him. He was being lifted, almost gently, toward the lattice of lightning slashing its way inside the tornado's core.

Faster and faster he flew, until all was chaos and noise. He no longer screamed. There was no point. In fact, it was at this point that a strange sense of calm acceptance overcame him.

If he were going to die, well, the thought had crossed his mind before. It was just happening a little more quickly than he'd originally thought; that was all. He supposed it was the ultimate proof, given the course of his life, that the universe indeed hated him in particular.

But before he could truly make his peace, the darkness deepened. To his surprise, he was still very much alive, with a field of endless black extending in all directions.

That was when a blue light appeared, like a distant star. And that star seemed to pull him closer, an ovoid plane that flashed with potential.

Justin tried to move, but he could do nothing to control his trajectory. He was heading straight for that light, whether he liked it or not.

By fate, or perhaps luck, or even a mixture of both, he was thrown right through.

1

IT ALWAYS STARTS WITH GOBLINS

"And now we come to goblins. Nasty little buggers. They might be small, but they'll stab you in the back, steal your boots, and eat your rations all before you've even drawn your blade. Best advice? Keep your eyes sharp, your coin purse hidden, and bring a friend—they love nothing better than a solitary mark."

Lord Captain Jorrik Stane
    —*The Mercenary's Field Guide*

JUSTIN BLINKED AWAKE to the faint trill of birdsong. Everything hurt, especially his head. Feeling it with his fingers, there didn't seem to be any external injuries.

It was just the mother of all headaches.

"Mylanta," he breathed. "What the hell happened?"

As his vision returned, he found himself in what appeared to be a forest. A thrill of fear coursed down his spine. He scrambled up, looking every which way, wild-eyed and afraid. Trees...trees everywhere. Where could that tornado have possibly carried him? Oklahoma had its share of forests in the eastern part of the state, but not in Enid, where he lived. That would have meant the twister had carried him a hundred-plus miles.

"Impossible."

The aroma of earth and wild things filled his nostrils, while the cool air touched his skin almost like a kiss. Despite the situation, he felt a strange sense of calm in the surrounding natural beauty.

"Okay. What is going on?"

That was when his eyes focused on something before him in the meadow, something he had completely missed in the confusion. It was a bright, glowing orb that swirled with every color of the rainbow, about the size of a crystal ball.

An ethereal, melodic hum emanated from it, and it rotated slightly on its axis, as if it were a miniature world unto itself.

It was just sitting there, waiting to be picked up.

So, he did exactly that.

He grabbed the orb, gasping as it reacted to his touch. A prismatic rainbow of light entered his body. Justin felt an infusion of power and potential that was equivalent to a rapturous experience on a mind-altering substance.

[Congratulations! You have found a Prismatic Core. Please select any class.]

The Voice echoed through his mind, smooth and resonant, its warmth both comforting and commanding. It didn't come from any direction but seemed to fill the air around him, like a story unfolding in the quiet.

In fact, it reminded him of Burt Reynolds, with an easy, confident drawl that made him want to lean closer, as if every word was a secret just for him.

Justin blinked as a holographic screen projected in front of him.

Six words floated in the air before him: Power, Coordination, Endurance, Intellect, Spirit, and Charisma. Underneath each of these headings were six smaller words. Scanning them, he saw things like

Warrior, Thief, Ranger, Wizard, Summoner, Merchant...and the list went on. There seemed to be about thirty or forty choices in all.

Suddenly, realization dawned. Justin had played enough video games to know exactly where he was and what was happening. There had been the tornado, of course, and that tornado had obviously knocked him out, sending him into a medically induced coma.

His brain, therefore, was recreating a video game, which shouldn't have been a surprise. After all, he had spent almost every waking hour playing one.

This, he supposed, was inevitable. All he had to do was play the game and wait for the docs to resuscitate him.

But then again, there had been that strange portal. A common trope to be sure, and arguably a cliché, but how else was an adventure like this supposed to get started? A tornado had worked for Dorothy and Toto, so why not him, Justin Talemaker?

He rubbed his pudgy hands in glee. This could actually be fun!

He noticed his hands were pale and freckled, the same hands he had in the outside world.

He frowned in consternation. Couldn't he be an elf or something? Why was he still the same overweight individual he was in real life? Wasn't the entire point of video games to escape, to be the hero for once instead of the failure staring back at him from the mirror?

Whatever the case, he could worry about it later. Aside from semantic differences, it seemed these "Core Attributes" were quite similar to many other games he had played. Power for smashing, Coordination for sniping, Endurance for tanking, Intellect for outsmarting, Spirit for...magicky stuff?

And Charisma? Well, there was something oddly satisfying about getting people to do what you wanted. But was it good enough for what appeared to be a survival situation?

After thinking about it for a while, there was only one real choice he could think of. He would be a barbarian of sorts wielding a claymore or warhammer. He didn't know why, but he always gravitated to such builds in the RPGs he played. There was something strangely calming about smashing heads in like overripe pumpkins. Although doing so in a game as realistic as this one might prove to be a bit of a different experience.

"Hmm..." he said, stroking his chin. "Decisions, decisions..."

He went back up in the list, his eyes locking on the Barbarian option. Then he scanned back down, finding himself at an impasse.

Did he *really* want to be a Barbarian? Maybe he could be an Alchemist or an Enchanter. Craft things, make money. That could be a fun direction. It wasn't *all* about raw power, was it?

Then again, selling things required people skills. Trying to talk to people, in his view, was about as useful as yelling into the wind. People had a knack for disappointing you, or worse, stabbing you in the back after you'd let your guard down.

Then there was magic. A Wizard, a Summoner, or a Druid.

He shook his head. Was a squishy "glass cannon" the way to go?

He needed to pick a class that was good for operating solo. Now, which class had the most solo survivability? Not just combat ability, but the skills to survive, make money, and so on.

As he deliberated, the memory of his disastrous raid surfaced. The panicked voices over Discord. The mocking laughter. Jorbo's dismissive tone as he kicked Justin from the guild. His inability to fight back with words.

"You've gotta learn to win friends and influence people, bro."

That was what it always came down to, wasn't it? People skills. The one thing he'd never mastered. Every job interview that went nowhere. Every conversation that died awkwardly. Every guild that eventually kicked him for "being unbearable."

His eyes drifted to the Charisma column. Bard. Merchant. Cleric. Diplomat. Thespian. All classes that required dealing with people.

A Bard would need to perform for crowds. A Merchant needed to haggle. A Cleric had to tend to a congregation. A Diplomat needed to, well, be diplomatic. And a Thespian? He'd rather die than get on any stage.

But then his gaze settled on "Socialite."

The description read: "Masters of social manipulation and charm, the Socialite excels at making connections, extracting information, and bending others to their will."

Justin snorted. Him? A Socialite? It was the exact opposite of who he was.

But then, wasn't that the point? To become someone different, someone better?

He thought of the countless times he'd fumbled social interactions. The way people's eyes would glaze over when he spoke. The cringe-inducing silence after one of his "jokes." All things that had caused him to retreat into his self-imposed isolation.

What if he could change all that?

He was tired of being the awkward loner. Tired of being kicked from guilds and friend groups. Tired of watching others succeed through connections while he remained isolated.

"In a world where everyone else seems to know the rules of social interaction except me," Justin muttered, "maybe it's time I learned those rules."

He reached out and decisively touched the Socialite option.

[Congratulations! You have chosen: Socialite. Your class excels in social situations, making connections, and gaining favors.]

[You now have a class and can access the Aethereal Interface!]

[Ten points have been added to your Power, Coordination, Endurance, Intellect, Spirit, and Charisma attributes. Level-up to unlock more attribute points!]

[Language stack added: Aranthian.]

Justin did a double take at that last message. The language had...changed to some strange form of runes, and yet he could read it perfectly.

[As a Socialite, you have unlocked your class skill: Poison Barb.]

Poison Barb. That sounded promising. Was it some sort of ranged attack?

He read the description that appeared before him.

Poison Barb: You know precisely what to say to inflict emotional damage on someone, staggering them or forcing them to hesitate, with a chance to stun based on your Charisma attribute. If your barb stuns them for at least three seconds, the cooldown immediately refreshes. The stun chance decreases with repeated use on the same target. (Cooldown: 2 minutes.)

"Wait, what?" Justin's excitement deflated. "So my special ability is...being *mean* to people?"

This wasn't what he had in mind when selecting a social class. He'd been hoping for charm, persuasion, and razzle-dazzle. Not insults.

"Okay, not the end of the world," he said. "Just the first skill of many, right?"

The mysterious Voice returned to him.

[You are now Level 0. Always remember that a well-placed insult can cut deeper than a blade. Good luck, Brave Adventurer.]

The Voice retreated, leaving him once again alone in the woods.

He was wondering what came next when a hideous screech resounded from behind. He let out a yelp, whirling around to face the sound.

Three short and nasty goblins stood before him, all bearing crude clubs. They had sharp, bat-like ears, oily green skin, and slobbering mouths bristling with jagged yellow teeth that seemed eager to taste him.

"Holy crap," Justin said. "Goblins! Why do these things *always* start with goblins?"

The reality of his situation hit him like a bucket of ice water. He had chosen a social class in a world where the first encounter was with monsters who probably couldn't even understand him.

"Yep. Should've gone with Barbarian."

He had to make do with his class skill. Justin activated Poison Barb.

It seemed to happen naturally, without having to press any sort of mental button. He directed Poison Barb at the lead goblin advancing toward him.

He felt himself filled with adrenaline, a sort of primal instinct rising within him. Words began flying out of his lips unbidden.

"You guys must have been born on a highway because that's where most accidents happen!"

The goblins looked at each other in confusion. Justin wasn't sure the goblins understood sarcasm, or even if they understood him at all. But it still caused them to pause.

Justin seized the moment and dashed through the trees as fast as he could. The goblins snarled from behind, giving chase.

He had a stride advantage over the goblins for sure, but he was very out of shape. The last time he'd been forced to run was in ninth grade P.E. class, and that was years ago. His breaths came out in pained wheezes. Did this fantasy world have asthma? He sure hoped not.

He swiped at the underbrush, pushing it out of the way, occasionally stealing glances over his shoulder. The goblins let out high ululating cries, their bloodlust driving them as they tore through the underbrush like feral dogs on a hunt.

Justin skidded to a halt, his heart dropping as he found himself teetering on the edge of a small cliff.

With a shriek, he tumbled over the side and began sliding down the steep slope. He cried out in pain, wondering if this would be how he died: fall damage less than twenty minutes in.

At last, he came to a stop on a dusty wagon track, still conscious and hurting from head to toe. The goblins stood on the cliff above, yelping in vexation, seemingly not wanting to follow him down.

Justin didn't understand why. They could easily end him in such an exposed state.

It took a moment for Justin to realize he wasn't alone. A shadow loomed over him, blocking out the sun.

Groaning, he turned his head—and froze. Whatever it was, it didn't look friendly.

2

NOT IN OKLAHOMA ANYMORE

—Vault Runner Tharic Wren,
 An Adventurer's Guide to Vaults

JUSTIN FELT SOMETHING POKE HIM, which he recognized as the shaft of a heavy weapon.

He squeaked and stood up, and when he got a good look at the one doing the poking, he wondered if he should run again.

The man stood tall and proud, his broad shoulders stretching the straps of his armor. His muscular frame was wrapped in a suit of gleaming steel. He wore white robes, with the crest of a fiery phoenix on the breast. His chiseled jaw was set in a determined expression, and his blue eyes regarded Justin with a sharp intensity. Every inch of him exuded a quiet confidence and readiness for battle, as if he were born to be a warrior. He was perhaps in his late thirties or early forties.

He was a man, Justin thought, who had clearly invested in his Power attribute.

At that moment, Justin realized the pain was all over his body. Nothing was broken, but the bruises on his arms and legs were deep, while his skin was covered in scrapes and dirt. His head throbbed, and a sharp pain stabbed his left shoulder.

The man stepped forward. "Here, lad. Try to stay still."

Before Justin could do anything, the man raised a gloved hand, which became wrapped in an aura of golden light. Justin felt the energy spread to him, cold and refreshing, like diving into a cool spring. His wounds, internal and external, were instantly healed. He looked down at his arms, amazed to see they were knitted anew.

For a moment, he was at a loss for words. "What in the...?"

"Bind Wounds. A basic healing spell all Paladins get."

"I see," Justin said. "My stars, that was...*magic*, was it not?"

The man frowned in confusion. "Yes. You've never seen a healing spell before? Well, I guess that's possible, but not likely."

Justin changed the subject. "Where am I? What is this place?"

The man frowned in confusion. "What do you mean? You don't know where you are?"

Justin realized, without having to be told, that this man didn't think this was a game. An NPC, maybe. Although if he were an NPC, he seemed to be a very aware one.

"What year is it?"

"I don't know what you're on about, lad, but you've clearly got your brains all mixed up from that fall."

"It was goblins."

The man scrutinized him for a moment, then chuckled. "Goblins, eh? Well, not everyone can be a Paladin, I suppose."

"I'm a Socialite."

The man laughed even harder, even wiping a tear of mirth. Justin merely frowned.

"Now *that's* the funniest thing I've heard in weeks."

"How is it funny?"

"Well, for one, you rarely find those types here in the Wildwood Forest. They're up there in the big cities, looking pretty and being useless." The man looked him up and down. "You've got at least one of those things covered."

Justin looked down at himself. "What do you mean by 'one of those things?'"

The man gestured to Justin's outfit. "That getup of yours. I've seen nothing like it. It's certainly not armor."

Justin looked at his outfit, realizing for the first time how out of place it must seem to this man. He was dressed in an Iron Maiden t-shirt, cargo shorts, and Crocs. Not exactly ideal for adventuring. To his embarrassment, he realized he still had a Cheeto stain on his gut.

"This isn't my usual attire," Justin said defensively, though it most certainly was.

The man raised an eyebrow. "Well, it's not doing you any favors out here. You might as well paint a target on your back."

Justin sighed. How was he going to get out of this mess? All he wanted was to log out of this "game" and get back to his real life.

"How do I log out?"

"Log out? What are you talking about?"

"I mean, this is a game, is it not? Am I on an RP server or something?"

"Listen, son," the man said, taking him aside, "I can tell your head got jumbled in that fall. It has happened to me far too many times to count. Why don't we join up and I can see you safely to Mistwatch? Maybe someone knows you there."

"Mistwatch?"

The man shook his head. "Just five miles up the track here. Where are you from?"

"Oklahoma."

"Ok-la-ho-ma?"

"Yes," Justin said earnestly. "Where the wind comes sweeping down the plain?"

"I have never heard of it. Funny name, that."

This was getting worse and worse. "This...isn't Earth, is it?"

"You mean Eyrth?"

"Yeah. I mean, no! Earth. Pronounced *Urth*, not *Airth*."

"You're a strange one, lad. Come on. We've got to get moving."

[Alistair has invited you to join his party. Do you accept?]

Seeing no other way out, Justin accepted the prompt with a mental push.

[You have joined Alistair's party. You are now refreshed by his Divine Aura, granting complete immunity to the Fear effect.]

Justin could only assume this Divine Aura was some sort of passive ability that benefited him as a member of Alistair's party. All he knew was it did little to ease the fearful knot that had formed in his stomach.

There was nothing to do but to get moving.

They were walking down the path for a few seconds when Alistair gasped. "Arion above!"

"What?"

"You're Level 0!"

"Yes. And?"

"You must've just gotten your class, then. What are you doing all the way out here?"

Justin recalled the tornado. He considered telling Alistair about the portal, but he didn't know the guy and it seemed crazy on the surface. "I'm not sure. I just woke up in the forest, got chased by those goblins, and here I am." Before Alistair could ask anything more, he peppered him with his own question. "How can you tell what level I am, anyway?"

"You can inspect anyone in your party. It will give you some basic information about them, such as their name, class, and level."

"Seriously?"

"Yes. I suggest you open your interface. That's the connection between you and the Aether, how you can look over your attributes and abilities. You *do* know how to do *that*, right?"

Justin was about to ask how when a simple thought summoned a "screen" before him. It seemed he was the only one who could see it.

To his surprise, he found that, indeed, he could see something akin to character screens he was used to in his games. It listed his name, class, and the six attributes the "Voice" had already introduced to him.

He had ten points in each attribute already. Somehow, he knew this was the default amount, what everyone started with.

On the projection, he saw an avatar of himself, along with his sweat, dirt, and Cheeto-encrusted clothing.

Justin Talemaker
    Class: Socialite
    Level: 0
    Experience to Level 1: 0/1

    Attributes:
        Power: 10
        Coordination: 10
        Endurance: 10
        Intellect: 10
        Spirit: 10
        Charisma: 10

    Skills:
        Poison Barb

That was all there was to see, at least for now. He closed the screen.

Justin considered the information above. If he was reading things correctly, it took a mere one experience point to get from Level 0 to Level 1. From that fact alone, Alistair had correctly surmised that he had just gained his class.

One thing Alistair didn't realize was that this reality had all the trappings of a fully immersive VRMMO, such as the kind Justin was familiar with from his web novels. But the longer this "game" went on, the more real it was starting to become.

Of course, Justin had always fantasized about this exact scenario as a way to escape his mundane life. But now, all he wanted to do was wake up from this nightmare.

And to top it all off? He was this bloody *Socialite* instead of literally any other useful and cool class.

They walked for a few minutes before Justin broke the silence, mostly to distract himself.

"So, what do you do, Alistair?"

"I'm a Paladin for the Church of Light," he replied, puffing out his chest.

"A Paladin? So, you fight evil and stuff?"

Alistair nodded. "That's right. I serve the Church of Light and smite any darkness that threatens the innocent."

Justin raised an eyebrow. "That's cool, I guess."

Alistair chuckled. "It's not all glamour and glory, kid. It's a tough job, but someone's got to do it."

"So why are you helping *me* out, then?"

Alistair shrugged. "I'm a Paladin. I help people when I can. It's who we are." Then he gave a devious smile. "And...helping the weak and innocent also gives me experience."

"Seriously?"

When Alistair nodded, Justin's mind raced with thoughts. He could help people, too, and get level-ups, along with new attribute points and skills.

Alistair laughed. "I see what you're thinking, kid. It doesn't quite work that way."

"What do you mean?"

"Well, depending on your class, you get rewarded for doing things related to that class. Paladins, for example, get experience for helping people, hunting the undead, and healing. I'm not sure what it is for Socialites, but you guys probably get experience for...well, *socializing*.

And not just any socializing, but making things go your way with your honeyed words."

"I see," Justin said, considering this. "Well, I suck at social situations. So, I'm screwed."

For a moment, he thought back to the horror show that was high school, along with the sadness that was his brief college experience before he'd dropped out because he couldn't get his Aether Quest addiction under control. He wouldn't have been surprised if he'd spent more of his adult waking hours in it than outside it.

He had always repelled people with his general attitude and appearance. It had made him quite bitter over the years.

Justin had accepted his lot with time. Video games helped a lot, along with eating. No one bothered him, and he bothered nobody. Plus, online, he could be anyone he wished.

But now, he was expected to socialize in a more real sense. And worse, there was no other way for him to advance in this world.

And he only had himself to blame.

"What if I had killed those goblins?" Justin asked. "Would that have given me experience?"

"You only get experience if the action performed harmonizes with your Core Attribute." It was like he was quoting from a textbook.

That sounded familiar. Hadn't the "System" voice talked about that? "What's a Core Attribute, exactly?"

Alistair shook his head. "That fall must have been worse than I thought. Your Core Attribute is what you're born with, One of the Six. Like I said before, you only get experience for doing things related to your class. That's just how it works and there's no way around it."

Justin could only feel mounting horror. "So, I *have* to talk to people? Then why am I not getting any experience from this conversation?"

"Well, probably because you haven't charmed or manipulated me yet."

"So, if I told you a joke, that would level me up?"

"Maybe. But you should be careful. The gods know when you're trying to fiddle with things, so it might not have the effect you want.

There need to be stakes, that's for sure. The bigger the stakes, the more the experience. But why don't you try it and see for yourself? Can't harm anything, and I love a good joke."

Justin thought hard, though nothing truly funny came to mind. He could only think of a joke his chemistry teacher had used as an icebreaker on the first day of tenth grade.

"Why don't scientists trust atoms?"

"Why?" Alistair asked.

"Because they make up everything."

Alistair frowned, clearly not getting the joke.

"Hmm. I've known a few Adams, and most have been upstanding people."

"No, *atoms*," Justin said. "They're these extremely small…forget it."

Apparently, they didn't know about atoms here, which made sense considering Alistair was using a war hammer and wearing heavy armor.

As the trees broke, opening into a valley surrounded by low hills, Justin spied a small town in the distance. The settlement was surrounded by a wooden palisade, smoke rising from chimneys dotting the rooftops. A Gothic cathedral rose from the town's center, many times higher than any other building. The multihued sunset only added to the idyllic scene.

"That's Mistwatch," Alistair said, pointing to the town. "You'll be safe there."

Justin nodded numbly.

They continued walking toward the town. Justin could see people going about their business: blacksmiths hammering away at metal, farmers tending to their crops, and children playing on the road. Justin watched, somewhat dazed. It was as if he had stepped back into medieval Europe.

As they entered the town itself, the cobbled streets were mostly empty. Most buildings were one or two stories, and a light fog had settled on the streets. Justin realized that was where the town had likely gotten its name. Not that he cared too much at the moment. Acceptance and the accompanying depression were both settling in.

Alistair led Justin toward an inn. A wooden placard swung in the wind, with a small, winged creature. The creature had a cherubic face and rosy cheeks. The placard read, "The Drunken Pixie."

"We'll stay here for the night," Alistair said.

Justin followed Alistair inside, and they were greeted by the warm glow of a fireplace and the sound of merry chatter. A group of travelers was gathered around a table, playing a game of cards. Most of the patrons looked up for a moment to size them up, some of those eyes lingering on Justin. He felt entirely out of place in his ragged clothing and general heft, neither of which was the norm in this society.

Justin kept his eyes forward as he and Alistair approached the innkeeper. She was a beautiful woman who looked to be in her late thirties with fiery red hair that left Justin a little flummoxed. She had a welcoming smile that put him at ease. Her hair was pulled back in a loose bun, with a few loose strands framing her face.

"Two rooms, please," Alistair said, walking up confidently.

"Right away," the innkeeper said. "That'll be ninety coppers. A full silver if you want dinner and breakfast on the morrow."

Alistair reached for his coin purse, handing over a gleaming silver coin.

"Thank you kindly," the innkeeper said, handing over two small keys. "The rooms are upstairs. Three and four."

She looked Justin up and down and smirked a bit. It was easy to understand why, from the dirt and tears in his sweat-crusted shirt. While his cheeks burned with embarrassment, he found he had nothing to say. Being embarrassed by pretty women was nothing new, so he would bear the shame in this world as much as in the last one.

As they made their way up the stairs, the events of the day hit him in full force. He felt a despair such as he had never known. Why was he here? Was any of this even real?

And if it was, how in the world did he survive?

Survival. Was that really the game here? Maybe if he died, he would wake up back home in Oklahoma.

Then again, maybe he was already dead from that tornado, and this was some sort of afterlife or weird quantum purgatory. It could be the universe's way of punishing him for playing games constantly instead of taking accountability for his life.

Even if that was the case, this new reality might be his only chance to live. Did he *really* want to throw that away?

Or maybe, just maybe, if there was a portal to this world, didn't it stand to reason that there might be a portal back?

"Are you all right, lad?"

Somehow, they had ended up in the hallway on the second floor. Alistair was looking at him with concern.

"Just tired, I guess."

"Get some rest. That's all you really need." He sniffed. "And order a bath." He reached into his coin purse and pulled out ten pieces of copper. "That should cover it."

"Do I just order it at the front?" Justin asked, not wanting to face the red-haired beauty again.

Alistair smiled, seeming to guess his hesitation. "While you're down there, maybe you can try to negotiate a lower price. Or make her smile. It looks like she's having a rough day. That might get you to Level 1. Wouldn't that be a positive spin on a bad situation?"

Before Justin could answer, Alistair left him with that as he went to his own room.

Justin looked at the coppers in his hand doubtfully and went down to the common room. Before he could second-guess himself, he headed toward the beautiful innkeeper, who was looking into what appeared to be a ledger.

Justin stood there a moment before clearing his throat awkwardly. "Excuse me."

She didn't seem to hear him.

"*Ahem.* Excuse me!"

His tone came out harsher than he had intended, and there was a moment of affront on her face before she replaced it with a professional mask.

Yes, this was going swimmingly.

"How might I help you, sir?"

"I was wondering if I could order a bath."

"You may," she said, not maintaining eye contact. "Twenty coppers for a man of your...*size*."

A few men sitting at a nearby table had a laugh at that.

Justin's cheeks colored, and he almost wanted to shout his protest, but he remembered what Alistair had said.

Negotiate.

He put on his best smile, which felt extremely fake. "Did I ever tell you how beautiful you are?"

"Thirty coppers."

"And irksome?"

From her stony expression, she wasn't going to budge.

"Never mind. I'll go find a river or something."

He turned to leave.

"Eighteen coppers," she said. "Best offer."

"I know it's not worth more than ten. So, why would I pay eighteen?"

She looked him up and down. "We'll need to use more water."

"Why's that?"

"You're bigger."

Justin couldn't believe this. "So, you're basing the higher price solely on my size? That's discriminatory!"

She shrugged. "It's business. Bigger bodies need more water."

"Well, if it's truly based on water usage, then I should pay less, not more."

She arched an eyebrow, as if daring him to go on.

Justin cleared his throat awkwardly. "What I mean is, because I'm larger, I take up more volume. So, you'd actually be using *less* water." He gave a sheepish smile. "That's basic arithmetic."

"Are you being smart with me?"

Justin could see the innkeeper was not amused by his comment, but he pushed his luck anyway. "Not at all. I'm simply stating a fact. You've already said the price is based on water usage." He forced a smile. "Plus, if I can get a bath for a price I can afford, well, I'll be less offensive on all fronts."

Justin didn't know where all this was coming from. The words just seemed to flow from him like water. In normal circumstances, he wouldn't let out more than a squeak around a woman of her beauty.

And to his surprise, his words were having an effect.

The innkeeper sighed and gave him a small smile. "You're persistent, I'll give you that. This is a fine establishment, and you are rather filthy. And you'll be using our towels. In normal circumstances, yes, ten is a fair price. But I can't let you bathe here for less than fifteen coppers."

"I don't have fifteen," Justin admitted. "But I have ten. I'll skip my breakfast tomorrow and we'll call it even." He patted his belly. "I've got plenty in the tank here, anyway. Deal?"

She considered for a moment. "Deal."

Justin handed her the coins and watched as she wrote something down in the ledger.

"Your bath will be ready in thirty minutes. We'll bring the water up."

"To the room? Isn't that heavy?"

"Don't worry about it, sir. Is there anything else?"

"Nothing," Justin said. "Thank you."

The innkeeper went back to her ledger. Justin couldn't help but feel a little proud of himself for negotiating a better price. It was something, however small.

[You have gained 1 experience point. Your experience stands at 1/1. Level-up available!]

He waited another moment, but nothing else happened. Why wasn't he leveling up?

He opened his interface, only to find the experience was 100% full. 1/1. Obviously, there was some other action he needed to undertake to level up. He would have to ask Alistair in the morning.

He headed up the wooden stairs and into his room.

3

FIRST STEPS IN A NEW WORLD

"Never underestimate an innkeeper. They may seem like humble hosts, but most know more than any king's spy."

—Dornal Flint,
  Lessons Learned the Hard Way

THIRTY MINUTES LATER, a copper tub came, hauled by several strapping young lads. They set it in the center of his room, along with a couple of towels. The tub was rather small, more of a giant bucket really, but just large enough for Justin to enter. They spent the next few minutes running up and down the stairs, filling the tub halfway. The final boy dropped a glowing stone in the cold water, inscribed with a couple of red runes.

Justin watched, amazed, as, over the next few minutes, the water warmed in response to the magical stone, creating bubbles in the process.

He locked the door and sank into the deliciously warm water. The warmth soothed his aching muscles, and he lowered himself into the water with a sigh of relief. The bubbles tickled his skin as he closed his eyes and leaned back against the tub. The stress of the day slipped away with each passing moment. He stayed in the tub until the water cooled.

He would have fallen asleep had it not been for the knock at the door. They were probably coming to take the tub back.

"Just a moment."

He got up and, to his surprise, found a pair of basic clothes waiting for him on his bed that he had missed before: tan breeches, a white shirt, socks, and boots. All seemed close enough to his size, which must have been rather difficult to procure. Justin assumed they were from Alistair. The man was truly too kind.

He got dressed and unlocked the door, and as he suspected, it was the boys coming to take the tub. Justin was grateful they didn't comment on the filthiness of the water. They managed to scoot it into the hallway without spilling a drop.

They also brought him some food: nothing fancy, just a slab of cold roast beef, cheese, bread, and a light ale.

As soon as they were gone, he scarfed down his food, never tasting anything so delicious, despite the simplicity of the fare.

After setting his plate in the hallway outside, he returned to the room's tiny bed and lay down. Such were the events of the day that he was instantly asleep.

Justin blinked awake only to find himself in a room that wasn't his. He had a moment of panic before he remembered everything that had happened. A groan escaped his lips, and he hid himself under the sheets.

And he would have stayed there had the Voice not entered his mind.

[You have reached Level 1. The world is your stage, and you've taken the first step in your performance. Charisma and wit will be your tools—use them wisely, for every conversation can lead to opportunity.]

Much to Justin's surprise, he felt a sense of accomplishment and purpose. Something that seemed to come from outside himself. And he realized he hadn't leveled up yesterday because it was waiting for him to sleep. It seemed to be how this System, or whatever entity controlled this reality, worked. He supposed for simplicity's sake he should simply think of it as "the System," or perhaps "the Voice," at least until he learned more.

[You have one attribute point to distribute.]

Justin opened his character screen and saw that he could place the point into any of his six Core Attributes. It was tempting to put it in power or endurance, as that might help his survivability.

But he knew he could not do so. He was a Socialite, and his strength was charisma. All of his skills would surely benefit from it, and in fact, he could not level up unless he used charisma-based skills, at least as far as what Alistair had told him.

He sighed, then locked the point into Charisma and confirmed.

Almost instantly, he felt his thoughts become clearer, and he sat up straighter. He wasn't sure if it was an effect of the stat increase or something else.

He looked into a mirror on the wall and was surprised to see his cheeks were a little less pudgy and his eyes less red. The fresh air and exercise had done wonders for his complexion. He wasn't good-looking by any stretch. Not even average. But he looked better than he did on his best days, of which, admittedly, there weren't many.

Was it exercise, or something else entirely?

Whatever it was, it was a step in the right direction.

[As a Level 1 Socialite, you have unlocked your class boon, **Magnetic Presence!**]

Magnetic Presence: People are more instinctively drawn to you, sensing an aura of trustworthiness or allure. As your Charisma grows, your presence can inspire loyalty in allies and unease in adversaries without a single word.

Justin rubbed his chin thoughtfully. In a world where he didn't know who to trust—or even how to survive—having people naturally gravitate toward him might not be such a bad thing. Trustworthiness was a currency he could spend, and if enemies were uneasy around him, maybe he could avoid some fights altogether.

It wasn't the smashing power of a barbarian or warrior, or the fireballs of a wizard, but it was a tool he could work with, something that would be useful in everyday situations. The more he invested in his charisma attribute, the more effective this "class boon" would become.

And for that matter, what was the difference between a skill and a boon? A question for Alistair, perhaps.

[Now go and make your mark in the world, Brave Adventurer. Your potential is boundless.]

With that, Justin felt the warm presence of the Voice depart.

"All right," he said, rolling his shoulders. "Time to see if this magnetic thing works."

Justin stepped back out into the hallway, just in time to see Alistair leaving his room, all decked out in gleaming paladin gear.

The paladin's face brightened at seeing him. "Morning. All cleaned up, I see!"

"I got to Level 1!"

"Well done, lad! You will always remember your first level-up."

Justin frowned. "Heading out?"

Alistair chuckled. "Yes, I'm afraid so. Zombies to slay and all that. But before I do, a parting gift…"

He reached into his coin purse and gave Justin five silver coins.

Justin's eyes widened. "Alistair, you don't have to."

"I know I don't. But something is different about you; that much I can see. I'd stay longer, see you on your way, but the Church keeps me busy. Maybe as a first step, you can ask the innkeeper for leads on work around here. Or better yet, visit the local cleric at the cathedral and see if he can do a bit of healing to help you with your memory."

"Good idea," Justin said. "Before you head out, how do levels work here, anyway? What's the difference between a boon and a skill?"

Alistair looked at him, marveling. "You *really* don't know any of this stuff, do you?"

Justin hung his head.

"Hey, it's all right," Alistair said, his tone softening. "Well, from birth, the gods know your strength, your purpose. All of us are born with the sacred Spark of Life of the Creator within us, and that Spark feeds your Core Attribute. You have a charisma core, Justin. For all your words about not being good with people, the gods think otherwise. It's up to you to build on your strength. You've handled yourself well so far. Who knows how far you can go if you try?"

Justin blinked at him, surprised by the encouragement.

Alistair gave a knowing smile and a shrug. "Trust your instincts. Words can inspire, cut, or heal, but only if you wield them with purpose. Arion guide your steps, Justin. And remember—charisma isn't just about talking. It's about making others believe."

With that, Alistair adjusted his shield and strode past Justin, his boots echoing down the stairs.

[Alistair has left the party.]

Justin felt a certain warmth leave him. At first, he thought it was a sense of sadness that he was on his own again, but he also remembered that it might have been Alistair's Divine Aura dissipating.

Whatever the case, he was on his own again. Level 1, in a new world, with no proper goals or motivations.

One thing was obvious, though. He had to learn more.

As he headed downstairs, he could only wonder what the day would bring.

4

EMOTIONAL DAMAGE

"Attributes are multipliers—amplifying what is already there. A fool with a high Power attribute will indeed strike hard, but a trained swordsman with less Power will hit even harder. Master yourself first, and your attributes will magnify talent into true greatness."

—Scholar Rindle Faelstorm,
  Class Fundamentals

"CHECKING OUT?" the innkeeper asked.

Justin nodded. "I'm wondering where I might get some basic gear. A coin purse, a map, a pack..."

"You'll want to go down to the market square," the innkeeper said. "There are plenty of shops that sell those sorts of things. You might also try the general store at the edge of town."

"Thanks," Justin said.

"One more thing," the innkeeper said. "If you want your breakfast, I can get you a bit of bread and meat before you head out the door." She gave him a warm smile. "Wait right here."

Justin nodded, wondering what could have inspired this change of heart. Maybe that one point of charisma had made all the difference, or even his new boon.

She came back with a baguette laden with meat and cheese. It would be perfect to eat on the road.

"Appreciate it," he said.

"In return, just point any new customers to the Drunken Pixie," she said with a parting smile. "I have a feeling you might go far. Good day."

Justin nodded and headed out the door. He was already out on the street before realizing he hadn't even asked where the market square and general store were.

He walked and ate, and the market was easy enough to find, just a street over from the inn. Dozens of shops and stalls lined the central square, along with the towering cathedral, quite lofty for a town of this size, with the same phoenix Justin had spied on Alistair's armor. It must have been the Church of Light. Well over a hundred people were gathered here, buying, selling, and haggling. The air was misty and cool.

As the innkeeper said, there were vendors selling many goods: food, clothing, and even weapons.

He spotted a store that looked promising and headed inside. A friendly-looking woman with wavy brown hair greeted him. He wasn't sure how far five silvers would carry him, but he already knew from fiddling with his interface this morning that one hundred coppers equaled a silver. And a hundred silvers equaled one gold.

"Welcome, traveler," she said. "What can I do for you today?"

"I need some basic gear. A coin purse, a map, and a pack for starters."

"You've come to the right place. We have everything you need."

She led him to a section of the store that was filled with backpacks, pouches, and other travel gear. Justin selected a sturdy pack and a small pouch to hold his coins. Despite their size, the shopkeeper assured him that both were enchanted to hold more than they appeared to on the outside. The pack, she also mentioned, was enchanted to prolong the life of any food placed within it and was popular with local hunters. He didn't think he would be doing any of that—he simply wasn't equipped for it—but it was good to know.

He also picked out a map that was enchanted to fill in details as he discovered new areas, and a few supplies, such as a pocketknife, flint and steel, a pot, a canteen, and some basic foodstuffs, on the storekeeper's recommendation. After that, there was little left to spend.

"Is there anything else you need?" the woman asked, handing Justin his change.

"A bit of information, perhaps," Justin said, stowing the coins in his new pouch. "If you have the time."

"Well, it's been a slow morning, so ask away."

"What can you tell me about the Socialite class?"

She frowned. "Well, I've *heard* of it, but I've met no one who *has* it. It's one of the basic charisma classes, of course. Everyone knows that. I think you'll find some in the big cities. Most of us with charisma cores learn something that's a bit more useful, if we have the means." She gave a sudden smile. "As for Socialites, we don't have much need for that around here. Like any other basic class, the Socialite class can be adopted on one's twentieth name day by anyone with a Charisma Core Attribute."

Twentieth name day. So, a person wasn't allowed to pick a class until they turned twenty. And, as he had suspected, the Core Attribute for the class had to match.

She looked at him a bit curiously. "Are you a Socialite, dear? If so, you're far from the courts of Belmora."

"Belmora? Where's that?"

She watched him strangely. "That's the capital of Aranthia. Quite far from here, but you can make it in a couple of weeks by walking the Silver Road heading southeast from Mistwatch. Before that, though, you'll come to Silverton, about fifty miles away. Not the biggest city by any stretch of the imagination, but there's a lot of work there in the mines. It's definitely someplace all the young ones want to get off to. If you're aiming for something bigger, well, as I said, Belmora on the Golden Gulf is what you want." She gave a playful smile. "Are you running from something, lad? Or chasing a girl?"

Justin smiled easily, the instinct seeming to come naturally. "Why? Are you interested?"

She gave a good-natured laugh. "Well, I do like 'em a bit on the heavy side, but you could do with a proper shave." Her smile softened. "You aren't *entirely* unhandsome, though."

"That's a green light if I've ever heard one."

"Green light? A...strange expression. Where are you from, dear?"

Justin played it off with a grin. "Oh, somewhere far and exotic. Where charm is a national export."

The woman chuckled, her eyes twinkling. He realized, with a start, that he was flirting. And more shocking—she was actually enjoying it. He couldn't remember the last time this had happened, if ever.

She touched his arm lightly. "You're too funny, dear. But much too young for me, I'm afraid."

"What do you mean? You don't look a day over thirty."

Her cheeks reddened. "Oh, stop! I am spoken for, after all. Is there anything else I can help you with, young master?"

He smiled graciously. "No, ma'am. Have a pleasant day."

As he walked out of the store, he pondered the conversation. Such flirtations were not his normal character, so he had to wonder if it was his class that was causing him to act this way. It was almost like an instinct.

[You have gained 2 experience points. Your experience stands at 2/200.]

Well, *that* was unexpected. He opened his character screen, and to his shock, saw that the experience requirement for level 2 was a full two hundred points, far more than the single point required to get to Level 1.

Well, he would get there. One day.

Out in the market square again, he retrieved his enchanted map and gave it a good look. It seemed to be highly detailed up to twenty miles, but after that, things became more nebulous, listing only major landmarks and settlements. Silverton was fifty miles away and was barely contained on the edge of the map. There was no sign of Belmora, so clearly, this was a local map. As he examined the map, his eyes nearly popped out of his head.

To his surprise, he could zoom in on the map and get a better sense of details, though it didn't reveal everything. He found Mistwatch, which was in the center of a place called the Wildwood Forest, in a country called Aranthia. The road to Silverton went southeast, over a range of hills, or perhaps even small mountains, called the Umber Range, with Silverton set in a pass within it. As the shopkeeper had said, it was about fifty miles. Fifty-two, to be exact.

He briefly examined other points of the map, but found there wasn't much information—just some cities, forests, hills, and mountains. The map was entitled "The Central Hinterlands."

"Interesting," he said.

He looked around, not sure what to do with himself. A sudden sense of loneliness and homesickness overcame him. He thought about his old life, how he had taken everything for granted there.

And now he was stuck here. Completely lost and overwhelmed.

He needed a goal. But what? Here, he could make his own life and his own destiny.

He took out a few coppers from his pocket, staring at them for a moment. He had a charisma-based class. Maybe he should try to make some money. Start a business.

Then again, he didn't have the Merchant class, and wouldn't get bonuses for owning a store or anything like that. It seemed all he could do was schmooze with people.

Could it get *any* worse?

Justin decided to head to an inn—a different one from before—to get some information. It seemed to be the thing to do in the games he played, so he didn't see why it would be different here. At the very least, it was something to do.

But as Justin walked down a random street, he couldn't help but notice how deserted it was. Skulking in the alley between two shabby buildings were two youths. They were both tall and thin, with greasy hair and scruffy clothes that looked as if they hadn't been washed in weeks. Their eyes flickered over to him, and they exchanged a few quick words Justin couldn't quite catch.

Justin headed for the open door of a nearby inn, but the two youths stepped out in front of him, blocking his path. One of them, who was tall with a pockmarked face, snarled at him.

"Hey there, Tiny. If you're lost, the pig pens are back on the farms over yonder."

Justin tensed up. He was all too aware that he had nothing but the pocketknife he'd just bought to defend himself. He could see the glint of greed in their eyes, and he knew they were after his newly purchased possessions.

Justin smiled as a line serendipitously came to him. "Lost? Just thought I'd take the scenic route and admire the local ambiance. But you two are really bringing down the local property value."

The second boy, shorter and skinnier, laughed. "Some sort of wise guy, eh? We saw you at the market square. You've got some silver on you, don't you?"

"Sorry. Fresh out of silver. But I have a pocketful of sarcasm if that interests you."

The boys didn't seem interested in his witty banter. "Hand over the silver, and we'll let you go," the taller one said, brandishing a rusty knife. "Otherwise, things are going to get ugly."

Justin realized there was only one way out, since handing over his goods was the last thing he wanted to do. He realized he had no choice but to use his Poison Barb skill. And his barb would have to be so good that it would render the first boy speechless for three seconds, allowing it to immediately go off cooldown so he could use it on the second boy.

That would give him enough of an opening to escape into the inn.

Justin activated Poison Barb, looking the two boys up and down, feigning boredom. He felt a surge of energy, as if he were tapping into some deep well of mystical power. Somehow, the Poison Barb ability allowed him to read his opponents like a book, to know exactly what to say to hit them where it hurt the most. He perceived that the tall boy was self-conscious about his ragged appearance, while the shorter one was ashamed of being bossed around by the older one.

"Ah, two scrawny weeds have sprouted from the cracked pavement." He eyed the taller youth. "And what is that? *Unwashed hair*? And are those garments you are wearing, or merely rags that have been scavenged from a garbage heap? I can smell the stench of your unwashed body from here, and truly, your presence is an offense to my eyes. I would not be surprised if they became infected by your foul visage."

The taller boy's eyes widened, and he seemed unsure for a moment. But after a few seconds, he scowled, and the shorter one couldn't help but chuckle nervously.

[Poison Barb refreshed.]

"You're going to regret that, you little—" the tall boy said, suddenly coming to his senses.

But before he could finish, Justin struck again. He was aware that the odds of stunning him again were lower, but as he saw it, he had no choice but to try. "Oh, I'm quaking in my boots! Do you want to know what *really* scares me, though? The thought of being stuck with your repulsive appearance for even a few more seconds. It's like you're trying to make me physically ill. I doubt even a rat would come near you for fear of catching something. You look like you crawled out of the sewer!"

Again, the boy watched him, flummoxed.

Good. It had worked.

[Poison Barb refreshed.]

As Justin took another step forward, with confidence he didn't know he possessed, he turned his attention to the shorter boy. "And you," he said, his voice low and dangerous, "you're just the tagalong, aren't you? Can't even come up with an insult of your own. Just do what your master tells you. How pitiful!"

The shorter boy flinched, his eyes darting nervously between Justin and his partner in crime.

[Poison Barb refreshed.]

Justin continued his barb chain. "You're nothing but a scared little mouse. But don't worry, I'm sure your big, tough friend here will protect you!"

By now, Justin had caused such a scene that a crowd had gathered. The taller boy took a quick look around and breathed a curse.

"Come on!"

He bounded down the alley, the shorter boy clipping at his heels.

Justin watched him go with a smirk, feeling a surge of satisfaction.

[You have gained 20 experience points. Your experience stands at 22/200.]

Justin shook his head. With the would-be attackers gone, whatever instinct had possessed him vanished, leaving his hands shaking.

Without further hesitation, he ducked into the inn.

5

A WORKING BOY

"If you're looking to hire a mercenary, heed this advice: a good mercenary won't talk too much about their exploits—those who brag about slaying dragons usually haven't survived a chicken coop. Check their gear: polished weapons and well-maintained armor are marks of a professional, not someone looking to pocket your gold and vanish. And finally, pay well, but not too well. Loyalty lasts only as long as the coin purse is heavier in your hand than in theirs."

—Captain Jennet Dane,
   The Definitive Guide to Mercenary Dealings

INSIDE, Justin found himself in a dimly lit common room. The fire in the hearth cast a warm glow on the wooden tables and benches that filled the space. A few patrons were scattered throughout the room, nursing drinks and conversing in hushed tones. The air was certainly different here than at the Drunken Pixie, but despite the shabbier interior, the owner seemed to keep the establishment clean and in good working order.

Taking a deep breath, Justin approached the bar, where an older man with grizzled hair and a bushy beard stood wiping a mug. He looked up as Justin approached, his eyes appraising.

"What can I get you, lad?" the man asked gruffly.

"Just a drink and some information, if you have it."

"Drinks are cheap. Information is pricier, depending on the request."

What kind of drinks did they have in a place like this? Probably not a Harvey Wallbanger.

Justin sighed. "Ale is fine."

The barkeep nodded, sliding a tankard of dark-hued liquid across the counter. "That'll be five coppers."

Justin fished the coins out of his pouch and handed it over. Taking a swig of the ale, he savored the bitter taste as it cooled his tongue. Judging by the price of the goods he had purchased, a copper seemed to have about the same value as a U.S. dollar. That would be his prevailing assumption until proven otherwise.

"I'm looking for some advice," Justin began. "I'm new around here, and I need to figure out a way to make some money."

The barkeep raised an eyebrow. He had no real reason to help him, but maybe his Magnetic Presence boon would come in handy.

"What skills do you have?"

Justin hesitated. "I'm a Socialite." He cleared his throat awkwardly. "Level 1."

"You have a class?" the barkeep asked, a bit surprised. "Well, that helps you out quite a bit. Take on a few skills and boons, and you'll be all right."

"You speak as if having a class is a rare thing," Justin said, taking another sip. "I thought everyone of age had a class."

The man looked at him as if he had grown a second head. "Well, classes aren't easy to come by. Maybe it's different where you're from. But by the time you're my age, and half your life is spent, well, the cons of going into debt for one outweigh the pros. Count yourself lucky, lad. You've got your whole life ahead of you."

Justin frowned. If classes were indeed rare in this world, maybe he should be careful about advertising the fact.

"Would there happen to be a library in town? There's a bit of information I would like to look up."

"Well, the Church is your best bet. I believe they have a clergyman with the Scholar class. Silas Penwell is his name. He'd be the one to talk to. But access to knowledge like that doesn't come cheap."

"Where I'm from, libraries are paid for by taxes."

The man chuckled. "Well, I haven't heard of that. Where are you from, anyway?"

Again, Justin had fumbled, and now he was stuck answering an awkward question. "Belmora," he said smoothly. "Anyhow, if you have any leads on a job, I could pay you back with further business."

The man shrugged. "Besides your class, do you have any other talents or education? Can you read and write? Can you do math?"

"I can," Justin confirmed. "I have some book learning, but truth be told, I don't have much in the way of practical abilities. But I *can* talk to people."

With that last part, it felt as if he were lying through his teeth. But who was to say that *wasn't* true? In his old life, he was a bumbling fool who couldn't string two words together to anyone who even slightly intimidated him.

But here, he had more important concerns. Talking was easier now, and his thoughts were strangely clear. Either it was the fresh air, his class, or the endless dangers making pesky things like social anxiety take a back seat. Now, he had anxieties of a different sort.

The barkeep considered this for a moment, stroking his beard. "Well, there are a few options that might suit you. You could look for a job as a merchant's assistant, helping with negotiations and deals, or balancing the books. Or you could try your hand at being a courier or a scribe. People are always in need of someone who can deliver messages or write letters."

"Hmm. That might suit me."

"It's not as bad as you think," the barkeep confirmed. "You've got something of an education, and that puts you ahead of most. Aim for something that gets you at least a silver a day."

"Is that enough to live on?"

"Maybe not in Belmora, where you're from. But here in Mistwatch, it's doable. If you want something a little more, the Royal Mail is always hiring couriers. It's dangerous, especially these days. In a town like this, the official mail only goes out once a fortnight. But sometimes people or businesses need their parcels faster and are willing to pay through the nose for it. You might make ten silvers a week doing work like that, up to twenty, depending on the danger and how many jobs you take on."

"Twenty? Now we're talking."

"Granted, a lot of your pay would have to go into financing your own coach, horse, and perhaps a guard or two. It's a hard business. My advice is to try to work *in* the post office. A lot safer."

"I can't just deliver parcels by myself? It can't be *that* bad."

The barkeep chuckled. "You'd just be asking for it, even on the roads. *Especially* on the roads. At least hire a guard."

Justin thought back to those goblins and realized the barkeep might be right. "Thank you for the advice; I appreciate it."

The barkeep waved a hand dismissively. "Don't mention it, lad. Just remember that sometimes, it's not what you know, but who you know. Make the right friends, and doors will open for you."

With that piece of wisdom, Justin finished his drink and left the inn. He had no friends, so that advice was probably useless.

Truth be told, he hadn't ever held a job in his life. His mom always got on him for that. She always told him to at least do something, even if it was working at McDonald's, but his pride would never allow it.

Looking back, he realized it would have been good for him. He'd gotten more sun and nature in the past couple of days than he had in the last couple of years.

Maybe even the last couple of decades.

Here, though, he didn't have to be his old self. He could be whoever he wanted, and there was no one to say boo. There was power and freedom in that.

He would start by making connections, forging alliances, and learning everything he could about the people and places around him. And he would begin right here in the town of Mistwatch.

He headed back toward the town square, looking at his map all the while. The town wasn't large, so it took about two minutes to find the post office.

He strolled through the front door, the bell above the entrance announcing his arrival. The room was simple, with a long wooden counter at the end. Behind it, rows of pigeonholes were filled with letters and parcels, each one meticulously sorted by destination. Brass placards labeled each slot with names like Silverton, Belmora, Windfall, Draegor's Keep, Caroway, and Highcliff. A middle-aged woman with a strict bun and spectacles looked up from her ledger as he approached.

"Can I help you?" she inquired, her tone brisk.

"I've heard you need workers," Justin replied, his voice steady. "I'm here to offer my services."

She arched an eyebrow, her gaze appraising him from head to toe, taking in his basic clothing. "Experience?"

Well, all those fetch quests in Aether Quest probably didn't count as experience, but Justin could pretend they did. He had to hope his 11 in Charisma was enough to carry him through.

He put on a confident smile. "Yes, madam. I've handled many tasks—delivering urgent messages, transporting valuable items through hostile areas, and navigating dangerous territories to complete critical assignments. I've worked for high-profile clients—merchants, mostly. Back in my last job, the routes weren't easy, but I made sure the deliveries were always on time and intact. As someone with the Socialite class, I always know the right words to get out of a hairy situation, and I'm skilled at handling high-profile clients."

The clerk listened, her eyes widening with a mix of surprise and concern as he spoke. By the time he finished, she looked almost wary. "Well, can you give an example of a hard assignment you've completed? Do you at least have a letter of reference?"

Justin hesitated for only a moment before replying. "Unfortunately, I don't have a letter of reference with me. My last employer was…somewhat secretive. They were involved in sensitive matters, and discretion was paramount. We agreed that any formal documentation could compromise that discretion. But I'm happy to tell you about one of my most challenging assignments."

Then, with skill he didn't even know he possessed, he wove an epic tale regarding a specific fetch quest from Aether Quest that he had to complete. "There was a time when I was tasked with delivering a rare vial of medicine to an orcish village deep in the mountains. The village was suffering from a terrible plague, and the medicine was their only hope. The path was treacherous. Blizzards and landslides made travel nearly impossible. But I knew the importance of my mission."

Justin watched in amazement as the clerk's bespectacled eyes widened while she was rapt by the story.

Good. This was going better than he had expected. Normally, he wasn't one to spin wild tales, but he could make an exception in cases of survival and, of course, landing a job.

"At one point, I was ambushed by a group of bandits who wanted the vial for themselves, thinking it was something valuable they could sell. I talked my way out of the situation, using my charisma to convince them it was cursed and would bring them nothing but misfortune."

That actually hadn't been what happened. In Aether Quest, Justin had used his "Hammer Storm" ability to make short work of the miscreants, but she didn't need to know that.

"Anyway, they let me go, and I continued on. Despite the odds, I reached the village just in time, and the medicine saved countless lives."

The clerk's expression softened as she listened to his story, her initial wariness giving way to a mixture of admiration and relief. She actually *believed* him. "Ye gods…that's quite the tale. Well, we're desperate for help, and most don't want to take the Silver Road these days…"

Sensing an opening, Justin swallowed hard and leaned in slightly.

"I'm aware of the risks, and I assure you, I've risked far more. There's no better person for the job than I."

"Well, I'd be remiss not to tell you first that we have something safer, if you prefer. I actually could use someone to do the sorting. My junior clerk quit last week."

"Pay?"

"Fifty coppers a day," she said evenly.

Justin's face fell. "That's poverty wages! I have a class, so I'm aiming for a silver a day. Just think of the value I can offer, especially as I unlock more abilities."

She chuckled drily. "Even I don't make that, young man! We need help, but we'll pay you the market rate for it. Any old Jack could do it."

"I'm not any old Jack; trust me. I want something more. I've got a fire in my belly, and nothing can stop me! Tell me more about this courier job."

She looked him over once more, then sighed. "All right. You mentioned experience working for high-profile clients, and your Socialite class would be helpful there. I've got an important parcel that needs to be delivered to Baron Valdrik in Silverton. Normally, I wouldn't give it to someone as untested as you, and without an official reference. But I'm getting desperate because he can be quite... demanding. You deliver it and head to the postmaster there, and you'll get five silvers. Sound good?"

Justin blinked. The Baron of Silverton? This didn't sound like a simple delivery.

But then again, if he were successful, it would give him a good amount of money. Five silvers was a considerable sum. With one job, he'd make ten times what he'd earn doing sorting. Walking fifty miles to Silverton would take two days at the most. Plus, it would get him to a bigger city where his class might be more useful.

Then again, the clerk had made the mistake of saying she was desperate...

"I'll do it," he said. "But I want ten silvers."

"Five," the clerk said firmly. "This rate is set by the client and is non-negotiable. Sorry."

No wonder no one had taken it yet. "Well, you mentioned no one wanted to take it, and it's time-sensitive. Either your client can wait, or he can raise his bid."

"I sympathize and actually agree with you. However, this client is particular that the pay be no more than five silvers. It's yours if you want it."

Justin sighed. "Very well. I'll do it."

She blinked in surprise before recovering. She handed him a small package, tied up with twine and sealed with red wax. The weight felt right in his hands. Plus, it got him paid more while getting him to a bigger city.

"That's your seal," she explained. "It's enchanted; once accepted by the intended recipient, it'll log with the Universal Ledger. Once that's done, head to the local post office for your pay." There was something in her eyes that suggested she knew he'd been stretching the truth. "Look, normally I wouldn't give this to you. A lot of couriers have gone missing lately. All of them have had one thing in common."

"What?" Justin asked, curious despite himself.

"They refused to hire help."

Justin smirked. "At these rates, I can see why."

The clerk was not amused. "The Mercenary Guild is just down the street. Please hire someone and don't be too picky."

Justin nodded, placing the parcel carefully in his pack. "Understood."

As he left the post office, the interface in the corner of his vision flashed with a new message.

Job Gained: The Baron's Parcel

Deliver the parcel to the Baron of Silverton. Upon successful delivery, go to the Silverton Post Office to collect your pay.

Pay: 5 Silver Marks

Experience: 50

Justin couldn't help but smile. This wasn't just about delivering a parcel—it was a challenge, a game.

Or at the very least, something to do. There was the risk, of course, but the prospect of five silvers and the experience points was too enticing to pass up.

He retrieved his map and made his way to the Mercenary Guild, just down the street.

So far, his interactions had granted him very little experience. He hadn't gotten any from his conversation with the clerk, probably because he hadn't negotiated a higher payment.

Soon enough, he arrived. The Guild was smaller than he'd expected, just a simple door that was open to the street. For a town the size of Mistwatch, it was a minor affair, quiet, with only two armored soldiers sitting at a nearby table, each nursing a drink. Both leered at him dangerously.

But sitting in the opposite corner, almost hidden from view, was a young woman, perhaps in her mid-twenties like him. She had a lean face, hawkish features, and hollow cheeks that spoke of more than a few missed meals. Her wide green eyes, framed by shoulder-length brown hair, watched him curiously. While the other two men wore heavy armor and carried swords and shields, she had nothing but disheveled clothing and several knives strapped to her belt.

Justin approached the main counter, manned by a burly orc with green skin and pointed tusks—a sight that threw him for a loop. It was the first time he'd seen a non-human in this world. Or really, *ever*, in this world and in his own reality. It should have surprised him, but it felt oddly natural.

As Justin cleared his throat, he felt the weight of battle-hardened eyes on him.

"What can I do for you, sir?" the orc asked gruffly, his expression disinterested.

"I need protection for the Silver Road journey. As far as Silverton."

"Very good. What kind of protection?"

"The good kind."

"Well, it can be had if your pockets are deep enough."

Justin considered for a moment. If he paid even two silvers, it would cut into his profits significantly. But it was still more than what the junior clerk position offered.

"I've got two silvers to pay," he began, trying to sound confident. "On arrival, of course."

Laughter erupted from the table where the two men sat, and Justin felt his cheeks burn.

The orc grinned, revealing more of his yellowed tusks. "Two silvers? You want your hire to fight with a twig? No one here will risk the Silver Road for anything less than five, especially these days!"

Justin had hoped to negotiate, but this was more than he'd expected. "I can go as high as two and a half."

The orc guffawed. "Sod off, little boy. This clearly isn't for you."

"Never mind, then. I suppose I'll have to go to Silverton on my own. Good day."

Justin turned toward the exit, feeling deflated. If the post office was only paying five silvers, the risk would make the job almost pointless if he hired help. He felt a surge of anger because the post office clerk clearly knew that but still foisted the unwanted parcel on him anyway.

He'd been played for a fool. This Baron had probably set a lowball bid, hoping some desperate rube would come along and take it. But that still didn't make sense, because if the Baron actually wanted the damnable package, wouldn't he set a reasonable bid to make sure it arrived safely?

In the end, Justin had to shake his head. People's actions didn't always make sense, but it was certainly aggravating when they affected him.

Emerging into the sunlight, he paused. Maybe he should just humble himself and take that sorting job at the post office.

But now that he had accepted the parcel, something about it felt strangely binding. It was a job, and a job had to at least be attempted. Otherwise, he'd be stuck with this parcel for the rest of his days.

Strangely, he didn't care about the Baron, but something about this package called out to him. It needed to be delivered, and he would be the one to do it. It was something to latch onto in this uncertain world. Plus, getting to a bigger town was his goal. A goal he couldn't fulfill so long as he stayed here in Mistwatch.

Just as he was about to turn around and head for the town gate, a hand grabbed his arm, and he nearly jumped out of his skin.

He spun around, meeting the intense gaze of the young woman from the guild. Her striking green eyes sized him up. Justin found her presence unsettling, but she didn't seem to mean him any immediate harm, despite the knives at her belt.

"Lila Fairwind," she said, holding out a hand with a winning smile. "Those guildies don't know an opportunity when they see one. I'll escort you to Silverton for three silvers."

Justin looked her up and down doubtfully. "Where's your armor?"

"I'm a Bard, Level 1," she said. "We don't use armor. I can tell you've fallen on hard times. We have that much in common." She drew one of her knives quickly, twirling it in her fingers. "Name?"

Justin's eyes widened slightly at the sight. "Justin Talemaker. Socialite. Are you good with those knives? You're Level 1, after all."

She smirked. "Well, it's a little-known fact that Bards are almost as good with knives as they are with music. Trust me, not a hair on your head will be harmed."

"Uh-huh," Justin said, still skeptical. "And you want three silvers?"

"It's a fair price. So, what do you say?"

He hesitated. The path ahead would undoubtedly be perilous. In most games Justin had played, Bards were known for their songs and musical skills, not martial prowess, but Lila seemed capable enough.

Plus, he had no other options.

"All right, here's the deal," Justin said. "I have half a mind to do it myself, but I'll be honest: I have little in the way of combat skills. But if I hire you for three silvers, there's no point in me doing the job. So, how about we split the money? Two and a half once the job is done."

Lila considered, then nodded. "Deal. You won't regret it!"

Justin hoped not. In the corner of Justin's vision, his interface blinked with a notification.

[You have gained 2 experience points. Your experience stands at 24/200.]

[Lila has requested to join the party.]

Justin accepted with a mental push.

[Lila has joined the party. You have assumed the role of party leader. You have shared a job with Lila: The Baron's Parcel.]

"It's official," she said, a bright smile spreading across her face. "Ready when you are."

"Let's move out," Justin said.

The unlikely duo set forth for the town gate.

6

CROSSROADS OF CHOICES

"People will argue all day about why the Creator turned His back on His Creation. Some say it was our wars, others our pride and greed, and a few whisper it was simply boredom. But perhaps the simplest answer is this: even gods know when they've made a mistake."

—Git the Bard,
  Ale-Stained Wisdoms

As JUSTIN and Lila made their way toward the town's southern gate, the hustle and bustle of the surrounding streets melded into a distant hum. The palisade walls were illuminated by the morning sun approaching noon. It had been a busy morning, and Justin wanted to get at least halfway to Silverton before the day was through so that they could arrive by evening tomorrow.

It was quiet at first and awkward. Justin wasn't sure of the proper protocol for hired muscle. Did they talk or ignore each other? He and Lila couldn't have been more different, at least on the surface.

Appearance-wise, she definitely wasn't disagreeable. He supposed his mind shouldn't go to such places, but there it was. He was a man, and men noticed things.

"So, a Socialite?" Lila began with a smirk, glancing sideways at him. "Can't say I've met one of those before."

"It seems to be a common sentiment."

"So, how does that work? Do you fight enemies with the power of charm and dinner parties?"

Justin couldn't help but chuckle. "Well, words can be as powerful as any sword. And trust me, social situations are difficult. You'd be surprised at how much damage a whisper can do."

Lila feigned a look of mock horror. "Please, spare me from your deadly gossip."

"Hey, don't underestimate the power of a well-placed rumor. It can break empires!"

"Well, you're Level 1, just like me. I think it's a little early to call yourself the 'Breaker of Empires.'"

"True enough," he conceded. "If you want to know the truth, I could hardly convince the innkeeper to fetch me a bath last night."

Lila laughed, shaking her head. "Really, though. A Socialite? You're obviously not from around here."

"It's a long story," Justin said. "You wouldn't believe me if I told you."

"Well, now I want to know even more."

"Alas, I must maintain an air of mystery, at least for now. Suffice it to say, my class is powerful in the right hands."

"Okay, Mr. Socialite, here's a question for you. What happens when words fail and fists fly?"

Justin smirked, adjusting his pack. "That's why I hired you, isn't it? I trust you are handy with those knives and that spinning move you did wasn't all just for show."

"You sound skeptical. Bards are far more capable in combat than you might realize. I don't just play with knives; I can make them fly as true as any Ranger's arrow."

"Is that so? It isn't all just singing and dancing?"

"Well," she said with a smirk, "I *am* a wonderful singer."

"So, what is your class skill?"

"Bardic Inspiration. It lets me boost any attribute by +2, and it applies to the entire party."

"That sounds useful. What about your Level 1 skill?"

"Well, you get a class boon at Level 1, not a skill. Mine is called Artful Precision. It enhances my ability to play instruments and handle knives."

"Sounds fitting. So, what's the difference between a boon and a skill, anyway?"

She looked at him strangely. Again, he suspected he was asking a basic question most everyone knew. "Well, a skill is something you actively use, if that makes sense. Most of the time it has a cooldown, so you have to be careful when and how you use it. Boons, on the other hand, work in the background, giving you a benefit without you ever having to lift a finger."

"I see," Justin said, nodding. "One is active, and the other is passive."

"That's right," Lila said with a smile. "Though a smart person knows how to make the most of both."

He set his thoughts on Lila's character, and to his surprise, his interface opened to give him more information.

Lila Fairwind
    Class: Bard
    Level: 1

That was all there was to see; Justin dismissed the information.

"I put my first point in Coordination," Lila said. "That should help my accuracy."

"I invested in Charisma, because it doesn't seem like I have many options," Justin admitted. "But in case things get rough, it's good to know I have you at my side."

She grinned, clearly liking the compliment. "And don't you forget it! Still, I must admit, it'll be interesting to see how your...*unique* skill set comes into play."

At that moment, Justin got the oddest sense that Lila was

inspecting his character. He wasn't sure how the thought had entered his mind, but he was certain of it. It was like the feeling of someone looking at him from a distance, but stronger.

"So, what are your class abilities?" she asked.

"Poison Barb is my class skill," Justin said. "It lets me inflict emotional damage on someone. My boon is called Magnetic Presence. It basically makes people want to help me."

"Huh," Lila said, raising an eyebrow. "So *that's* why I volunteered to save your sorry ass."

Justin smirked. "You say that like you regret it."

She chuckled. "Give me a reason to, and we'll see." She tilted her head thoughtfully. "What is this 'emotional damage' anyway? Do you insult someone until they cry, or...?"

"It's like a stun," Justin said. "Consider it a punch right to the heart and soul of a person. It's pretty amazing to see it in action."

Lila shuddered. "I'd rather get in a fistfight than have to deal with that."

Justin looked ahead, finding that somehow, they had already passed through the gate. The vast expanse of the Silver Road stretched out before them. In the distance, the Umber Hills waited, rising low out of the misty forest. Justin hoped to make it there by nightfall.

Their banter faded as they left the city behind.

The Silver Road stretched out like a ribbon through the dense Wildwood, leading Justin and Lila to the opening of a narrow, steep-walled canyon as the late afternoon dragged on. The trees overhead formed a thick canopy, their branches intertwined, blocking most of the sunlight. The sun had been warm and bright earlier but was now subdued beneath this verdant canopy. The distant chirping of birds and the occasional rustling of leaves were the only sounds accompanying their footsteps.

As they approached the mouth of the canyon, Justin motioned for

Lila to stop. He pointed to a bend in the road up ahead, where muffled voices reached their ears. Silently, they crept closer to get a better view and soon found themselves behind a massive boulder, using it as a vantage point.

A group of rough-looking men, unmistakably highwaymen by their worn-out leather armor and crude weapons, had surrounded an elderly traveler. The man's horse stood nervously to the side, its saddlebags being rummaged through by one of the robbers.

In the corner of his vision, Justin spied an alert. He set his focus on it, and it opened of its own accord. His heart raced as he read the message contained within.

Quest Available: Rescue the Waylaid Traveler

Recommended Party Level: 4

Average Party Level: 1

Risk Level: Almost certainly fatal! Proceed only if you have a death wish.

Description: Highwaymen are robbing an elderly traveler on the Silver Road. Will you be the beacon of hope in these perilous times and stand up against the oppressors? This quest is high-risk, but with significant risk comes a glorious reward.

Experience Points: 500

Rewards: Whatever items the robbers carry, plus any potential bounties on their heads.

Justin nearly gawked at those rewards. It would be enough to put him at Level 2 and then some, and the amount of loot could be quite a bit, likely far more than his current job.

Before he could tap the alert and accept, Lila grabbed his wrist, pulling it away.

"Are you *insane*?" she whispered. "There are four of them, and they look like they've been doing this for a while. We'd be killed!"

"But we can't just let them rob and hurt that man," Justin whispered back, torn between his sense of justice and the danger in front of him.

"I know, it's a hard thing to watch. But *one* dead is better than *three* dead. And I don't think your Poison Barb or my knives will be much use against those broadswords."

Justin immediately saw her point. This wasn't just a game. As far as he could tell, there were real consequences here. If he died, he *really died*. This might be his only chance at life. The will to live was a powerful thing, and Justin felt fear clutching his throat.

He decided, perhaps, given the circumstances, that it was best to stay on the sidelines.

The scene in front of them took a grim turn. After snatching all the man's valuables, one highwayman roughly pushed the traveler to the ground. Another unsheathed his dagger and, with a swift motion, ended the old man's life. It was quick and methodical. Clearly, they had killed before, and this group might even be the source of all the missing couriers.

The shock of witnessing the cold-blooded murder left Justin frozen, his mouth agape. The brutal reality of it hit him hard; this was clearly no game, but a ruthless environment where death lurked around every corner.

Lila's hushed whisper pulled Justin out of his daze. "We need to retreat. Now."

Without waiting for his reply, she turned and made her way deeper into the woods, away from the Silver Road. Justin, still trying to process what he had just witnessed, followed her.

They walked in silence for what felt like hours but was probably closer to minutes. The approaching dusk painted the sky with dark purples and blues.

Lila finally stopped in a small clearing, hidden by thick foliage. "We'll set up camp here for the night. We're far enough from the road, and those brutes won't find us in the darkness."

"Hopefully," Justin managed.

As they started setting up a makeshift camp, Justin spoke, his voice tinged with guilt. "We should have done something."

Lila looked up, her green eyes softening. "In a perfect world, maybe. But you've got to choose your battles. We wouldn't have stood a chance. I'm only Level 1, for the gods' sake. And you..." She paused. "Well, you have no fighting abilities at all, sorry. You hired me to protect you, and that's exactly what I'm doing."

Justin sat down, feeling the weight of the world on his shoulders. "This world...it's so *real*. The violence, the fear, the blood...I wasn't prepared for this! What happens if you get killed? Do you respawn somewhere, at least?"

Lila gave him a confused look. "Resurrection, you mean? Well, true resurrection isn't possible. But certain classes, like White Wizards, get powerful healing spells. It's said their magic can take even the smallest spark and fan it back to life. But as for what happens after...well, as an Adherent of the Light, those who place faith in the Creator and the Six Gods, and behave justly, will ascend to the Aether Realm upon death. Those who do not—like those men back there—are doomed to spend eternity in the Nether with Morvath, the God of Death. Others say it's all nonsense, and there is nothing but the Great Silence that cannot be heard. Whatever the case...I'm not ready to find out."

Justin remained quiet, not sure what to say. He could only assume, from the man's dying screams, that the pain was indeed very real. It solidified for him that this was a real place. A place where nature and the System itself, or its creators, were impartial observers and imposed their own rules over reality.

Of course, there was the third option he wasn't ready to entirely discount. That he was in a coma, or in some weird sort of purgatory he might wake up from someday. But with each passing hour, this idea seemed more unlikely. What dream was as realistic as this?

Lila offered a reassuring smile. "Look, every choice we make, whether to fight or flee, changes our path. The important thing is to learn and adapt. We survived today, and tomorrow we'll be smarter, stronger, and better prepared. We have our whole lives ahead of us. Let's not get caught up on something that was impossible to deal with."

Justin nodded, but of course, it was hard to be satisfied with that answer, even if he knew she was right. "That voice that talked to me when I got my class, when I leveled up...who is that?"

Lila watched him curiously. "Where did you say you were from?"

"I hit my head pretty badly a couple of days ago," Justin explained. "Plus, I just got my class."

The excuse sounded lame, especially since he had no visible injuries, but thankfully, Lila seemed to accept it. "That's the Voice of Veyrith. Normally it's just called 'the Voice.' Veyrith is one of the Three Manifestations of the Creator. Basically, anyone who has a class and access to the Aethereal Interface can hear it when you gain a new level."

"Yes, but why? Why are there classes and levels to begin with? Where does it all come from?"

"Well, all that's in the *Book of Life*. The Voice tests everyone with a class so that they can become stronger. So their cores can transcend the Mortal Realm through trial and choice."

The way she said that made Justin feel like she was reciting something. Something repeated so often that the words had completely lost their meaning. But for someone like him, it seemed like something very important.

The best he could figure it, leveling up was some form of spiritual purification. Hell if he knew.

Justin wanted to ask for more information, but Lila was already suspicious of him. Whatever questions he had, it was best to ask them slowly, over time. If he told her something completely crazy, like being from an entirely alternate reality, there was no telling how she might react.

Once again, getting access to a library would need to be one of his top priorities, so he could research things in peace without raising anyone's suspicion.

As night drew in around them, they opted not to build a fire, for obvious reasons. They just had to hope no monsters or unwelcome creatures found their way into their camp. Justin's stomach growled; he hadn't had a bite since lunch that day.

"I'll take first watch," Justin said. "No way both of us can sleep with those ruffians out there."

"No argument from me. I'm beat."

As Lila drifted off to sleep, Justin wondered how she could do it so easily. It seemed that death in this world was a constant companion, where the very act of reaching the age of twenty was a triumph, and much more than that, gaining a class.

It was enough to shift his perspective, at least somewhat.

The sounds of the Wildwood surrounded them, a symphony of the untamed wilderness. Justin found himself wondering about Lila. Like him, she must have just gained her class too, being only Level 1. What was her story? What was she doing in that Mercenary Guild, anyway?

He supposed those were questions that would have to be answered another time.

7

THE STAR OF ELARA

"The Star of Elara is the most famous tale to come out of Daeloria. Every year, would-be heroes don their armor and gather their companions, all in pursuit of the legendary Ascendant Artifact. Of course, for most, it's less about the artifact and more about an excuse to drink, brawl, and swap exaggerated tales of bravery. Yet, even as centuries pass, the allure of the Star endures, a beacon of hope—or hubris—that refuses to fade."

—Scholar Bela Nefar,
 Legends That Never Die

BY SOME MIRACLE, Justin stayed awake for the first watch, waiting about four hours before waking up Lila. Thankfully, she didn't complain, and he fell into a fitful sleep.

When morning came, he felt as if he had been hit by a truck. They had walked some fifteen miles out of town, and that wasn't counting the backtracking they had done.

Justin just wanted to sleep, but he knew they had a decision to make.

"If we keep going," Lila said, "we can't use the road. It seems those bandits went into the woods to the east. Right now, we're west of the road. Therefore, if we go south a few miles, we should come back onto the road and avoid any nasty fights."

"But how will we not lose our way?"

"Don't you have your map?"

"Yes, of course. I'd forgotten."

"We'll use that. Make sure we're heading due south until we're well past that canyon. Then we'll head east until we hit the road. Then we'll head south again, toward Silverton."

"Sounds like a plan."

They packed up their camp and began the day's journey. The walk was grueling, especially given Justin's exhaustion and the endless hills and foliage.

To enliven their spirits, Lila began singing, despite the risk of being overheard. Justin had to admit she had a sweet voice, somewhat thin and trilling, and striking chords in his heart. He couldn't help but have a little extra pep in his step. He wondered if it was her Bardic Inspiration ability and if she had chosen to enhance their endurance attribute.

A quick look at his character revealed that yes, indeed, his endurance attribute was now 12. While the rest of the numbers were black, endurance was green, likely to show that it was being modified by Lila's skill.

But then, after silence, Lila's voice took on darker tones as it spilled forth into a new song, weaving a tale of ancient love and loss. She sang of Elara, a radiant beauty whose presence enchanted Alden, a brave warrior. Alden promised Elara the Sapphire Star of Eyrth, a celestial gem of unmatched splendor. After a year-long quest, Alden returned triumphant with the Star, but their joy was short-lived. As they journeyed to Alden's homeland, they were ambushed by ruthless highwaymen. Alden fought valiantly, but in the chaos, Elara unleashed the Star's magic to save him, only for him to be struck down by a treacherous blow from one of the bandits he believed was dead. With his last words, he claimed that though the Star was broken, he would always keep her safe.

Elara continued on, guided by Alden's love and the remnants of the Star's power. She was ambushed by a cave troll in the Seraphim Range, and her prayer to the heavens was answered by a new star flaring to life in the sky above. With renewed strength, she vanquished the troll and found solace under the guiding star, now known as Elara's Star. This celestial beacon, Alden's promise of protection, led her to a place of peace, where she lived out the rest of her days, where the Star was buried with her.

When Lila's voice faded, it was nearly half an hour later, and Justin marveled at the picture that had been painted in his mind. It was almost as if he were watching a movie, but the melody of Lila's voice made it far more emotive.

A tear, unbidden, fell from his eye. "What was that song?"

"It's called "The Star of Elara." A very old, very famous story from my homeland. You can still see Elara's Star to this day. It's the brightest one in the night sky, and it points directly north. Useful if you ever lose your way."

"You've got a gift for singing."

Lila smiled. "Thank you. Some of it is the class, but I've always been told I'm a good singer."

"Well, *is* the story true? Is there really a Sapphire Star of Earth somewhere to be found? It sounds like it could be a powerful amulet of protection."

"Some go hunting for it," Lila said. "I have no doubt it exists somewhere. But in these darker days, very few adventure for it in particular. My country, Daeloria, used to host an annual festival where Hunters of the Star would set out every year. Mostly an excuse for adventurers to go off and carouse, but some truly wanted to find it. Most go searching for the Star in Kurath, the land where Elara is said to be buried. The story is at least a thousand years old, and probably more. If it has been found, none have said anything about it."

"I'm sure the Star is worth a fortune!"

"No doubt. But it's probably better to set our sights on more attainable goals. Like finishing this job."

"Of course," Justin said.

It grew quiet after that. Soon after the song ended, Justin felt his limbs grow tired. The going was slow, and it wasn't until late after-noon that they got back on the Silver Road, weaving its way through the hilly, forested landscape. The pair quickened their pace.

"There's an inn and a hamlet on the other side of these hills," Lila said. "In normal circumstances, travelers can reach Whispering Pines from Mistwatch with a single day of hard walking, and then get to Silverton the next day. As it stands, it seems the inn is the only safe place we can stay tonight."

"How much will it cost? I only have a few coppers left."

"Well, that's hard to say. The room and two meals will be at least sixty coppers. Maybe you can try to talk it down a bit with that silver tongue of yours."

"Or maybe you could sing to get us a discount," Justin said.

"Perhaps," Lila said. "It wouldn't be the first time."

Thankfully, they made it to the top of the hills without incident. Once they crested the rise, the misty Wildwood spread before them, and down a few switchbacks stood a cozy-looking inn with yellow-lit windows and a steeply thatched roof. Smoke curled out of the chimney, promising a warm fire. Such was Justin's hunger that the savory smell of stew and freshly baked bread set his mouth to salivating.

As they approached, Justin noted the wooden placard swinging in the cool breeze. "The Whispering Pine," it proclaimed in fanciful letters. Apparently, the inn's name was the same as the hamlet's. Even from outside the door, he could hear the mumble of voices beyond.

The pair entered. The inn's atmosphere was quite different from the Drunken Pixie back in Mistwatch. Instead of merriment and music, hushed conversations filled the room. The central topic soon became clear as they made their way to a table close to the bar.

"...brutally killed, right on the Silver Road!" one man proclaimed.

"He was a regular here, was he not?" a woman's voice asked.

"A regular? Brennan was my brother!" another woman squawked.

"...highwaymen getting bolder by the day! By Arion, what is Aran-thia coming to?"

The innkeeper, a pot-bellied man with mutton chops,

approached. "Evening. Were you two traveling on the Silver Road yesterday from Mistwatch?"

While his tone was curious, Justin caught the concern on his face.

Justin hesitated, deciding honesty was the best policy. "Yes, we were."

Whispers filled the room as more patrons turned their attention to the newcomers.

A stout woman with graying hair tied in a bun stood up. "Then you must have seen something! My brother was murdered. They left his body there on the road, the devils! Tell me you saw those responsible!"

Justin swallowed hard, feeling the weight of the room's eyes on him. He would have to play this delicately. "We...we didn't see the actual event. We heard voices and hid. I'm a courier, you see, new to the area. I was warned the road was dangerous, so I didn't want to take any chances."

The woman looked at him incredulously. "So, you saw *nothing*? *Did* nothing?"

"Well, not nothing," Justin said, realizing he'd have to give her at least something, or it would look suspicious. "We saw them leaving after...after they did what they did. Being just the two of us, we didn't want to get involved. We feared for our own lives. There were four of them, all well-armed with broadswords and leather armor."

Another man stepped forward, narrowing his eyes. His brown hair was styled in such a way, complete with a red cap, that Justin couldn't help but think of Lord Farquaad from *Shrek*.

"If you were on that road around that time, you must've seen something more than that!" the man demanded. "Are you sure you didn't recognize anyone?"

"They are new to the area," another woman interjected. "Remember?"

Lila spoke, her voice firm. "We understand your pain and anger. It seems this man—Brennan—was well-liked. But we truly didn't see anything beyond what we've just told you. Like any sensible person, we hid. It all happened so fast."

A tall figure stood up from the back of the room, dressed in a dark green robe embroidered with intricate patterns of silver vines. Over his shoulder, a quiver of black-feathered arrows was visible, complementing the longsword with an ornate hilt at his belt.

"Enough," the stranger said, his voice deep and gravelly. "The blame lies with the highwaymen, not these travelers. Accusations won't bring the dead back. They did what any of you would have done, and that's a fact."

The room was silent, save for the crackling of the fire.

The innkeeper cleared his throat and turned to Justin and Lila. "Apologies for the...interrogation. Emotions are high. Still, if you need a room, we have the space. I'll give you a special discounted rate. Half off. Just for tonight. That's thirty-six coppers for the room and two meals. Least I can do for the information, as little as it is."

"There's something more, now that I remember it," Justin said, realizing that giving any useful information might get them a free room. "We think we went off into the woods by that canyon, heading east. We got past them by doubling back and heading west off the road. We lost a whole day's progress because of it."

"That would put them out by Raven's Rock!" one man exclaimed.

"I don't know this area too well," Justin said. "Just thought that the info might be useful."

"We're grateful for anything," the innkeeper said.

"I'll be reporting that to the county sheriff," the woman said, the sister of the murdered man. "It's something!"

Unfortunately, the innkeeper didn't seem to have a mind to give them the room for free, but he had already left and was bringing back a couple of pints. "Thanks again. I know it's not much, but these drinks are on the house. Hopefully, justice will come of this."

[You have gained 6 experience points. Your experience stands at 30/200.]

Justin wondered for a moment why he'd gained experience until he realized that he'd navigated quite a prickly conversation. He'd balanced giving just enough information to satisfy them while not giving too much to make people suspicious of him and Lila. And he'd also defended their decision not to get involved, even convincing that stranger in the corner to side with them.

His Magnetic Presence boon was helping him once again, perhaps. Maybe being a Socialite had its perks.

He took a swig of the cool lager, feeling it was well-earned.

"Well," Lila said, "if you hand me eighteen coppers, I can go settle up with the innkeeper. I'm heading to bed. It's been a long couple of days."

Lila left to do just that, letting him know before she turned in that they were in room six, handing him a spare key.

Justin looked over in the corner, where the green-cloaked man was now smoking a pipe. Justin gave a grateful nod, which the man acknowledged and returned.

Justin wasn't going to stay long, not really relishing the thought of conversation when the stranger sidled over to his table. The man was tall and lean, with weathered skin that spoke of years in the sun and wind. His hazel eyes were sharp, and his dark brown hair was streaked with gray. He had a trimmed beard, and scars ran down his left cheek, hinting at past battles. To Justin, he was quite imposing.

The stranger took a moment to look Justin over, sizing him up. "You handled yourself well tonight. Few can navigate the emotions of a room with such...*precision*."

Justin raised an eyebrow. "Thanks for standing up for us."

The man chuckled. "Well, we Rangers have a way of seeing the bigger picture. Like you, I'm a stranger to these parts."

"I appreciate it," Justin replied.

The Ranger leaned in, his voice lowering. "The name's Eldrin."

"Justin."

"Pleased to meet you. I've been tracking these highwaymen for a while. By the Nether, they've become bolder with each passing moon."

Justin nodded. "From what we experienced, it's clear they are not just ordinary bandits."

"You're right. They're organized, have a leader, and worse, they're growing in number."

"Why are they allowed to exist like this? It seems like someone should have taken them out by now."

"Well, you're right. But we live in strange times. The mayor of Silverton has his hands full preparing for the upcoming autumn festival. He has a vested interest in keeping any hint of danger away from the public ear to ensure merchants and visitors still come. As for the Sheriff... let's just say his loyalties lie with those who line his pockets the most."

Justin frowned. "You're saying the bandits are paying him off?"

"Gods, no! I'm saying he couldn't give a flying fig unless someone were to light a fire under his arse. Trust me, that fire is not forthcoming. A lot of money flows out of Silverton. And money has the power to corrupt."

"I can see that."

"Point being, the roads will remain dangerous as long as those bandits are out there. Now, I've been planning to take them out for quite some time, but doing so alone would be risky, even for someone of my experience. You and your friend could be valuable allies. I perceive that you both have a class."

Justin wondered how he knew that. Maybe Rangers had some keen sense of insight not available to others.

Justin hesitated, taking a deep breath. "Look, Eldrin. I appreciate the confidence, but I'm a Level 1 Socialite. My skills involve persuasion and navigating social scenarios, not battle. Lila's just a Level 1 Bard. Are you sure we're the help you're looking for?"

Eldrin regarded him, seeming to size him up. "Well, once you've had as many years as I have under your belt, you learn that level isn't always a measure of potential. You navigated tonight with aplomb. With the right guidance and strategy, even a Level 1 can make a significant difference. And Lila might be a Bard, but I can tell she has the heart and spirit of a fighter. With my experience and your combined potential, we could bring these highwaymen to justice."

Justin looked into Eldrin's eyes, trying to gauge the depth of his belief. He thought of the parcel he was supposed to deliver.

"There will almost certainly be a reward," Eldrin went on. "I'm keeping my eyes on the quest board over yonder. With the information you shared tonight, it's only a matter of time before something becomes available."

He gave a nod toward the wall, a bulletin board filled with quests, bounties, and various odd jobs. A reward would be nice, but then he recalled the fear he had felt hiding from the highwaymen, the weight of the room's eyes on him, and the hopelessness of the woman who had lost her brother. It was by no means an easy decision.

But at last, he decided. The parcel could wait.

"Well, I can't speak for Lila. But if she's in, I'm in."

"Glad to hear it. Let me know in the morning. Sleep on it."

Eldrin left the table, heading upstairs to his room. Justin headed that way a few minutes later.

Justin turned the key in the brass handle. As he walked into the room, closed the door, and dropped off his things, to his surprise, Lila was lounging in a copper tub in the middle of the room.

Startled, he spun away. "Lila! Sorry, I didn't know—"

"Didn't know what?"

"That you were…"

He was about to say "naked and taking a bath," but it seemed she didn't get the point.

He cleared his throat. "Sorry. It's just that where I'm from, things are a bit…different."

She laughed, finally understanding. "Oh, I see. My mother always told me the people in Aranthia were a bit more conservative. Prudish, even."

"Prudish? It's not that. It's just…" He trailed off, not sure where he was going with this. Maybe she was right.

"In Daeloria, shared bathing spaces are common," Lila explained.

"I grew up with three brothers in cramped quarters. Privacy was a luxury we couldn't afford. Sometimes in bigger inns, they might have a separate bathhouse or bathroom that is segregated. But a small country inn like this? Almost never."

Justin took a breath. After all, he was in a new world with different customs, and they had just witnessed a murder together. He supposed such experiences tended to accelerate bonds between people. He supposed he should feel good that Lila trusted him to this extent.

Besides, this was hardly the strangest thing he had encountered since arriving here. He had seen *literal magic.*

He set his pack down, half-turning so that he could see her from the edge of his vision. "I talked to that man downstairs who spoke up for us. His name is Eldrin, and he's a Ranger. He has an interesting idea."

"What idea?"

Justin quickly recapped Eldrin's proposition to go after the highwaymen at Raven's Rock.

From Lila's face, Justin instantly knew she didn't like the idea. "Sounds risky. Are you sure that's smart? We barely escaped them last time, remember? Both of us are just Level 1. And we don't even know this Eldrin. How can we trust him?"

"He reminds me of someone I know."

"Who?"

"Aragorn, son of Arathorn."

"Ara-corn? What kind of name is that?"

"Never mind. Lila, how do you expect to level up if you never take risks?"

Lila's green eyes narrowed. "Careful with your words."

Without warning, she stood and reached for a nearby towel in one fluid motion. Justin politely averted his gaze until she had wrapped it around herself. Such was her matter-of-factness about it that he was starting to accept it as normal.

"The innkeeper only brought one tub of hot water," she said, gesturing to the bath. "You should use it before it gets cold."

She gave a slight smile. "After the day we've had, you could use it."

Justin considered this. In his old life, he would have been paralyzed by social awkwardness, but here, practicality and survival took precedence over discomfort. "Makes sense. No point in wasting warm water."

"I'll turn around," she offered, already moving to face away.

"Thanks," he said simply.

He made sure she was really looking away before undressing. He'd been overweight for most of his life, and it was always something he was insecure about. Lila was the exact opposite.

But it seemed all the body shame that existed in his own world, reinforced by mass media, was far more absent here.

It was a silver lining, however small.

He settled into the bath, finding it surprisingly soothing. It was exactly what he needed. He cleaned himself efficiently and dressed in some fresh clothes he had purchased in Mistwatch.

"All done," he said.

"We should catch some rest. We have a long walk ahead of us tomorrow."

She blew out the candle and rolled over in bed.

As Justin made himself as comfortable as possible on the floor, he reflected on how quickly he was adapting to this world's differences. Perhaps it was a necessity, or perhaps it was the strange bond forming between him and Lila after their shared experiences.

He cleared his throat. "Think about Eldrin's offer. We might do some real good and get some experience to boot."

It was a moment before she answered. "I'll think about it. But don't hold out hope. We have a job to do, remember? One that's practically guaranteed not to kill us."

Justin realized she had a point, but all the same, he hoped she would agree with him.

He didn't have the chance to think about it much longer because he fell asleep.

8

THE RANGER'S PROPOSITION

"Rangers are more than bow-wielding hunters. They are survivalists, pathfinders, and watchers of the wild. In the end, it is not the sharpness of their arrows but the sharpness of their instincts that keeps them and their party alive."

—Perseus Dalvik,
    Ranger of the Verdant Expanse

THE MORNING SUNLIGHT crept through the windows of the inn's common room, where Justin and Lila had seated themselves at a secluded table, their breakfast of fried eggs and toast on plates in front of them.

Eldrin wasted no time as soon as he came down the stairs, completely outfitted with his pack, bow, and longsword. He sidled up next to Lila on the bench.

"Eldrin Thornwood," he said with a winning smile. "I trust you've heard about my noble plan?"

Lila speared her toast with her fork, her eyes thoughtful. "I've heard about it, but I still have reservations."

"Well, I hope to put those to rest. I have much to say about the subject, and by the end, I think we can come to an agreement."

"We'll see about that," Lila said doubtfully.

Justin took a sip of coffee from his mug. "I'm all in. But if Lila wants us to keep moving, well, I won't lose sleep over it."

Eldrin said nothing about this; instead, he watched Lila for her reaction.

Her gaze was still uncertain. "I'm just a Level 1 Bard, Eldrin. I don't have the skills or the equipment to take on a group of dangerous men. This is too much, even if it comes with a reward."

Eldrin nodded, taking a moment to consider his words. "It's not just about the potential rewards, Lila. These highwaymen are causing chaos and pain to the county. The Mayor's too caught up with the coming festival, and the Sheriff? Well, I have my doubts about his intentions. We might be the only chance this hamlet has. Not to mention the dozen men and women that have disappeared over the past couple of months."

"You're appealing to the wrong thing," Lila said. "I'm very practical, and others' troubles don't trouble me. What's the reward for risking my neck?"

Eldrin smiled. "Thought you might ask that. Thanks to Justin's intelligence, the good innkeeper had enough information to make an official report to the Silverton Mercenary Guild. It is now an official bounty, tacked onto every quest board in the county, and maybe even outside of it. All the families of the victims have come together, and the reward for justice served is generous. And by fate or the gods' will, we are probably the closest party in a position to seal the deal. Yes, there's a risk with you both being at such a low level. But nothing ventured, nothing gained. Trust me, now that this is out there, these bandits won't last too much longer."

"As if I need further convincing," Justin said. "How much is the bounty?"

Eldrin smiled. "Eighty silver marks."

Lila's eyes widened. "Eighty marks? That's..."

"A lot," Justin finished.

Eighty silvers was sixteen times the amount the courier job was going to pay. True, the reward would be split among the three of them, but even so, it would go a long way to securing Justin's position in this new world.

"Here's what I'm thinking," Eldrin said. "Given my expertise and the fact I'll be pulling most of the weight, it's only fair, upon completion, that I get fifty. Each of you can have fifteen."

"That's not fair at all!" Lila said. "We're risking just as much as you! Maybe more since we're only level 1."

"Well, it has to be worth *my* time as well," Eldrin said. "Simply, this is a job I could do on my own. It wouldn't be as easy, but there it is. This job will take a solid two or three days to complete."

Each of them looked at Justin, wanting his opinion.

"Whatever's fair or not, what's important is that everyone feels valued," Justin said. "I understand your position, Eldrin. As you said, you will do most of the work. I'm a Socialite, so there's little I can do but lob insults at our enemies. However, it's premature to say we won't be doing as much work as you. No one knows how this will turn out, and it's quite possible it's far more dangerous than we realize. Lila is right. Since we are at lower levels, the risk to us is much greater. By that metric, perhaps we should get more."

Eldrin stroked his chin. "Yes, you have something of a point there, Socialite. But the fact remains, I'm the one who came up with the idea, and I will do most of the work. Can either of you bring yourselves to kill, even when you're in the right?"

Both Justin and Lila were silent at this.

Eldrin continued, "Fifty silvers is fair compensation for my role."

"But it's also important to keep everyone happy," Justin pressed. "And my instinct tells me you need our help, because I doubt you're purely doing us a favor. Maybe you can take half the bounty, while Lila and I split the rest."

Eldrin took a moment to think it over before guffawing. "Well, you have something of a point, too. It's not something I'd normally do, but as you said, it's important that everyone be happy with the arrangement. And time is pressing down on us. I'll concede. I'll take forty, with the remaining forty being yours and Lila's to split."

From Lila's expression, she didn't seem happy about this, but Justin agreed readily. "Deal."

"I'm glad that's worked out. However, I'm concerned about the potential for conflict over the loot if we don't hash out an agreement ahead of time. Assuming we succeed in our venture, whatever the robbers possess becomes ours. Absent any identifying information or core binding, it will be impossible to track down the original owners."

Justin assumed "core binding" meant items that were explicitly attached by the System, or gods, to an original owner, making them unusable for others unless, perhaps, that owner was deceased.

"That's a fair point," Justin conceded. "Assuming we can't agree, you'll get half the value of whatever loot we find, while Lila and I split the remaining half."

"That's a compromise," Lila said. "The fairest option is to split three ways, levels be damned."

"And while we argue about it," Eldrin said, "another party will nab the prize."

"A fair point," Justin said.

Lila seemed to consider for a moment, weighing her options.

"If we can come to an agreement," Eldrin said, "Justin will need a proper weapon. Perhaps you don't gain experience from fights, like Lila and me, but it's essential you have something to defend yourself with. I still have my old dagger; it's been with me through many battles. It's still in great shape, and a good weapon for a Socialite, at least until you can get a cane. You can have it."

Justin was touched. "Thank you, Eldrin."

He frowned in thought for a moment. A cane? Was his class supposed to be like a pimp or something, complete with a feather jacket and scarf? He put the thought aside for now.

"Now wait a minute," Lila said. "I still haven't agreed to anything!"

"An equal distribution of half the bounty," Justin said. "That gives each of us twenty silvers. Just imagine what can be done with that money, Lila."

Her green eyes became glazed as she imagined the possibilities before she seemed to think better of herself. "No use for money if you're dead."

"With Eldrin, we are in capable hands."

"It's the question of the big reward or the sure thing," Lila said. "Yes, I can throw knives in a pinch, but I'm supposed to be singing and spinning tales by the fire, not fighting!"

Justin realized that her hesitancy was less about fairness and more about confronting her fears. "I thought you said Bards were as good with knives as they are with music."

"I...I was just trying to sell my services! Which brings me to my main point. My job is to protect you, Justin. Which is exactly what I'm trying to do. That means keeping us out of fights and away from... strangers." She looked at Eldrin. "No offense."

"It's a fair point," Eldrin said with an amused smile. "I'm not well-known around here, but I've done a few jobs for the innkeeper. Ask him if you need a reference."

"Look. I understand it's risky," Justin said. "But this is a way to do some good *and* get paid for it. Imagine what you can do with that money, Lila."

Lila looked from Eldrin to Justin and back. Justin gave what he hoped was a reassuring smile.

Lila let out a breath. "I feel out of my depth. But...it seems Justin is sure about this, and the money *would* be nice. It would solve a lot of my problems." Finally, she smiled. "All right, you've got me. Eldrin gets half, Justin and I split the rest. When do we start?"

A blue notification ticked in Justin's vision.

[You have gained 4 experience points. Your experience stands at 34/200.]

Justin blinked at the message. Another negotiation handled with care.

"We leave now," Eldrin said, answering Lila's question. "When I join your party, you'll get the benefit of my party tactic, Pathfinder's Pace. Then we head for Raven's Rock."

"What does Pathfinder's Pace do?" Justin asked.

"Rangers have a natural affinity for traveling faster in the wilds, knowing just where to step for maximum speed. I think you'll find we'll be going just as fast through the wilds as on the roads, and sometimes even faster. You'll also be able to walk farther without rest."

"That's amazing," Lila said.

"What's a party tactic?" Justin asked.

"You unlock it at Level 5," Eldrin said, watching him closely. "It's basically like a boon, but it benefits the entire party. Party tactics upgrade automatically every ten levels after they're first adopted."

"I see," Justin said.

Eldrin shrugged. "It's the gods' way of getting us to work together, I suppose."

"Like a Paladin's Divine Aura," Justin said, proud that he actually knew something for once.

"Exactly like that."

"All right," Lila said. "Let's join up. Although Justin is currently the party leader."

Justin realized it was on him to invite Eldrin to join, and not only that, but to take over the party. He did so simply with a thought.

[Eldrin has joined the party and assumed the role of party leader. You now benefit from the expertise of his Pathfinder's Pace. Eldrin has shared a bounty.]

Bounty Received: Highway Justice

    Recommended Level: 4

    Party Level: 4

    Risk Level: Normal. Your party is suitably equipped to handle this bounty.

    Details: Recent reports show a group of highwaymen causing chaos in the county. They were last seen heading toward Raven's

Rock. A generous bounty has been posted by the Silverton Mercenary Guild, and families of victims have pooled their resources. The reward stands at eighty silvers for the capture or dispatch of the bandits.

Experience: 250 (500 if you capture the bandit leader, to be brought to the Mercenary Guild in Silverton for inspection).

Bounty: 80 silver marks to be divided among the party.

Loot: Whatever items the robbers carry.

"All right," Eldrin said. "Let's go after those bandits."

Justin grinned, relieved that Lila was on board. She gave a nervous smile.

As they walked out of the inn and into the cool morning air, Justin couldn't help but feel a bit excited. Yesterday, things had seemed all too real. Even if he knew this world was real now, it felt like a game at the moment.

And not only that, but the experience. Completing the bounty would easily put him at Level 2, while the harder option of apprehending the leader and bringing him to the Mercenary Guild would impart 500 experience points, which might even be enough to put him at Level 3.

They started north up the road, backtracking the way they had come.

And that was when something shot out of the sky and straight for Justin.

9

AMBUSH AT RAVEN'S ROCK

"In days of yore, the Silver Road was a mighty highway, stretching proudly from Silverton to Eribar. Along its length stood many prosperous towns, their markets bustling and their banners flying high. But now? Now it is little more than a dusty track, winding through ruins, trees, bandit camps, and the occasional hamlet clinging to life. The Silver Road is a somber tale, a stark reminder that the prosperity of today can wither into the poverty of tomorrow. Time, after all, is the only road with no end."

—Chronicler Ellisar Vain,
Echoes of Forgotten Glory

THAT SOMETHING soon revealed itself to be a bird of midnight black, its dark form cutting through the sunlight before alighting on Eldrin's shoulder. Its black feathers shimmered with hues of dark blue and purple, giving it an almost mystical appearance.

Both Justin and Lila watched the magnificent animal with awe, which looked at them both with its intelligent eyes.

"Shadowflight," Eldrin introduced, stroking the falcon's head tenderly. The bird nuzzled him. The bond between the two was obvious.

"You have a falcon?" Justin asked.

"Just as he has me," Eldrin said with pride, as they continued their way up the road. "Shadowflight is my bonded animal. Most Rangers get the privilege of choosing to bond with a wild creature. That creature becomes an extension of ourselves, sharing in our senses and even our emotions."

"I knew that about animal bonds," Lila said, "though I've never seen it in action."

Justin couldn't help but feel a pang of jealousy, looking at the bird, equal parts beauty and deadliness. He doubted he'd ever have a cool ability like that.

He set his mind on Eldrin's character, and some basic information popped up.

Eldrin Thornwood
    Class: Ranger
    Level: 10

Justin wondered if there was a way to see his boons and abilities, but despite trying, it didn't seem like it was possible.

"So, what kind of skills do you have?" Justin asked.

Eldrin looked at him matter-of-factly. "I have a mix of skills related to archery, pathfinding, trap detection, and potion-making. The Ranger is something of an eclectic mix, but it is useful for making a life in the wilds."

"I see," Justin said, impressed. "And will it be enough to deal with these bandits?"

"Of that, I have no doubt. I think it might be a good idea, at least temporarily, for us to form a party pact with one another."

"A party pact?" Justin asked. "What's that?"

"It's a formal agreement forged through the interface. It will allow us to better see each other's abilities and attributes. That way, we know what everyone in the party is fully capable of."

"Sounds like a good idea," Lila said. "Although Justin and I each have only one skill and boon."

"No matter," Eldrin said. "It will still be useful. And at any point, you can retract the agreement if you want to go your own way."

"I see," Justin said. "Let's do it then."

[Eldrin would like to form a party pact with you. Do you accept?]

Justin accepted with a mental push.

[Party pact formed with Eldrin Thornwood. You may now inspect Eldrin in greater detail.]

Justin did so immediately.

Eldrin Thornwood
    Class: Ranger
    Level: 10

Attributes:
    Power: 10
    Coordination: 15
    Endurance: 12
    Intellect: 13
    Spirit: 10
    Charisma: 10

Abilities:
    Skills: Ranger's Insight (0), Eagle Eye (2), Nature's Cloak (3), Hunter's Mark (7)
    Boons: Ranger's Intuition (1), Animal Bond (4), Nature's Bounty (6), Botanical Insight (9), Survival Instinct (10)
    Party Tactic: Pathfinder's Pace

Justin thought the information over. It seemed that even with the pact, he could not get specific information about each ability he had.

Still, it was easy to imagine Eldrin's uses simply based on the ability names. It seemed he got a mix of ranged combat bonuses, a stealth ability, plus things that helped him and his party survive in the wild. In short, it only reaffirmed Justin's decision to join him.

Eldrin continued leading the group northwest as morning passed into early afternoon. Once well past the hills, Eldrin veered eastward, entering the thick of the forest. Now things felt less like a game and more like reality. Those bandits had melted into these woods just yesterday.

As they moved, Justin felt a lightness in his step, realizing that despite the thick underbrush and uneven terrain, they were traversing the wilds as easily as they would a well-trodden path.

"You have a knack for picking the best way forward," Justin mused.

Eldrin chuckled. "That's my Pathfinder's Pace for you."

"You said that, but now I'm really believing it. Even my pack feels lighter."

Eldrin lapsed into silence. It probably wasn't wise to speak so loudly when danger was getting closer. Lila seemed more alert, always having a hand on the hilt of one of her throwing knives.

Without warning, by a stand of pines, Eldrin stopped in his tracks, raising a hand to halt the others. He bent down, brushing aside some reeds to reveal a large pit, its floor lined with wickedly sharp spikes.

"A common bandit trap," he whispered. "A single misstep, and one could find oneself impaled."

Justin shivered, thankful for Eldrin's sharp senses. With a gentle whistle, Shadowflight took to the skies, disappearing from sight.

"We'll let him scout ahead," Eldrin said.

"Now what?" Lila asked.

Eldrin held up a hand. Lila's voice had carried farther than she had probably intended.

He nodded toward some underbrush just a few steps away. "Over there."

They followed the Ranger, waiting in the gathering darkness without saying a word.

Minutes later, Shadowflight returned, landing deftly on Eldrin's arm without a single sound. Eldrin closed his eyes for a moment, his face a mask of concentration. Justin could tell he was communing with the animal.

"Four of them," he murmured. "Just as you said, Justin. They're camped out by Raven's Rock, cooking their evening meal."

Justin and Lila exchanged glances. The sun was descending, casting a golden hue over the landscape. Nightfall wasn't far off.

"They're half a mile from here. We can speak a bit more freely, though you would be shocked at how far sound carries in the Wildwood. It's a quiet forest, and the outcrops of rock can produce echoes that only amplify sound."

"What's the plan?" Justin asked quietly.

"We'll use the cover of night to our advantage. Shadowflight can distract them from above while I use my Nature's Cloak skill to approach undetected. I then set up a good ambush point and ensure my first hit lands true on their leader." He looked at Justin. "That's part of the reason I wanted you here. I need you to tell me what he looks like."

Justin hesitated for a moment, the image of the bandit leader forming clearly in his mind. "He's tall and broad-shouldered. He has a long, unkempt beard that's streaked with gray. A scar runs from his temple to his jaw."

Both Eldrin and Lila watched him, impressed. Even Justin was surprised that he could recall the face so easily. He had always struggled with remembering faces and even names. He wondered if it was a passive gift of his class, something not exactly mentioned by the Voice to him upon adopting it.

"Good recall," the Ranger said. "He won't stand a chance."

Lila gripped the haft of the throwing knife in her belt. "And if things go south?"

"That's what you're there for, Lila," Eldrin stated simply, meeting both their gazes. "You too, Justin. They'll do one of two things when their leader falls. They'll split, or they'll fight. I imagine the former is the most likely. You're there for backup in case they decide to charge me. You two can hold them off while I take more shots with my bow. With luck, neither of you will have to lift a finger. But battle plans never go off without a hitch; that's the reason I wanted backup. And of course, the bandit leader might have a class. We must be ready for any surprises."

"What surprises?" Lila asked nervously.

"That, we will have to see. Hope for the best; plan for the worst."

They ate a light meal as they waited for the full cover of darkness.

The moon hung high in the night sky, its silver light filtering through the trees of the Wildwood. They stood at the edge of the tree line, watching the meadow where the four highwaymen lay on their backs, all but one clearly asleep below a high, pointed cliff that could be none other than Raven's Rock. In the nighttime darkness, its shape was reminiscent of the dark bird, the cliff's point as sharp as a beak.

As planned, Eldrin activated his Nature's Cloak skill and melted into the shadowy dark grass like a wraith. Justin was shocked at how quickly he was lost to sight.

Justin and Lila remained in the shadows of the trees; there was no chance either of them would be spotted. Up above, Shadowflight circled, waiting for the Ranger's signal.

Justin waited, having long lost sight of Eldrin. His heart pounded in his chest while sweat ran cold down his neck. At any moment, Shadowflight would—

The falcon's high shriek sounded out of place in the night. Immediately, all four bandits roused, including the leader, who stood head and shoulders above the rest. He was perfectly open to Eldrin's shot.

Eldrin's bow twanged from somewhere in the distance, and then something quite unexpected happened. As the missile made its approach, it didn't land true in the bandit's chest. It only pierced his right arm.

"Ambush!" the leader roared, clutching the arrow.

The three other bandits drew their swords and charged into the darkness toward Eldrin.

"Come on!" Justin said, drawing Eldrin's dagger and heading out of the trees. "We can't let him fight alone."

Justin's voice was louder than he intended. Thinking he was the source of the arrow, the bandits immediately turned and sprinted his way. They would be upon him all too soon.

But that was when Shadowflight swooped down, his talons gripping the shoulder of the most laggardly bandit and digging in. The bandit screamed, flailing, but Eldrin took advantage of the distraction, rising from the underbrush and advancing like a shadow, bow drawn. This arrow shot true, directly into the man's heart. He crumpled, lifeless.

That left two more bandits. The first was charging toward Lila.

Not knowing what else to do, Justin willed himself to perform his Poison Barb skill, unsure of its efficacy in this situation. He got a lock on the bandit's face, and at that moment, gained insight into the perfect insult that would emotionally damage his opponent.

Justin cleared his throat. "Isn't it tragic that you'll never amount to anything more than a failed pawn, forever overshadowed by your more talented and handsome brother?"

Even Justin was startled by the scornful insult. There was something about his voice that wasn't exactly his. Without having to be told, he knew he had assumed the mannerisms and inflections of the bandit's shrewish mother.

The bandit froze for a heartbeat, his face blanching as if memories of childhood rivalries and endless comparisons were surging to the forefront of his mind. It was a wound, deep and painful, and Justin had just poured salt into it.

The comment didn't stun the bandit exactly, but it at least made him falter, giving Lila the second she needed to gather her courage. With a cry, she lunged forward and launched her throwing knives. They twirled through the air, one landing true right in his throat. The man's scream became a bloody gurgle as he went down.

Eldrin dispatched the last bandit with a clean, lethal shot.

[You have gained 20 experience points. Your experience stands at 54/200.]

Eldrin lit a torch and inspected each bandit to ensure they were truly dead. Justin watched, wide-eyed, his heart feeling as if it would beat out of his chest. It had all happened in less than thirty seconds.

Eldrin nodded toward the leader, who was still lying injured by the campfire.

"Come on," Eldrin said. "This isn't quite over yet."

They approached the bandit leader, whose eyes were closed. At first, Justin thought he was dead, too, but he was shocked to see that the man was still breathing.

Without a word, Eldrin quickly secured him with some rope, expertly tying his hands behind his back while attaching another rope around his waist, fashioning a makeshift leash. He finished by tearing up some old fabric and placing a blindfold over his eyes. The arrow that had pierced his arm was more like a dart, hardly lethal.

"You meant to shoot him in the arm," Lila said in realization. "You poisoned that dart, didn't you?"

"Aye. Duskbell flowers and the venom of the blue-spotted tree frog. He'll sleep all night and well into the morning. The poison will also stop infection in its tracks. Even dragging him along with a leash, we'll reach the Mercenary Guild in a couple of days and get double the experience for our troubles."

"Nicely done," Justin said, impressed.

"Yes," Eldrin said. "Even if they weren't supposed to come after you both like that, it all worked out in the end."

"Thanks for helping," Lila said to Justin. "But no thanks for drawing their attention."

Justin shrugged. "Win some, lose some."

"Let's see what we've got here," Eldrin said, looking around the camp. "Once we're done having a look around, it might behoove us to head back to the road rather than pass the night here. I don't think there are any more of them, but one can't be too careful."

"What about him?" Lila asked, nodding toward the bandit leader.

"It's but a mile to the road from here. And with my Pathfinder's Pace, we can bear him with ease." Eldrin paused thoughtfully. "One more thing. This bandit is a Level 5 Thief."

"Is Level 5 bad?" Justin asked.

"It's a bit higher than I expected, so we'll need to be careful toting him to Silverton. Sometimes, Thieves get skills that can help them escape a tight spot. Just something we need to be wary of. I'm confident that with Shadowflight keeping watch, he won't get far, even if he manages to escape."

As in agreement, the noble bird gave a dignified squawk.

They rummaged through the bandits' possessions. Most were worthless trinkets, and the weapons Eldrin judged too worn to be worth the weight. But among the valuable loot, they discovered a gold chain, an ornate silver dagger with a ruby-encrusted hilt, and a velvet pouch filled with twenty-four silver coins and seventy coppers.

"Not bad," Eldrin said, pleased. "But that knife is worth far more than the coins, especially if it's enchanted. From the size of that gem alone, it'll easily sell for eighty silvers or even more to the right buyer. If it's a nice enchantment, it could sell for a crown or even more. The chain will sell for about five silvers. Whatever the proceeds, I'll take half, and you two can split the rest."

Justin and Lila nodded in agreement. After seeing how tonight went down, Eldrin was right to say he required most of the compensation, especially if they got the bandit leader back in one piece. If anything, he was being quite generous in his dispersal of the loot.

The trio hoisted their unconscious captive, making their way back to the road. Justin felt a mixture of exhaustion and triumph. The rewards hadn't been settled yet, but if his calculations were correct, anywhere from forty to fifty silver marks was coming his way: twenty for the completion of the job, and an additional twenty-five or more from the sale of the loot and distribution of the coin. So new to this world, he couldn't even guess how he'd spend the money. The Baron's parcel seemed so inconsequential in comparison.

From Lila's smile, however, it seemed she knew exactly what to do with her reward.

Setting up a makeshift camp just out of sight of the roadside, they prepared to rest. Shadowflight perched on a nearby branch, on the very tree Eldrin was binding their captive. The bird's sharp eyes watched from above, ensuring he made no moves.

Eldrin nodded, satisfied, before starting a fire and settling down to sleep.

Justin watched him concernedly. "Are you sure your falcon will let us know if he wakes up?"

"That bandit isn't waking up till the sun has gone up a fair way," Eldrin said. "But if he wakes before that, you have nothing to fear. Shadowflight will do a far better job than any of us with those eyes of his. As you've seen, he's very capable."

Justin nodded, satisfied with that answer. "Good enough for me. Good night, all."

He slept with his back to the fire. When morning came, they would finish things up and start their journey to the Mercenary Guild in Silverton.

10

THE ROAD TO SILVERTON

THE EMBERS of the fire provided scant warmth as the chill of the morning settled around them.

Suddenly, a grunt broke the silence, followed by rustling noises as the bandit leader regained consciousness.

Justin awoke to the commotion to see him struggling against his bindings, thrashing about wildly while uttering a litany of curses. He moaned as his injured arm strained against the ropes.

Eldrin calmly approached him, blocking out the morning sun as he cast a shadow over the bandit leader's helpless form. "Listen closely. Escape is a fantasy you can't afford. In a few minutes, we're going to march down that road. You'll walk or face a fate much graver than Silverton's courtrooms." He motioned to the sky, where Shadowflight circled ominously. "Try anything, and my falcon up there will make sure you never get far. Plus, these ropes can get a lot tighter."

"Piss off, you fuck," the bandit said with a growl.

"Delightful," Eldrin said.

He forced a canteen to the bandit's lips. The man hacked and coughed, but eventually had no choice but to drink whatever was offered.

"Why waste water on the likes of him?" Lila asked.

"Not just water," Eldrin said. "I mixed in some mendleaf paste. It should make things go easier."

They ate a quick breakfast of smoked deer jerky and a handful of berries Lila had foraged, and flatbread heated on the rocks around the fire. Soon, they got on their way. Eldrin roughly undid the rope that held the bandit to the tree, giving him a little push for good measure. He stumbled and tripped in the dirt, and Eldrin roughly pulled on his leash to stand him up.

"Can't you at least take my blindfold off, you spineless lump of rotting toad guts?" the bandit retorted.

Eldrin smirked. "If you play nice, sure. But you have to earn it."

The bandit looked as if he was about to curse again but thought better of it.

"You learn quickly."

With the warning delivered, their journey south to Silverton resumed. By noon, they passed the top of the Umber Hills to find themselves back in Whispering Pines. Now, in full daylight, Justin could see the hills spreading into the distance, the first trace of red autumn gracing the leaves. On the horizon rose a line of low mountains, between two of which was a smoky spot. No one was about in the small village square; Justin figured they were probably out on their terraces on the sides of the hills, reaping the harvest.

"Silverton," the Ranger said, gazing into the distance. "One more night in the wilderness will see us there tomorrow morning."

Eldrin removed the bandit's blindfold, and Justin did his best to avoid the man's gaze, though he could feel his beady, hateful eyes leering at him. He was mindful of Eldrin's warning that he might have some ability that would allow him to escape. But the Ranger didn't seem concerned, so Justin told himself it was okay.

The rest of the day passed uneventfully. The bandit sunk into sulky silence, and by evening, they set up camp in a meadow off the road. They met a few travelers on their way, a lot of them with their eyes popping at their prize. None asked any questions.

Eldrin led them off-road, toward a meadow where they could take shelter. Shadowflight went off to hunt and keep watch over their camp. Eldrin forced the blindfold on again and tied the bandit to a tree; he complied because of a previous dosing of mendleaf water.

They were so fatigued that, after dinner, they all went immediately to sleep, even the bandit.

Morning dawned again, cloudy and colder than the day before. They broke camp quickly. As they approached Silverton, the landscape changed gradually. They saw more people on the roads, first farmers heading to their fields, then traders with their mules and carts. They passed a couple of hamlets, small clusters of houses built from timber, surrounded by fences of stacked stone.

The path eventually led them to the city's imposing stone walls. The gates stood open, guarded by men in uniform, a crimson tunic over chain mail, with a silver heron clutching a silver coin in its talons—a fitting emblem for the city. Each soldier bore a pike and wore a conical helmet. Justin could see that the city was built strategically within the pass, with its stone buildings and towering walls making it a fortress against any threats.

As they neared, Eldrin turned to Justin and Lila. "Silverton is key to the Aranthian Plain beyond, and currently, we're in the Aranthian Hinterlands. It's a stronghold, a beacon of security for miles."

Justin wondered why he was telling him this, but maybe the Ranger was suspecting he wasn't from around here at all. Not just Aranthia, but this entire world. Eyrth, Alistair had called it. Eventually, he was going to be found out.

As they passed through the gates, Justin marveled. The city bustled with activity, with the distinct sound of hammers and anvils resonating amidst the background hum of wagons and chatter. Stone and wooden structures, predominantly two and three stories high, spread out like a sprawling mosaic. Thin streams of smoke arose from the many smithies and workshops, speaking of a city that thrived on industry. Up the mountainside to the west, grand mansions stood overlooking the town, symbols of the elite and their affluence.

But what caught Justin's eye the most were the roofs. The beautiful bluish-purple tiles looked as though they were borrowed from an idyllic Eastern European town, reflecting the hues of the sky and adding an air of charm to the industrious city. The buildings' sides were probably once painted white, but years of smoke and soot had stained most of them gray.

Eldrin navigated the streets confidently, leading them to the Mercenary Guild toward the center of town, directly across from the cathedral in the main town square. The Guild was an imposing stone structure with tall, narrow windows and a great oak door that was probably always kept open during business hours. Above the entrance, a large emblem of a crossed sword and arrow shone in the morning light. It was clearly a larger affair than the one in Mistwatch.

As Justin entered behind Eldrin, Lila, and their catch, it was to the sight of a cavernous hall bustling with activity. The clinking of coins, murmurs of negotiations, and the shuffling of armored feet echoed through the chamber. Eldrin led their captive through the throng of mercenaries, bounty hunters, and guild officials. Justin could see the sidelong glances and raised eyebrows at their haul.

At the far end of the hall, seated behind a massive oak desk, was the Mercenary Master. He was a human with a stout frame, a weathered face, and sharp eyes that seemed to miss nothing. Eldrin approached with a confident stride, producing the bounty bill he had picked up back in Whispering Pines.

"Master Branton," Eldrin addressed the stout man with a curt nod, "we've brought the bandit leader, as specified in your bill."

Master Branton looked the captive over, his keen eyes taking in every detail. "Aye, he matches the description."

Without further ado, he motioned for a pair of armored men to take the bandit away. While the man was restrained, Eldrin unbound him, carefully coiling his ropes and placing them in his pack.

As the guards dragged the bandit off with a yelp, Master Branton reached into a drawer and retrieved a small pouch, which jingled merrily. "Your reward," he said, handing it to Eldrin. "Thank you for your part in securing the Silver Road."

As Eldrin counted the coins and doled them out, Justin felt a rush, an almost physical sensation, as a blue notification bar surfaced in his vision.

Bounty "Highway Justice" Complete!

Experience Gained: 500

Money received: 80 silver marks, to be distributed among party members by Party Leader Eldrin Thornwood.

Loot: One ruby-encrusted dagger and one gold chain, to be appraised and sold or kept, as decided by party leader Eldrin Thornwood.

[Your experience stands at 554/200. Level-up available!]

"Congratulations, all," Eldrin said. "Let's head outside."

Emerging from the guild, the trio found themselves back on Silverton's bustling streets. Curious, Justin took a moment to check his interface, his eyes widening slightly at the experience bar reading 554/200. A check inside his coin pouch also revealed he had just over thirty-one silvers. That number would go even higher once he completed his courier quest and paid Lila her part, and when he got his share of the sold loot from Eldrin.

Justin couldn't suppress a grin. Such was the experience he had gained that he was almost certain he'd get not one, but two level-ups on his next sleep.

"Just one good sleep away from leveling up," he said.

"Same here!" Lila gushed. "This was *so* worth it."

"Is there a way I can research the skill I'll unlock next?" Justin asked.

"You could try the local library," Lila answered. "They probably have a skill book for your class. But just be warned, progression isn't the same for everyone."

"What do you mean?"

Eldrin cut in. "Certain skills have a way of showing up for most everyone in a class. But there's also an element of randomness to it, or even skills that are completely unique to a person. Traditionally, you'll be presented with two skill choices for every prime number level you attain. A class will always grant a class skill upon adopting a class, and as far as anyone can tell, they give the same skills to everyone. Level 1 will always confer a class boon."

"Interesting," Justin said. "What influences which skills are presented?"

Eldrin shrugged. "Normally, lower-level skills are presented earlier, but this isn't always the case. Scholars have developed various formulae to denote how likely or unlikely a skill will be presented, but I wouldn't trust them as reliable. Basically, some are more common than others. If you're lucky, you might even get a an option for a "Rare Skill." They tend to be better than the non-rare options. Your actions can determine just what skills show up."

"That makes it dynamic," Justin said. "And what about boons?"

"Boons work a bit differently. For every non-prime level, you get to adopt a new boon. And every non-prime level thereafter, assuming it's not a multiple of a previously adopted boon."

Justin frowned. "Care to explain that one?"

"Take mine, for example. At Level 4, I got my first boon, Animal Bond. And at Level 6, I got my second boon, Nature's Bounty. But at Level 8—the next non-prime number—I didn't get a new boon. Rather, my Animal Bond boon upgraded to Improved Animal Bond, which gave me and Shadowflight additional benefits. For example, it increased Shadowflight's strength and recovery. When you adopt a new boon, you also have to consider how it might grow with you."

"Interesting," Justin said. "So, I have something to look forward to with every level-up."

"That's right," Eldrin said. "And you'll always get a new attribute point to distribute. And what's more, your actions will determine the skills and boons you're presented with." He nodded back toward the guild hall. "Take our bandit friend, for example. He had the Thief class; that much I could see. Well, if he made a lot of decisions to rob and murder people, he might have been presented with skills that helped him do that better and been rewarded with experience."

"Horrible to think about," Lila said.

"However, if he'd just burgled houses, then no doubt he would get skills related to stealth and lock picking, for example."

Justin wondered how it would work with him. "There's no point in researching ahead of time, then."

"You may, if you wish," Eldrin said. "Just don't expect things to work out as you expect! As often is said in Eyrth, 'The gods roll the dice, and mortals guess the numbers.'" He adjusted his pack. "About time I headed to the market to offload our loot. That'll give you two a chance to drop off that parcel. Why don't we reconvene at the Moonlit Alehouse later? Cozy place, just around the corner. They also have fine rooms available that won't break the bank."

"Sure, let me just check my map." Justin pulled it out, only to find it was completely blank. "What the hell? I thought this was a world map!"

Eldrin laughed. "It takes a lot of rare and magical objects, plus a top-level Enchanter, to create a Complete Dynamic World Map like you're talking about. I'm guessing the one you bought wasn't too expensive?"

"It was to me," Justin said. "A couple of silvers, if I remember correctly."

"A local map, then. The dynamic range usually doesn't extend beyond ten miles, but that's all most folks need. Beyond those ten miles, things get hazier."

Justin was learning more and more. "How much would a dynamic world map cost me?"

Lila whistled. "A lot. Even a blank map with dynamic capabilities is at least a gold crown. If you want one completely filled out, well, that's almost priceless."

"All that for just a blank map?"

"Well, it doesn't *stay* blank," Lila said. "You go to a local Enchanter, and most can add anything of note in their local area if they're worth their salt."

"Start saving," Eldrin said, "but in the meantime, if you need a map, a good local map will only put you back a couple of silvers in most places. In bigger cities it might run you three or four. But it's not worth it if you're not staying long." He pointed his feet away. "The tavern is just in the square over there. I'll head that way once I've found the right buyer for these items."

Lila eyed him suspiciously. "And what's stopping you from taking the loot and disappearing?"

Eldrin merely chuckled and slipped a finely crafted signet ring from his finger. "This should be enough collateral," he said, offering it to Lila. "It's enchanted and worth more than our haul."

Justin looked at the ring. While it didn't seem valuable, it was well-worn. Eldrin would surely be loath to part with it.

"Go ahead, keep it," Lila said. "I trust you."

"Lila and I had better take care of that delivery before it's dark," Justin said.

"Farewell," Eldrin said. "We'll celebrate tonight!"

[Eldrin has left the party. You are now the party leader.]

"Shall we?" Justin asked.

At Lila's nod, they moved through the bustling streets. Justin ducked into a tavern to ask a pretty barmaid about Baron Valdrik. He noticed her brief surprise at the question, and Justin got the sense that the Baron was a well-known figure here, perhaps not in a good way. It made his stomach churn a bit, but five silver marks were five silver marks, and a delivery was a delivery.

Once Justin was confident he had the right directions, he and Lila headed to the slopes of the western mountain bordering Silverton.

11

THE BARON'S OFFER

"What's the difference between an Elementalist, a Wizard, and a Sorcerer? Good question. An Elementalist's magic is inherent—awakened from the moment they absorb their core. A Wizard's magic must be earned through years of studying the Foundation Language of Arcanis and poring over dusty tomes. And a Sorcerer's magic? Well, let's just say they likely made a very poor deal with something they really shouldn't have been talking to in the first place."

—Saldran Merris
> *What They Don't Teach You at Magic School*

THE NARROW, winding streets of Silverton grew steeper as Justin and Lila made their way uphill. Indigo cobblestones gave way to staircases cut directly into the rock and adorned with vibrant flowers. Buildings became more spaced out, their architecture grander, and balconies lined with wrought iron that gleamed in the sunlight.

Before long, they left the bustle of the town below and were heading up a secluded pathway that twisted its way around a dense grove of pine trees. The air was fresher here, laden with the scent of mountain flowers and undergrowth. Justin felt his thighs burn a little from the incline but didn't want to admit it.

Perched atop a crest overlooking the city was Baron Valdrik's mansion, easily the largest they had seen. The impressive residence was crafted from gray mountain stone, its tall spires reaching toward the sky, while large windows, with ornate wooden frames, offered breathtaking views of the pass below. The property was surrounded by manicured gardens, a splash of color against the gray and green backdrop.

As they approached, they were met with an intricately wrought iron gate depicting a raven in flight, apparently the symbol of House Valdrik. A pale-faced guard, in a deep maroon uniform adorned with the same raven emblem, stood watch. He studied their approach with sharp eyes, but then, recognizing the seal on the parcel, pushed the gate open.

"This way, please."

As they approached, the mansion loomed large, its tall spires and Gothic architecture lending it a haunting air.

Once inside, they were led through a series of beautifully decorated halls. Gilded portraits adorned the walls, mostly idyllic scenes of nature. Justin could hear the distant sound of harp music, indicating some leisurely activity in a distant room.

But despite the displays of wealth, the air was thick, almost tangible, like they had walked into a room full of unseen watchers. Cold drafts seemed to come from nowhere, causing candle flames to flicker while sending chilling tendrils down Justin's spine.

The guard led them to a dim hallway, where thick velvet drapes were drawn, allowing only minimal light, while much of the ornate furniture was shrouded in white sheets, giving the impression of lurking phantoms. If this was truly the Baron's residence, it didn't seem as if he entertained much or even spent much time living here.

Baron Valdrik awaited them in a cavernous study, its high ceilings disappearing into shadow. He rose from an ornate chair, his tall stature made even more imposing by his finely tailored black velvet coat. A thin beard traced his sharp jawline, and his piercing gray eyes seemed to see right through them. His fingers, adorned with various silver rings, drummed a slow rhythm on the table's surface.

"Finally, the parcel," he drawled, his voice smooth but carrying an undercurrent of menace. He carefully examined the seal, then shot a lingering, probing look at Justin. "Took you long enough. I expected it days ago."

"Sorry for the delay, Baron," Justin replied, swallowing hard, feeling the weight of the Baron's gaze. "I hope it's to your satisfaction."

The Baron seemed to have already forgotten him when something about Justin seemed to catch his eye. He tilted his head, studying him. "Curious. A Socialite...reduced to errands? How peculiar. Tell me, from which esteemed family do you hail?"

Justin quickly tried to think of something acceptable. He remembered a town from his map. "The Caroway family. From the Western Hinterlands."

The Baron's eyes narrowed slightly. "The Caroways, you say? They must be a minor house, for I've never heard of them, although I've heard of the town. They raise swine there, do they not?"

"Yes, sire."

The Baron smirked and leaned closer, his probing gaze making Justin feel like an insect under a magnifying glass. "And you're now delivering parcels for Barons. Why waste your talents on such...mundane tasks?"

"We've both fallen on hard times," Lila said, trying to rescue him.

Valdrik's gaze shifted to her, and then back to Justin. "Unfortunate indeed. Perhaps, Mr. Caroway, I could offer you a position in my household. I pay well. Fifteen silvers a week for one of your class. I could use a Socialite like you; they are quite rare, even in a town of this size. You could gain valuable training to boot. However, should you accept, you'll be exclusive to me."

Justin felt a knot tighten in his stomach. The gloomy atmosphere, combined with Valdrik's intense scrutiny, made him desperate to leave. "I appreciate the offer, Baron. I'll...think about it."

Valdrik's eyes darkened. "I'm not used to being kept waiting."

Lila, sensing the growing threat, said hastily, "We must be going. We have another delivery."

Valdrik's eyes flickered to her, then back to Justin, before giving a slow nod. "Think about it. I could make a powerful friend, a gateway to reclaiming your old life. Those of us with charisma cores must stick together, no?"

"You have a charisma core, too?" Justin asked, unable to help his curiosity.

Valdrik smiled, revealing his sharp canines. "Yes, verily so. I'm more than a mere charisma core, though. I'm a Lexicant."

"What's that?" Justin asked before thinking better of the question.

"Well, we are a unique advanced class. Not everyone has heard of us. We combine the charisma core of a Socialite with the intellect core of a Wizard."

"You can combine cores?"

"Yes," the Baron said with a satisfied smile. "Certain cores can combine at Level 20 to create an advanced class. Lexicant is just one of many possible combinations. So naturally, I am always interested when I meet a Socialite, especially when it's not expected."

"I see," Justin said. "What can a Lexicant do?"

"Our claim to fame is speaking the Foundation Language of Vranthillis. It allows us to manipulate reality in...intriguing ways."

"Sounds cool!" Justin said.

"Anyway..." Lila said, pulling on Justin's shirt sleeve.

"I understand you must leave, but before you do, Mr. Caroway, I will have you know that there is much I can teach you. Some even say that Vranthillis can even become the gateway to other realities..."

Justin couldn't help but widen his eyes at that. Gateway to other *realities*? Did that include his own?

It was at that moment that Baron Valdrik produced an ebony staff, then chanted with an otherworldly resonance: *"Terinthial Lantra Vrakor."*

A chill passed through the room; the air was dense with the weight of those words.

"What does that mean?" Lila asked, startled.

"It means, 'You will go far,' though of course the translation is not exact. All words in the language have multiple meanings, depending on context. It's just a taste of Vranthillis for you."

From the coldness of his smile, Justin was sure the phrase meant something far more sinister.

"We should go," he said.

"Of course," Valdrik said easily. "Good day."

They quickly left, the heavy mansion doors closing behind them with an ominous thud. As they descended the mountainside, the oppressive aura of the mansion seemed to lighten, but Justin still felt uneasy.

Job Updated: The Baron's Parcel

The parcel was successfully delivered to the Baron of Silverton. To claim your reward, please speak to the clerk at the Silverton Post Office.

"Good riddance," Lila said, glancing back at the looming silhouette of the mansion. "We were lucky to get out of there alive." She glanced over at Justin. "I don't think you should take his offer."

"Yeah," Justin agreed. "He was...weird, to say the least."

"Best decision you'll ever make. I don't care *what* he pays."

They made their way to the post office at the heart of the bustling central square. White-stucco buildings with their customary roofs of indigo framed the area, while a central fountain in the shape of a gargoyle dominated the center of the plaza, water cascading from its outstretched wings. Market stalls were set up, selling goods from exotic fruits to woven fabrics. The sun had set over the western mountain slopes.

They entered the post office and approached the counter, where a middle-aged woman with her hair tied in a bun looked up, adjusting her round glasses. She could have been a sister to the clerk in Mistwatch. "Ah, what brings you?"

"We've completed the delivery to Baron Valdrik," Justin said.

"Let me check on that." She consulted a ledger, and to Justin's surprise, words shifted around, rearranging themselves in response to his presence.

"Very good," the clerk said. "The seal is no longer active." Reaching into a drawer, she pulled out a small pouch. "Five silvers for your service."

[Job Completed: The Baron's Parcel]

[You have gained 50 experience points, and 5 silver marks have been added to your inventory. The Aranthian Royal Mail thanks you for your service!]

[Your experience stands at 604/200. Level-up available!]

Justin counted out three silvers and handed them to Lila. "Your share."

"Excellent," she said, handing back two twenty-five copper coins. "This has been a productive trip!"

The clerk cleared her throat. "If you'd like any more work, I have a package that needs to be delivered to Belmora. It pays well."

"How well is 'well'?" Justin asked.

"Ten silver marks."

"It must be two hundred miles to Belmora," Lila said.

The clerk looked from Lila back to Justin. "Well, this one has been sitting for a while. The office will add an extra two silvers to get it out the door."

"With the roads as they are?" Justin asked, sensing weakness. "Better to make it five extra!"

"*Six*," Lila corrected. She looked at Justin. "This job we're splitting evenly."

The clerk sighed. "I'll have to talk to my boss about it. But I think we can arrange it. Come back tomorrow. It's here for you if no one else takes it."

"It will be," Lila said. "Let's move out. Eldrin's probably waiting for us already."

As they walked out the door, Justin couldn't help but feel light on his feet. They made their way through the crowded streets to the Moonlit Alehouse, the unnerving behavior of the Baron already a distant memory.

12

THE MOONLIT ALEHOUSE

"Never get romantically involved with a bard. They'll sing you the sweetest ballads, make you feel like the hero of every story...until you're not. Then you'll find yourself the villain of a tune that every tavern from South Cape to Land's End will be humming for the next decade. Don't ask me how I know."

—Dornal Flint,
Lessons Learned the Hard Way

AS EVENING FELL ON SILVERTON, Justin and Lila approached the Moonlit Alehouse, the soft glow of hanging lanterns and the faint strumming of a lute hinting at the merriment within. But as Justin pushed the heavy oak doors open with a muted creak, the full scale of the tavern's cozy grandeur greeted them.

Inside was a symphony of golden hues—honey-colored wooden beams stretching across the ceiling, supporting an array of chandeliers made of wrought iron, each holding glowing orbs that emitted a soft, moonlike glow.

The walls were lined with shelves of ornate bottles filled with liquids of every imaginable hue. Plush burgundy seating lined the perimeter, and in the center, rows of sturdy oak tables were surrounded by patrons engaged in animated conversation, laughter, and song. The majority were human, but mixed in there was the occasional orc. Musicians sat on a raised platform, drawing lilting melodies from lutes, flutes, and hand drums.

"Quite the place," Justin murmured, glancing around. His gaze lingered on a corner where a group played dice. Several cheered raucously as coins changed hands.

Lila nodded toward the counter. "I want to book a room. Care to join?"

Justin followed her, not sure if she wanted to share a room again, now that they could each afford their own, or if she merely wanted him to accompany her to the front, where the innkeeper waited behind the oaken counter.

Before he could ask her, the innkeeper spoke, taking them both in. "Looking for a room? It's a silver a night for a single, and two silvers if you want something bigger."

"Anything cheaper?" Justin asked.

"We have the dorm for fifty coppers a night. It sleeps twelve."

"No dorm," Lila said. "Do you have anything with double beds?"

"We have one left. That one's one silver and forty coppers."

Lila looked at him sidelong, smiling slightly. "Do you mind sharing again?"

Memories of two nights ago came flooding back, and before Justin could stop it, his cheeks were coloring. "Yes. That would be fine."

"Well, we have been through a lot together, haven't we? Might as well be comfortable."

At her suggestive smile, Justin felt his pulse quicken as he swallowed a nervous lump in his throat. It sounded like Lila wanted to celebrate with more than just drinks.

The innkeeper looked between the two of them, giving Justin a sly wink. "Very good. Will you be taking a bath or breaking your fast tomorrow?"

"Yes to both," Lila said. "And make sure the tub is big."

"Why big?" Justin asked.

Lila just smiled.

Even the innkeeper was having a chuckle at that. "Our largest tub is thirty coppers."

Lila nodded. "Bring it up just short of midnight."

"Yes, madam. It shall be done."

They settled up, Justin deciding not to question anything. Sometimes, the best thing to say was nothing at all.

That was when they were interrupted by a familiar voice. "Over here!"

Eldrin, seated in a dim corner, waved them over, his chiseled face illuminated by the glow of a nearby lantern. He was nursing a pint of dark, frothy ale, and by the look in his eyes, it wasn't his first.

"Another round for my friends!" Eldrin called out, raising his mug in salute. The serving girl promptly arrived, placing two more mugs filled with the same deep amber liquid. As Justin and Lila sat, the girl placed the mugs before them.

"To victory and spoils," Eldrin said.

"Victory and spoils," Justin and Lila echoed.

They clinked their mugs and drank deeply.

"Well?" Lila asked.

Eldrin flashed a smile and opened his coin purse. From it, he counted out thirty silvers for each of them. Justin's and Lila's eyes popped.

"A good haul," Eldrin said.

Lila looked to be near tears. "I never thought I would have such luck."

Justin took his share, adding it to his coin purse. Sixty-three silvers and some odd coppers earned over the past few days. A good haul indeed.

"It's yours," Eldrin said. "You'd think I was a Merchant from the way I haggled that man to give me a fair price."

The scent of roasting meats wafted in from the kitchen, making Justin's stomach rumble. Lila flagged down their server and placed an order for a sumptuous banquet: roasted fowl with a tangy berry sauce, seared venison steaks, and an array of fresh vegetables and seasoned potatoes, with rhubarb pie and whipped cream for dessert.

As they waited for their feast, the atmosphere grew more intimate, setting the stage for an evening of revelations and stories. For two hours they sat, talking, laughing, and eating as the evening deepened. Justin couldn't remember ever feeling such camaraderie. In his old life, he spent almost all his waking hours downstairs in a basement playing video games. He almost felt like an imposter here. After all, the warmth of this companionship in a single evening was more than he'd gotten in years.

The candlelit glow from the walls turned the cozy tavern into a realm of dancing shadows. The music slowed, turning more soulful, and conversations in the tavern seemed to hush a bit.

Eldrin, after sharing a tale of an unexpected rainstorm during one of his hunts, turned to Lila. "So, what about you? What's a lady like you doing adventuring with us misfits?"

Lila hesitated, her fingers playing with the rim of her mug. "It's...complicated."

"Isn't it always?" Eldrin said with a chuckle, taking another sip of his ale.

Lila exhaled, the weight of her past clear in her eyes. "I didn't want to get into this, but by the Nether, why not? I'm four drinks in, and both of you seem like the okay sort. And...it would be good to get this off my chest."

"You can trust us," Justin assured her.

She paused for a moment. "I did something very foolish. I...bought a class core on credit. I thought it would be a smart investment for the future."

Eldrin raised a brow. "That's a brave move. They cost a fortune!"

Justin didn't know exactly what they meant, but he nodded sympathetically. He wasn't quite ready to betray his ignorance yet.

She nodded. "I intended to buy a Merchant core. I already had a nice business; just general sundries, nothing fancy. I thought it would take me to the next level, you know? It belonged to my father before he passed." Her eyes became misty with remembrance before darkening. "But..." She paused, taking a deep breath. "I was swindled by my contact. I got a core all right, but it wasn't a Merchant core. It was a Bard core. I was so eager to use it I didn't even bother to read the rune inside. I just assumed it was okay. It was the right color, after all. But I'd signed the contract; as you know, Merchant cores are quite expensive. Well, I paid the Merchant core's price for the Bard core. By the time I realized the truth, it was too late. I had already absorbed it."

Justin leaned forward, his brow furrowed. "And now?"

Lila bit her lip, looking down. "I owe sixty crowns. Maybe more now, with the interest. A fortune I don't have. And every day, the interest grows."

Eldrin let out a long whistle. "Sixty golds? Who on Eyrth gave you such a hefty line of credit?"

Lila's voice was soft. "It wasn't always like this. Remember that business I talked about? It was my collateral. But such were my interest payments that I could no longer make the business work. They took bloody everything from me, and by the time I barely had a shirt on my back, I still owed. It didn't take long for them to send their thugs after me for the rest, but there was nothing left to give. So, I did the only thing I could do. I ran."

Justin studied Lila for a moment. "But you're only Level 1. This must have been recent?"

She merely sipped her drink, avoiding his gaze, neither confirming nor denying. "I've already said too much. It's been about a month since then."

"Daeloria to here in a month?" Eldrin asked, surprised. "You must have been running like the wind."

She was silent on this point. "Now the both of you know what a fool I am."

"You're not a fool," Eldrin said. "It's a story I've heard before. Everyone wants a class, and there are a lot of bad sorts who'll take advantage of that desperation."

"I should've known," Lila said. "With a Merchant core, I could have made it work. But now, I'm a Bard. So what if my core allows me to sing like a nightingale? That won't pay back my debts. I fear they will never stop hunting me. And if they find me..."

She trailed off, not wanting to say anything more.

"I know this might not be what you want to hear," Eldrin said carefully, "but you could set sail. Plenty of ships to catch in Belmora. Passage isn't cheap, but it's far cheaper than a debt you can't pay. I doubt they'll chase you as far as Calidon, especially if they know you have nothing to offer."

"To live among the orcs?" Lila asked, draining her glass. "It sounds like a lonely life."

After a somber moment, Eldrin cleared his throat. "Well, my turn, I suppose. I've been living in the wilds of Serenthel for the past seven years."

Justin remembered seeing the name on his map. It seemed to be the name of the entire continent of which Aranthia was a part.

"The thrill of the hunt, the chase of treasures. That's what I live for. I was running, too, though from something else. We won't go there. I imagine you'd lose a lot of your goodwill toward me if we did. Anyhow, my proper story begins five years ago, when it started snowing something fierce. That was a terrible storm."

"I remember that winter," Lila said. "Cold enough to freeze your blood."

Eldrin nodded. "Well, I was out in it in the Northern Umbers, of all places. Somehow, I made it to a cave for shelter. I went as deep as I could to escape it. That's when I saw something orange glowing in the darkness of the cave. I thought I was hallucinating. I didn't dare believe it could be what I thought it was..."

"...No," Lila said. "It wasn't a core?"

Eldrin nodded. "It was. Right there, in front of me. The Priests have always told me my Core Attribute was Coordination. And I knew enough to recognize it was a Ranger Core. Whether I'd sell it or absorb it wasn't even a question."

"Wait," Justin said. "Can someone explain to me more about class cores? I understand it's how you get a class. But you're talking as if your cores could only give you one class. I feel like I'm missing a crucial piece of the puzzle here."

Lila and Eldrin exchanged glances. Justin didn't care if what he was asking was common knowledge or if it made them suspicious of him. He had to know these things if he was going to make it in this world. At least long enough to get back out again.

Eldrin began. "All right, lad. I'm not sure how you've gotten this far in life without learning about this stuff. But a class core is a magical artifact. They are the only thing that allows you to gain a class. As long as the person is twenty years old and they have the Core Attribute to match the core, then they can absorb the core and gain the class, assuming they don't already have a class, of course."

"And they're incredibly rare," Lila added. "Most are bought up by the rich. Commoners like us have to get more creative. Loans. Pledging years of fealty to an institution or lord that will help us out. Even stealing them. They can rarely be found in the wilds, like what Eldrin was describing, or in the Vaults."

"Vaults?" Justin asked.

"Magical formations that arise from Eyrth's interaction with the Aether Realm," Eldrin explained. "Think of them as magical chambers filled with challenges and treasures. These Vaults can be anywhere, deep in forests, under mountains, even within cities or underwater. It varies. One might pop up for a week and disappear, while another can exist for years, decades even, without anyone ever clearing it. And they're highly dangerous, even the less challenging ones. But you'll know one when you see one. Better make sure you have powerful friends before you try your luck! It's by far the easiest way for an adventurer to die."

"Some even make a profession of it," Lila added. "They call themselves Vault Runners. Most don't live long, but those who do can become very rich. They take their profits and start businesses, and some even buy their way into nobility."

"Interesting," Justin said. The concept of "Vaults" sounded similar to dungeons from the games he had played. "How much does one of these class cores cost?"

Lila shrugged. "It depends. Anywhere from thirty to two hundred gold crowns, depending on rarity and demand. Some are even more."

Justin sat back, absorbing all the information. The tapestry of Eyrth's mysteries was slowly unveiling before him. And he realized just how little he truly knew.

After a deep sigh, Justin looked into his drink, swirling the amber liquid. "You know...what you mentioned about finding cores in the wild, that sounds awfully familiar. When I was in the Wildwood north of Mistwatch, I stumbled upon...well, something I can't explain."

Eldrin raised an eyebrow, his interest piqued. "What did you find?"

"It was an orb, shimmering with every color you could imagine, like a rainbow trapped inside a crystal," Justin said. "I picked it up, and it seemed to flow into me."

Lila's eyes widened. "You...you found a class core in the Wildwood? Just like that?"

Justin nodded, looking sheepish. "You said earlier that a core only contains one class, and it has to match your Core Attribute. Except this core allowed me to choose both my class and my Core Attribute. I thought it was normal, you know, since I'm new to all this, so I never brought it up."

Lila and Eldrin exchanged a glance, disbelief evident in their eyes.

"That's...extraordinary," Eldrin murmured.

Justin regretted mentioning it, feeling the weight of their disbelief. "I know it sounds strange, but it's the truth."

Lila leaned forward, her skepticism obvious. "See, the thing is, Justin, class cores only give one specific class. And it only resonates with those possessing the right Core Attribute. But what you're describing..."

Eldrin finished her sentence. "...sounds like a Prismatic Core."

Justin's brow furrowed. "Prismatic what now?"

The memory returned to him. The Voice had mentioned he had

absorbed a "Prismatic Core," but until now, he hadn't realized it had been anything truly extraordinary.

Lila's gaze was intense. "Prismatic Core. They're legendary artifacts, more myth than reality. Most people in Eyrth don't even believe they exist. Such cores allow you to choose any class you want. If you already have a class, well, you can make use of it once you reach Level 20 to gain any advanced class you want. You can pretty much customize your destiny."

Justin felt his breath catch. "How rare are they?"

"The stories say only four show up every year," Lila said. "During both solstices and equinoxes."

"When did you find that core, lad?" Eldrin asked.

Justin counted back the days on his fingers. "Let's see...it would've been..." He paused. "Four days ago?"

"September 21," Eldrin said. "The fall equinox."

"There's no way," Lila said. Her eyes were amused, expecting a punchline that never came.

Justin thought back to his choice of Socialite for his class. If he'd truly found this Prismatic Core that comes only four times a year, then he'd bungled the biggest opportunity of all time.

He could have been anything he wanted. A luxury others born in this world could only dream of.

But maybe he'd appeared next to that core for a reason. Somehow, he'd come into this world. Maybe the act of taking on the Prismatic Core had given him a Core Attribute to match. After all, he wasn't from here. As far as he knew, he didn't have a Core Attribute before that.

He kept this speculation to himself. "You know, thinking about it, maybe I just found a Socialite core in the woods. I don't know. I'm new to all this and hit my head pretty hard."

Eldrin and Lila exchanged glances again. It was the Ranger who spoke. "Justin, you should know us better than that. Both of us know you didn't hit your head. And you're asking questions that just about anyone would know. It's not easy to lie to a Ranger, but I also want you to know that neither of us means you any harm. If there's something you feel we should know, well, now is the right opportunity."

Justin hesitated, realizing he was on the cusp of a decision. Should he trust these newfound friends with his incredible story, which, in their eyes, would be even more unbelievable, or continue weaving tales?

He looked into their expectant eyes and knew he couldn't lie any longer. So what if this came back to bite him? It wasn't as if he was fighting for anything except the infinitesimal chance he'd get to leave this place someday.

"All right," he began, taking a swig of his ale. "You want to know the truth? This is where I'm really from..."

13

GHOSTS OF THE PAST

"And therefore, the Creator Supreme closed the Shining Gate to the Aether Realm and banished the races from its splendor, for they had been deceived by Morvath, the God of Death, who whispered false promises of dominion over life and eternity. And thus, the Aether was sealed, and the races were left to wander the shattered worlds, seeking the path they lost, never to return until their cores came unbound by the curse of death..."
—*The Book of Life*, Chapter VII, Verses 22–23

As Justin began his tale, the firelight cast a golden hue over their faces in their corner of the Moonlit Alehouse. The laughter and chatter around them seemed distant, drowned by the weight of the revelations and confessions he knew would soon pass his lips.

He began hesitantly. "I'm not...*from* here, I guess you could say."

"Not from Aranthia, you mean?" Lila said. "Yeah, we figured. So what? I'm from Daeloria myself, all the way past the Umber Range."

"You don't understand. I'm from another world entirely. Not from Eyrth."

Both of them frowned at him, confused. Eldrin broke the silence. "What do you mean, lad? There are other worlds, of course. Some say they host life; some don't. But I don't think that's what you mean."

"I'm from an alternate universe. I'm not sure if that concept exists here. A world without magic, classes, and levels. A world that's completely mundane."

He saw he was just confusing them more. As he suspected, this was all they knew. An entirely alternate universe where magic and levels were baked into the quantum fabric of reality. Justin didn't know how else to explain it to them.

"What's your world called?" Lila asked.

"Earth."

"That sounds quite similar to our world," Eldrin observed. "A coincidence?"

"I think this world is a part of mine," Justin said. "A smaller part. Except there is no escape. Then again, I could be wrong about that."

"No escape?" Eldrin said, laughing nervously. "You make this world seem like a prison!"

Justin realized that it could be the truth of things, at least from his reckoning, but didn't say as much.

"All I know is I was in my mom's basement, playing video games, and then a tornado came out of nowhere and swept me up. It threw me somewhere over the metaphorical rainbow, and somehow, I found myself here, right in front of that Prismatic Core."

Several heads at a nearby table turned at that. Eldrin looked in their direction, giving a winning smile. "He's drunk."

Justin realized he had been far too loud. "Sorry. Sometimes, I forget where I am."

"That's all right, lad. Listen. I'm not quite sure what has happened to you. I'm not willing to rule out magical means of memory erasing. It's been known to happen. There are certain rare potions that will do it."

"No, that's not right," Justin said. "If that's the case, how can I know anything about this other world? I mean, I'm talking about things that are so detailed that I couldn't possibly make them up."

"Things like what?" Lila asked.

"Where to even start with that? Over four billion years of history on our planet alone, of which humans have only been around for a small part. Countless empires have risen and fallen. Triumphs and tragedies. Mozart, Beethoven. Hell, Michael Jackson, Rihanna, and Bieber! Not to mention all the rest!" He looked at them helplessly. "Radiohead?"

"Who is this...Bieber?" Lila asked. "He seems a mighty lord of great renown."

"Oh, you wouldn't believe it! He's a proper bard, all right. Though this world is different, everything is recognizable as something that can be found in my world. It's like...someone from my world designed this place. I just don't know how I got swept up in it. I'm thinking that maybe I died and got sent here, or maybe all tornadoes have portals. Who can say? Maybe L. Frank Baum was onto something."

"Or maybe *on* something," Eldrin said with a smirk. "Whoever he is."

Both of them were looking at him as if he were crazy. Justin knew this had been a mistake. "Just forget it."

"I'll humor you," Eldrin said. "What was your class in your world?"

"There are no classes," Justin said again. It seemed hard for them to accept that fact. "I guess you could say I was a NEET."

"A NEET?" Eldrin asked. "Strange name for a class."

Justin shook his head. "It's not a class. It's short for not in education, employment, or training. Back in my old world, I didn't exactly have an...admirable life." He glanced up, assessing their expressions before he continued. "A NEET is someone who has just...given up. They do nothing and add nothing of value to society. That's what I did. I just sat in the basement of my mother's house. Sometimes, I wouldn't go outside for weeks. My only social interaction came from other members of my guild."

"Being part of a guild is good," Eldrin said approvingly. "It's important to forge connections with others to get ahead."

Justin frowned as he realized he and Eldrin were talking about two different things. "Maybe."

"I don't see how you can just do nothing," Lila asked, alarmed.

"Were you sick, maybe? Did you not have to hunt? Or sell things to survive?"

"Well, to say I did absolutely nothing is a lie. I spent most of my time playing video games."

"What are these 'video games' you speak of?" Eldrin asked, somewhat stumbling over the unfamiliar term. "Like dice or cards?"

"I don't know how to describe it. It's like a virtual world, I suppose. I spent all my time there because the real one seemed to have nothing for me."

Lila's eyes softened, a sympathetic smile gracing her face, even if it was clear she didn't understand the meaning of his words. "Justin, everyone has a past. It doesn't dictate who you are now."

He shrugged. "But it feels like it does sometimes. I was...a loser, Lila. I had no real friends. I was always made fun of, to where if someone actually was nice to me, I thought it was a trick. I have some stories there, but it would just depress me to tell them."

Eldrin leaned forward. "And these...video games, as you call them...became something of a refuge for you, given the misery of your life?"

That was a rather blunt way to put it. "Yes, exactly. I could be someone there, someone important, someone who mattered. But when the screen turned off, there was nothing. Just my face staring back at me from the black screen. And a silence so deep that it echoed inside my soul."

Lila reached across the table, her hand finding Justin's. "That sounds lonely, Justin. A kind of loneliness that shouldn't exist."

Justin's face twisted. The raw honesty of Lila's words struck deep. "It was."

It took everything he had not to cry. He couldn't let himself do that.

Eldrin's voice took on a nurturing tone, one that seemed to bring warmth and light to the cold corners of Justin's memories. "You said you lived with your mother. Did she not notice? Help you find another path?"

A bitter laugh escaped Justin. "I think she gave up on me. I could never meet her expectations. I mean, I don't blame her. Connor was always the golden child."

"Connor?" Lila asked. "Who is that?"

"My older brother. He was everything she wanted. Perfect. As long as she had him, she could stand me. And for my part, I loved him, too. He was the only one who seemed to see the real me. We would game together sometimes." Justin lowered his face. "But he died in a car accident when I was eighteen."

"A car accident?"

"A vehicle that moves fast in my world," Justin explained. "After that, my failures just reminded her of what she lost. Many times, I've had the sense that she wished it had been me."

There was a long, dark silence. Justin couldn't believe he had said so much. And he couldn't believe that they had the patience to listen to him.

"Whatever your past," Eldrin said, "you're one of us, Justin. Though we've only known each other for a few days, we have the bond of adventurers, no matter where our travels take us. When one member of the pack falls behind, it's for the others to make sure he can keep up."

"That's...not something I've ever experienced. I guess...I guess I never really had the chance to be anything else. Long story short, I've always been different, and maybe my parents didn't know what to do with that. They didn't guide me, didn't show me how to live in the real world. My dad passed away when I was ten. My mom...well, let's just say the light went out of her life not once, but twice. I don't blame her for what she was like."

"Well, no one knows everything," Eldrin said. "Every one of us is figuring this life thing out. By the Nether, you think *I* have it figured out? I've got my own demons. Like Lila, I'm running too."

"From what?" Justin asked, curious.

Eldrin shook his head. "I'd rather not talk about that. But fair's fair, though, right? I can tell you something about it, at least. Enough to give you an idea."

Justin and Lila waited quietly for Eldrin to continue.

"Like I've already hinted, I wasn't always a Ranger. I come from a...different life. One with responsibilities I didn't ask for and wasn't ready to bear. My family—they had expectations. Expectations I failed to meet."

"What kind of expectations?" Justin asked, but Eldrin shook his head.

"It doesn't matter now," he said. "I thought I could escape them, carve out a life of my own, free of obligations. For a while, I did. But the gods...they have a way of reminding you that freedom often comes at a cost."

Lila frowned. "What happened?"

Eldrin hesitated. "There was...a time when people depended on me. When I should have stayed, fought for them. But I didn't. I ran. I thought I could start over, leave it all behind. But no matter how far you run, some ghosts refuse to let go."

Justin's brow furrowed. "You mean you left them to—"

"I mean I failed," Eldrin cut in sharply, his eyes snapping to Justin's. "And that failure haunts me every day."

The words hung heavy in the air. Lila opened her mouth to speak but seemed to think better of it. Instead, she studied Eldrin.

"Maybe you didn't fail," she said gently. "Maybe you just...weren't ready. We can only carry what we're strong enough to bear."

Eldrin snorted, a bitter sound. "You make it sound so simple. But it's not."

They sat in silence for a moment. The crackling of the fire was the only sound between them.

"What would you do now?" Justin asked. "If you had the chance to...I don't know, fix it?"

Eldrin stared into the flames. "I don't know. Sometimes I think it's too late. This was years ago. That the damage is done, and all I can do is live with it. Other times..." He shook his head. "Other times, I think maybe there's still a way. A way to make things right. But that would mean facing everything I ran from. And I'm not sure I have the strength for that."

Justin nodded slowly, sensing that Eldrin had said all he was willing to say.

Lila's voice was soft but firm. "You're stronger than you think, Eldrin. Sometimes, the hardest part isn't facing others. It's forgiving yourself."

Eldrin's lips twitched into a faint, humorless smile. "Wise words, Lila. We'll see if they hold true."

Eldrin's story wasn't finished; Justin was sure of that. Whether he elected to say more remained to be seen.

Eventually, the weight of the night's revelations settled upon them, a gentle reminder that the world still spun, and time never stopped to mourn the lost years. Eldrin stood up, stretching his muscles.

"Let's break our fast tomorrow," he said. "With the sun, our spirits will be enlivened. There is always another day, right?"

It sounded somewhat hollow, but then again, Justin figured that maybe that was life. Sometimes, you couldn't escape the consequences of bad decisions, and just had to lie to yourself to keep going. He felt that in his core.

They parted ways, and Justin and Lila headed to their room. As they walked, Justin could feel nothing but a distinct lack of belief that this was real, that when he went to bed, he would wake up back in his old life.

It hadn't happened yet, but perhaps someday it would.

It *had* to, right?

Inside the room, the subdued light from a single lantern flickered. That lantern illuminated the bath Lila had ordered, a detail that Justin had completely forgotten about. It was still warm, its curling steam inviting.

Given the somber end to the evening, whatever mood there had been between him and Lila—that was, if he hadn't been misinterpreting things—had been completely killed.

But she surprised him by touching his arm. "You okay? That was some heavy stuff."

"It was," Justin agreed. "I hope Eldrin's okay. He seems so friendly. It's hard to believe he's ever done anything *that* bad."

Lila gave a sad smile. "Those who wear the brightest smiles often carry the heaviest sorrows."

Justin paused, considering her words. "That's...pretty profound. And kind of depressing."

"I'm a Bard. What do you expect?"

But before anything more could be said, there was a bump at the window. Justin was wondering if he had imagined the disturbance when another bump, more insistent, hit the windowpane again.

Lila went over, peering down. "Someone's down there."

Justin joined her, peering into the darkness of the alley below.

With a start, he realized he recognized the person down there.

And from the stern expression on that someone's face, something was terribly wrong.

14

THE MARK OF DEATH

"Six worlds, six attributes, six gods—Creation is obsessed with sixes. Perhaps the Creator found the number pleasing, or perhaps He simply lacked the imagination to go beyond it. Either way, beware the seventh of anything. That's where things get...unstable."

—Mystic Lorian Kavel,
   Patterns in the Divine

JUSTIN SLID THE WINDOW OPEN. "Alistair? What are you doing here?"

There was a moment's pause as Alistair the Paladin stared up at him in shock and disbelief. His white robes over his steel armor made him stick out like a sore thumb. "Justin? Is that you, lad?"

"Yes. Are you following me?"

Lila joined him at the window, and Alistair looked at each of them.

"I take it you know him?" Lila asked.

Before Justin could answer, Alistair cut him off. "Listen. Something's amiss. Can we meet in the alehouse below?"

"Can't this wait until tomorrow?"

"I'm afraid not. Your life is in question, boy. I won't say anything more. Hurry!"

Alistair headed out of the alley and toward the entrance of the alehouse.

"Your life?" Lila asked. "Sounds serious."

"He must be confused," Justin said. "I need to go down there."

"I'm coming with you," Lila said.

"Sure. What about Eldrin?"

"Ah, just let him sleep. From tonight, it seems like he's ready to go his own way."

The duo left the room and headed down to the tavern. There, it was mostly empty, with Alistair sitting alone in a corner. Justin and Lila joined him.

"So," Justin said, "what's this about me dying?"

"Careful what you say," Alistair said, his eyes scanning their surroundings. "You never know who might be listening."

"Okay then," Justin said, quieter. "Why are you following me? It's been a long day, and I would like to rest."

"I wouldn't be speaking to you if it weren't important, so I'll cut to the chase. I'm on a quest, bestowed by the Templars of Arion themselves."

"The Templars of Arion," Lila said. "Sounds serious."

"Aye, very much so. A necromancer is wreaking havoc in the County of Silverton. And I have tracked down an agent of the necromancer to this very inn."

As his piercing blue eyes settled on Justin, a silent accusation hung in the still air.

But before fear could fully grip him, Lila's voice rang out. "What, are you accusing Justin? Justin, the Level 1 Socialite?"

"Indeed, my Paladin's Sense detects an agent of darkness sitting at this very table. Death magic is emanating from you, Justin."

"You must be mistaken," Justin said. "And you are leveling a very heavy accusation. Besides, if you can detect this 'death magic' on me, then why didn't you notice it before, when you helped me at Mistwatch?"

"That's what I'm trying to figure out."

"I don't have time for this. I really need to get to sleep. I have a level-up to process."

Justin rose, but Alistair's arm shot out, keeping him seated with iron strength. He wasn't going anywhere tonight until he'd answered some questions.

"You must tell me everything that has happened since we last parted, Justin," Alistair said. "You must do so if you wish to prove your innocence."

"Where I come from, you have to prove that I'm guilty."

Alistair gave an amused smile. "That is not how things are done by the Templars of Arion."

"Is that a threat?" Lila asked.

"Nay," Alistair said. "But my sense has never failed me, and it has led me right to your window. There is more to you than meets the eye, Justin Talemaker."

Justin locked eyes with him and sighed. "You want to know what's happened with me? Well, I'll tell you, and you'll see I've done nothing wrong."

Justin caught him up on everything. It took half an hour or so, but soon, Alistair was up to speed.

But Justin couldn't help but notice that the Paladin's disposition had darkened when they had gotten to their interaction with Baron Valdrik.

Once done, Alistair seemed to think deeply, taking a deep draught from his mug.

"The puzzle is coming together."

"What puzzle?" Justin asked.

"It must be the Baron of Silverton," Alistair said. "He is among my top suspects. You mentioned him uttering words in the Foundation Language of Vranthillis. What were those words again?"

"I have no idea."

"What does Vranthillis have to do with anything?" Lila asked.

"Could be nothing. Could be everything. The language is mysterious, and there are very few Lexicants. But what few Lexicants *do* exist are somewhat known for dabbling in the darker arts, and some have even been known to take up necromancy. It's a path open to Lexicants, given the right conditions."

"Okay, but what does this have to do with me?" Justin asked.

"You mentioned that the Baron spoke in Vranthillis. My suspicion is that he placed a death mark upon you. A mark that would make you his to command upon your death."

Justin's eyes went wide. "Upon my death? Is he trying to murder me?"

"Well, there would be little other reason to place the death mark. It takes time to mature. Three risings of the moon, to be precise. If he did this today, then this would be your first night."

"I'm going to die in three days?" Justin asked, feeling as if he was going to pass out.

"Not from the mark itself," Alistair clarified. "It merely means that once you *do* die, the mark will make you controllable by the Baron. Bound to him in undead thralldom."

Lila looked at Justin nervously. "He *did* mention wanting you to work for him..."

"That's *worse* than dying!" Justin said. "There must be some way to stop it!"

"There is," Alistair said, "but it requires you to pay very close attention to me. Now, I came here to root out the evil in this town that has been festering. On the surface, it might seem a busy and prosperous place. But there has been a string of murders stretching back years, and the local government doesn't seem to want to investigate them adequately. The sheriff, unfortunately, has been bribed to look the other way."

"So we've heard," Lila said.

"That's where I come in," Alistair said. "The Church of Light sent me here to figure out just what's going on. And now, I've discovered that things are a bit too much for a single Paladin to handle."

"Well, what can I do?" Justin asked.

"Now, this death mark can be cured," Alistair said. "But the paths to doing so are far from easy."

Justin was filled with many conflicting emotions. Fear. Confusion. Skepticism. He wanted to trust Alistair, and yet he didn't *feel* any different.

The only thing that had felt strange was that sense of coldness when Baron Valdrik had spoken those words. If Alistair was right, the Baron was keeping tabs on him right now and was determined to finish what he had started. He suddenly felt exposed and unsafe, despite the comfortable aura of the inn.

"We need to wake up Eldrin," Justin decided. "If I'm really in danger, then he is too by association."

"Eldrin?" Alistair asked.

"A Ranger we met in Whispering Pines," Justin said. "We sort of fell in together."

"I can go get him," Lila said.

She went off, leaving Justin alone with the Paladin.

Alistair leaned forward. "If those two aren't to be trusted, simply say the word and we'll be off."

"I trust them."

The Paladin eyed him closely, then nodded.

Eldrin joined them at the table, surprisingly alert for the late hour. "What's this about Justin being in danger?"

"I have a death mark on me, apparently. Courtesy of Baron Valdrik."

Eldrin's eyes widened at that. He looked at Alistair. "You can confirm this, Master Paladin?"

"Aye. I cannot determine the nature of the mark, but given the certainty of there being a necromancer in this town, it cannot be anything else."

"And what is your suggestion? I suppose I must be in danger too?"

"All of us are," Alistair said. "There are only two ways for Justin to rid himself of this mark. The first is a near impossibility, taking down the Baron himself, who uttered the incantation. But if the disappearances of the past few years are any indication, it's not only the Baron we'd have to contend with, but also those working for him."

"You think he has a small undead army in his halls?" Eldrin asked.

"I'm certain of it," Alistair said. "And in fact, I suspect that army might not be small. Worse, Valdrik's level far exceeds anyone sitting at this table. There is no record, but he had to be at least level twenty to have access to the Lexicant class, and it's likely, given the bloody work in this town and its environs, that he must be much higher than that. More than a match for even me."

"Then why did you come here thinking you could take him down?" Lila asked.

"I didn't. I came to learn more."

"But how do I get rid of the mark?" Justin pressed. "You said there's a way."

"Yes," Alistair said. "You must come with me to the Templar Chapter House at Mont Elea. There, the High Priest of Arion can remove the mark. He's the only one I know who for sure out-levels the Baron and has access to the right kind of magic. It's about a hundred miles north of Belmora."

"That far?" Lila asked. "We can't cover such a distance in three days!"

"No, we cannot," Alistair agreed, leaning forward. "But I will be with you every step of the way, protecting you from any and all pursuit. Remember, the mark becomes active in three days, and it won't kill Justin outright. But it *will* allow the Baron to know exactly where Justin is. If he's close enough. We need to be well ahead of them when that time comes. What's more, once the Baron realizes *I'm* here, he will act immediately."

"Then we must leave now," Eldrin said. "Although, if all this is true, then surely the gates will mark our passing."

"There is a hidden way," Alistair said. "It's a mountain path located on the north side of the pass, by the silver mines. That way will be little watched, and if you're coming with us, Eldrin, all the better. Your Pathfinder's Pace will be vital to our escape. I assume you have that party tactic?"

"I do," Eldrin confirmed. "I stand ready to help."

"Wait a second," Lila said. "What do you think was in the parcel? Does it have anything to do with this?"

"Perhaps," Alistair said. "Or maybe it was just a coincidence that Justin was the one who made the delivery."

"Maybe the Baron uses these parcels to lure new victims into his manor," Eldrin suggested.

"That is also possible. But the point is, Eldrin is right. We must leave immediately. For whatever reason, he wants to enthrall Justin."

The only question Justin was left with was, "Why?" However, he doubted that the question could be answered by anyone here.

"I need to gather my things," Justin said.

"Let's reconvene in five minutes," Alistair said. "Try to hurry."

Justin and Lila rushed to their room. The darkness of the hallway seemed altogether threatening as he fumbled for the room key and unlocked the door. But everything inside was undisturbed, awaiting their arrival.

It only took a minute for Justin to pack, along with Lila. They both shared a look, slightly unbelieving of the situation, before they rejoined Alistair and Eldrin in the alehouse below.

But as soon as Justin came forward, he reached for the dagger on his belt.

Alistair and Eldrin were no longer alone.

15

FLIGHT FROM SILVERTON

"The first and most important rule of necromancy? Don't get caught. The second? Always have an alibi that doesn't involve graveyards after midnight."

—Merrik Duskbane,
    Reportedly said hours before he was flayed and burned alive.

STANDING with them was a group of heavily armed men, with no identifying markers that would attach them to any particular house or government. To Justin, the room felt much colder, and at least half of the men bore expressions completely devoid of humanity, their eyes carrying a dull, almost lifeless glint.

Justin didn't want to think it, but he knew that these men were undead. He felt fear twisting his stomach into knots just by being in their presence.

"Looks like the Baron didn't waste any time," Alistair commented dryly, his hand resting on the haft of his silver hammer. His posture was rigid, ready for a fight.

Justin could feel his heart pounding in his chest. Beside him, Lila held one of her daggers on her belt, her stance defensive yet ready to strike. Eldrin seemed ready to draw his longsword at a moment's notice.

The leader of the group, a tall man with cold, gray eyes, wearing leather armor and a dark cloak that seemed to drink in the surrounding light, stepped forward. "Well, well, Alistair of Drakendale," he sneered, his voice echoing strangely in the silent room. "Looks like you've been sticking your nose where it doesn't belong again."

Alistair didn't respond to him. His face was a stoic mask as he stared down the challenger, but the tension in the room seemed to increase tenfold.

"Justin, listen to me," Alistair said, his voice low. "I want you to take Lila and run. Fancy words won't do any good here. I'll hold them off."

"Not alone you won't," Eldrin said. His eyes flickered toward Justin. "I'll catch up with you later."

"No, we can't just leave you here!" Lila protested, but Alistair's stern gaze silenced her.

"This is not a request, Lila. It's an order. Now, promise me. You know where to go."

The moment hung in the air, and Justin could sense her uncertainty and then reluctant acceptance.

Finally, Lila nodded. "I promise."

The leader watched all this play out in silence. His gray eyes found Justin, looking at him with obvious disdain. "Seems like you've gotten yourself into quite a mess, boy. But not to worry. The Baron is quite merciful. It is you he wants, and if you come with me, you can save the lives of all your friends. He only wants to talk."

"If that's true, then why bring all these swords?" Justin asked.

"Justin, go!" Alistair ordered.

Alistair stepped forward, and with that movement, the tension snapped. Alistair and Eldrin moved with a synchronicity born of years of training. Alistair's hammer swept in a wide arc, felling the rightmost undead lackey, while the Ranger shot forward with adroit ease, engaging another of the undead minions in a series of swift and deadly strikes. The tall leader took a step back, drawing a long curved blade that, like his armor, seemed to drink in the surrounding light.

"Come on!" Lila said, pulling Justin's arm.

They sprinted toward the back exit. They burst into the night, the chaos of the battle echoing behind them. There was only a sliver of a waning moon, offering them the cover of darkness as they raced through the empty streets toward the eastern edge of the town. Justin had to trust Lila knew the way.

They ran as fast as their legs could carry them, their breaths coming in ragged gasps. The cool night air stung Justin's lungs, but they couldn't afford to slow down, even after the sounds of fighting had long ebbed. At this hour, the streets were mostly empty, and in the smaller alleys and byways Lila selected, no guards challenged their passing.

It wasn't long before they were weaving up some steps into the eastern mountain flanking Silverton, on the opposite side of the valley where Baron Valdrik had his mansion. Over here, it was mostly industry: mines, smelters, and forges that would be heavy with activity during the day.

"Where's that damn path?" Lila asked. "As if we're supposed to know where we're going!"

Justin didn't answer. It was much too dark to see. He wished he had nabbed one of the lanterns hanging in the inn, but it was too late for that.

They had barely taken a few uncertain steps into the darkness when a chilling moan pierced the silence. From the shadows behind them, an armored figure with a pike emerged, its movements jerky and unnatural. It was surely one of the Baron's minions, and it had managed to track them here, ignoring the fight back at the inn.

Justin's mind raced. His Poison Barb ability had always been his go-to in confrontations, but this...this was something else.

All the same, he had to try.

With a surge of adrenaline, he unleashed the most cutting insult he could muster at that moment, aiming it directly at the undead creature.

"Is this the best you can do? You move slower than a snail with a limp!"

The undead's only response was a continued, relentless advance, unaffected by the verbal jab. Clearly, this creature lacked the sapience of the undead speaker down in the inn. More than that, Justin's ability hadn't even been activated. The creature before them was completely immune to it.

But at least the barb caused Lila to wake up. She drew her throwing knives, the blades whistling with deadly intent. Despite the darkness, all three struck true, the last one in the neck.

But horrifyingly, the creature barely reacted; its hollow gaze was fixed on them as it extended its pike. The necromantic magic controlling the minion was not to be denied.

Justin felt panic set in. They were being cornered, their backs pressed against the cold stone of a forge.

"The head!" Justin said. "Go for the head!"

He was far too tired to run, but even so, he made a feeble bid to escape, pulling Lila along with him. He knew they couldn't keep it up for much longer.

They had only made it a few steps when something black shot down from the sky with a chilling screech, talons extended.

It was Shadowflight. There was a moment of fighting between the brave bird and the zombie soldier, and it wasn't long before the falcon disengaged, buying them another moment.

But another moment was all they needed. An arrow whistled through the air, piercing the undead soldier squarely through the head. The zombie stumbled and crumpled to the ground.

At the top of the steps stood their rescuer, his robes dark in the night and Shadowflight now fluttering on his shoulder.

"Eldrin!" Justin exclaimed.

Eldrin approached, offering a grim smile. "Night's not over yet, it seems."

A moment later, Alistair burst onto the scene, his silver hammer gleaming under the moonlight, his expression grim. With a mighty roar and a fatal swing, he delivered the final blow, crushing the undead soldier's head into oblivion with an overhead strike. It seemed Paladins were aware of the importance of the double tap.

Alistair, breathing heavily from the exertion, turned to Justin and Lila, his expression all business. "We need to move. The Baron's forces won't stop here."

"Why does he even care about me?" Justin asked.

"You're a loose end. This could crumble all of his ambitions."

Justin nodded, the reality of their situation sinking in. They were in the heart of a battle they had barely begun to understand, against forces darker and more powerful than they could have imagined. But with Eldrin and Alistair by their side, they at least stood a fighting chance.

"What have I gotten myself into?" Lila asked, working quickly to retrieve and clean her knives.

[Eldrin has joined the party. You now benefit from the expertise of his Pathfinder's Pace.]

[Alistair has joined the party. You are now refreshed by his Divine Aura, granting complete immunity to the Fear effect.]

[Alistair has assumed the role of party leader.]

No one answered Lila as Alistair led them into the darkness. Justin could hardly see anything, but the Paladin seemed to know the way. Before long, Justin realized they were in a narrow cleft, with a rough trail beneath their feet and nothing but the sliver of dark sky above filled with stars to light their way.

They kept climbing, Alistair setting a brutal pace despite his heavy armor and swirling white cloak. Eldrin brought up the rear, periodically turning to watch the trail behind. Shadowflight circled above, seemingly in communion with the Ranger.

Justin sucked in breath after breath; it never seemed to be enough. Even when they rose above the cleft, the narrow trail before them was engulfed in darkness. Silverton spread below them, hundreds of two- and three-story buildings looking deceptively peaceful and cozy below, more windows dark than yellow. The mountain slope soon became forested, and the dense foliage seemed to swallow them whole.

"Should've picked up that parcel while we had the chance," Lila grumbled.

Justin was far too winded to respond. But all it took was one thought of those undead minions, who likely didn't get tired, for him to keep moving. In his mind, he couldn't help but see Baron Valdrik's cruel visage leering at him.

Three nights. He had three nights. His only hope was to reach Mont Elea and pray whoever was there could really help him. He wanted to ask if there would be any bad side effects of the mark, but he simply didn't have the breath to ask, and no one else was talking.

They ran in bursts, walking only when Justin and Lila could not keep pace. At this point, Alistair cast some sort of light spell that illuminated the immediate space around them, which made the going much easier. Justin supposed Alistair judged that the cover of the forest would block the light from spreading too much.

"What's that magic?" Justin asked.

"Some sort of spell, Creator's Light, I think it is called," Lila said. "Paladins get some basic healing and support magic."

Over the next few hours, they wrapped around the mountain, and Silverton was left behind. Before them spread a forested valley filled with many hills.

"The trail ends here," Alistair said. "Eldrin, would you take over and lead with your Pathfinder's Pace?"

"Of course," Eldrin said.

Eldrin, leading the way, seemed to navigate the terrain with an uncanny precision that only a Ranger of his caliber could possess.

"Keep close," Eldrin instructed, his voice low. "The night is full of more than just shadows."

Lila, despite her fatigue, managed to smile at Justin. "He always talks like he's quoting from an ancient tome, doesn't he?"

Justin remained quiet at the joke, finding that he was simply too tired to respond.

Eldrin's Pathfinder's Pace was remarkable. Just as when they went to Raven's Rock, it allowed them to traverse the rough, uneven ground at a pace Justin wouldn't have thought possible. The natural obstacles that should have slowed their progress seemed almost to melt away before Eldrin's expertise.

However, as the hours wore on, even Eldrin's skillful guidance couldn't ward off the exhaustion that clung to Justin like a second skin. His legs felt like lead, while every step was an effort of will. The adrenaline that had fueled him thus far was waning, and the emotional weight of his revelations at the alehouse, combined with the physical toll of their escape, was catching up.

Finally, noticing Justin's staggering steps, Eldrin called a halt. "We'll rest here." He gestured to a shallow cleft in the hillside that would offer some protection from the elements and concealment from any who might be pursuing them. "We'll have to trust our enemies can't pick up the trail, and for Shadowflight to keep watch. It's only the latter of which I'm certain."

"Do you believe your Pathfinder's Pace has not adequately covered our tracks?" Alistair asked.

"I'm certain it has," Eldrin replied. "However, against the power of a high-level Lexicant and necromancer, it can be difficult to predict the future."

On that ominous note, they settled into the cleft, the ground hard and unwelcoming beneath them, but Justin was too tired to care. Lila and Eldrin busied themselves with setting up a minimal camp, while Alistair stood watch, his gaze scanning the darkness. He allowed his Creator's Light to dissipate.

As Justin lay down, the ground beneath him seemed to spin. He closed his eyes, and within moments, the exhaustion overtook him, pulling him into a deep, dreamless sleep. His last conscious thought was a mix of gratitude for the safety of the moment and a lingering worry about what the dawn would bring.

16

A NEW SKILL

"Over the millennia, countless kingdoms and empires have risen and fallen across the face of Eyrth. Each has clung to the vain promise that one day, they might reclaim the glory of the Ethereal Era. But such a promise can never be fulfilled. Why? Because magic, for all its power to create and build, is equally—and tragically—the greatest agent of destruction. The higher civilization soars on the wings of magic, the more devastating its fall when those wings inevitably burn."

—Chronicler Ellisar Vain
   When Empires Fall: A History of the Aftermath

As soon as Justin felt the first bit of consciousness, the Voice entered his mind. Or at least, what Lila called "the Voice." He supposed if he was in this world, too, perhaps he should think of it in the same way.

[You have reached Level 2. A new day has dawned, and despite the challenges you have thus far faced, you feel hopeful for the new day ahead.]

Much to Justin's surprise, he actually did feel hopeful, though he had no real reason to, given the circumstances. As when he reached Level 1, the feeling seemed to enter from outside himself.

[You have one attribute point to distribute.]

His interface sat open before him, waiting for him to place his new point.

Justin considered whether it might be beneficial to put it in Endurance to increase his survivability and perhaps even help with the long marches ahead.

In the end, he heaved a sigh and locked his point into Charisma.

[Your Charisma is now 12.]

Almost instantly, he felt a lightening of his spirit that was hard to quantify, too subtle to put into words.

[As a Level 2 Socialite, you have unlocked your next class skill. Choose wisely—there is no going back!]

Justin looked through both of the skills that were presented to him.

Dazzling Display (Rare): Once a day, channel the charisma of legendary figures you have encountered, adopting their gravitas, movements, or manner of speech, enthralling those in your presence. This effect deepens as your Charisma grows.

Justin thought it over. The first thing that caught his attention was the "Rare" marker, something he had yet to see. That told him that this skill, in particular, might be quite powerful.

He examined his other option:

Tantalizing Miasma: Exude an indelible aroma that enchants those around you, boosting your Charisma by 5 for five minutes. (Cooldown: 4 hours)

As the morning light filtered through the dense canopy, Justin mulled over each skill with quiet intensity.

Dazzling Display and Tantalizing Miasma—each skill whispered potential, each a tool that could shape his path in this world.

Dazzling Display seemed like a beacon in the chaos, a flare shot to momentarily gain a crowd's attention. Its once-a-day limit underscored its potency. In a world where swords and spells decided fates, could a charismatic display sway the balance? Distraction could mean the difference between safety and peril. A sudden, captivating gesture could provide the critical seconds needed for escape or to turn the tide of a negotiation.

Then, there was Tantalizing Miasma. Unlike Dazzling Display, it could be used once every four hours, which made it more useful in that way. The +5 boost to Charisma was reliable, and that it hung around for an extra five minutes was nice. But, unlike Dazzling Display, it seemed less of a guarantee to get what he wanted and more of a slight advantage.

In a land governed by alliances and enmities, words could be as sharp as any blade. The Tantalizing Miasma skill offered the opportunity to forge connections, to unravel intentions, and perhaps even to unveil secrets hidden behind layers of diplomacy or deceit. He could imagine himself in a social situation with a lot of people, like a party, where this skill would be incredibly useful.

Justin pondered his past life on Earth, filled with missed cues and misunderstood intentions. He thought about the loneliness that had gnawed at him, the isolation of not quite fitting in. Here, in Eyrth, was a chance to rewrite that narrative. To be someone who not only belonged but thrived.

He considered the future, too. Encounters with bandits, negotiations with potential allies, and perhaps even audiences with royalty lay ahead. The path of a Socialite was not to overpower but to weave through society's fabric, influencing threads one conversation at a time. Words could topple kingdoms or build them more surely than a single sword.

Tantalizing Miasma felt like the right choice. However, Dazzling Display felt like the more interesting choice and also like more of a sure thing. Plus, there was the Rare modifier, telling Justin that the skill could be quite powerful, even if he didn't understand how it worked in practice.

With a decisive mental click, Justin selected Dazzling Display.

[You have chosen: Dazzling Display. May your poise and flair become your destiny.]

As he stood, stretching muscles sore from the night's exertions, Justin felt a newfound confidence. He was still a Socialite, yes, but increasingly he was becoming one well-equipped to navigate the complex tapestry of Eyrthian society. Or was it Eyrthi society?

Assuming he ever made it back to society.

With a nod to himself, he rose to face the day.

"You too, huh?" Lila asked with a smile.

Justin turned, surprised to see that not only was she awake, but that Eldrin and Alistair were breaking camp.

"Yeah!" Justin said. "I'm Level 2 now!"

"Wonderful!" Lila said, beaming. "Me too!"

Justin quickly checked his interface.

[Experience to Level 3: 404/250 (Level-up available!)]

He frowned. "I have enough experience to be Level 3, so why am I not?"

"You'll have to sleep again, and it needs to be real sleep, not just a nap. You can't do two level-ups in one night."

"What defines real sleep?"

"The gods, of course! Now, what skill did you get?"

Justin told her his decision, and she looked impressed. "Dazzling Display! That sounds pretty useful."

"What's your skill?"

She concentrated, as if reading something in the air. "Rhythmic Barrage: Unleash a flurry of knife throws, with each successive hit increasing damage based on a percentage of your Coordination attribute. The barrage can chain up to six times."

"That sounds like it could be powerful!"

"That's why I picked it. Could've come in handy last night. Now I've just got to get me some more knives to throw..."

By now, Eldrin and Alistair were putting out the night's fire. With practiced efficiency, the entire camp was picked up. Shadowflight was nowhere to be seen and was likely scouting behind them for signs of pursuit.

"What about breakfast?" Lila asked. "Leveling makes me hungry."

"Enjoy those early levels," Eldrin said with a wink. "Progression takes longer the higher you go."

"What do you mean?" Justin asked.

"Levels start off unlocking quite quickly," Alistair explained. "For example, it takes just one point to go from 0 to 1, and only 200 points to go from 1 to 2. After that, the experience requirement for each level increases roughly by 30%. So, in practice, it's quite easy to reach Level 10, but beyond that it gets tougher. Which is why you won't find very many people who are Level 20 and beyond."

"How many levels are there?" Justin asked.

"Most say 40 is the limit, but if there are any of those, there aren't many."

"We should get moving," Eldrin said, passing around some cheese and bread. "We'll eat on the trail."

Not a few seconds later, he was blazing a rapid trail through the bush.

The morning sun cast shadows through the trees as Eldrin led them deeper into the wilderness. The air was crisp, laden with the scent of pine and damp earth. Birds chirped their morning songs, providing a soundtrack to their journey. It seemed they were well into the mountains now, though Justin supposed they might fairly be called tall hills.

So far, there were no signs of the Baron and his minions. Justin hoped it would stay that way.

Eldrin's Pathfinder's Pace was nothing short of miraculous. Despite the uneven terrain and dense underbrush, they moved quickly and efficiently. Justin marveled at how effortlessly Eldrin navigated the forest, avoiding obstacles and finding the best paths with ease. Every so often, Eldrin would stop, raising a hand to signal them to listen or observe a particular detail—a broken branch, a footprint, or the distant call of an animal.

Justin and Lila kept close behind, their eyes scanning the surroundings for any sign of danger. Justin wasn't sure how much good he was doing, but he figured it was better to look busy.

As they walked, he couldn't get rid of the sinking feeling in his stomach. Just the idea that the Baron had marked him for death made him feel a sense of dread, even if nothing was different physically. Alistair brought up the rear. From time to time, he'd call out the general direction for Eldrin to go, and the Ranger would dutifully find the most efficient path there.

As the hours passed, they encountered various wildlife—deer grazing in a clearing, a family of rabbits darting into their burrows, and even a majestic stag that watched them curiously from a distance. Despite the situation, Justin felt a sense of wonder at the natural beauty around him. It was a far cry from his previous life. This reality was just as real as his own, almost to the point where he was wondering if his world was the dream. Thoughts of his old life still came to the fore, but as the days passed, as this world took firmer hold, it was starting to feel more distant.

Occasionally, they would come across strange runes etched into the bark of trees or carved into broken masonry along their path. Clearly, this area had once hosted buildings, or even entire cities, now reclaimed by nature. Eldrin would pause to examine these markings, his brow furrowed.

"What are those?" Justin asked.

"Markers left by past travelers," Eldrin said. "They often denote areas of significance or hidden dangers."

"Hidden dangers?" Lila asked. "Like what?"

"That remains to be seen."

"I think we must have taken a wrong turn," Alistair said. "I've traveled these lands before and have never run across these markings."

"The Umber Range has many hidden pockets and secrets," Eldrin said, somewhat mysteriously. "One could spend years here and not uncover a quarter of them."

"You've led us astray, Ranger?"

"Nay. This is a faster way to the Guardian Pass. It's much safer."

Alistair gave a grunt. "I hope so. Lead on."

As they continued, the forest began to change subtly. The trees grew taller and denser, their branches forming a thick canopy that filtered the sunlight into dappled patches on the forest floor. The air grew cooler, and a strange tension seemed to permeate their surroundings. Justin almost wanted to describe it as electricity, but it wasn't that. It was some form of energy. Magic, maybe.

All he knew was that he didn't really like it. It felt like someone, or something, was watching him.

By late afternoon, they reached a small stream, its clear water bubbling over smooth stones. They paused to refill their canteens and rest for a moment.

"Are you sure we're going the right way?" Alistair asked.

"Yes," Eldrin confirmed. "I've been in this forest before. Its magic will make anything undead think twice before crossing through it."

"It feels...weird," Justin said. "I hope we pass it soon."

"It shouldn't be long," Eldrin said. "We're making good time." He glanced up at the sky. "If we keep this pace, we should reach the outskirts of the valley by nightfall."

"Good," Alistair said, his eyes scanning the horizon. "The farther we get from Silverton, the better."

They moved on, the land sloping upward slightly. No one spoke, and an hour later, the silence was broken.

"The pass to the Aranthian Plain beyond should be coming up shortly," Eldrin said. "We can make camp on the other side."

But as they made a final bend around a cliff, Justin didn't see a pass at all. A narrow canyon greeted them, at the end of which stood the entrance to a cave. A barrier of light covered the cave's entrance, affixed with runes that glowed faintly.

Justin and Lila gasped at the sight, while Eldrin and Alistair looked grim.

"Is this some trick, Ranger?" Alistair said. "You had better take care in how you answer!"

"This is no trick," Eldrin answered. "This is the pass. I know these lands like the back of my hand. This is surely not a cave."

"What are you talking about?" Justin asked nervously.

Alistair heaved a sigh. "Alas. It would seem, for better or worse, that we have stumbled upon a Vault."

The party stood for a moment, considering. When Alistair had talked about Vaults, this wasn't what Justin had in mind. He'd imagined decrepit castles, ancient ruins, and temples inside a volcano. Standard RPG fare.

This cave—or Vault—looked perfectly ordinary, aside from the barrier of light covering it.

Justin cleared his throat. "Didn't you say Vaults were highly dangerous, Eldrin?"

"Very much so."

"We should turn back," Lila said, her face pale. "This is far too dangerous for people like me and Justin."

"I concur," Alistair said. "What's the fastest path around?"

"We'd have to do a fair bit of backtracking, since we've already come so far up the slope," Eldrin said. "But to go back would also be risky."

"Risky, how?" Justin said. "Riskier than this Vault? That's hard to believe."

At this moment, there was a dark flutter of movement that fell from the sky as Shadowflight perched on Eldrin's shoulder. The Ranger communed with the bird for a moment, his expression grave.

"They're getting closer. Fifteen men, some undead, some not. They are a mix of soldiers and mages, with Gareth at the helm."

"Arion above," Alistair said. "It's worse than I thought."

"We have to remember that every step backward is a step closer to them. Despite the failing light, we were quite exposed going up the mountain here. If any member of their group has a class that grants enhanced sight, they might have been able to see us up here, though I've done my utmost to cover our tracks. So, the question becomes, is there time to choose another way?"

"Is there another way?" Alistair asked. "If this Vault has sprung up on the pass, then the pass is closed to us anyway. We have no choice but to turn back, no?"

"Not necessarily," Eldrin said. "Hypothetically speaking, if we were to clear this Vault, it would disappear, allowing us to continue on our journey through the pass."

"I know how Vaults work," Alistair said, almost grumbling. "However, clearing the Vault would take time. Assuming we are successful, the Baron's minions might be awaiting our exit."

"The pass itself is quite long," Eldrin said. "About five miles. Worst case, assuming the Vault takes up most of the space on the path, we would have a five-mile head start on our pursuers, assuming we can come out the other side. My guess is, given the Vault's location, that option will be open to us. And once we enter the Vault, its magic will prevent anyone else from following after us. That should give us enough time to make it to Highcliff. From there, we can push on, picking up the Queensroad to the Gulfway, and then north to Mont Elea."

"I say it's too much of a risk," Alistair said. "And yet, going back could be even worse if your falcon has the right of it. The soldiers I can handle, but even a mage or two could tip the scales."

"The longer we talk here, the more we're trapped," Lila said. She glanced at Justin. "What do you think? Should we give it a go?"

Justin hesitated, weighing their options. The Vault could be a faster route, but it was also filled with unknown dangers. Plus, at least in the games he was used to, dungeons were cleared by damage-dealing characters, tanks, and healers, and most assuredly not Socialites. What good would he be? Alistair and Eldrin would be carrying them all, most likely. Even Lila had the benefit of her knife-throwing skills.

What was he supposed to do, dazzle his enemies with small talk and charm them into submission?

He glanced at Alistair and Lila, seeing the concern etched on their faces.

"I don't know," Justin admitted. "It's risky. What if we run into something I can't handle?"

Alistair nodded in agreement. "It's true. Vaults are unpredictable. We could find ourselves in more trouble than we bargained for. And once we enter, there are two ways out. Clearing it, or dying."

Putting it in such a way made Justin feel a cold dread.

"There are different types of Vaults," Eldrin said. "Some are static. The dangers and challenges within are the same, no matter the composition of the party. Some, however, are dynamic. That means they are calibrated for the levels and classes of the people who enter. They will be a challenge, but are set up to be achievable."

"The trick is, how can we tell which one is which?" Lila asked.

"That's the thing," Alistair said. "We can't really. If we were to go closer, we'd get a sense of what to expect inside from the Vault description, but that's hardly a guarantee."

"I imagine there would be treasure," Justin said. "Right?"

"Assuredly," Eldrin said. "Given the danger pursuing us, I say we press on. It's the most direct route, and something tells me that this Vault may have formed for a reason. It's entirely too coincidental."

"That's speculation!" Lila said. "If there's another option, what is it? Justin and I are incredibly vulnerable. To go in would be irresponsible!"

The Ranger shrugged. "We would need to backtrack about an hour and then head north. In another week, there will be another pass, harder to cross. We will be greatly slowed since our supplies won't stretch so far. While we need to stop and eat, the undead have less need for sustenance. Their progress will be slowed in the daytime, true, but at night, they can travel faster than even we can.

Seven days would be enough, perhaps, for them to catch up entirely. Not to mention that it takes us close to orcish territory."

Eldrin paused for a moment, seeming to sense something the others could not. Lila opened her mouth, but Eldrin held up a hand, pointing his ear down the mountainside.

"They're close now," he whispered after a moment. "Maybe a mile behind us. It seems the decision has been made for us."

Justin swallowed and felt his heart miss a beat. He reached for Eldrin's dagger at his belt, though he supposed the dagger was his now.

Alistair's face was grim. "Well, I am a Level 25 Paladin, and one would think that counts for something. Eldrin, though you are Level 10, you fight well beyond your abilities. Between the two of us, we should have no trouble clearing this Vault's trials. Indeed, as you said, we have little choice." He turned to face Lila and Justin. "Stay close, and no harm will befall you."

Justin and Lila both nodded shakily. Reluctantly, the party moved toward the entrance of the cave. The ancient runes flared to life as they approached, casting an eerie glow on everyone's faces.

Vault Discovered: The Guardian Pass

Recommended Party Level: 12

Average Party Level: 9.75

Risk Level: Highly Dangerous! Your party is below the recommended level. Disaster, dismemberment, or death is likely. Proceed with utmost care!

Description: The Guardian Pass once bore witness to a great battle between the Guardian Force of the Kingdom of Valoria and the Shadow Empire. Within its depths, your party will face trials designed to test your resolve, unity, and courage. Can you and your daring party rewrite history and turn around an impossible battle?

Rewards Upon Completion:

Experience: Scaled to party member level.

Guaranteed Bronze-Tier Item: For each party member.

Chance for a Silver-Tier Weapon: For one party member.

[Do you accept the Vault's challenge?]

Despite the danger of the situation, Justin couldn't help but feel a strange thrill. It almost felt like he was playing a game in his mom's basement again. Almost.

"We'll let Alistair lead," Eldrin said.

"Stay close to me," Alistair said. "I should vastly out-level everything here, so as long as you are near, we'll make it out in one piece."

Justin surely hoped so. "Lead the way."

Alistair gave a firm nod.

Justin felt a mental push to accept the Vault's challenge. He knew everyone else was receiving the same prod, and the challenge would only begin once everyone had confirmed their willingness to undergo it.

Lila sighed. "Well, here goes nothing."

[Your party has accepted the challenge of the Guardian Pass. May courage be your guide and your resolve your shield. And remember, don't discount the power of a single whisper. Good luck, Brave Adventurers.]

Justin felt something like a mental click in his head.

In tandem, the four party members passed the threshold of light and into the Vault.

17

FOLLOWING A HUNCH

"The Vaults are a mystery. Some claim they are the Creator's test, a chance for mortals to prove their worth and ascend their cores. Others whisper they are Morvath's cruel playground or Nyriss's Seeds of Chaos. Still, others say any divine being can spawn a Vault for their own inscrutable purpose. Whatever the truth, one thing is certain: the gods may create the Vaults, but it's fools who keep walking into them."

—Vault Runner Tharic Wren,
  An Adventurer's Guide to Vaults

To Justin's amazement, as they passed through, the cave was completely replaced by what he assumed to be the pass, just shy of full darkness. Two mountain peaks rose on either side, cloaked in shadow, while the weather had become colder. The sky above was completely clear and full of stars, where before it had been quite cloudy. Justin wasn't sure what was going on, but it probably had something to do with the magic of the Vault.

In the distance, Justin spied what looked like the light of many campfires, along with pavilions and tents, and shadowy figures moving about. Eldrin sent Shadowflight off to explore, and the dark bird was almost instantly lost to the sky above. But Justin didn't need the creature's intel to know what he was looking at. Even at a distance, it looked like something off the set of one of his favorite TV shows, *A Throne of Games*.

"An encampment," Alistair said. "This must be the Valorian Guardian Force."

"What do we do?" Lila asked. "Is the battle about to start?"

"Only one way to find out," the Paladin responded. "I imagine we're expected to offer our services to them, to turn the tide in an otherwise hopeless battle against the Shadow Empire."

"Valoria lost this battle," Eldrin said grimly. "Once, their cities completely filled the valleys of the Umber Range."

"That's what those ruins were, then," Justin said. "How did they lose the battle? That information might come in handy if we are to reverse history."

"Unfortunately, I've heard the tale before, but the details of exactly how they lost elude me. All I can say is Valoria was a small kingdom, hardly able to withstand the might of the Shadow Empire. The Empire went on to rule the entirety of Serenthel for the next four centuries."

"And we're expected to stop that somehow?" Lila asked in disbelief. Justin could see just how pale her face was under the moonlight.

"I would assume so," Alistair said. "But remember: this is not an actual recreation of history. This Vault is Level 12 and, as such, it should be perfectly possible to clear for our party. The only thing we can do is find out more."

They stepped into the light of the camp and were greeted by a somber scene. Soldiers dressed in heavy bronze armor sat around fires, spears and shields never far away. The martial technology seemed akin to Ancient Greece; steel armor, such as the kind Alistair wore, likely hadn't been discovered yet, or at least wasn't widespread. The soldiers were sharing quiet conversations in a strange tongue that Justin couldn't at first understand, but after a moment, in a strange burst of knowledge likely supplied by the Vault itself, he understood it as well as his own native English. They were over a thousand years in the past, so it made sense that the language was different, especially if this Vault was doing its best to correspond to a real historical event.

The soldiers were casting glances at the darkening sky.

"Aye, they'll attack tonight," Justin overheard one of them say. "Mark my words."

"They'll wait until morning," another disagreed. "They don't know the pass like we do, and they stand to lose too many men."

"They say they have fifty thousand. Fifty thousand, against our one thousand. I don't think the Empire cares about the loss of life; they'll want to end this as soon as they can, especially with our reinforcements a day away. You watch."

"A bright ray of sunshine, aren't you, Darian?"

Darian flashed a dark smile, and Justin didn't much like the look of him, though he couldn't have explained why. "Is there any point in saying otherwise? I welcome death and will fight to the last drop of my blood, just like any other Guardian. But we'd be fools to deny the truth. Soon, the Shadow will cover all of Serenthel. Mayhap death would be a mercy compared to what our wives and children will have to endure in the coming weeks."

"I'm done with you," the other soldier said in disgust. "If I truly have only a few hours left, I don't want to spend them with you."

"It matters not," Darian said with a dark chuckle. "I need to take a piss anyway. Mayhap the last one of my life."

Darian stood and left while the other nameless soldier simply sat, thinking dark thoughts.

Just hearing their conversation made Justin feel a sense of impending doom. Clearly, morale was incredibly low, and it wouldn't take much for the men to break.

They clearly had their work cut out for them.

They stayed out of the light of the fires, Alistair picking a path to avoid the soldiers who were still eating dinner. In this way, they made their way to the center of the camp, where what appeared to be the command tent stood. Two guards in full bronze armor, with spears and shields, stood outside, crossing their weapons at their approach.

"Who goes there?" the taller of the two said. "State your business or be gone!"

"Spies," the other guard said.

"We are no spies," Alistair said. "We've come to offer our aid in these dark times."

Only now did the soldiers seem to register his garb, their stance relaxing a bit. Their eyes seemed to go wide at his steel armor. "Sir Paladin. Forgive me. I didn't notice your robes at first. Has the Church of Light at last responded to our call for aid?"

"It has," Alistair confirmed. "I must speak with your commander at once."

"Where are the rest?" the other soldier said. "It's not just you, is it?"

"Alas, this was all they could spare," Alistair said. "But I assure you, I am here to fight, and if necessary, die for your cause."

"Bold words, Paladin. Better one Paladin than none, I say. They say the Shadow Empire is bringing the undead to this battle, so your aid will be much needed."

The second soldier took in the rest of them. "And who are your companions? A Ranger, I see, and that is well enough." He said nothing more as his eyes ran over Justin and Lila doubtfully.

"Friends and allies. Stronger than they appear, I assure you."

"For Valoria's sake, I would hope so. Wait here."

The soldier ducked into the tent, and not a moment later, came back out.

"You may go in. Commander Thalon is expecting you."

"I thank you," Alistair said. He nodded to the rest, and they ducked inside.

The commander's tent was spacious and well-organized. A large wooden table dominated the center, covered in maps and battle plans. The walls were adorned with black weapons and armor, many filled with wicked points. Justin could only assume the armor had once belonged to the enemy. Dim lanterns hung from the tent poles, casting a warm, flickering light that contrasted with the cold tension in the air.

Commander Thalon had the appearance of a grizzled veteran, with several scars marring his face. He was dressed in intricately carved bronze armor that suggested the shape of a stag. A few of his officers stood silently by, also in bronze, with stags carved into their breastplates. The animal was likely the emblem of Valoria.

From the empty goblets and plates with bones and trace scraps, Justin got the sense that they had been in here a while. Thalon watched the maps, deep in thought, seeming to search for a solution that wasn't there. His sharp blue eyes lifted as they entered, immediately taking in Alistair's presence with recognition and respect. He didn't seem to see anyone else.

"Sir Paladin," Thalon said. His voice was weary but commanding. "I had expected at least nine more of your brethren to heed our call to arms. At least, I got news this morning that the Chapter House of Ulua was withdrawing from the Seraphim Range and seemingly abandoning Valoria to its fate. Do you come bearing more ill tidings, or that hammer of yours?"

Alistair stepped forward. "My hammer, my lord. Though we are few in number, I would like you to take heart. We are here to offer our assistance in your battle against the Shadow Empire."

Thalon gave a dry chuckle. "Take heart? I know not if you mock us, but all of us here know the truth. This is to be our last stand against the Shadow. I have fought against them nearly since my first memory. The mountains have ever been Valoria's shield, even as other kingdoms have fallen around us. But it would be easier to stop a glacier with the palm of one's hand than the inevitability approaching us now."

"Maybe so," Alistair said. "But if we can win this battle, your country might have at least a few more years of freedom, and perhaps be able to secure favorable terms of peace. It is our intention to fight by your side, whatever the case. This battle can still be won, and I must ask you to have faith in Arion's plans."

"Arion. Yes. Some of the men are saying Arion is weak, blasphemy or not. When the Shadow is so strong, along with their Dark God, how can a man of faith not question? All of Calidon they hold, and it would seem Serenthel is next."

"Save these unwholesome thoughts for another time, my lord," Alistair said. "We are here to discuss strategy. My skills and abilities can stand up to the Shadow Empire's minions, and Eldrin the Ranger, who stands next to me, is not to be discounted."

"And these two?" Thalon asked, eyeing Lila and Justin. "They seem rather ill-suited to battle." His eyes seemed to dismiss Justin entirely. "There is yet time to flee to the Seraphim Range if you are fleet of foot."

"We are here to fight, too," Lila said. "Such as we can."

Justin nodded grimly, though he felt his stomach sink a bit at the thought. "The men's morale seems quite low. Perhaps I can give a speech or two. Try to encourage them."

"A Charisma class?" Thalon said. "Are you a Bard or perhaps a Diplomat?"

"A Socialite."

"Hah!" Thalon barked a laugh that seemed genuine. "The men will have a laugh at that! We need a good joke before we march to our doom."

Justin's cheeks colored, but he said nothing.

"Time is limited," Alistair pressed. "I am here to lend my knowledge of military strategy. Sometimes, a fresh pair of eyes is all it takes to find a solution."

"Perhaps. But if you can scrounge a solution from this muddled mess, many songs and stories will be dedicated to your name!"

"It is not my glory I'm worried about, but that of Arion. He has not abandoned you, Commander. Have faith, and we will come out on the other side."

"Maybe so, Sir Paladin. May I ask your name?"

"Sir Alistair of Drakendale."

"Drakendale. I've never heard of it, but I pray that it is indeed far from the threat of the Shadow Empire."

Justin was beginning to feel worse than useless. "Perhaps Lila and I can explore the camp a bit. Maybe we can find something out."

"Of course," Alistair said. "Don't stray too far. Return at once if you ever come under threat."

Lila watched Justin curiously, but in the end, she followed him out. Once out in the cold night, she rubbed her hands together. "I did *not* dress appropriately for this Vault!"

But Justin was already watching the campfire where they had passed the two soldiers and their grim conversation. Darian was still gone, while the other he'd been speaking to sat alone, staring into the flames.

"Don't discount the power of a single whisper," Justin mused.

"Hey," Lila said. "That's what the Vault description said, right?"

"It *has* to mean something. Come on."

He headed for the soldier, taking up a seat on a nearby stump without waiting for an invitation. He was a wiry man with a thick mustache, along with sharp features and short, cropped hair. His bronze armor, though scuffed and worn, was meticulously maintained. He had an honest face, at least by Justin's estimation.

"Good evening," Justin began. "Dark times for Valoria, eh?"

The man looked back into the fire, letting out a sharp breath and choosing not to respond.

It probably hadn't been the best thing to lead with.

"Who was that guy you were talking to back there?" Justin asked. "Darian, was it?"

This at least provoked an answer. "Yeah, that's his name. Shifty fellow. Never much liked him. He's gone now, and that's good enough for me."

"I'd hoped to speak with him," Justin went on. "Has he come back to camp yet?"

"Netherfuck if I know," the man said.

Justin blinked at the expletive. Damn, he'd have to remember that one for a rainy day.

Finally, the soldier looked up, seeming to take them both in. "What are you both doing out here? Squires to the sir in the tent?"

"Something like that," Justin said. "However, with the way things are looking, it would seem we're going to die like the rest of you."

The man gave a dark chuckle at that. "Well, if you were to head back west, I'd keep my lips sealed." He eyed their weapons. "There's not much those knives can do against the Shadow Empire's armies."

"Well, we're here to stay, for better or worse. Would you happen to know where Darian is bunking?"

"Why? What's it to you?"

Justin shrugged nonchalantly. "Nothing. We're just going around to talk to the men, see if we can boost spirits. He seems to be especially dispirited."

"Good luck in that," the man said. He looked at Lila. "And what's your contribution?"

"I'm a Bard," Lila said simply. "Have you heard the tale of the Star of Elara?"

The man's face softened into a smile. "Aye, who hasn't? What I wouldn't give to find that amulet! We could use a bit of protection right now." He paused for a moment. "My name is Georgius, by the way."

"Georgius," Lila said, softening him up with a smile. "Well, Georgius, tell my friend here where Darian went off to, and I wouldn't mind entertaining you with a song or two. And maybe even one you haven't heard of."

"Hmm," Georgius said, considering. "Well, I can't guess why you'd want to talk to that odd fellow, but I can't turn down a song from a pretty lass. Skip the Star of Elara, though. Why don't you pick something a bit happier?"

"I'd be glad to," she said. "This one's a song from my childhood. Of happier times when there was no Shadow Empire to worry about."

"What's it called?"

"Echoes of the Sunlit Glen," she said.

Lila cleared her throat and started singing, and her voice was so sweet that despite its softness, it carried throughout the pass. In no time at all, grizzled men started gathering to watch. First, there were just a few, and then there were dozens. Their eyes were hungry for any sort of hope, any reason to fight. Justin could hardly describe it, but there was definitely some sort of bardic magic in the air.

The ballad was one of peace and prosperity, conjuring in Justin's mind memories of simpler times. Images of green fields and clear blue skies entered his mind unbidden as Lila's voice wove a vivid tapestry. Clearly, Justin wasn't alone, from the way all the men hung on her every word. No doubt, this was an effect of her Bardic Inspiration skill.

As the final notes faded into the night, the soldiers remained silent for a moment, lost in the reverie Lila had conjured, some even with tears in their eyes. Then, one by one, they began to clap, a slow, appreciative sound that grew into heartfelt applause. For a brief moment, the fear hanging over the camp was lifted.

Meanwhile, Justin searched among the men for Darian, but he was absent.

One of the soldiers called out, "Do you know Valor of the Fallen?"

Lila frowned in confusion. "No. I don't. It might go by a different name in my land."

The man quickly hummed the tune in a deep bass, and Lila nodded in recognition.

"Ah. That one's called The Heroes' Last Stand where I'm from. I do know it. And I'll be happy to sing it if anyone can tell me where Darian went off to."

"Darian?" said a thickset man with a square face, close to the fire. "I saw him walking toward the northern slopes, where we have the latrine. About fifteen minutes ago."

"Thanks," Lila said.

As she started the new song, Justin headed north. He knew it was north because of what Lila had told him about the Star of Elara. It was blue and bright in the northern sky before him.

As Lila's voice faded with distance, Justin exited the perimeter of the camp, smelling the latrine long before he found it. On the way, he grabbed a torch to light his path. He wondered when the Shadow Empire forces were supposed to attack, and it made him nervous to go off on his own. He remembered Alistair's warning to stay close and fully realized that what he was doing was stupid.

And yet the hunch was too strong to ignore. Lila knew where he was going and would catch up later.

When he reached the latrine, he found that it was completely empty. If Darian had already come back to camp, they must have missed each other in the darkness, sometime before Justin grabbed the torch. But for some reason, he didn't think that was why.

Possessed by he knew not what, he trekked beyond the latrine, toward a small stream that ran at the base of the north side of the pass. He forded the water at the easiest point he could find in the darkness. The water was horribly cold, but he kept moving, hoping it wouldn't get too deep.

Thankfully, he pulled himself from the other side, having only gotten wet up to his hips. As he lit the way, he noticed a trail of water leading up the slope.

Someone had been up here, and quite recently. It had to have been Darian.

Justin considered his next move, only to hear splashing in the stream behind him. He felt a thrill of fear, but it was far too late to put out his torch. Whoever was down there had already seen him. He reached for his dagger.

"It's me," Lila said. "What on Eyrth are you doing up here?"

He waited for her to catch up before responding. "I think Darian came this way. There's no reason for him to be up here unless he's up to no good."

Lila noted the trail. "Well, he'd have about fifteen minutes on us, assuming he's not out there watching from the darkness right now. Where do you think he's headed? Sounds like he was ready to split."

Justin already had something of an idea. History had been one of the few subjects he'd enjoyed in school, and he sometimes even listened to history-related podcasts while he gamed. And this situation was definitely tickling that part of his brain.

"Let's follow his trail. There's something to this."

"We can always turn back if it's nothing, right?" Lila asked. "Besides, you need me to watch your back."

"Appreciate it."

The duo set off into the darkness. It didn't take long for the water trail to disappear, but there were still boot prints from time to time. Justin was no tracker, but it was impossible to miss the impressions. Darian could have easily stepped on the many rocks to more easily cover his tracks, but the man was in a hurry.

The question was: Why?

After five minutes, it became clear they didn't need to follow the tracks anymore because they were on some sort of trail.

"Interesting," Lila said.

"Just as I thought," Justin said. "I *knew* something was off about him."

"What about him was off? He's a deserter, clearly. Someone who knows the land. It hardly changes the equation, right?"

"I would say the same thing," Justin said. "Except we're in a Vault. He has nowhere to desert *to*."

"True," Lila said. "So, where is he going?"

"The Shadow Empire's camp," Justin said. "Where else? And if the Shadow Empire doesn't know about this trail, that could be the thing that tips the battle."

Lila's face paled as she considered the implications. "Yes, I can see that. We need to hunt him down before he reaches that camp!"

"Let's move," Justin said.

With that, they followed the trail as fast as their feet could carry them in the darkness.

18

A DANCE WITH DEATH

"The Kingdom of Valoria was a small, often forgotten nation of mountain folk—isolated, hardy, and strong. Under the leadership of Skanderhart, they held their ground far longer than anyone thought possible against Belshar the Nightbringer. To some, their defiance was proof that the gods had not yet abandoned the Faithful to the God of Death and his dark champion. But I would argue differently. Valoria's unlikely story of endurance is not merely one of divine intervention, but a parable. Sometimes, it is the smallest things—an arrow in a chink, a pebble in a wheel—that bring even the mightiest to their knees."

—Chronicler Erinal Gallant
  Truths Hidden in Myths

JUSTIN WANTED to leave the torch behind. It seemed too risky to be seen. However, there was no way they would go fast enough to catch up with Darian without it, especially considering the unfamiliar path.

On the other hand, Justin worried that Darian might see them pursuing and either pick up his pace or, worse, get off the trail and ambush them.

Eventually, they ditched the torch. It took a few minutes for their eyes to adjust to the darkness, but the risk of being seen was just too great.

Besides, the moon and stars were bright enough to lend some light, though Justin tripped more than a few times.

As the trail continued, it seemed Justin's original hunch was right —it led to the enemy army's camp. They were traveling due east, and at many points, they came right up to the cliff that overlooked the pass.

The going was rough, and it was clear this trail was mostly used by animals, perhaps mountain goats. Despite that, there was more than enough room for two men to march abreast. Assuming the Shadow Empire used it tonight, the Valorians would have an ugly surprise for them in a few hours.

"How did you figure all this out?" Lila asked. "It seems like a lucky guess."

"Well, I'm not sure I really figured it out, per se," Justin said. "I just felt like something was off about Darian. When he left the fire and said, 'It matters not,' I thought that was a weird thing to say for someone about to face his death. Second, Georgius had a low opinion of him, calling him shifty and strange, which matched my assessment. And finally, this is where my knowledge of history came in handy."

"What knowledge?"

"Well, in my world, there was a battle similar to this one, called the Battle of Thermopylae. I won't bore you with the details, but a group of elite fighters, called the Spartans, defended a crucial pass against the much larger Persian Empire. They were doomed to die, but their end was hastened when a goatherd showed the Persians a hidden path, allowing them to surround the Spartans. Instead of using the pass as a chokepoint, they were forced to defend multiple angles."

"I see," Lila said. "So, Darian is our goatherd."

"I believe so. This trail can lead nowhere but to the enemy camp.

In exchange for selling out the Valorians, he wants to save his own skin and maybe turn a profit."

"Makes sense. But should we really be doing this part alone? We're getting too far from camp. We've probably walked a mile with no sign of him. What if we're too late and run into the Shadow Empire?"

"There's still time to catch him, maybe," Justin said. "And if we're too late, we've probably already failed the Vault anyway."

"We'd better run," Lila said. "Our eyes should be fully adjusted."

As they picked up the pace, there was still no sign of Darian, and within half an hour, they'd hit a turn that took them around the mountain, only to reveal a vast camp before them, many times larger than that of the Valorians, lit with hundreds of fires and tents. Perhaps even *thousands* of fires, considering the camp followers. The camp sprawled out like a small city, with rows of tents in neat formations and sentries patrolling the perimeter. Shadows flickered across the canvas of the tents as soldiers moved about, their armor dark in the night. The low murmur of voices and the occasional clink of metal filled the air. Beyond the camp, the land sloped downward, revealing a rolling plain interspersed with low hills.

"That's an army if I ever saw one," Lila said. "Seems Darian is already inside. It would be too risky to keep going. There's no way we can catch him and escape with our lives."

Justin was considering this when a shadow fell from above. He nearly screamed, but it was only Shadowflight, perching on a nearby branch and regarding him curiously. Fear instantly changed into happiness; the bird certainly had a knack for showing up at just the right times, probably a product of the animal's keen sense of sight.

Justin addressed the noble creature. "Tell Eldrin to head north of the latrines. There's a hidden path here that the Shadow Empire is going to use to attack the Valorians."

Justin wasn't sure if the bird understood, but before he could even ask, Shadowflight flew off without so much as a screech. Within minutes, he would perch on the Ranger's shoulder, relaying the message.

Or at least, Justin hoped so.

"It's the best we can do," Lila said.

Justin and Lila were about to do just that when a sudden bright light shone, temporarily blinding them and accompanied by a shout.

"Halt! In the name of the Eternal Sovereign!"

The language used differed from Valorian, harsher and more guttural. As Justin's eyes adjusted, he noticed several guards approaching until, within seconds, eight soldiers had him and Lila surrounded. Likely, this was an advance party sent to check out the pass for themselves.

Justin realized, with a sinking heart, that the Vault had meant for them to pursue Darian from the get-go. He wanted to kick himself for not acting on his hunch immediately.

The soldiers loomed, decked out in heavy black armor with spikes on the shoulders. Each soldier bore a pike, except for one who was dressed in black robes, a sort of light spell hovering above his head. That was a magic user if Justin had ever seen one.

Justin did his best to plaster on an amiable smile.

He was a Socialite, so it was time to socialize.

"Oh, am I glad to see you guys! We have urgent information about the Valorian forces that could change things entirely. We're working with Darian."

The two soldiers in front of Justin, the mage and a soldier whose armor was more ornate than the others, exchanged skeptical glances.

It was the latter who spoke. "And who are *you* supposed to be?"

"I'm Justin," Justin said. "Justin Talemaker, Socialite Extraordinaire. And this is my partner, Lila the Bard. I've been undercover with the Valorians and have gathered key intelligence on their defenses. Intelligence that may save thousands of Shadowian lives tomorrow."

Justin internally winced at his use of the word "Shadowian," but thankfully, the soldiers didn't seem to think anything of it.

"A Socialite and a Bard," the mage drawled, his voice cold and his thin lips curled downward in distaste. "Well, if there's one thing your kind is good for, it's spinning tales."

Lila seemed to be frightened out of her wits, so Justin knew it was on him to respond. He was strangely calm, perhaps an effect of his increased Charisma attribute.

He just had to keep talking.

"We've been gathering information in the guise of entertainers. It's the perfect cover. No one suspects a Bard and a Socialite, trying to earn their keep from those doomed to die, anyway." He gave a slimy smile. "And if we thieve a silver here and there, well, who's there to cry boo?"

"Just get on with it, Socialite," the mage said. "My patience wears thin. What is this key intelligence?"

"I will speak to no one but the commander of this army," Justin said. "Whoever he may be."

"There's no time for that!" the mage said. "I'm Zaramund Dar'Karesh, Arch-Mage of the Nihilan Order. I need to make sure this is worth the General's time. Give us something so that we know you're not playing us false. How far away are the Valorian reinforcements? What are their exact numbers? Telling us this would prove your loyalty to the Empire. And who knows? Mayhap a few silvers might find their way into your pockets."

"About three days away," Justin lied. Maybe if they bought it, they'd be less inclined to attack early, though it wasn't likely. "I can't say how many, but enough to bog things down for the Shadow side, for sure. And at least ten Paladins to boot."

"Ten Paladins, you say?" the captain asked. "Our spies must be sleeping behind Valorian lines."

Even Zaramund seemed disturbed by this. "What about their magical forces? Are they deployed near the front, or are they keeping them in reserve?"

"That, I can't say. Commander Thalon has been shifting them around of late."

"What do you think, Captain Varus?" the mage asked the senior officer.

"Something's not adding up, that's for sure. Why didn't Darian say anything about you?"

"That's easy," Lila said, coming to her wits. Her voice was filled with indignation. "He hoped to take the entire reward for himself, but this was always our teamwork that pulled this off. He left us without a word."

"I see," the Captain said. "Well, perhaps it's time you headed back to camp. The attack will begin soon." He turned to a soldier next to him. "Take them to the supply tent and see that they get paid...*appropriately.*"

"Of course, Lord Captain," the man said, with a sinister smile that Justin didn't much like. "Follow me."

"The Empire thanks you for your service," the Arch-Mage said with a thin, cold smile. "Now off with you before we change our minds."

Justin tried to repress the lump that was forming in his throat. Instead, he returned his own smile and gave a half bow. "It was our pleasure, m'lords."

With Shadowflight likely relaying the news to Eldrin even now, there was only one thing he and Lila had to concern themselves with: escaping with their necks intact.

They walked a couple of minutes into the darkness in silence, and it didn't take long for Justin to realize they were not going toward the Shadow Empire camp. There was only one reason for that. They were being marched off to be killed, somewhere out of sight and out of mind. He could only wonder why they hadn't killed them on the spot. Perhaps the captain wanted to avoid alarming the troops with the presence of spies or dissenters, or maybe they intended to interrogate them further before disposing of them.

As Justin was racking his brain for a way out, the soldiers came to a sudden stop. As they turned, brandishing their pikes, he knew they only had seconds left.

He exchanged a quick glance with Lila. Her aim had to be true. But Justin could at least give her a better shot.

Immediately, Justin directed his Poison Barb ability at the leader, analyzing his face and discovering the perfect emotional wound to exploit. This had to stun him, or they were both dead.

Justin felt his body fill with an anger and viciousness he had never known. It was as if he were channeling the spirit of someone who had once been unbelievably cruel to the leader. The words flew from his lips furiously.

"You know why your captain keeps you in the shadows? Because even he knows your mother sold you for less than a pig's trough and that you're nothing but a bastard dog licking at the Empire's boots for scraps!"

The man stopped short, completely stunned. Before the other men could react to the insult, Lila's hands were flashing. One knife flew, then another, whistling through the air and burying themselves in the soldier next to the stunned leader.

[Poison Barb refreshed.]

The other men, finally waking up to the threat, thrust their pikes forward. Justin and Lila danced out of the way, heading toward the gap created by the leader. Justin hurled another insult, locking onto the Shadow soldier closest to them.

"You couldn't fight your way out of a brothel, and even a whore wouldn't waste her time on that nub of yours!"

The man stopped short, even throwing a hand over his heart, as if he were truly in pain. The leader, surprisingly, was still stunned and even shaking a bit. From the jerking of his leg, it seemed he was trying to move but was failing.

Lila threw the rest of her knives, all but three clinking off their armor. The final one buried itself in the most laggardly soldier's neck.

Two down, two to go.

[Poison Barb refreshed.]

By now, the leader was coming to his senses, along with the other soldier whose manhood Justin had insulted. His Poison Barb had gone off cooldown, but with both soldiers advancing, there was no time to lob another insult.

"Attack, attack!" the leader screamed. "Kill them!"

They had one chance left. Justin wasn't sure how Dazzling Display would get them out of this, but he had no choice but to try.

He activated the skill. As with the Poison Barb, it felt as if his entire body were taken over.

Like a puppet on strings, he had no control over what happened next. He started moonwalking in an extravagant fashion as a spotlight from seemingly nowhere shone down on him.

"Hee-hee!" he cried, his voice booming ridiculously loud, as if amplified by a stadium's worth of speakers.

The two soldiers gawked at Justin, their jaws dropping. Their weapons sagged, their expressions a mix of confusion and disbelief. They were definitely dazzled, especially as streamers of light shot from Justin's person in a flashy display.

From the corner of his vision, Justin saw Lila rushing to grab her discarded knives.

Justin kept moving, though he felt the power of the move waning.

Then the spotlight went out.

Justin let out a labored breath. "Hee?"

The two men, waking from their trance, charged with a defiant roar, pikes extended. But Lila hurled her knives, felling them both with expert throws.

It was long past time to run. After Lila had retrieved her weapons, they stumbled into the darkness toward the pass.

"By the gods, that dancing was something else!" Lila said.

As they ran, Justin could only wonder just why it had happened. It was beyond random.

But as he thought about it, maybe it wasn't so random at all. Perhaps the Dazzling Display skill had scrounged Justin's brain for all his knowledge of entertainers, allowing him to channel what he had seen.

The skill had definitely been designed for a person who didn't have access to all the media of the Internet age.

Justin smiled. This could be *very* useful.

"We need to be careful," Justin warned. "I don't know who else saw the Dazzling Display."

"We might have the entire Shadow Empire army tracking us down," Lila said. "You did right in choosing that skill. I'm not sure how else we could have escaped."

Justin suppressed a shudder. Maybe Tantalizing Miasma would have been enough to smooth-talk his way out of the situation, but then again, maybe not. He was just glad to have taken Dazzling Display.

At last, they made it back to the trail, taking the switchbacks up quickly. In the distance, there was no sign of the Arch-Mage's light. Surely, he was on the trail somewhere. Or, if they were lucky, they had merely come onto the trail to confirm its existence before reporting back to their commander.

If it were the latter, they would have a chance of getting back to the Valorians.

As they ran up the trail, Justin could spy torchlight in the general area where their skirmish had taken place in the pass below. Clearly, they were being hunted, but they had enough of a lead to make it back. There was no way to hide the location of the hidden path, but assuming Shadowflight warned Eldrin in time, the Valorians could at least be apprised of the danger.

As these thoughts raced through Justin's head, a sudden bright light shone on the trail ahead, like a miniature sun. And that sun was approaching them fast.

Justin felt the fireball's heat warming the air, and there was nothing he could do but grab Lila and jump for the safety of a nearby boulder. Just in time, they reached shelter before it could incinerate them. The fireball exploded on the trail about twenty feet behind them, its heat licking their backs.

"Shit," he said.

Now, they were trapped, with the Shadow Empire's Arch-Mage on one side, who certainly out-leveled them mightily, and the entire Shadow Empire army behind them.

And worse, Justin had none of his abilities left to use, aside from Poison Barb.

"You're going to have to make those knives count," he whispered.

"I can use Poison Barb, but for it to work, I have to get a lock on that mage's ugly face."

Lila whispered back. "Justin, how can we possibly stand against him? Even if Charisma isn't his main stat, he almost certainly has a few points in it. Perhaps enough to resist the insult."

"We have to try something. Here's the plan. I'll duck out and try to get a read on his face and use Poison Barb. You wait till I'm done before coming out with those knives. Assuming I can stun him, you can take him down easily enough."

She looked unsure, but they were all out of options.

"All right," she whispered. "I can try to boost your Charisma with Bardic Inspiration, too. Arion protect you, Justin."

Justin released a breath, trying to focus. Then, with a single nod to Lila, he stepped onto the path and ran forward, likely to his death.

19

A BRIEF LESSON IN MAGERY

"There are eight elements—four physical, four spiritual—each under the purview of the Eight Old Gods. This is a truth universally acknowledged, even among the Adherents of Light. And yet, we mages are expected to worship the New Gods of the Church of Light, as if their favor grants us our powers. I know not how the Old Gods have the patience to tolerate such folly, but I pray that patience doesn't one day run out. For when gods tire of mortals, it is mortals who pay the price."

—Elementalist Velar Thayne
  Magic in the New Age

JUSTIN CHARGED DOWN THE TRAIL, his heart pounding in his chest. The uneven ground caused him to trip over his feet, but he caught himself.

He tried to focus on a face in the darkness, but there was nothing. Why wasn't another fireball heading his way?

That was when a familiar voice called out. "Hold your fire! It's Justin."

Justin's eyes widened in relief. It was Eldrin. As he came closer, the Ranger materialized from the darkness, along with a group of three mages, all wearing the violet robes of the Guardian Force.

Justin turned his head. "Lila! You can come out. It's Eldrin."

Lila appeared from behind the boulder, marching up the trail to join them.

Eldrin watched them both with a quizzical expression. "What in Arion's name are you doing up here? Alistair and I have been looking all over for you!"

"Shadowflight didn't tell you?"

"He only told me about the path. We came up here to block it."

Justin frowned, wondering why the falcon hadn't relayed that crucial bit of info. Maybe it was because Justin hadn't directly told the bird to do so.

"We followed Darian all the way to the Empire's camp," Justin said. "He was that soldier from earlier who was a real Debbie Downer."

Eldrin frowned at the colloquialism but seemed to understand what Justin meant. "And?"

"We couldn't stop him in time. We also ran into the Shadow Army's Arch-Mage, though. Some dude named Zarathustra or something."

"Zaramund," Lila corrected.

Eldrin's eyes widened. "The Arch-Mage? And you lived to tell the tale?"

"Yes. Thanks to Lila's knives and my sharp wit."

"And Justin's dance moves," Lila put in.

"I feel there is a story for the ages there, but we really must be moving. Alistair is preparing the army while I've taken all the mages with access to earth magic to bury the pass here. It's all but certain the Shadowists will attack tonight."

Shadowists. So that's what Shadow Empire folks were called. Maybe Justin calling them "Shadowian" had been the slip that had given them away.

Eldrin turned to one mage, who looked sheepish. "And you," he said sternly, "almost killed our allies with that fireball. Be more cautious next time."

The mage, a tall male with a bald head, bowed in apology. "I'm sorry, Sir Eldrin. I thought they were the enemy."

Eldrin sighed, nodding. "That's understandable, but just be careful." Eldrin continued. "Right, let's continue our work." He directed his attention to the mages. "We need to collapse this path. Shadowflight has already scouted the key points, and this is the first. Collapse all these key points, and that should slow them down long enough for reinforcements to arrive this evening. Now, do all of you have access to the terra-shift spell?"

"Yes, all three of us do," the lead mage said, a woman with close-cropped hair and stern green eyes.

"There are twelve points Shadowflight identified. As long as you have the aether reserves for it, I'd like to hit all twelve."

"It should be no issue," the woman said. "We are Elementalists of a decent level."

Eldrin nodded. "Right, then. Let's get started. Stand back!"

The first mage, the woman, began her work. Her hands became wrapped in an aura of green light, which she directed at the slope above the path. The ground trembled as the spell took effect, rocks and earth shifting and burying the path before them. Justin did his best to keep standing as the ground shifted beneath his feet, but the force was mostly targeting a loose stand of rocks above the path.

Within seconds, the trail ahead was rendered unusable.

"Let's keep it moving," Eldrin said.

They retreated a quarter of a mile before Eldrin directed the same mage to bury another part of the pass. The work went far more quickly than Justin had believed.

As they walked to the next point of interest, Justin turned to Lila. "So, what is an Elementalist? A class?"

"Yes, it's a mage class. Elementalists have a Spirit Core. They get access to the Elemental School of Magic: Fire, Water, Air, and Earth."

"That's original."

"How do you mean?"

"Oh, nothing. Are there other kinds of mages and magic?"

"Of course. Mage is the catchall term for any class that uses magic as its primary base of skills. You see, some classes—like Paladins—are mainly physical but also have access to Lesser Life and Harmony spells, and as such, are not considered mages. There are many types of mages, each commanding a different school. Most mages have either a Spirit or Intellect core. Spirit cores tend to use aether to power their magic, while Intellect cores tend to use Cants. Basically, utterances tied to various Foundation Languages that shift reality itself."

"I see," Justin said. "Can you break down the main types for me?"

"I mean, there are a lot. I don't even know them all. There are Elementalists, as we've already said. Then there are Wizards, who have an Intellect Core. They learn their magic from books and dusty tomes. Most have to go to school to learn their spells, which are based on the Foundation Language of Arcanis."

"What about Vranthillis?" Justin asked. "That's the Foundation Language Valdrik was talking about."

"Vranthillis seems to be unique to the Lexicant class, because I'd never heard of it. Arcanis is what most Wizards use, and it can only be understood by them. That's advanced stuff, though."

"Elementalists, Wizards...anything else?"

"Quite a few. Spiritualists, Summoners, Illusionists, Enchanters, Druids...I'm forgetting a few."

Again, Justin felt a sense of missed opportunity. He could have been any of these classes, but at the time, Socialite had felt like the right call. Maybe it had stemmed from feeling vulnerable after his expulsion from the guild.

Without that...his would have been a different story.

"What about White Wizards? You mentioned them once. Are they different from regular Wizards?"

"They're an advanced class. They get access to the best healing spells and support spells, basically."

"Interesting. So, to review, a mage is just a general term for a magic user."

"That's right. When you say White Wizard or Fire Elementalist, you're being more specific. But both are mages."

"Fire Elementalist? Is that an advanced class?"

"Technically, no." Lila rolled her eyes but couldn't hide a smile. "It's a Focus chosen by an Elementalist if they develop their Fire Magic at the expense of others. In that case, you'd call them a Pyromancer."

"Erm...what's a Focus?"

"You don't know *anything*, do you?"

Justin shrugged. "I've been here less than a week. Cut me some slack!"

"True." She leaned back, crossing her arms. "Okay. A Focus is something you choose at Level 10 that influences how your class develops. It shapes your entire progression. Think of it like a class specialization."

"That actually sounds kind of cool. What's yours?"

"Well, I don't have one yet. I'm only Level 2, like you. But for a Bard like me, the main Focuses include Singing, Instruments, Acrobatics, Dancing, Storytelling, Juggling, or something similar. But it's not like you get to pick just *any* Focus. The choices you're presented with are based on the actions you've taken since you absorbed your class core."

Justin frowned. "So, what will determine mine?"

"That's the mystery, isn't it? If I had to guess, you'll get something that involves annoying people with questions."

"Maybe I'll get a Detective Focus or something. What's Eldrin's Focus, you think? He's Level 10. Why can't I see it on the interface?"

"You can't see another person's Focus. They just have to tell you. Most of the time, people are private about it."

"Why?"

Lila chuckled at Justin's excitement, but her expression grew a touch more serious. "Focuses are personal. They reflect the choices someone has made, their path, their experiences. Sharing that with someone means revealing more about yourself than you might want to. It's not just a skill—it's a declaration of who you are. Or the person you hope to become. And if the wrong sort knows it, it gives them a key to defeating you."

Justin raised an eyebrow. "So, it's like asking someone for their deepest, darkest secret?"

"Not quite *that* dramatic, but close enough. If someone wants you to know their Focus, they'll tell you."

Justin tilted his head. "I understand all that, but wouldn't it help the party if everyone knew what each other was good at?"

"Depends," Lila replied. "Sometimes, a Focus reveals a flaw or a compromise. Like a Fire Elementalist giving up their connection to other elements. Other mages will know how to better counter them. Or take the Baron. He might have a Focus that helps him do shady stuff."

"Makes sense when you put it that way."

There was so much to learn, but already, they had arrived at the next location. Justin and Lila hung back while the pass was buried, and they moved on to the next one.

By the time the female mage had exhausted her mana reserves, the next mage took over.

Shadowflight came from nowhere, landing adroitly on Eldrin's shoulder. The Ranger inclined his head toward the falcon, nodding.

"They're on the move," he said, his face grim. "Both through this path and the main pass. We need to hurry."

Justin felt a surge of determination. "Let's go."

They worked quickly to bury the rest of the pass. When the final mage had buried the last bit of the trail, Justin felt assured that they had done all they could.

The group made their way back to the Valorian camp. Eldrin led the way, his sharp eyes scanning their surroundings for danger. The mages followed, their faces set in concentration as they prepared themselves for the upcoming battle.

Back at the camp, the atmosphere was tense. Soldiers were preparing for the impending battle. The mages left to join their division while Eldrin led Justin and Lila to Commander Thalon's tent.

As soon as they entered, they found Thalon, his senior officers, and Alistair.

"There you are!" Alistair said. "We feared the worst."

"It will take more than the Shadow Empire to stop us," Justin said.

"You can tell us about it later," the Paladin said. "What of the path?"

"Buried, as best as we can," Eldrin informed him. "These two were the ones who got the message to Shadowflight just in time."

"You have Valoria's gratitude," Commander Thalon said. "But I will save my thanks for when we stop the Shadowists dead in their tracks." He turned to his officers. "There's nothing left to discuss. Prepare the troops for battle."

Eldrin turned to Justin and Lila. "You two need to stay out of the way. Neither of you is equipped for frontline combat."

Justin nodded, though a part of him wanted to argue. "We understand. We'll stay back and do what we can to support."

"We can run messages if needed," Lila said.

Eldrin nodded his thanks. "You've already done much. It would be a shame to throw it all away."

"Good luck, Eldrin," Justin said.

With that, Eldrin left with Alistair, Thalon, and the rest of the officers, leaving Justin and Lila alone in the tent.

"So, I guess we just twiddle our thumbs now?" Justin asked.

"Maybe we can find a good vantage point," Lila said. "I noticed a wooden watchtower of sorts out there. It might be a good place to see what's going on."

"Sounds like it would make us an excellent target for the enemy's mages."

"The mages will be focused on the front lines, not us," Lila said. "At least, I would hope so. Either way, I want to know what's going on. If things get dicey, we can always get out."

Justin almost wanted to tell her it would be much safer to stay right here, but he thought better of it. He was curious to see what a battle from above looked like, complete with mages, fire spells, and the undead. He'd get to see something no human from his world ever would.

"All right, Lila, you've sold me. Lead the way."

20

THE PALADIN'S STAND

"Necromancers tend to be beings of the shadows, preferring to weave their magic unseen and unheard. It is this secrecy that makes them the object of so much fear. But what is far more terrifying is the Necromancer who no longer feels the need to hide. The Necromancer who grows so powerful that the shadows can no longer conceal them, and nations begin to bow, not in reverence, but in trembling submission. Fear not the Necromancer who hides, but the one who deems themselves powerful enough to walk unscathed in the Creator's light."

—Arlan Kaive, High Templar of Arion
   Defending Against Practitioners of the Dark Arts

JUSTIN AND LILA found the platform easily enough, climbing to the top. There, they had a commanding view of the pass before them, along with the regiments of Valorian soldiers arrayed in a line. From the torchlight, it was easy to see that they completely covered the pass wall to wall. Purple standards with a silver stag were interspersed among the organized regiments, their bronze armor dull in the predawn light.

Along the ledges on both sides of the pass, contingents of archers, crossbowmen, and ballistae were stationed, and somewhere in there, mages were mixed in. Justin knew if the Valorians were wise, they would keep them hidden so that they wouldn't become targets.

They waited there in the frosty early morning for a very long time, even as the sun rose. Justin wondered why the Shadow Empire wasn't attacking yet, when their undead would be less affected by the sunlight, but maybe they were counting on the shade of the mountains covering the ground of the pass, at least through the morning.

Justin was wondering if the battle would ever start when there was a rumbling in the ground.

From around the bend in the pass, they came. Thousands upon thousands of black-armored foot soldiers, their collective dull roar filling the pass. The Valorian forces held their ground at the top of a slight incline at the narrowest part of the pass.

Soon, the Shadowist forces came to a stop just outside the range of the Valorian mages and artillery.

The dawn made details more discernible. Hundreds of black flags with a crimson serpent coiled around a golden sword waved in the cold mountain breeze, while on the Valorian side, purple flags with the silver stag stood ready to defend. Alistair was easy to pick out among the Valorian troops, standing in shining armor, his white cloak swept by the breeze, his war hammer seeming to glow despite the lack of sunlight in the pass.

Justin realized for the first time that he had never actually inspected Alistair's character, nor sought to form a pact that would allow him to see his skills and boons.

He set his thoughts upon it, having nothing better to do. There was a moment's pause, as if Alistair were considering the proposal.

But, after a moment, Justin received a notification.

[Party pact formed. You may now inspect Alistair in greater detail.]

Justin immediately looked at his information.

Alistair of Drakendale
Class: Paladin
Level: 25

Attributes:
Power: 18
Coordination: 13
Endurance: 15
Intellect: 13
Spirit: 15
Charisma: 16

Abilities:
Skills: Paladin's Resolve (0), Divine Strike (2), Heavenly War Cry (3), Leap of Faith (7), Invoke Blessing (11), Righteous Whirlwind (13), Arion's Shield (17), Arion's Hammer (19), Crusader's Stand (21), Lay on Hands (23).
Boons: Paladin's Sense (1), Holy Training (4), Consecration (6), Bulwark of Faith (9), Sacred Tactics (10), Paladin's Grace (14), The Blessing of Arion (15), Paladin Magery (22), Holy Fervor (25).
Party Tactic: Divine Aura (5)

"Holy cannoli," Justin said. "Did you ever look at Alistair's information?"

Lila laughed. "You're just now looking at that? I made a pact as soon as we left Silverton."

Justin shook his head. "How is it even possible to level up that high? It would take tens of thousands of experience points. Maybe even hundreds of thousands. And here I am, excited to get five hundred in one go. I don't even know what any of those abilities do!"

"It's hundreds of thousands of experience points," Lila said. "Men like Alistair are a rare breed. We might have actually been okay not chasing Darian, all things considered. That's how strong he is."

"Damn," Justin said. He did some mental math. If Alistair started with ten points in each attribute, like him, that meant he had unlocked thirty attribute points.

It should have been twenty-five since only one was gained per level.

"Is it just me, or does Alistair have extra attribute points? Is that from his gear?"

Lila shook her head. "He has thirty because once you adopt an advanced class, you get two points per level instead of one. We don't get to see what his gear is doing for him."

Justin's eyes widened. "Oh. Got it."

Lila smiled. "You're in for a treat. Just sit back and watch the show."

Justin hoped it was that simple. Thinking back, it was no wonder the goblins hadn't wanted to mess with Alistair that day on the road. He'd also noticed each of his boons had a number beside them. Justin supposed that was the level they were first adopted.

Justin watched the Paladin, who now had an aura of divine light surrounding him. The other men around him were laughing and joking, taking heart from his mere presence.

And then, with no warning at all, low horns blew, and the Shadow Empire's armies charged en masse, with no regard for life. Well, at least from what Justin could see, they had no regard for *unlife*. The unmistakable stilted shambling of the first wave of attackers was something he'd seen countless times in zombie films. Only these zombies were wielding weapons and wearing black spiked armor. There were even skeletons mixed in, glowing with a shadowy aura. Death Magic, Justin could only assume. The hordes of undead ran past woodpiles the Valorians had prepared in advance.

The Elementalists began their attacks at once, shooting fireballs at the woodpiles, instantly lighting them up and creating a wall of fire, cutting off the attackers from further support. Many of the undead were instantly lit with flames.

Alistair was a beacon of divine power amidst the chaos. His war hammer gleamed as the undead attackers crashed into the Valorian shield wall. Alistair swung his hammer, which somehow spread curious, golden flames upon each strike, reducing the zombies to ash. The undead around Alistair recoiled. They didn't seem to fear anything, but something about those magical flames clearly terrified them.

"The Flames of Life," Lila said in awe. "It's a kind of life magic that wreaks havoc on the undead."

Alistair pressed forward, his hammer a blur of righteous fury. Each strike was accompanied by a flash of light, the impact sending shockwaves of the Flames of Life through the ranks of undead, many of them even being set ablaze. Those not set aflame were instantly reduced to ash.

The undead shrieked and writhed as the sacred flames consumed them, their decaying forms crumbling to dust even as they spread the holy fire through their ranks far beyond Alistair's position.

A group of skeletal warriors advanced toward him, their bony fingers clutching rusted weapons. Alistair met them head-on, spinning in a tight circle, war hammer sweeping out in a deadly arc. The skeletal warriors shattered under the force of his attack, their bones disintegrating into a fine powder.

A giant zombie, twice as tall as Alistair, lumbered toward the Paladin, its massive frame covered in tattered remnants of black armor. Alistair was not intimidated, wailing on it with several hits, driving it back before swinging his weapon with all his might, the head of the hammer glowing like a meteor about to make impact. The hit was cataclysmic, the zombie's chest caving in with a sickening crunch before the divine energy erupted from within, obliterating it entirely.

The undead forces continued to pour in, attempting to overwhelm Alistair, but the Paladin was relentless. Even as the Elementalists continued to rain fireballs from above, Alistair let out a mighty war cry.

"Arion's Light, guide my hands!"

The shout and its echoes reverberated within Justin's very bones. If he were on the other side of that, he would have pissed himself.

A golden wave of invigorating energy spread out from Alistair, boosting the strength of nearby Valorian soldiers. Emboldened by the Paladin's presence, they fought with renewed vigor, surrounded by a golden aura, cutting down the undead with ease.

Alistair's armor deflected blows from the few undead that struck him. The mages' fires had somewhat died down by now, allowing more Shadow Empire forces to pour through, with human regiments now mixed in among the undead.

Alistair summoned a shimmering golden barrier. During this time, in between knocking back a fiercer breed of undead that attacked with feral tenacity, he focused on healing his comrades.

The Elementalists' fire spells were slowing. According to Lila, it seemed they were working with a pool of aether they all started with, which they had to wait to recharge.

The archers and crossbowmen on the slopes of the pass, along with the ballistae, rained death on the enemy. Some missiles even seemed to be enchanted with fire magic, exploding on impact. Justin watched as one burst among a cluster of zombies, scattering their remains.

Justin could hardly believe his eyes as Alistair went right back into it, rallying the beleaguered Valorian troops. He was a one-man army. The undead that dared to come near him were swiftly dispatched, their ranks thinning under his relentless onslaught. The Shadowist humans seemed to be more cautious, and when they did attack, they threw a volley of javelins first before charging ten at a time, pikes extended. Alistair still held his own against them, usually supported by some Valorian soldiers or missile fire from above.

And so it was that the battle ebbed and flowed, stretching into the late morning. The initial momentum of the Shadowist forces faltered. The Valorians didn't gain ground, merely defending their position against the vastly superior foe. And despite the thousands of dead Shadowists, more kept coming down the pass, their numbers never seeming to end.

Most of the undead, it seemed, had been dispatched, and Justin recognized them for what they were: cannon fodder. Very few of the

Valorians had fallen in the initial wave. Indeed, there were so many fallen Shadowists that they formed a wall of corpses. New attackers had great difficulty in even mounting an assault on the Valorian front lines because of this.

As morning passed into afternoon, Justin felt a wave of exhaustion. He had been up all night and all morning, and he wondered what Baron Valdrik's soldiers were doing, what seemed like another world away. Were they just waiting outside the Vault? It seemed so distant when the situation at hand felt so real. Justin had become fully invested in this battle, even if he knew it was a scenario set up by the Vault.

Of course, it was easy to be fully invested when one's life was on the line.

Justin glanced toward the hidden path, sighting a line of black-armored soldiers on the northern slopes. It seemed they were stuck about halfway; they were still clearing the obstacles the mages had set up, but too slowly. Justin knew the Shadowists must have diverted a lot of their mage resources to clear the path because so few mages had challenged the Valorians directly on the field of battle. Without that, this battle might have turned out differently. It seemed the Shadowists were still hoping to set up a flank before the Valorian reinforcements arrived.

Battle rejoined in earnest in the middle of the afternoon. The battle line was getting tired, and the Valorians had few fresh troops to switch in. Around late afternoon, a sudden volley of fireballs was shot by the Valorian mages, a pivotal resource that must have been kept in reserve for a surprise attack. It annihilated an enormous chunk of the Shadowist army. But that chunk was almost instantly filled in with fresh troops, of which there seemed to be no end.

"Come on," Lila breathed. "Survive. Just a couple of hours longer!"

To Justin's dismay, the Shadowists were making quick progress on the secret path, while the front lines were being pushed back in the main pass, slowly but surely. If the mages at the pass joined with the rest of the Shadow Empire forces, it would spell disaster for the Valorians.

"Where are those damn reinforcements?" Justin asked.

"We might have to fight ourselves," Lila said.

That was when Justin noticed a large boulder being hurled from the direction of the hidden path, sailing through the air, seemingly in slow motion.

Right for their watchtower.

"Run!" he shouted.

Seeing the danger, Lila reacted instantly, going for the ladder, with Justin close behind. One after the other, they slid down the rungs, never minding the splinters and pain. Justin brought up the rear, reaching the bottom just as the boulder made impact. The tower immediately started crumbling as he ran as fast as his feet could carry him. He just barely escaped being caught in the wreckage of the heavy timbers.

They didn't stop running until they had reached the command tent, which had been set up as a makeshift hospital. Mages with healing magic were doing their best to triage the wounded. There was more blood than Justin had ever seen in his life, men wailing in pain, crying for their mothers. It was a far cry from the neutered wars he had experienced in his video games and favorite movies.

Justin looked at his palms, scraped and somewhat bloody. The pain was very real. But, considering the situation, it could have been much worse.

"We stayed up there way too long," Lila said.

Justin was about to respond when he heard cries of alarm coming from the western portion of the camp. A massive fireball shot into the air, almost like a miniature mushroom cloud.

The Shadow Empire forces had gotten through the hidden path, or perhaps some mages had gone on ahead, seeing that time was limited.

Justin was about to run when, in an alley between two of the larger tents, he spied the last person he wanted to see.

It was the Arch-Mage Zaramund, his pale face bloodied and his eyes bloodshot, his black robes tattered. He gave a sinister smile that made Justin's skin run cold.

If this world had boss room music, Justin realized it probably would have started playing right now.

"The shadows may falter, but the darkness within us never dies," Zaramund said. "Today, Valoria falls."

21

VALOR OF THE FALLEN

"The Shadow Wars are long behind us, and for the most part, zombies are a grim tale to scare children. I assure you that they do exist, though you are not likely to run into one. But on the off chance you do encounter one of those shambling horrors, remember the most important axiom of all: always go for the head. Anything less, and you're just wasting time you probably don't have."

—Priestess Allania Destius,
    Forgotten Threats and How to End Them

JUSTIN TRIED to think of an insult for his Poison Barb ability, but the words caught in his throat.

Lila, thankfully, didn't hesitate. She started lobbing her knives at the Arch-Mage, each successive knife shining brighter, an effect of her Rhythmic Barrage ability. The first two blades buried themselves in his chest, hardly slowing him down, while the last four also struck true, each one knocking him back further. The final knife landed in his abdomen, and the Arch-Mage actually grunted.

But despite this, he still stood, his face hardly registering pain.

Weren't mages supposed to be physically weak? In Zaramund's case, apparently not.

The knives fell from him as sinews of dark magic knitted his wounds, repairing them almost instantly.

Justin was still frozen as Zaramund raised his arms, becoming surrounded by a dark aura of shadowy magic.

That was when groans emanated from behind.

Justin spun around to see dead Valorian soldiers rising from their cots near the command tent. The Healers screamed and fled, none apparently having offensive magic to counter them. The reanimated bodies jerked and twisted, effusing dark magic, their eyes glazed over with death.

They hobbled toward Justin and Lila, about a dozen in all.

Justin charged for Zaramund, dagger out, but Zaramund raised his hand, completely stunning him with terror. Justin somehow knew he was under the Fear effect, but maybe Alistair was too far away to protect him with his Divine Aura.

Justin could think of nothing but the undead soldiers creeping closer with each passing second, and yet, he was unable to do anything to counter the spell. Lila could do nothing either, having run out of knives to throw.

After five seconds, Justin broke from the stun. It was far past time to run, but escape was impossible. The undead were closing in, forming a wall that was impossible to break. The zombies stumbled to a stop, likely at Zaramund's command, a noose ready to tighten.

Zaramund's hands then glowed darkly with a new spell. "And now, Socialite, you will become mine. In body. In spirit. In death. Behold the power of Death Magic!"

The air around Justin grew cold, similar to the chill he had felt at Baron Valdrik's mansion; only this coldness was deeper, seeping into his bones.

Until that coldness was rebuffed mightily.

Zaramund's face twisted in rage. "Who...who has marked you for death already?"

Activating his Poison Barb ability, the perfect insult came to

Justin. "Someone far more powerful than you ever will be! You thought taking up necromancy would make you strong. But no. You are still as weak as that helpless, scared child abandoned on the streets of Karadesh, mewing for the mother who told him she'd be back. She's never coming back, Zaramund. Never."

Zaramund's eyes widened, and he stood completely stunned. In his gray eyes, it was as if he had gone back in time, reliving the terror of his childhood. The undead stood still, receiving no further orders from their master.

"Come on!" Justin said.

The duo sprinted between two of the undead soldiers who made no move to attack.

[Poison Barb refreshed.]

Zaramund recovered from Justin's stun, howling in rage. As one, the undead stumbled after them, even as Zaramund began casting a new spell, one Justin was sure would pull no punches and end them for good.

But that was when Eldrin swept in, appearing from around a tent with his longsword drawn. He blazed by, and Justin and Lila turned to see the Ranger cutting through the ranks of undead with several deft and deadly strikes. Faster than Justin would have believed, Eldrin felled three of them in quick succession, slicing their necks clean through.

Zaramund's spell was interrupted when Lila threw a knife, not one of her own, but one retrieved from nearby. It took Justin a moment to realize it was his own dagger, the one gifted to him by Eldrin. Despite not being balanced for throwing, it struck true, landing right in the Necromancer's shoulder. He grunted, but this time, there was no dark magic to mend his wounds. Perhaps that had been a once-a-day skill or spell.

Meanwhile, Eldrin continued fighting the undead while Zaramund started a new spell, raising more zombies from fallen corpses.

Justin focused on the Necromancer's face, lobbing another hasty insult, one so pathetic it did absolutely nothing.

"Hey Necromancer, your magic sucks!"

The insult failed to even get his attention. Justin madly searched for some sort of weapon to help Eldrin, who was quickly becoming overwhelmed, when out of nowhere, Alistair entered the fray, jumping in with a gravity-defying leap. His war hammer glowed with divine fury.

Zaramund had enough time to widen his eyes and raise a thin, cadaverous hand, just as Alistair's hammer came down, instantly smiting Zaramund into a mixture of pulp and ash.

With Zaramund's death, the reanimated dead collapsed to the ground.

Alistair turned to Justin and Lila. "Are you okay?"

Eldrin groaned, clutching his side. Alistair came over, throwing out a hand and casting Bind Wounds, the same spell he had used on Justin back on the road when he'd first come to Eyrth.

When the golden magic faded, Eldrin looked up and nodded his thanks.

As the dust settled, a sense of relief washed over Justin.

Alistair's clothes and armor were both dirtied and bloodied as he regarded the party. "The Shadowist mages have broken into the camp. As long as we stick together, there's still a chance we can—"

The blaring of a horn echoed throughout the pass. This was not the low horn of the Shadow Empire forces. It was high, trilling, and triumphant.

Lila jumped for joy. "The reinforcements. They're here!"

Justin felt his spirits lift. "Hell yeah!"

They ran toward the sound of the horns, only to see the first lines of fresh Valorian troops with purple banners marching toward the camp. Within minutes, soldiers in gleaming bronze armor were pouring in, along with mages who started cleaning up the leftover Shadowist magic users. And among them were not only mages, but several Paladins in steel armor and white cloaks, not to mention several other classes Justin couldn't name.

Alistair, instead of joining the battle once again, allowed himself a smile. "We've made it. Can't you feel it?"

They headed back for the front lines, where Justin watched in amazement as the Valorians, spirits lifted, began pushing back immediately. Within minutes, the Shadowist lines were breaking, especially under the assault of multiple Paladins and Elementalists with fresh fire spells.

As for the hidden path, more reinforcing Valorian mages rained death against it, using a combination of throwing boulders and fireballs. Even at a distance, Justin could see the Shadowist soldiers trying to flee, but such was the treachery of the trail that many fell to their deaths.

It was all over in a matter of minutes.

Half an hour later, Justin, Lila, Eldrin, and Alistair stood before Commander Thalon within the throng of celebrating soldiers. Thalon's smile was so wide that Justin thought it seemed likely to split his face.

"Gods be praised!" he said. "Arion has not abandoned us to the Shadow!"

"Not on this day, nor any day, my lord," Alistair said. "We must always trust in His plans."

"I didn't believe you at first, but now I know you were right, Sir Paladin. Because of you and your companions, Valoria will live to fight another day. Thank you. Thank you, from the bottom of all our hearts."

Suddenly, the scene paused, the image of smiling soldiers freezing in time. Slowly, the surrounding setting faded, replaced by the mountain pass of modern day under starlight. There was nothing but dirt, trees, and a thin path snaking its way around the bend in the distance, the same bend which, hours ago, had swarmed with Shadowist soldiers.

"You have passed the Trial of the Vault of the Guardian Pass," Thalon intoned solemnly. "Alas, would that your party were here a millennium ago in our hour of greatest need! But now, the spirits of the Guardian Force can rest easy, knowing how things might have been."

Justin listened solemnly, taken in by the moment. From the somber expressions of the others, it seemed they were of a similar mind. Even Shadowflight, perched on Eldrin's shoulder, was silent, not even ruffling his feathers.

"Your party has fought bravely, and each of you is owed one bronze-tier item, while one of you will be rewarded with one silver-tier weapon." First, Thalon turned to Alistair. "To Alistair the Paladin, I gift the Ring of Valor, which will boost your Power and Endurance by 10% when targeted by three or more foes."

Alistair nodded graciously, accepting the proffered purple ring, which seemed to be crafted from pure amethyst. "I thank you, Commander Thalon."

Thalon turned to Eldrin, and in his hands appeared an unassuming pair of leather boots, supple and well-made. "To Eldrin the Ranger, I gift the Boots of Silent Steps. They are enchanted to make nary a sound, no matter how hard they press down or what they find underfoot."

"A wonderful prize," Eldrin said, taking the boots. "My thanks."

Thalon then turned to Lila, producing a gold-chained amulet with an amethyst gem crafted in the likeness of a knife. "And for Lila the Bard, who fights with knives, I gift the Amulet of Everblade. When you throw a knife, hold out your hand, and after fifteen seconds, it will return directly to you, provided it is within a hundred feet."

Lila's eyes widened as she took the amulet. "That's pretty damn handy. Thank you!"

Next, Thalon turned to Justin, and he felt the weight of the Commander's blue-eyed gaze. He produced an unassuming silver ring. "And for Justin the Socialite, I gift the Ring of Hygiene. Once a day, become perfectly clean in body and apparel, and get your hair cut and groomed to your exact specifications."

Justin accepted the ring with shock, almost in dismay, as he inspected its properties.

The Ring of Hygiene
Type: Accessory
Tier: Bronze
Dapper's Touch: Once per day, become perfectly clean and groomed to your exact specifications.

He put on a smile, but it was hard not to be disappointed. The others got cool weapons and gear, and he just got free haircuts and showers for life?

Surely he didn't stink *that* much.

It was only made worse because Lila looked like she was stifling laughter.

"Thanks," Justin said, hardly able to keep the glumness out of his voice.

All the same, he slipped on the ring.

[Do you wish to bind the Ring of Hygiene to your core?]

Justin hadn't expected that, but it made sense. He intrinsically knew the action would make the ring truly his. No one else could use it as long as he was alive.

Justin did so with a mental click. He felt its potential, but for now, he decided not to use it, even if he was filthy.

Thalon stood back, surveying the party. "And now, the ultimate prize. A silver-tier weapon for the one the Vault has determined to be the most valuable character—"

"—If it's me," Alistair said, interrupting, "I withdraw from consideration."

Thalon regarded him coolly. "It was not you, Sir Paladin."

Alistair's eyes widened at that, but he said nothing.

Again, Thalon's eyes went to Justin, and he felt a thrill enter him.

"Justin Talemaker," he said. "It is by your brave deeds, insight, and decisiveness that the battle was won at all. Trusting your keen Socialite's instinct, you read the malcontent soldier Darian like a book, following him to the Shadow Empire camp, a detail missed by all other party members. Though you couldn't prevent him from delivering the fateful message, you at least told Shadowflight, who relayed it to Eldrin, who was able to block the hidden path in time. You also deftly handled the Arch-Mage Zaramund with skill far beyond your abilities as a Level 2 Socialite, aided, of course, by Lila the Bard. Alas, Darian the Treacherous, in real life, betrayed the Kingdom of Valoria to the Shadow Empire, revealing the path he himself walked as a youth as the son of a goatherd. He betrayed his country, and as his reward, he enjoyed a rich life thereafter. At least, until four years later, he hanged himself from the rafters of his Belmoran manse."

Justin felt a chill at those words, swallowing a nervous lump in his throat.

"Justin Talemaker," Thalon began again. "The Vault has determined that your contributions have made you the worthiest of the silver-tier weapon." Thalon held out his hand, and within it materialized, seemingly from the Aether, a beautiful cane of pure ebony, about four feet long, with an amethyst as large as a fist on top, carved in the likeness of a stag's head.

Justin's breath caught, and even the others' eyes went wide.

"The Cane of Valoria," Thalon said solemnly. "As soon as you wield this cane, you will be granted a permanent increase of 1 to any attribute of your choosing. Besides this permanent increase, you will gain an additional +1 boost to Charisma and Intellect when wielding this cane. Unlike many weapons, the Socialite's cane can be used both as a bludgeon and a spear, for it has a retractable top that, with a swift press of a button, reveals a sharp knife, about six inches long, with a blade enchanted to never go dull. Also, when wielding the

Cane of Valoria, you gain access to Gentleman's Rebuff. With Gentleman's Rebuff, you will instinctively block the first hostile attack directed at your person, physical or magical, once per day, by any character, monster, or creature up to Level 20. This reflects the brave defense the Valorian soldiers made, both in this Vault Trial and in real life."

"Whoa," Justin said.

"A silver-tier weapon with the properties of a gold," Alistair mused. "My congratulations, lad."

Eldrin nodded appreciatively, while Lila looked amazed.

"The Cane of Valoria is yours, Socialite," Thalon intoned. "Wield it with poise and aplomb."

Justin accepted the cane, eyes wide. It was lighter than it had first appeared.

His interface lit up with information as he regarded the cane.

The Cane of Valoria

> **Type:** Weapon
>
> **Tier:** Silver
>
> **Class Restriction:** Socialite, Diplomat
>
> **Heroic Ascension:** Upon core binding, gain a permanent +1 to any base attribute. This enchantment can only be used once.
>
> **Valor of the Fallen:** The heroes of the Battle of Valoria lend their gravitas and cunning while you wield this cane, granting you +1 to Charisma and Intellect.
>
> **Gentleman's Rebuff:** Block the first hostile attack directed at you once per day by any character, creature, or monster up to Level 20.

"Now we're talking," Justin said.

A free attribute point and an amazing defensive enchantment? This more than made up for the Ring of Hygiene. The +1 to Charisma and Intellect was icing on the cake.

[Do you wish to bind the Cane of Valoria to your core?]

Justin mentally agreed, and he felt the cane become one with him.

[The Cane of Valoria has granted you a one-time boost to any base attribute of your choosing. You now have one attribute point to distribute.]

For Justin, it wasn't even a question. With a mental click, he locked it into Charisma.

[Your Charisma is now 13.]

Unbidden, he gave the beautiful cane a twirl and a quick button tap, exposing the knife at its tip from the mouth of the stag. His eyes widened as he almost fumbled it. He pressed the button again, retracting it. This would indeed come in handy, but he still needed to learn how to use it effectively.

Thalon stood back, taking in the entire party. "Well done, Brave Adventurers. The Trial of this Vault is over. The Vault has also sensed the danger to your Party from those who await your exit. However, you may continue enjoying the Vault's safety as you continue out the other side of the pass. But this boon will not last forever. Once again, the Kingdom of Valoria thanks you—not for saving it, for it can no longer be saved. It thanks you for giving it a cherished memory, so that its inhabitants can rest easy knowing that faith in Arion isn't misplaced. Fare thee well."

And with that, Thalon faded, and the Voice came to Justin, speaking as if in benediction:

[The Vault honors your triumph. Now go forth, with courage in your hearts, strength in your limbs, and wisdom in your minds.]

[The Trial of the Vault is complete!]

[Experience Gained: 1,000]

[Your experience stands at 1,404/250. Level-up available!]

Justin blinked at that experience notification. During the entire Vault, he wondered why he hadn't gained anything, especially for his use of Dazzling Display. Perhaps the experience from Vaults was given as a lump sum toward the end.

The air was now warmer than before, telling Justin they were back in the modern day. A thin veil of green magic covered the pass overhead, through which the stars could be seen.

"That was something," Justin said, examining his new weapon. "What a productive Vault!"

"It turned out well," Alistair said. "Congratulations, all."

Eldrin had already changed into his boots, giving them a few steps. Indeed, not a sound was made. He nodded in satisfaction.

Lila put on her amulet. She threw one of her knives, embedding it in the bark of a nearby pine, then held out her hand. She waited for fifteen seconds, and sure enough, the knife spun backward, its hilt landing in Lila's outstretched palm.

"Nice," Justin said.

"That Vault was much closer than it seemed," Eldrin said, "but we survived."

It was at this point that a message interrupted Justin's interface:

[Warning: the protective magic of the Vault will dissipate in one hour.]

"We'd better get moving," Alistair said. "I know it's been a while since our last rest, but there can be no rest until Highcliff. And if we push ourselves, we can make it by morning, especially with Eldrin's Pathfinder's Pace. The daylight will slow down our undead friends, giving us a chance to rest."

"We'll be safe there?" Justin asked.

"The Aranthian Plain beyond is less forested," Eldrin explained. "There aren't many places for the undead to avoid the sun. They'll be reduced to hiding during daylight hours and making up time at night. Plus, the undead can hardly show themselves on the Queensroad. They'll either have to journey off-road or leave them behind."

"We go," Alistair said. "If we don't hurry, this will all be for nothing."

Dutifully, they followed the Paladin. After seeing the way he was fighting, Justin had to wonder if he might have been capable of taking on all the Baron's men on his own. Perhaps that in itself was too risky; Alistair's strength during the battle might have been deceptive, since he was mowing down mobs of low-level undead, against which he had strong bonuses, anyway.

It was also likely that Baron Valdrik would have sent minions which, working together, could feasibly bring down a party like theirs.

With that unwholesome thought, they headed due east, toward the eastern exit of the Guardian Pass. Justin used his cane as a walking staff, and as such, found the going much easier. Indeed, these days there was less weight to carry around. He had dropped at least ten pounds since entering Eyrth.

As they walked, Justin summoned his character screen:

Justin Talemaker
>   **Class:** Socialite
>   **Level:** 2
>   **Experience to Level 3:** 1,404/250. (Level-up available!)

>   **Attributes:**
>>   **Power:** 10
>>   **Coordination:** 10
>>   **Endurance:** 10
>>   **Intellect:** 11 (Base 10+1)
>>   **Spirit:** 10
>>   **Charisma:** 14 (Base 13+1)

Attribute Buffs:

The Cane of Valoria: +1 to Charisma and Intellect.

Justin closed his interface, pondering his new items and abilities. It was a lot to take in, and he could only hope he would survive long enough to explore their capabilities.

22

THE ROAD TO HIGHCLIFF

"They say the Creator gifted mortals the classes to elevate their cores from the 'Imperfect Mundane' to the 'Holy Aetshereal.' Well, here's my take on it: perhaps the Creator wasn't giving us a gift but a leash. Classes define what we can become—but they also limit what we can dream of being. Maybe the Creator feared what we would achieve without them."

—Orvel the Apostate,
    Challenging the Divine Narrative

JUSTIN and the rest of the party reached the eastern edge of the Vault. They passed through the green, shimmering veil of magic, officially exiting and stepping into the eastern edge of the pass.

He was struck by how silent it was, how empty, with no sign of the battle from a thousand years ago. The tranquility was almost eerie compared to the chaos they had just endured.

The land was dark, but the skies had cleared, leaving enough moon and starlight to see the Aranthian Plain spreading below them. It was mostly empty, aside from a few small hamlets, but in the far distance, Justin spied what appeared to be a medium-sized town built on a plateau of sorts, quite high off the plain, the tallest building being, unsurprisingly, a Gothic cathedral that no doubt belonged to the Church of Light. A thin river, dark in the night, made a bend around the plateau, seemingly heading east.

By morning, if all went well, they'd be safe within the city's walls.

Alistair pointed it out. "That's Highcliff. Our next stop."

"We're getting close, then?" Lila asked.

Alistair chuckled. "Oh, no. We're just getting started."

Justin was absolutely exhausted. They had been up for about two full days. "I can't *wait* to get some sleep."

"You'll be waiting a while longer," Eldrin said grimly. "It will take the greater part of the night to get down the pass, and we must keep walking all morning. By then, we will have made it."

"I'm so tired I'm liable to fall," Lila said, looking down the thin, steep trail doubtfully.

"I've got just the antidote for that," Eldrin said. He reached into his pack, taking out a vial of a mysterious dark liquid. "Grimroot Extract. Made from the Grimroot plant and a few other secret ingredients. It'll keep you wide awake. For a time, at least."

"That concoction is unlawful in Aranthian territory," Alistair said. "I will not partake, but I will not stop you from doing so if you deem it best."

Justin almost refused, but in the end, decided he probably needed it. If this would get him safely down the trail, he would quaff it gladly.

Eldrin took a shot of it first, and he handed it to Justin. "Half a mouthful. No more or less."

Justin nodded. "Bottom's up."

The thick liquid tasted bitter and earthy, but it wasn't too disagreeable.

As Lila took her own drink, the effect on Justin was almost immediate. His eyes widened as he felt strength return to his bones. His exhaustion melted away, replaced by a heightened sense of alertness and energy. His steps felt lighter, and his mind was clearer.

"Hippity-hoppity, let's go!" Justin exclaimed.

Lila giggled giddily.

"We've tarried too long," Alistair said, his voice grave. "Let's go."

They began the treacherous climb down the rocky path, where they had to be careful not to slip. Every step was a potential hazard, and Justin constantly looked down to avoid missteps. But the increased focus of the Grimroot Extract meant his footing was sure, aided by the Cane of Valoria. They had maybe a two-hour head start on Baron Valdrik's minions.

Alistair lit the way with his Creator's Light spell, casting a warm, golden glow that illuminated their path. Eldrin's Pathfinder's Pace kept them moving swiftly and efficiently. Eventually, the land evened out into a pine forest, the dense canopy above them filtering the moonlight into faint beams.

They were heading east, making good progress when a chilling set of howls filled the air. The sound sent a shiver down Justin's spine, and he instinctively moved closer to Lila.

Shadowflight fluttered from the forest's canopy, having returned from scouting. The bird landed gracefully on Eldrin's shoulder. The Ranger inclined his head toward him.

"A pack of dire wolves," Eldrin said, relaying the falcon's message. "Ten in all."

"Dire wolves!" Lila exclaimed. "Dear gods!"

Alistair frowned deeply, concern etched on his face. "What are dire wolves doing so far south of the Seraphim Range? We need to pick up the pace."

"No picking up the pace can outrun a pack on the hunt," Eldrin said grimly.

All the same, the group increased its speed, but the dire wolves were relentless, their piercing howls growing louder and closer.

"We must at least get out of these woods," Alistair said. "I need room to maneuver my hammer."

Thankfully, it wasn't long before Eldrin led them to a wide meadow. They stood in the center, awaiting the creatures that couldn't be far. It was only half a minute before Justin spied the predators' eyes glinting in the darkness from the trees, their forms hulking and menacing. Justin felt fear course down his spine at the sight as they stalked closer.

"Stay in the center," Eldrin commanded, hand on the hilt of his longsword. "Lila, Justin, be prepared to defend yourselves if necessary. Alistair and I should be enough to dispatch these."

Lila readied her knives while Justin clutched his cane. He felt his heart rate increase. Between a dire wolf's jaws was not the way he wanted to go, and he knew, from his size alone, they would probably find him a decidedly delicious morsel. He definitely wouldn't be getting involved unless he absolutely had to.

The dire wolves were enormous, their fur bristling and matted, with eyes glowing an eerie yellow in the moonlight. Their growls resonated deep and guttural, a sound that seemed to vibrate in Justin's very bones. Their teeth were sharp and white, and their breath was visible in the frosty night air, coming in puffs as they circled closer.

Justin wondered why Eldrin wasn't shooting his arrows, but perhaps it was because it would take too long for him to transition from the bow to his longsword once battle was joined. For whatever reason, the Ranger elected to stand, blade at the ready.

Justin could feel the tension in the air. He gripped his cane tightly, his heart pounding.

Alistair stepped forward, his war hammer raised high. "Stand firm," he called out. "We'll get through this."

One of the dire wolves lunged, and Alistair met it with a powerful swing of his hammer, the blow landing with a sickening crunch. The wolf yelped and was thrown back despite its enormous size, but the others were undeterred, closing in from all sides.

Eldrin's blade moved swiftly, landing true and felling another of the beasts. Lila's throwing knives flashed in the moonlight, finding their mark in a white-furred wolf. On the sixth blade, the beast fell into the grass. Lila backed away, hands extended to retrieve her blades.

One dire wolf had eluded both the Paladin and the Ranger, and it looked mean and hungry as it readied itself to lunge at Justin. Poison Barb or Dazzling Display would do nothing against this creature.

Justin was wondering just how to attack when, faster than he would have believed possible, the dire wolf pounced, teeth flashing. By instinct, Justin raised and twirled his cane, instantly rebuffing the attack and sending the dire wolf staggering back with a pained yelp.

[Gentleman's Rebuff has shielded this attack!]

Pumped full of adrenaline, Justin seized the moment, dashing forward while extending the cane's hidden knife, stabbing the dire wolf just under the neck before it could recover. The creature gave a hot exhalation of breath as Justin twisted the blade and pulled it out, dripping red blood. The creature lay in the grass, giving a few more pained wheezes before settling into death.

Justin backed away, just in time for Eldrin, Alistair, and Lila to come to his side. Looking around, the remaining dire wolves were fleeing the scene, leaving six of their brethren scattered in the meadow.

Immediately, Alistair cast Bind Wounds on Lila, who had somehow gotten a bite wound on her arm. The golden magic wrapped around the bloody mess, doing a decent job of healing it.

The silence that followed was only broken by the rustling of the wind through the trees and a few chilling howls.

"We need to keep moving," Eldrin said, his voice urgent. "There could be more of them, and the Baron's men will not be pausing."

With Alistair's light guiding them once more and Eldrin's pathfinding skills leading the way, they continued eastward toward Highcliff. The forest ended just as dawn tinged the eastern horizon. They were half-running, half-walking. The effects of the Grimroot Extract had long since dissipated, meaning Justin felt like a dead man. He didn't even have the energy to look over his shoulder to see if they were being tailed. Thankfully, the dire wolves were sticking to the forest.

Almost as soon as they'd entered the plain beyond the trees, farms took over. They hopped stone fences, walked through fields of wheat and rye yet to be harvested, and followed the thin dirt tracks lined with hedges. They even passed through a couple of hamlets, their progress sped by narrow wagon tracks. In the early hours, they even passed a few farmers heading out to the fields. Around a bend in the path, Justin caught sight of Highcliff, which seemed much taller now that they were out of the mountains.

"Almost there," Lila said.

"Just...keep walking..." Justin said between breaths.

At last, the dirt road joined a stone-paved road, an actual highway at least fifteen paces wide. Somehow, Justin knew it was the Queensroad mentioned by Eldrin before the Vault, and it was much more impressive than the dirt road connecting Mistwatch to Silverton. He got the feeling that they had entered the main part of Aranthia, where infrastructure was a bit more developed. Somehow or another, he was still set on getting to Belmora and seeing what opportunities the big city could offer a Socialite like him.

But, for now at least, survival took precedence. That, and the task of getting rid of this pesky Death Mark.

As they approached the plateau upon which Highcliff was situated, they passed ambling carts making their way both in and out of the city. It was late morning by now, and Justin could barely keep himself from keeling over. They crossed a sturdy stone bridge that spanned the river Justin had spied earlier from the top of the pass.

Unfortunately, they had a long series of switchbacks to ascend to reach the plateau upon which the city was situated. Justin was absolutely filthy, coated in dirt, sweat, and even some blood from the fight with the dire wolves, as were the others. They got more than a few looks from the traders and farmers they passed on the way.

At last, they came before the tall iron gates of Highcliff. The guards at the gate, bearing spears and shields, were dressed in sky-blue tunics beneath their armor, which had the sigil of a soaring eagle on their breasts. Both guards cast them curious glances but didn't stop them from entering. Justin imagined it was not the first group of adventurers they had seen.

The city beyond was bustling, far busier and more crowded than any Justin had seen thus far. Most buildings were of red brick, lining a wide central avenue of cobblestone. These buildings were four or five stories tall, hinting at a prosperous city that had been developing for quite a while. Shops and stalls of various sorts lined the streets, offering everything from fresh produce, meats, and baked goods to clothing, jewelry, and books. Blacksmiths hammered away at anvils, and the scent of fresh bread wafted from bakeries. Townsfolk filtered in and out of the various stores, perusing the wares on display in the street carts. Inns and taverns beckoned travelers with open doors, while iron lampposts dotted the sidewalks.

Justin noticed metal tracks in the center of the streets with horse-drawn streetcars serving as mass transit, adding to the sense of activity. Two of these streetcars wandered through the streets, both filled with people, some even hanging off the sides. The air was filled with the chatter of townsfolk going about their day.

They finally came to a cozy-looking inn of three stories near the center of town; its metal placard, swinging in the breeze, proclaimed it to be The Silver Stag. Its sign featured a gracefully leaping stag against a backdrop of what seemed to be pure silver. The inn had a welcoming exterior with large, clean windows, flower boxes brimming with colorful blooms, and a well-kept façade.

"Here we are," Alistair said, his voice filled with relief. "Let's get inside. Gregory, the innkeeper here, is a friend of the Templars of Arion. We'll be safe."

With that, Justin, Lila, and Eldrin followed the Paladin into the inn.

23

THE SILVER STAG INN

"Beware the northern woods, for nothing escapes a direwolf pack on the hunt. Their howls are the only warning you'll get, and by then, it's already too late. In those moments, you are no longer a traveler—you are prey."

—Ranger Rowan Lightfoot
Tales of the Savage North

As they entered the Silver Stag, the warmth and comfort of the interior immediately embraced them. The common room was spacious, with polished wooden tables, a roaring fireplace, and the aroma of hearty food wafting through the air. At this time of day, it was mostly empty.

A friendly innkeeper behind the counter, a middle-aged man with graying hair, greeted them with a smile, addressing Alistair. "Sir Alistair of Drakendale. It is a pleasure to see you again. Be welcome to The Silver Stag. Will you and your entourage be staying the night, or merely taking lunch?"

"Staying the night," Alistair said, retrieving his coin purse and producing three fat, five-silver pieces. "Lunch, dinner, and breakfast on the morrow, and four of your finest rooms."

"Very good, sir. To confirm, this will not be on the Chapter House's credit?"

"No, sir. Off the books. The extra is for your discretion."

"Of course, sir," he said, almost giddily. "All of you seem tired and worn, but The Silver Stag is the finest establishment in all Highcliff. If you cannot find rest, succor, and peace here, then you can't find it anywhere." He turned his head back. "Martha! Prepare a swift but full luncheon for four guests in the private dining chamber." Then, back to Alistair. "Will you take ale or wine?"

"Wine, but make it well-watered," Alistair said. "We've been walking all night through the wilds, and we plan to rest as soon as we have had lunch."

"Indeed?" the innkeeper asked, surprised at this. "Well, after your meal, we can prepare four tubs for you, so that you might wash the night's trials away. You can count on our discretion, Sir Alistair."

"I thank you, Gregory."

"Please follow me to the dining room."

The innkeeper led them swiftly through the common room toward a door leading into the rear of the establishment. Thankfully, what few patrons there were sat far from the counter, so there was no chance of Alistair's words being overheard.

They entered the private dining room, a cozy chamber with a large oak table set for four. The walls were adorned with tapestries depicting hunting scenes, and a chandelier with candles cast a warm glow. They settled into cushioned chairs. Within minutes, a generous meal was set before them: roasted chicken, fresh bread, a variety of cheeses, and a hearty vegetable stew. Cool, watered wine was poured, and Gregory left them to their meal.

The four attacked their plates ravenously. Once done, Justin was so full that he was about to nod off, a feeling aided by the wine's gentle buzz. From Lila's heavy eyes, it seemed as if she were in the same boat.

The innkeeper returned. "Your baths and rooms are ready. If you're ready, I will take you there myself."

"Very good," Alistair said.

They rose from their seats, following the innkeeper up a set of stone steps. Everyone was too tired to even talk.

"Here they are," the innkeeper said with a smile, once they had arrived at the end of the hall. He handed them four small brass keys. "At The Silver Stag, we have a dedicated bathroom for each floor. You shall find it halfway down the hall, separated by gender, of course. Is there anything else I can do for you?"

"Nothing, good innkeeper," Alistair said. "Thank you."

"If you have dirty laundry, it is not too late to begin the early afternoon wash. I can have Martha return it to you by evening if you set it outside your door within the hour."

"Of course," Alistair said.

The innkeeper gave an accommodating bow before retreating down the stairway.

Once Gregory was gone, Alistair took the others in. "We'll be safe here through the night. I'll be able to detect any trace of Death Magic if it comes too close to the inn. Those thralls of Valdrik are better suited for hunting overland than blending into a city like this. If we leave tomorrow when the sun is bright, we should get a sizable head start on them."

"They will be lying in wait for us on the Queensroad," Eldrin pointed out. "By now, they've surely figured out where we're headed, especially considering the company we're keeping."

"That is something we must discuss, perhaps this evening, when our heads are fresher for rest." Alistair's gaze took in Justin and Lila. "You two can bathe first."

"Don't have to tell me twice," Lila said. She then frowned. "Just realized I don't have a change of clean clothes. Is it safe for Justin and me to go out and buy a few things?"

"Not a chance," Alistair said. "We must stay in the inn until it's time to leave. It's far too dangerous."

She pouted a bit but didn't argue. She was probably too tired for it.

"Let's go," Justin said. "You'll have clean clothes tonight, Lila."

"I guess."

As they headed down the hallway, Lila looked down at the Ring of Hygiene on Justin's right index finger. "What I wouldn't give for one of those right now! The guy said it cleaned your clothing too, right?"

"He did," Justin confirmed. "But a hot soak is just what I need right now."

"I hear that."

They entered the bathroom, and as the innkeeper had said, there was a partition to separate the two. Justin thought back to what Lila had said about bathing customs. Apparently, here in Highcliff, modesty was a thing.

On the men's side were three steaming copper tubs, and on the women's side, just one.

Justin bathed quickly. Once dried off, he left Lila there and returned to his room. Alistair and Eldrin had vacated the hall, though he could hear their voices talking low through the door.

Slowly, he crept up and pressed his ear to the oak. There was nothing at first, and for a moment, he believed he had been discovered.

That was when their conversation resumed. Justin heard Alistair speak first.

"You're right that Valdrik's men are likely waiting for us on the Queensroad. We have to be ready for that."

"Aye, they'll be expecting us to head straight to Belmora before heading north to Mont Elea. It's the fastest route. But it will also be the busiest, and that can be a sure shield. There are regular patrols of the Queensguard every few hours, and the Baron will think twice before trying something."

Alistair sighed. "I fear the Baron is desperate. He knows there's little time left before we reach Mont Elea and may risk a direct confrontation, even if we opt for the Queensroad. After all, if we make it to Mont Elea, his schemes will be foiled. And, of course, I'd rather avoid unnecessary bloodshed, especially if it puts Justin and Lila in danger. That incident with the dire wolves was far too close. Not to mention the Vault."

"Aye, all that's true. There's an old trader's road that breaks off from the Plainsway to Draegor's Keep. It's less traveled, and if need be, we can head east overland and lose them in the wild. My thinking is Valdrik's men might not think to look for us there, and by the time they realize where we went, it'll be too late for them to catch up."

There was a pause before Alistair spoke again, his tone contemplative. "That could work. But what of supplies? We'll need provisions for the extended journey, and there are few villages up that way. That would take us through the Wilderlands of Baelor. That's rough country."

Eldrin's voice was reassuring. "We can stock up here in Highcliff, of course, which will see us a good part of the way. The hunting is good in the Wilderlands. It might slow us down a bit, but we won't want for anything. Winter is still two months away. Enough time to make Mont Elea before the hammer falls."

"It will take at least a couple of weeks longer than the obvious path," Alistair said. "And let's not forget, after the Wilderlands, there's the Brackenbog. One false step will see you sinking to your death. There are at least fifty miles of that before we reach the Gulfway. And if winter comes early, as it did five years ago, that alone could be enough to end us."

"Aye, all true. Two poisons, pick one. The faster Queensroad or the less-traveled route."

Alistair seemed to consider this. "All right. First light, we'll head to the market. We'll need supplies, whatever path we choose. We need to be discreet, though. Valdrik surely has eyes here." There was a pause. "What is it about the boy that the Baron would go through all this trouble? It's not just about me reporting him to the High Priest."

Eldrin hesitated for a moment. "That, I can't say. His story is...interesting. You should ask him."

"Humph. Perhaps I will, Ranger. But for now, rest is best. Both he and the Bard will need it for the long road ahead."

"Do you think she'll want to go her own way? If she does, would the Baron try to track her down?"

"That's hard to say. My guess is he'll put all of his resources toward finding Justin and me. Lila is not a concern of his. I will put the decision to her tomorrow, or perhaps this evening. She deserves to have a choice. Though it's clear she sees something in the young man."

"Aye, that she does." Eldrin's voice took on a more serious tone. "I'll keep an eye out for any suspicious activity."

Alistair's voice softened slightly. "Thank you. Your skills have been invaluable on this journey. However, like Lila, I know Valdrik is not your fight. When we make Mont Elea, I'll ensure you are properly rewarded."

"If what you've just told me about Valdrik is true, Paladin, then I would do this for free. However, the money would be welcome."

Justin heard movement within the room, so he pulled away from the door and crept down the hallway toward his own room. Thankfully, the floorboards made nary a sound.

He wondered at the part of the conversation he had missed, what Alistair had told Eldrin about Valdrik. He felt left out, and he wondered why this information wasn't for him or Lila. Clearly, Alistair esteemed the Ranger far more, perhaps because of his age or abilities.

Justin returned to his room, the exhaustion at last becoming impossible to ignore. He fell asleep to the sound of creaking wheels, horses, and distant conversations.

When Justin awoke, the evening light bathed the room in hues of gold. The noises of the city could still be heard, but they had softened somewhat with the fading of the daylight. He resisted the urge to fall back asleep, even if that was all he wanted. His head was throbbing something fierce, either from exhaustion or perhaps an aftereffect of the Grimroot extract. His bones were aching, and his muscles were stiff.

As he sat up in bed, the Voice entered his mind.

[You have reached Level 3. As you awake to greet the evening, things feel as if they are coming together...slowly. You know you'll get there, one step at a time.]

Justin felt reflective as he pondered his journey so far. Instead of resisting the introspection, he bathed in it for a few minutes until a new message broke him from his reverie.

[You have one attribute point to distribute.]

For the first time, Justin felt he faced a tough decision on where to distribute the point. So far, he'd gone all in on Charisma, which made sense for his character. As a Socialite, all of his bonuses depended on that attribute. At least, as far as he knew.

But after getting stunned twice by Zaramund and having a close call with the dire wolves—not to mention all the hard travel that required Endurance—he was torn. Maxing out Charisma as much as possible would make sense if he were in a large city, where he could count on guardsmen to keep the peace.

For the foreseeable future, at least, it didn't seem like that would happen. If Alistair and Eldrin's conversation was any sign, they had a long, tough road ahead of them.

His Cane of Valoria already granted him a +1 boost to Intellect and Charisma, which was nice, but he had the distinct feeling it wouldn't be enough.

So, that begged the question: where to put the point?

He could do with a boost in either Power or Endurance, which would help his survivability. From the conversation he'd overheard, if they ended up going up this Plainsway, or even running into Valdrik's men along the Queensroad, it might be the difference between life and death.

And yet...it still felt wrong.

He sighed and locked the point into Charisma.

[Your Charisma is now 14.]

And just like that, the tension of having made the wrong decision evaporated. Besides, he had plenty of banked experience points. If he really needed to put a point in something else next time, he had the full freedom to do so.

[As a Level 3 Socialite, you have unlocked your next class skill. Choose wisely! There is no going back.]

Justin considered both skills that were presented to him.

Dandy's Swagger: Perform a captivating strut that immediately fills you with confidence and swagger, increasing your resistance to the Fear effect. You and your allies gain +2 to Charisma for one minute, while enemies receive a -2 Charisma malus. This strut can halt conversations and cause enemies to hesitate, or, with a mocking flair, gain their attention. (Cooldown: 3 minutes)

Tailored Compliment: Deliver an endearing compliment that can soften hearts of stone! Recipients of the compliment treat you as if you have +5 Charisma for the duration of the conversation. (Cooldown: 2 minutes)

Justin pondered both skills, weighing their pros and cons with careful consideration.

Tailored Compliment seemed straightforward and powerful. The ability to craft a perfect compliment and gain a +5 Charisma boost could be invaluable in negotiations or when trying to gain favor with a specific person. And it would definitely be useful.

Dandy's Swagger offered a more dramatic and immediate effect. It would not only fill Justin with confidence, but also grant him +2 Charisma. Not only that, but it also inflicted a -2 Charisma malus on hostiles. That was an effective 4-point differential, making enemies more vulnerable to a Poison Barb. There was a clear synergy between the two skills: Dandy's Swagger to soften up their Charisma resistance so that Poison Barb would land more effectively.

While not as specific and powerful as a +5 Charisma Bonus, Dandy's Swagger had the potential to turn the tide in larger social confrontations and even in battles. The ability to halt conversations and make enemies hesitate was particularly intriguing, as it could create openings for strategic maneuvers or escape—something Justin could have sorely used several times. Then again, it said it could also be used as a way of getting attention, only adding to its utility. The cooldown of three minutes was slightly longer than Tailored Compliment, but it was still reasonable, given the power of the move.

Justin reflected on his journey so far. The Vault had tested his mettle in ways he hadn't expected. He had faced Zaramund's terrifying presence, endured the treacherous climb down from the Umbers, and survived the dire wolf attack. Each challenge underscored the importance of not just Charisma, but presence and confidence. The ability to make enemies hesitate could be the edge he needed on the unpredictable and dangerous path ahead.

Dandy's Swagger aligned with the essence of his Socialite class. It was about more than just words; it was about presence, confidence, and the ability to command attention.

He locked in Dandy's Swagger.

[You have chosen: Dandy's Swagger. May your strut own every room you enter.]

Instantly, Justin felt a surge of confidence wash over him as the knowledge of the skill entered him. He knew he had made the right choice. The road ahead was uncertain, but with his new skill, he felt more prepared to face whatever challenges came his way.

He went to the mirror, looking at his unkempt, almost wild hair. Despite this, he was shocked by the transformation.

He hadn't lost ten pounds, as previously supposed. He had lost at least twenty, and maybe even as much as thirty.

It wasn't just exercise and fresh air. Something else was going on, too. Maybe it was his class or Charisma attribute, or perhaps both.

His face was thinner. His double chin was still discernible but reduced. A jawline was taking shape, and it was magnificent. His facial hair was a right mess; he hadn't taken care of himself in months, and it was even worse now. He looked better than he had in years, perhaps all the way back to his childhood.

He observed the silver Ring of Hygiene on his finger. Perhaps it was time to test out its capabilities.

He wasn't sure how it worked, but he looked in the mirror, imagining a clean-shaven face and a classic haircut, with a modern twist. He wanted the top to be long enough to have some volume to create a slight wave, parted to the right. Overall, he wished for a clean, polished look, but with enough length on top to style it a bit.

As soon as he was done with that image, he confirmed it with a mental click. An aura of yellow light surrounded him, making it impossible to see just what was happening. After a moment, it dissipated, and Justin stared in astonishment at his reflection.

His auburn hair was perfectly styled, just as he had envisioned, with the top long enough to boast a gentle wave, neatly parted to the right. His face was clean-shaven, highlighting his newly defined jawline, and his skin seemed fresher, almost glowing with health. The transformation made him look years younger, a stark contrast to the unkempt appearance he had grown accustomed to over the past years.

There in the mirror stood not merely Justin Talemaker, former NEET, recluse, and dweller of basements. There stood a proper gentleman: well-groomed, revitalized, brimming with confidence and, yes, even aplomb.

With a satisfied nod to his reflection and a sly wink, for he couldn't help himself, he twirled his cane and stepped out of the room, his stride carrying the weight of his newfound self-assurance, his cane clacking merrily on the wooden floorboards.

For the first time, he looked and felt every part of the Socialite.

24

A FORK IN THE ROAD

"There is something peculiar about the capitals of once-great empires. When the need for endless ambition and conquest dissolves, these cities often transform into places of festivity and indulgence. It's as though, freed from the need to take themselves so seriously, they finally learn to enjoy life. Highcliff has traded its banners of war for banners of revelry. Here, the ghosts of its former glory drink alongside the living, toasting to an empire no longer burdened by greatness."

—Chronicler Ellisar Vain
  When Empires Fall: A History of the Aftermath

JUSTIN STROLLED DOWN THE HALLWAY, cane tapping against the wooden floor, punctuating the rhythm of his newfound confidence. He nearly bumped into Lila, who was coming up the steps.

She stopped dead in her tracks, her green eyes widening as she took in his transformation. "Justin! Is that really you?"

Justin couldn't help but grin. "Yes, of course it's me." He gave a small, playful bow. "Just a bit more...*polished.*"

Lila laughed, the sound filling Justin with warmth. "Polished? You look like you've stepped out of a bard's tale!" She blinked, seeming to remember herself. "I mean, compared to before."

As Justin struck a pose, her gaze lingered on his clean-shaven face and styled hair. Her smile brightened.

It was almost as if she were *checking him out*, of all things.

"Lila...are you okay?"

She blinked, seeming to come out of a haze before giving a nervous laugh. "Yes, of course! I'm just glad you woke up. I was getting bored. Did you level up?"

"Yep," he said. "Level 3, baby!"

"Same here!" She frowned in confusion. "Though I'm no babe."

"Oh, you're not?" Justin asked with a wink.

She giggled. "So, what skill did you take?"

Justin took a step back. "Watch this!"

Before she could react, he activated Dandy's Swagger. With a flourish of his cane, he began an eye-catching strut, his movements exaggerated yet elegant. His entire body glowed with yellow light, and he moved like a panther on the prowl. The mere movement filled him with unbridled confidence.

Lila's eyes sparkled as she watched, and as if in reaction to the move, she joined in, mimicking his movements, even her steps syncing with his in a spontaneous, playful dance that echoed through the hallway.

Their laughter and footfalls attracted attention. Eldrin and Alistair emerged from their rooms, likely to see what the commotion was, their expressions a study in contrast. Eldrin's face broke into an amused grin, while Alistair remained unsmiling, his brows furrowing slightly as he watched the impromptu performance.

"Quite the moves, Justin," he remarked dryly. "I trust this new... *energy*... will serve us well on the road ahead?"

Justin and Lila slowed to a stop, their smiles lingering.

"Absolutely!" Justin said. "A little flair can only help, right?"

Eldrin laughed. "That's the spirit! We could use a bit of lightness in our step, especially with what lies ahead."

Alistair merely nodded, his skepticism clear but not voiced

further. Justin knew the Paladin had a lot on his mind. Indeed, Alistair seemed far more somber of late than at their initial meeting on the road to Mistwatch. The stress of protecting them from Baron Valdrik was weighing on him heavily, and he saw Justin's shenanigans as a needless risk that could get them all killed.

Justin realized he might have never had this insight without the recent Charisma boost. He was far more able to read the room and the expressions around him in a way he never had before. He assumed a properly modest expression.

Alistair nodded toward the stairs. "Dinner should be served soon. It would be a good chance to discuss our plans for the road. And please, for all our sakes, try to keep the dancing to a minimum."

"Yes, Sir Paladin," Justin said. "After you. Respectfully."

The Paladin watched him grimly before heading down the stone steps. Eldrin gave him a neutral look and a shrug, while Lila just winked, her steps light and teasing.

Justin let out a breath, following with his head held high.

The large oak table in the private dining room was set with a hearty meal: roasted venison, herbed potatoes, fresh bread, a variety of cheeses, and a bowl of cool, watered wine. Alistair, Eldrin, Lila, and Justin settled into their seats, the earlier mirth replaced by a more serious air as they prepared to discuss the road ahead. They ate quickly, sensing that Alistair wanted to get started as soon as possible.

Once the dishes were cleared, Alistair waited for the door to close before reaching into his pocket, producing a rolled map, which he spread out on the table. Justin's eyes widened at the sight. This map looked far more complete than his, seeming to have dynamic capabilities over all of Serenthel, the continent they were on. Alistair, with a tap of his hands, zoomed in on the map, with Highcliff in the bottom left corner and the Golden Gulf on the right.

Along that coast were three points of interest: Belmora in the south, Mont Elea in the center, seemingly on a small island just off the coast, and Draegor's Keep, a fortress town bordering both the ocean and the Seraphim Range, a large mountain range running along the northern edge of the map. All three were connected by a single road running along the coast, appropriately named the Gulfway. There were also many other cities, towns, and landmarks, all clearly labeled, but it was far too much to take in at the moment.

"We have two choices before us to reach Mont Elea," Alistair began, his voice low. "Each holds its own set of advantages and perils." His hand traced a line, extending from Highcliff across the Aranthian Plain, along which there were several modestly sized towns, toward Belmora. "The Queensroad is the fastest route, patrolled and relatively safe, but it is also where Valdrik's men will expect us to travel. They could ambush us, despite the Queen's regular patrols. Eldrin and I suspect he is desperate." Alistair's brow furrowed as he ran a hand along a thinner road snaking its way northeast from Highcliff. "The Plainsway, though less traveled, will take us to Draegor's Keep if we take this old trader's road that breaks off from it. And from there, the Gulfway goes south to Mont Elea. The road is rough. It's dirt in most places, and there are fewer chances to resupply. And of course, patrols are rare. This course would take at least a month longer than going to Belmora and then north along the Gulfway."

"Why not go up the Plainsway a bit and cut across?" Lila asked. "Seems that's the most direct route, and we have Eldrin's Pathfinder's Pace."

Eldrin came out of his silence. "That would take us through the Wilderlands of Baelor. Any settlements there are not on a map, and it's rife with bandits and other dangers. The forests are thick, the hills unforgiving, and the streams are many. I've been there a few times, but I spend most of my time in the Aranthian Hinterlands. Some of this ground would be new even to me. Pathfinder's Pace will help, but it is no substitute for a well-established road."

Lila frowned as she considered this.

Alistair watched her, and her eyes rose to meet his gaze. "Lila, there is something we must discuss."

"What?" she asked, her voice thin.

"Whatever path we choose, it will be fraught with hardship. You've been invaluable, and while the Baron has seen you with Justin, he is not after you in particular. Eldrin and I have judged that the Baron will put most of his resources into pursuing us to Mont Elea. If you wish to go your own way, this might be your last chance. Of course, you would be wise to never tread in the County of Silverton for the rest of your days. If we take the Queensroad, I suggest you take the Plainsway. If we take the Plainsway, you could find a hamlet near here and lie low for a few weeks before deciding where to go next. If you decide to leave, no one here will think less of you. I'm ready and able to supply you with a modest amount of silver to ensure your safety."

Justin tried not to look at her, so as not to influence her decision. He saw Alistair's point, but Lila was the one he was closest to. And she was his friend—and perhaps there was a chance for something more.

It would sadden him greatly to lose that, but perhaps it was for the best.

Lila's eyes narrowed in thought, then she shook her head. "I'll stay with the group." Her tone left no room for doubt. "I'm aiming for Draegor's Keep, and no matter which way the party goes, it's on the way. After Mont Elea, I might take a couple of days' rest. They say the mountain is beautiful, and the Blessing of Arion is not to be missed by anyone who is faithful to the Six."

Alistair nodded, respect clear in his eyes. "Very well. We would welcome your company, Lila."

Justin felt a sense of relief. He wondered more about "the Six." Lila had mentioned the six gods before, along with the Creator. He supposed Arion was one of these six. More questions for later.

"With that settled, which way should we go?" Justin asked. "What are the risks of both?"

Eldrin gave a coy smile. "You should know that as well as we do, Justin."

From the stares he and Alistair were giving him, he had not been as stealthy as he thought.

"What are they talking about, Justin?" Lila asked.

"All right, I'll admit it. After my bath, I heard them talking, and I got a little nosy and eavesdropped. What about it?"

"Never underestimate a Ranger's senses," Eldrin said. "Even the quietest eavesdropper leaves a trail."

Justin nodded. "Okay, point taken. It seems from what you guys talked about, the Baron is sure to ambush us somewhere on the Queensroad, despite the regular patrols of the Queensguard. The Plainsway, and then cutting across this Wilderlands place, would be rough going. And I heard something about a bog that's sure to kill us. It seems there's a third way now, going all the way to Draegor's Keep via the Plainsway, and then south on the Gulfway. This way would take the longest, and I assume it might be hard to travel with winter coming on."

"An accurate assessment," Eldrin said.

"Queensroad all the way," Lila said. "It's hard to see the Baron trying to attack us with so much security there."

"Simple Queensguards will be nothing to the soldiers he is sending after us," Alistair said grimly. "As long as there is nothing to tie them back to Valdrik, we will be ambushed."

"You can just take them out, right?" Justin asked. "I saw how you fought in that battle. Plus, you took care of their men easily enough at the alehouse."

"Nay," Alistair said. "Lieutenant Gareth—that's Valdrik's pasty lieutenant you saw at the Silverton alehouse—escaped our fight. There's no doubt he's in charge of the expedition hunting us down."

"How did he escape?" Lila asked.

Alistair paused, seeming to weigh his next words carefully, as if he were wondering whether he should even say them. "Lieutenant Gareth is a Shadowblade. One of their key skills makes escaping a prickly situation quite easy."

Justin felt his blood run cold. "Shadowblade? Sounds dangerous!"

"I kept it from you—didn't want to scare you out of your wits. But maybe it's good that I say as much, just to show you what we're up against. It's an advanced class, meaning that Gareth is at a minimum of Level 20, but he is not more than I am. I could sense the stain of

Death Magic upon him, which means he is at most equal to my level, which is 25."

"Death Magic," Justin said. "That would mean he's undead, too."

"Valdrik's most trusted soldiers are," Alistair said. "Normally, Valdrik would keep such men behind the scenes. He wouldn't want to risk a Paladin or mage detecting Gareth's undead status. So, the fact that he's bringing him into the open only proves his dedication to taking us out."

"Shadowblade," Lila said. "I've never heard of that class."

"It's the combination of a Warrior Core and a Thief Core," Eldrin said. "Shadowblades are favored as assassins, masters of both open combat and covert operations. They combine the raw strength and combat techniques of a Warrior with the stealth, agility, and cunning of a Thief. They excel in hit-and-run tactics, infiltration, and striking from the shadows, making them versatile fighters capable of adapting to any battlefield situation."

"Dear Gods," Lila said. "And if Alistair hadn't come along at the right time, we would have been murdered in our sleep!"

"That, or worse," Alistair said. "I had him cornered, but he doesn't fight fair. Shadowblades get a skill called Cloak of Shadows. They can become invisible once a day, and he used the invisibility to get rein-forcements. And you can bet those reinforcements are a well-honed team. While Lieutenant Gareth's retinue won't be Level 20 or above, each member likely has a class and is highly capable."

Justin almost wished Alistair had kept his mouth shut. Even now, all he could think about was where this Lieutenant Gareth was. Perhaps he was sneaking in the shadows of the city even now, looking for an opening.

"You should take heart," Eldrin said. "In a way, a Paladin is the perfect counter to an undead Shadowblade. Their chief ability is striking from the shadows, something they can't do if Alistair can sense the Mark of Death upon them. At best, Gareth can use his invisibility to escape. However, that means you can't stray too far from Alistair. He can detect Death Magic within a quarter of a mile or so, and that feeling only becomes stronger the closer an undead gets to him. Just stay close and you'll be safe."

Justin nodded shakily. Despite Eldrin's words, it certainly didn't *feel* as if he was safe. If Alistair was so adept at detecting Death Magic, he should have detected Gareth approaching the Moonlit Alehouse back in Silverton.

"Not to denigrate your abilities, Alistair," Justin said, "but I have to ask. If you can detect Death Magic, then how was Gareth able to approach the Moonlit Alehouse in the time it took me and Lila to get our stuff from our room?"

"Bad timing," Alistair said. "They moved through the streets quickly, but thankfully, I was able to gain their attention and lure them into the alehouse itself. If not for that, they might have gone straight for your rooms."

Justin felt a chill at those words. "So, what are we deciding? Is it not possible that they are trying to block both the Queensroad and the Plainsway?"

"That's fully possible," Eldrin said. "Whatever the case, they are probably watching the city closely and will know what choice we make, no matter what. But the fact remains, they must position their forces somewhere well away from Highcliff, somewhere with shelter from the sun." Eldrin pointed to Alistair's map, at a small forest south of the Queensroad. "My best guess is they're lying in wait there, while they've taken a few of their human soldiers to keep watch over the city for any sign of us leaving. There are three ways into Highcliff: the North Gate, the East Gate, and the West Gate."

"Will they be watching all three?" Lila asked.

"Probably. But the West Gate is the least likely to be watched."

"That's the one we came in from, right?" Justin asked.

Alistair nodded. "Could be our best move to leave through that one. It would be unexpected."

"Of course, it doesn't matter if we're tailed trying to buy supplies tomorrow," Eldrin said. "But if there's any sort of trouble, I'll root it out. A Ranger has a keen sense of observation."

That was something Justin could attest to personally.

"Well, that's our plan, unless otherwise stated," Alistair said. "Leave by the West Gate and head for the Plainsway."

"As sound a plan as any," Eldrin said. "We could even cut across the woods north of town to hit the Plainsway, so that we're not so obvious. It'll take longer, and of course, there's the risk that the Baron's men are actually camping there. But if we suppose right about the Queensroad, the woods to the north should be clear."

"Shadowflight can watch our backs," Justin added. "Right?"

"Aye. His eyes are sharper than any of ours. We can adjust as needed. Good plans are like rivers; they bend and flow as needed."

"Is it possible we can hire some mercenaries?" Lila asked. "I know it's expensive, but this is our lives we're talking about. And if the Baron is really bad news, whatever they cost would be a pittance in comparison."

Alistair shook his head. "As well as the Templars compensate me, even I can't afford the number of mercenaries we'd need to travel safely from Highcliff to Mont Elea. And even if I could, there are other problems."

He gestured outward. "First, even in a town as large as Highcliff, I doubt we'd find enough willing fighters. We wouldn't just need a few extra swords—we'd need a hundred or more, and if not that, mages to counter the Baron's own spellcasters. And even if we *could* find them, getting that many battle-ready mercenaries on short notice, all willing to work for us with no questions asked? Unlikely. Such things take time to put together. Time we don't have."

Alistair paused in thought before continuing. "And say we *do* manage to scrape together a company. Mercenaries fight for coin, not loyalty. A clever enough enemy—like the Baron—could simply outbid us. He has a rich prize in Silverton and can easily afford it. We'd spend a fortune just for them to turn on us at the worst possible moment."

Justin frowned. "That's a good point."

Alistair nodded. "Then there's the matter of subtlety. Right now, we're a small group that can move quietly. Hiring a mercenary company is like lighting a beacon. Soldiers mean supplies, wagons, moving more slowly, and with less flexibility."

Lila sighed. "So it's not just about the money."

"No," Alistair said. "It's about survival. And to survive, we need to be shadows, not a small army marching to its own execution."

"Well said," Eldrin agreed.

Justin considered all this, realizing Alistair had the right of it. In video games, hiring a few mercenaries was simple. They were basically NPCs who would obey without question.

It was naive to think it would be the same here.

"Given the potential dangers of being watched," Alistair continued, "I must insist that we retire early this evening. Highcliff, while bustling and seemingly safe, could harbor spies or worse. I don't believe Gareth would risk himself, owing to my abilities, but that doesn't mean he won't contract someone to do the watching or killing for him."

Justin's shoulders slumped a bit. He'd hoped to relax a bit this evening, have a bit of a talk with Lila, maybe even go out with her. There would be no chance for quite a while, and if she intended to go on to Draegor's Keep without him, there might never be a chance again.

Alistair seemed to read his intent, his normally stony features softening somewhat. "As a minor concession...the common room downstairs will remain available to you. It should be safe enough. If Gregory sees anything suspicious, I'll be the first to know. And for Arion's sake, stay inside and don't stay up too late. We have an early day tomorrow."

Eldrin grunted in agreement. "It's settled then. At first light, we will venture to the market for supplies. We'll keep a low profile, purchase what's necessary, and prepare for the longer journey along the Plainsway."

"Just to be clear," Lila asked. "Are we going to Draegor's Keep first, or are we cutting across the Wilderlands of Baelor?"

"The former, if possible," Alistair said. "I'll take the early snows of the Seraphims over the unknown dangers of the Wilderlands and the Brackenbog." The Paladin gave a firm nod. "Good night."

As the strategy meeting adjourned, Justin felt a mix of anticipation and apprehension. But most of all, he was relieved by Lila's decision to stay.

Alistair and Eldrin rose from the table, heading to the door that would lead to the stairway. Clearly, both had a mind to retire early.

Lila caught Justin's eye. She nodded to the opposite door, the one that led into the common room. "I'd say we've earned a drink or two."

He followed her out the door and into the common room of the Silver Stag.

25

OF GOBLINS AND KARAOKE

"Enchanters are the invisible architects of civilization. Without them, the tools we depend on—lamps that never dim, pitchers that purify water, swords that cleave through steel—would be mere dreams. They do not just enchant items; they sustain society itself. And all of it is made possible by the Aether Crystals, the lifeblood of their craft. Yet, the power they wield is a double-edged blade. If the crystal trade falters, as it has in the past, the world as we know it would once again crumble into chaos."

—Arwin Drell
Threads of Magic and History

Within a minute, Justin and Lila were sitting down with pints of cool ale. The common room of The Silver Stag was lively, almost full given the lateness of the hour. The patrons were a mix of working people, dressed in simple, practical clothing, and a few richer folks, adorned in finer fabrics and jewelry. This eclectic mix told Justin it was popular among all crowds. The buzz of conversation meant that whatever they talked about wasn't likely to be picked up in their little corner of the common room.

"So," Justin began. "You're from Daeloria, huh?"

Lila smiled. "Yes. What of it?"

Justin smiled, sipping his lager. "Just curious about this world. What's it like?"

"Well, the food is divine, the wine is the best in Serenthel, and, of course, the maids are the prettiest."

"I believe it. It must be quite different from here."

Her face fell a bit. "Yeah, that's an accurate assessment."

He smiled. "I've been wondering. How did you end up at that Mercenary Guild in Mistwatch?"

She chuckled. "Pure desperation?"

"Fair enough. There has got to be more to it, though."

"Well, I needed the money, and the more well-off folks hire a guard or two to travel the Silver Road these days. I thought that might be a good opportunity."

"So, you're telling me they let you into the guild as a Level 1 Bard?"

"Gods, no. I was actually waiting to be interviewed. But when I heard your story about needing to go to Silverton, I leapt at the opportunity."

"And the rest is history," Justin finished.

"Pretty much. Of course, I miss home. But I don't miss those thugs coming after me."

"Where was the last place you saw them?" Justin asked. "Surely, they wouldn't chase you this far."

"I saw them last in Stonehaven, a mountain town in the Umbers. It's the border between Aranthia and Daeloria. I lost them by paying a farmer to hide me in the hay bales of his cart. I haven't seen them since."

"Do you think they're still chasing you? All this way?"

"I don't want to take the chance. They followed me all the way from Eribar to Stonehaven, over two hundred miles. My debt is pretty sizable. And it grows larger every day."

"Yes, but at some point, the expense of sending thugs after you for hundreds of miles can't be worth it."

"You're right." She took another sip from her mug. "I...may have insulted the one who sold me the Bard Core. So, it's more than owing money. It's personal."

"What did you say?" Justin asked.

Lila smirked. "I told him he had the face of a troll and the manners to match. Not my wisest decision."

"Damn," Justin said. "That'd do it."

"That's why I'm heading for Draegor's Keep. It's at the butt end of nowhere, at least as far as Aranthia is concerned. They say it's cold and rainy, the opposite of Daeloria. I think it's the last place they'd look for me. If all goes well, perhaps I can make a life there. And if push comes to shove, well, it's a port. I can hop on a ship and head to Calidon."

"Calidon," Justin said. "That's another continent, isn't it?"

Lila nodded. "Mostly orcs live there, at least in the western half. But there are human enclaves. It wouldn't be a simple life, but at least I'd keep my kneecaps."

"An important consideration, to be sure. So, your goal is to strike it rich and pay off the debt?"

She laughed a bit at that. "Well, not that it will ever happen. But if I make that kind of money, it's probably best to start over somewhere. Even if I paid it back...I'm not sure I would be completely forgiven. Not without making some other gesture."

"This guy you borrowed from...he must have a delicate personality."

"He's tougher than old leather. It's about maintaining an image. And if the cheeky store owner got away with something, it ruins his credibility." She sighed. "No, I'm afraid Daeloria and I have parted ways. At least for a very long time."

Lila drained the rest of her mug, her eyes going up to an open archway that seemed to lead into a separate common room. "I just noticed that over there. I wonder where it leads."

Justin turned around. "It seems to be another room."

He noticed patrons flitting back and forth between the two spaces. When Lila rose and headed that way, Justin followed her lead.

Gregory, the innkeeper, gave them a knowing nod but said nothing as they slipped through the archway.

They were met with another common room, cozy and warm, with a more intimate ambiance than the Silver Stag. Clearly, it was another inn, or perhaps simply a tavern, connected to the Silver Stag. Another archway lay on the other side of this tavern, leading to another one.

"Seems all the inns here are connected, likely to share customers," Justin said. "It's a cool arrangement."

"Cool?" Lila asked, arching an eyebrow.

"It means it's an interesting and fun setup. It allows people to explore different vibes without having to step outside."

"Oh, I see!" she smiled with mischief. "Well, maybe we should explore, then. Alistair said it's all right as long as we stay inside."

Normally, Justin would have disagreed. But the lively atmosphere of the inn's patrons, combined with the pint of ale and, of course, the smile of a pretty girl who seemed to be interested in him, was a potent combination that could hardly be denied. "I don't see the harm. Just an hour of exploring."

"Maybe two," Lila said with a giggle.

Justin knew he was as good as lost now, but sod it. They'd run from terror to terror for days on end. Would having a little fun kill them?

Well, he realized the answer to that might actually be "yes," but at the moment, it didn't seem to matter.

They got another drink in the tavern connected to The Silver Stag, which was apparently called The Whispering Willow. It wasn't as busy, so they sidled over to the next one, which was down a set of steps and called The Thirsty Fox. Here, they ordered a spiced cider, a specialty drink that was warm and comforting.

By now, they were beyond buzzed. Somehow or other, Lila had grabbed his hand as she led him from place to place, and she hardly let go, an arrangement Justin was quite happy with. Back in his old life, he was rarely—if ever—invited for a night out, so in his mind, he was making up for lost time. The danger of Valdrik's men, and even the threat of the undead Shadowblade, seemed far away from the lively atmosphere.

As long as they stayed within a quarter of a mile of Alistair, things should be okay. Or so his thinking went.

After a couple of hours, Justin lost track of just how many inns they'd visited and how many drinks they'd had. Each inn had its own unique charm and specialty, creating a vibrant tapestry of experiences, a kaleidoscope of faces, laughter, music, and revelry. Highcliff, it seemed, was a party town. They sampled exotic ales, spiced wines, and honeyed meads.

And as they wandered, Justin couldn't help but notice people were drawn to him and Lila like moths to a flame. The women watched Lila with jealousy, while some men looked at him in challenge. More still wanted to be his friend, buying him even more drinks. No matter where he went, he was Mr. Popularity, a crowd forming around him, eager to hear his stories. The attention, which he had lacked so much in his former life, was downright addictive.

"And then," Justin said, gesturing dramatically with his cane, "the dire wolf lunged at me, but with a swift flick of my wrist, I sent it sprawling back!"

The patrons gasped and cheered, hanging on his every word. Lila's eyes sparkled with amusement and pride as she watched him command the room, hanging on his arm. That was worth more than any amount of attention he was getting.

Justin wasn't sure how it happened, but at some point, there was a stage in this one inn that called for its guests to come up and sing. He supposed it was something like medieval karaoke. Lila sang a lively drinking song to the crowd's roaring approval. Afterward, she insisted they sing a duet, a song from his world.

He tried to say no, but she wasn't taking no for an answer.

"Come on! You have an entire world of music that doesn't exist here. What's the best duet from your world?"

"Well, the best is subjective," Justin said.

He thought of some common duets. "Shallow," "Endless Love," "A Whole New World."

None felt right, though.

Then, a smile came to his face. "Wait. I've got just the one. But are you sure you can learn it quickly enough?"

She looked insulted. "Justin, I'm a Bard. Sing all the parts for me, and I can figure out the rest."

"Well, don't say I didn't warn you when I hit those low notes and the floor starts vibrating."

So that was how, in the dim corner of the Frosty Mug Tavern, Justin started teaching her "Islands in the Stream."

He wasn't sure why he chose that song in particular. Maybe it was the warmth and comfort of it, the sense of two people finding each other. Or maybe it was the sense of sailing away, adrift in a new reality, complete with magic, goblins, necromancers, classes, and even enchanted canes.

Whatever the case, Lila was right. Her Bardic class allowed her to pick it up with surprising ease, with Justin only having to sing each part a couple of times for her to get it down. This was even considering translating the lines into Aranthian.

Lila even borrowed someone's lute and was pretty good at picking out the right chords, which gave it a decidedly medieval flair. She had the acumen and ear of a professional musician.

"Okay, I think we're ready," Justin said, unbelieving of how fast it had come together.

"Don't look so shocked," she said with a wink. "Level 3 Bard doesn't mean Level 3 talent."

She drew him on stage, and within a minute, they were facing a half-interested crowd.

"This is a new song of our own we've just cooked up," Lila announced.

Lila began strumming the gentle, steady rhythm that captured the song's warm, heartfelt mood perfectly.

Even edified by liquid courage, Justin was a bit nervous. But then he remembered his Dandy's Swagger skill infused confidence.

So, he activated the skill, spreading his arms wide with his cane in hand, as if in benediction. He was surprised at the effect. Most of the bar went quiet as he eased into his role.

Justin began with a rich, deep voice. He wasn't a *bad* singer, but he wasn't the best either.

When Lila joined in with her part, she easily stole the show. Justin did his best to stay in key, and their voices actually blended together quite well.

At one point, when he stumbled over a lyric, she smoothly improvised, making it sound like it was meant to be that way all along.

The crowd warmed to the performance, far more so than Justin would have guessed. Several patrons started swaying in their seats, some couples even standing to dance in the corners of the tavern. By the time they reached the chorus a second time, a few voices in the crowd had even joined in. A grizzled man at a corner table raised his tankard in appreciation, nodding in time with the music.

When they sang the final notes, their voices blending together in perfect harmony, the tavern erupted in hearty applause, accompanied by the pounding of mugs on tables.

There were several cries of "Well done!" and "Another!" but Justin shook his head. It was time to wind down for the evening.

As they headed to the bar, an appreciative patron bought them both a round of frosty ales. They sat, and after the first sip, they shared a look.

"Well, I think we killed it," Justin said.

"Yeah, I think so too."

"Ready to turn in after this round?"

"Just one more inn," she said. "There's no harm, right?"

He laughed. "You're like the Energizer Bunny."

She smiled suggestively. "I'm not sure what that is, but I do like to hop. Given the right circumstances."

Justin nearly spat out his drink at that one. The way her eyes were staring at him made it hard to resist.

"All right, one more," he agreed. "But you have to promise."

He looked at her lips, which looked especially inviting in the light of the muted lanterns. Lila only widened her smile. Justin touched the side of her face gently. She closed her eyes, and at that moment, he wasn't thinking about the fact that he had never even kissed a girl.

All that was about to change. Within seconds. His heart raced, his face just inches from hers...

But just before he closed his eyes to give himself to the moment, he saw, from the corner of his vision, a sight that almost frightened him completely out of his wits.

Sitting on the barstool next to Lila—right behind her, in fact, previously missed because of its small stature—was a goblin. It had long ears, a pointed nose, and wide golden eyes—both of which were looking directly at Justin.

Yep, it was a goblin all right. But there were several differences between this goblin and the ones that had chased him in the Wildwood. It had a slighter figure while it wore finely tailored clothing with a bow tie, suggesting it was a goblin of means, and it had white, almost icy-blue skin. It sported a number of jeweled piercings on both of its ears.

Lila turned to see what had gotten Justin's attention; though when she saw the goblin, her expression wasn't one of fear, merely curiosity.

Before they could say anything, the goblin spoke, his voice surprisingly smooth. "Good evening. Forgive me for interrupting, but I can't help but notice that cane of yours. Quite the piece you have!"

Justin, deciding the goblin wasn't a threat, exchanged an annoyed glance with Lila before nodding. "Yes, it is. What's it to you?"

The goblin, with two hands, took a swig of his frosty ale. The pint glass was almost bigger than his head. Justin would have laughed, but something about the goblin's manner was quite serious.

"You're a Snow Goblin," Lila said, her words slurring a bit. "From the Seraphim Range, right?"

The Snow Goblin nodded sagely. "Yes, quite! We aren't often seen in human lands, but this inn is quite accepting of non-humans. More so than others, anyway." He extended a long hand, his nails curled and painted gold. "My name's Gribble Frostfang. Of Clan Frostwalker."

Justin shook the goblin's hand, trying to ignore the way its sharp nails felt on his wrist. "I'm Justin, and this is Lila. Is there something special about my cane?"

"Yes, quite special," Gribble said. "You see, I'm an Enchanter of respectable level, and I have a skill that allows me to see an item's enchantment just by looking at it. Yours, simply, has a very interesting property. Where did you get it?"

Justin hesitated for a moment, knowing he probably shouldn't share, but often, booze does the talking when the speaker shouldn't. "I found it in a Vault!"

Gribble's eyes widened with interest. "A Vault, you say? Fascinating! You see, I could tell there was something special about that cane the moment I saw it. It's not so much the +1 to Charisma and Intellect. A nice bonus, but nothing too unique. I see that it also grants a free attribute point upon core binding. That is an extremely rare enchantment called Heroic Ascension. It's one I've been searching for all my life to find."

"Really, this old thing?" Justin asked, examining his cane. "I suppose you want to buy it from me?"

"Yes, very much so," the Snow Goblin said seriously. "It matters not if it's core-bound; I can break down the cane and discover the enchantment, and with luck, replicate it. No doubt, recreating it would require many expensive and rare components. But the rewards, for both me and you, would be great."

"I see," Justin said, ready to find a way out of this conversation. "I'm afraid the cane isn't for sale."

The goblin's white, bushy brows lowered for a moment before resuming its former friendly expression. "Of course, I'd be willing to pay. Handsomely."

"How handsomely?" Lila asked.

"For an enchantment of this rarity," the goblin mused, "ten gold crowns aren't out of the question."

It was hard for Justin not to react. Ten crowns? That was over ten times the amount of money he had on him.

Lila whispered in his ear, "I'd take that deal in a flash."

Justin was considering it until he remembered something that was general knowledge, at least where he came from. Never take the first offer.

"Your offer is...generous," Justin said. "However, I'm not sure of the value of the cane, since you're the first one to make an offer. I would need to get it appraised separately."

"I know just about every appraiser in this town," the goblin said eagerly. "I'd be happy to arrange it."

Justin smiled. He wasn't born yesterday. "I think not, Mr. Gribble. I appreciate the offer, but really, we must be going."

Justin rose, with a look at Lila to say to get up too. Reluctantly, she stood up.

"Twenty crowns?" Gribble asked. "I'll pay up front, right now."

Then, the goblin reached into his purse, laying the fat, golden coins on the bar top, one after the other. The coins glowed with an inner light, attracting a lot of attention. But no one made any move to grab them.

"Justin...?" Lila asked, whispering in his ear. "Take. The. Money."

Justin felt himself relaxing, almost giving in.

And yet he knew he was being played. Maybe it was his Charisma, but something about the goblin's manner was throwing him off.

They needed to leave now.

He grabbed Lila's hand firmly to let her know he was serious. "I thank you for your offer, Gribble, but I'm afraid the cane isn't for sale. Have a pleasant evening."

He walked firmly away, at first dragging Lila before she fell in beside him.

"What are you doing?" Lila asked, almost angrily. "You could have been rich. Rich!"

"Lila, the cane is worth more than that. Plus, I can tell something is off about him. We need to get back to our rooms."

But just as they were about to enter the adjoining inn, four swarthy men wearing leather armor, each bearing a club, blocked their path.

Gribble appeared from the side, all of four feet tall, apparently having followed them through the crowd. The crowd shrank back at the impending confrontation.

Gribble put his hands behind his tailored coat. "I'm afraid, Mr. Justin, that my offer stands and cannot be refused. Take my money or take something much worse."

"Are you making me an offer I can't refuse?" Justin asked with a smirk.

The Snow Goblin gave a yellow smile full of pointy teeth. "Yes. That's an...apt description, Mr. Justin. Don't mind if I steal that for the future."

Justin twirled his cane while Lila reached for two of her knives.

"Gribble, you're about to see just why you don't mess with a gentleman."

26

SWAGGER AND SHADOWS

"The Creator and His gods know every person's purpose and their strengths, for to each is accorded their Core Attributes, a reflection of the soul's divine design. These attributes guide the path set before them, shaping their role in the Tapestry of Creation. But let no one forget: while the Creator grants the foundation, it is the will of the bearer that builds upon it. Purpose is not a gift freely given—it must be earned through trial and choice."

—*The Book of Life*, Chapter 12, Verses 7–10

As the men advanced, Justin activated Dandy's Swagger. Instantly, he felt the power of the skill enter him, filling his limbs with strength and confidence, with even the haze of his drunkenness fading.

With a preening strut, he brandished his cane, his body glowing with a yellowish aura. The toughs paused in their tracks while the inn's patrons watched in awe, some even mimicking his movements. Some came closer, making fists, apparently ready to come to his defense.

The first tough, a burly man with a tattoo on his neck and a sneer that could curdle milk, shook his head, snapping out of his hesitation by swinging his club.

But Justin, with a fluid move that belied his experience, side-stepped the blow, swatting the man's club away.

[Gentleman's Rebuff has shielded this attack!]

The tough's eyes widened at the adroit maneuver, which Justin followed up swiftly with a Poison Barb.

"You swing like a drunkard trying to swat a fly!"

The man growled, the words making him hesitate for a moment. It was all Justin needed. He was no master of cane combat, but all he knew was that he had the initiative. Buoyed by the confidence of Dandy's Swagger, he brought the cane down on the tough's wrist, disarming him with a pained yowl. In the same motion, he jabbed the cane's tip into the man's midsection, knocking the wind out of him. As the tough doubled over, Justin gave a quick strike to the back of his head, sending him to the floor like a sack of potatoes.

Lila, meanwhile, performed a graceful flip, evading an attack from the second brawler with ease. She landed lightly on her feet, a triumphant grin on her face. As she aimed her knives, the man raised his hands placatingly, bowing out of the fight. Lucky for him, Lila spared his life.

The third and fourth thugs closed in, but Justin's Dandy's Swagger had inspired some of the tavern's patrons. A brawny man, the same one who had been moved to tears, grabbed a chair and swung it at one thug, while a group of women threw their mugs at the other. The room erupted into chaos, with other patrons joining the fray to defend Justin and Lila. Justin knew it wasn't just his Dandy's Swagger, but the fact he and Lila had warmed up the crowd with their epic duet.

With the remaining toughs facing down multiple opponents, the rest of the fight was quite elementary. Justin twirled his cane again, delivering a series of blows that kept them off balance. He knew he had to keep up the momentum, not to give up until the fight was done. With the growing mob of tavern patrons, their opponents could hardly defend themselves.

"Come on, you lot," one of them said. "This isn't worth the goblin's coin!"

The bullies pushed their way through the crowd, leaving behind the one who had been knocked out cold. Gribble's eyes watched in mounting horror. With a squeak, the agile creature beat a hasty retreat, slipping through the crowd. He had lost himself in a matter of seconds.

[You have gained 10 experience points. Your experience stands at 1,164/325. Level-up available!]

Breathing heavily, Justin turned to Lila. "Well, that was something."

The muscled patron who had thrown the chair approached Justin. "Are you all right, lad?"

"Yes, completely fine. Thanks for the assistance."

"Don't mention it. I don't enjoy seeing bullies like that pushing people around. Especially ones as good at singing as you!"

"Hey!" the barkeep shouted. "Are you two going to pay for all this? I'm down a chair and several mugs!"

It was too little, too late to prevent property damage, but Justin laid a couple of silver coins on the bar. "Hope that covers it."

The barkeep waved them away. His features softened somewhat.

As they left the establishment they were in, heading back to The Silver Stag, Lila laughed. "I'd say that was a resounding success!"

Justin smiled. "It's not a night out unless you've been kicked out of the bar, right? By the way, what was that move you did?"

Lila's eyes sparkled with excitement. "I forgot to mention it. I unlocked a new skill, Acrobatic Tumble. It increases my evasion by fifty percent for three seconds, and by one hundred percent when targeted by classes of equal or lower level. The cooldown is only thirty seconds."

"Impressive," Justin said. "Seems like it came in handy!"

"Speaking of moves, the way you handled that cane was a work of art! I would never have thought—"

Her words were interrupted when a hand roughly grabbed Justin's shoulder, yanking him into a booth. He scarcely had time to yelp.

But once he saw the one doing the pulling, he relaxed. "Eldrin? What are you doing here?"

The Ranger was nonplussed, the cowl of his hood hiding his features in shadow. "You draw far too much attention to yourself, Mr. Talemaker."

Lila sat down with a smile, joining them. "We're just having a bit of fun, Eldrin. Life isn't all death and despair."

"You're completely drunk! What's gotten into you both?"

Neither of them had a response. They had been caught red-handed, acting like immature children.

"Just got caught up in the moment, I guess," Lila said.

"I'll say. Alistair will know all about this tomorrow morning."

"Are you going to rat us out?" Lila asked.

"Nay. But the good innkeeper, Gregory, will. But all that is beside the point."

"And what are you doing up so late?" Justin asked.

"I've been hard at work; of that, I assure you."

For the first time, Justin noticed that Eldrin's pint was barely touched. "Doing what?"

"Shadowflight returned to me on the rooftop just an hour ago. He's informed me that every gate—including the West Gate—is being watched. It seems they've paid men to mark our passing, no matter which way we choose."

"Then we're stuck," Justin said, sobering at the news. "Right?"

"That's what I've been trying to figure out. I've been asking questions—casually, mind you—and I've discovered something interesting."

"What's that?" Lila asked.

"As you know, Highcliff is built on a plateau. That's where the name comes from. But did you know that, in the past, it was its own city-state? And not only that—the city was far larger than it is today, extending well beyond even the plateau. It has been reduced in the last few hundred years by several wars and the shifting of trade routes, until two hundred years ago, it became part of the Aranthian Queendom."

"Interesting," Justin said. "But why the history lesson?"

"Only to say that the city hosts a grand network of catacombs beneath it that belies its modern-day size. And those catacombs extend well beyond the current city limits, given the city's storied history."

"Catacombs?" Justin asked. "So, we can use these catacombs to get out?"

"That, I can't say. From what I've gleaned, it's a strong possibility. Either way, it seems to be our only option with the gates under constant watch."

"Have you told Alistair about this theory?"

"Not yet. I was about to head that way when I picked up on the commotion coming from the Frosty Mug."

"What about the market?" Lila asked. "Don't we need to get supplies?"

"It would be too much of a risk now. Food can be found on the road, and in the worst-case scenario, going without for a few days is a small price to pay to ensure our escape. As for the catacombs, they're accessible from the Church of Light. Using Alistair's rank, we might convince the High Cleric there to let us in. Hopefully, by the time our pursuers know what's happening, it will be too late for them to give chase. And even if they figure out the puzzle, there are likely to be multiple exits, giving us options."

"Will it be far enough from town to make a difference?" Justin asked.

"Almost assuredly. Assuming those passages aren't buried."

The three seemed to consider the possibilities. Justin had sobered up considerably, both from the conversation and the fight. However, Eldrin was right. They had already attracted too much attention—and enemies. Getting out without being seen was crucial.

"One thing is for sure," Eldrin said. "We need to get some rest. It must be an hour after midnight. We will wake early, before first light."

Justin nodded. "Sounds good. And again—we're sorry."

Eldrin nodded. "Life is filled with choices, and tonight, yours could have cost us dearly. Let's hope tomorrow brings wiser decisions. Now, get some rest. I'll be there shortly."

As Justin and Lila made their way back to their rooms at the Silver Stag, the common rooms were much emptier. The "success" of the night had been dampened by the danger they had put everyone in. It was hard not to feel guilty. Even Lila seemed glum.

"I'm sorry," she said, once they had made it to the stairs. "All this was my idea."

"I was a willing participant," Justin said. "This is on both of us."

"It's too easy for one thing to lead to another. I was having fun for the first time in months."

"Years for me."

They paused halfway up the stairwell as she took his hands.

"There's one other thing. I...want to apologize. I've acted like a proper ass this evening."

"What do you mean?"

She hesitated a moment. "I think we've gotten a bit carried away with...well, whatever is going on between us."

The silence stretched between them uncomfortably. There had been handholding, arm-locking, and sultry looks. Not to mention certain words spoken and an almost kiss that had been foiled.

"I understand," he said. "You want to focus on the road ahead, right?"

"It's not that," she said. "I'm just not ready, I suppose. I'm not sure how I feel yet. You're my friend, Justin. I don't want to ruin that."

Justin was quiet, not sure what to say.

She must have sensed his disappointment. "You misunderstand me. We've passed the point where it could've meant nothing. That point happened, I think, after Silverton. It's not right for me to encourage things that aren't possible. We…have a lot at stake." She sighed. "Gods above, I'm no good with words…"

Justin watched her green eyes, and to his surprise, he could read her like a book. Whatever words she was speaking now, several facts remained. She'd held his hand, had nearly kissed him, not to mention the outright flirtation. Yes, there had been a few drinks involved, but Lila had said similar things without alcohol.

She just wasn't sure, and that was natural. Plus, she was right. It made little sense to pursue things when they had to focus on getting to Mont Elea in one piece, and Eldrin's warning had been a wake-up call.

Feelings and relationships gummed things up. And he couldn't be the one to do that. Not while things were uncertain.

"I agree," he said. "There's nothing to forgive. Friends?"

To his surprise, she leaned into him for a hug.

"Thank you, Justin."

He let her go when he heard the single creak of a floorboard at the top of the stairs.

"Is that you, Alistair?" Justin called.

Silence.

Lila suddenly grabbed his hand, and not a moment later, someone was dashing down the steps above them, blade drawn.

Justin and Lila flew down the stairs, making the bottom landing as the assailant behind them gave chase.

Justin twirled around, brandishing his cane. The would-be assassin, a young man barely out of his teens holding a pair of daggers, threw his entire body into the attack, both blades out. Justin, by instinct, extended the cane's blade, raising it just in time to impale the young man through the stomach. The assassin stopped short, both blades falling to the floor.

He was finished off by two of Lila's knives flying, burying themselves in his neck. The assassin went down. It all happened in less than ten seconds.

Not a moment later, a set of heavy footsteps thudded down the stairs above, Alistair rushing onto the scene, a short sword—what

Justin supposed to be his sidearm—in his right hand. Meanwhile, Eldrin swept in from the common room, longsword drawn. Lila held out her hands, and her knives returned, one by one, perfectly clean. Her expression was grim as she regarded the body before her.

Justin watched the dead assassin, the blood draining from his face. The assassin had bungled it, a creaky floorboard having given him away. Without that, he and Lila might've been done for. The mere thought of it made his stomach churn.

They had been lucky. Insanely lucky.

Alistair came to stand next to them. His gaze took in all three of them. "We must away immediately, before Gareth learns of this failure."

Several inn patrons had emerged from their rooms and were gathering at the bottom of the stairs, gasping at the bloody sight. Not a moment later, Gregory appeared in his pajamas, apparently sensing the commotion. His eyes widened upon seeing the dead body before taking in Alistair.

Before the innkeeper could even speak, the Paladin was giving orders. "Coordinate with the Church of Light in the morning regarding this...unfortunate incident. Tell them I sent you. They should offer protection in the coming days. I'm afraid you may need it."

The innkeeper's face was pale, but he nodded. "I will do so, Sir Paladin."

Eldrin came up to join them on the landing. In a low voice to Alistair, he said, "I've found a way out. One that is safer."

Alistair gave the barest of nods. "Let's gather our things. Then to the private dining room."

Within two minutes, all four of them grabbed their packs and equipment and were gathered in the dining room downstairs.

Once they were alone, Eldrin spoke. "Shadowflight has informed me that all the gates are watched, with no means of passing unmarked. Luckily, my night's work has been productive. There may be a way out of the city using the catacombs beneath it."

"The catacombs," Alistair said. "Yes, of course. I don't know why I didn't think of it."

"They're often forgotten about," Eldrin said. "And it's been a tumultuous few days. Of course, there's no guarantee they will actually lead out of Highcliff, but owing to the city's history, the probability is quite high."

"Most cities have sewer mains," Justin said. "It wouldn't be pleasant, but that's a possibility too."

"And one I've considered, but that way is also likely to be watched, since it leads directly to the river," Eldrin said. "The catacombs, at least, have multiple exits that lead far from the city."

"What's the next step?" Lila asked.

"We need to speak to the High Cleric. He's likely to be sleeping at this hour, but getting inside the cathedral itself should prove simple enough. And it will offer some measure of safety. Once we're inside the catacombs, we can find some place to pass the night safely. Sleep, unfortunately, is a necessity."

"And we are unlikely to be pursued there, given the Life Magic enchantments every cathedral has," Alistair mused. "It's a brilliant play."

"When do we go?" Justin asked. "I assume now?"

"Yes," Eldrin said. "I've already charted a course that will get us close. We can simply weave through the various taverns that surround the city's main square. There is one street we'll have to dash across, but I've already scouted a spot the lampposts don't quite reach. If we stick to the shadows and move quickly and quietly, we can hop the fence into the cathedral's courtyard. From there, we should be able to break in, or better yet, Alistair might have a way of getting us inside."

"Sounds like a plan," Lila said. She stifled a yawn. "Gods, I'm beyond tired!"

"We should be able to rest in the next hour or two," Eldrin said. "If the plan is good to Alistair, then I say let's move at the first opportunity, before the City Watch gets involved."

Alistair considered for a moment. "It's a plan. Lead the way, Ranger."

Eldrin nodded. "Then follow me. And try to do so quietly. Once they figure out the assassin is dead, it won't be long before they send another, perhaps in even greater numbers."

The Ranger headed out from the private dining room. Alistair nodded at Justin and Lila to follow, intent on bringing up the rear.

Justin and Lila exchanged a glance before following.

27

THE SANCTUARY'S SECRET

"Which pantheon is more powerful—the Old Gods or the New? A question that has baffled Scholars, Priests, and Clerics alike for centuries. But the answer, my friend, is simple: the most powerful gods are the ones currently pointing a divine spear at your chest. Worship accordingly."

—Vennick Tallow
Practical Theology for the Everyday Fool

THE INN WAS QUIET NOW, the few remaining patrons whispering in hushed tones. The aftermath of the fight and the appearance of the assassin had sobered everyone up considerably.

Eldrin led the way through the interconnected taverns and inns, weaving through darkened hallways and shadowy common rooms. Justin marveled at how the Ranger moved so silently, likely thanks to his Boots of Silent Steps. Lila followed close behind, her steps also light. Justin did his best to imitate them, but the occasional creak betrayed his presence. Alistair, in his heavy armor, was the loudest, but that couldn't be helped.

They emerged into the final tavern, a place called The Moonlit

Rest, which was dimly lit by a few flickering lanterns. The patrons here were asleep at their tables or quietly talking in corners.

Eldrin motioned for them to stay close as he approached a side door, his eyes scanning the street beyond. He turned to the others. "Ready?"

Justin nodded, gripping his cane tightly, while Lila gave a quick nod, her eyes alert and focused now. The shadowed path they needed to take was clear: about ten steps across the cobbled street to the wrought-iron fence. Beyond lay a dark courtyard filled with trees, with the shadowy spires and buttresses of the cathedral looming above. The half-moon gave the scene a menacing air. He tried not to think about what might be out there in the darkness.

Eldrin opened the door just enough for them to slip through one by one. They stepped into the cool night air, the street empty and silent. The iron fence of the Church of Light's courtyard loomed ahead, its spiked top casting long shadows in the moonlight.

"Over the fence," Eldrin whispered. "Quickly and quietly."

Justin glanced at the fence, then at Lila. She gave him a determined look before stepping up to the iron bars. With surprising agility, she climbed over. Justin followed, his hands gripping the cold iron as he hoisted himself up and over with a boost from both Eldrin and Alistair. Eldrin and Alistair were over the fence in moments. Justin was surprised Alistair could do so in his heavy armor, but he supposed that was what the Power Attribute was for. His landing was hard, his armor clanking.

Once inside the courtyard, they moved swiftly across the cobblestones, heading for the side doors of the cathedral, up a set of stone steps. Those doors were quite grand, considering they weren't the main entrance.

Eldrin reached the doors first, testing them gently, but they wouldn't open. Alistair then approached, placing a gauntleted hand on the wood. A glyph shone briefly at his touch, creating the shape of a radiant phoenix surrounded by a hexagon of six lights in the colors of red, orange, yellow, green, blue, and purple. Somehow, Justin knew those colors each represented an attribute. The heavy wooden doors swung open with a faint creak.

"Stay close," Alistair said, his voice a low rumble in the quiet night. "The next step is to find the High Cleric. He's likely in the undercroft."

They slipped inside, the sanctuary of the Church of Light illuminated by the soft glow of floating enchanted crystals. The air was cool and still, the silence reverent. The vastness of the space, dimly lit and filled with shadowy columns, made Justin feel as though anything could jump out at them. From Lila's wide green eyes, it seemed she was having similarly dark thoughts.

Eldrin led them through the main hall, past rows of empty pews and grand stained-glass windows that depicted scenes of fantastical creatures, Clerics healing the wounded, Paladins fighting monsters, and what had to be Arion himself, God of Power. He was portrayed as a tall, muscular figure with flowing hair and a serene expression, holding a war hammer that emanated red light.

At the end of the hall, a smaller, nondescript door led to what had to be the undercroft. Alistair led the way, knocking softly. The sound was barely audible in the stillness. Justin thought they would never get an answer when a narrow metal grate opened, revealing a sleepy-eyed Cleric peeping out.

"What is it at this hour?" he asked groggily. Then, seeing who was speaking, he straightened and unlatched the door, swinging it open. "Sir Paladin! You must be here about the bill."

Alistair frowned in confusion. "What bill?"

"The one sent to Mont Elea by High Cleric Theophilus. We've been waiting for months!"

Everyone looked at each other, puzzled.

Alistair cleared his throat, his presence commanding even in the dim light. "I am Alistair of Drakendale, Paladin Brother of the Mont Elea Chapter House. I've been away from the Mont for many months now, so I know nothing about a bill. We seek an audience with the High Cleric. It is of utmost importance."

The Cleric's eyes widened. "Of course, Sir Paladin. Please, give me a few moments."

They waited in silence for about three minutes, those three minutes seeming to stretch into eternity for Justin. At last, the Cleric returned.

"The High Cleric will see you at once; I can take you to him directly. I'm Brother Eamon, by the way."

"Eamon. Lead the way, Brother."

They followed Eamon through a series of narrow corridors, and when the undercroft door was shut behind them, latched, and even barred, Justin felt much safer. Perhaps the Brother had sensed something in the Paladin's manner that had inspired him to redouble the door's security. While Justin was certain that nothing had marked their passing in the street's darkness, it was nice to be as safe as possible. It had taken all of two minutes for them to leave The Moonlit Rest and get inside the cathedral with hardly any sound.

If that wasn't good enough, he didn't know *what* was.

Instead, he turned his attention to the gray stone walls, adorned with tapestries and portraits of what seemed to be past High Clerics, all wearing crimson robes and pointy, conical hats. Finally, they arrived at a humble oaken door, which Brother Eamon knocked on softly.

"Come in," a voice intoned from the other side.

Brother Eamon opened the door, stepping out of the way, revealing the High Cleric, an elderly man with a flowing white beard and piercing blue eyes, who sat at a large wooden desk. The office was modestly furnished, with a few chairs and shelves lined with ancient tomes and religious artifacts.

Despite the late hour, the High Cleric seemed alert and composed. "Sir Alistair. I've read your name in official dispatches, of course, so it is with great pleasure that I can meet you in person, despite the late hour. Brother Eamon has informed me you haven't come about the bill, but I can't imagine any other reason you'd arrive at such a time."

Alistair stepped forward, bowing slightly. "High Cleric Theophilus, I wish I could say that was true; however, as Brother Eamon said, we've come for another reason. We seek refuge and safe passage out of Highcliff. Our enemies are closing in, and we believe the catacombs beneath the city may offer us a way out."

The High Cleric studied Alistair for a moment, frowning slightly. "Enemies? What enemies?"

"The tale would take too long to relate, and to be perfectly candid, the less you know, the safer you will be."

The High Cleric gave a dark chuckle. "Ah, cloak and dagger, is it? Very well, I won't press for details."

"This is no joke, High Cleric. I don't believe our pursuers would follow us here, as we covered our tracks carefully, thanks to the Ranger here I've contracted. I will say this much. The Life Magic infused in the cathedral's stones will serve as a sure guard against the ones coming after us."

"I catch your meaning," the High Cleric said darkly. "Grievous news indeed, and I sense no lie in your words, though you keep strange company for a Paladin. Whatever ails you, you have come to the right place."

He studied them briefly, and to Justin, it seemed his eyes lingered on him the longest. Perhaps he could sense the stain of the Death Mark upon him, just like Alistair. With a start, Justin realized that this would be the third rising of the moon since he had received it from the Baron. The very thought made his stomach queasy.

"I will do what I can to help," the High Cleric continued, interrupting Justin's thoughts. "Such is my charge to all of Arion's faithful. Should we write to the Mont, as little good as that would do?"

"I'm going there with all speed, High Cleric," Alistair said. "I must be the one to deliver the message."

"Of course. I don't mean to stick my nose into a Paladin's business. I only wish to help."

"And I am grateful for it. So, will you grant us access to the catacombs?"

The High Cleric gave an ironic smile. "Yes, I am happy to. However, I regret to inform you that the catacombs are... *closed*."

Justin felt a tinge of fear at those words. Was this Theophilus playing them false?

Alistair frowned. "Closed? What do you mean? The dead must be interred, no?"

"Indeed, they must."

"It is too late for riddles, High Cleric," Eldrin said, perhaps a bit too gruffly.

The High Cleric, with patience, faced the Ranger. "Perhaps it's better to show you what I mean than to tell you. I would let you be the judge. Follow me."

The High Cleric rose from his desk, his plain crimson robes seeming to glow as he moved. Justin knew Cleric was a class with access to healing and support magic. A Paladin came from the combination of a Cleric and a Warrior core, which likely meant Alistair outranked him, but the High Cleric was probably a highly placed Church official in his own right, of a decent level and capability.

Theophilus led them from his office and down another corridor, where a heavy door was barred twice. The High Cleric removed the bars, opening the door to reveal a small, dusty chapel, quite intimate, likely for the private use of the Church's staff. It was so dark that Alistair had to cast his Creator's Light, as no floating crystals lit its interior. The air was cool and musty, and it was obvious the chapel wasn't being maintained.

And, of course, why would a small chapel like this need to be barred? To Justin, it certainly seemed spooky. Almost haunted.

They passed rows of dusty pews, some laced with cobwebs, until they reached the back where, behind the altar, a set of steps led downward to a small chamber of stone, at the end of which stood a heavy stone door.

And before that door stretched a green barrier of light, flickering with mysterious runes. Justin's skin went cold at the sight.

At their stunned silence, the High Cleric gave a sad smile. "Now you see why I've been eagerly awaiting a team from the Mont to arrive. The Vault first appeared four months ago, and it has only grown stronger since."

Alistair's face was pale. "And they have done nothing? What Level is it now, High Cleric?"

"Level 13," he said somberly. "It began at Level 8, which is far beyond our capabilities as a church. I hope your party is equipped to face such dangers."

Thirteen. So, this Vault would be even tougher than the Guardian Pass, if only slightly. And, of course, the nature of the danger could be very different.

"What do you think?" Eldrin asked the Paladin.

Alistair gave an ironic laugh. "Never have I seen so many Vaults gather from the Aether! And always in the very place we must be going. Something tells me the gods are playing with us."

The High Cleric watched the Paladin neutrally. "The gods test us for strength and faith, Sir Paladin, so that we may learn to rely on them."

"Of course," Alistair said, his voice tinged with annoyance. "And I suppose you didn't want to put out a general call to clear it, wanting to keep it within the Church?"

Theophilus nodded gravely. "Yes. If the Church is viewed as weak, it would harm our reputation. After all, ours is not the only faith competing for the hearts of men these days. But you need access to the catacombs, and I need someone within the Church to clear it. This may be the providence of Arion himself."

"Indeed," Alistair said, his voice tired. "I hope you'll forgive us, Theophilus, but it's been an eventful week. If it's not too much trouble, we would camp here in the chapel. Assuming the Vault hasn't broken containment."

"It has not," the High Cleric said, "but I would urge you to reconsider. Though it hasn't broken containment, it could do so at any moment. Though it's rare for a Level 13 Vault, it has happened."

Justin frowned at yet another concept to learn about. "Broken containment?"

Eldrin took it upon himself to explain. "When Vaults become too strong, or have stuck around too long, they can begin releasing nasty things. Monsters, mostly, but sometimes even diseases or curses. The risk is quite low for a Level 13 Vault, but not unknown."

"Indeed," Alistair said. "Then again, there is no safe place for us in all of Highcliff, and this one seems to be about the safest. The Vault should stay passive, at least for one more night."

The High Cleric looked at Alistair as if he were crazy, but in the end, he conceded. "Of course, I will leave the decision to you. Tomorrow, I can have Brother Eamon bring some breakfast and general supplies. It seems you could use both."

"That would be most appreciated."

The High Cleric gave a small bow. "I know not from what you flee, but I will have you know you are safe here. All are welcome in the Church of Light; we are ever a bastion against Death and Darkness. Take what rest and respite you can, and let me know tomorrow if you wish to exorcise us of this curse."

Alistair nodded. "I shall do so. Thank you, High Cleric."

"Unfortunately, given the danger of the Vault, I must bar the chapel for the night. I will post Brother Eamon by the door just in case."

"Do what you must, High Cleric," Alistair said. "Good night."

He withdrew, leaving the party alone. When the chapel door was closed, Justin could hear two heavy bars being placed behind the door. It was like two nails being driven into a coffin.

"Glad I'm not claustrophobic," Lila said.

They made camp in the chapel above, setting up next to the heavy oak door. Within minutes, their bedrolls had been spread out.

"Let's sleep," Alistair said. "I can keep the first watch."

"I'll take second," Eldrin said. "Wake me in three hours."

With that, Justin, Lila, and Eldrin had settled down to sleep.

Despite his exhaustion, Justin had difficulty drifting off. The thought of what might be released from the Vault was unnerving. He could only imagine the many horrifying creatures that might emerge from the darkness: spectral wraiths, monstrous beasts, or even curses that could afflict them. The weight of the unknown pressed heavily on his mind.

In the end, sleep won out. He took some solace in knowing that Alistair and Eldrin were well qualified to keep watch, and the fact that he would gain a level from his banked experience, which could prove crucial for the challenges ahead.

28

DECISIONS BEFORE THE DOOR

"The Unitary School would have us believe the Creator Supreme is three beings in one—a Supreme Architect, a Daughter Made Flesh, and a Disembodied Voice. Tell me, then: is a Craftsman his tools? Is an echo the same as the mountain it bounces from? The Solitary School holds, as ever, that Ayla was mortal while Veyrith is but the Creator's will. To worship them alongside the Holy One is to kneel before shadows while calling it Light."

—Edran Volis
   Reflections of the Pure Light

JUSTIN AWOKE STILL TIRED, but that changed in an instant when he heard the Voice in his mind.

[You have reached Level 4. Your charm and wit mark you as a rising star on the grand stage of life. With your growing mastery of presence, there is no telling how far you might ascend.]

Justin felt the inspiration of those words, despite the dangers he knew lay ahead.

[You have one attribute point to distribute.]

Justin, at least this time, felt no temptation to put the point elsewhere. He locked it into Charisma.

[Your Charisma is now 15.]

Justin nodded, satisfied. Now it was time to unlock his next ability.

[As a Level 4 Socialite, you have unlocked your next boon. Choose wisely—there is no going back.]

Justin checked out both options that were presented to him.

Basic Cane Proficiency: With a touch of flair, you wield your cane as more than a mere accessory. Unlock basic techniques, allowing you to defend yourself with poise and fend off minor threats with confidence.

Effortless Eloquence: Whether in a ballroom or a battlefield, your wit never falters. The perfect phrase springs to your lips just when it is needed most, turning conversations into opportunities and obstacles into stepping stones.

Justin stared at the two options hovering in his interface.

On the surface, Effortless Eloquence was the obvious choice. It was flashy, undeniably in line with his Socialite roots, and promised an edge in any social encounter. And in a world where the wrong word could get you killed, a little extra social grace never hurt.

But as he mulled it over, a seed of doubt crept in. How would Effortless Eloquence hold up when steel was drawn and the time for clever quips gave way to the brutal reality of combat? Justin found himself in that situation right now.

Then there was Basic Cane Proficiency. The description sounded more like something a fencing instructor would teach to an amateur on their first day. Couldn't he just learn that on his own with the right teacher?

But the practicality was undeniable. Eyrth was a dangerous world. His cane had been his lifeline a few times already, and he had only just acquired it. And the boon would improve itself every four levels, allowing him to skip the hassle of training. Once he made it to Level 20, it stood to reason that he might be a master of cane combat without ever putting in an hour of practice.

This boon promised to shore up a glaring weakness. His cane wasn't just a weapon; it was a part of his image, his style. If he was going to carry it, he might as well wield it with confidence.

Justin exhaled slowly, the decision settling in his chest. "Sometimes, a gentleman has to get his hands dirty."

[You have chosen Basic Cane Proficiency. A Socialite's weapon is an extension of himself: elegant, versatile, and always ready. Your cane is no longer a prop—it is a promise.]

As Justin felt the Voice depart, he summoned his character screen to see how close he was to Level 5 and his next skill.

Justin Talemaker
> **Class:** Socialite
> **Level:** 4
> **Experience to Level 5:** 839/420 (Level-up available!)

Justin closed the interface. Now, he knew exactly what Eldrin meant when he said the first level-ups came quickly.

Assuming Justin could keep himself alive, he would reach Level 5 and even Level 6 in no time at all.

Justin rolled over to find that Lila was also waking up. No doubt, she was Level 4 too.

"Coordination again?" Justin asked.

She shook her head. "Endurance, this time."

"Whoa. Don't go too crazy!"

"This Vault has me scared," she said. "Please tell me you put your point in Power or Endurance this time."

Justin felt unsure of himself for a moment. He'd locked it into Charisma without hesitation, but maybe Lila was right. They had a Level 13 Vault ahead of them, after all.

"Charisma," he admitted. "I just can't help myself."

"You're going to get yourself killed. Plus, Endurance will make travel easier. I can carry more stuff now!"

"Great! Would you mind taking the cookpot for me?"

"Ha. *Hilarious*, Justin."

"Did you get a new boon?"

Lila nodded. "It's called Harmonic Amplification. It doubles the buff of my Bardic Inspiration."

"Wow. So +4 to any attribute?"

She nodded. "That's right. Should come in handy, right? Though I'm not sure Alistair will want me to belt out a song in a quiet crypt..."

Justin chuckled at the image of it. "Speaking of...where *is* Alistair?"

"Checking out the Vault. I think they want to get started."

"It's decided, then?"

"Seems like it. All out of options."

Justin supposed that much was true.

He and Lila ate quickly, also packing the supplies the monks must have dropped off. That Justin hadn't even noticed their coming only spoke to his exhaustion.

Once packed, they headed through the chapel, which was still unnerving, even with Alistair's light spell he'd set to float in the nave. He wondered if the rate of deterioration had been hastened by the proximity of the Vault. Four months couldn't make things look *this* bad.

Justin and Lila went down the steps, finding both the Paladin and the Ranger just a few feet away from the Vault entrance. Both of their expressions were quite severe, more so than Justin would have expected, even given the situation.

"Is something wrong?" Justin asked.

The two exchanged a glance before Eldrin addressed Justin. "It would be easier if you just examined the Vault yourself."

Justin and Lila looked at each other before approaching. As soon as Justin did so, the Vault description appeared before him.

Vault Discovered: The Crypt of King Alaric

    Recommended Party Level: 15

    Average Party Level: 10.75

    Risk Level: Extremely Dangerous! Your party is significantly below the recommended level. Catastrophic consequences, including severe injury or death, are highly probable. Proceed with extreme caution!

    Description: The Crypt of the High King Alaric, within the famous and beautiful Catacombs of Highcliff, has been corrupted by the dark rituals of the Cult of Morvath, the God of Death.

    Once a place of rest for the beloved King, a renowned and powerful White Wizard, the crypt has become a haven for death and darkness. The cultists have raised the venerated dead with necromantic magic while twisting King Alaric's spirit toward unwholesome ends.

    To clear this Vault, you must defeat the Cultists, allowing the King's spirit to rest easy. The challenges within will test your resolve to confront your deepest fears and the vilest sorcery.

Rewards Upon Completion:

    Experience: Scaled to each party member's level and individual contributions.

    Guaranteed Silver-Tier Item: For each party member.

    Chance for a Platinum-Tier Artifact: For one party member.

    Treasure: Ten gold crowns to be divided among the party.

[Do you accept the Vault's challenge?]

Justin stepped back, his face pale. "Recommended Level 15? What the hell? I thought it was supposed to be 13!"

"It changed overnight," Eldrin said somberly.

Alistair was still quiet, still not having spoken. Justin had never seen him so solemn. It was easy to see he had been weighing the pros and cons of entering versus turning back, perhaps for hours.

"I have another level up to process," Justin offered. "Lila, too. If we rest here another day, get our bearings, we might enter the Vault in a better position. I stand to unlock a new skill."

"The risk is too great," Alistair said. "We're likely to wake up and discover this Vault is Level 17. Perhaps even Level 20 or more."

"It's growing exponentially," Eldrin said. "As you said last night, Alistair, it would seem the gods are playing with us."

"We have no choice but to enter," he whispered. "No choice. A Level 20 or more Shadowblade and all his classed followers, all knowing exactly where we are. Or the trials of a Level 15 Vault. The answer is straightforward, but it's not easier to decide."

"We must prepare ourselves as best we can," Eldrin said. "I have some potions that can help edify Justin and Lila and improve their survivability. Combined, they'll increase Endurance and Power for a short time. They can use it if we ever get into any dangerous situations."

"Those kinds of potions aren't cheap, Ranger. But I fear we have no choice."

Eldrin reached into his pack, producing several vials and handing them out to both Lila and Justin. "Only drink them at need. The gray one, Ironroot Essence, will boost your Power by 2 for one hour. The red one, Heartwood Elixir, will boost your Endurance by the same. You have one of each. It's all I have."

Justin nodded. "Thank you, Eldrin. I'll put them to good use."

Lila nodded. "I'm scared, but I have my knives and my new amulet. Both should come in handy for this Vault."

Everyone was silent as they watched Alistair, who still seemed to be at war with himself.

"I fear most for the safety of you three. Nothing here should trouble me, but the challenge is to get through while losing no one. Even I could quickly become overwhelmed if caught unawares."

"Not too late to turn back, if you judge it best," the Ranger said. "It is at least daytime now. That should provide some shield against the undead out on the open road."

"Nay," Alistair said. "We are here, and we have no choice. The strength of this Vault could easily become overwhelming, threatening not just the Church of Light, but all of Highcliff. It is our duty to clear it before it can become an even greater threat."

"Not to mention the rewards," Lila said. "Let's not forget that."

"Aye, a consideration, to be sure," Eldrin said. "I'm surprised a platinum-tier artifact is being offered in a Level 15 Vault. At most, you'd see a gold at this level, and rarely at that."

"Maybe the gods are trying to tempt us," Justin said.

Eldrin grunted. "I wouldn't put it past them."

"And a guaranteed silver-tier item to boot, not to mention the gold," Lila said. "I say we go for it."

Justin wondered at Lila's confidence, but if last night was any sign, money was a huge motivator for her. Which made sense, given her debts.

"Plus, Alistair has bonuses against the undead," Justin added. "I'm with Lila."

Alistair let out a breath. *"The wise know that the inexperienced speak loudly, for they have not yet faced the trials that temper steel into strength."* He turned to face Justin and Lila, his blue eyes haunted. "We must proceed with caution and resolve."

"Lead the way, Alistair," Eldrin said.

The Paladin took in the entire group. "This will be our most difficult trial yet. Follow every order without question. Not only do our lives depend upon it, but perhaps the lives of hundreds or even thousands of residents of Highcliff. Our High Cleric friend did a foolish thing by not nipping this in the bud, reputation or not, and now he's in a terrible bind. We must always remember: reputation is dust when considering the lives of the innocent, who hold the sacred spark of Life gifted by the Creator."

The others nodded solemnly. Justin realized there was no one better to follow into this Vault.

"We're right behind you, Alistair," he said. "We'll do everything you say."

Alistair gave a curt nod. "That is well. My first order is to stay behind me. Eldrin, you bring up the rear. Let's approach. When ready, accept the Vault's invitation."

Lila gave a firm nod. "Without risk, there is no glory or gain."

Justin nodded. While Lila seemed confident, he couldn't kid himself. This one would be a doozy, and that was putting it lightly.

As soon as he was about five paces from the Vault, a notification appeared.

[Welcome, Brave Adventurers. The Crypt of King Alaric lies within. Do you accept the Vault's challenge?]

Justin clutched his cane tightly, hesitating only a moment before giving his mental assent. As soon as he did so, the stone door was thrown back, revealing a long, decrepit staircase descending into darkness, the only illumination being various magically lit candelabra placed at irregular intervals within alcoves in the walls. A cold, dry wind, smelling of must and decay, escaped into the chapel.

[You have accepted the Challenge of the Vault of the Crypt of King Alaric. May courage be your guide and your resolve be your shield. Good luck, Brave Adventurers, and remember: a life welllived is the greatest treasure of all.]

As one, the party of four entered the Catacombs of Highcliff.

29

DESCENT INTO THE CATACOMBS

"The catacombs of Highcliff are often overlooked as one of the world's great wonders—a mistake born of ignorance. Its twelve levels, masterful pillars, and the Hall of Heroes with its Hundred Statues are marvels of craftsmanship. Yet, it is also a tragedy. The builders, at the height of Highcliff's glory days, made the perennial mistake of all great empires. They believed they were creating an eternal legacy, never imagining a time when no one would remain to tend it."

—Chronicler Ellisar Vain
　　When Empires Fall: A History of the Aftermath

THE PARTY BEGAN its descent into the Catacombs of Highcliff, down a long, winding staircase carved into ancient stone. The steps, worn smooth by countless years, spiraled downward into the darkness. Within minutes, the candelabras had extinguished themselves, leaving only Alistair's Creator's Light to illuminate the path ahead. As they descended, the air grew cooler and heavier, carrying the faint mustiness of long-sealed tombs.

Justin observed the ancient carvings and inscriptions along the walls depicting the history of Highcliff. Scenes of battles, peace treaties, and moments of royal court life unfurled before him, offering glimpses into a past long gone. Quite a few seemed to show a fair-haired king sitting on a throne, wearing vestments of sky blue, bearing a scepter in his hand and a crown upon his head. Of note was also a glittering amulet that shone with the six lights of each attribute, those lights depicted with various colored jewels etched into the artwork. Though Justin couldn't say for sure, he was certain the figure presented was King Alaric himself.

The descent felt interminable, each step echoing softly in the enclosed space. Justin couldn't shake the feeling that something was watching them from the shadows.

Finally, after what felt like an eternity, they reached the bottom, and the party looked around in awe at a vast hall of marble and pillars. So vast was it that Alistair's Creator's Light couldn't even reach the ceiling, nor see too deeply into the forest of columns.

"Major Moria vibes," Justin said.

"A place from your world?" Lila asked.

"Yeah, I guess you could say that."

Alistair turned his head back, giving them what Justin could only describe as "the look." Justin resolved to keep his lips sealed.

The hall was breathtaking, a testament to the grandeur of a bygone era. Eldrin had mentioned Highcliff was once a rich trade city with a grander past, but Justin hadn't expected this. High ceilings soared above, supported by intricately carved marble pillars, each a masterpiece of craftsmanship. Statues of ancient heroes and imposing gargoyles lined the walls, their glinting ruby eyes seeming to follow the party's every movement. The floor was a mosaic of variously colored marbles, meticulously depicting scenes of Highcliff's past royalty, many dedicating themselves to King Alaric's life. He led armies into battle, offered mercy to the defeated, and embodied ideals of justice and compassion.

And in nearly every representation, he wore that same amulet with the six colored jewels.

"What is that amulet he's wearing?" Justin whispered, unable to help himself.

No one answered him, and Justin figured that was their way of getting him to shut up.

Along the columns were sarcophagi on raised pedestals, the last resting places for the nobility and heroes of Highcliff, each adorned with inscriptions and carvings telling of their deeds and lineage. Scanning a few of the lines, they seemed to be written in an archaic form of Aranthian. They were hardly decipherable.

While the hall's splendor was undeniable, there was a pervasive chill, an unease that hung in the air. Justin was certain it had something to do with the cultists and their Death Magic.

Speaking of...where were those Cultists, anyway? Justin had so many questions, but he had to keep them to himself. This God of Death was definitely not a part of the Pantheon of the Church of Light. Bad guy material, then. Maybe the foil to the Creator, whoever they were.

At last, the columns seemed to end, a square doorway of marble appearing at the end of the hall. Justin couldn't perfectly decipher the writing above it, but he definitely recognized the word "Alaric." They were heading the right way.

As they proceeded, the temperature seemed to drop further. Shadows danced ominously in the corners of the room, flickering from the orb of light shining above them.

Eldrin turned to them all, letting them know that something was about to happen. Justin remembered his class boon, Ranger's Intuition, which gave him an uncanny knack for knowing when danger was imminent. Justin gripped his cane tightly.

It was then that the first signs of movement caught Justin's eyes—shambling figures emerging from the darkness between the pillars and mausoleums. Stumbling into view were skeletal warriors, their bones clad in ancient, rusted armor, along with zombies, whose decayed flesh barely clung to their frames. The undead, with hollow eyes and jerky movements, were surrounded by an aura of darkness, bearing weapons as aged and brittle as they were.

The party sprang into action. As Justin twirled his cane, Alistair leaped and landed directly in the middle of the mob, instantly drawing their attention. As they charged at him, he let out a roar, swinging his hammer in a wide arc that instantly smote the first wave of attackers. Flames of Life covered their bodies, a truly awesome sight. As they screeched in dismay, Justin felt no heat from those flames. Apparently, they only affected the undead.

With the pressure taken off the rest of the party, the others engaged. Lila's knives flashed, focusing on the zombies' heads. Justin used his cane, finding the blade was quite effective at stabbing through the zombies' faces or just below the base of the skull. Despite his fear, it was easy to fight when all the attention was off him. The movements seemed to come easier, likely a product of his Cane Proficiency boon. Eldrin swung his longsword, easily lopping off the heads of skeletons and zombies alike.

The air was filled with the sound of clattering bones and the dull thuds of falling corpses. As the last of the undead crumbled, the party took a moment to catch their breath. Looking around at their handiwork, there were at least thirty or forty undead. Without Alistair, who'd racked up well over half of the kills, it was obvious the party would have been overwhelmed.

"Glad we have a tank," Justin said, trying to lighten the mood.

"Is everyone all right?" Eldrin asked.

"Not a scratch," Lila said. Her knives had already been retrieved and were secured in the holsters strapped to her thighs.

Justin raised his hand as if he were in a classroom. "Um, question. So, if a zombie bites you or something, do you turn into a zombie too?"

The others looked at him in confusion.

"Nay," Alistair answered. "It requires Death Magic to be turned, and you must first be dead yourself. However, with the Mark given to you by the Baron, this would be your fate should the worst happen. Although your undeath would be markedly...different."

Different, how? Justin was afraid to ask, his stomach twisting just knowing there was a worse fate than becoming a zombie. It had been three risings of the moon since receiving the Death Mark. While he didn't feel any different, he was all too aware of it.

"Then I just have to stay alive."

"The Six willing," Alistair said.

"And the Creator," Justin added.

Alistair frowned at this, and Justin wasn't sure why. Perhaps invoking the Creator's name was out of place or disrespectful in this context. So many questions about this world, too few answers. If he had a pen and paper, he could make a long list.

Whatever the case, the immediate threat had been neutralized.

"We are getting closer to the crypt itself," Alistair said, his voice low. "Stay by me."

The others nodded and proceeded through the doorway, down a wide, curving staircase that led deeper into the catacombs.

Justin soon realized that this staircase, circling down into darkness, gave access to lower levels of the catacombs, each deeper than the last. From time to time, Alistair would pause at each landing, reading inscriptions that detailed who exactly was buried on each level. But each time, they continued down to the next level, deeper and deeper underground. The first levels seemed more crowded, filled with the remains of commoners, their skeletons clearly visible in loculi within the walls, with the next levels becoming more ornate, with more generous tombs and individual details.

Clearly, the lower one went, the more important the deceased were. And it became easy to guess just where King Alaric would be laid to rest, given his importance.

As they descended, Eldrin held up a hand to signal that danger lay ahead.

They rounded the final spiral as quietly as possible, finding before them a smaller chamber, dimly lit by a few flickering candles. In the center stood a female figure clad in black robes, on the front of which was embroidered a skeletal hand grasping a wilting white flower, which had to symbolize the God of Death. She was chanting in a low, guttural voice in some indeterminate tongue, and before her lay a row of six corpses adorned in richer clothing and robes.

The Cultist of Morvath was completely oblivious to their

entrance, engrossed in her dark ritual. The surrounding air crackled with dark magic.

Quick as a flash, Eldrin raised his longbow, nocking an arrow. At a nod from Alistair, he let loose with a twang. The arrow flew true toward the cultist's head.

But somehow sensing the intrusion, the cultist cast a ward of dark magic, and the arrow clattered to the stones beneath her feet.

Alistair charged, giving a running leap with his hammer extended. From the distance and speed with which he jumped, Justin knew he had to be using a skill of some sort. Just as the Cultist raised her arms, ghostly apparitions issued from the bodies before her, swirling as she stepped back.

"Wraiths!" Eldrin warned.

The wraiths were ghastly, their spectral forms shifting between solidity and intangibility. They bore grotesque faces, which Justin could only assume was a macabre mockery of their former selves. Their semi-solid forms hinted that physical attacks *might* work, but it might be difficult to inflict damage.

Alistair landed hard among the specters, drawing their attacks. Flashes of red light glanced off his armor as the wraiths attacked him. The Paladin brightened his Creator's Light, which slowed the wraiths' movements.

Eldrin wove among the specters, his sword doing some work, but the attacks were mostly ineffective. Lila threw her knives from a distance, each one sinking into one of the closer wraiths. The knives only seemed to annoy the creature, which turned its attention to them. Justin stood next to her, cane twirling, as the specter floated toward them.

"Justin!" Lila cried.

The wraith advanced, and with a bloodcurdling screech, lunged at Justin, ethereal jaws agape.

His Gentleman's Rebuff was still on cooldown, so Justin had to make the best of it. He raised his cane, keeping his eye on the ghost as he gave his weapon a mighty swing. Much to Justin's surprise, he knocked the wraith back a suitable distance, the weapon's tip flashing yellow.

Eldrin spun fiercely, wailing on the creature with his sword. He drew the wraith's attention, but from the look of things, it seemed to be an even match.

Justin charged forward, joining in Eldrin's attack.

Lila's voice pierced the din. "Justin, Eldrin, duck!"

Justin immediately dropped to the stone floor, and as soon as he did, six whistling knives flew overhead, each burying themselves in the wraith before sinking through its body and clattering to the floor. The wraith advanced toward Justin, who stood between it and Lila. Justin gave it a strong thwack with his cane. While the attack connected, flashing yellow at the point of contact, it did little. The entity floated forward, surrounding Justin with its frigid, spectral force.

Justin felt a horrible cold and despair such as he had never known. Just as his vision began to go dark, a strange sensation surged within him—a resistance that, miraculously, forced the wraith back with a screech.

Justin had no time to ponder this; he followed the wraith, which was now outright fleeing from him.

With newfound confidence, he chased it down, slapping it repeatedly with his cane.

"Take that! And that, foul specter!"

The wraith screeched in both pain and fear, especially as Justin cornered it in the chamber. He wailed on it repeatedly, rage fueling his attacks, until it was reduced to almost nothing. Destroying it took far longer than Justin would have liked. Again, his cane flashed yellow with each strike, and it took him a moment to realize that it was from the enchantment. Lila's knives and Eldrin's sword seemed to go through the wraith at least half the time, not finding purchase.

Eventually, the wraith collapsed into a puff of blue smoke.

Justin, panting, turned around to find that the rest of the wraiths had already been dealt with, a low blue fog hanging over the stones. The cultist's head had been smashed to a pulp, thanks to Alistair's hammer. Alistair was watching him curiously, while Eldrin nodded in respect. Lila's green eyes were wide.

"It was afraid of me!" Justin exclaimed.

Alistair came to stand by him. "It would seem it feared the Baron's Mark. Wraiths like this feed on the living, draining the Spark of Life from one's core. If successful, the victim is doomed to become just like them. The Baron's Mark of Death may have helped you, at least in this situation. It is not you they fear, but him."

It was a sobering reminder of just how powerful the Baron was. Justin suppressed a shudder.

"This happened with Zaramund, too," Justin mused. "Maybe it's a blessing in disguise."

"It is no blessing, I assure you," the Paladin said. "Now fully mature, the Mark will be detectable by the Baron himself if he gets close enough. Given the extent of the situation, it wouldn't surprise me if he made his own way to Highcliff soon. We must be well away from the city before that happens."

The party took a moment to regroup. The air was thick with the acrid tang of the specters' remains, which were thankfully now dissipating.

"Glad we got that taken care of," Justin said. "Where's our prize?"

Eldrin snorted. "Prize? We're just getting started, lad."

Justin frowned. "Wait. That wasn't the boss fight?"

"Nay," Alistair said. "That was a lackey at best, a Death Mage of middling level. About equivalent to Zaramund, if I had to guess."

"Zaramund was the boss last time."

"We are now in a Level 15 Vault," Eldrin said quietly. "The 'boss,' as you put it, is now just another goon."

Justin gulped. "Yikes."

For the first time, Justin took stock of just what the Cultist had been defending. They stood before a grand door, wrought of what seemed to be pure gold. It was a magnificent piece of craftsmanship and art, intricately carved with scenes from King Alaric's life. The images depicted his coronation, his battles to defend Highcliff, and moments of wisdom where he sat in council, dispensing justice and mercy. Above King Alaric himself was a majestic eagle in flight, the symbol of the City of Highcliff.

Above the door, an inscription read:

> *Here lies interred Alaric,*
> *Good King of Highcliff:*
> *A King Just and Balanced,*
> *Beloved of the People.*
> *Guardian of the Realm,*
> *Protector of the Peace.*
> *Wise Wielder of the Magic of Life,*
> *In Death, he doth rest with Honor.*
> *Never shall his like be seen again.*

The door stood slightly ajar, a sliver of darkness visible through the crack.

Alistair sighed sadly. "They say Good King Alaric was one of the most powerful White Wizard to live on Eyrth, and besides that, that he had mastered the blade. It is ill indeed that the Cult of Morvath has so perverted his legacy."

"Arion willing, that won't be true for much longer," Eldrin said.

"Aye, Ranger," Alistair said. "The Six will it so."

Justin remained silent, still shaken from the battle. He still couldn't get over the fact that they hadn't even reached the main boss yet. Once again, he'd only survived by luck and forces beyond his control. His Gentleman's Rebuff was gone, and the Death Mark had kept that wraith from absorbing his life force.

But maybe there was something to this Death Mark. Despite what Alistair said, it might allow him to take risks the others couldn't, at least regarding monsters that wanted to feed on his so-called "Spark of Life."

It was something to keep in his back pocket, perhaps.

At last, Alistair shifted on his feet, steeling himself for what lay ahead. "I don't know what lies beyond this door, but I know it will test us dearly. Lila, Justin; remember your potions. Take them as soon as the final battle starts. I would take no risks."

"Will do," Justin said.

Lila's response was a firm nod.

"We stand behind you, Paladin," Eldrin said. "Lead on."

Alistair started forward, slipping through the crack through which a cold draft wafted, carrying the faint smell of decay mixed with an oddly sweet scent. Justin shivered.

It was as if death itself lay just beyond this door, waiting for them to step through.

30

PUZZLES IN THE CRYPT

"Adventuring is a hard business. The Vaults promise riches, glory, and relics of untold power, and every would-be hero dreams of claiming them. But when you factor in the cost of travel, the endless supplies of potions, splitting the loot, and even bribes and dues paid to local officials or guilds, the whole endeavor starts to look less like a heroic quest and more like a reckless investment. For every adventurer who strikes it big, ten more come back broke or broken—or not at all."

—Vault Runner Tharic Wren,
  An Adventurer's Guide to Vaults

AS THE PARTY stepped through the golden door, a short passageway led into a vast chamber with an austere feel. In the center of the stone floor was an empty square, with a slight depression about three or four inches deep. There were six rectangular slots in that square, like missing jigsaw pieces. On the left and right-hand walls were six rectangular stone reliefs, each depicting a scene from Alaric's life.

Eldrin was the first to approach the panels, surveying them. Justin and the rest followed.

"What are we supposed to do?" Justin asked.

The Ranger frowned. "It seems we need to arrange these reliefs on the wall in the correct order to proceed."

"What kind of order?" Lila asked.

"Chronologically, I would assume."

Justin took his time examining each scene. The first clearly depicted some sort of war or battle filled with chaos and conflict. Alaric's face was grim as he faced an army with his sword raised high and golden magic covering his other hand. He wore the same amulet Justin had noticed upon first entering the catacombs, with the six colored jewels.

The second relief showed the king much younger, receiving a crown and scepter, with subjects bowing before him. Again, he was wearing the amulet.

The third showed what appeared to be a death scene, the king lying peacefully with flowers, surrounded by mourners, and, of course, the amulet around his neck.

The fourth showed Alaric sitting on his throne, surrounded by scholars, warriors, and citizens, with a crown of jewels set in gold, along with the amulet.

The fifth showed Alaric and the amulet shaking hands with a foreign ruler, the scene radiating calm, with doves flying in the background alongside the Eagle of Highcliff.

Last of all was a scene of what had to be his birth, or perhaps the birth of one of his own children, showing the royal family rejoicing. The resemblance of the baby to Alaric in the other images was striking, but not definitive.

"These look familiar," Lila mused at last.

Eldrin nodded, his expression thoughtful. "Yes. I remember seeing all of them as we descended. And I'm certain they were shown in a particular order. An order we must recreate on the floor over there."

"This isn't familiar to me," Alistair said. "I was looking out for threats. If I had known..." He trailed off, clearly regretting not paying closer attention.

"So, left to right on the floor over there," Justin suggested. "Pictures 1-3 will go on top, and 4-6 will go on the bottom."

"That's right," Eldrin confirmed. He approached the birth scene. "This one seems likely to be our first."

"How do we know it's first?" Lila asked, her voice tinged with concern. "That could be him as a father with the birth of a son."

Eldrin pondered this. "Well, the background shows symbols of new beginnings and prosperity, which are traditional for birth scenes. You can see the rising sun, a common emblem for the start of life, and the abundant flowers and green vines, which often symbolize growth and potential."

"Damn, Eldrin," Justin said. "Did you take an art history course?"

He cracked a smile. "Never underestimate the value of a well-rounded education, even for a Ranger."

"He's also not wearing the amulet in that one," Justin said. "He is in all the others."

"More to the point and definitive," Eldrin said. "The amulet is clearly important to him."

"This begs the question," Lila said. "What happens if we get this wrong? Instant death?"

"That's hard to say," Alistair replied. "Something bad, that's for certain."

"Okay, birth first. Then what?" Lila asked.

"Likely the coronation scene," Eldrin said. "He looks quite young there."

"Birth and then coronation," Lila repeated. "Death, obviously, would be last. Which leaves the war, the one with the scholars, and the one where he's shaking hands."

"He's likely brokering a peace in the handshaking one," Justin suggested. "That would naturally come after the war. The doves are an obvious symbol of peace."

"I think you're right," Eldrin agreed. "So, I think we have the right of it so far. We just need to place the court scene."

Lila thought about it. "It could be a council debating going to war, which would place it third."

Justin considered this. "Highcliff is known for its Golden Age, right? That scene could represent the prosperity and wisdom that followed the war. There are scholars in it, after all."

Eldrin thought about it, weighing the merits of both arguments. "The court scene seems more like a time of peace and governance, possibly before the war. Let's place it there."

Justin didn't agree, but he also didn't want to be a pedant. There were merits to both arguments. "Let's give it a go, then."

They moved the panels into position, everything going smoothly for the first two scenes. However, when they placed the third panel, it instantly popped out, as if the grooves were rejecting it.

"Uh-oh," Justin said.

A loud rumble shook the chamber, followed by hidden doors sliding open, unleashing a horde of zombies and skeletons into the room.

"Brace yourselves!" Alistair shouted, drawing his hammer.

The following moments were pure chaos. Justin found himself face to face with a skeleton wielding a rusty sword. He parried the blows with his cane, doing his best to keep it at a distance. With an adroit maneuver, he knocked the skeleton's head off, but not before a zombie grabbed his arm, taking a vicious bite with sharp teeth.

Justin screamed as red-hot pain seared up his arm. Lila was there in an instant, her knives flashing as she buried them both in the back of the zombie's head.

Justin felt himself being pulled to the center as his three companions surrounded him. Blood gushed from the wound as his vision went hazy. The sight and smell of blood seemed to drive the undead into a frenzy. It was all Justin could do to keep his feet.

About a minute later, the rest of the undead had been taken care of. As soon as the threat was neutralized, Alistair turned, wrapping Justin's wound with golden magic. It felt as if he had been plunged into ice water, but it brought relief as his flesh was knitted anew.

All the same, he felt a burning sensation just beneath his skin. He tried not to think about what nasty bacteria might have been lingering in that zombie's decaying mouth.

Eldrin pushed a potion into his hand, green in hue. "Draught of Veridian. It will fight off even the most potent infections."

Justin downed it; the taste was truly vile. "Thanks." He chased it with a swig of water from his canteen, the aftertaste stubbornly clinging on.

The group was panting, exhausted, and Justin could still feel the sting of the wound. Hopefully, Eldrin's potion would do its work.

"We got it wrong," Eldrin said, frustration clear in his voice. "But now we know that one likely comes after the War Scene and the Peace Scene."

"Let's move these bodies off the puzzle," Alistair said. "Then we can proceed."

They did so, Justin not relishing the task. This time, they had to get it completely right. He might not survive another fight like this.

"War is next," Eldrin said, confidence returning. "I'm sure of it."

"Let's do it," Alistair agreed.

They moved the war piece into place, and it clicked agreeably.

"Yes!" Lila said.

"Not out of the woods yet," Justin said.

"Peace," Eldrin said, moving the corresponding panel into place. As expected, it clicked in perfectly.

Now, only the court scene and the death scene remained, and it was pretty easy to figure out the order. They moved the court scene into place, and it clicked perfectly. Finally, they placed the death scene.

Once all the pieces were in place, the entire puzzle glowed green while the sound of stone grinding against stone filled the chamber. The door at the far end of the room began to open.

Justin smiled, relieved. "We did it!"

Eldrin wiped the sweat from his brow. "Barely. One more mistake might have finished us."

Lila managed a small smile. "At least we got it right before the end."

Alistair nodded. "It's time to move on. This is just going to get tougher."

They followed a short corridor into another vast chamber, this one illuminated by a soft, ethereal glow. The light seemed to emanate from a massive statue at the far end of the room. The statue depicted King Alaric in a regal pose, his expression stern and noble, as if gazing down at his subjects with both wisdom and authority. In his right hand, he held a sword pointed downward, its tip aimed at a spot just above where a person's head might be.

The chamber was eerily silent, the only sound being the faint echo of their footsteps on the stone floor. As they approached, Alistair's Creator's Light revealed a gruesome sight previously missed in the room's shadowy corners: five dead cultists, their bodies bloody and contorted, as if they had been impaled by an unseen force. The blood pooled beneath them was dark, weeks or even months old. Their collective smell was musty, with a faintly sweet scent of decay.

Justin's stomach churned. "This doesn't look promising."

Alistair nodded, his expression grim. "There's no telling what dark magic might be at play here."

The party stood in a semicircle around the statue, from time to time eyeing the lifeless cultists warily. Suddenly, a green aura formed beneath the sword's tip, expanding into a circle large enough for a person to stand in. As the aura brightened, an ethereal voice echoed through the chamber, clear and commanding:

> *"A gift unasked; some get less, others more,*
> *It binds us all from first to final door.*
> *But the only question for which you should care,*
> *Is whether you've spent me with joy or despair?"*

The riddle hung in the air. It was unmistakably King Alaric, or rather, his spirit.

Eldrin was the first to speak. "It seems we must answer the riddle to proceed. But we must choose our answer carefully. The fate of these cultists suggests the consequences of a wrong answer."

Alistair nodded. "Indeed. It seems we have as many chances as we have party members. Although losing anyone would be grievous."

Lila glanced at the cultists, her expression set. "I'll go first. Alistair and Eldrin are more pivotal to clearing the Vault."

"What about me?" Justin asked. "Arguably, I'm less pivotal than you."

Lila ignored the question, and he didn't like that. He felt a pang of fear at the thought of losing her.

"Lila, we need to think this through. If I die, at least I'll still be alive...in a manner of speaking, assuming the Baron's Mark makes me undead."

"That is not a possibility," Alistair said grimly.

Lila shrugged. "If I get it wrong, at least we know what not to say."

Eldrin considered the riddle, frowning. "Whatever the case, we can probably discuss it among ourselves, as one of us must enter the light to give an answer."

"True enough," Alistair said. "Any ideas?"

Justin pondered it. Normally, he was pretty decent at riddles, but of course, coming up with an answer with someone's life on the line had a way of muddling things. The riddle felt like it should be obvious, but the answer eluded him.

"I'll start," Eldrin said. "The riddle speaks of something given to everyone, binding us all together. It could be something like time, or perhaps fate."

Alistair shook his head. "No, it must be something more personal. Can time be said to be truly a gift, or fate?"

"Fair points," the Ranger conceded.

Lila stepped forward, her face thoughtful. "Maybe it's money. Everyone gets different amounts, and it definitely influences how we live our lives. It's certainly influenced how I've lived mine. You'd be a fool to spend it poorly and wise to spend it well, either giving you joy or despair."

Eldrin nodded. "That's a possibility. But does money really bind us all together? There are societies that do without money. In that way, the riddle doesn't fit."

Alistair spoke up. "It could be duty or responsibility. We all have different duties, and our lives are often shaped by them."

Justin listened, his mind racing. Each suggestion seemed plausible, yet something about them felt off. The line about joy or despair particularly stood out to him. But an hour ticked by, and then two. They couldn't afford to spend more time on this riddle with the Baron's men skulking outside the city walls. Thankfully, there didn't seem to be any sort of time limit.

By now, Gareth had certainly figured out they were no longer staying in the inn, and they hadn't left the city. Eventually, they'd put two and two together, erasing their advantage.

At last, Alistair's face relaxed. "It's money. It must be."

Everyone looked up, considering it. Indeed, of the couple of dozen answers they'd contemplated, it seemed to fit best. Money was a common element in all their lives, and perhaps at the time the riddle was devised, they hadn't considered other cultures that didn't use it.

Justin, however, couldn't shake the feeling that money was too materialistic for someone like Good King Alaric. And yet, he had nothing better.

"Shouldn't we think about it some more?" he asked. "This is important. A life is on the line. Lila's life."

"Time is pressing," Alistair said. "We've dedicated two hours to this riddle, and we can scarcely dedicate one more. If we think it out any longer, our brains are liable to turn to mush."

"That's better than one of us dying."

"Better than all of us dying," Lila said. "The Baron's men can't be given any more time to find us than they already have."

"That begs the question," Eldrin said. "Who will answer? You mentioned yourself, Lila, but to make things fair, I would let fate decide."

He produced a silver mark from his pocket. On one side was the head of some unknown historical figure, while on the other, a hexagon denoting the Six Attributes. The Ranger gave a playful yet sad smile. "Heads or tails?"

"So, to be clear, the winner is the one who goes to answer?"

"Yes," Eldrin said.

"Tails," Lila said.

As soon as the word escaped her lips, Eldrin flicked the coin up, allowing it to land on the stone.

When tails stood revealed, Justin's heart dropped.

Lila only smiled. "It's only fitting. Money was my answer, and money decided it."

The Ranger smiled. "Good luck."

No one said anything, and she turned slowly and walked toward the green aura. Justin wanted to say something, anything, but the words were caught in his throat. Deep down, he knew the answer was wrong. He needed to think quickly. His heart pounded, and he felt as if he might throw up.

In seconds, Lila would be dead. He knew it.

He ran up to her. "Lila!"

She slowed, but didn't stop walking, set on her goal. He caught her by the arm.

She tried to shirk his grasp, but he didn't let go.

"Justin, you must let me go."

"Please. There are things I'd like to say first."

Tears welled in her eyes. "You're making this more difficult than it needs to be."

"I know. Will you give me just a moment?"

She gave the barest of nods. "Yes. As long as you let me go after you're done."

"I will," he promised. Now what? He hesitated, struggling to find the right words. "Some people make life worth living. Life is hard enough as it is, but it's the people we share it with that bind us together. None of us asked to be here, but because we are..." He trailed off. "It's people like you who make life worth living."

"Stop," she said. "How am I supposed to do this when you say things like that? It has to be me, Justin."

He smiled. Before she could respond, he brushed past her toward the aura.

He had it.

"Justin!" Alistair ordered. "Justin, stop this instant!"

"Sorry," Justin said, a determined edge in his voice. "That's one order I'm going to have to disobey."

He heard the Paladin's armor clanking as he ran forward to restrain him, but Justin was too close now. He stepped into the green aura and was locked in.

Alistair reached the edge of the light and, with a quick swing of his hammer, tried to break it. The weapon only rebounded and clattered onto the stone floor.

"Justin, you know not what you've done!" Alistair said. His blue eyes were fearful, close to tears, even. "If you die…"

He trailed off, not finishing.

Eldrin just looked at him in shock, and it seemed like death itself was written on his face. Only Lila's face was filled with hope.

Like Justin, she knew the answer, and unlike the others, she knew he knew.

But he wouldn't know for sure until he answered.

Justin turned to face the statue, feeling the weight of the moment. He looked up at the sword, just inches from his face, and smiled.

"Life."

There was a brief silence, then the sword lifted, and a resounding click echoed through the chamber as the doorway beyond was unlocked and rolled back. The green aura vanished, and the others looked at him in awe.

"Life," Alistair said, a note of admiration in his voice. "Of course, it's life! What I swore to defend. So simple. So elegant…it fits the riddle perfectly."

Justin nodded, relief washing over him. "Alaric was a White Wizard, and the riddle talks about something everyone has, though to different extents. The true value of life isn't in wealth or duty but in how you live it. More than that—these cultists serve the God of Death, the ultimate perversion of everything Alaric stood for. It makes sense they guessed wrong five times. Life was the only answer that fit every part of the riddle."

Eldrin hummed thoughtfully. "Well-said. The question of joy or despair speaks to the quality of one's life, not just the material aspects. Good King Alaric would have valued life more than anything else, including money." He gave Justin a respectful nod. "Sharp thinking, lad."

Lila, looking pale but relieved, embraced Justin. "How did you figure it out?"

He smiled, shaking his head. "I didn't. I just wanted to stop you and started talking to drag it out. That's when the answer came to me."

"Well, this isn't over yet," she said. "But it's a good start."

Justin had another epiphany. Even the Vault description hinted at the answer: "a life well-lived is the greatest treasure of all."

"Let's press on," Alistair said. "We should save our congratulations for when the Vault is cleared, and Alaric's spirit rests easy. I think the last trial is before us."

The air around them felt lighter, as if a heavy burden had been lifted. The door behind the statue now stood open, revealing a passageway leading to the next chamber.

They advanced, Alistair in the lead with his hammer, Eldrin with his bow, Lila with her knives, and Justin with his cane.

It was time to clear this Vault and get the hell out of Highcliff.

31

A KING AND QUEEN

"Summoners are the most dangerous class to mortal civilization. They don't merely gamble with their own souls—they gamble with ours as well. For when the chains of their summoned entities slip, as they eventually do, it's never just the Summoner who pays the price."

—Erynal Sharion
  A Treatise on the Magical Classes

As the party stepped into what Alistair had suggested was the last chamber, they were met with a scene of solemn grandeur. The room was vast, dominated by a majestic sarcophagus at its center. A dark, pulsating energy surrounded the sarcophagus, casting a sinister glow over the room and filling the space with an eerie hum.

The malevolent force at work sent a shiver down Justin's spine. This was the heart of the crypt, the final resting place of the great King Alaric, now desecrated by dark rituals.

Yes, Justin mused. Classic Boss Room material.

At the foot of the sarcophagus stood a figure cloaked in dark robes, facing away from the party. A stream of dark magic tethered him to the sarcophagus. As they approached, the figure turned, revealing a gaunt, pale face with eyes that glowed with cold, malevolent light. His robes, like the other cultists', bore the insignia of a skeletal hand grasping a wilting white flower, and he grasped a dark staff, at the head of which was a red demonic skull.

"Who dares disturb the meditations of the Dread Summoner Malachor?" he intoned, his voice low and menacing.

"Great," Justin muttered. "He refers to himself in the third person."

Malachor's eyes narrowed as he smiled faintly. "Ah, a fellow practitioner of the Magic of Death! Why would one such as you ally yourself with these...life-loving fools?"

"I'm not really a practitioner of Death Magic. More of a dabbler, really."

Malachor looked like he was about to blow some more hot air, so Justin figured it was the perfect opportunity to down his potions.

He reached into his pouch, uncorking the first of them. The pop echoed loudly through the chamber, along with Justin's gulps. The Ironwood Essence tasted almost like blood.

As he put the empty vial back, Lila followed his example, probably realizing this would be her last chance to edify herself for the fight.

Next, Justin downed the Heartwood Elixir. This one was woody but had a pleasant bite, even with notes of umami.

As both potions worked, he felt strength and power enter his limbs. "Ah, much better! Now, where were we?"

Malachor's expression darkened. "Such insolence! Well, you wouldn't be the first. As if a couple of potions could save you! All of my companions perished to bring me here, but it was a small price to pay. They have joined my Master in the Nether Realm, while I have gained an even greater prize."

"You talk too much," Alistair said, stepping forward with his hammer.

But Malachor raised his hand, sending him flying back with a telekinetic push. Alistair recovered quickly, hammer in hand, ready to strike.

"Fool! The Vault grants me this moment to speak, and you will listen. Behold!"

With a dramatic gesture, the sarcophagus burst open. The party stepped back as an amulet—the same one Justin had seen in the artwork—floated from the skeletal neck of King Alaric. The amulet affixed itself around Malachor's neck as dark magic swirled around him.

"Lo! I now possess the Amulet of Equilibrium, King Alaric's most treasured artifact, the source of his power and wisdom." As he held up the Amulet, its six colored gems glinted ominously in the dim light.

The party tensed, uncertain of the artifact's power, but Justin was sure it was formidable.

"With the power of the Amulet, I will transcend mortal limits. Weep now, foolish Life Worshippers, as I summon a servant fit for a king's tomb!"

Malachor raised his hands, chanting in a guttural, otherworldly language. The air itself darkened as a portal opened, revealing an abyss of pure black. From this void, a monstrous form began to coalesce.

A towering undead demon emerged, its skeletal wings stretching wide as it let out a bone-chilling roar. It was a grotesque fusion of a giant skeleton and a zombie, with a fetid face and torso that combined exposed bones with patches of decaying flesh. The creature's eyes burned with green fire, casting an eerie glow around the chamber. In one clawed hand, it wielded a massive, jagged sword.

There were no pithy words Justin could muster to downplay the situation. He felt a moment of panic, even pissing his pants slightly, as the demon's wings fluttered, filling the chamber with an aura of death and decay. The very air seemed to rot under its presence, making it hard to breathe.

Justin glanced at his companions; their faces were set in grim determination. This was it. Within seconds, the battle would begin.

With a flourish and a decidedly evil laugh, Malachor lowered his hands, and the demon advanced on its insect-like legs.

Alistair led the charge, his hammer glowing with holy light as he struck the demon's legs with a wide, sweeping attack, attempting to bring it down quickly. The demon screeched as several legs were lopped off and engulfed in holy flames. The demon swung its jagged, oversized sword, but Alistair surrounded himself in an aura of golden light, tanking the blow entirely. His hammer then glowed with red, latent power as he slammed it into the demon's midsection. The demon reeled from the impact as Alistair followed it up with several further strikes, sending waves of holy fire rippling through the monster.

As Eldrin loosed arrows and Lila threw knives, Justin wondered what he should do.

So, he activated his Dandy's Swagger, strutting like a peacock in full display. Yellow magic surrounded him, infusing his allies and temporarily boosting everyone's Charisma. It seemed useless in a direct fight, but it was something—perhaps the only thing he could do without risking immediate death.

But maybe it wasn't entirely useless because now Alistair was fighting with increased confidence, while Lila and Eldrin moved with more vigor.

Justin couldn't help but crack a smile. Alistair had been wrong. The solution wasn't less dancing. It was *more* dancing.

And not only that, but Justin felt an insane surge of confidence from the skill. Twirling his cane, he edged closer to the beast, positioning himself behind Eldrin and Lila, who were continuing to deal steady ranged damage while Alistair took on the role of the tank.

Malachor, meanwhile, lurked behind his demon, casting dark magic to support it, presumably healing or buffing it. A classic Summoner, then, Justin thought derisively. Hiding in the shadows and letting his minion take the hits was *not* how a gentleman should fight.

If there were a way Justin could sneak up on Malachor, this fight could be over in a jiff.

Reel it back, he thought. The swagger is making you a bit too confident.

Instead, Justin stood next to Eldrin, who was shooting arrows with uncanny accuracy, targeting the demon's eyes and joints. Lila moved with a dancer's grace, darting around the demon, her knives flashing as she aimed for weak spots. She deftly avoided the demon's sword and wings, and every time she ran out of knives, she simply held out her hand to recall them.

Justin remembered that his swagger would also give the demon a Charisma malus. With his +1 boost from his Cane of Valoria, his current Charisma was actually at 18—a respectable number. Coupled with the demon's -2 Charisma penalty, perhaps a well-placed Poison Barb would be just the ticket.

Justin cleared his throat. "What are you, a failed science experiment? I've seen scarier things on a haunted house ride at the county fair!"

The demon seemed to hesitate for a moment, probably more confused than anything else. But this hesitation, however slight, allowed Alistair to land a pivotal hit, driving the demon further into the chamber's corner.

But despite their combined efforts, the demon was incredibly resilient. Its tough, leathery hide and Death Magic defenses, bolstered by Malachor, deflected much of the damage. Alistair's hammer, though powerful, seemed to have a limited effect, while Eldrin's arrows often glanced off without penetrating. Lila's knives, while more effective, couldn't be thrown fast enough to make a significant impact.

The battle raged on for at least another thirty minutes, each member of the party pushing their limits to bring down the formidable foe. Alistair was doing what Paladins did best: tanking, with clutch heals on himself and others, while dealing a respectable amount of damage. Justin had to remember, despite the demon's size and ferocity, it was still only Level 15, while Alistair was Level 25.

In a way, the fight was going about as well as it could.

Of course, as soon as Justin had this thought, it all started coming apart.

Alistair landed what should have been a decisive blow, his

hammer crashing into the demon's chest. The demon collapsed on its scuttling legs, ceasing all movement. Eldrin prepared to finish it, drawing his sword and charging.

But that was when the demon's form began to crackle and distort, its body convulsing violently before exploding into a swarm of wraiths. The ghostly figures, about thirty or even more, quickly filled the chamber, their eerie moans echoing off the walls.

The wraiths darted toward each member of the party, at least seven or eight to a person. Justin, standing back and having dealt no physical damage during the entire fight, was totally ignored.

But maybe that wasn't a bad thing. Perhaps now was the time to go after Malachor and end the fight once and for all. If the Summoner died, so would his summons. Or at least, so Justin thought.

But alone, Justin couldn't hope to face Malachor. Despite being a Summoner, Malachor still had plenty of spells at his command, for which Justin had little resistance.

He needed to use his Charisma to turn the tide, but how?

With mounting dismay, Justin realized things were not going well at all. The party's weapons were passing through the wraiths with limited effect. Even Alistair was overwhelmed by sheer numbers. Lila and Eldrin struggled against the onslaught, their movements slowing.

Now off cooldown, he activated Dandy's Swagger again—his comrades were overdue for a morale boost.

Justin's strut was angry, almost violent. He even did a few twirls, his cane arcing through the air and tracing trails of yellow magic. He was bursting with confidence, his Charisma once again boosted to 18 while all these nasty wraiths were getting a -2.

But, of course, this was not enough on its own, for he had one last trick up his sleeve.

Justin bowed his head. It was up to him now.

And Freddie Mercury.

Why Freddie Mercury? He couldn't say. It was just the first thing to pop into his head as soon as he activated his Dazzling Display skill.

He wasn't sure if it was going to work, but as far as charismatic individuals, well, Freddie had to take the cake.

As the spirit of Freddie Mercury infused into Justin, he felt a surge of magnetic energy. The move's power, he knew, was going to be much more than when he had previously used it. Justin felt the raw charisma and stage presence of a rock god coursing through him. He spread his arms wide, a confident grin on his face, and belted out in a commanding voice that filled the chamber.

"Ayyyyyyyyyyyy-oh!"

The very stones shook with this mighty emanation. And not only that, but a sparkling yellow aura rippled through the air, infusing the surrounding wraiths.

The specters paused, their attention snapping to Justin. They seemed strangely captivated by the unexpected display, their forms flickering in response.

Alistair, Lila, and Eldrin all looked at Justin as if he were a madman or a hero.

It seemed the wraiths needed a bit more coaxing.

"Ayyyyyyyyyyyy-oh!"

The second call seemed to do the trick. They shot toward him as if of one mind, their ethereal faces twisted in confusion and anger.

"Get Malachor!" Justin shouted, as the skill's power left him. "This won't last long enough to—"

But then the wraiths were upon him, one after another. Justin felt an intense coldness unlike anything he'd ever experienced, a coldness that seemed to freeze his very soul. He imagined that this feeling must be what it was like to float at the edge of the universe.

But he only felt it for a moment. Once again, as before, Justin felt the internal resistance, the repelling magnet that was the Death Mark.

The wraiths let out a high, discordant screech and recoiled from him, their ghostly forms scattering. Justin gawked in amazement.

By the Six, it had worked. It had actually worked.

Malachor, witnessing this unexpected turn, was visibly shaken. "No! This isn't how it was supposed to be!"

The path to Malachor was clear. The party, as one, turned their focus to the Dread Summoner. Alistair, Eldrin, and Lila advanced, weapons at the ready, while Justin, still glowing with the aftermath of his Dazzling Display, moved with renewed confidence, brandishing his cane.

Malachor's dark eyes widened in fear. He cast quick spells to empower the wraiths that were still scared witless and finally cast a dark shield around himself.

The wraiths, bolstered by Malachor's magic, regained some of their cohesion and surged toward the party, but they were disorganized and weaker than before.

But the party pressed their advantage. Alistair led the charge, his hammer ablaze with the power of his attack. He easily shattered the dark energy shielding Malachor. Eldrin shot arrow after arrow, each one finding its mark in the Summoner's body. Lila's knives flashed as they embedded themselves in Malachor from head to toe.

Malachor made no sound, despite the pain he must have surely felt. Blood stained his clothes and dribbled from his cadaverous face. Dark tendrils of energy snaked around the Summoner's body, attempting to heal him, but there was no way he could take this amount of damage.

To add insult to injury, Justin gave him a few hard thwacks on the head for good measure. The Summoner fell, and with his sure death, the wraiths eddied out of existence, creating a thick, icy fog on the floor.

As the echoes of the battle faded, the dark energy that had once surrounded the Summoner, the central sarcophagus, and the amulet itself had dissipated.

Against all odds, they had done it. The Vault was clear, and Malachor had been vanquished.

Now, it was time to claim their just rewards.

32

THE TREASURES OF ALARIC

"The Faithful always ask, why would anyone willingly embrace the God of Death? It is easier than you would think. Some seek to defy their own mortality. Others see in Morvath a grim kind of mercy—a release from the pain of existence. Others see it as an easy path to power. And then there are those who simply relish in the cruelty of their master. Whatever their reasons, one thing is certain: the Cult of Morvath thrives on desperation. And desperation is a currency the world is never short of."

—Issander of Duphal
  Altars of Shadow: A Study of the Nether Gods

A SOFT GREEN aura emanated from the sarcophagus. Justin watched in surprise as the Amulet of Equilibrium, which had been around Malachor's neck, suddenly lifted into the air and floated back toward the sarcophagus. The amulet settled around the neck of a spectral figure that was now rising from the stone tomb.

It was King Alaric, adorned in the royal attire he had been depicted wearing in the carvings. He had shoulder-length blonde hair and piercing blue eyes. The amulet, now gleaming with a soft, violet light, hung around his neck. His eyes, wise and kind, scanned the party, and he smiled warmly.

"Brave Adventurers," King Alaric's voice was deep and resonant. "You have freed my spirit from the dark ritual of the God of Death that sought to bind me. For this, you have my eternal thanks."

The party stood in awe. For the first time since entering the catacombs, Justin relaxed.

"As a token of my gratitude, I bestow upon each of you a gift matched to your valor," Alaric continued. "A silver-tier item, one guaranteed for all party members."

With a wave of his hand, an armlet appeared before him, a beautifully crafted piece of silver adorned with intricate engravings of swords, shields, and eagles. It gleamed with a faint blue light.

"To Alistair the Paladin," the King intoned, "I present you with the Armlet of the Eagle. It is a silver-tier arm piece that will bolster your Endurance by +2 while reducing the duration of negative status effects by 30%, allowing you to stand strong in the face of danger."

Alistair accepted the armlet with a solemn nod, slipping it onto his wrist. "Thank you, Your Majesty. I will wear it with honor."

Alaric waved his hand again, producing a longbow made from sleek, dark wood, polished to a high shine. Its string was a silver thread.

"And to Eldrin the Ranger," the King continued, "I gift the Bow of Eagle Sight. Made from the finest Ebonwood, it will upgrade your Eagle Eye skill to Eagle Sight while wielded, allowing you to see things at great distances, as an eagle would. In addition, the bow grants a +2 boost to Coordination."

Eldrin's eyes widened in admiration as the bow floated toward him. He tested its balance, giving a pleased nod. "A fine weapon, indeed! Long have I coveted an enchanted weapon that would have the power to bring down ethereal enemies. Thank you, Your Majesty."

King Alaric nodded regally, next producing a delicate ring made of a fine, woven silver band set with a small orange gem, fashioned in the shape of an eagle. "And to Lila the Bard, I gift the Ring of Eagle

Strike. It will confer the boon, Eagle Strike, when you wear it, which increases your attack speed by 20% when using throwing weapons. It will also confer additional nimbleness in playing stringed instruments, such as lutes, guitars, harps, or dulcimers."

Her eyes widened as the ring floated toward her, and she instantly slipped it onto her right middle finger, a slight orange aura surrounding her person. "This will serve me well. My thanks, King Alaric."

Last of all, the King raised his hands, and a beautiful long blue coat materialized, with golden trim that glowed subtly. The emblem of Highcliff, an eagle in flight, was embroidered on the back.

"And for you, Justin the Socialite, I gift the Coat of Highcliff's Elegance. It's of a kind that might have been worn by the nobles of my court. But unlike many enchanted coats Socialites wear, this one provides a bonus not for Charisma. It gives you +1 to Coordination and Endurance, perfect for a gentleman on the go. The coat also contains an Enchantment of Featherweight, which reduces its weight when you wear it, helping with mobility and reducing fatigue during long journeys."

Justin's eyes widened as the beautiful coat floated toward him, and when he reached for it, the luxurious fabric felt soft under his hand. The magic of the Vault supplied a description of its enchantments.

The Coat of Highcliff's Elegance
>   **Type:** Chest Piece
>   **Tier:** Silver
>   **Class Restriction:** Socialite, Diplomat, Merchant
>   **Highcliff's Elegance:** +1 to Endurance and Coordination.
>   **Featherweight:** Greatly reduces this coat's weight without sacrificing its quality.

He immediately put it on.

[Do you wish to bind the Coat of Highcliff's Elegance to your core?]

Just gave a mental affirmation, and just like that, he felt its effects as soon as he donned it over his shirt. He felt hardier and nimbler, and such was its lightness that he almost felt like he wasn't wearing it at all.

"This is incredible. Thank you, Your Majesty!"

Lila turned to him, giving a thumbs-up.

There was a moment of silence, as they knew what came next. The dispersing of the platinum-tier artifact.

King Alaric smiled warmly. "These gifts are but a small token of my gratitude. But the true prize is the very amulet I'm wearing around my neck. It is called the Amulet of Equilibrium. In life, it was my most treasured possession, but the tale of its acquisition is sad."

King Alaric seemed to collect his thoughts. Justin knew they were in for quite the speech.

"As a young man, my father took me, along with some of his strongest knights, to the Seraphim Range after hearing rumors of the return of the Vault of Aeternum. Many brave and talented people perished trying to claim its treasures. At last, our party ventured inside, facing a creature of unimaginable power, the Elder Shadow Wyrm, a being of pure darkness and malice, whose progeny were causing much grief in northern Serenthel. The battle was fierce, and many of our company fell, including my father. However, through great skill and even greater luck, we brought the beast down at last."

Alaric continued. "Although the Vault did not deem me worthy of the Amulet of Equilibrium—I was still young, after all—it was given to me by Sir Garrick Stormblade, one of my father's most loyal knights, a Spellsword of great renown. He was loyal to my father above all others. As he handed me the amulet, resisting its call to power, Sir Garrick said, 'Use this well, young prince. Let it bring pride to your father's memory and wisdom to your rule.' As Sir Garrick said, my father was a wise man, and I resolved to honor him by seeking wisdom myself. I used the Amulet of Equilibrium toward this end, and I used it to boost my Intellect greatly, granting me insight beyond my years, bringing me fame, wealth, and power.

"However, such power attracted many enemies. The amulet's unique abilities made it a highly coveted prize. Only by my death could it become unbound from my core, allowing it to be wielded by another. With the enhanced Intellect the amulet granted me, I led my small kingdom to victory, subduing many threats. My plan was to pass the amulet on to my son, but tragically, he passed away before me."

Alaric paused sadly for a moment before continuing. "Therefore, I ordered the amulet to be buried with me, locked within my crypt, for I could not trust any other to wield its power. I ordered the magically enchanted key to be thrown into the sea. However, there must have been some treachery after my passing, and somehow, by and by over the centuries, the key fell into the hands of the Cultists of Morvath, who used it to unlock my tomb. Here they remained for months, using their fell magic to unbind my sarcophagus of the mighty Life Magic that protected it. All of this explains why, despite this Vault being only Level 15, such a priceless treasure is available and why the cultists were so desperate to get it."

While all this was interesting, it didn't tell Justin what the amulet actually *did*, as well as who would receive it.

But he knew that it would be coming soon.

The spirit of King Alaric looked at each party member thoughtfully. "The amulet, of course, is the platinum-tier artifact I will give to one of you. In life, there was no one I trusted with it, but one of you has shown the courage and wisdom necessary to wield its mighty power. Indeed, I have watched your deeds and weighed your contributions ever since you first entered this Vault."

The party exchanged glances, each wondering who Alaric would choose.

"Each of you has shown remarkable courage and skill," Alaric began. "Your combined efforts have freed my spirit and cleansed this sacred place. Let us reflect on your individual deeds."

He turned first to Alistair. "Alistair of Drakendale, your steadfast bravery and unyielding faith have been a pillar of strength for your comrades. Your leadership and holy hammer protected your allies and struck down the darkness that sought to consume us all. You have been a staunch defender of Life, and your wisdom has been invaluable to this party's success."

Alistair bowed his head. "Thank you, Your Majesty. It is my duty and honor to serve and cleanse this place of darkness."

Next, Alaric looked at Eldrin. "Eldrin Thornwood, your keen eyes and sharp aim have been crucial in this battle. You navigated the challenges of this Vault with insight, recalling the details of my life in the murals you observed with accuracy. You were wrong only once, while the cultists got it wrong several times, arguing and bickering over the proper order. Not only that, but your arrows found their mark when it mattered most, and your strategic mind has aided your companions. Your generosity in giving your companions your potions, precious indeed, is noted."

Eldrin nodded, a faint smile playing on his lips. "I did what I could, Your Majesty. I'm glad to have played a part."

Turning to Lila, Alaric's expression softened. "Lila Fairwind, your agility and resourcefulness were clear at every turn. Your deft movements and quick thinking kept the group safe, and your precision with your knives proved essential. You faced danger without hesitation, and your courage was a beacon of hope. You were also the first to offer to answer the riddle, at the risk of your own life."

Lila met his gaze, her eyes bright with emotion. "Thank you, King Alaric. I'm just glad I could help."

Finally, Alaric's gaze settled on Justin. His expression grew contemplative, as if weighing something deeply. "Justin Talemaker, you have displayed an extraordinary talent for inspiration. Your... *unique abilities*...are unlike anything we have seen in this world. And perhaps that is because you learned them from another."

Justin's eyes widened at this, wondering how Alaric could know that. But maybe, as a spirit, he had access to knowledge that mortals didn't.

Alaric continued. "You turned the tide in the party's favor, especially when you faced the wraiths. There was a moment, however small, when all thirty-six wraiths attacked your very core, from which they hoped to drain your Spark of Life. Such an attack would have ended even the strongest member of your party within seconds."

"By the Six," Alistair said, his face pale.

"You didn't know if it would work, but you did so anyway, perhaps not knowing that if it failed, you would have suffered a fate worse than death, joining the Demon Zalthor of the Nether Realm from which the wraiths issued. Not only that, but you discovered the answer to the riddle. You gambled everything for the chance to save your friend, Lila. That took great bravery, even if you were confident in your answer. Your actions, though unconventional, were pivotal to the group's victory."

At all this, Justin felt a flush of pride. "I just did what I thought was right. It was a team effort."

King Alaric nodded. "Indeed, it was a team effort. Yet, in every challenge, there is one who stands out, whose actions are critical at a key moment. You all have shown great valor and wisdom, but the Amulet of Equilibrium requires a bearer who understands the value of balance, both in power and in life."

He paused, letting his words sink in. "Justin Talemaker, I bestow the Amulet of Equilibrium upon you. It holds a rare Enchantment, called Unbound Ascension. When you wear the amulet, the hard cap of raising a single Attribute to more than twice the average of all other Attributes is waived."

Justin's eyes widened at that. He hadn't known that it was a restriction, which meant that upon reaching Level 10, assuming he went all in on Charisma, he wouldn't be able to place a point in it. He supposed the enchantment was useful, but he couldn't imagine any character, much less him, reaching that point.

"That's not all," King Alaric said. "For it contains a unique enchantment for which the amulet is famed, the likes of which cannot be found in all the Realms of Eyrth." Alaric paused, probably for dramatic effect. "This enchantment is called Grace of the Six. Grace of the Six takes your highest base Attribute and divides it by six. The resulting number, rounded down, is then applied to all your other Attributes."

"Whoa," Justin said, unable to help himself. Even the others gasped at that.

It seemed busted. But maybe that was the power of a platinum-tier artifact. And because of the dynamic nature of the enchantment, it would remain useful at all levels.

Right off the bat, it would grant Justin a +2 to all other attributes that were solely lacking, ten levels' worth. And once he got to a higher level, say 24, it would grant a +4 in all other attributes. And since only one attribute point was granted per level, with rare opportunities to get a free one here and there, that was powerful. *Extremely* powerful. Even Gribble the Snow Goblin had pointed out that the free attribute point he'd received from the Cane of Valoria was extremely rare.

"The Amulet of Equilibrium is yours, Justin Talemaker. You have shown that strength does not solely lie in physical might or magical prowess, but also in the courage to inspire and protect others, even at significant risk to oneself. Use this amulet to continue guiding and uplifting those around you. But be warned: If you raise your highest base attribute to more than twice the average of all others, the amulet cannot be removed except by death."

Justin considered this warning soberly. This wouldn't be an issue for a long time. The more important consideration was whether it would make him a target. The Enchanter class, it seemed, could see what enchantments certain items had. Some blessings could become curses and liabilities.

But all the same, the risk seemed to be worth it, at least for now. He had until Level 10 to decide if he wanted to change his mind by taking it off. That was when he'd get to raise his Charisma attribute to 21.

The amulet floated gently toward Justin, the six-colored jewels glittering in the light of the glowing sarcophagus. As it did, he could see more detailed information regarding it.

The Amulet of Equilibrium

Type: Artifact

Tier: Platinum

Relic of Life: This artifact cannot be bound by those with a Death Affinity.

Grace of the Six: The Six Gods smile upon your singular dedication to mastery. Divide your highest attribute by six, then apply the result to all other attributes.

Unbound Ascension: Let no being, god or mortal, stand in the way of your progress. All attribute caps have been lifted, but be warned: if you raise a base attribute to twice the average of all others, the Amulet of Equilibrium cannot be removed.

His eyes widened as it settled around his neck with a soft violet glow.

[Do you wish to bind the Amulet of Equilibrium to your core?]

To his surprise, Justin hesitated. Once the amulet was bound, it would be his, and he knew others might want to kill him for it once they recognized its power, as they had wanted to kill King Alaric. He could at least keep it hidden under his shirt, offering some measure of protection.

But as he considered it, the pros far outweighed the cons. He had risked himself greatly to clear this Vault, and he deserved a just reward.

Justin immediately gave his mental assent.

He frowned. Nothing had changed.

[Core-binding failed. The Amulet of Equilibrium cannot be bound to those with a Death Affinity.]

Justin's heart sank. Death Affinity? What in the blazes was that?

Then he realized the truth. "This Mark. This damn Mark!"

What he had half-jokingly called a blessing was now a glaring obstacle. A Platinum Artifact was right here, around his neck, but he couldn't even use it. The frustration was beyond visceral. It was almost maddening.

King Alaric noticed the change in Justin's expression. His eyes softened. "This situation is...unprecedented. I had considered giving the amulet to another. However, I chose you, Justin Talemaker, knowing the Mark was not something you sought. It is a foul doing of Death Magic, so powerful that the gods—for whatever reason—are treating you as if you are a practitioner of Death Magic yourself."

Justin's voice was tight with frustration. "Nothing could be further from the truth. So, I really can't use the amulet's benefits?"

Alaric nodded solemnly. "The Amulet of Equilibrium is a Relic of Life, and as such, it cannot be bound by those aligned with Death. The Mark of Death has shifted your alignment. However, this is not an insurmountable obstacle. Removing the Mark will take away your Death Affinity and allow you to use the amulet."

Lila placed a comforting hand on Justin's shoulder. "We'll remove the Mark, Justin. That's the whole reason for this quest, right?"

Justin forced a smile, but inside, the frustration churned. At the beginning, he'd never dreamed he would be the one to get the reward. Alistair, as a Paladin, was far more deserving. But the amulet could have been Justin's way of enhancing his meager abilities to contribute to the party more effectively.

Now, it was a reminder of the dark mark he carried and the influence of the Baron.

Eldrin looked at him with sympathy, while Alistair's face was grim.

King Alaric's voice broke through his thoughts. "Take heart, Justin. It seems your friends are committed to removing the Mark. This challenge is an opportunity to prove your strength and determination, to become even more worthy of the amulet."

"Do I have to give it back?" Justin asked.

King Alaric shook his head. "No. It was given to you, and that cannot be undone. You may keep it for yourself until you can remove the Mark, or you can give it to another."

Justin's face fell. "That's probably what I'll end up doing. I'm just a Level 4 Socialite, and I can't even use it. If this is a Relic of Life..." He turned to Alistair. It wasn't easy, but he lifted the Amulet of Equilibrium from his neck. "Alistair...would you take it?"

Alistair's blue eyes regarded the mighty prize, and Justin could see his desire for it. He reached for it but did not take it. He simply closed Justin's hands over it.

"It's yours, Justin. And I swear that you will get to wear it one day and wield its power. It's one more reason to keep going for Mont Elea. The gods would not have given you this amulet if they didn't want you to have it. They would test you first, so that you can prove you are truly worthy."

Justin nodded, putting the amulet back around his neck. "I'll do everything I can to be worthy of it, then."

Alistair gave a respectful nod.

King Alaric smiled warmly. "Your ties of friendship are commendable. It is in these bonds of strength that we can rise above ourselves and achieve greatness." He nodded, satisfied. "And though it might seem a small prize in comparison, as promised, each of you shall receive 2.5 gold crowns, a substantial sum, to aid you in your future endeavors."

[2 gold crowns and 50 silver marks have been added to your inventory. You now have 3 gold crowns, 11 silver marks, and 24 copper pieces!]

Justin whistled. "That's a lot of pints."

"Thank you, King Alaric," Alistair said, bowing deeply. "Your generosity is unmatched."

"Thank you," the others echoed.

King Alaric's form shimmered, his time in the mortal realm drawing to a close. "You have my eternal gratitude. Should you ever find yourselves in Highcliff, know that my spirit watches over you."

"Good King!" Alistair said. "If I may ask one question before you fade to the Aether Realm. Is there a way to use the catacombs to leave Highcliff to the north?"

Alaric nodded, his form growing faint. "Indeed, there is a passage that leads to the northern outskirts of the city. Follow the path through the Hall of Heroes, two levels up. You will find a hidden passage behind the statue of the First King. Fare thee well, Brave Adventurers."

With a final, grateful smile, King Alaric's spirit dissipated. The silence was soon interrupted by the Voice.

[The Vault honors your triumph. Now go forth with courage in your hearts, strength in your limbs, and wisdom in your minds.]

[The Trial of the Vault is complete!]

[Experience Gained: 750]

[Your experience stands at 1,589/420. Level-up available!]

And just like that, it was over. Justin looked around the tomb, finding that all traces of the fight, including Malachor's body, were gone.

Everyone crowded around him to check out his prize. The prize that would not give him its benefits.

"Tough luck, Justin," Lila said. "It's a beautiful thing."

"Congratulations, lad," Eldrin said. "We'll make sure you get to Mont Elea and get that Mark removed."

Justin nodded numbly. Mont Elea was a long way off yet.

Alistair's blue eyes regarded the amulet. "I am certain now the gods' hands are in this. They watch over you, Justin, and that is the greatest gift of all. We will do everything we can to ensure you are free of the Mark."

"The gods watch us all, do they not?" Lila asked.

"Yes, of course," the Paladin responded. "And yet, it is clear there is something about you, lad. Eldrin said you had a story, and an interesting one, but that will have to wait for another day. We must leave Highcliff at once."

The others nodded.

"Lead the way, Alistair," Justin said.

As the Paladin did so, Justin frowned in thought. Despite the others' words, he only felt sick. Part of the appeal was seeing the numbers go up. The more they went up, the better. The Amulet of Equilibrium would have been a way for his numbers to go up significantly.

In a way, he almost wished it had been Alistair to get it. Then he wouldn't be feeling this pain.

Lila sidled over, wrapping an arm around him. She didn't say a word, but Justin appreciated the comfort.

He looked at her, forcing a smile. "I should be grateful. I'm richer than I've ever been, got a spiffy coat, and have friends to watch my back. Yet I can't stop thinking about what I *could* have had."

She smiled. "It's human nature. Think of it this way, though. It will make it all the sweeter once you have that amulet working."

"Maybe," Justin said.

The party continued out of the dead king's crypt, reaching the main part of the Highcliff Catacombs. One day, he determined he would get to bind the amulet to his core. It was another reason to keep going. To keep fighting.

He followed Alistair and the rest up the spiral staircase.

33

THE HALL OF HEROES

"Ask yourself this hypothetical: if the gods did not exist, would your life be any different? Would you labor less? Suffer less? Pray less for things that never come? If the answer is no, then perhaps you have already proven their insignificance. For what kind of gods shape a world where belief or disbelief makes no difference to the faithful? And don't tell me 'They give you power if you have a class.' I say instead that they give you a leash. Either way, is it really so bold a claim to say that we should live—and die —by our own hands, not theirs?"

—Orvel the Apostate,
  Challenging the Divine Narrative

THE PARTY LEFT King Alaric's crypt, returning to the main part of the Highcliff Catacombs. The air was cool, and the only sounds were the echoes of their footsteps on the stone floor. Despite the disappointment of the amulet, which Justin had already hidden under his linen shirt, it felt good to be finally moving on. Hopefully, they could escape without Lieutenant Gareth or his followers being any the wiser.

They followed Alistair up the wide spiral staircase. Strangely, the corpses and the cultist's body were gone. Was their desecration of the tomb merely a conjuring of the Vault itself? Justin couldn't say. Certainly, the amulet in his hand felt genuine enough.

It didn't take long to ascend two levels, and upon turning, they entered a vast hall of white marble that seemed to stretch on endlessly. Alistair's light spell pushed back the darkness effectively, revealing the Hall of Heroes. The walls were lined with ancient sarcophagi, many bearing the coat of arms of the soldiers in question: a lion rampant, a stag and oak, a silver fox, among many more.

The air was laden with the scent of old stone and earth, mingled with the faint, musty odor of age. Dust lay thick on the floor and surfaces, while broken pots and urns evidenced grave robbers. Highcliff, a city in decline, could no longer protect its venerated dead.

As Justin passed the silent statues, though he never knew these soldiers, he felt a renewed determination to prove himself worthy of the amulet. He'd never imagined himself to be a hero, but somehow, that was the way his story was shaping up. Courage, sacrifice, honor —all had been foreign concepts to him. But now, with some help and by sheer necessity, perhaps they were qualities he might one day embody, even if he was only a Socialite.

Eldrin seemed to note the detailed craftsmanship of the carvings. "Every hero has a story, though few of these are remembered today. And right now, each of us is writing our own story, one step at a time."

To Justin's surprise, Alistair didn't shush him. Maybe with the disappearance of the Vault, it was safer to speak.

"Do you think the spirits of these heroes are still watching over Highcliff, Eldrin?" Justin asked, curiosity piqued. He would have thought the idea laughable in his own world, and yet not even an hour ago, he had spoken to a ghost.

Alistair was the one who answered. "In a way, yes. The deeds and sacrifices of the past shape the present. Their spirits inspire us, reminding us of the values they fought for. We honor them by striving to uphold those ideals."

Justin couldn't help but feel that the heroes were watching over him, urging him onward. It was easy to believe certain things were impossible, but this very hall was a reminder that heroism could be found even in ordinary places. Perhaps even in a Socialite.

Maybe Justin couldn't use a sword, wear heavy armor, or fight in a battle the way Alistair could, but he had his own personal fights. Like getting rid of the Death Mark.

The question became, though, what came after that? He couldn't say. He supposed his next big goal should be to find a way home, but he didn't know what was involved in that. Did he need to find another tornado? He remembered the blue portal that had brought him here. If one had brought him here, it stood to reason one could bring him back. Maybe it was as simple as finding that meadow west of Mistwatch.

He missed home. He had never gotten to figure out what had happened to his mom, and he felt a pang of guilt that these days he hardly spared his old life a thought.

Every day, the past was slipping further and further away...

"Still thinking about the amulet?" Lila asked.

Justin forced a smile. "Yeah, I guess."

Lila smiled encouragingly. "Don't worry. We'll remove that Mark. You deserve to use that amulet, and we'll make sure it happens."

Justin nodded. "Thanks."

The party continued through the Hall of Heroes in silence, the passage eventually ending at one last hero at the end of the hall. This statue stood twice as tall, its imposing figure dominating the space. The placard declared it to be a representation of King Eldred I, the first king of Highcliff.

The party paused for a moment to examine the statue.

Alistair looked at it admiringly. "He rebelled against the Shadow Empire nearly six hundred years ago. He's not called the First simply because he's the First King of Highcliff. He's called the First since he was the first to stand up and declare Highcliff's independence, inspiring others to do so as well. Indeed, it is because of his bravery that we even reckon our years, at least here in Serenthel. It has been nearly six hundred years since he threw off the Empire's shackles, inspired by the Prophecy of the Six Gods. The Six whom we worship to this day."

"567 A.R.," Eldrin said, adding context for Justin's benefit.

Justin swallowed. That number alone told him that this world was vastly different from his own. Even something as simple as a different way of counting time changed everything.

"Despite Eldred's influence, his reign did not last long," Alistair said. "But if not for him, perhaps the Shadow Empire would never have fallen, and Morvath would still reign supreme. It's a lesson for us all."

"What lesson?" Lila asked. "If you stand up, you're the first to die?"

"Nay," Alistair said. "Sometimes, all it takes is one good man, one brave deed, to change the course of history. The gods smile upon that. And now, the People of Highcliff will remember him as long as the city exists, and perhaps even beyond."

Justin watched with a feeling akin to awe. The statue depicted Eldred in full armor, a great sword in one hand and a shield emblazoned with the Highcliff eagle in the other.

"End of the line?" Justin asked.

"Let me have a look," Eldrin said.

The Ranger walked around the statue, finding a narrow crevice behind it. A rectangular recess could be seen in the darkness there, on which he pushed. Sure enough, the recess spun, a cloud of dust falling from above.

"Like clockwork," he said with a smile.

"Let's move on," Alistair said.

They squeezed behind the statue and went through the recess, finding a narrow passage beyond, of simple stonework and no further adornment. The air was cooler here, carrying a faint draft from somewhere ahead. They followed the narrowing corridor until they reached a set of stone steps leading upward into the unknown.

Justin felt himself becoming nervous. This was the moment they'd been waiting for—emerging from underground. Would it be to safety or danger? Now that the Vault was gone, the catacombs were relatively safe. It was easy to imagine them hiding in here for a long time, if not for Baron Valdrik being able to sense Justin's Mark.

Only time would tell what awaited them on the surface. Justin watched Eldrin closely, knowing that his Ranger's Intuition would be key here.

Alistair led the way, his light spell casting a soft glow on the steps as they climbed cautiously. The air became noticeably cooler as they ascended.

After what felt like an eternity of climbing, they reached a simple stone door, cleverly disguised to blend in with the surrounding stone. The door was made of the same material as the walls, with intricate carvings mimicking the natural rock formations around it. Alistair pushed the door open, revealing a narrow exit that led outside. Sunlight flooded in, momentarily blinding Justin.

The party emerged onto a hillside, Justin's eyes taking a moment to adjust to the late afternoon sun dappling the forested landscape. The cool breeze was a welcome change from the stale air of the catacombs; the temperature had dropped significantly since their time underground.

The leaves of the forest were changing, many already yellow and red, some even borne by the wind. From their vantage on the hill, Justin could see the northern countryside, a mix of rolling hills and woodlands, with the foothills of the Umber Range to the northeast. Nearby, the ruins of a disused watchtower stood sentinel. The view was breathtaking, yet the sight of the ruins brought a sobering reminder of the impermanence of all things.

Alistair slammed the door shut behind them, and Justin marveled at how well it blended in. There was no chance that the Baron's men could find this, even if they were trying.

"We must keep moving," Eldrin said. "Shadowflight should be returning soon with information."

They headed downhill and into the thick of the trees. Looking behind, there was no sign of Highcliff; the hills blocked Justin's view. All was quiet as they blazed a trail through the forest, the ground giving way underfoot to Eldrin's guidance.

It seemed that they had made it, but Justin wouldn't rest easy until they were a few days out from Highcliff with no sign of pursuit.

As they traveled northwest, Eldrin scanned the area, sticking to the bases of the hills. They had walked about a half-mile when the Ranger held up a hand and crouched, signaling the others to do likewise.

Justin kneeled, feeling a chill that had nothing to do with the temperature. He wanted to ask what was wrong, but he simply watched Eldrin's gaze, which was focused on the sky.

Moments later, Shadowflight appeared, circling above before swooping down to land on Eldrin's arm. The bird's urgent movements conveyed an obvious message: trouble was coming.

"The Baron's men are close," Eldrin said, his voice tense. "They expected us to come out this way. They must have figured out where the secret passage came out."

Alistair frowned. "How long do we have?"

"Minutes, maybe," Eldrin replied quietly. "We need to decide our next move, and fast. We can't hope to outrun them."

"Why not?" Justin asked.

"If we go forward, we'll run into them. Go west, and we'll reach the River Marin, which is too wide for us to cross before they catch us. The hills are too steep to climb effectively."

"We need to find some high ground," Lila suggested. "Eldrin can ambush them with his new bow. I can come at them with my knives. Alistair, you can draw their attention."

The Paladin was already shaking his head. "It won't be enough, Lila. Now, you must remember your vows to follow my every order. I want no arguments."

The others were silent, waiting for Alistair to speak. Justin's heart raced.

"The best chance for us to escape is to split up. Eldrin, you lead Justin and Lila west toward the Umber Range. You'll be able to cross the river and lose yourselves in the woods if I can give you enough time."

Eldrin nodded, his face set with determination. "The terrain is rough, but it's our best shot."

Justin shook his head. "Alistair, you can't mean this. What are you supposed to do?"

As Alistair met his gaze, a calm resolve in his eyes, Justin already knew the answer. "I can handle them, Justin. My only job is to buy you time. Eldrin knows these lands and the way to Mont Elea. The most important thing is to keep you safe and out of the Baron's hands."

Justin frowned, frustration bubbling up. "Why am I so important? What aren't you telling me?"

"There's no time, Justin. Just know that the Baron wants you for a reason, and we can't let him get his hands on you. Now go, before it's too late."

Lila opened her mouth to argue further, but Eldrin placed a reassuring hand on her shoulder. "Alistair knows what he's doing. We need to trust him."

At that moment, Justin saw some movement in the trees, downslope from where they were.

As much as he hated it, the Paladin was right. He would buy them time. Maybe even enough to escape.

Justin couldn't imagine Alistair dying. He didn't know what he would do without him.

"Stay safe," Alistair urged, looking each of them in the eye. "Stick together and keep moving." Alistair's sharp blue eyes settled on Justin last of all. "You've come so far already—don't let this setback define you. Keep going, for all of us."

With that, he stood and walked downhill, hammer in hand, doing nothing to hide his presence. Eldrin waited a moment, keeping his palm outward to signal them not to move. Justin wondered why they weren't moving yet until he realized Eldrin wanted to make sure Alistair had all the enemies' attention first.

"Now," Eldrin said.

Eldrin, Lila, and Justin turned and started heading west, crouching low and moving swiftly. Before they lost sight of him completely, Justin turned, glimpsing Alistair on one knee, saying a quick prayer, even as Gareth and his men advanced toward the high ground he had picked out.

The Paladin's words echoed in his mind. *All it takes is one good man, one good deed, to change the course of history.*

It wasn't long before the sounds of battle echoed off the hills. The clashing of steel and the shouts of men filled the air. Justin's stomach twisted with worry. The Umber Range was now in sight, the forest ahead promising cover and safety as long as they got enough of a head start.

They ran through the trees. Despite Alistair's words, Justin knew this would probably be his last stand.

Alistair stood firm as Lieutenant Gareth ascended the hill. The Paladin had chosen a sunny spot, knowing it would weaken the undead Shadowblade. And yet, possessing a level above twenty meant Gareth likely had some resistance to sunlight. It certainly didn't seem to slow him down as he approached in his dark armor, his eyes cold and calculating.

Flanked on either side were more soldiers, an assortment of warriors and mages, about twenty in all. Half bore the stench of fully realized Death Marks, while the others were still mortal, loyal to Morvath and the Baron by choice. The air grew colder as they neared. Alistair felt the weight of their malice, like a dark cloud settling over him.

He glanced around, taking in the scene—sunlight dappling through the sparse trees, the gentle rustle of leaves in the breeze, and the distant cry of a bird. It was a beautiful fall day. Alistair's heart ached, knowing this might be the last time he saw such simple beauty. The Creator was truly good.

He thought briefly of Justin, Lila, and Eldrin, praying they were far enough away by now. The gods were watching over them; he had to believe that.

He tightened his grip on his hammer, feeling its familiar weight. There was no way he could survive this, but he could delay Gareth and his soldiers long enough for the others to escape. He drew a deep breath, centering himself in the light of Arion, God of Power.

"That's close enough, Lieutenant," Alistair called out. "In the name of Arion, tread not another step, lest you wish to taste my hammer."

Gareth's expression was cold and mirthless. "This need not come to blows, Alistair. The Baron only wants the boy."

"He won't have him. So long as I draw breath."

Gareth's gray eyes narrowed. "Oh, you won't be here for too much longer, I assure you. You are a foolish man, Alistair. Why die for the likes of him?"

Alistair felt a surge of anger. "Your master didn't tell you?"

"He did. The boy is important. More than you could ever know. To bring him to Mont Elea is a doom far worse than any that the Baron could conjure. I'm the only man he has entrusted with this task."

"You're not a man, Gareth. Not anymore."

Gareth chuckled, the sound devoid of warmth. "It irks you to see me more powerful than you ever could be. Those prattling Priests of Arion have nothing over the power of Death."

"You are a traitor, a thief, and an apostate," Alistair retorted. "You left the Templars because you craved power and glory, no matter the cost. You sold your soul to darkness."

Gareth's expression darkened. "Typical take for a Life-loving fool. I am more powerful than you could ever imagine. And I'm about to prove that fact to you, brothers though we once were."

Alistair glanced at the soldiers behind Gareth, noting their unease. "If you wish to prove the power of Death, why not a duel? Life against Death. We are of a similar level, Shadowblade, so the fight would be fair."

Gareth laughed openly, the sound echoing across the hillside. "Do you take me for a fool, Alistair? I see now what you're doing. You would speak and speak until the sun falls, and the moon rises over us all. Even knowing the night would make me even more powerful. Your aim is not to defeat me, but to slow me down."

"You were never known for your brains, Gareth. You are simply Valdrik's tool, nothing more. But it is not too late to disavow him and his Dark Master. There are ways to turn back to the Phoenix of Light."

Gareth's smile faded, replaced by a sneer. He drew his long, curved blade, a weapon that seemed to absorb the surrounding light. Alistair could feel its coldness, the chill of the grave, and smell the stench of Gareth's Death Mark, fully realized, wafting toward him. The other soldiers drew their weapons.

"You will not be speaking much longer," Gareth said, his voice low. "Morvath take your soul!"

With a roar, Gareth shot forward, fast as a shadow cast by a setting sun. Alistair raised his hammer, perhaps for the last time.

If this was the end, he would make it count. He felt no fear—only a deep, abiding peace.

It was up to the gods now.

34

ACROSS THE MARIN

"No one truly knows why the mighty Ilvari Elves fell. Most would blame the Orcish Confederation and their endless wars over the fate of Serenthel. Some would blame the Verdant Plague. But if you ask me, the answer is simpler: it's hard to see the blade coming when your nose is so far in the air. Pride cuts deeper than steel."

—Ellisar Vain
  The Rise and Ruin of Empires

JUSTIN STRAINED HIS EARS, catching the last echoes of clashing steel and shouts, now distant and faint. Each fading sound sent a pang of guilt twisting in his gut. He wondered, against all hope, if Alistair could survive. If he did, would he be able to find them again?

While the first answer was a maybe, the second answer was almost assuredly a "no." There would be no way for Alistair to catch up. If he found them later, it would have to be in some predetermined spot. As far as Justin knew, the only spot that would be possible was Mont Elea itself.

No one spoke as they ran. Eldrin set a grueling pace, and both Lila and Justin fought for air as the miles passed. The forest closed in around them, the trees thickening and the underbrush growing denser. The sounds had completely faded by now, leaving only the rustle of leaves and the distant call of a bird. It was getting darker, too. Sunset was two hours away if Justin had to guess.

After another hour of relentless running, Justin's legs felt like lead. His lungs burned, and each breath was a struggle. Just when he thought he couldn't make it any longer, they emerged from the dense forest to find themselves on the rocky banks of the River Marin. The river was wide, its waters rushing with a swift and powerful current. The surface was broken by swirling eddies, hinting at hidden dangers beneath. The river's chill seeped into the air, adding to the exhaustion that clung to Justin like a heavy cloak.

Eldrin was the first to speak and was already wading into the water. "We need to cross." The current tugged at him, and he looked back, his eyes concerned. "It's not too deep here, but the current is strong. We'll have to swim partway."

Justin shook his head, fear tightening his chest. He put his hands on his knees to catch his breath. "I...don't think I can make it. I'm beyond exhausted."

Even Lila, thinner and in better shape than he was, nodded in agreement.

Eldrin frowned, regret clear in his expression. "If only I had more Heartwood Elixir..."

"There's the bridge to the south," Lila said. "The one we crossed to get into the city. It can't be that far."

"About two miles," Eldrin said, frowning in thought. "Not far at all."

"What's the problem, then?" Justin asked.

"If Gareth brought all his men with him, then yes, it's perfectly possible to cross it. But if he left anyone behind, it would be an obvious point to block off. Gareth started with about twenty men following him out of Silverton. And if that assassin in Highcliff was any sign, he's hired a few more since coming here. The bridge is too much of a risk."

"I can't swim this," Justin said. "It's too wide. Too fast. And it's getting dark."

"And the water is cold," Lila added.

Eldrin nodded. "Yes, that is a danger. There's a ford ten miles upriver, but that's a long way. I'd rather do this part of the river while there's still daylight. There should be enough time to cross and lose them."

"This is taking us in the opposite direction of Mont Elea," Lila said. "They probably don't expect us to cross the river at all."

"I'm hoping so," Eldrin said. "But I'm not making any assumptions until I'm sure we've lost them." He took a deep breath, his expression settling into firm determination. "We head north to the ford. With my Pathfinder's Pace, we can stay ahead. The ford will be shallower, yes, but it will also be darker and colder. We won't have time to build a fire until we've gone at least a few miles west. And the ford will only work if Alistair has bought us enough time."

Justin wondered what had happened. It had been at least two hours by now, so the fate of the battle had long been decided. For all his strength, Justin couldn't imagine Alistair surviving against twenty classed soldiers, one of them a high-level Shadowblade. All they could hope was that he'd put enough of a dent in their numbers to slow them down.

"Let's move, then," Justin said.

As they marched north along the riverbank, the sun continued its descent, casting a golden glow over the Umber Range. It was a beautiful sight, the forests silent, the wind sighing through the trees. The leaves rustled, already turned into shades of red and gold. Justin couldn't believe that somewhere in this peaceful forest, someone was pursuing them. As the temperature continued to fall, Justin was grateful for his new coat.

As the setting sun finally disappeared behind the mountains, it plunged the forest into inky darkness. Justin's imagination ran wild, every rustle and crack of a twig was a potential threat. His thoughts wandered to Alistair, hoping desperately that the Paladin had somehow escaped.

As they went upriver, the terrain became rougher, with the river flanked on both sides by tall cliffs. The trees seemed to close in, their branches intertwining above them, creating a canopy that blocked out the stars. Justin felt a creeping fear, not just of the darkness but of the unknown dangers it concealed. His mind conjured images of dire wolves and even malevolent spirits lurking just out of sight, watching their every move.

For hours, they traveled in silence. It was far too dangerous to run, so they walked quickly. Eldrin's Pathfinder's Pace was indeed a boon; even in the darkness, they moved steadily, though not as fast as if it were day. As adrenaline faded, the exhaustion of the day's events hit Justin with full force.

About a couple of hours after they headed north, Justin jumped when Shadowflight flapped down from the branches above. They took their first break as Eldrin relayed the bird's news.

"They're at the river now," he said, turning to the others as Shadowflight fluttered away to do more reconnaissance. "A couple of hours behind us. They're debating which direction we went."

"And Alistair?" Lila asked.

Eldrin went silent.

"Look," Justin said. "You don't have to protect us, Eldrin. We deserve to know the truth."

Eldrin nodded sadly. "He fell. But not before he took half of them down with him."

The news was like a punch in the gut, even if it was expected.

"He's the only reason I'm here," Justin said. "I will miss him."

"We must keep moving," Eldrin said firmly. "We can mourn him once we've reached safety. That won't be for a while yet."

"Will they be able to track us?" Lila asked.

"Hard to say. Shadowflight will let us know soon, I'm sure. We're not far from the ford. We must keep pushing."

They continued on, Justin's thoughts spinning. He couldn't help but wonder if there was something else he could have done. But no matter what, he kept coming up short. All he could feel was guilt that the Paladin had to give his life for him. How could he ever be worthy of that sacrifice?

After what felt like an eternity, Eldrin turned toward the cliff, weaving a path down to the water. The river here was narrower but still swift and deep in places. It was difficult for Justin to tell, even with the moon and starlight. He told himself just to follow Eldrin, and he would be all right.

Eldrin didn't pause, going straight from rock to rock without hesitation. Lila was graceful, easily tracing the Ranger's footsteps. Justin was far less so, splashing into the water more than a few times, and it would have been even more so had it not been for his cane.

About halfway across the river, they could no longer step on stones. The water, icy cold, came up to Justin's chest, numbing his limbs. It felt like needles pricking his skin, each breath catching in his throat as the chill seeped into his bones. His muscles ached and stiffened with every movement, and he could feel his body growing sluggish. Lila's head was barely out of the water, and Eldrin held her firmly so that the current wouldn't carry her away while grasping a fallen log for support.

Soon, both Eldrin and Lila emerged from the deep part of the ford, entering some shallows that came up to their waists. Justin followed, the current tugging at him, threatening to sweep him away.

Eldrin held out his arm, which Justin barely grasped. He was pulled from the water, using his cane for support, finding purchase on the rocky bottom. The feat would have been hard enough if well-rested. But by this point, they had been traveling all night while exploring the catacombs all morning and afternoon. Not to mention the draining fight against Malachor and his demon.

After all that, it was a wonder Justin didn't simply drop dead.

Together, they waded through the last of the rushing water, stumbling and slipping, but finally reached the other side. They collapsed on the riverbank, panting and shivering from the cold. It was hard to guess the temperature, but it was cold enough for their breaths to make clouds.

"We need to keep moving," Eldrin said. "I know that's the last thing you want to hear, but it won't take long for hypothermia to set in. We need a fire, shelter, and rest. Then we must press on."

Justin was too tired to argue. He almost wondered if death itself was preferable to the misery he now felt.

It was at that moment that he remembered the Ring of Hygiene. Its description said that once a day, he could become perfectly clean and groomed to his exact specifications.

Perfectly clean. Did that include becoming dry?

There was nothing to do but try. He set his thoughts on the ring.

Instantly, yellow light surrounded him, and not even a moment later, he was dry from head to toe.

The other two looked at him, astonished.

"What did you do?" Eldrin asked.

"The Ring of Hygiene," Justin said. "One of us needs to be kept from freezing."

He took off his coat, placing it around Lila. He wasn't sure what good it would do, but she needed it far more than he did.

"Quick thinking," Eldrin said. "Let's move."

Eldrin continued on, with Justin and Lila close behind. The trees on the opposite bank provided some relief from the breeze, but not much.

"Do you know any place we might shelter?" Lila asked, her teeth chattering, her body hunched. "I...can hardly even walk..."

The coat seemed not to be doing her much good. She was cold and wet underneath it, which would continually sap her strength.

"Just a few miles more," Eldrin said. "The further we get from the ford, the better off we'll be. If they don't know we're headed here, they will soon."

"Lila might not make it a few miles, Eldrin. We need to think about starting a fire."

She didn't respond, only shivering uncontrollably. Justin knew that at these temperatures, it didn't take long for someone who was soaking wet to get hypothermia. He had the advantage of having a bit of extra padding on top of his dry clothing. Lila, in contrast, was scrawny and would lose heat much more quickly.

They continued for another ten minutes before Lila came to a stop, collapsing to her knees.

"Eldrin, we need a fire," Justin said. "This is getting dangerous."

"Stay here. Keep her as warm as you can for now."

Already, the Ranger was wandering off into the darkness. Justin didn't know what for. All he could do was grasp Lila, do whatever he could to warm her up. It didn't seem to do much good. He placed their packs on her back and covered them both with dead leaves. It wasn't much, but it was better than nothing.

"It'll be all right," he said. "You'll be warm soon."

A few minutes later, Eldrin came back. "Created something of a shelter. It's not much, but there's plenty of underbrush. I've already prepared a fire."

"Wonderful," Justin said. "I think we need to carry her."

They did so, along with Lila's pack. It wasn't easy to carry all that weight while following the Ranger through the almost pitch darkness. How the man navigated strange territory without the aid of a torch, he couldn't guess.

Justin was surprised when Eldrin brushed some branches aside and found a low ledge beneath which a small, smokeless flame crackled merrily. It wasn't large, but he could already feel its warmth. Various branches had been piled thickly in front of it, obscuring the fire from view. Even with the flame, there was no way to spot it unless you were within ten feet of it.

"Stay here," Eldrin instructed. "Get Lila out of her wet clothes and wrap her in anything dry you have. Keep her as warm as possible, as close to the fire as you can without burning her. Keep her awake and give her small sips of water, but no food just yet. Hypothermia can be tricky. I'll be back soon. I need to backtrack a bit to make sure our trail is covered. Rest is necessary, but mark my words, they will be in the vicinity within the next few hours, and morning at the latest. I shouldn't be more than a quarter of an hour. If I am, get some rest and don't wait for me."

Eldrin ducked out of the makeshift shelter and quickly disappeared into the night.

Justin worked quickly to follow the instructions. Lila wasn't even shivering; her face was pale, and her lips were blue. He retrieved a fresh change of clothes from his pack. Though he hadn't specified that the pack be waterproof when he'd bought it in Mistwatch, it seemed to have done a good job. All of his things were mercifully dry. He worked quickly to remove Lila's wet clothing. Her skin was ice cold, and he worked as fast as his own shaking hands allowed. Even if he was dry, the plunge in the Marin had taken a lot out of him. He also removed her socks and boots, then dressed her in his own dry clothing.

He offered her a bit of water, but she was too weak to even do that.

With Lila settled, he changed into dry clothes since his clothes had gotten damp from holding her. He set all the wet articles near the fire to dry, laying them on flat stones.

Justin stayed near her. Now that both of them were dry, she would warm up much more quickly. Lila revived slowly, her color gradually returning as the warmth seeped into her body. She shivered—a good sign—and her breathing steadied. She even smiled weakly at Justin, who nodded encouragingly. He wrapped her in his new coat, which had dried significantly, then sat beside her, feeding the fire with more kindling while ensuring it didn't get too big. He offered water, and this time she took a few sips.

At least an hour passed. Lila was asleep now, and Justin was nearly there too. Eldrin had still not returned, which worried him. He'd said a quarter of an hour, and it had been far more than that. If they had lost Eldrin as well as Alistair, Justin wasn't sure it was a blow they could ever recover from.

He would be back before morning. He was sure of it.

Justin carefully broke off some more deadwood for the fire. He resolved to stay awake, but the warmth of the flame and the day's events were too much. He fell asleep right where he was sitting, leaning back against the ledge.

Eldrin faced a hard decision. Well, perhaps not so difficult as it was inevitable.

Checking their trail, it became clear that they hadn't traveled far enough to create a significant gap between them and Gareth's soldiers. The trail they'd left from the river was still too fresh, making it easy to follow.

Eldrin backtracked, using his keen Ranger senses to identify and address the telltale signs of their passage. A broken branch here, boot prints in the earth there, a path cleared through beds of leaves…all these things told a story that was all too easy to put together, even for the inexperienced.

He worked swiftly and efficiently in the darkness, years of experience enabling him to erase all traces of Justin and Lila's trail. After about an hour, he found himself by the river, faced with a choice: return to Justin and Lila and hope for the best, or absolutely ensure that the two of them could escape before meeting up with them later.

The choice was hard, but it was also easy. Eldrin picked a stand of rocks downriver from the ford that would provide decent cover, then sat vigil. As the wind picked up, he was grateful for an enchantment on his clothing that ensured it dried quickly. It was practically a must for anyone who spent a lot of time in the wilds. While he had been as wet as Lila at first, he was fully dry within ten minutes.

Shadowflight returned, landing lightly on his shoulder. The bird conveyed its news.

"Closer than we'd like," Eldrin muttered, his voice low. "Much too close."

Half of Gareth's forces had fallen to Alistair's hammer, but the Shadowblade Lieutenant remained alive and determined. The onset of the night would only strengthen the undead soldiers under his command.

The falcon's report confirmed Eldrin's decision. Lila was too weak to continue, and they were beyond exhaustion. Even Eldrin, with his hardier constitution, felt his energy waning. Continuing the journey as a trio was impossible.

He needed to mislead their pursuers. It was their only chance, and he was the only one who could do it. Telling Justin his true intentions might have caused a needless argument. He had to trust the two of them to do the right thing in the morning and keep going.

Eldrin had already prepared a false trail, subtle enough to require a keen tracker but noticeable enough to be found, leading right to his position. It was their best chance to misdirect their enemies.

The Ranger didn't have to wait long. Movement on the cliffs revealed Gareth's group. They made no effort at all to conceal their presence, speaking to their confidence.

Or, Eldrin thought, their hubris.

Slowly, stealthily, Eldrin raised his new Bow of Eagle Sight. His Nature's Cloak skill kept him hidden, while the poison he'd applied to his arrow, Nightshade's Kiss, was the most potent he possessed.

The best moment to strike would be when the Shadowblade was crossing the river at the ford's deepest part. Gareth was tall enough that his shoulders and head would both be exposed, at least for a moment.

As silent as a phantom, the Ranger waited.

After about fifteen minutes, the soldiers began crossing the dark Marin. Gareth, as the leader, took the rear, just as Eldrin had hoped.

Even with Eldrin's abilities, it wouldn't be an easy shot. He was relying on his class skills to ensure accuracy, but luck would play a part, too. He waited for the wind to calm, his focus sharpening. The forest seemed to hold its breath.

The first soldiers were already fanning out, exploring the rocky western bank. Eldrin waited just a moment longer for the Shadowblade to step into the deepest part of the river. He waited for Gareth to fully perform the action to ensure his arrow would intersect the Shadowblade's path perfectly.

He loosed the arrow. It flew swiftly, almost invisible in the night. At first, it looked as though it might miss, but then the wind shifted slightly, guiding the arrow to strike Gareth's shoulder, the least protected area in his otherwise dark armor.

It landed true, and the Shadowblade slumped.

There was no sound, no scream. Panic erupted among the

soldiers. Eldrin fired several more poisoned arrows, no longer bothering to hide himself. Some hit, causing confusion and chaos. With luck, it would create a couple more dead bodies.

A fireball lit up the night, aimed in his general direction. Eldrin ducked behind the rocks, the heat from the explosion warming his back.

Now it was time to lead them on a merry chase. He melted into shadowy trees, leaving a few breadcrumbs for his enemies to follow. Alone, he could move much faster. He was in no danger of getting captured.

Eldrin had no illusions. The poison wouldn't kill Gareth; it would only slow him down while the mages dealt with the wound. Gareth's rage would drive him south along the west bank of the Marin. He would never suspect that Justin and Lila were hidden less than a mile to the north.

By the time Gareth figured out the deception, Justin and Lila would be far away, possibly heading west for the Umber Range or along the bank to Darkstream Crossing thirty miles upriver. Whatever path they chose, he planned to lose his pursuers and reunite with Justin and Lila later on.

The only thing he feared was that they might choose to go north into the Darkwood, aiming directly for Windfall. That forest teemed with monsters too dangerous for two low-level Charisma classes to handle alone, and there was an old protective magic in those woods, courtesy of the Ilvari Elves who used to live there. It was quite easy to lose one's way.

There were a few reasons they might choose that path. The first might be out of sheer ignorance, or their fear of staying too close to the river. They might also decide that the Umbers would take them too far from their original goal.

Whatever happened, Eldrin would do his best to find them.

After all, the life of a Ranger and a Paladin was a small price to pay to prevent a greater calamity.

35

A CHANGE OF PLANS

"Scholars divide the classes into four categories: damage, utility, healing, and tanking. Damage classes are the blades, striking swiftly to fell enemies. Healers are the lifeline, mending wounds and lifting spirits. Tanks are the shields, standing firm against overwhelming odds. Utility classes are those who sustain the society others fight to protect. No single role can shoulder the world alone; each is a vital piece greater than the sum of its parts."

—Professor Loryn Thalyn
  Lectures on Class Synergy

WHEN JUSTIN WOKE UP, it was full daylight. His muscles ached fiercely from the previous day's exertion. The surrounding forest was still, the air crisp and silent.

Justin almost jumped when the Voice entered his mind. In all the chaos, he had forgotten he was due for a level-up.

[You have reached Level 5. You're learning to navigate the complexities of Eyrth with grace and cunning. No longer content to be a mere spectator, you aim to become a key player, a beacon of influence.]

Justin found the words ironic. As a Socialite, he *should* have been leveling up with his charm and social skills, not out adventuring. Here in the cold forests of Northern Aranthia, the courts of Belmora seemed a world away.

Another notification flashed before him.

[You have one attribute point to distribute.]

Given the increasingly frail hope that one day he would be able to use the Amulet of Equilibrium, he allocated it to Charisma.

[Your Charisma is now 16.]

[As a Level 5 Socialite, you have unlocked your Party Tactic: Refined Aura.]

For this level, there would be no choice. But Justin looked forward to whatever his party tactic was, something that apparently all classes got at Level 5.

Refined Aura: Your mere presence inspires confidence and poise in those around you. You and all party members gain +1 to Charisma as long as you are present.

Justin smiled. It felt nice to get not just one attribute point, but two with this level. And not only that, every other party member would benefit from a +1 to Charisma.

[Remember, true presence isn't putting on a show. It is accepting who you truly are.]

As the Voice departed, he opened his interface.

Justin Talemaker
   Class: Socialite

Level: 5
Experience to Level 6: 1,169/550 (Level-up available!)

Attributes:
Power: 10
Coordination: 11 (Base 10 +1)
Endurance: 11 (Base 10 +1)
Intellect: 11 (Base 10 +1)
Spirit: 10
Charisma: 18 (Base 16 +2)

"Not bad," Justin muttered, closing the screen.

Justin stood, and as he moved, his steps became more fluid, each motion carrying a subtle, almost imperceptible elegance. His Refined Aura seemed to ripple outward, casting an aura of quiet confidence around him.

Yes, something had definitely changed.

Justin looked around the campsite. Lila was still sleeping, utterly exhausted from yesterday's ordeal, while there was no sign of Eldrin at all. The emptiness left by the Ranger's absence made Justin uneasy. He had promised to be back in a quarter of an hour, and it had been at least eight hours, judging by the sun's position.

Justin didn't want to think about what could have possibly happened. It certainly had something to do with Lieutenant Gareth, but the fact that he and Lila were still alive suggested that Eldrin had been successful in covering their tracks.

He wasn't sure what to do, but they were on their own, at least for now. The Ranger had said not to wait for him, but the prospect of striking out in the wilds alone, with no guidance whatsoever and a high-level Shadowblade hunting them down, was nothing short of terrifying.

He felt torn between waking Lila and letting her rest longer. In the end, he shook her awake.

She stirred, blinking against the harsh morning light.

"Eldrin's gone," Justin whispered.

Lila suddenly became alert, sitting up. "Gone? What do you mean?"

"Process your level up first," Justin said. "We can talk about it in a few minutes."

Lila did so, apparently going through the motions quickly. "Done. So, what happened?"

"He left last night, saying it wouldn't be fifteen minutes."

Her face paled. "So, what do we do now? Go look for him?"

"Before leaving, he said that if he didn't come back, we should move on."

Lila shook her head. "I don't like that one bit. Did he leave us?"

Justin shook his head. "No way. After everything, you think he'd bail?"

"Well, the other option is worse. If he hasn't returned, that would mean he's..." She trailed off. "I'm sorry. With Alistair, and now Eldrin...the thought is too horrible to entertain."

That Eldrin, along with Alistair, was dead would make their situation beyond hopeless. Both men had sacrificed so much for him, and worse, Justin didn't understand the reason.

"He's a Ranger," Justin said. "Maybe he wanted to cover our tracks a bit more. Make sure we really couldn't be found."

"You'd think he would have returned, though," Lila said. "Something is definitely wrong."

"If he didn't come back, it was for one reason. It would endanger us in some way. Maybe Gareth and the rest were closer than we thought. Maybe he had to create a false trail or something. Lead them away."

"Huh. Yeah, that could be it. I prefer that theory over anything else." She frowned in thought. "If that's the case, though, eventually they'll catch on that they've been fooled. And turn right back around."

"That has to be why. He intends to catch up with us later. He has Shadowflight. That means that once he shakes them, he can use his Pathfinder's Pace to catch up to us. It might take him a few days, but he'll manage it."

"Either way you cut it, we're on our own for a while. We need to put some ground between us and Gareth.

It was a terrifying proposition. Alistair and Eldrin had been the ones keeping them alive so far, and Justin couldn't imagine just the two of them—neither of them a combat class—surviving the wilds of this forest. Not with dire wolves and maybe even worse.

"Okay," Lila said. "So, the question is, what's our plan? Where do you think Eldrin planned to go?"

Justin shrugged. "I don't know. Maybe he didn't even *have* a plan. All we know is that eventually, he was going to turn east, which would lead to the Plainsway. Right?"

"I would suggest an alternate plan," Lila said. "The Plainsway plan happened way back in Highcliff, and I would argue that things have changed."

"Okay. I'm listening."

"The closest big city besides Highcliff, of course, is Windfall," Lila said. "But it's about a hundred miles to the northwest. Not exactly the way we want to be going. But leading out from Windfall is the Northway, a well-established road that runs just south of the Seraphims. Assuming we can reach Windfall, we can head east from there on the Northway. It's less expected by our enemies. We could take that road all the way to Draegor's Keep, and from there, head south to Mont Elea. Better yet, in Windfall we can resupply and blend in. Without Eldrin, we can't hope to live off the land. We have plenty of gold. Enough, perhaps, to buy a carriage the rest of the way. Disguise ourselves as nobles, maybe."

"That would be nice," Justin said. "Much faster."

"The distances are too great for just the two of us to walk all the way to Mont Elea without Pathfinder's Pace," Lila said. "But the downside is, the roads are going to be more dangerous. If we lose them in the forest, they know we'll pop out on a major highway eventually. Worse, if we're slogging in the wilds too long, they have time to set up a spy network in every major city we might think of going to. I say we try to make Windfall as quickly as we can, before anyone there is on the lookout for us. We're not truly safe until we reach Mont Elea."

Justin was quiet. Again, he couldn't help but wonder just what about him was so important. Alistair knew something, and for that matter, it seemed Eldrin did too.

What about Lila? Did she know something, too?

"Did either of them say why the Baron wants to get me so much?" Justin asked. "Why place his Death Mark on me in the first place?"

"If there's a reason, it was never said to me," Lila said. "Clearly, from the first, the Baron saw something useful in you. Maybe it has something to do with your past. This other world you're from."

"But how would the Baron even know about that?" Justin asked. "It doesn't make sense. And if he didn't want me to escape, he could have trapped us before we even walked out the door."

Lila thought for a moment. "Well, there's more to this than we understand, that's for certain. Perhaps he was content to let you leave and learn more first. He had no reason to suspect you'd ever discover the Death Mark, and Alistair's timely arrival put a major kink in his plan. Clearly, he had his eyes on you from the moment you left."

"Maybe," Justin said. "We should eat first. I'm starving."

They broke out a quick breakfast of hard cheese, dried fruit, and strips of salted meat. Justin tried to ignore how little food was left in the pack. Getting to Windfall on empty stomachs might prove a tricky proposition.

"So, what's your party tactic?" Justin asked.

"Unified Cadence," Lila replied. "It gives the party a 5% boost to damage and healing anytime I sing."

"That sounds like a nice bonus," Justin said. "And it makes a big difference when spread across a lot of party members."

"We should get going," Lila said. "We've been talking too much already. And...thanks for helping me out last night. Not my best moment."

"No problem. I was only saved by the Ring of Hygiene. Apparently, it dries you off as well."

"Supremely useful," Lila agreed, though her brow furrowed in concern. "Maybe that's why Eldrin never came back. Do you think it was the cold that did him in?"

"It's hard to imagine that," Justin said. "If that's the case, I think the Baron's men would have discovered us by now."

"Maybe," Lila said, a hint of uncertainty in her voice.

"Eldrin will find us, you'll see. For now, our only goal is to head north. Are we sure we don't want to backtrack to the road after a few days? This forest looks like rough going."

"We can discuss it later. To be honest, I'm not sure what the country is like between here and Windfall. I know it's a lot of hills and a lot of forests. Hopefully, nothing too scary lives in them. Right now, the important thing is getting some distance."

"One thing at a time," Justin said. "Shall we?"

They packed up quickly, burying the ashes of their fire, which were already cold. He felt a pang of anxiety as they left their shelter, but there was no avoiding it. The forest awaited.

The trees loomed tall and dense, their branches forming a thick canopy overhead. The air was still, the only sound being the crunch of leaves underfoot. Justin took out his map. Though they were far outside its range, the enchantment would still point them north.

They kept walking, the underbrush thick with ferns and brambles. The ground was uneven, littered with rocks and fallen branches, making their progress slow and arduous. The lack of Pathfinder's Pace was all too clear. They were working twice as hard for half the miles.

The sun climbed higher in the sky. From time to time, Justin glanced backward, seeing no signs of pursuit. The River Marin flowed off to their right, perhaps a couple of miles away. There was nothing but trees and hills in all directions, and no sign of the Plainsway.

The forest seemed to close in around them. Without Eldrin and Alistair's comforting presence, the woods felt more sinister. Justin couldn't shake the feeling of being exposed, with no one to guide or protect them.

"Damn," Justin muttered. "This is rough. Would it be a bad idea to sing a song to give us a bit more Endurance?"

"Yes," Lila said firmly. "Absolutely."

They kept plodding on through the afternoon. It seemed too quiet, as if the world itself were holding its breath.

"Probably time to think about shelter," Lila suggested, as the sun neared the top of the western mountains. "Before it gets too dark."

As they crested the next hill, Justin scanned the landscape to the north. About half a mile away stood what appeared to be a decrepit watchtower. The stone structure was weathered and crumbling, with ivy creeping up its sides. The roof had partially collapsed, leaving jagged edges silhouetted against the sky.

"Is that too obvious a hiding spot?"

"Looks like a sure shelter to me," Lila said. "Either way, I don't think they know we've gone this way and we're a whole day ahead at this point."

"Someone else might think it's a good place to shelter," Justin said.

"No smoke," Lila said. "We can sit here for a few minutes and see if anything is moving."

It was good enough for Justin. He was certain Eldrin would have discouraged it, but with Eldrin absent, they had to do what they thought was best. They weren't covering their tracks effectively, anyway. They just wouldn't go to the top of the tower, where their movements might be visible from a distance.

They watched for a while, and it seemed the place was empty, at least from the outside. Nothing moved around it. It was the best they could hope for as the sun started sinking closer to the top of the Umber Range in the west.

It took another thirty minutes to reach the tower's base. The surrounding terrain was uneven, with stones and rubble scattered about. The air was cooler, and the shadows lengthened. A broken path led out north from the tower, accompanied by crumbling stone fences. That path quickly became lost in the northern forest. At least the journey tomorrow might not be so bad, assuming the path continued in the same direction. Justin assumed this place must have once been part of the Kingdom of Highcliff, having since fallen into ruin. Perhaps there would be a town or hamlet to the north where they could resupply.

"Nothing but to go in," Lila said. "We should be careful. Make sure we're the only ones here."

The tower was especially quiet. If it were a bandit's hideout, they would have made their presence obvious by now. Or so Justin's thinking went.

Justin gave his cane a twirl; the movement was fluid and confident.

"Show-off," Lila said with a smirk.

Her smile vanished when, as soon as they breached the open threshold of the tower, a sudden explosion of crimson light sent them sprawling back. Justin was momentarily stunned, and it took a couple of seconds before he could come to his senses.

Whatever this attack had been, Gentleman's Rebuff hadn't blocked it.

"Stay where you are," a gruff voice commanded. "Or the next blast won't be a warning."

Justin looked up, his eyes widening. The figure before them was definitely not what he expected.

36

THE UNLIKELY WARDEN

"There is a quiet beauty to the northern forests of Aranthia—a haunting beauty, really. Beneath the silent boughs of the Northwood, you are as likely to stumble upon the ruins of an age long forgotten as you are on a pristine grove untouched by mortal hands for centuries. It is a beauty born of time and decay, where nature reclaims what was once lost and whispers to those who dare to wander. Perhaps beauty is not meant to be seen, but simply to exist, waiting patiently for the rare souls who choose to seek it."

—Pallin Longstride
  Echoes of the Wilderlands

JUSTIN'S HEART RACED, brandishing his cane and preparing for whatever might come next. Lila stood beside him, her hand subtly resting on the hilt of a throwing knife.

In the dim light at the top of the stone steps stood an orc, and one unlike any he had ever seen. This orc was younger, which Justin could tell from his smooth skin and lack of wrinkles. He sensed the orc was not just young but likely a teenager. It was something about his bearing, the lack of assurance. His skin was a distinctive shade of gray, contrasting with the few green-skinned orcs Justin had encountered before. He stood around six feet tall, with a lean build that suggested agility rather than strength. His amber eyes flickered with a mix of caution and uncertainty.

The orc held a basic wooden staff and wore gray mage robes that were frayed and patched in several places, which also evidenced red bloodstains. His black hair was short and unruly, and his tusks were small, barely protruding from his lower lip. A distinct brand was visible on his forehead, a circular mark with two intersecting lines. Despite his initial aggressive stance, the orc's posture was not that of a warrior ready for battle but rather that of someone hoping to deter trouble without causing harm.

"Stay where you are!" the orc commanded again, his voice gruff yet tinged with nervousness. "There's plenty more where that came from!"

Justin raised his hands slowly, signaling peace. "We're not here to fight."

He took a moment to observe the young orc, noting the signs of fear and uncertainty in his eyes.

Lila glanced at Justin, her eyes questioning, but Justin was confident in his assessment. Perhaps it was his heightened Charisma, but he could read the young orc like a book. The orc was far more scared than they were and didn't want any trouble.

Justin took a careful step forward, maintaining eye contact. "My name's Justin." His tone was soothing. "This is Lila. We're just looking for shelter for the night. We didn't mean to intrude. What's your name?"

The orc's grip on his staff tightened, his eyes darting between Justin and Lila. There was a moment of silence, and Justin could see the internal struggle in the orc's eyes.

"You...you shouldn't be here," the orc stammered, his voice lacking the previous intensity. "This place...it's not safe."

Lila raised an eyebrow. "Not safe? From what?"

The orc hesitated, searching for words.

Justin sensed an opportunity. He made his voice as gentle as he could. "Look. We're not here to cause trouble. Are you alone?"

"I'm warning you!" the orc said, raising his staff. "My friends will be back anytime! You don't want to be here when that happens."

Justin knew it was a bluff. "You don't look like someone who wants to fight. And we just want to talk. Can we do that at least?"

The orc's shoulders slumped slightly. To Justin's surprise, his words seemed to reach him, and he looked down, avoiding their gaze. "Fine. What is it you want? Say it and then be on your way. I...I could still make you leave. You'd best remember that!"

Justin nodded, understanding the underlying fear and loneliness in the orc's words. "We won't stay if it's a problem. I was thinking maybe we can help each other out. We've been through a lot, and it seems like you have too. We have food. We'd be happy to share it."

The orc licked his thin, gray lips, unable to hide his interest. "I'm not hungry. I've got plenty to eat in here."

Already, Lila was reaching for her pack, producing her supplies. "We're happy to share. No pressure."

The orc looked up, his amber eyes meeting Lila's. There was a flicker of something—hope, perhaps, or maybe just a desperate need for connection. But he was still guarded, not willing to share more. Justin sensed this hesitation, recognizing it from his own experiences of feeling out of place and misunderstood.

"We've all got our stories," Justin continued. "And sometimes, it's easier to get through them together. You don't have to tell us everything, but maybe we can start with your name?"

The orc hesitated again before finally sighing. "Kargan," he said, his voice barely above a whisper. "My name is Kargan."

Justin smiled warmly, sensing a breakthrough. "Nice to meet you, Kargan. Why don't we sit and talk? Eat some dinner? Maybe we can figure out a way to help each other."

Kargan nodded slowly, the last remnants of his defensive stance fading away. He seemed to relax slightly, though there was still a wary look in his eyes. He wasn't ready to fully trust them yet, but at least he would talk.

"I'll eat. After that, I'd kindly ask you to get on your way. This tower is mine."

"No problem," Justin said. "We can eat right out here if you'd like."

Lila handed out the food, a simple meal of bread, cheese, and dried meat, and Kargan tore into his portion, eating it in under half a minute. Justin felt a pang of sympathy for the orc, and Lila's green eyes widened with pity.

"You poor thing," she said quietly. "What are you doing out here all alone?"

Kargan clenched his fists on his staff, looking like he was about to defend himself, but something about Lila's voice just caused his stance to soften. Then, before Justin knew it, Kargan became wracked with sobs. He cried for a solid minute or two, and all Justin could do was watch him. Comforting him felt too risky at that moment.

"We're here for you," Justin said gently, once the sobbing had subsided a bit. "Let's get inside at least, get a fire going. It'll cheer you up."

Kargan nodded at last, seeming to recognize that these two strangers didn't mean him any harm.

They retreated to within the tower, where a low fire had burned down to coals. Kargan stoked it with the base of his staff, adding a couple of logs. Then he gave a harsh sniff, wiping his nose with his robes. "I...apologize for that. It was...weak of me."

"No need to apologize," Lila said. "Sometimes, you just need to cry it out. Gods know I've done it plenty of times in the last few weeks."

Kargan gave a singular nod, the flames dancing in his amber eyes. "I suppose you want to know what a young orc like me is doing way out here, away from the clan halls."

Justin didn't push for more, knowing that prying would just close Kargan off further. Sometimes, the best thing to say was nothing at all. He knew this intrinsically, but he didn't know where the knowledge had come from. Conversation wasn't just push and pull. Sometimes, conversation was simply sitting still and allowing truths to settle.

After a few minutes, Justin cleared his throat. "How about we tell our story first?"

"If you'd like," Kargan replied, his tone neutral.

"I'll be honest," Justin began. "We're on the run from some bad types. We think they'll be headed this way in a day or two."

"Hmm. Thanks for the information. Why are they chasing you?"

"That's a long story. We're not thieves or anything. Just in the wrong place at the wrong time."

"Heh. I can relate to that."

"What do you mean?" Lila asked.

"It's the story of my life." Kargan paused for a moment, reflecting. "Being born a gray-skin is bad enough, so I'm used to being alone. You probably know that we orcs value Power and Endurance above all." He gave a bitter laugh. "Well, you can see from my stature, I'm hardly larger than a grown human."

"You're still strong," Lila protested. "Very!"

"Not for an orc," he said. "I've given up on the idea that I'm going to be a mighty warrior. There's smithing, of course, but to make armor like we do, it requires raw strength. Master Grudak didn't want to apprentice me unless I could get my hands on a Craftsman Core. Not likely. Such cores only go to the strongest of the brood, not a runt like me."

"The way you talk about yourself," Lila said. "It hurts my heart, Kargan."

"Does it? Well, I'm used to it, you might say. Sorry if I've made you uncomfortable. We esteem ourselves the way others esteem us. The clan is like a forge that shapes its children. If you don't fit the mold, you end up discarded."

Justin felt a burst of realization. "Is that what happened to you, Kargan?"

The orc was silent for a long time, and from that silence, Justin knew he had hit the nail on the head.

"A gray skin. A mage. A weakling. I suppose it wasn't hard to figure out."

"Mages are powerful, though," Lila said. "You knocked us back a good five paces!"

Kargan laughed bitterly. "Powerful? My clan would say I'm weak to use such a spell. Magic is for the weak, for those who can't wield a hammer or war axe, who can't shape armor or shields or useful tools. Magic is not for the orcs. Orcs are only born with Power or Endurance Cores. Magic isn't even a consideration."

"But you're a mage," Justin said. "How is it possible for you to be a mage if orcs have only Power or Endurance Cores?"

"That's...a long story."

"Well, we have time," Lila said. "I mean, only if you want to share it. It might take the burden off your shoulders."

Kargan stared into the flames doubtfully. "I've been out here a long time. Over a month now. You two are the only ones I've seen. Maybe...maybe it's not a bad idea."

"How'd you become a mage?" Justin asked again. "Orcs really only have one of two Core Attributes?"

"That's right," he said. "In return, we are hardier than other races. And stronger. And we can see well in the dark. It's give and take, I suppose. Humans can take on any core. It's kind of your thing."

He took a deep breath, weighing his decision to share. Justin and Lila waited as Kargan began his tale.

The orc stared into the flames, his expression a mix of bitterness and resignation. "I suppose it all started with the raid. Our clan often sends out raiding parties to claim resources and, occasionally, magical items from nearby territories and Vaults. It's not unusual; it's just the way things are done among us orcs. We prize Power and Endurance, and whatever we can use to enhance those is worth the risk. Might is right, mostly."

He paused, looking down at his hands, which were wrapped around the staff. "There was this Vault in the mountain valleys to the northwest of here—a place of ancient magic, dangerous but filled with treasures. The clan elders decided it was worth the risk, and they sent a party to clear it out. I wasn't part of the main group; I was just there to assist with carrying supplies and doing the menial tasks the warriors couldn't be bothered with."

Kargan's voice grew softer, and he seemed to withdraw into himself. "Inside the Vault, they found a core. A Blood Warden core. It's a rare type. It's one of two mage cores that use the Endurance Attribute, the other being Blood Mage. The Blood Warden core grants the ability to protect and heal—supportive magic, really. Not the power we orcs value. Sometimes, some of the lower-caste women will take it on, but even then, they have to live far away from the clans and aren't allowed to marry or bear children. They downright look down upon the Blood Warden class. It uses one's very Life Force—a sacred thing to us orcs—spending it to create wards and healing spells and stuff. Basically, it's not in keeping with Gor'Thaak, so it's tolerated at best."

"Gor'Thaak?" Justin asked.

"The Duology," Kargan explained. "I suppose humans know little about it. It's our god, I guess you could say. Male and female rolled into one. Male for Power, Gor. Female for Endurance, Thaak. If it doesn't follow Gor'Thaak, well, it's probably outright heresy. Though Blood Warden is an Endurance class, it directly attacks one's Life Force to heal and protect, so it is sacrilege."

"I see," Lila said.

Kargan nodded. "We orcs have little respect for magic anyway, and those who use it are often seen as weak or untrustworthy. It's not in keeping with Gor'Thaak. The clan was disappointed with the core, especially given the blood that was spilled for it, but given its rarity, they thought it would fetch a good price in the market, even if it wasn't useful to us. Failing that, one of the lower women would be forced to take it on. Despite the class being reviled, the elders are wise enough to understand it has its uses in healing the sick and injured."

He swallowed hard, the memories clearly painful. "But then, as we were leaving the Vault, we were attacked. A pack of dire wolves, led by an alpha wolf twice the size of a normal one. It was chaos. The warriors fought bravely, but we were outnumbered and surprised, and the party was weakened from the raid. I...I panicked. I didn't know what to do. In the chaos, I was bitten badly on the arm." Kargan held up his right arm, but there was no injury to speak of. "One warrior drew the beast away from me. Somehow, I found myself alone, hiding in the baggage cart with the core. It was glowing, pulsing with energy. I was certain we were all going to die, and it was the only way I'd get to live. I knew it was forbidden. But all the same... I felt it calling to me. So...I absorbed it."

Kargan looked up, his eyes reflecting the flickering firelight. "And for the first time in my life, I heard the Creator's voice. I felt something like acceptance for the first time in my life. The core bonded with me as if it had always belonged. It was like nothing I'd ever felt before—a rush of power and energy. As a Level 0, of course, I had nothing but my main class skill, Blood Aegis."

"What does that do?" Justin asked.

"It's what you ran into when you approached. It creates a dome of protection, knocking anything back that gets too close. Plus, anyone inside gets boosted healing from me. It will get more powerful as I level up."

"That does sound powerful," Lila said. "What's your class boon?"

"That one is called Forge of Life. You see, because Blood Wardens use their very Life Force for their spells, we need to recover it more quickly than others. Forge of Life gives us fast natural healing."

"Sounds useful," Justin said.

Kagan continued his story. "Among the cart, I found this old staff among the loot. Somehow, I knew it would work to focus my magic. Because of Blood Aegis, I felt brave enough to contribute to the defense. I wouldn't say I turned back the tide, but for the first time, I felt like I was contributing to the clan. Some part of me hoped the others would see that, too." His shoulders slumped. "Of course, it was too much to hope for. To them, I had stolen the core. And worse, I had become something they despised: a mage. A male Blood Warden. It's like an oxymoron to the orcish clans. There is no deeper shame among us."

Justin felt a deep sympathy for Kargan's plight, understanding the pain of being ostracized for being different.

Kargan clenched his fists, his gray knuckles turning white. "They took me back to the clan for judgment. The elders were beyond furious. My parents...they looked like they wanted to die from shame. The elders accused me of treachery, of dishonoring our traditions. For going against Gor'Thaak. My father and mother spoke not a word in my defense. In their eyes, I could see the truth. I was no longer their son. The elders...they said I had tainted myself with magic. I was no longer fit to be part of the clan. They exiled me, cast me out with nothing but the clothes on my back and this staff. And of course, this brand you see on my forehead, so every other clan knows what I am. A mage and an exile. They let me keep the staff. I'd already bound it to myself, so it was of no use to them."

Kargan's shoulders slumped further, the weight of his story clearly bearing down on him. "I've been out here ever since, trying to survive on my own. The magic is useful, but it can't replace the life I lost. I just...wish I could go back. I don't know what possessed me to grab that core. I just...I just wanted to belong, I guess. To help. For once in my life."

Justin's throat clamped up, but he knew he had to be the one doing the comforting. Lila looked as if she wanted to hug Kargan, but she was also restraining herself.

"You just wanted to help," Justin said. "You said you did it to save yourself, and that's true. But deep down, all you've ever wanted was to help others. That's why the core called to you. Religion can be funny. They're just a collection of traditions that are wrapped up and given a name. They might be useful for the time in which they were written. But times change. That might sound like heresy to you, but clearly, you want to use your powers to help people."

Kargan nodded, sniffling a bit. "That...speaks to my soul."

"What level are you at now?" Lila asked.

Kargan grunted. "Just Level 2. There are few opportunities to practice my magic out here. That spell that knocked you back is one of the two I have. It also helps hide anyone inside of it, like if you're camping out in the wild."

"It's pretty powerful already," Lila pointed out. "That can come in handy out here. That's why this tower seemed empty from a distance. The spell was concealing it."

"What's your other spell?" Justin asked.

"Sacrificial Armor," Kargan said. "It lets me take some of my Life Force and use it to protect myself for a while. Or an ally. Useful, I'm sure, but I haven't had the chance to try it out in a fight."

"I'm not trying to offend, but it's crazy to say that you're not strong," Justin said. "It's not just your class, Kargan. It's your desire to help others. This tower is the last place you should be."

"It is the place society has deemed fit for me."

"There are orcs out there in the world," Lila said. "I've seen them. I've even seen some with similar brands on their foreheads. You aren't unique in being exiled."

"They could be criminals, or worse," Kargan said.

"Or they could be just like you," Justin pointed out. "Either way, what do you plan to do once you run out of supplies?"

Kargan didn't have an answer for that. Something told Justin that he intended to starve himself.

"Listen," Justin said. "I'm an outsider, too. I have been for my whole life. I also have a class that many people find useless. It doesn't feel great to be called that."

Kargan nodded in recognition. "What class is that?"

"Socialite."

"Ah," Kargan said. "I see how others might say that it's useless."

Lila couldn't stop herself from snickering.

"My point exactly," Justin said good-naturedly. "I've made the best of it. If I could be a badass Blood Warden who got to cast blood magic, I'd do it in a heartbeat. That said, this class has surprised me. It's gotten Lila and me out of some tough spots. The point being, you never know your worth until you try. And sometimes, people's beliefs prevent them from seeing your value. It just means you haven't found the right people yet."

"The right clan," Kargan finished. "Yes. I see what you mean." He frowned a bit. "This…is a lot to take in. And it's rather late. I've…probably shared too much. It's weak to share feelings."

"You did just fine," Justin assured him. "And sharing your feelings isn't a weakness. Vulnerability can be a sign of strength."

Kargan frowned, as if the concept were foreign to him. "That… makes little sense."

"Think about your magic," Justin said. "You take your Life Force, which weakens you, right?"

"Yes."

"And you apply that Life Force elsewhere, creating strength. It's like that."

"Hmm. Maybe there's something to it."

It was quiet for a while after that. Lila yawned.

"We should get some rest," Justin said. "Before we do, though, I'd like to make you an offer."

"An offer? What do you mean?"

"Lila and I could use someone like you. We're heading for Windfall. We've…lost two of our friends recently."

Kargan's expression became somber. "My condolences."

"They were our guides. I'm not sure we can find our way alone out here. You're probably not safe to stay in this tower for much longer, anyway."

"I have my Blood Aegis; I can manage."

Lila leaned forward. "No disrespect, but with the ones chasing us, that won't cut it. You need to come with us for your own safety. Windfall could use someone with your abilities, Kargan. The Mage Guild is widespread over all of Serenthel. It wouldn't be easy, but there is a place for you in the world. I know it."

"Would they help a Blood Warden like me?" he asked. "Our magic works…differently. From what I've researched, many people distrust it, even other mages. *Especially* other mages. It's Blood Magic, so technically, it's Chaos Magic."

"Chaos Magic?"

"One of the four Spiritual Elements," Kargan said, looking at him strangely. "Like Death Magic, its casting is banned in most of Serenthel. It's a different school, if that makes sense. And it's frowned upon at best."

Justin wasn't sure he totally understood, but he got the essence of what Kargan was saying. "The world is a big place, Kargan. Not everyone will understand or accept you, but there will always be those who value what you can offer. The right people are out there; it's just a matter of finding them. Windfall could be a start."

Kargan nodded, contemplating Justin's words. "I know the way to Windfall. I...could take you there. Maybe." He shook his head. "I'll have to sleep on it."

"Of course," Justin said. "If you're ready to sleep, we can head back outside, as promised."

Kargan shook his head. "No need for that. Both of you have been generous. Among my people, it's often said: Better to share a fire than to burn alone. For the first time, I'm realizing it's not just about fires." He stood. "Let me recast my ward. It'll keep weaker creatures away and do a good job of hiding us, at least until morning. It might help hide us if enemies head this way."

"We would be grateful," Lila said. "Thank you, Kargan."

The orc nodded. "Don't mention it."

The orc took a few steps away, raising his arms wide, staff in hand. He gave a pained grunt as an aura of crimson light spread from him, quickly fading into the night. Justin felt a sense of peace. It was subtle, but recognizable. An effect of the spell, he was sure.

"Did...that hurt?" Lila asked.

Kargan had his hands on his knees, wincing in pain. "Just a bit. But it's worth it for the safety. Plus, I'll recover quickly." For the first time, his lips upturned in a smile. "Nice to get triple the experience for protecting two more people instead of just me."

Justin and Lila got out their bedrolls, settling down for the night on the opposite side of the fire. Kargan watched the flames, seeming to ruminate.

"Good night, Kargan," Justin said.

The orc grunted in response. "Night."

As the conversation ended, Justin received a notification.

[You have gained 20 experience points. Your experience stands at 1,189/550. Level-up available!]

Justin realized the experience had come from winning the young orc's trust. A less experienced person might have fumbled it.
Justin closed his eyes and was soon asleep.

37

NORTHWARD BOUND

"They call blood magic wicked, as if morality is anything but a matter of perspective. So what if my power flows from the Nether, where Death and Chaos reign? A world without Death is stagnant, and a world without Chaos is lifeless. And in the end, who's to say the Aether is any holier when it too feeds on the struggles of the living?"

—Blood Mage Vaelith Sarn
  Crimson Truths

JUSTIN WOKE up to the first rays of sunlight falling through the broken roof of the tower. As soon as he had his first conscious thought—that the fire was low—the Voice entered his mind.

[You have reached Level 6. Setbacks are inevitable, but by keeping your eyes on the horizon, you will find that each step becomes easier.]

Justin thought that was an apt way to describe things. The Voice seemed to change its little "encouraging notes" to him based on what was going on in his life. It was intelligent, then, or at least self-adapting.

He remembered what Kargan had said about it—that it was the Creator. Lila had said something about it being "the Voice of Veyrith."

He would have to ask Lila about that later when he got the chance.

[You have one attribute point to distribute.]

It wasn't even a thought anymore. He locked it into Charisma without hesitation.

[Your Charisma is now 17.]

[As a Level 6 Socialite, you have unlocked your next boon. Choose wisely—there is no going back.]

Justin looked over both options.

Polished Footwork: With every step, you are always exactly where you need to be. Your ability to keep time and rhythm greatly improves your dancing, while in combat, you gain a 10% increase in your movement speed.

Add Injury to Insult (Rare): Nothing cuts deeper than a sharp tongue followed by an even sharper blade. While any enemy is under the effect of your Poison Barb, you deal an additional 50% damage to them.

Justin's eye immediately lit upon the "rare" marker. He had already gotten a rare skill, but now, he might be adding a rare boon to his collection. He wondered if he was just getting lucky, or if something else was influencing it.

First, he considered Polished Footwork. It looked more generally useful, its advantage being that it didn't rely on Poison Barb to be effective. Combat speed didn't mean just hitting faster but also having the ability to reposition or even escape entirely.

Justin was also intrigued by the possibility of becoming a more natural dancer. It was a talent that took years to master, so getting a leg up on it would certainly be nice. True, it wouldn't do him any good out here, but if he ever found himself in that sort of situation, well, it was a nice boon indeed.

Add Injury to Insult, on the other hand, was even more tempting. It was an opportunity to shore up a major weakness. The boon didn't say Justin had to stun an enemy with his Poison Barb. An enemy merely had to be suffering its effects. From what he could tell, Poison Barb always did *something*, whether that was causing hesitation or making an enemy stumble. Under the auspices of the boon, that would count as being "affected" by it.

The 10% boost to combat speed was nice, but in Justin's mind, it was clearly outclassed by the possibility of hitting 50% harder, even if the window for dealing extra damage was somewhat narrow.

[You have chosen Add Injury to Insult. The art of conversation is not merely a matter of charm; it's knowing how to wield words as weapons. May your words be salt in the wound.]

With those words, the Voice departed.
As with every level up, Justin summoned his interface.

Justin Talemaker
    Class: Socialite
    Level: 6
    Experience to Level 7: 639/720

For the first time since Silverton, Justin didn't have enough banked experience to get a level up on his next sleep. The experience requirements were already getting much larger.

His quick rise to Level 6, however, was all because of running into two Vaults and having Alistair and Eldrin do most of the legwork. True, he'd found pivotal ways to contribute that had earned him the experience, but he knew Vaults were dangerous places usually not suited to characters of his class.

Most Socialites probably had to level up the old-fashioned way: schmoozing, manipulating, lying, bargaining, charming, networking, flattering, and persuading. Justin had done little of that upon entering Eyrth, but he had the feeling that more of that would be in his future.

With a beefy base 17 in Charisma, modified to 19 with the Cane of Valoria and his Refined Presence party tactic, with a possible 21 when activating Dandy's Swagger, he would be a massive social force, at least among unclassed individuals, and even among classes that had invested little in their own Charisma Attribute.

Of course, most of that was useless out here in the wilds, but it wouldn't be that way forever.

Or so he told himself.

Lila was next to wake up, taking on a look of silent rumination. If she was anything like Justin, she would have her own last level up to process.

Once done, she turned to face him. "New boon. Descant Defense."

"Oh? And what does that do?"

"Basically, anytime I sing, it reduces damage to the party by 5%. Plus, anytime I start a new song, it casts Minor Regeneration on the entire party."

"Is that a healing spell?"

"Yes, a small one. But every little bit helps. It only lasts fifteen seconds, though, and I can only switch songs once a minute to keep it going. I figured, combined with Unified Cadence, we're getting 10% damage reduction across the board."

"That sounds like it will help a lot!" Justin said. "Since it's a boon, it just works automatically, right?"

Lila nodded. "That's right."

"What did you put the point in this time?" Justin asked.

She smiled. "Charisma. I'm a Bard. Time to do bardic things."

Kargan continued sleeping, snoring softly by the fire. Clearly, the young mage had become more comfortable with them. Justin and Lila prepped breakfast, something hot for the road, but not even the smell was enough to wake the orc.

"Teenagers," Justin said.

The word seemed to rouse Kargan, who rolled over and blinked his eyes drearily. "Huh?"

"Time to eat," Justin said. "Do you like oatmeal?"

"Sure, I do," Kargan said.

He immediately tucked in, clearly still ravenous. He would have eaten more, but at least he left some for Justin and Lila.

After eating, Justin looked the orc up and down. "So, have you thought about our offer?"

Kargan grunted. "Yes. I'll go with you. At least as far as Windfall."

"Yay!" Lila said. "You've made the right choice."

"Not much of a future here, anyway. The food is tough enough to forage already, and it'll get even worse come winter. I was thinking about what you said, Justin. Maybe there's a place for me in Windfall. It never hurts to try, right?"

"Glad to hear it. Let's make it official."

Justin mentally invited Kargan to join his party.

[Kargan has joined the party.]

"Whoa," Kargan said. "A Charisma buff. And Lila's Unified Cadence looks like it'll be useful, too."

"We should all make a pact with each other; that way we are familiar with each other's abilities," Justin said. "It'll come in handy to know what we're all capable of if we run into trouble."

Kargan didn't seem comfortable with this. "Err...is that really necessary at this point? I can just tell you what I'm capable of. It's not much."

Justin exchanged a glance with Lila. She didn't seem to think it was strange that Kargan was unwilling to share. On the contrary, from her amused expression, perhaps Justin was being a bit too forward in his request.

"Sorry if I made things awkward," Justin said. "Sure, that works."

Kargan cleared his throat. "Well, it's not much, to be honest. Like I said, my class skill is a spell called Blood Aegis. Basically, it creates a shield that repels all damage around me. Anyone inside it benefits from increased healing from my spells. Plus, it helps to hide whatever is inside, as long as they're already undetected, if that makes sense. It's useful for traveling in the wilds and such. It's not foolproof, but it helps."

"Got it," Justin said.

"Then there's my class boon, Forge of Life. That increases my natural healing by a lot. Which helps, since I cast blood magic spells."

"How fast is a lot?" Lila asked.

Kargan looked at her seriously. "Well, for example, I accidentally cut myself with a knife while cutting some meat the other day. It was pretty deep. The wound healed in under a minute."

"Wow," she said. "That's amazing!"

"That's blood magic for you," Kargan said. "And a lot of people don't like it."

"Well, you have nothing to fear from us," Lila said. "I'm a pretty practical person, and most Daelorians are pretty liberal about these things. Maybe you should consider moving there."

"Hmm. I've heard as much. I guess I will consider it."

"And the last one is a shield, right?" Justin asked. "Sacrificial Armor?"

Kargan nodded, his tusks protruding. "That's right. This one is a specific shield spell that covers one person. It mitigates all damage until it runs out." He shrugged. "That's it. At least for now. I'm pretty close to Level 3, thankfully. I'm not sure what my next spell will be. Hopefully, I'll find out soon. For now, it seems like my class is meant to absorb a lot of damage."

"Interesting," Justin said. "It's rare to see a mage who takes on the role of a tank."

"I'm not sure what my role is yet, to be honest," Kargan said. "Just learning as I go. I'm confused about your skills, though, Justin. Lila seems to be a standard damage dealer with those knives. I can see she's a Bard from my interface, but it doesn't seem that your class gives you many combat-related skills."

"I have my cane for that," Justin said, giving it a flourish. "You'd be surprised how much damage this can do."

"Hmm." The orc didn't seem convinced. "Anyway, there's an old path that leads north from here. I actually followed it down from the mountains. It's rough going at points, but it beats heading into the wilds. I remember there being a fork in the road, so when we find it, we can choose the path that leads north to Windfall. From there, it's just a matter of heading for the Northway, and then to Windfall from there."

Justin remembered seeing the path. "Any towns on the way? We need to resupply."

"There are none in the Darkwood itself. There's Darkstream Crossing on the eastern side of the forest, about twenty miles northeast. If you're being chased, and they know you're up here, that's the next natural spot for them to check."

"No, thanks," Lila said. "Is the Darkwood dangerous?"

"This area has always been pretty wild, at least by human standards," Kargan said. "Plenty of monsters, but most of them aren't too bad, at least if the warriors from my clan are anything to go by. Apparently, they get tougher closer to the Umber Range toward the west. There's also Greenhollow on the northern side of the forest. More of a farming hamlet, really, but we can probably trade for food there with the locals. It's about thirty-five miles north, at a guess. The next big town after that is Windfall, and of course, a few smaller towns in between."

"Lead the way," Lila said.

They stepped out of the front threshold, the day already bright.

Kargan looked at the tower he'd spent the last month in, regarding it for a moment.

He then turned to face north, his gray mage's robes swirling in the breeze.

Silently, the trio set off down the path. Justin wondered about Eldrin's fate. He struggled to imagine anything happening to the Ranger. He was too wily for that.

Alistair, however…

He pushed the thought from his mind as they hiked into the hills covered by the Darkwood, following the path cut by the overgrown road.

As morning gave way to afternoon, and afternoon to early evening, the forest grew thicker, the air filled with the scent of damp earth and decaying leaves. The trees loomed larger, their ancient trunks gnarled and as big as buildings. The sunlight struggled to penetrate the dense canopy, casting the forest floor in an eerie twilight. It was hard for Justin not to feel dwarfed by it all.

"I can see why they call this the Darkwood," Lila said.

Her voice seemed muffled, as if the surrounding trees were absorbing it.

"It's an old forest," Kargan said. "Part of Aranthia, technically. It hasn't been maintained in well over a hundred years."

"No monsters yet, at least," Justin said.

Lila eyed the sides of the trail warily. "Let's hope it stays that way."

The trio walked in silence. The road was somewhat overgrown, but it was surprisingly clear given its age. Every time Justin checked his map, they were still heading north.

"How is this trail even here?" Justin asked. "It hasn't been maintained in over a hundred years, right?"

"That's easy," Kargan said. He pointed to a worn, smooth stone covered in ivy on the side of the trail. It stood about four feet tall. "See that?"

"Sure. I've seen several of them."

"They're Shield Stones. Ten per mile. And each one has been heavily enchanted to keep vegetation from reclaiming the path. Of course, the magic weakens over time. Eventually, this path will be taken over by the forest."

"Interesting," Justin said.

The forest became silent again. Just minutes ago, there had been birdsong and the usual chirps of small mammals. All that was gone now. Justin gripped his cane tightly, while Lila reached for her knives and Kargan held his staff with both hands. He couldn't help but notice how deep the shadows were on the sides of the path. Anything could be lurking in there.

That's when Kargan came to a sudden stop, grunting in pain as he created his Blood Aegis. A translucent crimson circle, about twenty feet across, surrounded them.

Justin was about to ask what was going on when, from the darkness, a low growl rumbled. Justin strained his eyes, trying to pinpoint the source.

That was when Justin saw it—two glowing red eyes glaring at him from the shadows.

"I knew I saw something," Kargan said.

"I saw nothing at all," Lila replied, her voice thin.

"Orcs have excellent night vision," Kargan explained.

Justin swallowed. Without their new ally, he and Lila would have been caught by surprise.

It crawled forward to the edge of the ward and into the dim light of the path. Justin could only describe it as an oversized badger, its fur a dark, mottled gray that perfectly blended into the forest floor. Muscles rippled beneath its pelt while sharp, curved claws dug into the forest floor. Its mouth hung slightly open, revealing rows of razor-sharp teeth.

"I hope he's by himself," Lila said.

"Shade badgers are solitary hunters," Kargan replied. "The thing is trying to size us up right now."

Justin took his cane, waving it in a wide arc. "Go away! We're big and scary predators."

The monstrous badger's response was to let out a low snarl, crouching as if preparing to pounce.

Lila, poised with her knives, watched the beast intently. "What's the plan?"

"Hammer and anvil," Kargan said. "If it breaks through the ward, let me get in between. Justin attacks from the left, Lila from the right."

The badger lunged at them with a sound somewhere between a hiss and a growl. It struck the barrier, causing a ripple of energy. The beast recoiled, flipping over and snarling in frustration.

Lila unleashed a flurry of knives, each one finding its mark on the beast's tough hide. The badger roared in pain, its red eyes burning with rage. It clawed at the ward, and at last broke it.

Kargan advanced, giving a heavy grunt as he became surrounded by an aura of crimson magic. Blood covered his gray skin, but already, the wounds were knitting themselves together. The beast lunged for Justin, but Kargan stepped into its path, knocking it back with his staff.

Lila had recalled her knives and was throwing them again. Black blood mottled the beast's fur, and it slunk toward Lila with surprising speed. Kargan shifted his position, blocking it and taking the hit with his Sacrificial Armor.

But Justin knew that armor wouldn't last forever. He approached from behind, extending the knife from his cane's tip, stabbing the badger deeply. It whirled and extended its claws, slashing more quickly than Justin would have believed. With inhuman swiftness, Justin parried, knocking the creature back with a shriek.

[Gentleman's Rebuff has shielded this attack!]

Kargan's shield was petering out, and with another pained grunt, he created a new veil of armor. His very skin was dripping blood, his form hobbled and travel robes stained, but despite this, he stood directly in the beast's path as it charged Lila again, who was once more preparing to throw her knives.

Justin, once again, came from behind, determined to end the badger. It was slowing, blood loss finally dampening its ferocity. Justin stabbed at it repeatedly, and the creature recoiled at each strike. Kargan beat it down with his staff, while Lila took two of her knives, now recalled, and buried them both in the badger's neck from behind.

Only then did the beast grow still.

The three fought to catch their breath. Kargan lowered his staff, his breaths labored, his body drenched in both sweat and blood. Justin could see open wounds marring his skin. Wounds that, even now, were slowly knitting themselves together. The crimson light of his armor faded, leaving them standing in the dim forest once more.

"Are you okay?" Lila asked Kargan.

The young orc nodded shakily. "Yeah. That's my first proper fight, not counting the dire wolf attack."

"You did great," Justin said. "That badger was positively radioactive!"

"I've never heard that term," Kargan said. "But sometimes, when a Vault is near, its magic will affect the local wildlife. It'll turn animals into monsters, or it might spawn monsters itself."

"We're not going into a Vault," Lila said.

"No, it wouldn't be wise," Kargan said. "But an isolated forest like this would be the perfect place for one to spawn." His gaze took in both of them. "We should try to find a safe spot to set up for the night. My ward should allow us to sleep somewhat peacefully."

"Unless another one of those things attacks," Lila said, glancing nervously around the darkening forest. "That one broke your ward!"

"My ward will repel weaker creatures and monsters for sure," Kargan said. "Against something like that, though...I need to get stronger."

Justin glanced around warily. "We were probably better off going to Darkstream Crossing, huh?"

"Maybe," Kargan replied. "Either way, Greenhollow shouldn't be too far north. It might be safest to walk through the entire night."

"I'm so tired," Lila said. "But it doesn't seem like we have a choice."

As they continued their journey through the Darkwood, Justin couldn't help but feel a growing respect for the young orc. Kargan might still be unsure of himself, but he had proven his worth by protecting them from that monstrous badger.

But something told Justin that the horrors of the Darkwood weren't through with them yet.

38

THE DARKWOOD

"There is a certain magic in the Darkwood—and not the kind that comforts. As the Ilvari elves' power and influence dwindled, their curiosity for the forbidden grew. They once held their faith in Lathalon, Goddess of Life, as their highest virtue. Yet their fall is a sobering reminder: when desperation beckons, even the proud and devout will kneel before the darker forces."

—Arastine Duvret
  The Shadows of Elvenkind

THEY WALKED ANOTHER HOUR, following the winding trail through rougher and rougher terrain. Night had fallen, and were it not for Kargan's Sacrificial Armor, which cast an eerie crimson aura around them, they would have had no light at all. It almost functioned like infrared vision, given the hue. The armor dissipated every five minutes, forcing him to cast it again, almost always accompanied by a grunt of pain.

Despite this, Kargan seemed unfazed, accepting it as part of his duty. Justin felt bad for the guy. He wondered if he ever got used to it.

As they ventured deeper into the Darkwood, Justin's sense of unease only grew. The towering trees seemed to press in on them. Strange sounds echoed through the forest—unfamiliar bird calls, the rustling of unseen creatures, and the occasional low growl that sent shivers down his spine. A faint mist crept along the forest floor.

They hadn't come upon a fork in the trail, as expected. Justin was afraid that they had missed it in the darkness.

"We need to get well away from that Vault, wherever it is," Kargan said, his voice tense.

"I'm afraid we're getting *closer* to it," Lila said, her eyes darting around.

It was at that moment that Justin noticed an angry buzz. Flying right before them was what appeared to be a giant wasp.

Kargan immediately reacted, casting Blood Aegis just in time to send the insect reeling back. Lila let loose two of her knives, both finding their mark. The monster landed with a sickening splat.

"This is the Forest of Death," Justin said.

They had no choice but to keep going. Justin was afraid to even get out his map, which would mean dropping his concentration. Any lapse in alertness could end in their deaths.

He just had to trust it was still leading them north, that they had taken the right turn.

Another hour passed. Kargan set a fast pace. They went up and down hills, across small streams, as the narrow path took them higher in elevation.

"We're getting closer to the Umbers now," Kargan said, his voice low. "Too close."

At last, after what he guessed to be midnight, Justin saw a light through the trees. Hope rose in his chest. "*Please* tell me that's Greenhollow."

"It's green," Lila said. "I'll give it that much."

Indeed, the light had a green hue to it, not what would be expected of a small village. The light belonged to something else, and Justin already had an idea of what.

His worst fears were confirmed when they rounded the path, coming face-to-face with what looked like a broken wall covered in vines, the trees of the Darkwood interspersed with broken stone buildings and towers. It was hard to tell in the darkness, but it looked like the ruins of an ancient city, long claimed by the forest.

The entire area was surrounded by a green veil of magic that made a dome over the ruins. The stone structures and towers were covered in moss and vines, crumbling with age, yet still holding a ghostly majesty. The trees had grown through and around the buildings, their roots and branches intertwining with the stone, a hauntingly beautiful blend of nature and architecture.

Kargan surveyed the scene with a furrowed brow. "I...can't believe it. We've definitely come too far west. Justin, have you been checking the map?"

"Not for a while, no. I've had my eyes peeled for that path you mentioned."

"We must have gotten sidetracked," Kargan said in frustration. "We're way off base here."

"Well, where are we then?" Lila asked. "Because this city looks big, ancient, and scary."

Kargan shook his head. "I...can't be sure. But if I had to make a guess, this would be the ruins of Eldareth. But Eldareth doesn't *exist* anymore."

"Eldareth?" Lila asked tentatively.

"It was an Ilvari Elven city, truly ancient. As in, over two thousand years old, ancient. The clan elders always tried to avoid this area. It is said to be completely swallowed by the Darkwood."

"Damn," Justin said. "There are elves? You mean tall and pointed-eared elves? And I'm just *now* learning this?"

"Yes, but they aren't around anymore," Kargan said. "They were known for being strong with magic and quite advanced. Of course, there hasn't been an elf left in Serenthel in at least fifteen hundred years, and all of Eyrth for a thousand or more."

Justin felt a pang of sadness. "So, they're all dead?"

"Yes. If this is really Eldareth, we've *definitely* strayed too far to the west. It's said to be located in a hidden valley that sort of carves its way into the Umbers. There was a big war between elves and orcs back in the day. The elders say that the elven spirits are especially violent toward those of my kind."

Justin frowned. "Can't we go around it? Or turn back?"

Kargan shook his head. "The trees are too thick to go around. We'd lose too much time. Besides, the city occupies a pass that cuts right through the Umbers. You see, the mountain range sort of veers east here instead of north and south for a small section. We're in that part now, called the Serpent's Bend. So, the fastest way would be to go through it. Unless we want to backtrack and see where we missed the turn."

"We didn't miss any turn," Lila said. "I've been watching the trail closely this entire time. I think the magic of the forest is playing tricks on us."

"You're saying the road changed?" Kargan said. "This is the same path I followed down from the mountains. And I definitely didn't run across this place."

"If it's the same path, then why did it lead here?" Justin asked. "Can magic really switch the direction of the trail? Wouldn't these shield stones prevent that?"

Kargan grunted. "They would have, assuming we stayed on the right path. I don't know about you, but I haven't seen a shield stone in miles."

"If we go back, it could change on us again," Justin said. "I think we should check this Vault at the very least. If we read the description, we're not actually committing to anything."

"A Vault in a city like this one will be far beyond our party's abilities," Kargan said. "We might camp in front of it tonight, assuming it's low enough in level. But we'd need to head back into the forest tomorrow and take our chances. The important thing is we need to make sure we keep pointing north, even if we have to go off trail."

"You said the city is in a pass," Lila said. "What's on the other side?"

"The Northwood," Kargan said. "Much gentler terrain, to be sure. The path to Windfall would be fairly clear, admittedly."

"Maybe we should check out the Vault first," Lila said. "Who knows? It might be doable."

Kargan sighed, clearly not liking this. "It doesn't hurt to learn more."

As they approached what appeared to be the entrance to the city, a large archway covered in ancient runes, a notification appeared before Justin's eyes.

Vault Discovered: The Fate of Eldareth

 Recommended Party Level: 8

 Average Party Level: 4.667

 Risk Level: Extremely Dangerous! Your party is well below the recommended level. Some challenges may be difficult, perhaps even fatal.

 Description: Eldareth, once a flourishing city, now lies in desolate ruin. However, the city's ancient magic endures, offering adventurers a rare glimpse into a forgotten past.

 Over two millennia ago, during the twilight of the Age of Wonders, the Elven Kingdom of Ilvaria and the Orcish Confederation were embroiled in a brutal war over the fate of Serenthel. Despite the splendor of the past, it was a dark time for Ilvaria, especially as the war dragged on with no clear resolution.

 Your party must assume the role of a diplomatic delegation sent from the Orcish Confederation to offer terms of peace, with neither side gaining or losing ground or resources in the deal. The Vault is only cleared when King Thalion and Queen Alaria agree to enter peace talks with the Orcish Confederation.

 This challenge is not solely political. It may also lead to physical confrontations if the party cannot convince both monarchs. It demands both sharp intelligence and a capable hand.

 Rewards Upon Completion:

 Experience: Scaled to party member levels and individual contributions.

 Guaranteed Bronze-Tier Item: For each party member.

Chance for a Silver-Tier Item: For one party member.

Treasure: One golden crown to be divided among the party.

[Do you accept the Vault's challenge?]

Kargan turned to Justin and Lila, his expression serious. "This is it. If we go through, we're committing to this. There's no turning back from the moment you enter a Vault."

Justin took a deep breath, glancing at the foreboding ancient structures before them. "Looks like we have little choice. Let's do this. Level 8 is less than anything we've done so far."

"Right now?" Lila asked incredulously. "I'm beyond exhausted, and we don't have Eldrin or Alistair to breeze through it anymore. And need I remind you, both of us are only Level 6 and a Charisma class?"

"Are those your friends?" Kargan asked curiously.

Justin and Lila both nodded somberly. So far, they hadn't told Kargan anything about Alistair or Eldrin. Everything was still too fresh, and Justin hadn't even had time to process things.

Justin broke the silence. "Let's camp out in front of the entrance, then. At Level 8, this Vault isn't making monsters anytime soon. There must've been another Vault in the forest doing that. We're probably safe to camp here as long as Kargan has his ward up."

"Hmm," Kargan said. "True enough. It's late. We should definitely take a rest while we have the opportunity. Plus, I have enough experience to unlock my next spell, which could prove vital."

"That's what we'll do, then," Lila said. "We can make a better decision tomorrow morning."

"I'll take the first watch," Kargan said. "We can't count on the ward to completely protect us."

"I can grab second," Justin said. "Wake me in a few hours."

"I'll take the last one, then," Lila said.

As they settled down for the night, Kargan created his Blood Aegis. Justin could only hope it gave them some measure of protection. They ate a hasty dinner, each lost in their thoughts, with the ancient city looming behind them.

This Vault would prove a challenge to them for sure, especially with Kargan being at such a low level. Then again, from what Alistair and Eldrin were describing, it seemed all Vaults started at a low level and grew more powerful over time.

As such, perhaps this Vault was still quite new. Over the centuries, perhaps numerous Vaults had been cleared from these ruins dozens of times by various adventurers, the scenarios encountered within different each time.

They laid out their bedrolls near the entrance. Justin lay down and stared up at the starry sky. Lila rested on her side, her knives within reach.

Justin could only hope it wasn't a long night.

39

BEFORE THE RUINS

"Nestled in the northern foothills of the Umbers lies Eldareth, an elven metropolis that, at its height, eclipsed anything existing in Serenthel today. It is now a forgotten ruin overtaken by the Darkwood, seen only by the most daring—or foolhardy—of adventurers."

—Kaelion Myris,
   Ilvaria: A Lost History

THE MORNING LIGHT filtered through the dense canopy of the Darkwood, casting an eerie glow on the ancient ruins of Eldareth. Justin stirred awake, feeling the chill of dawn and the cool earth beneath him. He glanced around to see Lila already awake, stoking a small campfire. Kargan was still asleep, snoring softly.

They had made it through the night in one piece, and that was about the best he could ask for.

For the first time since Silverton, Justin had no level-up to process. He got up and stretched, trying to reduce the tension in his muscles. Though it was daytime, the dimness was downright eerie.

He moved closer to the fire, where Lila handed him a piece of bread.

"Morning," she said, her voice low. "We're getting a little low on supplies, unfortunately."

"Morning," Justin replied, taking a bite. "Well, once we get to Windfall, we'll dine like royalty." He looked over at Kargan, who was still asleep. "We should wake him up."

As if on cue, Kargan stirred, blinking groggily as he sat up. "Huh?"

"Time to eat," Justin said, handing him some food. "Hope you like bread. It's all we have left."

Kargan nodded, taking the offered meal. "It's fine."

As they ate, Kargan was quiet, lost in thought. Justin guessed he was probably choosing his level 3 skill.

After a few minutes, Kargan's short tusks stuck out a bit in what Justin assumed was an orcish smile. "New spell," he announced with pride. "Vital Surge. It lets me use some of my Life Force to heal myself or a party member."

"That's great!" Justin exclaimed. "It will definitely come in handy if we decide to explore the city."

"Is that the way we're going?" Lila asked. "We've had our share of close calls already."

Before they could discuss it further, a sudden rustling from the trees caught their attention. Justin stood up, his hand instinctively reaching for his cane. From the shadows emerged a figure—half-man, half-horse. It was a centaur with a brown coat, holding a short bow designed for rapid firing, along with a quiver full of arrows at its side. Its pale face was framed by a mane of dark hair, and its green eyes glowed with anger.

Before Justin could say anything, the centaur was already drawing an arrow and letting it fly. Thankfully, it was knocked back by Kargan's Blood Aegis, which was still standing strong.

Lila was already moving, while Kargan quickly cast a fresh ward. The arrows kept coming, pelting the barrier constantly. It wasn't long before even this new version petered out entirely.

The centaur moved with astonishing speed, firing on the move. Kargan moved quickly to recast the barrier, but in the interim, an arrow flew right toward the group and lodged right into Lila's shoulder, causing her to scream in pain.

"Get behind me!" Kargan roared, abandoning the creation of a new aegis.

As the orc stepped between Lila and the centaur, and Justin moved behind him, Kargan cast Sacrificial Armor, surrounding himself in a blue barrier. Even as arrows were knocked back by his magical shell, Kargan turned to Lila and roared with pain as he cast magic anew. A flash of crimson light surrounded her, and the arrow slipped from the wound as the flesh beneath knitted together, leaving nothing but the blood that had stained her shirt. Her eyes widened at the sight.

Kargan's entire body was sweating blood, riddled with wounds, even as he turned to face the centaur, staff in hand. His magical armor was already weakening from the continuous barrage of arrows. He needed time to recover.

Justin felt worse than useless. There was no way that centaur would let him even get close enough to attack with his cane. Even with Sacrificial Armor covering him, the centaur could easily outrun him.

"I can't keep this up forever," Kargan said, his voice strained. "We need to think of something."

Justin thought of his own skills. Poison Barb *might* work, but did the centaur even speak the same language as him? Dandy's Swagger would provide a small morale and confidence boost, but it was questionable how useful that was. There was Dazzling Display, of course, but if Justin used it now, it wouldn't be available again until tomorrow, and he might need the move for the Vault.

In the end, Justin activated Dandy's Swagger, strutting forward and twirling his cane. A yellow aura surrounded him, infusing itself into his allies. An unbridled, cocky confidence filled him.

Kargan glanced at him. "What on Eyrth are you doing, Socialite? Now's not the time for dancing!"

But he'd gotten the centaur's attention, which had apparently taken the strutting dance as a threat. Justin decided now was the perfect time to lob a Poison Barb.

"Nice shooting! Did you train with the village idiot, or are you just naturally this bad?"

The centaur apparently understood the message all too well, its cheeks flushing with anger. It began firing only at Justin, who did his best to dance out of the way. One of the arrows he *couldn't* dodge, but thankfully, it didn't matter. His Gentleman's Rebuff kicked in, swatting the arrow aside like a fly.

[Gentleman's Rebuff has shielded this attack!]

Kargan stood between Justin and the centaur, tanking the hits with a newly conjured Sacrificial Armor spell. He quickly followed this with a new Blood Aegis. He stumbled a bit, blood dripping off his skin and even staining his robes. He definitely couldn't keep this up forever.

"Now, Lila!" Justin shouted.

Lila seized the opportunity, lobbing her knives. The centaur stumbled, three of Lila's six knives hitting right in its flank, causing it to rear up on its hind legs as it let out a horse-like scream.

When it backed away into the trees, Justin thought it was retreating.

But then, two *more* centaurs burst from the underbrush—one with a sword and shield, the other with a bow.

"This...is bad," Justin muttered.

Kargan was panting for breath, his form slumped. The new centaurs wasted no time in joining the attack, the sword-wielding one charging toward the outside of the freshly conjured aegis while the two archers continued to rain arrows on it. The new aegis wouldn't last long against the barrage.

Kargan gritted his teeth, already preparing a new aegis in anticipation of losing the current one. "We need to retreat into the Vault!"

Just as they were about to make a break for it, a pained scream echoed from the forest. Justin looked up to see the original centaur archer falter and fall to its knees, an arrow embedded just below its left arm. Two more arrows then were buried in its side.

From the trees, Eldrin emerged, bow in hand, his face a stern mask of concentration. The sight of their friend arriving in the nick of time filled Justin with a surge of relief and hope such as he had never known.

"Eldrin!" Lila shouted.

Eldrin quickly shifted his aim to the remaining centaur archer, which was already backing away into the Darkwood. Eldrin fired in rapid succession, bringing the second beast down.

The centaur swordsman, still attacking Kargan's new Blood Aegis, suddenly switched tactics and charged at the Ranger. Eldrin had enough time to shoot another arrow before diving into some underbrush, barely avoiding the creature's charge.

The Ranger needed help, even if it was only a distraction.

"Now!" Justin yelled.

They ran forward to engage. The centaur cut its losses and fled into the Darkwood, screaming furiously while beating at its shield. Maybe it was calling for reinforcements.

Eldrin watched the centaur's retreat, not breaking his defensive stance until he was sure it was gone. Then, he put his bow on his back and approached the trio, his eyes noting Kargan's presence.

"What in the gods' names are you doing here?" he demanded, though his tone held more relief than anger. "The Darkwood, of all places?"

Justin, still catching his breath, managed a tired smile. "Nice to see you too, Eldrin."

"They'll be back with more," the Ranger said. "I hope that Vault there isn't too high a level."

"It was Level 8 last night," Justin said. "Though we haven't had the chance to check it this morning. Where did you go? We were worried sick!"

Eldrin ignored the question for now. "All of you are lucky to be alive. It's my fault, I suppose, for not warning you about the Darkwood."

"I'll say," Lila said. "How did you find us so easily?"

"Shadowflight. And you left a trail that would put a drunken elephant to shame."

"Thanks," Justin said. "Any news about Gareth?"

Eldrin gave a coy smile. "Let's just say they won't be a problem."

Lila's eyes widened. "You killed them?"

"No, of course not. I led them south along the Marin. They've probably figured out the ruse by now, and when they do, they'll probably head for Darkstream Crossing. From there, they'll have to spread themselves thin trying to figure out where we're going. The point being, we should be safe to head to Windfall. That's the closest city of note."

"That was our plan," Justin said. "We should've gone to Darkstream Crossing instead."

"Aye, but there's no use lamenting the path not taken. Our new goal is Windfall, and from there, getting the rest of the way to Mont Elea."

"That's what we figured," Justin said. "Apparently, this city is the fastest way through."

"Aye," Eldrin said. "If this Vault is still Level 8, it's doable. However, without Alistair, we'll need to be on our toes. I'd take this over the Darkwood and centaur ambushes any day. Nasty, brutish creatures."

"They'll be back any moment," Kargan said.

At this voice, Eldrin regarded him, putting out a hand in greeting. "Eldrin Thornwood."

"Kargan Durzag," he said, taking the hand cautiously.

"Clan?"

Kargan was silent. "It's...complicated."

"A Blood Warden," Eldrin said with respect. "That's quite a rare class."

"And you're a Ranger, unless I miss my guess. I'm just here for a time. Until Windfall."

The sounds of movement and distant war cries from the forest showed that time was pressing.

"About time we entered that Vault," Justin said. "Mind taking over the party before we do, Eldrin?"

"Aye. Let's approach."

Justin invited Eldrin to the party and mentally offered him the role of party leader.

[Eldrin has joined the party and assumed the role of party leader. You gain the expertise of his Pathfinder's Pace.]

As they walked toward the Vault, Justin set his focus on Eldrin's character, noticing that he had earned a level and a new skill called Falcon's Mark.

Justin closed Eldrin's character information. "That Falcon's Mark looks interesting!"

"Haven't had the chance to test it out yet," Eldrin said. "Basically, it lets Shadowflight spot for me, allowing me to shoot into places I couldn't otherwise see."

"That sounds useful."

"I'm sure it is." Eldrin's eyes turned to the Vault. "Let's approach."

Even as the sounds from the forest increased, Kargan cast a new Blood Aegis, having mostly recovered from his wounds. It would buy them a bit more time to review the Vault description in case arrows came flying at them.

When they were within a few paces of the city's open gate, Justin received the information.

Vault Discovered: The Fate of Eldareth
> **Recommended Party Level: 8**
> **Average Party Level: 6.5**
> **Risk Level:** Dangerous! Your party is below the recommended level. Proceed with extreme caution.

[Do you accept the Vault's challenge?]

Good, it hadn't gone up in level while all other details remained the same. Justin immediately gave his mental assent. With Eldrin leading the party, there was no reason to delay.

Kargan, however, seemed to hesitate, watching the broken gates of the city with worry.

"It'll be all right," Lila said reassuringly. "You're more than capable."

Kargan sighed. "No choice, huh?"

"Unless you wish to fight an entire centaur herd," Eldrin said.

"No. That, I do not." A moment later, Kargan nodded.

[You have accepted the Challenge of The Fate of Eldareth. May your courage be your guide and resolve be your shield. Good luck, Brave Adventurers.]

Justin was surprised to see another notification flash across his interface.

With that, the party entered under the broken gates of the city as one.

40

INTO ELDARETH

As soon as they passed through the green veil of magic, the city was no longer in its ruinous state but appeared to be at the height of its power. They stood on a wide boulevard paved in pure white marble, the median lined with tall trees that shimmered with a soft, ethereal glow. Tall, curving buildings rose on either side, none shorter than five stories, with many as high as ten. The streets were filled with tall figures in flowing, vibrant robes, and—Justin noticed—pointed ears. Their skin tones ranged from pale silver to deep emerald. The sky was pure blue, the weather warm, even balmy.

Kargan looked around, eyes wide. "I never dreamed I would see an elf in all my days."

"They're not real," Lila said.

"Yes, but they might as well be," Kargan replied.

"Okay," Lila said. "What's the plan? We're supposed to be a delegation from the Orcish Confederation, so we need to find the King and Queen. How can we do that?"

As they stepped forward into the city, Justin couldn't help but notice that the Elves were shrinking back from them. He realized it wasn't he, Eldrin, and Lila they were afraid of, but Kargan. That made sense, considering they were at war with the Orcs.

It didn't take too long for two guards to approach. They wore green, natural-looking armor that seemed to be woven from living vines and leaves, and they carried staves made from a white, almost silvery bark. Each had green skin, along with platinum-blonde hair hanging down to their waists.

"There you are!" the leader said. "They told us to be on the lookout for the delegation, but the fact that you've snuck right past the walls doesn't bode well for the Gate Wardens."

To Justin's shock, the words came out in the language that must have been Ancient Ilvari. It sounded melodic and slurring, but he understood every word.

He was even more surprised when Eldrin responded in the same language. "Indeed, we are representatives of the Orcish Confederation. Please take us to the King and Queen. There is no time to waste."

"Just the four of you?" the other guard asked. "And our enemies would insult us to send an orc! The delegation was to be entirely neutral."

"I'm not from the Confederation," Kargan said.

"I see," the guard said. "Well, maybe so. It would seem you're a mage, and the Confederation doesn't look too kindly on them."

Justin cleared his throat. "The Confederation wishes to show its good faith, knowing the power of the Ilvari mages. It has been a long and terrible war, and they are eager to sue for peace."

The first guard scoffed. "I'll say, especially after how badly we beat them at the Battle of Eryndor!"

"Please," Eldrin said. "Lead us to the palace."

"We will do so at once."

Within a minute, a contingent of Ilvari guards in similar natural armor, all bearing staves, had boxed them in and were escorting them up the main thoroughfare. The city was far larger than anything Justin had seen so far. This had clearly once been an important city. The towers rose like skyscrapers, even connecting to each other in graceful, arched bridges. Blending in with the buildings were beautiful trees with wide and graceful limbs. Passersby watched them with distrust, their gazes lingering especially long on Kargan.

But for all of these wonders, Justin's eyes widened in shock as he saw something that he could only describe as a bipedal, armored dinosaur with emerald-green skin being ridden by an Elven warrior. It was about the size of a horse, and from the lack of looks, it was not a strange sight.

At Justin's look of confusion, Eldrin leaned over, speaking in Aranthian while also watching the creature. "That's a thera. Its kind has been extinct in Serenthel for as long as the Elves."

Justin had to wonder. If society had been this advanced two thousand years ago, what had caused it to...well, *stop* being so advanced? War? Plague? Random meteor strike? Yet more questions he didn't have the answers to.

At last, they rounded a bend and found themselves before a palace that seemed to be a series of giant interconnected trees, with branches and leaves gleaming silver and similarly silver bark shining under the sun. Its canopy spread wide, falling over the stones of the plaza on which they stood.

The guards led them up a set of marble steps, right through the open entrance of the main tree, where the grandeur only increased. The walls were lined with tapestries depicting scenes of Elven history, and statues of great Elven heroes stood in alcoves, their eyes watching the party as they passed. A magnificent fountain rose in the middle, depicting some great Elven king on the back of a unicorn.

Finally, they entered a grand hall. The space was vast, with high ceilings supported by columns that were, in fact, living trees with golden bark, their branches arching overhead to form a natural canopy. The air was filled with the scent of blooming flowers and the soft hum of magical energy.

They passed dozens of nobles dressed richly, and all Justin could think of was that these people—if they could indeed be called people—no longer existed and hadn't for two thousand years. More than that, their entire race had been wiped out by...*something*. Perhaps by this very war the Vault had tasked them to end.

Within a moment, the guards had brought them before the King and Queen, both of whom sat on thrones made of intertwined vines and precious stones. The King's eyes, green as emeralds, surveyed them with interest. He had long, silver hair that flowed down his back and a strong, dignified face. The Queen's eyes, the same hue of amber as Kargan's, held a mixture of curiosity and caution. She had dark, flowing hair and a serene presence.

Justin remembered their names from the Vault description: King Thalion and Queen Alaria.

The hall was utterly silent as the monarchs looked down at them from their thrones. Justin had to remind himself this was only a Level 8 Vault, and that they were more than capable of handling whatever was thrown at them. At least, they should be in theory.

At last, King Thalion's voice broke the silence, deep and resonant. "Speak."

Eldrin took a humble step forward, lowering his head. "My king and queen..."

The Queen raised a bejeweled hand, instantly stopping him. "No, I want to hear from *him*."

To Justin's surprise, she was looking right at him.

Justin cleared his throat. "Me, Your Majesty?"

"You dare question me, Socialite? Where is your respect?"

Justin recognized why she was singling him out. Somehow, she knew all their classes, and as the Socialite, she expected him to be the one to speak.

And come to think of it, why *shouldn't* he? He had the highest Charisma of anyone in the party.

Eldrin seemed to recognize this, gracefully taking a step back.

It was up to Justin now. He gave a winning smile, hardly even feeling the gazes of the Elven nobles upon him. In fact, it seemed the more eyes that were looking at him, the more confident he felt.

This was not his normal personality. It was definitely something to do with his Charisma attribute, or perhaps his Magnetic Presence boon.

"Your Majesties," he said, his voice clear and commanding. "My name is Lord Justin of House Talemaker, and with me are my associates, Lord Eldrin, Lady Lila, and Lord Kargan. We have come on a mission of peace from the Orcish Confederation, eager to end the long and terrible war that has ravaged both nations and Serenthel at large."

The Queen's eyes narrowed as she looked at Kargan. "An Orc mage in our midst is an unusual sight. Is this some idea of a joke from our enemies, Lord Justin?"

Justin held her gaze steadily. "It is no joke, Queen Alaria. It is only proof that it is possible for an orc—the dreaded enemy—to come within the hallowed walls of Eldareth itself and conduct himself worthily."

To Kargan's credit, he stood straighter, having a noble bearing. He seemed to understand that this was all an act.

Justin continued. "We desire to end the bloodshed and find a path to peace. We understand the pain this war has caused, but we believe that through diplomacy and mutual respect, we can forge a new and brighter future for both sides."

The court murmured among themselves, their suspicion clear. Despite Justin's eloquence, Kargan's presence seemed to cast a shadow over their intentions. He wondered if that was by the Vault's design, or whether things would have been easier without the orc in their party.

King Thalion raised a hand to silence the court. "Of course, peace is desired by all. But when so many have died, and the borders remain the same as they ever were, the sacrifice of tens of thousands of Elves will have availed nothing. We cannot accept peace unless we receive something in compensation."

Justin wished he *could* give something to the Ilvari, but the Vault description was clear. No land or resources could change sides in the peace deal.

Justin's face became solemn. "Peace is better than the alternative, my king."

"What alternative?"

Justin paused, weighing his words. Either what he said was a significant risk, or it would end up effectively making his point. "It's been said that every empire falls as the ages turn. But when historians look back on the ruins of the past, they point to the reasons this or that kingdom fell, and what might have been done to prevent it. Sometimes, larger societal shifts are to blame, under the control of no single being in all of Eyrth, but a zeitgeist all moving in the same direction that can hardly be averted."

Zeitgeist. Yes, the Charisma Attribute was definitely doing something to his words. And much to Justin's surprise, everyone was listening closely.

"At other times," Justin continued, "one can point to a single action, a single ruler, who set the course of future events in such a way that collapse became inevitable. A single decision, or lack thereof, can act as a trapdoor through which a kingdom crashes and burns."

The King smiled. "And you would say that I'm that king, Lord Justin?"

"The powerful often cannot see what is apparent to all those who do not hold power. The humble farmer, whose house has burned, whose family has been killed, has already lost his kingdom. Multiply that by a hundred times—a thousand, or even more—then you discover that a kingdom does not derive its power from its rulers, but from the ruled. Make no mistake. If this war is allowed to continue, and both sides waste themselves on each other, either the entire continent devolves into anarchy, or space is made for a third player to enter and eat the carcasses of those who remain."

The hall was incredibly silent following these words. His

companions were looking at him strangely, maybe feeling that his speech was out of character.

But perhaps it *wasn't* out of character. Perhaps he was simply stepping into his role for the first time.

"Your words are well spoken, Lord Justin," King Thalion said at last. "Of course, the danger of running out of resources and soldiers is real. But words alone are not enough to prove your sincerity, or that of the Orcish Confederation. In these times of war, we cannot afford to trust so easily."

The Queen looked at the King. "But Lord Justin's words are as good as a prophecy. The Ilvari Elves are mighty indeed, but there are certain truths that even our people cannot escape. It might be said one day, 'Here once ruled the Ilvari; their cities were powerful, their magic mighty, and their craft great. And yet, they are nothing more than a memory, because they didn't know how to make peace with their enemies.'"

The King's face firmed. It was clear they didn't see eye to eye on this.

"That may be true," the King said at last. "But if we were the first to cast aside our staves, it would expose our necks to the Orcish enemy. It's only been fifty years since they even learned to write. Unlike our people, they do not abide by treaties and laws. Their word is only good for a generation until the next forgets it and takes up the hammers and axes of their fathers."

"The Orcish Confederation is sincere in its offer of peace," Justin said. "In the halls of their Clan Elders, they recognize the need for change in their society."

"I imagine they do," King Thalion said. "We dealt them a mighty blow at Eryndor. A blow for which we deserve compensation."

"Or," Queen Alaria said, "in our hubris, we overreach and find ourselves with a string of losses and erase all of our gains. The war was faring poorly before our timely victory, my king. It might be best to take the peace while we can. A leaf knows the wind, but a fool trusts the breeze. Let us get out ahead, before the wind shifts."

Justin could see that his words had convinced the queen already. The king was the main holdout.

And yet, Justin knew he had pushed enough already. Anymore, and the king might become even more stubborn. His wife, after all, had already gone against him in front of the entire court.

At last, King Thalion sighed. "I cannot trust you, Lord Justin—or more accurately, the ones you represent. We've made peace in the time of my father, and still, they come raiding down from their mountain halls. Why should we ever trust them?"

"My King," Queen Alaria said. "We must lay down our pride. We have already lost so many young soldiers. How can our kingdom hope to recover if we lose even more?"

The tension between the two only seemed to increase. Justin was wracking his mind for something to say to save the situation when the silence was broken by an unknown voice resounding throughout the hall.

"Why not let the gods decide?"

A warrior stepped forward from the shadows, clad in silver armor that gleamed like the moon. His eyes were cold and calculating, fiercely blue, and his skin was the same color as his armor.

"Lord Seraphiel," the King said, a smile tugging at his lips. "Would you challenge these envoys who have come in peace by laws centuries old?"

Justin frowned. "If this is some trial by combat, we aren't interested."

"And yet," Lord Seraphiel said, "the King and Queen are at an impasse. In times of old, if the monarchs could not agree on a matter, it was left to the gods to decide." He turned to the King and Queen. "With your permission, your Majesties?"

The King nodded regally, while the Queen waited a moment, clearly not liking this. Yet she also nodded.

Lord Seraphiel smiled, the picture of confidence as he turned to face the party. "I am Seraphiel Thalarion, of the very Eryndor that won the great victory a fortnight ago. My land has suffered greatly at the hands of the Orcs, and I would die long before I ever made peace with the overgrown goblins."

Kargan's short tusks protruded further at that, but he kept silent, even as his amber eyes burned with anger.

Lord Seraphiel gave a mocking smile as he looked down on Kargan. "That you bring one of these savages into our hallowed halls is the greatest insult."

Kargan was about to speak, but Justin raised his hand.

Justin smiled. "Really? I'd have thought the greatest insult would be your complete lack of manners. If anyone is behaving with savagery, it's not Lord Kargan, but you, Seraphiel. But I suppose one can't expect much from someone who compensates with such... *shining armor.*"

A couple of nobles tittered in the background, but most seemed interested in how Seraphiel would react. Clearly, the man had a reputation for violence.

Seraphiel puffed out his chest. "Trust me, my dear Socialite, I shall not be the one found lacking. With the permission of the good King and Queen, I say we settle this in the arena. Me, against the four of you."

Justin activated his Dandy's Swagger, strutting forward with exaggerated grace, puffing out his chest mockingly while twirling his cane. His movements were fluid, a gross exaggeration of Seraphiel himself. Gasps of alarm echoed through the hall, though some laughed nervously. Seraphiel's expression turned to one of disgust and anger.

Justin followed it up with a Poison Barb. "Well, my good Seraphiel, if your combat skills are as sharp as your wit, then we have nothing to fear."

Seraphiel became momentarily stunned, his face red as he fought for words to speak. A couple of nobles gasped in the background.

"That settles it," Seraphiel said, finally recovering. "By the good grace of the King and Queen, this will be no simple contest, but a fight to the death. The four of you against me and my thera, with the Goddess Lathalon herself as witness! I can see by those *implements* you call weapons that you are warriors of great renown." His voice was dripping with sarcasm. "If you can prove your strength by spilling my life's blood, the bravest and most powerful warrior in the Kingdom, then I swear by the Good Goddess herself that the Ilvari Elves will enter peace talks with the Orcish Confederation."

Eldrin, Lila, and Kargan looked at Justin. The Ranger nodded, and somehow, Justin knew that was part of the Vault's challenge. While he had failed to convince both the King and Queen, there was still a way to complete the Vault.

To do that, they would have to face this warrior. It was four against one. Two, if they counted the Elven warrior's thera.

Justin looked at the King and Queen. "Do we have your word that you'll honor the terms given by...remind me again...your most powerful warrior?"

"Of course," the King said, somewhat miffed. "No elf can make such a vow and live to break it."

"Then we accept your challenge, Seraphiel. Upon our victory, the Ilvari Elves will gain two gifts: peace with the Orcs and the absence of one fool. I must admit, it's difficult to say which is the greater blessing."

"Very well," Seraphiel said, his voice measured. "We will see how empty banter avails you on the battleground. I can't wait to crush you beneath the claws of my thera."

The courtroom broke into a flurry of whispers.

The Queen's gaze softened slightly as she looked at the party. "May the Goddess be with the winner."

"The trial will begin in one hour in the courtyard arena," the King declared. "You had best prepare yourselves; Seraphiel is indeed my strongest warrior."

In the next moment, Justin and the rest were escorted out of the throne room. His mind raced as they walked. He wondered what else he could have said to convince the king before things came to blows, but it was too late for that.

He just had to believe that the four of them had what it took.

41

TRIAL BY COMBAT

"For all the Ilvari elves' triumphs in the arts and sciences, perhaps their most fearsome accomplishment lay in the bond between rider and thera. The beast's brutal strength was nothing without the precise commands of its Elven master, and together, they moved as if guided by a singular will. It was not just a beast on the battlefield, but a deadly symbiosis of intellect and ferocity—a weapon the world has not seen since."

—Kaelion Myris,
   Ilvaria: A Lost History

Within the hour, Justin, Eldrin, Kargan, and Lila were gathered in a circular arena within the palace. The ring was vast, with high stone walls encircling a sandy floor.

The seats around the perimeter were packed with the Elven population, and Justin had to wonder how so many could get here on such short notice. Scanning the faces of the crowd, the general mood seemed to be a mix of curiosity and disdain.

Ornate banners hung from the walls, depicting a silver tree on a field of gold. The sunlight streamed down through the open roof, casting a golden glow over the combatants.

So far, their opponent had yet to show up.

"So, what's the plan?" Justin asked. "Should I start off by hurling an insult or two?"

Lila let out a disbelieving laugh. "Haven't you done enough of that already?"

"It might make him blind with aggression," Kargan said. "That could go one of two ways. Whatever the case, someone needs to take the hits. I suppose it must be me."

"You are too low-level for that," Eldrin said. "You might survive for a while, but the Vault would not make this one versus four unless Seraphiel proved to be a fair challenge. It would make more sense if you functioned as a healer."

High above, Shadowflight circled the arena, his dark violet feathers almost black against the bright sky. Eldrin glanced up at his falcon with a slight nod, as if confirming some silent arrangement between them.

"Hmm, you might have a point there," Kargan said. "Well, what's your idea, then?"

"I will take on the role of tank, fighting with my longsword. My higher level will prove key. You will keep me healed with your Vital Surge, and if possible, maintain your Blood Aegis to improve the power of your healing. And of course, that Sacrificial Armor spell you have. As long as I can draw his attention and keep him focused on me, we should be able to beat him. I'll do everything I can to bring down his thera. Once he loses that, he loses his advantage."

"I could use my Blood Aegis to start off," Kargan said. "Maybe we can bait him into charging us, then I can set up the spell quickly. It should knock him back, or at least stagger him a bit."

"Hey, that's a good idea!" Lila said. "But will it work on someone as strong as Seraphiel?"

"We'll have to see," Eldrin said. "It's certainly safer than my trying to take on both the beast and its rider. Assuming this works, focus everything on Seraphiel. He's going to be the weaker of the two."

"Either way, that monster is going to be quick," Justin said. "What if it goes around you and attacks us directly, Eldrin?"

"In that case, Kargan is the second line of defense. Lila can stay behind him and throw her knives with ease."

"What about me?" Justin asked.

Eldrin thought for a moment. "You can join the melee if you judge it safe. While fighting is not your forte, you are Level 6 now. Just try to stay back if Seraphiel focuses on you. And of course, your Dazzling Display and Dandy's Swagger could prove pivotal in distracting the enemy. And if you can stun him with your Poison Barb, all the better."

"And Shadowflight?" Lila asked.

"He'll be our eyes from above," Eldrin replied. "He can dive in to distract at critical moments, but I'd rather keep him as a last resort. Seraphiel's thera might see him as a snack otherwise."

"Sounds like a plan," Justin said. "It's easy to fluster a blowhard like Seraphiel."

"That can be a good thing or a bad thing," Eldrin said. "Either way, your skills have proven pivotal in every Vault so far. Just play it safe. I don't want you risking yourself too much. While this Vault is only Level 8, we shouldn't let that make us too confident."

"Eldrin," Kargan said. "If we need to switch out the tank role, there's no shame in it. That bow of yours could probably do even more damage than your sword."

"Sensible," the Ranger said. "If I need to swap positions, I'll let you know."

With the plan set, they continued to wait for their opponent's arrival.

At last, the iron gate at the edge of the arena raised foot by foot, and out came Seraphiel atop his thera, which was also covered in silver armor. It loped gracefully to its position on the other side of the arena. Seraphiel twirled his staff, his silver hair and armor making it difficult to tell where his skin began and where the armor ended. He gave a cocky, self-assured smile as if this trial were already decided.

The crowd erupted in approval at his entrance. Nobles shouted his name, their faces alight with admiration. It didn't seem to matter what he was fighting for. Justin could only assume that the majority not only supported their champion but also wanted to continue the war with the Orcish Confederation.

"I want to wipe that stupid smile from his face," Lila said, twirling her knives.

The announcer, a tall elf, stepped on top of a podium over the gate from which Seraphiel had emerged. His robes were deep green, embroidered with silver thread, and his presence commanded the attention of the crowd. His voice washed over the arena like rolling thunder.

"Welcome, noble spectators, to this rare trial by combat! Today, we witness a challenge of great significance. On one side, we have Seraphiel Thalarion of House Eryndor, a warrior of unparalleled bravery, whose deeds in battle have become legend. His skill with the staff is unmatched, and his courage knows no bounds. He rides his mighty thera, Aravath, a beast of formidable strength and speed."

At the mention of its name, the thera opened its wide mouth, giving a beastly scream that revealed rows of needle-pointed teeth.

Justin felt the vibration in his bones. He tried not to wet himself as he had with the other Vault trial. But in case he did, well, that was what the Ring of Hygiene was for.

"And on the other side," the announcer continued, his voice dropping slightly, "we have a delegation of Mysterious Strangers from the Orcish Confederation. They stand before us in defiance, hoping to prove the sincerity of the dastardly Orcish Confederation. If they win, the Ilvari Elves have agreed, under the eyes of the Goddess Lathalon herself, to enter peace talks with the Orcish Confederation. If Seraphiel wins, the war will continue until the last breath is drawn. Anything goes in this fight. May Lathalon, Goddess of Life, watch over the valiant!"

The crowd's reaction was mixed. Some booed, others remained silent, while the rest watched with keen interest.

The announcer lowered his hand, signaling the start of the battle.

From high above, Shadowflight let out a piercing screech, as if announcing his own readiness for battle. Seraphiel's thera glanced up momentarily, distracted by the sound.

Seraphiel wasted no time, immediately kicking his beast into a charge and twirling his staff. Kargan gave a guttural yell, creating a Blood Aegis just in time to deflect the creature's assault. The beast gave a pained scream as it was thrown back by the aegis, along with Seraphiel, who went flying through the air.

Justin's eyes widened. Damn, that was easy.

"Charge!" Eldrin called.

Justin didn't immediately follow in Eldrin's footsteps; instead, he activated Dandy's Swagger, performing a little jig and cane twirl.

Some in the crowd laughed, others jeered, thinking he was insulting the great warrior, but he didn't care. What mattered was that he was infused with confidence, giving him the bravery to charge forward.

Already, Lila was tossing her knives at the beast, which was blocking her view of Seraphiel. Its hide and armor were so thick that the knives simply clattered off.

Seraphiel clambered up from the dusty ground, running to mount his thera again, which had intercepted Eldrin before he could reach the elf. Unable to get around the beast, Eldrin started attacking it with fury. Seraphiel was approaching from the side for a flanking attack, and Justin rushed to meet him before he could catch Eldrin unawares. The elf was none the wiser about Justin's approach, apparently still rattled from his fall.

Eldrin whistled sharply, and Shadowflight plummeted from above, talons extended. The dark falcon raked across Seraphiel's face just as he was about to swing at Eldrin's back. The elf warrior cried out, momentarily blinded as he swatted at the bird, which deftly twisted away and soared back up.

Edified by his Charisma bonus, and Seraphiel still under a Charisma malus from Dandy's Swagger, Justin hurled his first Poison Barb as he moved in.

"Getting flanked isn't part of your strategy, I take it? So much for being the best warrior in the city!"

Seraphiel froze in his tracks. It was enough of a distraction for Lila to throw a fresh round of knives at him. Five in a row all clattered off his armor, but the sixth found purchase in his right thigh, sneaking in through a gap in his armor. Such was the nature of Justin's stun that the elf couldn't even scream.

[Poison Barb refreshed.]

Justin began his attack, twirling his cane and giving the Elf Warrior a few good thwacks, his staff ensconced in a yellow light. He wondered why it was doing that until he realized his new boon, Add Injury to Insult, had activated. Indeed, he was hitting Seraphiel hard enough to make dents in his armor.

He was about to finish him off with a solid thump to the skull when something charged into him from behind.

Justin's vision immediately darkened, and when the pain hit him, it was searing hot and extreme. He arced above the dirt of the arena and landed with a graceless thud. His side was wet, pouring out blood.

Immediately, a refreshing coolness surrounded him, and it was as if his wound were frozen solid. He scurried to get up and defend himself, but the thera was already focusing on Eldrin, while Seraphiel was limping along to aid in his mount's attack.

Already, the fight was bloody and not going according to plan.

Justin, still reeling from the pain, at least had his wounds knitted together.

He hobbled forward, once again going on the offensive. He wondered if Dazzling Display would do any good here, but right now, no one was in immediate danger, and it would only place all the focus on him when he needed a break.

He would use the skill when the time was right.

Justin ran right through the perimeter of Kargan's newly cast Blood Aegis and felt himself refreshed and edified by it. Both Seraphiel and his mount were fighting fiercely within the bounds of the ward. Justin charged at the thera, stabbing deep into the dinosaur's exposed flank, which was fleshier than its tough exterior. The creature gave a high shriek, wheeling around and swiping with its armored tail. Justin was hit so hard that he immediately went flying back.

He landed hard on his side, and once again felt himself surrounded by refreshing coolness. He scrambled up to see that Kargan was struggling, his body coated with blood from his healing exertions. But both Seraphiel and his mount were focusing on Eldrin again, who was doing all he could to hold off both with his longsword and limberness. The Ranger had already taken some hits, and Justin knew he couldn't keep it up forever, nor could Kargan with his healing.

Shadowflight dove again, this time targeting the thera's eyes. The beast reared back, snapping its jaws at the air as the falcon narrowly escaped its teeth. The momentary distraction gave Eldrin just enough time to roll away from what would have been a devastating bite.

"Good work, Shadowflight!" Eldrin called out.

It was at this moment that Lila started singing, even while throwing more knives, using her Bardic Inspiration ability. Her voice rose above the din of battle, clear and melodious, weaving a song that seemed to dance in the air. The lyrics, which Justin couldn't even catch in the chaos, were swift and light, urging quickness and grace.

Justin felt himself more limber, and he realized she was edifying the party's Coordination Attribute by +4. This gave him a breath of fresh air, enough to have another go at it.

Instead of attacking the thera, Justin went for its rider. He lobbed another insult, hoping that his Charisma was high enough to make the stun stick.

"Nice moves! Did you learn them from a children's puppet show?"

Seraphiel's face contorted with fury, the words cutting deep into his pride. Eldrin seized the moment, stabbing the elf warrior right through a gap in his armor, where Justin's earlier cane work had made way. Seraphiel's eyes went wide as he sank to his knees. Justin followed it up with a series of quick strikes, ending with extending the blade and slicing the elf's neck.

The crowd gasped in shock and awe, never having expected their champion to fall so soon.

"Lila," Justin called. "Switch to charisma!"

He was going off script a bit, but thankfully, she understood perfectly what was coming. She changed tunes to something inspiring and playful, boosting his Charisma by +4.

And not only that, he felt a refreshing coolness surround him. He recognized it to be Lila's new boon, Descant Defense, triggering to give him some light healing.

It was at this point that Justin activated his Dazzling Display, knowing that he needed some way to distract Seraphiel's thera, which would no doubt become enraged by its master's death.

When the legendary actor Russell Crowe entered Justin's mind, he wasn't even surprised. He simply accepted it, taking on the actor's aspect, grabbing the fallen warrior's staff, and throwing it into the surprised crowd, just below where both the king and queen were sitting.

"Are you not entertained?" he shouted.

The whole stadium seemed to go still, sucked into the performance. All but Justin's companions, who continued to assault the thera, which was also watching Justin, unable to tear its gaze away, even as it was being attacked.

"Are you not entertained? Is this not why you are here?"

The Dazzling Display ended, and time itself seemed to resume.

The thera roared, attacking with renewed vigor, going straight for Justin.

"Eeek!"

Justin dove to the side, in time for Kargan to approach with a crimson shield of Sacrificial Armor. The beast, however, was still targeting Justin, who was running for all he was worth. The thera's jaws extended, and Justin performed an adroit dodge just as its sharp teeth clamped together.

Thankfully, Lila had switched back to her Coordination song. Without that, he doubted he could have avoided the attack.

He slid behind Kargan, who tanked the hits of the thera's jaws and claws. Eldrin began unleashing arrow after arrow, almost all landing true in the exposed gaps of the beast's armor.

Shadowflight, seeming to sense the thera's weakening state, made one final dive. With incredible speed, the falcon slashed at the creature's already wounded eye, drawing blood and an agonized howl. The thera thrashed its head wildly, disoriented and half-blinded, creating the perfect opening.

By now, the creature was a bloody mess and was slowing down.

Now was the time to drive the nail into the coffin. The party came together, surrounding the thera. With coordinated strikes, it was only a matter of time before it dropped to the dust. With a final stabbing of his longsword right below its exposed neck, Eldrin ended the beast once and for all.

The thera made no sound as it finally slumped into the red-tinged dirt.

As the party backed away, the crowd erupted into a mix of shock, cheers, jeers, and boos, witnessing what they perceived as an incredible upset.

Shadowflight descended to perch on Eldrin's outstretched arm. Eldrin stroked his companion's head once, a silent acknowledgment of their victory.

The announcer's surprise was obvious as his announcement sounded over the entire arena. "It's over, it's over, the fight is over! The Mysterious Strangers of the Orcish Delegation have won!"

Justin looked into the stands in a daze, battered but not beaten. A wall of sound beat against him. Many in the crowd had been won over to their side by his Dazzling Display. Even now, they were chanting, "Strangers! Strangers! Strangers!" until the cry took the whole arena by storm.

Was this what victory felt like?

Whatever the case, it was time to claim their just rewards.

42

ARENA LOOT DROP

"The Battle Arena is an oasis of barbarity in a sea of civilization, and the perfumed elves drink from it as greedily as a drunkard does from the mead bowl."

—King Erymandis I of Kurath,
    A Letter to Queen Saldra

THEY STOOD on the arena floor for a few minutes before the gate opened, through which the Elven King and Queen entered.

They approached, watching the party with respect, the noise of the crowd ebbing to allow them to speak. Thalion was the one to address them.

"This result was...unexpected. But I stand by my vow made before the entire court and the Goddess Lathalon herself. We will enter peace talks with the Orcish Confederation."

It was at that moment that the magic of the Vault faded, revealing the ruins of the surrounding city. The once-grand arena was now a desolate space overgrown with trees, its stone structures crumbling and covered in moss and vines. Yet the King and Queen, now ethereal ghosts, remained before the party, their regal forms shimmering in the late morning light.

Queen Alaria smiled. "Thank you, Brave Warriors, for saving our kingdom from certain doom. In truth, of course, this pointless war extended for another generation, until the Verdant Plague put an end to the fighting on both sides, beginning a Dark Age that would not lift from the continent for another five hundred years. And it was during this time that the Elves' numbers were reduced to only a few scattered clans, which in the end were hunted down by the Necromancer-Lords of the Shadow Empire."

The ghostly King Thalion stepped forward. "You have proven your worth and valor, Brave Adventurers. Though our time has long passed, we honor the promises made within the Vault. For your courage and skill, you each shall receive a just reward: one bronze-tier item for each party member, and one silver-tier item for the party member deemed most worthy."

Queen Alaria extended her hand. Within it materialized a pair of elegant boots, with golden embroidery of vines. The Queen smiled kindly and looked at Justin. "These boots were once given to our ambassadors. Normally, they would be given to someone of the Diplomat Class, but their benefits can be enjoyed by anyone with a Charisma core. Your Charisma and presence were enough to sway me, if not my husband. While wearing them, they will grant you +1 to Endurance and will always remain dry, no matter the weather, and even if you completely submerge them."

As the boots floated toward Justin, he inspected them.

Ilvari Ambassador Boots

> **Type:** Footpiece
>
> **Tier:** Bronze
>
> **Core Restriction:** Charisma
>
> **Aether-Fortified Leather:** +1 Endurance.
>
> **Dry Stride:** These boots are completely waterproof, keeping its wearer's feet completely dry in all conditions.

The Endurance boost would be welcome, making travel and pure survival all the easier. At first, he thought the enchantment that kept them dry was useless, since he already had the Ring of Hygiene. But as he thought about it, he realized they actually were still useful because the enchantment would *always* keep the boots dry, and not merely once a day.

"Thank you, Queen Alaria." Justin gave a respectful bow.

She nodded regally. With another wave of her hand, she produced a pair of fingerless leather gloves with the same golden embroidery of vines on the cuffs.

"These are the Ilvari Gloves of Precision," Queen Alaria said. "They will grant +1 to your Coordination and Endurance."

The gloves floated toward Lila, and she instantly donned them. "Thank you, Your Majesty."

Next, the Queen produced another pair of finely crafted gloves, their material darker than Lila's, made from finely crafted leather. "And for Eldrin the Ranger, these are the Ilvari Gloves of Alchemy. They will give a modest increase to the potency of your crafted potions and poisons."

Eldrin received them, wasting no time in donning the enchanted gloves. "I thank you, Queen Alaria."

And for the final bronze-tier item, Queen Alaria summoned an amulet fashioned from a dark, polished stone set in a silver frame, with intricate Elven runes etched along the edges. "This is the Blood Warden's Seal. Its enchantment will allow you to cycle your blood flow more easily with the Nether, slightly increasing your Life Force regeneration. You will also not have to worry about blood staining your clothing, so long as you wear it."

Kargan's amber eyes widened as the amulet floated toward him. He immediately put it on. "Thank you, Queen Alaria."

Finally, the ghostly King Thalion came out of his silence, looking at Kargan. Justin must have missed it, but at some point, he must have created the majestic wooden staff adorned with glowing Elven runes. "Kargan Durzag, you landed pivotal healing spells while bravely defending your companions and were at points near death itself for the amount of Life Force you channeled. Your performance far exceeded that which should be expected of a Level 3 Blood Warden. As such, the Vault has determined you most worthy of the silver-tier item. This is the Staff of Blood Aegis. The first Blood Aegis of any fight will not require any Life Force. It also grants you +2 to Endurance."

The staff floated toward Kargan, and he accepted it. "King Thalion. You humble me. My thanks."

"And of course, there is the prize money for winning the fight itself. One golden crown to be split among the party."

Justin then received a notification.

[25 silver marks have been added to your inventory! You now have
3 golden crowns, 36 silver marks, and 24 copper pieces.]

The King and Queen looked at the party with a mix of pride and sorrow. It was the latter who spoke. "May these enchanted items serve you well in your future endeavors. Know that the spirits of Eldareth will always remember your deeds here today."

With that, the ghostly monarchs faded, their forms becoming more translucent with each passing second, until they were at last gone.

The Voice entered Justin's mind.

[The Vault honors your triumph. Now go forth with courage in
your hearts, strength in your limbs, and wisdom in your minds.]

[The Trial of the Vault is complete!]

[Experience Gained: 350]

Birdsong once again warbled through the trees, while the green veil of magic still spread overhead. It would protect them for a while, long enough, hopefully, to escape the ruins of the city through the north gate.

Eldrin looked at Justin, a rare smile crossing his usually stoic face. "Not bad for a Socialite," he said, clapping Justin on the back.

"Not bad at all," Justin said with a smile.

Kargan was examining his new staff, something that would be of benefit not just to him, but to whatever party he found himself a part of in the future. On top of that, he had gained a new amulet that would increase his Life Force regeneration while keeping the blood from staining his clothing. For his class, that was a practical necessity.

Justin was already putting on his new boots while casting aside the old ones. The old boots were unenchanted, gifted to him by Alistair long ago on his first night in Eyrth. He almost didn't want to leave them behind because of that, but they were extra weight, and the Paladin would have understood. They were beyond all saving anyway.

[Do you wish to bind the Ilvari Ambassador Boots to your core?]

Justin gave his assent and immediately felt the benefit of the Endurance enchantment. They would be perfect for long marches.

Justin quickly summoned his character screen to check his experience.

[Experience to Level 7: 989/720 (Level-up Available!)]

Justin closed his screen, finding that everyone seemed to be ready to continue the march north.

"We must pass through the rest of the ruins," Eldrin said. "From there, we'll come out into the western extent of the Northwood, a far gentler forest than the Darkwood. From there, we can either head east-northeast and resupply in Greenhollow, or head straight north, living off the land."

"Which will be faster?" Justin asked.

"It depends on the hunting," Eldrin said. "But pushing directly for Windfall will probably be faster."

"Let's do that, then," Lila said. "We can't risk Gareth getting there first."

"I agree," Eldrin said. "With Pathfinder's Pace, we're likely to make it there in three days of hard walking."

Kargan nodded. "Let's move then."

As they walked through the forested ruins, Justin couldn't help but notice how much easier it was to move. The underbrush almost seemed to melt out of Eldrin's way as they proceeded forward. He had missed his Pathfinder's Pace.

Justin walked beside Kargan. "Congrats on the new gear."

"Thanks," he said gruffly. "You too, for those boots."

"You earned it," Justin said. "I'm glad we found you in that tower. It would have turned out differently otherwise."

Kargan nodded. "Let's just keep our eyes on the goal, Socialite. You've surprised me, too. That thing you did where you got the thera's attention...what was that?"

"It's a skill I have called Dazzling Display. It's quite powerful."

"No doubt," Kargan said. "Without that, that creature might have overwhelmed us." He looked at his staff doubtfully. "Maybe I shouldn't have been the one to earn this."

"Far from it, Kargan," Justin said.

At that point, he almost told him about the Amulet of Equilibrium, but thankfully, he thought better of it. While Kargan was probably trustworthy, it just wasn't worth the risk.

Things were looking up again. The Vault was cleared, the Darkwood left behind, and Eldrin was back in the party, leading them resolutely north.

And when Justin slept next, he would get to process his next level up. Since level 7 was a prime number, he would be getting his first proper skill since level 3. It was a lot to look forward to.

The only thing that was missing was Alistair. Somehow, they'd have to learn to manage without him. The thought was unimaginable. Justin still couldn't believe the Paladin was gone.

It was only proof of just how dangerous their enemies were and how important it was to stay ahead of them.

The party marched north through the ruined city in silence. Within the next hour, they had reached the ruined north gate, exiting into the Northwood beyond.

43

TRUTHS UNVEILED

"At each prime number level, you're offered two new skills to choose from. At every non-prime number level, two boons are offered, unless the level is a multiple of a previously adopted boon, which ascends to a higher tier. And every fifth level always unlocks your party tactic. There is talk, of course, of so-called "rare abilities." You might earn one of these; two if you're lucky. But what few people know—or dare to believe—is that there might be tiers beyond that. Mythic abilities are so rare that those who unlock one are said to be touched by the gods themselves."

—Johanna Ravenhair,
   Leveling and Luck: The Reality of Rare Power

THE WOODS NORTH of the ruins of Eldareth were much kinder than the Darkwood. Gently rolling hills met them, with tall pines and spruces, as they headed north under the guidance of Eldrin and his Pathfinder's Pace. The Umber Range remained to their left, and any streams they came across were shallow. Justin had no issue keeping his feet dry with his new Ilvari boots. Even when the water rose to his calves, it was magically repelled from entering. Beyond useful.

Shadowflight returned with news around mid-morning. Eldrin relayed the bird's message.

"Gareth and the rest have figured out the ruse. They are heading northeast, toward Darkstream Crossing. They should make it in a day. From there, they'll probably travel northeast on the Plainsway. After that, only the gods know."

"How long will it take them to get to Windfall?" Lila asked.

"Five days at the earliest," Eldrin answered. "Thankfully, they don't know that's where we're headed. On the Plainsway, they'll have no opportunity to turn west until they come to the Northway. We should be two days ahead of them by the time we arrive."

"Enough time for a well-earned rest and resupply," Justin said.

"And maybe some shopping," Lila added.

"I'll allow one night at most to be on the safe side," Eldrin said. "Unfortunately, we can't go east on the Northway without risking running into them."

"So, we need to head off the trail again," Lila said. "Well, we're used to that by now."

Eldrin nodded. "There are back roads we can take north of Windfall, but that would take us into the foothills of the Seraphim Range. It will be cold, of course, and there will be some nasty creatures up there."

"Nasty creatures," Kargan said. "Glad I'll be gone by then."

"Might put our coin to work and fill out some missing gear while we're in town," Eldrin continued. "Windfall is a grand city, famed for its markets. I suspect we can't find much better except in Belmora or Eribar."

"Eribar?" Justin asked, looking at Lila. "That's where you're from, right?"

She nodded. "It's the capital of Daeloria." Then, to Kargan, she said, "Careful what you say. I was hired as a guard, and I still haven't found a way to gracefully extricate myself from this situation."

Kargan grunted. "Well, I'll admit. That Vault was quite profitable. But I'm going to need to earn a lot more to make this worth it."

"So," Justin said, trying to get the conversation back on track, "I guess the plan is to cut east using these back roads before coming back down to the Northway?"

"That's the idea," Eldrin said. "We'll have to go at least two solid weeks before risking the Northway. It's hard to say what Gareth's next move will be. Either he spreads his men out to find us, or he simply heads toward Mont Elea, setting up somewhere on the Gulfway to intercept us. The latter would be simpler but would require more patience on his part."

"It would make more sense for you guys to head straight there, then," Kargan said. "Avoid Windfall and keep your lead."

"Yes, that's an option. But that would bring us quite close to him, since he's already farther east. I'd rather not run the risk. His skills are far beyond what any of us can deal with."

"Why not head to Draegor's Keep?" Lila asked. "It's a port, and we have the money to hire someone to ferry us down to Mont Elea. That would keep us off the Gulfway."

"Not a bad idea," Eldrin said, "but we're risking the foul weather of the Seraphic Sea. The wind blowing down from the mountains can be treacherous as the season turns cold."

"We can play it by ear, too," Justin said. "There's no need to decide right now."

He remembered Lila saying she was going to stop at Draegor's Keep. From there, it would just be him and Eldrin. But that was still a while away, so he wasn't too worried.

What he *was* worried about was what happened after Mont Elea. It was still weeks away, months even. Once he got the Death Mark removed, then what? Would the Baron really leave him alone?

Somehow, he doubted it, but hopefully, he would have the protection of these Templars.

Justin tried not to think about things too much, but it was impossible for questions not to form in his mind. They ate a light lunch since they were getting low on food before continuing north.

Around early afternoon, Eldrin motioned them down at the top of a hill. At first, Justin thought there was something wrong until, at the bottom of the incline, he spied a large wild boar rooting around in the underbrush. The creature was sizable.

Eldrin took his time, his movements deliberate as he nocked an arrow. It wasn't an easy shot, but Justin was confident he would get it, especially when Shadowflight fluttered down in a nearby tree. The Ranger would certainly use his new skill, Falcon's Mark, to ensure a perfect hit.

With a steady hand and a keen eye, Eldrin released the arrow as Shadowflight circled above, striking the boar cleanly behind the shoulder, piercing its heart. The animal fell swiftly, ensuring it didn't suffer too much.

"Nice shot," Lila said, impressed.

"We'll set up camp near our kill," Eldrin said. "It'll take the better part of the day to prepare the meat."

It took them ten minutes to actually reach the fallen boar and another two hours to butcher and prepare the meat. First, Eldrin used his knife to bleed the boar, ensuring the meat would not spoil quickly. Next, he skinned the animal, removing the hide in one piece to sell in town later. He then gutted the boar, removing the entrails and setting aside the liver and heart for cooking. Once the boar was fully dressed, they cut the meat into manageable pieces, separating the loins, ribs, and haunches.

The task was laborious, but the reward was worth it; they were down to some stale bread and perhaps one meal of oatmeal, so the meat would be welcome sustenance, providing enough to feed their party for a week, if not more.

They set up a makeshift fire pit using stones they found nearby and gathered dry wood and kindling from the forest floor. Eldrin had a steady flame going within minutes.

They crafted a spit from sturdy branches, skewering the larger pieces of meat and positioning them over the fire. As the meat cooked, they turned the spit slowly, ensuring even roasting. The sizzle of the pork and the aroma of roasting meat were tantalizing. For the smaller cuts, they fashioned a grill from green branches, placing it over the fire and laying the ribs and loins on top. The meat cooked to a golden brown, the fat dripping into the flames and creating bursts of savory smoke.

Eldrin seasoned the liver and heart with salt and herbs from his pack, then wrapped them in large leaves and placed them directly in the embers to cook. The liver and heart would be ready first, providing a quick, nutritious meal while the rest of the meat roasted to perfection. Neither would have been Justin's first pick in his old life, but hunger had a way of changing a man's opinion.

By twilight, Kargan had cast Blood Aegis and everyone had a full belly. They wrapped the remaining meat, about twenty-five pounds' worth per person, in cloth and secured it with rope, using Eldrin's salt to preserve it. Justin's pack was also enchanted to extend the shelf life of perishable food, and apparently, so were the others. It seemed to be a common enchantment, not too expensive to shell out for.

As Kargan and Lila settled down to sleep, Justin and Eldrin stayed awake. The Ranger was smoking a pipe thoughtfully, staring into the flames. Justin would have slept, but too many questions were bouncing around in his mind. Questions for which only Eldrin had the answer.

"Eldrin, can we talk a bit? Away from the camp."

The Ranger looked up. "Sure thing, lad."

They stepped away from the fire, a suitable distance away, but still in sight.

"What's on your mind?" Eldrin asked.

Justin gathered his thoughts. "I have questions. I know I wasn't supposed to be listening at the door at the inn, but the point is, I was, and I heard some things. Things I'd like answers to."

Eldrin nodded. "You want to know what the Baron saw in you, no doubt."

Justin nodded. "Yes. It seems extreme to go through all this trouble over a low-level Socialite. Why did he set the Death Mark on me in the first place? Did Alistair tell you anything?"

"He told me what he cared to tell me," Eldrin said. "I've deduced a fair bit on my own. We were going to tell you when the time was right. But of course, things went sideways..."

"The time is right now, Eldrin. I deserve to know."

The Ranger let out a smoke ring, watching it dissipate into the frigid night. "I expect that you do."

Justin waited patiently. He knew Eldrin wasn't hesitating. He was just trying to figure out the best way to deliver the information.

"As for why he placed that Death Mark on you, Alistair and I agreed that he probably didn't know what he had," Eldrin said. "At least, not at first. He saw you were isolated and alone, and no one would go looking for you. Plus, you have something of a rare class. That can be useful to a man like Valdrik."

Justin frowned in thought. "He assumed I was nobility. I made up some name."

"He's probably heard of every major and minor house in Aranthia, and even beyond its borders," Eldrin said. "If he didn't recognize yours, he saw through the fabrication. He simply saw an opportunity and jumped on it. As for the rest...he didn't figure that out until later."

"What do you mean, 'the rest?' I get that I have a rare class, but surely it can't just be that."

Eldrin nodded. "You're right. Normally, when someone is killed and then raised by a Necromancer, they are mindless, compelled to obey their master. Think of those zombies that attacked us back in Silverton, or the ones we fought in the catacombs. Terrifying in large numbers, but they have no mind or will of their own."

"Okay. So what would make me different?"

"You have a class. That changes everything. You would still be enthralled to the Necromancer, but you'd still have a mind and a will of your own. But a part of the master will always live there with you. You can't do anything that's against your master's wishes. Do you follow?"

Justin swallowed. "I believe so. Wouldn't other people know I'm undead?"

"It would become pretty obvious. Most classed undead, for that reason, stay away from towns and live at the beck and call of their master. Valdrik's men, for example, probably reside somewhere deep in his mansion or in the mountain behind it. At the same time, there are some undead who can hide their condition. They will get a boon that allows them to blend in. It probably wouldn't slip by a proper Paladin or a high-level Priest who has the ability to detect the undead, though."

"I see," Justin said. "So, I would be an undead Socialite. And that's valuable to him."

"My best guess, with you being a charm-based class and undead, is that you would meet the requirements to become a vampire. They are one of those forms of undead I mentioned that can blend in with the living. That would be incredibly useful to a man like Valdrik."

"A vampire?" Justin asked, horrified.

"Possibly. Some of these things are beyond me, admittedly, but Alistair mentioned it."

"Okay, that begs the question. If he *really* wanted to take control of me and make me his little vampire servant, why allow me to leave his mansion in the first place? That seems like a dumb move."

"It wasn't dumb. It was very astute. You were turning in a job for the post office. If he apprehended you, they would see the parcel was accepted, but the courier never came for payment, and that wouldn't be updated in the Universal Ledger. And if there's anything the Royal Mail takes seriously, it's the Universal Ledger."

"Makes sense," Justin said. "But at the same time...it doesn't. I mean, he killed Alistair over this. He's a Paladin, and when he turns up missing, that'll lead to questions."

"Again, you're right," Eldrin said darkly. "There's more."

Justin waited as Eldrin gathered his thoughts.

The Ranger continued. "One of his men was certainly there that night at the Moonlit Alehouse, listening to every word. My greatest failure was not noticing it; I was too deep into my drinks. No doubt, that spy was learning everything he could, so that the Baron wouldn't lose track of you."

Justin's eyes widened. Of course, that made sense. It was chilling to think about.

"The Baron was forced to move faster when Alistair got involved," Eldrin went on.

"That's another thing," Justin said, interrupting. "When Gareth saw Alistair, it seemed he knew him. Do you know anything about that?"

"They trained together at Mont Elea two decades ago," Eldrin said. "They were friends once. Gareth...took a different path. I can't speak to the reasons."

"Huh," Justin said. "That sounds like a story."

"Aye, it does. But you were asking what else Valdrik saw in you. Well, you should know yourself. You said it loud enough for half the tables to hear."

"The Prismatic Core," Justin said in realization.

The Ranger nodded. "That's right. They're rare—beyond rare. And you don't know what a person would do to get their hands on one. Unlike other class cores, which disappear when someone dies, Prismatic Cores simply become unbound, available for anyone to use again. At some point, after changing hands a few times, they run out of power and disappear altogether. Even so, if people figure out you have one, you're going to be hunted down."

Justin felt the blood drain from his face. "I was an idiot."

"Maybe," Eldrin said. "You were also a little drunk, and you didn't know better. Then Alistair got involved. That's why the Baron made his move despite the risk. Of course, if he kills you, you'll be enthralled by him. But my thinking is that he'd rather destroy you entirely to gain access to your Prismatic Core. At first, maybe it was about getting a useful new servant. The core just upped the stakes."

Justin suppressed a shudder. "How much is a Prismatic Core worth? From what little I understand, it gives you any class you want. Valuable, to be sure, but is it really something to murder someone for?"

"Well, I'll answer the easy one first. There's no way to quantify how much a Prismatic Core is worth. For one, most people don't think Prismatic Cores exist. Such a thing is beyond price. It might be worth more than the entire Queendom of Aranthia to some."

"I feel like I'm missing something."

"Well, for one, it gives anyone an extra Core Attribute and a class. Try to think of the implications of that, lad."

Justin thought about it. He didn't think he was stupid, but he was coming up short.

"I can only think of what it did for me. I had no Core Attribute or class to begin with. The Prismatic Core gave me both."

"Yours is a special case. I assume you'll get to choose your second Core Attribute upon reaching Level 20, same as others. Or you might get nothing at all. You're not from here, so I can't say. What I can say is that every human on Eyrth is born with one of the six attributes. And when they reach twenty years old, they have to pick a class core to match. It's the Creator's way of balancing us."

"I have to admit, I'm still lost. I don't understand why the Baron would want my Prismatic Core. After all, he already has his advanced class." Justin thought it over a bit. "Unless my Prismatic Core would give him *another* Core Attribute and class on top of what he already has."

From Eldrin's grim expression, Justin realized he'd hit the mark, or was at least close. "That's what we're trying to prevent. Normally, such a thing isn't possible. You get two Core Attributes, one at birth and one at Level 20, if you manage to reach it. You don't choose the first one, but you do choose the second one. A Prismatic Core bypasses all that. It would allow Valdrik to take on a *third* Core Attribute and unlock a class even more powerful than the one he already possesses. An Ascendant Class."

"Ascendant Class? What's that?"

"The most powerful tier of classes," Eldrin said. "It's said to be only possible with a Prismatic Core and an Advanced Class. Four Prismatic Cores are said to pop up a year, and most go undiscovered. They only appear in Eyrth's most dangerous Vaults on either a solstice or an equinox. Only a handful of people in all of history have actually been documented to have an Ascendant Class. One of them was the head of the Shadow Empire, Belshar the Nightbringer. His Ascendant Class was something called the Eternal Sovereign Class."

"Eternal Sovereign. Sounds powerful. And...evil."

"Powerful enough for him to rule his empire for centuries, never aging, until he was finally overthrown and destroyed."

"What happened to *his* Prismatic Core?" Justin asked.

Eldrin shrugged. "Who knows? At this point, it's faded to the Aether or someone else has it. Maybe it's yours. That's how rare they are."

Justin shuddered to think about it. "Could it really be?"

"It's not likely," Eldrin said. "The way you described coming upon it is...strange. Did you really just find it in a meadow? There was no Vault, no other dangerous enemies around?"

"I went through that portal, got knocked out for a while, as far as I can tell. When I woke up, I saw it there. So I grabbed it. There was nothing more dangerous than a few goblins, which came later. As soon as I picked it up, I heard the Voice, and it gave me the option to choose any class. When those goblins came out of the trees, I panicked and selected the Socialite class."

"I see," Eldrin said, his brow furrowing in thought. "And after you selected Socialite, did it give you a Charisma core to match it?"

Justin nodded. "It did."

"Hmm." Eldrin was silent for at least half a minute, stewing over Justin's story. "It almost sounds as if..."

As he trailed off, Justin watched him closely. "Almost as if what?"

But Eldrin, infuriatingly, didn't answer him. "It's beyond belief, lad. Alistair said the gods had their hands in this, and now I believe it. Paladins have a sense for these kinds of things, even if they don't understand them entirely."

Justin frowned. "So, if a Prismatic Core gives a new Core Attribute and any class, does that mean if I had found another class core first, and *then* the Prismatic Core, I could have taken an Advanced Class early?"

Eldrin shrugged. "Maybe. But I've never heard of anyone taking an Advanced Class before Level 20. But that doesn't mean it isn't possible."

Justin gave an ironic laugh. "Just my luck, huh? It was basically wasted then. Instead of getting two Core Attributes from the get-go, I only got one."

"Well, think of it this way. It's still better than no class core at all. And you couldn't have known that at the time. You should still get your second Core Attribute at Level 20. Well, I can't be really sure you will, but it's hard to imagine that not being the case."

"It feels like a missed opportunity," Justin said. "Just like taking on the Socialite class instead of something more useful."

"Now, your class definitely has its uses. You should know that as well as I do. No one class can do everything, and we cover for each other's weaknesses."

"I suppose," Justin said. "So I have to wait until Level 20 for the second Core Attribute."

"That's the most likely outcome. That's a long way off, but it means all you have to do is find another core that's compatible with the Socialite Class. Either way, none of that matters unless we can get the Baron off your back."

Justin sighed, his shoulders slumping. "I won't be safe for the rest of my life, will I?"

"Well, your secret is safe with me and Lila. I have a keen eye for character, and she's a good one." He paused thoughtfully. "If I were you, though, I wouldn't tell anyone else. I doubt Valdrik is telling anyone, either. He'll want the prize for himself."

"There's the one who overheard the conversation in the tavern."

Eldrin gave an ironic smile. "That man is dead. I guarantee it. Either that, or he's *undead* and completely beholden to the Baron."

Justin swallowed. The cold logic made sense. "Do you think Gareth knows?"

"I can't say. My guess would be no, but anything is possible."

"So, that leaves the Baron and possibly Gareth," Justin said. "But there's no way we can bring either of them down. I'm just a Level 6 Socialite right now."

"Well, we'll get there when we get there," Eldrin said. "The goal is getting to Mont Elea and getting the High Priest of Arion to remove the Death Mark. From there...well, we'll just have to see. Whatever the case, never tell anyone about the core. I guarantee you'll regret it."

"I should still get an advanced class early," Justin said. "It just...feels like I'm being punished a bit."

"Punished?" Eldrin chuckled. "Hardly. Having a class is something most people never get. They say only one out of a hundred ever gets one. It opens doors for you that don't exist for most."

Justin understood his point. "Still."

"It's also possible that even *if* you found the Prismatic Core first, the Creator would still require you to reach Level 20 first. The truth is, your situation has probably never happened before." He cleared his throat. "Well, maybe you weren't the first."

"What do you mean?"

"Well, it's a long story. But there was a woman thousands of years ago. People here in Serenthel call her Ayla. She basically saved all of Creation. She's a special case, though, and nobody agrees on a lot of the details. She basically became a religion, what you know as the Church of Light."

"*She's* a religion?" Justin frowned. "Then why haven't I seen her anywhere? In art, I mean."

Eldrin gave a mysterious smile. "Have you seen that phoenix all over the churches, on Alistair's armor?"

"Is that her?"

"That's right. What they say she became. Anyway, it's just a story. And in part because of that story, they say Prismatic Cores carry the blessing of the Creator Himself. I can't say if it's true, of course. But certainly, you've attracted some strange happenings. For example, we've run across three Vaults in the last week, and I don't think that's a coincidence. Some might say it's the Creator's luck."

"That's not luck!" Justin protested. "We almost died every single time."

"Think of it this way. Normally, the only person who'd even have access to a Prismatic Core would be someone who *wants* access to advanced Vaults and treasures. The Prismatic Core would be a way of getting that. It's also said to influence the rarity and power of items you receive from Vaults, and even in the presentation of rare skills and boons at level-ups. It's worth more than the possibility of an Ascendant Class."

Justin thought it over. Yes, it would make sense. They had run across three Vaults, and even Alistair had mentioned that it was strange. Then there had been the enchantment on his Cane of Valoria that had given him a one-time boost to his base Charisma. Gribble the Snow Goblin had mentioned the extreme rarity of that enchantment, to the point where he had sent some goons after him. Even Alistair mentioned that the Cane of Valoria, a silver-tier weapon, had the properties of a gold-tier weapon.

None on its own was definitive proof in isolation, but altogether, it painted a picture.

For the moment at least, Justin was more worried about Baron Valdrik. He was already incredibly powerful. It wasn't just his class, but the power and soldiers under his command.

What was his game, anyway?

"What does Valdrik want?" Justin asked. "Not my core, I mean. He's a Necromancer. That's not a class, is it? He's already a Lexicant."

"Necromancer is not a class," Eldrin confirmed. "It's called an Aspect. Kind of like a Focus, but not really. It's not anything you unlock by leveling, but rather by undertaking certain actions."

"Certain actions? Like what?"

"Such as pledging your core to Morvath, the God of Death. Or doing some other nasty things."

"Oh."

"As for what Valdrik wants, we don't know. Alistair came to Silverton to find out where the bodies were going, and it all pointed back to the Baron. The Baron getting his hands on your Prismatic Core is just about the worst thing that could happen. The last thing we want is to face a tyrant with that kind of power."

"So that's what he wants? Power?"

"What else could it be? The more thralls he has, the more experience he gets. That was how the Eternal Sovereign got his start back in the day, and it's why all power-mad fools are drawn to Necromancy.

The trouble with budding Necromancers is getting caught too early. That's what we have the Templars of Arion for, and they are quite effective at rooting out Death Magic practitioners. But if you don't catch the Necromancer in time, it can get bad, really fast."

"How bad?"

"Well, the Nightbringer started the Shadow Empire. Turns out, it's easy to conquer all your neighbors and create an empire spanning two continents when you have access to an Ascendant Class and can easily recycle dead soldiers, even if they don't fight as effectively as the living. Not to say Valdrik will be like that, but with Alistair dead, we're all that is left to deliver the news to the people who can actually do something about it. That's why I'm risking my neck for no guaranteed payout."

At last, Justin felt as if he understood Eldrin's motivations better. He was a good man, but helping Justin was also in his best interest. It seemed he truly believed every word he had spoken.

That terrified Justin, but there was nothing else he could do. He was stuck in this world with no way out. So there was nothing left but to see it through.

"Thanks for everything," Justin managed. "I have more questions, but this is already too much to take in."

"Aye, that it is. But for all the doom and gloom, remember that not everything is about levels, skills, and classes. There are the choices you make. You become those choices. Every day, we face decisions, and those decisions shape us. Always do the right thing so long as it's in your power. Attribute boosts aren't everything; your own strengths *do* matter. If you work hard, you can punch above your weight."

Justin nodded, letting out a sigh. "It doesn't feel that way, but I get your point."

The Ranger clapped him on the shoulder. "Let's get some rest. Tomorrow is another long day."

As they returned to the fire, Justin's mind buzzed with the new information. The road ahead was dangerous, but at least now he understood the stakes better. And he understood why Alistair and Eldrin had hidden it for so long. It was a lot to absorb.

He felt motivated, as he never had before. It was a reason to get stronger. Maybe he was a Socialite, but tomorrow was a new dawn and a new level-up.

Level 7 might not be much, and Socialite might be a maligned class. But all the same, Justin resolved to become as strong as he could.

As he settled down on his bedroll, the fire at his back, he reached for the Amulet of Equilibrium. Assuming he could keep boosting his Charisma and get the Baron's Death Mark removed, the Amulet would do a lot of work on its own, boosting his other attributes far beyond what they had a right to be.

So far, it had only been about survival. And it was going to continue being about that for a long time.

But one day, with luck, he would be strong enough to punch back.

And he looked forward to seeing Baron Valdrik's face when that happened.

44

A RARE SKILL

"If you want someone to do something, forbid it. If you want them to believe a lie, make it taboo."

—Lord-Orator Dain Verris,
  The Art of Influence

JUSTIN STIRRED awake to the smell of pine and the sound of birdsong.

And, of course, the Voice informing him of his next level.

[You have reached Level 7. You are becoming more competent, yes. But with increased competency comes the budding realization of just how much you truly don't know.]

Justin thought the description was apt, given the revelations of the previous night. But a part of him wondered whether the Voice was trying to tell him something else. Or was he reading too much into it?

[You have one attribute point to distribute.]

Justin immediately willed it into Charisma.

[Your Charisma is now 18.]

Justin smiled. He knew exactly what came next.

[As a Level 7 Socialite, you have unlocked your next skill. Choose wisely—there is no going back.]

As the options populated before him, his eyes widened. He didn't have just one but *two* rare skills to choose from. Maybe Eldrin was right about the advantage of the Prismatic Core.

Intimidating Lean (Rare): True charisma doesn't always play nice. Adopt a domineering posture that inspires fear and subservience, even when you have nothing to back it up. Its power scales with your Charisma attribute. (Cooldown: 1 hour)

A Solid Thwack (Rare): Strike with ultimate precision, dealing 20% extra damage and inflicting Daze for 10 seconds, interrupting your target's current action or skill. They cannot use it while Daze is active. Restricted to canes or bludgeoning instruments. (Cooldown: 3 minutes)

Justin considered his options.

Intimidating Lean felt like a bad guy ability, and yet there were plenty of situations where its use would be highly apparent. Sometimes, people just could not be convinced to see things your way, and preventing a greater disaster required actions that were morally dubious. He was especially intrigued by the part that said he didn't *have* to follow through on his threat. It would inspire fear regardless, but it still felt "icky" to use. Definitely not his style.

Even if he didn't like the idea, he had to respect its use case. The fact that it was a "rare" skill told Justin it was highly effective.

But then, there was A Solid Thwack. It would be a solid skill to add to his rotation. Extra damage was nothing to sneeze at, but a guaranteed way to interrupt an enemy's action was an absolute must. The cooldown of three minutes was quite long for a combat move, but saving the skill for a known powerful attack was probably the best way to play it.

It required him to be close to the enemy, and for the attack to land, but to him, there was no comparison. It was an attacking move, and combined with his new Add Injury to Insult boon, it would deal even more damage.

With a mental click, he confirmed his selection.

[You have chosen A Solid Thwack. When words fail, let your cane do the talking.]

A warm sensation washed over him as the skill was integrated into his being.

As with every level up, Justin summoned his character screen to check how much experience he needed to reach the next level:

Justin Talemaker
    Class: Socialite
    Level: 7
    Experience to Level 8: 269/940

    Abilities:
    Skills: Poison Barb, Dazzling Display, Dandy's Swagger, A Solid Thwack
    Boons: Magnetic Presence, Basic Cane Proficiency, Add Injury to Insult
    Tactics: Refined Aura

A long way to go to Level 8, then. But when he did get there, he stood to upgrade to the next tier of his cane proficiency.

Justin came out of his concentration to find that someone had already served him some pork, while most of the camp was packed up.

"There you are," Lila said. "You were just staring off into space for a few minutes."

Justin was already digging into his meal. "Did you get a new skill?"

"I did. It's called Encore Performance. It refreshes the cooldown of any one of my skills."

"Hey, that sounds like it would come in handy. Does it have a cooldown?"

"Ten minutes," Lila said. "It's something that will grow with me, too. If I unlock truly powerful skills down the line with long cooldowns, I'll be glad I took this one."

"Absolutely," Justin agreed. "Look, this is something of a strange transition, but I've been wondering. So that Voice we hear is 'Veyrith,' right?"

"Yes," Lila asked, looking at him strangely. "What about it?"

"Well, I was wondering. Can the other gods talk to us, too? I know Arion is the God of Power, but are there gods of the other attributes?"

Kargan watched him from across the fire. The orc still didn't know Justin's history, or lack thereof, in this world. Justin really needed to be more careful with what he said.

Lila answered, "Well, they don't talk to us in the way you might think. But they can speak in signs, or in dreams. Certainly, classes have more direct connections to the gods, but most wouldn't claim to speak to them directly. Veyrith is basically how the Creator communicates with us. His spirit, if you will."

"A Holy Spirit," Justin said. "I know some things about religion."

"Yes, that would be apt, but people usually call Veyrith the Ethereal Voice. Or 'Voice' for short. But as for your question about the Six Gods, Arion is the God of Power, like you said. But there's also Thalora, Goddess of Endurance; Elyndra, Goddess of Coordination; Vesperis, God of Intellect; Lioran, God of Spirit. And finally, Zephyra, Goddess of Charisma. But together, they make up the Six."

"I see. It seems like Arion is the most worshipped, though."

"In this part of the world, yes. But go to the central part of Serenthel and you'll find that Vesperis and Lioran are more popular. In my country, Zephyra is highly favored, while in the south of Aranthia, Thalora and Elyndra are most popular. However, all are part of the Pantheon of the Church of Light, equally esteemed for what they provide."

"What about the Creator?" Justin asked. "Is he above all of them?"

"Yes. I guess you could say he is the highest deity of all, on a higher plane than the Six. The Six are who you talk to when you want something. The Creator is just not someone you talk to, you know? He's too important for average people like you and me."

"I see," Justin said. He supposed it was like Catholics praying to Mary as an intermediary, or perhaps a saint. The concept wasn't wholly unfamiliar to him.

And yet, it was something of a contradiction. The Voice talked to anyone with a class when they leveled up, and yet, apparently, it was impossible to talk back.

Well, he supposed religion was nothing if not confusing, whatever reality one found themselves in.

"What about your new skill?" Lila asked. "I forgot to ask."

"Well," Justin said with a smile, "it's rare."

Lila's eyes widened, and even Eldrin's and Kargan's ears seemed to perk up at that.

"Rare?" Lila asked. "Tell me!"

"It's called A Solid Thwack. It lets me interrupt an enemy's skill and deal extra damage."

Kargan grunted with approval. "That could be a game changer. Interrupt skills are pretty rare."

Eldrin nodded. "We will see how it comes into play. If you are presented with a rare skill, it's almost always worth taking it, except under specific circumstances."

Justin didn't see the point in telling him that the other skill had been rare, too. It was further proof that his Prismatic Core was definitely shaping his destiny.

Besides this, Kargan revealed he had reached Level 4 and now enjoyed a new boon called Sanguine Infusion. It basically made all his wards, shields, and aegises heal slowly over time as well.

Justin frowned. "That sounds cool!" He cleared his throat. "So, uh, what's the difference between a ward, a shield, and an aegis, anyway?"

Thankfully, Kargan didn't find this a strange question. "A ward is basically an active effect that covers a certain area. It affects anyone within it. It can be either a good effect or a bad effect, depending on the use. A shield, on the other hand, is purely for defense. It can block physical or magical damage, but usually both. Finally, an aegis combines the properties of both. It normally shields an area around the caster in a dome, granting protection to anyone under it while also giving positive boosts. Naturally, it's the most expensive of all three."

"I see," Justin said. "Thank you for explaining."

"No problem," Kargan said. "I'm still learning this stuff, too. We orcs aren't exposed to magic much."

"Makes sense," Justin said.

He joined the party in the morning preparations, which were almost done.

"We'd better leave," Eldrin said. "We've got a long way to travel yet."

As they set out north, leaving no trace behind, the forest welcomed them with its natural beauty. The trees stood tall and proud, their leaves rustling gently in the breeze. Sunlight danced through the branches, casting dappled patterns on the forest floor. Birds flitted from tree to tree, their songs creating a soothing symphony.

"This forest is so beautiful," Lila said. "It's hard to believe we were fighting for our lives yesterday."

"That's the nature of our journey," Eldrin replied, his eyes scanning the surroundings. "One moment, we're in danger; the next, we're in a natural paradise. It's the balance of our world."

Justin took a deep breath, savoring the crisp, clean air. "I could get used to this."

They walked in companionable silence for a while, each lost in their thoughts and the tranquility of the forest. They were heading north, toward Windfall, and for now, the journey was as important as the destination.

Here, it seemed danger was far away, so Lila invoked her Bardic Inspiration, boosting their Endurance. Almost immediately, Justin felt strength infuse into his limbs, pushing him to the top of a steep incline. Lila's voice stilled once everyone had made it to the top.

Justin was met with majestic views of the surrounding forest and the Umber Mountains to the west. To the north, he could spy vast mountains in the distance that dwarfed the glorified hills to the west of them. The peaks were jagged and towering, capped with snow that glistened in the sunlight. Wisps of clouds clung to the upper reaches, while lower down, dark green forests blanketed the slopes. Waterfalls cascaded down the mountainsides, their mist catching the light and creating rainbows.

"The Seraphim Range," Eldrin said. "Aranthia's northern border and the tallest mountains in this part of the continent. Windfall will be somewhere over there."

He pointed to the western arm of the mountain range, where they met the Umbers.

"Looks like a lot of elevation to gain," Justin said.

"Yes. We'll be out of the Northwood soon. I'm certain there is a village or two on the way in the foothills. Come. We need to keep moving."

The forest thinned out slightly, revealing the faint outline of an old, overgrown trail winding through the trees. Eldrin, unsurprisingly, was the first to spot it. He knelt down, brushing aside some undergrowth to reveal a path that looked like it hadn't seen regular use in years.

"Look here," Eldrin said, his voice thoughtful. "Looks like an old trail."

Justin peered over his shoulder. "Do you think it's safe to follow?"

Lila glanced around, her eyes scanning the surrounding hills. "It's this or continue bushwhacking. This trail could save us a lot of time and energy."

Kargan nodded, but his brow was furrowed. "But what if it leads us into trouble? We don't know where it goes."

Eldrin inspected the trail, noting faint but recent footprints. "Someone has used this path recently. It's overgrown but not completely abandoned. I think it's safe enough."

Justin looked at the others, seeing the mixture of curiosity and caution on their faces. "All right, let's follow it. We should be careful, though."

As they walked along the trail, the signs of wildlife became more apparent. Deer tracks crisscrossed their path, and bird nests perched high in the trees. A fox den nestled among the roots of an old oak tree. Its occupants peered out curiously before retreating into the shadows.

"Seems like this trail is a lifeline for the local wildlife," Eldrin observed. "We should be in good company."

The trail gradually led them to higher elevations, and soon they found themselves at a vantage point overlooking a vast valley. The scene before them was breathtaking: a river wound through the valley below, its waters sparkling in the midday sun. Along the banks of the river was a small village nestled among a stand of trees, filled with sturdy houses and thatched roofs, a water mill, and small surrounding fields growing winter wheat.

"Is that the Marin?" Justin asked.

"It is," Eldrin confirmed. "Much smaller this far north, even though we're only a hundred miles from Highcliff."

"Can we go to that town?" Lila asked. "I'd kill for a warm bed to sleep in."

"It should be safe enough," Eldrin confirmed. "I imagine it would be impossible for them to have sent anyone up into this isolated valley."

In the distance, the Seraphim Mountains rose majestically, their snow-capped peaks and blue glaciers glistening against the clear blue sky. Cascading waterfalls tumbled down the mountainsides.

"Wow," Justin breathed, taking in the panoramic view. "This is incredible."

If he had a button that would take him back to his old life, he might hesitate to press it, at least at the moment, just because of this vista. If every day could be like this rather than running for his life, he'd see the appeal of staying here.

"It's been years since I've been up this way," Eldrin said. "The Seraphim Mountains are one of the most beautiful sights in all Serenthel."

"What's on the other side?" Justin asked.

Eldrin shrugged. "The Everwood Forest, and beyond that, the Frostplain, which is tundra. Very dangerous lands. Too much for even a Ranger like me, at least in most parts. Dire wolves, frost trolls, frost elementals, wraiths, frost giants, and even ice drakes, if you're truly unlucky. Far safer on this side. There is one large city, called Kaldrath, on the Ghostly Sea, but it's a long journey and not worth the effort."

They took in the scenery, the grandeur of the mountains filling Justin with a sense of awe. The cold air carried the faint scent of pine and the distant sound of rushing water.

Kargan observed the mountains, but it seemed nothing new to him. It was probably a common sight for him.

"We should get moving soon," Eldrin said eventually. "But let's take a few more minutes to enjoy this. Moments like these are rare."

The group nodded in agreement, savoring the serenity of the mountains for a little while longer before they had to continue their journey down into the valley.

45

THE PINE AND HEARTH

"Regarding the Scholar class, many would ask, 'Why do you need a class to read books?' What they fail to understand is the sheer depth of what Scholars can achieve. They can store memories with perfect clarity, absorb a page at a glance, and the most practiced can even recall entire libraries with a thought. They analyze patterns, predict outcomes, and wield logic as deftly as any warrior wields a blade. But the most important truth of all? Information is power. As they say, swords win battles, but knowledge wins wars."

—High Scholar Arden Keln
  The Codex of Essential Truths

BY LATE AFTERNOON, they had reached the small town on the Marin. The day had turned quite cold, and Justin was sure it was below freezing. This was confirmed as a light snow fell. It only spoke of how quickly they had climbed in elevation over the previous two days.

It was hard to guess this town's population, but Justin supposed it probably held about two or three hundred people. Farmers in the fields gave them friendly nods as they passed into the town's main drag, a dirt road lined with sturdy stone buildings with thatched roofs, all letting out gentle plumes of smoke.

Justin saw the people bundled in warm clothing, their breaths visible in the crisp air. Children scurried about with rosy cheeks, and elderly folk sat on porches, knitting or whittling wood, nodding as they passed. Already, a layer of white was being added to the quaint town.

A few stores caught Justin's eye: a general store with a wooden sign swinging in the breeze, a blacksmith hammering away at his forge, a potion shop with colorful vials displayed in the window, a tailor, a butcher, and a watermill turning slowly by the river's edge.

At the end of the town stood a two-story building, the only one in town, that had the look of an inn about it. Its stone walls were weathered but sturdy, while ivy crept up one side, adding a touch of rustic charm. The windows were framed with dark wooden shutters, and the thatched roof looked recently repaired, shedding light snow as it fell. Lanterns hung from the eaves, casting a warm glow. A sign above the door read "The Pine and Hearth." Indeed, on the inn's left side was a tall white pine tree, for which the inn was likely named. The inn looked inviting, with smoke curling from its two chimneys and the sound of laughter and the merry piping of a flute faintly audible from inside.

Justin had never seen a more welcoming sight. Lila's steps were lighter, but Justin couldn't help but notice that Kargan looked unsure. Indeed, everyone in this town was likely to be human. Justin hoped the orc wouldn't face prejudice.

"You'll be fine," Justin said. "You're with us."

Kargan gave a slow nod but said nothing.

Eldrin opened the sturdy front door, throwing it back. They were greeted by a rush of warm air and the comforting aroma of roasting meat and fresh bread. The common room was inviting, with wooden beams overhead and a large stone hearth crackling with a welcoming fire. Villagers and travelers alike filled the room, conversing while enjoying the bard's lively tunes from a corner. Wooden tables and chairs were scattered about, almost all occupied by groups. Justin was surprised by the nearly full common room, but perhaps that was due to the weather.

A pretty barmaid with rosy cheeks and a warm smile wove between the tables, carrying trays laden with mugs of ale and plates of hearty food.

As they headed for the counter, the innkeeper, a stout woman with graying hair pulled back into a tight bun, greeted them warmly. "Welcome to the Pine and Hearth. With the festival, space is limited. It's forty coppers for the dorm. A silver and twenty if you want something larger."

"Nothing in between the two?" Justin asked.

"We're out of our smaller rooms," she replied with a sympathetic smile. "We've got two big ones left, while we still have a few cots in the dorms."

"We'll take the two larger ones," Eldrin said. "Are they next to each other?"

"Yes," the innkeeper said. "They also have the option for a larger, private bath brought directly to your room. It's thirty coppers per room."

"We'll take it," Eldrin said. "Around ten this evening works for the bath."

"Very good, sir. Will you be taking dinner this evening? If so, it'll be twenty coppers a head, and thirty if you'd like drinks."

"Yes to food and drinks," Eldrin confirmed.

The innkeeper had clearly perfected the art of the upsell. "That'll be four silvers, twenty coppers."

Eldrin slid over a fat, five-silver coin. "Extra for your discretion. If you see anything strange, would you be so kind as to let us know?"

"Of course, sir." She slid across two brass keys. "You'll be in rooms 11 and 12, with a westward-facing view."

Justin did a quick mental calculation, giving Eldrin one silver and twenty-five coppers, as did Lila and Kargan.

"Let's drop our stuff off first," Eldrin said.

They headed up a narrow wooden staircase to the second floor. The corridor was dimly lit, the floor creaking at their passage. They found their rooms at the end of the hall. Inside, they were cozy and well-furnished, though simple. Each had a sizable bed with thick quilts, a small writing desk, and a wooden chest for belongings. A small iron stove, already prepared with wood, promised to keep the rooms warm and cozy as the night turned colder. The windows looked out over the snow-covered town, offering a picturesque view of the white-dusted rooftops and the pine tree beside the inn.

Eldrin placed his pack on the chest in one room and turned to the others. "We should get situated and then head back down for dinner. It's been a long day, and we deserve a good meal."

"So," Kargan said. "Who's with whom?"

"You can stay with me," Eldrin said. "I imagine it's been a while since you've felt a comfortable bed, and a Ranger is just as comfortable on the floor."

"Let's go drop off our stuff, roomie," Lila said to Justin.

Justin and Lila did so; though, out of habit, Justin kept his cane, as well as the trusty dagger Eldrin had given him long ago. "Flip a coin for the bed?"

She watched him strangely. "There's room for both of us. It's not like that small one in Whispering Pines."

"I see," Justin said.

"Or would you rather sleep alone?"

"It's just that sleeping together has certain...implications."

Lila laughed. "Sometimes, I forget how modest you are. It's cute. As long as you don't snore or hog the quilts, we won't have any issues."

"Well, if you're okay with it, I am, too."

"Great. Let's head downstairs. I'm starving."

With that settled, they headed back to the common room. Eldrin and Kargan were already waiting, sitting at a prime corner table not too near and not too far from the hearth. A glass window behind them revealed an increase in snowfall and the rushing rapids of the River Marin.

Justin and Lila settled in. The barmaid soon approached, a woman likely in her late thirties. Her cheerful demeanor instantly put even Kargan at ease. Her chestnut-brown hair was tied back in a neat bun, and her bright blue eyes sparkled above a light dusting of freckles across her nose.

"Welcome to The Pine and Hearth, travelers," she greeted, her eyes lingering on Eldrin a moment longer than on the others. "Here for the Autumn Festival, or just passing through?"

"Passing through," Eldrin replied smoothly, his tone warm and charming. "Though from the lovely ambiance, it feels like a grave misfortune to leave so soon."

The barmaid giggled like a girl twenty years younger. "Yes, many come for the fresh mountain air. Even though it's gotten unseasonably cold, that hasn't stopped the people from piling in. What's your pleasure? Food, drinks, or both?"

"What's on the menu?" Eldrin asked, leaning forward slightly to give her his full attention. "A hearty stew would do wonders for me."

"We've got a delicious venison stew, freshly baked bread with rosemary butter, roasted pheasant, spiced apple tarts, and a selection of sharp cheeses. For drinks, we have our famous honey mead, blackberry wine, and a strong ale brewed right here in town."

"Just bring out everything you can. I'll try the mead."

"Blackberry wine for me," Lila said.

"Ale," Kargan said.

"Same," Justin said.

The barmaid flashed a smile, her eyes taking in Eldrin most of all. "Of course. You won't be disappointed with any of it. If you need anything at all, I'm here. I'll be back with your meal shortly. I'm Mira, by the way."

She gave a quick bob and headed for the kitchen, casting a glance over her shoulder.

"So, *that's* how a Ranger flirts," Lila said playfully.

Eldrin chuckled, a slight blush coloring his cheeks. "Just being polite, Lila. Nothing more."

"Polite?" Justin asked with a wink. "She said 'anything at all,' Eldrin."

Eldrin chuckled while Kargan remained silent, apparently

uncomfortable with the conversation. It was hard for Justin to remember that he was just a teenager sometimes.

Within a couple of minutes, Mira brought their drinks back, and Justin couldn't help but notice that Eldrin's was in a larger mug than theirs, perhaps by a few ounces.

"Enjoy," she said.

Once she was gone, Lila gave Justin a knowing smile as he regarded Eldrin. "Who knew Rangers had rizz?"

Eldrin took a swig of his mead. "Rizz?"

"It's what the kids from my lands call charisma."

Eldrin shrugged with a smile. "I wouldn't be a Ranger if I didn't know how to leave a mark."

Justin grinned, a teasing line coming to mind. "Just make sure it's the right mark, Eldrin. We don't want her tracking us down later with a broken heart."

Lila joined in with a playful glint in her eye. "Yeah, we're already being chased by a Baron, but a woman scorned? Far more dangerous."

Even Kargan couldn't help but laugh.

Eldrin smiled and leaned back. "If I leave a mark, it's because I know how to cover my tracks. No broken hearts, just fond memories."

They laughed as the lively chatter of villagers and travelers filled the room with a comforting hum. For the first time in days, Justin felt himself truly relax.

Lila's attention was drawn to the dartboard in the corner. "Anyone fancy a round?"

"I'm game," Justin said.

Kargan, however, seemed more interested in a dice game going on a few tables over. He was already standing up to look.

"Enjoy yourselves," Eldrin said. "I think I'll hold our table."

Justin followed Lila to the dartboard, watching as she picked up the darts and handed him the red ones. "You know how to play, right?"

He eyed the board, which seemed no different from his own world. "First to zero wins, right?"

Lila nodded, a mischievous glint in her eye. "I have to warn you, though—I'm pretty good."

Justin raised an eyebrow. "Oh? Well, I'm not so terrible myself."

Her smile widened. "How about we make it interesting with a little wager?"

"What were you thinking?"

"Ten silvers."

"Whoa, what about honor and glory?"

She laughed, her eyes sparkling. "What's the matter? Afraid to lose to a girl?"

"Not at all. It's just...you've got skills that enhance your throwing. Hardly seems fair."

She pretended to consider it. "All right, how about this? If I win, I get the spot closer to the stove. If you win, you get a kiss. Deal?"

Justin couldn't help but smirk. "Sounds like you win either way. You either get a kiss from a devilishly handsome guy like me, or you get the warmer spot."

She tilted her head, her smile playful. "So, what will it be? I promise it won't be just a peck on the cheek."

Mocking a wipe of sweat from his brow, Justin pretended to weigh his options. Truth be told, he liked it cool when he slept, so there wasn't much to lose. "All right, you're on."

Unsurprisingly, it turned out Lila was the far superior darts player. They laughed and joked as they took turns. Kargan, meanwhile, was still watching the dice game, his curiosity piqued by the enthusiastic cheers of the players. He was already reaching for his coin pouch to place some bets.

Justin glanced over at the bar and saw Eldrin chatting up Mira, the two of them sharing a quiet conversation. So much for guarding the table, though Justin supposed their drinks were doing a good enough job of that. The barmaid was batting her eyes and even leaning forward to enhance what was already quite abundant. Eldrin's demeanor was relaxed, his smile genuine as he listened to her talk. Mira's laughter rang out occasionally, and she seemed to enjoy his company as much as he enjoyed hers. He was telling her some amusing story or other. Clearly, Eldrin had a lot more experience in the ladies' department than he did.

After a few more minutes, as everyone took their seats, Mira set the food down with a flourish, her eyes twinkling.

"Enjoy. If you need anything else, just let me know." She gave Eldrin a special smile before heading back to the bar.

Justin dug into his food. The stew was savory, the bread warm and crusty, and the pheasant perfectly roasted. The spiced apple tarts provided a sweet finish, their flavors a delightful blend of cinnamon and nutmeg. Justin felt himself relax further after he had downed a couple of pints.

Justin, edified by alcohol, mingled with some locals, learning the name of the town was, fittingly, Pinecrest, and that Windfall was about a two-day journey north on the dirt road leading out of town. He learned Windfall was a large city of stone, built into the mountainside, filled with staircases and tunnels intermixed with the buildings themselves. It was a border city, guarding the Wind Pass between Aranthia and Daeloria. Justin regretted he wouldn't have more than a day to explore it. From the sound of things, it would be the largest city he'd seen so far, Eldareth notwithstanding.

He also learned that, apparently, the Autumn Festival was a countrywide holiday in Aranthia and not just in Silverton. Justin listened as Eldrin and Kargan discussed their plans for the next day's journey while Lila hummed along with the bard's tune.

As the night wore on, the common room emptied somewhat, and the fire in the hearth burned low.

"We should get some sleep," Eldrin said. "Long day tomorrow."

Justin nodded, stifling a yawn. It was nice to relax after they had been through so much. "Thanks for allowing this, Eldrin. We needed it."

The Ranger nodded. "Well, rest is important. Just be careful what you say and who you speak to."

Justin nodded, but the warning made him second-guess every conversation he'd had that evening. He didn't feel like he'd revealed anything important, but maybe his questions about Windfall would be enough to raise suspicions should Gareth's company find themselves in this place. Certainly, their party would be remembered.

Justin supposed Eldrin was counting on them staying ahead. Gareth coming here probably wasn't too likely if he was going on the Plainsway, as Eldrin supposed. Either way, Shadowflight would return tomorrow with more information on Gareth's whereabouts.

"I'm off to bed," Kargan said. "See you all in the morning."

"Same here," Lila added with a yawn. "Time for a bath and then straight to sleep. Goodnight, everyone."

Both Lila and Kargan headed upstairs, leaving Justin and Eldrin alone in the common room.

Eldrin took out his pipe, lighting it as the barmaid wiped down the counter, though it was already spotless.

Justin hesitated, not wanting to intrude on whatever plans Eldrin might have, but also not wanting to walk in on Lila having a bath. He hoped the Ranger understood his need to linger a little longer.

"Well," Eldrin said, exhaling a puff of smoke, "Gods willing, it will be a peaceful night for everyone."

Justin's gaze drifted to the barmaid. "Looks like you're on your way to a relaxing evening. Lila's yet to give me that kind of look."

Eldrin chuckled. "Patience, lad. A night's distraction is one thing, but the best things take time. The path to someone's heart isn't always straightforward. Lila cares about you—you've seen that. Who knows? If you want it, this could be the start of something real."

"She's hard to read," Justin admitted. "One minute, it seems like she's into me, and the next, she pulls back."

"She's afraid," Eldrin said, his tone wise. "Show her you care, not just with words, but with actions. Be there for her, especially when it's tough. Trust grows in those small moments. A woman like Lila—she's worth the effort. But you've got to go at her pace. It's something of a dance, true. Look for the answers, and they have a way of revealing themselves."

Justin nodded, taking Eldrin's words to heart. "Thanks. I'll keep that in mind."

Eldrin smiled, his eyes twinkling with a mix of mischief and wisdom. "Now, get some rest. Tomorrow's another adventure."

Justin watched as Eldrin approached the barmaid, his demeanor relaxed and confident. The Ranger had a way with people that went beyond mere charisma—it was a natural ease, a blend of experience and self-assuredness. Justin realized he still had much to learn.

As the night deepened, the inn grew quieter, with the crackling fire casting a warm glow over the room. Justin finished his drink and stepped outside for a breath of fresh air.

Justin took in the snowfall, which was layered a good three or four inches by now. He stepped from beneath the awning to get a better look at the street when he noticed something out of the corner of his eye.

There, sheltering in the eave next to one of the inn's lanterns, was a bat. It wasn't any usual bat, but one that was a good two or even three times larger than a normal one, with fangs to match. And unlike any other bat Justin had seen, it seemed to have decent vision, for its black, beady eyes had locked right onto him.

Justin immediately got his cane out, but with a high screech, the bat fluttered off on leathern wings. Within seconds, it was flying into the snow.

46

WHISPERS IN THE DARK

"The Ranger class is most often associated with bonded birds—hawks, falcons, or even eagles. But any creature of sufficient intelligence and manageable size will do: dogs, cats, foxes, bats, and even certain breeds of rats or pocket drakes have served as loyal companions. I even heard a tale of one particularly ambitious Ranger from Ebon Valdra who bonded with a hatchling kraken. It worked out surprisingly well—for a few years. That is, until one fateful night when the kraken decided that its master's boat looked far more appetizing than the fish it was catching."

—Ranger Rowan Lightfoot
  Tales of the Savage North

ELDRIN IMMEDIATELY CAME out on the porch, arrow nocked. In one fluid motion, he pulled the string to his ear, sighted his quarry, and let loose. To Justin's utter amazement, the arrow landed true, and the beast spiraled to the ground, crashing into a snow pile.

Mira was just behind him, her eyes wide with shock. "What was that about?"

Eldrin lowered his bow. "Nothing of consequence. I'll be back inside shortly."

She looked as if she wanted to speak, but then nodded. "Okay."

When she went back inside, Justin looked at Eldrin. "Is there something I'm missing? That bat was big and scary, but I don't think it meant any harm. Probably after the warmth of that lantern there."

"On the contrary," Eldrin said. "If it had reported to its master, we'd find all our gains erased."

"Erased? You mean that thing was working for Gareth?"

"Working for someone in his party, certainly. Agents of Morvath like to use Blood Bats, carrion birds, and sometimes even rats to do their spying and run messages. If allowed to live, we'd have no hope of eluding our pursuers."

"Why didn't Gareth send this bat to follow us from the very beginning?"

Eldrin smiled grimly. "Shadowflight is more than capable of taking care of overly inquisitive animals. A bat like this wouldn't dare show itself unless it was certain Shadowflight was far away. Which he is at the moment, to keep track of Gareth's movements."

"I see," Justin said. "Well, it's a good thing you were quick."

"Ranger's Intuition," he said. "We should be safe to sleep through the night."

"What if they have another bat like this?"

"It's almost certain they have at least a few. Agents of Death are not shy about expending lives in pursuance of a goal, but all the same, creatures like these don't grow on trees. They must be trained for months, even years. When this one doesn't report back, they'll likely know Windfall is our goal. But it'll be a few days before that information becomes obvious. There's still time. We just have to be on our toes."

Justin swallowed. "I'm glad you're with us, Eldrin."

"Go get some rest, lad. It's probably best to stay inside for the rest of the evening."

Justin went inside, heading upstairs to his room. When he knocked, Lila was quick to answer.

"Took you long enough," she said, her brown hair damp. Seeing his face, she looked at him with concern. "What's wrong?"

Justin relayed the news. Lila listened, her expression grave.

"Damn. Just when I thought things were getting easier."

Justin nodded numbly. Once again, he was struck by the horrible truth that this just might be the rest of his life. What was supposed to be a relaxing evening was turning out to be the opposite.

"Take a bath," Lila said. "You'll feel better for it."

"I'm not really up for it. I'll just use my ring."

Justin didn't have time to bathe anyway. There was a knock at the door, which Justin answered as several young men came to take the water away. In the process of its removal, they spilled not a single drop with practiced efficiency.

Justin set his thoughts on the Ring of Hygiene, and within seconds, he was completely clean, every trace of dirt, dust, sweat, and grime removed from his person and clothing. He went to the mirror and was shocked to see his reflection.

In the few days since Highcliff, he had lost at least another twenty pounds, and his features were even more pronounced. It was like looking at another person, someone he didn't even recognize. He was down at least fifty pounds since his first day on Eyrth, if not more.

He touched his face. "It doesn't seem possible."

"I think it's a property of your class," Lila said, standing beside him and looking at his reflection. "Just don't let it go to your head."

Why would Lila say that? The only conclusion was that there was a reason it *might* go to his head. It reminded him of something Alistair had said on the day they met, something about Socialites "looking pretty and being useless." He wondered if it was a property of his Magnetic Presence boon. If this was Level 7, what would he be like at Level 11, or even Level 15?

Assuming he got that far, of course. It was nice to lose all the weight and become better-looking; it would make things go easier in this world. It was a certain, brutal fact of life that looks mattered in getting favors from people. Plus, there was the practical consideration of it being far easier to hike hundreds of miles and fight more effectively when there was less of him to carry around.

"Time to sleep," he finally said, feeling his exhaustion. He was probably thin enough to not overcrowd the bed too much, which was a startling fact in itself.

He drew the curtains closed, taking a glance out into the snowy darkness before doing so. Nothing moved in the streets aside from the falling snow. With luck, it would stay that way.

Lila had already settled into bed. She blew out the candle, leaving only the red embers of the iron stove supplying warmth. Justin wasn't sure of the etiquette for sharing a bed with a woman he wasn't romantically involved with but had at least *some* feelings for. Either way, he decided it was better than sleeping on the cold floor, and Lila seemed to expect it. Despite their earlier bet, she had chosen the spot by the window, farthest from the stove.

Of course, as he slipped under the quilts, it was impossible for his mind not to go to certain places. Sharing a bed with someone you were attracted to had implications, at least where he was from.

Whatever those implications were, Lila didn't seem too concerned about them. Her leg was already touching his, and she was doing nothing to move it away.

He closed his eyes, resolving to fall asleep, and such was his exhaustion that he almost did so until he heard her voice, soft in the darkness.

"You know, for what it's worth, I'm glad you're here. I know this isn't your world, and you'd probably go back if you had the chance."

Such sentiments expressed openly were rare for Lila. He wasn't sure what to say. He didn't even know if he *would* go back at this point. Yes, this world was dangerous, but what did he have to go back *to*? His basement and his video games?

"It's been a strange journey," he finally said. "It's hard to imagine going through all this without you."

"Remember what I said back in the stairwell? About things being complicated?"

"Of course."

"Well, maybe it doesn't have to be so complicated. Maybe we just take things one day at a time and see where it goes."

Justin thought it over. Of course, a large part of him wanted to say yes. It seemed they got on well together. And there was his obvious attraction to her.

And yet, there were certain realities getting in the way. Being chased by someone wanting him dead, for example. Someone who wanted either his soul or his Prismatic Core, and perhaps even both.

If they got together, that meant the relationship would escalate physically. As much as he would enjoy that, he wasn't sure he was truly ready for it, given the circumstances.

"If Eldrin had been just a few seconds slower, that bat would have gotten away," he finally said. "With my life on the line, is it really worth the pain?"

It was quiet for a while. Uncomfortably so. It wasn't a rejection per se, but a question.

At last, she answered. "I guess we'd just have to have faith that things could one day go back to normal."

"Do you have faith?"

"I'm not sure. I could have left a long time ago. I thought about it, but it felt wrong."

"You don't have to stay for my sake. What made you decide to stay? It can't just be about getting this Blessing of Arion at Mont Elea."

It was a question he should have asked a long time ago, but such was the nature of their journey that it never came up. Quiet moments like these were rare, and it seemed he never got to savor them.

She considered. "To be honest, I don't know. At Silverton, I thought we might go as far as Belmora before parting ways. Somewhere out there, those thugs are still after me. Maybe it's not as dangerous as your situation, but I can never stay in one place for too long. My plan is still to get to Draegor's Keep. But now I think I'm willing to go as far as Mont Elea. At least to see this whole thing through."

"Well, if these Vaults keep popping up, you'll be able to pay off your debts in no time," he said.

She snickered. "Yeah, right. I have three crowns and a few silvers to my name. Better than no crowns, of course, but with the interest, I probably owe close to seventy by now."

"Well, after Mont Elea, maybe we can revisit this."

Lila was quiet. "Mont Elea is a long way away. It might never happen."

Justin knew she had a point, but it seemed nothing more than a fantasy right now. That Lila was even having these thoughts meant she wasn't just into him. She really did like him and was just waiting for him to make a move.

The expectation was a bit terrifying, and Justin didn't know what to do with it. All his life, he'd told himself that he wasn't good enough for anyone. It was hard to overcome those mental blocks in a single night.

"I've said too much," she said.

Justin's mind raced, his emotions swirling in the dark. He wished he knew how to answer her, but the right words were elusive.

Finally, he spoke, his voice soft and sincere. "You didn't say too much. I'm glad you shared all that with me. I guess I'm just not used to having someone care about me. I'm grateful. I feel the same way about you, for the record. I'm just afraid of getting emotionally involved when so much is on the line."

"Are you not already?"

She had him there. "Well, *more* emotionally involved."

"I get that."

"I don't know what the future holds. This world is unpredictable. There are so many dangers we still have to face. Having you by my side makes everything better. Maybe we can take it one day at a time, like you said. But maybe we can wait until things are safer before getting more serious." Justin took her hand to show his sincerity. Then, remembering Eldrin's words, he added, "The best things take time."

She hesitated a moment before answering. "I know. You're right."

"There's still something I need to tell you. Last night, I talked to Eldrin while you and Kargan were asleep."

"Oh?"

"I wanted to know what the Baron sees in me. Why he's going through all this effort."

Justin shared what he had learned, and Lila listened quietly. If she was going to be following him, she deserved to know the truth.

She was quiet for a while, absorbing the information. "That's terrifying. I've heard of Ascendant Classes before, but it's more like a legend to most people."

"It's all possible if he catches me," Justin said. "And just hearing that...it made me feel completely hopeless."

She squeezed his hand. "It's not hopeless. Maybe it feels like that, but the fact that we've gotten this far is a blessing from the gods themselves. Maybe Alistair was right."

"About what?"

"They're watching over you. That's what the cores are. People say they are a connection between us, the gods, and even the Creator. The classes are their gifts to us, and you carry a Prismatic Core, the best kind there is. Some people say that it doesn't just give you any class you want. It gives you the blessing of the Creator himself."

"That's what Eldrin said, too. I'm not sure if I believe him."

"I mean, think of everything that's happened since you found it. Alistair walking on the road, just in time to save you from goblins. An offer of help from me, when you were laughed out of the Mercenary Guild. Finding Eldrin in that inn, having his skills to keep us ahead of our enemies. Alistair getting you out of Silverton just in time. And finding not one, but *three* Vaults, all of which gave us the resources we needed. I could go on." She paused, letting it sink in. "It doesn't make you invincible, of course, but it gives you an edge. As long as you can stay alive, Justin, time is on your side."

Justin wondered if she had a point. Eldrin had said much the same thing. "There were a lot of unlucky things that happened, too. I picked up a parcel that was addressed to a creep. Then there was the Death Mark. Alistair dying..."

"Maybe," Lila said. "But wouldn't you rather believe you were lucky?"

It was a nice idea. Hopefully, it was true. Either way, Justin mentally noted to learn more about it when he had the chance. He had to admit it would explain a lot of the fortunate "coincidences" that had happened. Lila was right about Alistair. The Paladin had even mentioned he'd never seen so many Vaults spring from the Aether.

"You've given me a lot to think about."

"It's too soon to give up and feel hopeless. In a couple of days, we'll be in Windfall, and our options will open up. You'll see."

The exhaustion of the day was now hitting him in full force. "Thanks, Lila. Let's get some rest."

"All right. Good night."

Justin soon fell asleep.

47

WINDFALL

"Windfall is a city of layers. First, there is the city proper, where most of its residents scrape by. Beneath that lies the Undermarket, a seedy refuge for the poor when the northern storms roll in. Above it all, perched on the Heights, are the manors of the wealthy aristocracy. But then there are also the layers of time. The elves first claimed the land as a trading outpost. Then came the dwarves, who built the imposing black walls and towers. Men came last of all, who saw little need to improve what already stood. The name, too, holds layers. The Wind Pass funnels biting gales through the city, and many are shocked by its brutality. Yet 'Windfall' also reflects the dream of fortune that draws traders, hagglers, and hopefuls to this improbable bastion of the north. Windfall is a city built on the promise of riches, a promise that lures many to forget the stark impracticality of settling in such an unforgiving land."

—Chronicler Vidorik Crestingfall
  Cities of the Wild Frontier

JUSTIN AND LILA headed downstairs to the common room, where Eldrin and Kargan were already eating a breakfast of hearty porridge, fresh bread, and slices of cheese.

They quickly ate and went to return their keys.

"Thank you for staying with us," the innkeeper said. "Safe travels."

Leaving the inn behind, the party stepped onto the snow-lined street, the first gray tinges of dawn lighting the eastern sky.

The sky was a clear, pale blue, the air crisp and carrying the scent of pine. The world was quiet, aside from the hammering of an anvil down the street at the town's smithy.

Eldrin broke the silence. "With Windfall just two days away, it might be best to resupply there."

Lila smiled. "*You're* in an awful hurry to leave."

Justin glanced back at the inn, where Mira was looking through the window. The effect of "fond memories," he supposed.

Eldrin shot Lila an annoyed glance. "I know what you're implying. But with that bat yesterday, I'm not taking chances. Best to keep our lead."

"Of course," she said brightly. "Following your lead, Mr. Ranger."

With a grunt, Eldrin pointed his feet westward and was walking just about as quickly as he could without running. Justin smiled while Lila stifled a laugh. Kargan, oblivious, kept marching.

The road quickly took them out of town and up a steep incline that angled toward the Umbers, which took about an hour to ascend. Then they started through the dense forest, where towering pines stood like silent sentinels. The only sounds were the crunch of snow underfoot and the occasional call of a distant bird.

Eldrin led the way with his usual grace, his Pathfinder's Pace making the trek easier for everyone. While the skill was intended for travel off the road, the depth of the snow was such that they were all stepping more lightly, hardly even sinking into the drifts.

The River Marin stayed to their left, much thinner than it was by Highcliff or even Pinecrest, as the landscape shifted to rugged canyons. The path narrowed, flanked by steep rock walls that echoed their footsteps. The river's gentle murmur accompanied them.

Justin found himself lost in the journey's rhythm, the steady pace and the beauty of the natural world once again taking his breath away. Growing up in Oklahoma, he was used to wide plains, and he had little reason to travel far. He remembered a vacation to the Rockies when he was a kid, but such was his life that he'd been nowhere more exotic than that.

They only passed a few people on the way: a farmer and his mule and cart, a single adventurer wearing fur-lined armor, a longsword, and a shield, who nodded pleasantly, and an older man who had the look of a pilgrim about him, wearing light armor, a cloak, and holding a walking stick.

They reached a fork in the road. The main road continued on into a valley, while a narrower path led further west, snaking up the mountainside of the Umbers.

"Left is faster for experienced travelers," Eldrin said. "Though the climb won't be easy."

"We need to save as much time as we can," Kargan said. "Lead on."

The climb began in earnest as they reached the mountainside. The elevation increased, and the air grew thinner and colder. The snow was thick on the ground, crunching under their boots with each step. Lila edified their steps with her Bardic Inspiration.

Eldrin's expertise was invaluable here, guiding them through the most treacherous parts with ease. They hardly had to pause and catch their breath, Justin realizing he no longer needed to. Apparently, like the real world, it was possible to get stronger and hardier without enhancing one's attributes.

The view of the valley below grew more magnificent with each passing hour. By early evening, they found shelter in a cave by a stream, the water almost thin enough to be stepped across. Eldrin set up a small campfire, its warmth a welcome relief from the chill, while Kargan cast Blood Aegis, the crimson magical barrier shimmering before fading into invisibility. They sat around the fire, eating leftover boar and enjoying the rare moment of peace around a shared fire.

It was then that Shadowflight returned. The dark falcon landed silently beside Eldrin, its keen eyes reflecting the firelight. Eldrin listened intently to the news the bird brought, a dark expression on his face.

"Gareth is heading northeast on the Plainsway," Eldrin said finally. "As expected. We'll keep Shadowflight close by in case there are other spies."

They settled down to sleep, the fire's warmth and the spell's protection providing a sense of security in the cold wilderness. Such were the exertions of the day that Justin was instantly asleep as soon as he closed his eyes.

The next day dawned clear and bright. Over a hasty breakfast, Kargan revealed he had earned enough experience to reach Level 5. He earned a party tactic called Blood Pact, which slightly boosted the passive healing of all party members.

Once they broke camp, Eldrin set a brisk pace, pushing them to cover as much ground as possible. The path continued to wind upward, the terrain becoming rougher and more challenging. Justin's legs ached with the effort, but he kept moving, knowing the pain would only strengthen him.

By late morning, they reached a ridgeline, and Windfall came into view in the far distance. Even from afar, Justin could tell the city was quite large. Built into the mountainside, the city was carved from pure stone, its formidable walls glistening in the sunlight. Such were the sheer sides of the terrain it occupied that Justin could see the strategic importance of the city, a thriving waypoint between two countries, and likely the only sizable pass in Northern Aranthia. There were multiple tiers, and it seemed the city occupied each side of the pass, stone towers rising high into the air, covered with snow.

The sight filled Justin with a renewed sense of purpose. They were getting closer.

Lila came to stand beside him. "You're seeing my country for the first time. That's Daeloria on the left, Aranthia on the right."

Justin saw that the terrain to the west of the mountains, Lila's home country, was far rougher and less forested, while on the right, the pine forests were thick, at least where there weren't farms or pastureland.

"Feeling nostalgic?" Justin asked.

She shrugged. "Well, I've never been this far north. Where I'm from, the Sapphire Coast, the climate is far more agreeable."

They descended in elevation, passing through narrow mountain valleys and coming across quaint mountain villages. Justin took in the sights with a mix of awe and curiosity. The villagers watched them pass with a mix of suspicion and interest, their lives seemingly untouched by the turmoil that plagued the world beyond their snowy enclave.

As evening approached, the formidable walls of Windfall loomed ahead. The city was imposing, a fortress of stone standing resolute against the encroaching darkness. Intricate Gothic carvings were etched into the walls, while stone gargoyles stood vigil on crenellations. Guards dressed in black, fur-lined coats, with a griffin emblazoned on their chests, patrolled the walls bearing halberds and crossbows. Snow fell once again, the flakes swirling in the wind and adding to the sense of urgency.

"People built this?" Justin asked in awe.

"Only some of it," Eldrin said. "Windfall is an ancient city, but it has been continuously occupied to various extents over the centuries. It was first built in the time of the Ilvari elves, but even then, it was only a small waypost. After the elves abandoned it, the dwarves occupied it, creating most of the grander buildings you can see today, vastly increasing its scope. Like modern-day Aranthia, it served as its border, with orcish lands to the west, now occupied by Daeloria."

"There are no orcish countries left today?" Justin asked.

"Not in Serenthel," Eldrin answered.

"Man," Justin said. "The orcs have the short end of the stick, huh?"

Kargan grunted. "Some of it was self-inflicted, but when the Shadow Empire came to power, the orcs fled to the mountains to hide. And there they have remained, mostly."

"Interesting," Justin said.

He wanted to ask if they could stay longer. He could really get lost in a city like this.

"I know a decent inn here," Eldrin said. "It will make the perfect stop until the next leg of the journey."

Justin and the rest followed Eldrin through the bustling streets. For the first time, Justin noticed the city's remarkable diversity. The population wasn't solely human—at least one in five was an orc, and even among the humans, there was a striking variety of skin tones and cultures. Aranthia, from what Justin had seen so far, was predominantly fair-skinned, but the size and influence of Windfall had clearly drawn people from all corners of the world.

With a start, Justin realized he hadn't encountered many people with darker skin since arriving on Eyrth. There had been a couple in the taverns of Highcliff, but here in Windfall, he saw many, dressed in vibrant, richly colored clothing, with the air of successful merchants.

For the first time, he realized that this was his first proper city, cosmopolitan and easily over a hundred thousand people, if not more. Stalls selling exotic spices filled the air with tantalizing scents. Merchants peddled wares from distant lands: gleaming dragon-scale armor, intricate clockwork devices, and shimmering crystals that pulsed with inner light. A blacksmith hammered away at a sword, sparks flying in the crisp night air, while a street performer juggled flames to the delight of a gathered crowd.

Eldrin led them past an apothecary with a window display of dried herbs and glowing potions, and a bakery that exuded the warm, inviting aroma of freshly baked bread and pastries. There was a magical emporium that seemed to offer self-stirring cauldrons and quills that wrote on their own. The scene was a blend of the familiar and the fantastical, each corner revealing something new and intriguing.

At last, Eldrin turned down a staircase that led into some sort of tunnel. To Justin's utter surprise, a wide underground avenue was filled with even more shops and narrow alleys, all lit with magical lamps. The subterranean city had a distinct atmosphere, more shadowy and secretive. They passed by a shop selling dark cloaks and hooded garments, another offering lock-picking tools and dubious trinkets. Another potions shop offered a variety of brews in murky bottles.

"What is this place?" Justin asked.

"It's the Undermarket. A city all on its own. And probably the safest place for us to stay."

"Looks sketchy," Lila said, observing a few beggars asking passersby for money.

"It's only for one night," the Ranger said.

After a few minutes of wandering through seemingly random alleys and staircases, they came to a narrow door, no different from any other. When Eldrin knocked, it unlocked on its own, revealing a surprisingly well-appointed space within. The interior was cozy, with plush chairs arranged around a roaring fireplace. A sturdy wooden table occupied the center of the room, laden with food and drink. Soft, ambient lighting from enchanted lanterns cast a warm glow.

The stone counter was manned by an orc with a broad frame and a tusked grin, his green skin weathered and marked by scars that spoke of a warrior's past. His eyes, sharp and alert, sparkled with recognition as he looked up.

"Ah, my favorite Ranger! What brings Eldrin Thornwood to the Mountain's Embrace?"

"I wasn't sure you'd remember me, Gorn," Eldrin said.

"I remember almost all my guests," the orc said with a chuckle. "The ones that make an impression, anyway."

"Do you have a suite available?"

"It just so happens I do. It's five silvers a night. Of course, food and drink are included in the price."

Justin's eyes popped at the price, but Eldrin didn't hesitate, laying down six silvers.

"For my discretion, and to bring you news of any potential danger?" Gorn asked, his tone amused. "That's what you said last time."

"You know me too well."

With a grunt, Gorn handed over two keys.

Eldrin leaned on the counter. "On that note, any special news?"

"Not really. Of course, there's the Festival going on. It makes the streets more packed than they would be normally. We've got peddlers from all across Serenthel trying to catch every stray copper they can, and not always by the rule of law. And of course, with the increased traffic comes increased crime. The Watch can hardly keep pace with the thefts and pickpockets."

"Sounds dangerous," Lila said.

Gorn chuckled. "Well, it's nothing too bad. Just got to keep your wits about you, but that's the same for every big city."

Eldrin nodded. "Very good. Please keep me apprised of any new information or...strange guests."

"Of course," Gorn said. "We don't put up with any unsavory types here at The Mountain's Embrace. Your suite comes equipped with its own private bathroom and plumbing. If you need anything at all, simply let me or one of the staff know. It's a pleasure to host you again."

"Thank you," the Ranger said. He turned and nodded to everyone, their signal to go stash their gear.

They headed down a short corridor toward the very end where a heavy wooden door stood, which looked quite secure. Eldrin unlocked it and pushed it open, revealing the suite within. The room was carved directly from the mountain itself, with stone walls and floors that gave it a solid, enduring feel. Despite the ruggedness, the suite was elegantly furnished with plush furniture, creating a harmonious blend of solid edges and comfort.

A dining area occupied one corner, complete with a sturdy wooden table and chairs. The two sizable bedrooms were each equipped with plush beds, soft linens, and ample storage space. The bathroom was a marvel, featuring running water and a large bath basin carved from a single slab of stone, with copper taps for both hot and cold water.

It was easily the nicest inn room Justin had ever stayed in, and wouldn't look out of place in his own world at an upscale resort.

"I have to say, this is impressive," Lila said.

Kargan stashed his stuff. "I think I'll try to introduce myself to the local Mage Guild. It's still not too late, I imagine, and I'd better move since all of you plan to head out tomorrow."

Of course, Justin knew this moment was coming. He just hadn't expected Kargan to leave so soon. "You sure don't want a good night's rest and to head out in the morning? I'm sure you're hungry, too. Why not eat first?"

"I would, but it's best that I make contact as soon as possible. If I can establish some connections, I'll be better off."

Eldrin gave a respectful nod. "Well, if you need a place to stay tonight, you know where to find us. I'll be the first to say, if this doesn't work out, you're more than welcome to continue with our party. Your skills have proven quite formidable."

The orc nodded. "I...appreciate that. There's a decent orc population here, so I think I'll be fine."

"Do you need help finding the guild?" Justin asked.

"I'll be fine on my own," Kargan said. "I appreciate everything. Truly."

"Good luck, Kargan," Lila said sadly.

He gave a firm nod. "My thanks. It was a real adventure. More than I bargained for, but an adventure all the same."

When Kargan closed the door behind him, Justin received a notification.

[Kargan has left the party.]

As the notification faded, Justin felt a strange sense of unease. He trusted the orc's abilities, but the city's vastness and unfamiliarity weighed on him. He hoped Kargan would be safe and that their journey would continue without further complications.

A few minutes later, their food was delivered, a thick stew brimming with chunks of tender beef, root vegetables, and wild mushrooms, all seasoned with aromatic herbs that Justin couldn't quite identify. Alongside it was a loaf of crusty bread, perfect for sopping up the rich broth, and a selection of local cheeses with a distinct sharpness that balanced the meal beautifully.

Despite the delicious spread, the mood was dreary with Kargan's absence. His shields and healing would be missed, and it meant that they would have to tread far more carefully in the future.

Once finished eating, Eldrin addressed them somberly. "In a city like Windfall, most stores will be open late, especially on account of the Festival. It would be safer to do all our shopping tonight rather than tomorrow so that we can get an early start. While I don't believe it's possible for Gareth and his company to reach Windfall until late tomorrow night, at the earliest, it's best to play it safe and leave early tomorrow morning."

"What sort of things do we need to buy?" Justin asked.

"There are no major cities between here and Draegor's Keep. There may be small towns along the way, but nothing like this. This is a prime opportunity to fill out your missing gear, healing potions, and the like with that gold earned from the Vaults. Our travels are certain to take us off the trail. As for food, our packs are enchanted to allow the meat to last as long as we need it, and we should have it all eaten within a couple of weeks."

"Is it too risky to hire a coach?" Justin asked. "Lila mentioned the possibility."

"Very much so," Eldrin said. "It would be the first place Gareth and his retinue would check. We have no option but to go off trail, north of the Northway, for at least a couple of weeks, as previously discussed. It is tempting to rush things, but it's far better to be safe. We'll have to start very early tomorrow, and if it weren't for the need for rest, I'd keep going well into the night."

Justin deferred to Eldrin's expertise. "Makes sense."

Lila was silent, and Justin got the sense she didn't like the idea.

"I can take care of the essentials," Eldrin said. "You two just worry about finding some gear. Look for things that enhance survivability. Lila, perhaps you can find a pair of enchanted knives, for example, to replace those basic throwing knives you have and better armor."

"I suppose I have money to burn these days," she said.

"Don't spend everything, but it would be wise to spend most of what you have. Belmora is the closest city that will have better options. Both of you should also consider warmer clothing, perhaps enchanting your current gear to provide a bit of heat. A headpiece is often overlooked and can provide a significant bonus to any class, so keep an eye out for that. Of course, if you can't find the enchantment you're looking for, you can buy something to your liking and take it to a local enchantry. There should be a dozen of them in a city this size."

"You can do that?" Justin asked.

Eldrin nodded. "Of course. It isn't cheap, depending on the work and the expertise of the Enchanter, but it's a valid option."

"So, how does gear work, anyway?" Justin asked. "Is there a limit to how much I can wear?"

"Yes," Eldrin said. "Until Level 10, you can equip up to six different pieces of enchanted gear—doesn't matter what they are; you just get six slots."

"And after that?"

"It increases with level. Nine slots at Level 10, twelve at Level 20. And as far as I know, it doesn't increase any more after that.

Justin frowned. "Okay...so let's say I found a ring that gave me +5 Charisma. And for argument's sake, let's say I bought six of them. Could I just stack them all and charm a bank into giving me all their money?"

Eldrin chuckled. "You could try. But first off, a bonus that strong isn't exactly common. You'd be lucky to find a ring that powerful—if you did, it'd likely be rated platinum-tier. And second, rings and accessories don't usually boost attributes like that."

"Except for my Amulet of Equilibrium," Justin pointed out. "If it were working properly, that is."

"Right, but that's an exception. Even then, it doesn't give a flat bonus—it adjusts itself based on the highest attribute. That's different from just stacking raw Charisma. More than that, if two different accessories give the same effect, only the strongest one counts while each successive accessory gives 50% less. By the time you get to your sixth ring, it's not worth it anymore."

"Got it," Justin said. "But let's say I still went all in on rings, each with a different effect. I could just wear regular armor, right? Or even normal clothes?"

"You could," Eldrin admitted. "But you'd be making a huge mistake. Enchanted gear isn't just about bonuses—it's also way more durable than mundane armor. It repairs itself, resists damage better, and even adapts to the size of the wearer."

Justin raised an eyebrow. "So what you're saying is that my silver-tier coat is basically as strong as steel?"

"Maybe not quite that strong. A silver-tier steel breastplate will always be stronger than a silver-tier coat, but a silver-tier coat is loads more flexible. But you'll find that your silver-tier coat has a knack for knocking back or redirecting mundane weapons, and even bronze-tier ones. It's not foolproof, but it gives you some measure of defense that a mundane piece of armor wouldn't."

"Makes sense."

"Now flip that logic around. If you're wearing mundane armor and someone attacks you with a bronze-tier sword. That blade will hit harder and be more likely to cut through it. Especially if it has an armor-piercing enchantment."

Justin exhaled. "Damn. So gear tiers actually matter that much?"

"Yes. Enchantments make all the difference, which is why even bronze-tier gear costs a fortune. Even a simple pair of bronze gloves can cost a crown or more, depending on the nature of the enchantment."

Justin remembered his earlier theory that a copper piece was equivalent to about a dollar. That would mean anything that cost a gold crown was about $10,000.

It was easy to see why most people couldn't afford even bronze-tier gear, and why Vaults were highly sought after, even given the stakes.

"All right," Justin said, "so stacking rings is a bad choice."

"Well, not always. Mage classes often stack accessories. But then again, mages tend to hang back and cast spells; in ideal scenarios, they aren't on the front lines taking hits. But even then, they have to be careful, because some weapons have 'Accessory Dispelling' enchantments that can cancel out the effects caused by an opponent's accessories. So if you rely too much on accessories, you're just setting yourself up to get countered. But of course, it depends on the situation."

Justin nodded. "Okay, so armor slots actually serve a purpose."

"That's right," Eldrin said. "Generally speaking, chest pieces boost endurance, while head pieces protect against status effects. Leg pieces help with speed, while gloves improve grip and blocking. It's not always the case, but that's generally how it works."

"What about weapons, though?"

"Weapons are different," Eldrin said. "You can only attune one at a time unless you have a boon that allows you to dual-wield."

"Wait," Justin said, "but you have a bow and a longsword. So you can swap mid-fight? You don't have a dual-wielding boon."

"Well, anyone can switch their weapon attunement mid-fight. But it takes a few seconds to switch. So if Lila had two sets of throwing knives with different enchantments, she wouldn't be able to swap fast enough to use both enchantments back-to-back and stack bonuses. Unless, of course, she picked up a boon that let her do that. She'd have to throw all of one set first, then let the second attunement take hold before throwing the next set."

Justin rubbed his chin. "I think I've got it. So the real key is balance."

"Exactly," Eldrin said. "If you go all in on one thing, you're painting a target on your back. Another thing. You can't wear two chest plates or a helmet over a hat. You can put them on, sure, but you'll only benefit from one enchantment per slot. Accessories are the only things that don't technically have a limit. They're sort of like wild cards."

Justin smirked. "So, no stacking two pairs of gloves."

Eldrin snorted. "Nope. One set of gloves, one set of boots, one chest piece, one helmet, one leg piece, and one arm piece...just like any normal person would wear. That said, armor enchantments are not to be confused with utility enchantments."

"Utility enchantments?" Justin asked. "This is just getting more complicated."

"No, this one is actually pretty simple to understand. Utility enchantments don't confer the bonus directly to your core. They work mostly on the piece of gear itself. For example, Cold Resistance is a utility enchantment. It'll naturally warm a piece of gear for freezing weather. But even someone without a class could put that on and benefit from it."

"My boots have a Dry Stride enchantment," Justin said. "Is that the same thing?"

"Precisely the same thing. Your Ring of Hygiene, however, is specifically attuned to your core. Anything you have to actively use, by definition, is not a utility enchantment. Nor is anything that directly affects your attributes or abilities."

"Got it. Sorry for all the questions. It's just my nature to try to find a loophole."

"Trust me, if there were an easy way to break the system, people would have figured it out centuries ago."

Lila yawned. "Is the info dump over yet?"

"I think so," Justin said. "Unless you want to hear my theory on how to get infinite money using enchanted spoons."

"No, I do not."

"Okay, hear me out. What if you had a spoon enchanted to always refill with soup? You could fill up however many bowls you wanted. Start a food stall. Use the profits to enchant even *more* spoons."

She rolled her eyes. "We're wasting time. Instead of talking about enchanted clothing, or enchanted spoons for that matter, how about we go out there and buy some gear?"

"Good idea," Eldrin said. "Long story short, be on the lookout for your missing gear slots. But accessories will do in a pinch." Eldrin passed Justin the spare key. "Note where we are before heading out. This place isn't easy to find."

"Got it, Eldrin," Justin said.

"And try not to stay out too late," Eldrin said. He gave a knowing smile. "I know a big city is an exciting place to be, but Gorn is right. It can be dangerous, especially given the festivities. Keep focused on your goal and always watch your back. Any item with an enchantment must be core-bound immediately; otherwise you're just asking to be robbed."

Eldrin saying that only reminded Justin of his Amulet of Equilibrium. It was well-hidden under his clothing, but for now, the item wasn't bound to him. Not yet, anyway. He briefly considered leaving it in the room, but the risk seemed too great.

They left the suite and headed out of the front of the inn, finding themselves back in the Undermarket. They followed Eldrin through the narrow underground alleys, Justin noting the turns required before they came to a set of steps that led to a town square above, one so busy that it had to be the center of the city.

The square was a riot of color and activity, with festival decorations hanging from every available surface. Strings of lanterns crisscrossed the open space, casting a cheerful glow. Stalls and carts were lined up in neat rows, selling everything from food to trinkets to clothing. Performers entertained the crowds with music, juggling, and acrobatics, their laughter and cheers adding to the festivities.

Dominating the square was a magnificent clock tower built on the side of the northern mountain. Its face was illuminated by intricate, glowing Aranthian numbers.

The air was frigid, and thankfully, the snow had stopped falling.

"If you get lost, just find your way back here," Eldrin said. "Try to be back in The Mountain's Embrace before midnight. Off to your right, you'll find Market Street. It should have everything you need."

And with that, the Ranger left Lila and Justin on their own to complete their shopping, weaving through the crowds.

The bustling streets of Windfall were a lively scene to explore, and Justin was looking forward to it. Vendors shouted their wares, colorful banners fluttered in the icy breeze, and the smell of roasted chestnuts filled the air.

Justin took it all in. It was hard *not* to be excited, to not forget that danger might be around every corner.

"We better get our shopping done fast, Lila," he said. "I really don't want to risk...hey!"

She was already taking off toward a wide staircase, on either side of which were bustling shops. With a sigh, he ran to catch up.

48

SHOPPING SPREE

"Have you ever wondered why we level up in our sleep? It's no accident. Consciousness is the one thing we carry between waking and dreaming. It is the thread that ties our scattered selves together. Perhaps the Creator chose this quiet moment for our growth because consciousness, untethered from the distractions of the day, burns brightest in the dark."

—Scholar Rindle Faelstorm,
    Class Fundamentals

JUSTIN at last caught up to Lila as she was standing before a shop. From the swinging placard in the shape of a lute, Justin could see it was named "The Melodic Armory." Beneath the shop's name was a subtitle, "Instruments and Gear for the Budding Virtuoso."

The storefront was vibrant, with musical notes and engravings of performers intricately carved into the wooden façade. The windows displayed an array of finely crafted musical instruments, enchanted gear, and stylish attire for bards, all gleaming under the soft glow of enchanted lanterns.

"You're quick," Justin said, catching his breath.

"Come on," she said, her eyes sparkling with excitement. "Let's go inside."

They entered. The warm air was filled with the soft strains of an enchanted harp being played in the background. The interior of the store was a bard's paradise, with rows of instruments, racks of clothing and light armor, and shelves filled with various enchanted items.

Behind the counter stood the shopkeeper, a stout man with a bushy red beard and twinkling eyes. He wore a brightly colored tunic and a large, feathered hat. He gave them a welcoming smile.

"Welcome to The Melodic Armory," he said in a jovial tone. "I am Bertram Merriwether, the owner. How can I assist you today?"

"We're looking for some specific items," Lila said, stepping forward confidently. "I'm looking to round out my gear with some bronze-tier pieces."

"Ah, a Bard seeking to enhance her craft!" Bertram said, his eyes lighting up. "You've come to the right place. Are you looking for clothing to enhance your musical skills, or something more fitting for a Bard on the go in a dangerous world?"

"Definitely the second one," she said.

"Well, we have a respectable collection of Bardic armor and weapons. Which would you like to see first?"

"Weapons, definitely. I fight with throwing knives."

"Of course. I would be pleased to take you to our knife section."

Without waiting for an answer, Bertram led them to the back of the shop. Shortly, they reached a section filled with throwing knives displayed on velvet cushions. Lila's eyes were drawn to a set labeled "Echoing Knives." Apparently, some sort of magic was placed on the weapons that allowed Justin to see more information about them.

Echoing Knives (Set of 6)

    Weapon: Throwing Knives

    Core Restriction: Coordination, Charisma

    Tier: Bronze

    Sharper Focus: +1 Coordination

Resonant Echo: Percentage chance, based on your Charisma attribute, for an attack to hit twice, either on the same target or a different one.

Price: 1 Golden Crown, 50 Silver Marks

"These look perfect!" Lila said, picking up a knife and testing its balance.

"They've got some other sets as well," Justin said, looking through the section.

"These look like the only bronze-tier ones," she said. "The rest are five crowns or more! I'll take these. They're much better than what I currently have."

Bertram nodded approvingly. "Excellent choice, my lady. These will serve you well and deliver excellent value. Like all enchanted blades, they shall never lose their edge and can even deal with ethereal enemies. After all, finding the best stories means going to dark places. Are you still in the market for some light armor? Or more travel wear?"

"Light armor," Lila said without hesitation. "Though I must admit I'm on a budget."

"I have just the thing. Please follow me."

Next, Justin and Lila followed Bertram to the armor section, where he stopped before a complete set on a mannequin called the Minstrel's Leather Ensemble. It contained a piece for the chest, legs, arms, and feet. The set was practical yet stylish, with intricate embroidery and lightweight, reinforced leather perfect for a Bard on the move.

Justin inspected the armor's description:

Minstrel's Leather Ensemble

Armor Set: Leather armbands, chest armor, cuirass and greaves, boots, and gloves.

Class Restriction: Bard

Tier: Bronze

Leather Ensemble: +1 to all attributes when worn as a complete set. If one piece is removed, the set enchantment is broken.

Utility Bonus: Cold Resistance

Price: 2 Gold Crowns

Justin nodded approvingly. That was a decent set for Lila. Plus, the Cold Resistance would be great for the weather.

"What is a set enchantment?" Justin asked. "That wasn't covered in my crash course."

"It's a cost-saving measure," Bertram explained. "Oftentimes, enchanted armor will be sold in full sets to save on magical components. This allows me to pass those savings onto you. The downside is, of course, that if you remove one piece of armor in favor of something else, you'll lose the set enchantment. The armor will still protect you, of course, but it will be no better than mundane gear. The Cold Resistance enchantment will still function, since it's a utility enchantment."

"I see," Justin said.

"Needless to say, this armor boasts decent protection for the traveling Bard at an affordable price. Two crowns are a bargain, especially considering the lady can walk out with this set today."

"This should round out my gear nicely," Lila said, examining it. "Except I can't get both it *and* the knives..."

"Can we work out a deal, Bertram?" Justin asked.

The shopkeeper's face became one of regret. "Alas, though this is one of our more affordable sets, a lot went into the crafting of it. Bardic armor is highly specialized. This is actually the only one we have left. The price, as it stands, is about as competitive as I can get."

Justin nodded thoughtfully. "I understand. But what if we take both the daggers and the armor? Surely, you could give us a small discount for buying both?"

Bertram stroked his beard, considering. "I appreciate loyal customers, and I do have some room for negotiation, especially for a Bard who might bring more business my way with tales of my fine wares. Let's see...I might reduce the price by twenty-five silver marks as a favor to you, in return for repeat business."

Lila looked crestfallen. If her wallet was anything like Justin's, it was probably enough to bleed her completely dry.

Justin saw an opening and pressed further. "How about three crowns for both the armor and the knives? That way, we can walk out of here today with everything we need, rather than having to leave something behind. In return, we will spread the word of your generosity and excellent service. It's a win-win for both of us."

Bertram chuckled, clearly amused by Justin's persistence. "You drive a hard bargain, young man. However, that cuts my margins quite thin."

It was at this moment that Lila reached into her coin pouch, producing three fat golden coins. Bertram paused his speech and cleared his throat.

"Ah, very well! I know that trick, and by the gods, it has worked on me! Very well. I'll let both go for three crowns, but only because I can see the potential for future business with you two. Your next purchase will have to be at full price."

"Deal!" Lila said, grinning.

Bertram nodded approvingly. "Excellent. Let me gather the items, and I will meet you at the counter."

They waited while Bertram returned with the gleaming knives and the full ensemble. "That will be three golden crowns."

Lila paid without hesitation, handing over the three fat gold coins she had received from the Crypt of King Alaric. Once the money had been exchanged, Bertram gave a pleased smile.

"Very good. Would you like them wrapped, or would you like to wear them out of the store today?"

"I can wear them. Do you have a changing room?"

"Yes, in the back."

Lila looked at Justin. "I'll be right back."

As she left, Justin was left alone with the storekeeper.

[You have gained 50 experience points. Your experience stands at 319/940.]

Justin couldn't help but smile at the negotiation handled with care.

"So, this Cold Resistance enchantment..." Justin said. "Is there a way to add it to my current clothing?"

"Yes, there is," Bertram said. "There's a good enchantry up the street that does fine work, called The Arcane Thread. A warming enchantment is necessary to live and work in a town like this, at least for the chest piece."

"We'll check it out," Justin said, though his attention was already drawn to something else. Above the counter, within an enchanted display case, he noticed two glowing yellow orbs, each marked with a rune resembling a harp.

"Are those Bard Cores?" he asked, intrigued.

"Aye, that they are," Bertram replied with a nod. "Are you interested?"

Justin shook his head. "I'm a Socialite, so I can't take it on until Level 20."

"A pity," Bertram said, his tone sympathetic. "Though, even then, you wouldn't be able to use it."

Justin frowned. "What do you mean?"

Bertram gave him a curious look, as if Justin had just revealed a glaring gap in his knowledge. "Well, you don't unlock your second Core Attribute until Level 20. Most people never do, given the difficulty. But since your first Core Attribute is Charisma, your next will be something different. So, you'll have to choose a class core that aligns with that new Core Attribute."

"Oh, right," Justin said, trying to cover his slip. "I knew that."

Bertram chuckled softly. "Of course, sir."

"Just out of curiosity, how much does one of those cost?"

Bertram shrugged, his expression noncommittal. "Thirty crowns."

Justin raised an eyebrow, sensing there might be room to negotiate. "That's quite a sum. Hard to see how starving artists could ever afford that. Do you require payment upfront?"

"I do," Bertram confirmed. "Although some secure financing from a bank, that's usually only possible if you already have substantial resources. Unfortunately, most can't afford a class core unless they already come from wealth. A Bard core is actually on the cheaper side compared to others."

"Where do class cores come from? Vaults, right?"

Bertram nodded. "Aye, most are found in Vaults, though they can also form in areas with high magical concentrations. The potential to sell cores drives many a Vault Runner, but, of course, that's impossible without a class to begin with. And since Vaults can't be cleared alone, the profits have to be split among the party. The riches can be great, which is why so many are drawn to the life of a Vault Runner—fame, fortune, or, often enough, doom. It attracts the spoiled children of wealthy merchants and lords, at least until they're ready to settle down. Some, though, never leave the life—they get addicted to the wealth and the thrill."

"I can see that," Justin said. "What level Vault should I be looking at if I want to find a class core?"

Bertram considered this for a moment. "It depends. They can appear in Vaults as low as Level 10, but rarely, and they're more likely to be the grand prize. They become more common in Level 15-20 Vaults, but even then, it's no guarantee. Beyond that, they drop like candy. But at those levels, adventurers drop like flies."

"Good to know. Thanks for the info, Bertram."

The shopkeeper nodded with a smile as Justin headed to the back of the store. A couple of minutes later, Lila emerged, completely decked out in her new outfit, with knives holstered three to a side. The Minstrel's Leather Ensemble fit her perfectly, its practical design stressing her natural curves. The Echoing Daggers glinted at her hips, ready for action.

Justin was surprised by his reaction—there was just something about a woman in leather that he couldn't quite ignore.

Lila twirled and struck a playful pose. "Well? Is it too much?"

Justin finally found his words. "No, it's perfect. You wear it well."

She smiled. "Well, as long as you like it."

"Let's head to the enchantry up the street," Justin said. "I want to see if I can get my gear ready for the cold weather."

As they passed the door, Bertram gave a noble bow. "Thank you for your business. May your songs always be filled with joy and your adventures grand."

"Thank you!" Lila said brightly.

As they headed back out onto the stone street, the temperature seemed to have dropped while they were inside The Melodic Armory, and the cutting mountain wind didn't help matters. Justin suppressed a shiver. It was high time they headed for The Arcane Thread.

"Wow, this warming enchantment is a game changer!" Lila said. "I've always wanted one, but I've never had the money to justify it. And in Daeloria, of course, it rarely gets cold enough to need one."

"Can't wait until I have one of my own," Justin said.

They headed up the stairs built into the street, quickly finding The Arcane Thread and ducking inside. The interior of the small shop was incredibly quiet. The shop was filled with bolts of fabric, enchantment materials, and a variety of enchanted garments hanging from racks. Shelves lined the walls, holding jars of glowing powders, shimmering liquids, and radiant crystals of multiple hues.

Standing at the counter was a Snow Goblin, though this one was clearly female and looked quite different from Gribble back in Highcliff. Her skin was a pale blue, and she wore a neat, tailored outfit with a pair of spectacles perched on her nose. She looked up as they entered, her eyes sharp.

"Welcome to The Arcane Thread," she said in a calm, measured voice. "How can I assist you this evening?"

"I was hoping for a Cold Resistance enchantment on my coat here," Justin said. "Is it doable?"

The Snow Goblin gave a derisive sniff. "Doable? It's quite elementary, my dear human. I am the best Enchanter in town, and to be frank, normally such a thing would not be worth my attention. Only, business is slow this evening. Allow me to examine your coat, and I can give you the price."

Justin went to remove it before realizing that in doing so, his amulet would be even more visible. "I'll just do this outside. Be right back."

The Snow Goblin's eyes narrowed, but she made no comment.

Justin rushed outside, finding a small unoccupied alley. Looking each way, he took off the amulet and pocketed it before removing his coat and returning to the enchantry.

Without a word, he handed it to the Snow Goblin. "Sorry about that. It won't be terribly expensive, will it?"

The Snow Goblin looked nonplussed. She produced a pair of what looked like jeweler's glasses, except they glowed with a golden aura, and examined the coat as if it were a dirty thing. Indeed, it had patches of dirt and snow on it. Justin realized he could have had it cleaned with his Ring of Hygiene, but it was too late for that now.

"Yes, I see," the Snow Goblin said. "The Coat of Highcliff's Elegance. The Highcliff's Elegance Enchantment confers +1 to Coordination and Endurance, while the Enchantment of Featherweight makes the coat quite light, making it an excellent choice for travel. The Featherweight is your only utility enchantment, so the attribute boost is immaterial insofar as the enchantment's complexity." The Snow Goblin removed her glasses. "This can be done for twenty silvers."

It was a lot more than Justin expected. "I was expecting it to be about five."

The Snow Goblin looked miffed. "*Five*? Well, there are the material costs, the interactions with the original enchantment that must be accounted for, and not to mention the price of my expertise. If I charge something of a premium, then it's only because you want the job done right. Unless you would like to go to Jackie's Jinxes for the bargain treatment?"

"Assuredly not."

"Then it will be twenty silvers and about five minutes of your time, if you can spare them. I take payment upfront."

Justin sighed, handing over the coins. "Here you are."

She immediately set to work. The Snow Goblin took a small, blue-glowing crystal from a shelf and placed it on the counter. She then picked up a vial of shimmering liquid and a small brush. As she worked, she murmured incantations under her breath, her hands moving with practiced expertise. She dipped the brush into the liquid and drew intricate runes on the inside lining of the coat. The runes glowed brightly for a moment before fading into the fabric. The magic of the crystal seemed to resonate with the runes, blowing a low, chilly breeze in the enchantry.

Next, she placed the crystal on top of the coat and pressed her hand down on it. The crystal pulsed with light, and a soft hum filled the room. Justin watched as the runes reappeared briefly, glowing in harmony with the crystal. The glow spread across the entire coat, and then, with a final whisper from the Snow Goblin, the light faded completely.

"It is done," she said, handing the coat back to Justin. "The Cold Resistance enchantment is now in place. You'll find it to be quite effective. Now keep in mind this is a *utility enchantment*. It will keep you warm from the environment, but *not* if it gets far too cold or wet. It will also do little if an Elementalist shoots you with an ice spike. It's sad I should have to spell that out, but there it is."

Justin slipped the coat back on, feeling a warm tingle spread through him. "Thank you. This is perfect."

The Snow Goblin gave a curt nod. "May your travels be warm and your path clear. If you need any more work done, please come back."

When they returned to the street, Justin hardly felt the effects of the cold weather wherever the coat provided coverage. The effects of the new enchantment were well worth the Snow Goblin's derision.

"You're right," he said to Lila. "Game changer."

"Last thing on the agenda," Lila said. "We need to find your items."

"Do you really think they have a store here specifically for Socialites?"

"Eldrin seemed to think so. We just have to find it."

Before they set off, Justin ducked back into the same alley as before, taking out his amulet and putting it back on, ensuring it was well hidden beneath his coat. It didn't feel truly safe until it was secured around his neck.

The two of them set off up the street.

49

THE ELEGANT ENCLAVE

"A skilled Merchant can turn a famine into fortune, a war into wealth, and a single coin into a kingdom."

—Guild Master Garrick Valdrey,
  The Merchant's Manifesto

SURPRISINGLY, it didn't take long for them to find what they were looking for. Lila was the first to catch sight of a shop where the swinging placard declared it "The Elegant Enclave." Like The Melodic Armory, it also contained a subtitle: "Finery for the Discerning Gentleman."

The storefront was adorned with intricate woodwork and gilded accents. In the windows were mannequins dressed in elegant clothing, brandishing canes and wearing accessories that shone under the soft glow of enchanted lanterns. Almost all wore top hats, while one wore a white fedora with a purple ribbon and a peacock feather. Rich velvet curtains framed the displays, and a subtle fragrance of polished wood and fine fabric wafted from the open doorway.

"Come on," she said, pulling his arm.

As they entered, the interior of the store was even more opulent than the exterior suggested. Plush carpets in deep burgundy covered the floor, and the walls were lined with dark mahogany shelves displaying an array of finely tailored clothing and gleaming accessories. Chandeliers hung from the ceiling, casting a warm, inviting light over the space.

Behind a polished counter stood the shopkeeper, a tall, thin man with impeccably groomed hair and a meticulously trimmed mustache. His clothes were of the highest quality, a tailored suit that spoke of both wealth and taste. He regarded Justin and Lila with a critical eye, his nose slightly upturned as if he were perpetually sniffing something distasteful.

"Welcome to The Elegant Enclave," he said in a smooth but slightly condescending tone. "I am Reginald Fairfax, the proprietor of this establishment. How might I assist you this evening?"

"We're looking for some specific items," Justin began, feeling slightly intimidated by Reginald's haughty demeanor.

"Of course," Reginald replied, his tone suggesting that he doubted they could afford anything in the store. "Do let me know if you require any assistance in selecting the finest attire and accessories for a gentleman of taste."

From the look Reginald gave him, it was quite clear that he believed Justin didn't have any taste.

As they wandered the store, Justin whispered, "I don't want to give this blowhard my business."

"Don't take it personally. He's probably trying to stoke your pride, make you feel like you can't afford anything. That way you'll want to prove him wrong."

"That...makes no sense."

"It's an old trick. Some of the high-end stores in Eribar do the exact same thing. So, what pieces are you missing? Let's focus on that."

"Well, a headpiece and an arm piece for starters, and a leg piece. And maybe a second accessory, since the amulet..."

He trailed off, realizing he had already said too much.

"Let's find a decent headpiece first."

Justin headed for the hat section, where each item was placed on a stand with an enchantment that displayed a brief description through his interface, along with the price, much like The Melodic Armory. His eyes popped at the prices. There was nothing less than ten gold crowns, and items as high as twenty-five.

"I think we're in the wrong store," Justin said.

Reginald, who apparently had sharp ears, caught every word. "You find yourselves in the Gold section. For clothing of...humbler tastes...please make your way to the Bronze items section in the back."

"Thank you," Lila said, turning back to Justin and rolling her eyes. "Let's see what they have."

They went to the back of the store, where the prices were more agreeable, but still quite expensive. There were only a couple of hats with a price Justin could afford. One was a fedora of sorts, called the "Sentry's Fedora," that conferred a +1 to Endurance and nothing more, along with a utility enchantment of "Dust Repel," which kept the hat free from dust and dirt, on sale for 75 Silver Marks.

Also on sale for seventy-five silver marks was a so-called Dandy's Cap, with a long, red feather.

Dandy's Cap
> **Headpiece:** A stylish cap with a long red feather.
> **Core Restriction:** Charisma
> **Tier:** Bronze
> **Dandy's Charm:** +1 Charisma
> **Price:** 75 silver marks

"Is this really all they have?" Justin asked. "It's kind of sad."

"Seems like it," Lila said. "I'd go with the Dandy's Cap. Charisma is what helps you most, plus the Dust Repel enchantment is not useful at all, especially with your ring."

He reached out to touch the feathered cap, and as soon as he did so, a sort of alarm went off, high and trilling. Justin took his hands off the hat, and it went away.

Reginald came into the back room, turning up his nose. "Please, sir, hands off the merchandise. If you wish to make a purchase, simply tell me."

"Sorry," Justin said.

With a derisive sniff, Reginald returned to the front.

"What an infuriating man," Justin said. "Dandy's Cap it is. Time to find a leg piece and an arm piece."

They made their way over to that section, but there was only one bronze-tier item in Justin's price range, the Squire's Armlet. Apparently, Socialites were expected to be loaded and go for silver-tier and higher items. It was a simple armlet of bronze to be worn on the upper arm.

Squire's Armlet
> **Armpiece:** A bronze piece that grants a modest strength boost.
> **Core Restriction:** Charisma, Power
> **Tier:** Bronze
> **Squire's Resolve:** +1 Power
> **Price:** 75 silver marks

"Nice," Justin said. "Something to help my physical strength, at least. Now if only I could test it out on Reginald..."

Lila gave him a playful punch. "Behave yourself. So, that's the Squire's Armlet and Dandy's Cap. That's a crown and fifty marks. That leaves you how much?"

"After enchanting my coat, I have about a crown and fifty marks left. Damn, being a gentleman is expensive!"

"I already saw their leg pieces," Lila said. "There's nothing cheaper than three crowns."

"Well, I'll have to stick with my normal pants for now. They've served me well so far. What about accessories?"

"All too much. Looks like this is all you can afford."

Justin sighed. "So be it. Let's check out."

They went to the front, where Reginald pretended not to see them until Justin cleared his throat and tapped his cane a few times.

Reginald looked up. "Yes?"

"We'd like the Squire's Armlet and the Dandy's Cap," Lila put in.

Reginald appeared to be bored. "That shall be one crown and fifty marks."

"Can we negotiate a bit on the price?" Justin asked, trying his best to sound diplomatic.

Reginald raised an eyebrow, clearly amused. "Our prices are quite firm, sir. We pride ourselves on the quality and exclusivity of our merchandise. We are, after all, the only Socialite clothier in Windfall specializing in superior clothes for the gentleman of means. As such, it would be unseemly to offer discounts."

Justin wasn't ready to give up. "I understand that, but surely there's some room for negotiation. We're buying multiple items, after all. And let's be honest, the quality of the enchantments leaves a lot to be desired. A little flexibility on the price would go a long way in earning our repeat business."

Reginald's expression didn't change. "As I mentioned, our prices reflect the superior quality and fashion of our items. Any common enchanter can slap an effect on a set of rags, if they so choose, but where's the *style* in that? At the Elegant Enclave, you are not just buying the enchantment. You are buying an image. However, if you purchase from us today and return for future needs, perhaps then we can discuss more favorable terms."

Justin felt a flicker of frustration but kept his tone even. "How about meeting halfway? I'll happily pay a crown and twenty-five silvers for the Dandy's Cap and the Squire's Armlet. That's still a substantial sum, and it shows our commitment to quality."

Reginald's eyes narrowed slightly. "Your offer is noted, sir, but it does not align with our pricing policies. If we lowered our prices, then we would lose our exclusivity, and we have never been known to give a discount, or indeed, have needed to offer one. The price remains at one crown and a half. I assure you, it is more than fair for the value provided."

Justin sighed, fishing the coins out of his pouch. "All right, fine. But this isn't how I usually do business."

Reginald gave a curt nod, clearly pleased. "Thank you for understanding. Would you like these items wrapped?"

"No, that's fine," Justin replied, handing over the money.

It pained Justin greatly to hand over the coins. Within a minute, Reginald had returned with both items.

"Here you are, sir. Is there anything else I can help you with today?"

"No," Justin said. "Unless…" He'd been about to ask if they sold patience to deal with snobs, but looking at the display case behind Reginald, he saw another yellow core, this one with a rune that resembled a cane. "How much for that class core?"

Reginald smiled thinly. "One shard."

Justin frowned. "One what now?"

Lila leaned over. "A platinum shard. Worth a hundred crowns."

Justin's eyes widened. "Nobody can afford that!"

"Well, it seems you certainly did," Reginald observed. "Unless you acquired your Socialite core by…other means?"

"What are you implying?" Justin said with a huff. "Know your place, sir! This is not how you should treat a paying customer who has asked you a simple question!"

The man actually smiled at that. "Ah, there's the Socialite in training! Please come back any time. The Elegant Enclave stands ready to serve all the discerning gentlemen of Windfall and its environs." Then, donning his spectacles and going back to his ledger book, he said, "Good night."

But suddenly, his head snapped toward Justin's chest, right at the amulet he was wearing, or rather, the golden chain that was clearly visible below his collar. Justin felt his skin grow cold.

"My, what a fine piece that is! I mean, it's not often one sees a platinum-tier artifact on the streets of Windfall. And not core-bound!"

The man seemed to take in Justin anew, as if looking at his next meal, but Justin was over it. "You had your chance, Reggie. Come on, Lila. Let's go."

"Wait!" the man said, the plea in his voice stopping them short. "At least hear me out. Are you in the market to sell it? I can offer a very good price." He gave a devious smile. "Or perhaps you'd prefer to trade? How would you like an outfit composed of all silver-tier items, hmm? A complete set? And perhaps a gold-tier cane of your choice?"

Now, *that* was a tempting offer. Justin had been dead set on refusing the man whatever he asked, but he just had to consider this one. From what Justin had seen of silver-tier items so far, they all came with at least two Attribute Points and an enchantment that was almost always useful. And as for a gold-tier Cane of his choosing, it would certainly be better than the one he currently had, which was silver-tier.

Justin's mind raced as he considered the offer. Silver-tier gear would be a significant upgrade, making him far more effective in almost every situation. The gold-tier cane would likely enhance his abilities even further, giving him an edge that could make a real difference. The practical side of him screamed to take the deal; after all, the amulet was powerful, but there was no guarantee he would ever get to use it, at least not soon.

But then he thought about the amulet's true value. It was more than just an item. It held boundless potential for the way he was building his character. Trading it away felt wrong, like giving up a part of himself for short-term gain.

Besides, how had Reginald known about the amulet and its value anyway?

"And here I was, thinking I was hiding it well," Justin said.

Reginald smiled. "I must admit, I didn't notice it at first. But it's difficult for something like that to escape the eye of an experienced Merchant like me."

"A Merchant?" Lila asked. "And you run a shop for Socialites?"

"It's my niche, you might say. But the item you carry, sir, holds great value. I made a costly mistake; I underestimated your means, something I don't do often. If you prefer money, well, it can be arranged. I can give you an enchanted promissory note to take with you to the bank tomorrow morning, and they'll pay you in cold hard coin. I know you aren't from here; I know all my customers, and my reputation is impeccable. But perhaps we can come to an agreement, one gentleman to another."

"How much are you thinking?" Justin asked.

"That...must be decided. I think one platinum shard is a reasonable starting point." He nodded toward the display case behind him. "Or, if you prefer, I can trade you for the core."

Lila's eyes widened at that. Justin only felt sick. The Snow Goblin back at the Frosty Mug had been willing to break his kneecaps over his silver-tier cane and twenty crowns.

What resources did a Merchant like Reginald Fairfax have?

"I'll consider it, Reginald. But you have insulted me greatly."

The shopkeeper's smile faded slightly. "The offer stands, should you change your mind. If the number is disagreeable, I'm sure we can—"

"You forget that being a gentleman is not just about style or money, but about manners. You made a big mistake, Reginald. Huge! Count yourself lucky if I ever return. Good day."

"Sir, if I may be so bold—"

"I said good day!"

In a huff, Justin ushered Lila out the door and closed it firmly. The jingle of the bell was practically frantic.

As they walked, Lila glanced at Justin. He remained quiet, deeply disturbed by the exchange. He was wondering if he had made a huge mistake. If Reginald was good for it, then that kind of money was game-changing. Even a Level 15 Vault had only gotten him 2.5 gold crowns. He'd have to run forty of those to reach a hundred crowns. Or rather, a platinum shard.

"Justin..." Lila finally managed. "Why did you do that?"

He shook his head. "I...I don't know. He just made me so mad!"

"I know. He made me mad, too. But assuming this is a legitimate number, that kind of money, if used wisely, can set someone up for life."

"I...think I've had my fill for the evening," he finally said. "The last thing we need is for Reggie to send some goons after us."

Lila nodded. "I understand. Maybe we can talk about it. When things have cooled off."

"You want me to sell it, don't you?"

Lila looked as if she wanted to respond but decided not to. "We can talk about it later."

Justin wanted to talk about it now, but he knew that it was the anger inside him. "You're right, Lila. I'm sorry."

"It's natural," she said. "Let's get some rest. We'll feel better for it."

First, Justin decided to don his new gear. He placed the Dandy's Cap on his head while also slipping on the Squire's Armlet, binding both items to his core.

That just left one clothing slot, a leg piece, and with one and a half crowns to his name, there was probably somewhere in this city he could buy something suitable.

But as they were walking down the street, Justin couldn't help but notice another person approaching, exuding an air of pompous confidence. The man was impeccably dressed in a dark, tailored suit with silver embroidery along the cuffs and collar. He was tall and lean with brown hair falling to his shoulders, with upward-twirling mustachios. His headwear, a tall top hat, sat at a jaunty angle. He twirled an ornate cane with a ruby head shaped like a fire-breathing dragon.

A beautiful woman hung on his arm, dressed in a flowing, green gown that accentuated her graceful figure. Her blonde hair was styled in intricate curls, and she wore a delicate pendant around her neck that sparkled with enchantment. The man's eyes locked onto Justin with a mixture of curiosity and challenge.

The stranger halted in front of Justin, raising an eyebrow. "Well, well, what do we have here? A fellow Socialite, I presume?" His voice was smooth but carried an undercurrent of condescension. He flourished his cane in a grand gesture, the weapon so tall that it could almost be called a staff. "I must say, your ensemble is quite...quaint."

Justin felt a spark of annoyance but kept his composure, his voice dripping with sarcasm and boredom. "Justin Talemaker. And to whom do I owe the pleasure of this...grand introduction?"

"Lord Percival Harrington, of the same house. Talemaker is not a house I'm familiar with, I'm afraid. Mayhap there's some obscure reference to it in some forgotten tome in the public library."

Justin smiled. Apparently, he wasn't the only one who had access to Poison Barb, but his Charisma was too high to take the hit. "You seem quite proud of that cane, Lord Harrington. You know what they say. The bigger the cane..."

Percival smirked, tapping his cane on the ground. "Indeed. It's gold-tier; not everyone can have one, as you should well know." He gave a haughty laugh. "But I see you've managed to acquire a few items of note yourself, if items they can be so-called." His aristocratic nose, wrinkling in disgust, told Justin just what Lord Percival thought of those items. "Tell me, are you familiar with the art of the 'Social Duel,' Mr. Talemaker? It's a sophisticated contest, not for the faint of heart or the..." He cleared his throat. "Poorly dressed."

Before Justin could respond, Percival activated what had to be his Dandy's Swagger skill. The air around him shimmered yellow as he took a step back, exaggerating his bow while holding the brim of his top hat.

Then, Percival spun, his blue eyes thunderous. "I challenge you to a duel of wits and charm, good sir! Let's see who among us truly embodies the essence of a gentleman."

"Beat his ass, Justin," Lila said.

Percival's lady companion crossed her arms and narrowed her eyes at Lila, clearly not liking her words.

Justin felt the familiar surge of confidence as he activated his own Dandy's Swagger skill in response. He twirled his cane and strutted like a peacock before performing a low bow to the delight of the gathering crowd, most of whom were applauding. Percival's lips curled downward in distaste.

"Challenge accepted, Lord Harrington. Let's see who outshines whom."

50

THE GENTLEMAN'S GAUNTLET

"It is a grave mistake to underestimate the combat prowess of a Socialite. A cane or umbrella might seem an innocent accessory, but you'll quickly learn otherwise when their reflexes prove swift, and the cane's head reveals hidden danger. Even a simple kerchief can become a weapon in their hands—thrown in a swift, elegant maneuver to blind an opponent before they can react. Yes, Socialites are known for gallivanting and dancing, but that same grace often translates into footwork sharp enough to outmaneuver even the most seasoned soldier."

—Master Duelist Callan Veyl
Tactics of the Charisma Classes and How to Counter Them

WHAT HAPPENED NEXT WAS something Justin could scarcely have predicted.

He heard the Voice, and it seemed that only he could hear it.

[Lord Percival Harrington has challenged you to a social duel using his Rare Skill, Gentleman's Gauntlet, and you have accepted! Lord Harrington has wagered his platinum-tier headpiece, the

Top Hat of Mental Clarity. Please wager an item of platinum-tier or higher.]

The Top Hat of Mental Clarity, or at least a vision of it, appeared before Justin. It was a sleek, midnight-black headpiece with a lustrous sheen, perfectly tailored for a gentleman of high society.

He read the item's description.

The Top Hat of Mental Clarity
Headpiece: A sleek top hat that grants critical status immunities.
Tier: Platinum
Core Restriction: Charisma
Unflappable Resolve: Grants complete immunity to mind control, fear, berserk, and intimidation effects.

Justin blinked. Complete immunity to four status conditions that could utterly cripple him?

Justin wanted that hat. He needed that hat.

[**Please select an item to wager.**]

Justin tried to wager his Dandy's Cap, but he instantly felt the Voice's rejection.

[**You must wager an item of platinum-tier or higher.**]

Of course, the only platinum-tier item Justin possessed was his Amulet of Equilibrium. And it seemed there was no way out of this challenge.

Justin had made a foolish mistake. The anger he had felt from the shopkeeper had been misdirected at this random person, and now he might be the one paying the price.

And yet, if he won, he would get an awesome piece of gear, one that would be perfect for his character.

So, he just had to win. He had no choice.

[You have wagered the Amulet of Equilibrium.]

The Amulet of Equilibrium
  Accessory: A rare artifact that has been blessed by the Six.
  Tier: Platinum
  Relic of Life: This artifact cannot be bound by those with a Death Affinity.
  Grace of the Six: The Six Gods smile upon your singular dedication to mastery. Divide your highest attribute by six, then apply the result to all other attributes.
  Unbound Ascension: Let no being, god or mortal, stand in the way of your progress. All attribute caps have been lifted, but be warned: if you raise a base attribute to twice the average of all others, the Amulet of Equilibrium cannot be removed.

Justin saw Percival's eyes widen at that. "Splendid!"

[Upon victory, the loser's core-binding, if already applied, will be nullified and bonded to the victor's core. All cooldowns have been reset and reduced for the duration of the duel, and all cooldowns will reset upon the conclusion of the duel. May the most distinguished gentleman prevail!]

And just like that, the duel began. Glowing yellow boundaries flickered, creating a circle about fifty feet across, on the edge of which a thick crowd had gathered to watch and cheer.

Percival began with a flourish, strutting around Justin with exaggerated elegance. "You must forgive my surprise, Mr. Talemaker. I could not resist challenging you, for I didn't expect to see a fellow Socialite with such... quaint taste."

Justin smirked, activating his Dandy's Swagger. He mirrored Percival's strut with added flair, his movements smooth and confident. "Quaint? Says the man hiding behind an accessory, hoping no one notices he's just an overdressed pretender. Keep clinging to that hat, Harrington—it's doing more work than you are."

The crowd laughed, enjoying the exchange of barbs.

Percival's eyes narrowed, clearly annoyed. "Well played, but let's see how you manage...this!"

He leaped into the air, performing an acrobatic flip before landing gracefully on one knee, his cane held high and even releasing a spout of flame from the dragon's mouth. The crowd erupted in applause.

Justin wasn't fazed. He focused his energy and activated his Poison Barb ability, his words laced with a biting edge. "Impressive gymnastics, Harrington. Did you learn that in a circus?"

Percival's eyes gleamed with mischief. "Tell me, Mr. Talemaker, does your tailor specialize in mediocrity, or is it a personal choice? From that garb, mayhap you don't even have a tailor!"

Justin countered with his own Poison Barb. "That's rich, considering your attire appears to be rummaged from a garbage heap in the Undermarket."

The lord's eyes narrowed, and Justin realized it was best to insult his style. But Percival recovered quickly, twirling his cane while performing a series of graceful, dance-like moves. He used a skill that temporarily blinded him with a flash of light before reappearing in a new, more impressive pose in another location. Justin had to admit that it would be handy to have.

But now it was time to bring out the big guns. Justin felt a surge of confidence as he activated his Dazzling Display. It was time to see how this upstart dealt with a rare skill.

The surrounding air shimmered yellow as the legendary rapper Eminem entered his mind. Justin's stance shifted, becoming more aggressive, his gaze intense. He felt the raw energy of Eminem's charisma infusing within him, giving him a razor-sharp edge.

With a quick breath, Justin launched into a verbal diss, his words cutting through the air like a knife, even as a sick beat manifested from the Aether to lock in the rhythm:

> *"You strut like you're hot, but you're just a façade,*
> *You're not a real player, just a fraudulent mirage.*

> *Talkin' up a big game with your cane and your suit,*
> *But when you step up to me, I'll render you mute.*
> *Think you look sharp? You're dull as a butter knife,*
> *Livin' a life of luxury but can't handle real life.*
> *You flash that cane like it's something profound,*
> *But I'm the Talemaker, and I'm taking you down.*
> *Your cane might spit fire, but it fails to inspire,*
> *A circus act on a wire, destined to crash in the mire.*
> *Your attire's like trash, and your style's a joke,*
> *With a grace as subtle as a sledgehammer stroke.*
> *Your legacy is empty, as short as a sneeze,*
> *Your fashion is forgettable, like a fart in the breeze.*
> *I'll leave you in ashes, your wit's slow as molasses,*
> *If you outclass me, it's as the King of the Asses.*
> *'Cause I'm the King of the Ring, the lyrical beast*
> *And you're just pretender, soon to be deceased.*
> *At the hands of my rhymes, was there ever a doubt?*
> *Harrington, your time's up—I'm knocking*
>   *you out!*

As Justin's Dazzling Display ended, the crowd gasped and then roared with approval, captivated by the unexpected display of lyrical prowess. Justin, with amusement, realized he just might have invented rap in this world.

But much to Justin's surprise, Lord Harrington gave a smug smile, spreading his arms wide while giving his cane a stylish twirl. The yellowish aura surrounding him told Justin that he was using the same skill, or something similar. His voice came out stuffy, dripping with superiority.

> *"Hark! It's Harrington, I'm the original Socialite,*
> *But for a fool like you, it's time for me to ignite.*
> *Why am I wasting time on a basement dweller,*
> *While you rot in the dark, I'm the high society*
>   *feller.*

I can smell your stink from here, no money, no
  fame,
No women to your name—oh my, what a dreadful
  shame!
Now if you'll excuse me, let's switch up the game,
My rhymes are so tight, even in a different frame.
If you can't roll like me, you won't get no baddie,
I've got a new lady every night, they all call me
  Daddy.
You've never had a lady, it's a painful joke,
'Cause I'm about to faint from that foul reek you
  evoke.
You're just a sweaty rube with no real friends,
Unless you count the relief that you get from your
  hands.
You're a faker, a loser, a joke on repeat,
Too busy with games to stand on your own two
  feet.
You're as fat as a bat, gorging on lard,
And your style's so wack, even your lady's on guard.
If you don't know how to treat her, simply send her
  to me,
I'll take her to paradise with my Cane of Destiny."

As Lord Harrington's words echoed, he raised his fire-breathing cane high, sending out a spout of flame. The crowd fell into a stunned silence, absorbing the venom of his verbal assault.

Then, like a wave crashing against the shore, the crowd erupted into a chorus of cheers and jeers, divided between admiration for Harrington's cutting wit and sympathy for Justin.

Justin gave a placid smile, but he was a storm inside. Harrington's disses had hit very close to the mark. And yet, Harrington's rhymes relied more on crude personal attacks rather than creative wordplay.

This was far from over. It was time to take this creep down.

Justin stepped up the duel with a series of stylized, choreographed attacks with his cane. His moves were precise, highlighting the elegance of his Cane of Valoria. Lord Harrington responded, his moves quick and bold, the dragon's head periodically spouting plumes of flame.

Justin dodged gracefully and countered with a mix of West Side Story-inspired dance fighting, cane twirls, and finger snaps, once again activating his Dandy Swagger. He even landed a few light hits. The crowd watched in awe as the two Socialites danced and fought with finesse.

Lord Harrington attempted to finish the duel with a grand finale, combining his Dandy's Swagger and another light-blinding move. He aimed to outshine Justin with a flurry of cane strikes and pirouettes.

Justin, feeling the surge of confidence from his own Dandy's Swagger, used his Poison Barb for a final, cutting insult.

> *"They say money can't buy class—thanks for*
> *proving it true.*
> *All that wealth you flaunt just highlights what's*
> *missing in you."*

Justin performed a moonwalk, and the crowd's reaction was electric.

Lord Harrington gave a superior smile as he puffed out his chest.

> *"Mock my money, but it has you beat.*
> *While I dine in palaces, you're stuck in the street."*

There was a scattering of applause, but the words didn't fare well with the local population, who knew the weight of hard-earned coin and the sting of struggle. The crowd's initial enthusiasm dimmed, their cheers for Harrington's retort less spirited.

Harrington's superior smile faltered, realizing too late that while his wealth might command attention, it could not command respect.

There was a moment's pause, the tension thick in the air, as both duelists awaited the final verdict.

[The Gentleman's Gauntlet has ended. And the winner is...]

The crowd erupted in a thunderous roar, their voices blending into a cacophony of shouts and cheers. Cries of "Talemaker!" and "Harrington!" echoed around the circle. Justin realized the winner would be based on crowd reaction. Everyone watched the two enchanted items floating high above the heads of the crowd, surrounded by an aura of yellow magic.

And then, both items shot toward Justin. The crowd's cheers surged to a fever pitch as Justin felt a surge of triumph. Justin grasped both items, one in each hand.

To Lord Percival's credit, he managed a smile and a respectful bow. Justin returned Percival's bow with a flourish.

[Congratulations! As the victor of the Gentleman's Gauntlet, the Top Hat of Mental Clarity has been bound to your core. The Gentleman's Gauntlet has ended!]

As the Voice departed, Justin donned it immediately, removing his Dandy's Cap. The headpiece's enchantment instantly became one with him. He would lose the small Charisma bonus of the Dandy's Cap, but in turn, he would receive complete immunity to four crippling status effects, and he now had a piece of gear that likely wouldn't be outclassed for a long, long time, if ever. Given the enchantments, it would remain useful throughout his entire journey, depending on the enemies he might face.

As Lila joined him, Percival straightened and approached, his demeanor stiff. "Well played, Mr. Talemaker. I underestimated you—something I rarely do. It's a pity to lose the chance to win that mighty amulet."

Justin forced a smile, but he realized the amulet might be more of a liability than an asset. Given the circumstances, selling it might be the smarter choice. He wondered how Lord Harrington even knew he had it—until it hit him: Harrington probably *hadn't* known. When Harrington used his Gentleman's Gauntlet skill, he wouldn't have been able to stake his platinum-tier headpiece unless Justin had a platinum-tier item of his own. Of course, being a wealthy snob, Harrington could afford to risk losing something so valuable more easily than Justin could.

It had been foolish to accept the duel in retrospect, but luckily, Justin's skills had been enough to carry him to victory, though he had a feeling that it had been close. Without Harrington's stumble at the end, it might have been a different story.

Lord Harrington's paramour stepped forward, her smile enchanting. There was something beguiling about her that went beyond her beauty, to the point where Justin wondered if some sort of skill was being used on him. "My, that was quite the spectacle!" She gave her brilliant green eyes a calculated flutter.

"Mr. Talemaker," Lord Harrington said, "allow me to introduce my consort of the evening, the lovely Lady Catarina. Like us, she is also a Socialite."

"Clearly, you are a gentleman of great renown, Mr. Talemaker," she said, her voice dripping with flirtation. "What was that spoken poetry you did? It was so...evocative."

"It's called rapping, my lady." He indicated Lila. "This is my own consort for the evening, the Lady Lila Fairwind."

To her credit, she eased into the role with a smile. Justin was glad she was good at playing the part.

Lord Harrington's gaze took in Lila, his eyes twinkling with interest. He offered a charming smile. "Miss Fairwind, is it? A name as lovely as the breeze that carries it. I must say, Mr. Talemaker, you have an eye for fine company. Tell me, Miss Fairwind, do you often find yourself swept into such intriguing spectacles? If not, might I suggest you make a habit of it? Your presence would undoubtedly elevate any gathering."

Lila's smile remained playful, but her tone was a little sharper than usual. "I can't say I'm normally swept up in spectacles, Lord Harrington, but when I am, I make sure they're worth my attention. And as for elevating gatherings—well, I'd say that's more a matter of who's present, not just who's invited."

Lord Harrington chuckled. "A fair answer!" The glint in his eye made it clear he was enjoying the game. "Miss Fairwind, it seems you are as discerning as you are beautiful. A rare quality, I must say, for beauty is common. Perhaps we can agree that the best gatherings are those where the right company finds its way, regardless of the invitation." He bowed slightly, a gesture of playful deference, as if acknowledging that Lila had won this particular exchange.

Lila raised an eyebrow. "Oh, I'm sure many find beauty to be common, Lord Harrington. But discerning company—now that's something worth seeking out. As for the right company, well, I'm afraid you might have to work a little harder to prove you're part of it."

Harrington gave a good-natured laugh. "Well, I do hope you'll allow me to keep trying, Miss Fairwind. After all, a challenge is half the fun, isn't it?"

"A challenge, yes, but one that is earned, not assumed."

"I'll admit, it seems I've underestimated you. But don't worry—I'm not one to back down from a challenge."

Catarina gave a tittering laugh. "Oh, stop, Harrington. He can prattle on all night if you let him, and he won't stop until he finds a way to get his cane wet on his newest object of affection."

Harrington raised an eyebrow at Catarina's interruption, giving a small, dramatic sigh. "Ah, Catarina, always so quick to cut to the chase. But surely you can't fault a man for appreciating beauty wherever he finds it?"

"That depends on whether you believe beauty is something to be conquered or if it's more of a discovery, my lord," Catarina answered. "I must align myself with Miss Fairwind on this matter, I'm afraid."

If Justin allowed it, these nobles would never stop yakking. He was ready to leave, but he was also curious about how Harrington had picked up rapping on the fly. Some part of him wondered, as he had before, if there were other "players" from Earth in this world. If someone could rap, it might be a good clue that he wasn't alone here.

"It's pretty impressive you were able to rap without ever having heard it before," Justin ventured. "I was definitely feeling the heat of your rhymes."

"Likewise, my good man. I'm quite adroit at social situations, to be sure, but I must admit I had the benefit of a rare skill called Social Mimicry. It allows me to copy a social or rhetorical technique and then add it to my repertoire. Beyond useful for a Socialite like me."

"I'm sure," Justin said, a bit disappointed.

"You, Mr. Talemaker, are more than a curiosity," Lord Harrington went on. "You are clearly a man with remarkably interesting stories. I would be remiss not to invite you—and your lovely companion, of course—to our little Fall Celebration at the Harrington House."

Lady Catarina leaned in toward him, her voice laced with meaning. "Do consider joining us, Mr. Talemaker."

Lila shot her a death glare as Justin responded. "We'll consider it."

"Splendid," Lady Catarina said. "We Socialites must really stick together. Our class is so unfairly maligned! Simply follow this street to the end, and you'll find the Harrington House. I hope to see you there. There will be stimulating conversation and other delights for those who have a mind and taste for them." She gave an alluring smile.

"You'll be needing this, my good man," Lord Harrington said, proffering a piece of gilded paper. A quick scan revealed it to be an invitation. "Simply hand it to my footman tomorrow morning upon arrival. Good night!"

As the lord and lady walked away, a notification appeared before them.

Event: The Harringtons' Fall Extravaganza

You've been invited to the social event of the season at Lord Harrington's estate. Rub elbows with the rich and ridiculous, eavesdrop on scandalous gossip, and survive the whimsical plots of the upper crust. Dress like your life depends on it and brace yourself for a day full of surprises and delights! It starts at 9 a.m. sharp and carries on until the last champagne flute is empty.

Rewards:

Experience: Scaled to level and participation (and ability to dodge scandals).

Loot: Sweet-talk your way to exclusive treasures and rare finds. Only the cleverest leave with more than just memories!

"Are you seeing what I'm seeing?" Justin asked.

"Yes," Lila said, with trepidation. "The answer is no. We're leaving tomorrow morning, remember?"

At Justin's silence, she just arched her eyebrows.

"Seriously? *I'm* being the responsible one for once? What happened to keeping a low profile? There were at least two hundred people watching you here on the street, preening like a peacock!"

Justin knew she had a point. "All right, fine."

"Smart move."

Justin followed Lila into the underground market, still bustling despite the late hour. In fact, it seemed even busier.

Justin looked over at Lila, whose expression was tense. "So, you're not jealous or anything, are you?"

She looked surprised. "Jealous? Why would I be jealous? I'm just...concentrating."

"You seemed a little peeved at Lady Catarina."

"Her?" she scoffed. "She's a lady only in name, trust me."

Justin chuckled. "Well, Harrington clearly has an eye on you."

She blew a raspberry. "That's different."

"Different, how?"

"Because, Justin, if I wanted attention, I'd go for someone who actually knows how to keep it interesting."

"Someone like me, huh?"

Lila smirked. "Well, you *do* have your moments. When you're not annoying me."

"I think you mean charming."

Lila was about to respond, but out of nowhere, Justin felt impelled to turn around and raise his cane in defense. A throwing knife clattered to the ground.

[Gentleman's Rebuff has shielded this attack!]

Standing in the alley was a shadowed figure, a wiry man with a hooded cloak. He had another knife ready. Beside him materialized another thug, this one burly with a bald head and wielding a crossbow.

Lila's reaction was instant. Her new Echoing Knives whistled through the air, striking true with impressive speed. Justin's eyes widened as three of the knives embedded themselves in their targets before they dislodged and flew again, striking new spots on the assailants' bodies or even hitting the other thug. The Resonant Echo enchantment was already paying dividends.

But Justin could hardly watch, for on the other side of the alley, two more toughs appeared. One was lean, with a wicked scar across his cheek, bearing a quarterstaff. The other was a hulking brute with a sword and shield, his muscles bulging under his leather armor.

Justin gave his cane a practiced twirl as he quickly lobbed a Poison Barb at the attacker with the staff.

"Still clinging to that pole? The mentor who gifted it gave up on you. Maybe you should too."

The wielder of the staff froze in his tracks, eyes wide with shock.

Justin wasted no time in engaging the fighter with the sword and shield. He parried his first strike, taking care to maintain his distance.

[Poison Barb refreshed.]

Though his Poison Barb skill had gone off cooldown, the quarterstaff wielder was still stunned.

As such, Justin decided to hurl an insult at the swordsman. "Come on, big guy. Swing that sword like you're trying to impress the girl you could never get."

The man wasn't stunned, but he did stumble a bit. Justin activated a Solid Thwack, giving him a swift upward jab that knocked his shield aside. Justin noticed a yellow flash of light at the point of impact, the move hitting far harder than expected, an effect of his new boon, Add Injury to Insult. With a spinning sweep of his cane, he took the man's legs from beneath him. Justin finished him with a precise strike to the temple.

The staff-wielding street tough recovered, but by then, Lila had retrieved her knives thanks to her Amulet of Everblade. She unleashed them once more, and the knives danced through the air, finishing off the final attacker.

Lila's face was pale as she retrieved her knives. "Come on. We need to find Eldrin."

As they ran back to the inn, Justin could only wonder how Gareth's men had found them so soon. Whatever the case, it looked like they were on the run again.

51

ELDRIN'S GAMBIT

"Strength bends steel. Magic bends reality. But charisma? Charisma bends people.

—Lord-Orator Dain Verris,
    The Art of Influence

ONCE BACK AT the Mountain's Embrace, Justin and Lila hurried to their suite, only to find that Eldrin wasn't there.

"Great," Justin muttered. "What do we do now?"

Lila was unusually silent while her face was paler than usual.

"I'm rattled too, Lila, but we need to figure out our next move. If those guys were in the alley, it means they know we're staying here."

"Those weren't Gareth's men," Lila said.

Justin frowned. "What do you mean? Was it Reggie?"

She shook her head. "I...recognized a couple of them. That wiry man with the knives—I saw him back in Stonehaven. They're the ones who were sent after me."

Justin's eyes widened. "For your debts? How did they track you down here?"

She sank into a chair, looking defeated. "I don't know! Maybe it was bad luck, or they spotted us in the street. They must have come straight to Windfall from Stonehaven instead of going to Mistwatch. There were three routes they could have taken to follow me, and I guess they chose the northern one."

"Was that all of them?" Justin asked, concerned.

Lila nodded numbly. "Yeah. Now I can never show my face in Daeloria again."

"Maybe they'll be smart enough to leave you alone now," Justin suggested.

Lila laughed bitterly. "Yeah, right. They'll want to make an even bigger example of me now."

At that moment, Eldrin entered the room with his pack. Apparently, he had been doing some shopping, too. His brown eyes appraised them both. "Those bodies in the alley—anything to do with you two?"

"They're the men after Lila," Justin explained. "She says that's all of them."

"Did anyone see the fight?" Eldrin asked.

Lila shook her head. "I don't think so. They tracked us from the street and waited until we were alone."

"Well," Eldrin said, his tone serious, "it pains me to say this, but Windfall is no longer safe. Those bodies are going to draw far too much attention."

Justin knew he was right, but the thought of leaving the inn's relative safety was unsettling.

"What's the next step?" Justin asked.

"That's what we need to discuss. It's certain the Baron and his men know we're in Windfall. And given Windfall's location, we have only a few options left, none of them good. The obvious choice is going east along the Northway, but that would almost certainly put us on a collision course with Gareth and his men."

"You mentioned there were back roads leading off from the Northway," Justin said. "Is that not the plan anymore?"

"Shadowflight has reported that Gareth is well on his way to Windfall. They have horses now."

"Dear gods," Lila whispered.

"They must have picked them up in the last few days," Eldrin said. "That said, it's greatly speeding up their journey."

Justin frowned in thought. "If they could have afforded horses this whole time, why wait until Darkstream?"

"Well, horses wouldn't have been much use in the Umbers north of Silverton. While we were in Highcliff, they expected to keep us contained. Once we slipped through their grasp, they knew they needed to catch up, and horses were the only way to do that."

"How long until they're here?" Justin asked.

Eldrin shrugged. "Probably by evening tomorrow, based on Shadowflight's information."

"Then we have time if we leave right now and walk through the night," Lila said. "Only...I'm exhausted."

"Perhaps," Eldrin said. "But I'm no longer optimistic about our chances of going east. We could make it to the first back road, which leads to a town called Highcross, by early morning. However, Gareth will expect us to do that. He knows we won't confront him directly on the Northway, so the odds of him sending riders that way are high."

"What can we do, then?" Lila asked. "There's the western path toward Daeloria, but that takes us far from our goal, and if they have horses, they'll catch up."

"It wouldn't be a good move," Eldrin said. "Even if I'd told you to hold off on gear in favor of purchasing horses, that path would take us too far from where we need to go. Also, we'd have to circle back to Mont Elea. The only way to do that would be to take the Umber Road down to Stonehaven, and then east—"

"Right back through Silverton," Lila finished. "I'm no equestrian either."

"Same," Justin added.

"As I thought," Eldrin said. "The next option is backtracking. We could head south, then east across the Marin, the Plainsway, and into the Wilderlands of Baelor. Of all the ideas mentioned so far, this one is the best. However, once Gareth realizes we haven't gone east or west, he'll know we've gone south and cast a wide net. We'll have to break through that net to have a chance. But of all the options, this one offers the best odds."

"Then that's what we'll do," Justin said. "Even if I don't like the idea of going backward."

"We could try hiding in plain sight," Lila suggested. "The Undermarket is complete chaos. We could find somewhere to hide until we're sure they've moved on."

"I've thought of that, too," Eldrin said. "But it won't help us if the Baron gets involved."

"Because of the Mark," Lila said, deflating. "Well, there goes *that* idea."

From Eldrin's silence, Justin could tell he was considering something different.

"What? Is there another option?" Lila asked. "I can't imagine what."

"There is," Eldrin confirmed. "I was talking to an orc in a tavern here in the Undermarket. Thalgar's Tunnel is open again—something I didn't think would be possible for years."

"Thalgar's Tunnel?" Justin asked. "What's that?"

"The dwarves used to make their home in the Seraphim Range. Windfall was only a small outpost of their vast kingdom, primarily for trading with us 'sky dwellers.'"

"I thought Windfall was an Elven city back in the day," Justin said.

"It was, but none of the buildings survived from that time. The dwarves built over the ruins about seven centuries ago, but their true glory was the Kingdom of Drakendir, which lay deep within the mountains. They died out about four centuries ago."

Justin smirked. "Let me guess—they delved too deep?"

Eldrin looked at him, surprised. "Aye. Did something similar happen in your world?"

"You might say that."

"Well, as you guessed, as their kingdom expanded, so did the depths they explored, where terrifying creatures lurked. While the Drakendir dwarves eventually fell, they at least collapsed most of their tunnels to prevent the surface from being overrun. This wasn't always successful. Goblins didn't exist in Serenthel until five hundred years ago. One tunnel, called Thalgar's Tunnel, was the main highway that led from Windfall to the Everwood beyond the Seraphim Range. From there, one can access the Drakendir Kingdom. The Aranthian army has kept the tunnel open over the centuries, for the most part. Though it has been periodically closed when monsters found their way through. Thalgar's Tunnel has been completely sealed for the last two decades, but it has been operational again for the last month with no deaths reported."

"And you want us to use this tunnel?" Lila asked skeptically. "It leads to the Everwood, north of the Seraphims. You said those lands are too dangerous, even for you. And then there's the question of where we go after that, and whether this tunnel is truly safe."

"My plan isn't to go into the Everwood," Eldrin clarified. "The Baron would expect that. My idea is to find a passage into the Drakendir Kingdom and navigate our way back to the surface from there. A way to dodge Valdrik entirely."

Justin found the plan immediately suspect for a litany of reasons. "How do we even know the way into this Drakendir place is open?"

"It's not," Eldrin admitted. "We'd have to bribe a watchman to let us through. The old passages to Drakendir have either collapsed or are sealed off with gates. There's one gate, about a third of the way into the tunnel, that adventurers have been using to access high-level Vaults that have been growing undisturbed for centuries. A hefty bribe is customary for those wanting to trek down there."

"High-level Vaults?" Lila asked, alarmed. "No, thank you. I've had my fill of low-level Vaults."

"We wouldn't be going into any Vaults," Eldrin said. "The trick is avoiding the monsters those Vaults are spitting out."

Justin swallowed. With his Prismatic Core, he was almost certain they would encounter a Vault or two.

"For the sake of entertaining this truly terrible idea," Justin said, "I know you've been to a lot of places, Eldrin, but I'm sure you've never been to Drakendir. How are you supposed to guide us through it? Where are we even supposed to end up?"

Eldrin took a deep breath. "I understand your concerns, Justin. Reliable maps of the old Dwarven tunnels are exceedingly rare, if they exist at all. The best we have are rough sketches and oral accounts passed down through generations, but nothing is guaranteed. These tunnels are ancient, and time changes things. That said, I've spoken to some adventurers who've recently made the journey and stumbled upon a Vault, which they cleared. After a few pints, I got the information I was after. Their Vault was Level 17, but they didn't explore too deeply. Ideally, we'd stay close to the surface to avoid the worst dangers. They claimed the main passage through Thalgar's Tunnel is straightforward. They encountered no trouble; the only fighting they did was inside the Vault itself."

Justin tried to ignore the ominous feeling in his gut. He knew how these stories turned from the media in his own world. They would face the unknown dangers of Drakendir or the known dangers of Gareth and his retinue.

"The goal is to get us far enough north that Gareth's reach is diminished," Eldrin continued. "Drakendir, while dangerous, takes us through a region Gareth's forces are unlikely to follow us into. The Drakendir Kingdom was vast, with many exits to the surface, some of which open into remote areas within the Seraphims. Once we're out, Gareth's men won't have a chance of finding us before we reach Mont Elea. Their best shot is ambushing us on the road near the Mont, but with so many Life Magic practitioners who can detect the Servants of Morvath, that would be risky for them. Windfall is Gareth's last chance to catch us, and he knows it."

"How is this a better idea than backtracking south?" Justin asked. "At least there, we know what we're getting into. Could we not go south and then cut west across the Umbers? That way we avoid Gareth's net to the east."

Eldrin leaned forward, his eyes locking onto Justin's. "That wouldn't be a bad idea...except for the orcs. Most are peaceful, but their clan halls want nothing to do with humans. Some, on the other hand, are extremely warlike. Trust me, you don't want to run across an orcish warband or be spied on by one of their scouts."

"Point taken," Justin said.

"Which leaves Drakendir," the Ranger continued. "We can't outrun Gareth forever in the open, but underground, in the tunnels, we can throw him off our trail for good."

It was a tantalizing promise, but Justin couldn't shake his doubts. Looking at Lila, he could see she had similar reservations.

"We're talking about going into a potentially monster-infested area with no guaranteed way out," Lila said. "Why not head straight north through the tunnel, come out into the Everwood, and then head north to Kaldrath? From there, we could make it to Draegor's Keep by ship."

"That would be a nearly impossible journey," Eldrin said. "With luck, we could make Kaldrath in two weeks, but by then, winter will be coming on. No sane captain will want to sail the Ghostly Sea under those conditions—if it's not completely iced over by then. By the time the water thaws in the spring, Gareth will have had more than enough time to corner us. We'd be forced into the tundra, and that's a death sentence. Even with enchanted clothing, surviving out there would be difficult."

Lila nodded, her expression grave. "That's what I feared."

"Do we at least have an escape plan if things go south in Drakendir?" Justin asked.

Eldrin nodded, though his expression was grim. "I've thought about that. The best escape plan in the tunnels is knowing when to retreat. If things go south, we'll backtrack to the last known safe point—the entrance to Drakendir itself. From there, we can head north to the Everwood. It's not ideal, but it's better than returning to Windfall."

"And once we're in the Everwood?" Lila asked.

"I wouldn't head for Kaldrath at that point. I'd find a quiet spot in the Everwood to overwinter. It would be risky, not just because of Gareth, but also because the monsters north of the Seraphims are of an entirely different breed. Even the roads up there aren't safe. But with luck, the hunting could be decent, so we could survive until spring. Then we'd strike east and hope for the best. It's that or return to Windfall and hope Gareth is gone."

"I don't like that option," Justin said. "I need to get rid of this Death Mark quickly. Is the High Priest of Arion really the only one who can remove it?"

"Alistair seemed to think so," Eldrin said. "The Arcane University in Belmora probably has a White Wizard strong enough to contest the Baron's mark, but getting there is just as difficult, if not more so—and seeking that kind of help always comes with a price. The High Priest is the only person in Northern Serenthel I'd bet my life on being strong enough and motivated enough to remove it."

"There goes that idea," Justin said.

Eldrin met Justin's gaze, his voice steady. "This isn't a perfect plan, Justin. It's a calculated risk. But honestly, we don't have many options left. If we're careful and smart about it, we can get through this. And if worse comes to worst, we'll fight our way out."

Justin let out a sigh. "You mentioned meeting some adventurers in the tavern. Do you think anyone else would go with us? Safety in numbers."

"I wouldn't trust anyone with something so important," Eldrin said. "And finding someone suitable would take time."

"How about Kargan?" Lila suggested. "It might not be too late to catch him."

Justin brightened. "That's a great idea! He has excellent night vision, and he can heal us. Plus, that armor spell of his casts a good amount of light. It's a good backup in case our torches go out."

Eldrin considered the idea. "I wouldn't be against it. We'd have to ask him, though. He's still only a Level 5, so his healing powers will be limited. But he has definitely proven his usefulness. That said, should he accept, it's only fair that we compensate him fairly. And even more importantly, out of respect for him, we need to share exactly what he's getting into."

Justin considered this. It was a risk, but he understood Eldrin's point. It was only fair that when, and if, Kargan made his choice, he had all the facts. Justin had a good read on Kargan, or at least he thought he did.

"I'm all for it," Justin said. "He's probably more useful than I am in combat. Where's the Mage Guild, anyway? Maybe we can still catch him."

"It's getting late," Eldrin said. "The Guild will certainly be closed to outsiders by now. But we can try. It's close to the entrance to Thalgar's Tunnel. Just don't get your hopes up. The Mage Guild is a better place for him than with us. And he's young. We have to ensure his interests as much as ours."

"Of course," Justin said.

Lila stifled a yawn. "After a long day walking, the last thing I want is to keep going, but it looks like we're out of options."

Their conversation was interrupted by a knock at the door. Eldrin instantly became alert.

"Probably Gorn," he said. "Let me handle this."

52

A PARTY OF FOUR

"The Mage Guild is something of a misnomer. By definition, a mage refers to anyone who can wield ranged magic—be they a Druid, Summoner, Wizard, Elementalist, or even a Priest. Yet the Mage Guild of Serenthel accepts for training only those with a Spirit Core. Wizards, with their own esteemed universities, have no interest in the Guild's restrictions, but the deliberate exclusion of certain branches of magic has not gone unnoticed. To many, it is less a matter of standards and more an aversion to what many deem to be...unnatural."

—Isaran Drel,
A History of Magic in Serenthel

Justin had a gnawing sense of unease as he watched Eldrin approach the door. His hand instinctively tightened around his cane, and for a fleeting moment, he considered stopping the Ranger from answering. But Eldrin moved with the certainty of someone who knew what to expect, and to Justin's relief, when the door creaked open, it was indeed Gorn, the orcish innkeeper.

Gorn's usually stern face was etched with concern. "Eldrin, you need to get your people out. The city watch is prowling outside the inn, asking too many questions. They're getting ready to knock on doors. It's only a matter of time before they poke around in your business."

Eldrin's eyes narrowed as he absorbed the information quickly. "Looks like it's time for me to sneak out the back, like the last time I was here."

Gorn grunted, his tusks protruding slightly. "Well, that's why you pay me extra, isn't it?"

Eldrin turned to Justin and Lila. "Grab your things. We're leaving."

Justin hadn't even unpacked, so it was a simple matter of slinging his pack over his shoulder. Lila and Eldrin were equally quick, their movements efficient and silent.

Gorn was already leading the way down the stone hallway, his heavy footsteps surprisingly quiet. He guided them through the kitchen, which, at this late hour, was deserted, the lingering smell of roasted meat and spices the only sign that it had been busy earlier. The orc opened a door at the far end, revealing a dark, narrow passage that led into the Undermarket.

One by one, they slipped through. Without another word, Gorn shut the door behind them and locked it, his expression grim.

Eldrin took the lead, guiding them swiftly and silently through the winding alleys of the Undermarket. The labyrinthine network of passages was dimly lit by flickering lanterns. After a few twisting turns, Justin was completely disoriented, with no idea of which direction they were heading.

The Undermarket was still bustling, even at this hour. Stalls and shops lined the narrow passageways, offering everything from exotic spices and "rare" artifacts to dubious magical services. A fortune teller sat at the entrance of a small tent, whispering cryptic predictions to a nervous customer. A shadowy figure offered enchanted trinkets from beneath a dark hood. The air was thick with the scent of incense, mixed with the sharp tang of something unidentifiable but vaguely unsettling.

To Justin, the people who inhabited this underground world were just as varied as the goods on display. Some were hunched and furtive, their faces hidden beneath hoods or masks, while others swaggered confidently, their expressions daring anyone to cross them.

Finally, they emerged onto the frigid streets above. The transition from the crowded, oppressive atmosphere of the Undermarket to the cold, quiet streets of Windfall was jarring. Here, the only sounds were the distant clatter of a horse's hooves on cobblestone and the occasional murmur of voices from a nearby tavern. Few festival revelers were out this late, at least in this part of town.

They crossed a small square dominated by a statue of a griffin, its wings outstretched as if ready to take flight. Beyond the statue loomed an imposing stone structure, cathedral-like in its grandeur. The Windfall Mage Guild stood tall, its gothic spires piercing the night sky, its arched windows glowing faintly with the light of magical wards. A pair of heavy oak doors, reinforced with iron, marked the entrance, flanked by statues of stern robed figures holding staves.

They approached the Guild's entrance, climbing up a short stoop. Eldrin took the lead, knocking firmly and taking a few steps back as snow swirled down the street.

They waited at least a minute until a small grate opened in the door, revealing the face of a mage with a ring of gray hair.

"The Mage Guild is closed to outsiders for the night," he announced in a firm, no-nonsense tone. "You must return at eight o'clock tomorrow morning if you have business."

Eldrin, undeterred by the lukewarm reception, stepped forward. "We're looking for an orcish mage named Kargan. He came by earlier today. Can you tell us where he might be?"

The man's eyes held a hint of recognition. "An orc named Kargan was indeed here earlier." His voice was laced with disdain. "But we contest the identifier of 'mage' that you attach to him. He was rejected by the Guild. The Council does not accept practitioners of blood magic."

A flicker of anger crossed Eldrin's face, but Justin was glad that he kept his tone measured. "Do you know where he went?"

The man considered for a moment. "I saw him heading east down the street, but that was hours ago. I guess he was searching for a less reputable establishment."

Eldrin turned to Justin and Lila. "Let's go. We might still catch up with him."

Without wasting another moment, they turned and headed east down the street, leaving the Mage Guild behind.

The streets were mostly empty, this quarter of the city having the look of a residential district with basic shops and businesses beneath on the street level, almost all dark for the night. They passed a few taverns that were still open, but they, too, were nearly empty.

But as Justin's eyes wandered toward a nearby tavern, he glimpsed something through the frosted window. There, sitting alone at a small table, was a figure that might have been Kargan, though it was difficult to be sure with the frost warping his shape. He was hunched over, nursing a drink, his shoulders sagging.

"Look," Justin said, pointing. "That has to be him."

Eldrin followed Justin's gaze and spotted Kargan through the window. His brow furrowed in concern. "That's him, all right."

Without another word, they made their way to the tavern's entrance, pushing open the heavy wooden door. The warmth inside was a welcome relief to the desolate streets outside. The air was thick with the smell of ale, mingling with the smoke from a crackling fire in the hearth. The tavern was dimly lit by flickering lanterns that did little to push back the gloom. Most of the patrons were drinking alone.

Justin noticed a few eyes glance their way, but most of the customers were too preoccupied with their own affairs to pay much attention. The tavern had an air of quiet resignation, as if it were a place where people came to escape their troubles, if only for a little while.

Justin's heart sank a little as he saw Kargan more clearly. The orc's hands were wrapped around a large mug as he stared down at its contents. His amber eyes were dull, while his expression was one of deflation.

"Kargan," Eldrin called out softly as the group approached the table.

The orc looked up, his eyes focusing on them with a hint of surprise. "Eldrin? Justin, Lila? What are you doing here?"

"We've been looking for you," Eldrin replied, taking a seat opposite Kargan. Justin and Lila followed suit, sliding into the chairs beside him. "We heard what happened at the Mage Guild."

Kargan's expression darkened, and he let out a bitter chuckle. "Mage Guild. You've been following me?"

"Only because we need to ask you something," Eldrin said.

Kargan drained the rest of his mug. From the dazed look in his eyes, it was far from his first one. "So, you heard they don't consider me a 'real mage.' I should have known before showing my face there. Blood Magic isn't magery, according to them. Now, who knows what I can do? Maybe there's some blacksmith that'll apprentice me. That's the job for orcs, right?"

Justin felt a pang of sympathy for Kargan. He could see the frustration etched on his face, the anger at being rejected not just for his abilities, but for who he was. Thus far, that had been the story of his life.

"They're idiots," Lila said, her voice firm. "Blood magic or not, you have real power, Kargan. They're just too blind to see it."

Kargan shook his head. "It's more than that, Lila. It's not just about power. It's about control. Blood magic...well, it scares people. They don't like what they can't control, and they can't control me. Besides, I doubt their curriculum has anything that can help me develop my abilities. I'd have to go underground for that."

Eldrin leaned forward. "We don't care what kind of magic you use, Kargan. You've already proven yourself to us. We're heading out soon, and we could use your skills. Come with us."

Kargan looked at him, the spark of interest flickering in his eyes, but it was quickly overshadowed by doubt. "Where are you going? You make it sound like you're not planning to head east anymore."

"We're heading through Thalgar's Tunnel," Eldrin explained. "It might be our best shot at getting out of Windfall unnoticed. Who knows? We could find some rare treasures down there, and you'd have the chance to build your skills."

"Rare treasures? You won't find them in the Tunnel." His eyes widened in realization. "Wait. Unless you mean to head down to Drakendir..."

Eldrin gave a slow nod. "We do. But Gareth's men will be here tomorrow evening, and they're on horseback. We hope to use the tunnels around Drakendir to come out someplace safer where we can stay undetected. It'll be dangerous. That's why we need someone with your abilities."

"You mentioned treasure. That would mean going into a Vault. I've heard about them opening up the tunnel, but the dwarf cities have had two decades to fester. The Vaults down there will be way beyond our abilities. I need a guaranteed payout, not something that'll get me killed."

"I'm happy to share in whatever we might find, but it's possible we could come away with nothing. In that case, the three of us agreed to make sure you are justly compensated."

"A job, then," Kargan said.

"It's better than whatever this is," Lila said, looking around the tavern. "Don't you want to spend time with people who respect your abilities?"

Justin watched as Kargan mulled over the offer, his fingers tapping lightly against the side of his mug. He could see the internal struggle in the orc's eyes—the desire to prove himself against the fear of more rejection and failure.

"Are you sure you want me along?" Kargan finally asked. "I'm only Level 5."

"And with each level up, you'll become even more capable," Eldrin said.

Justin leaned forward. "We're stronger together, and we need all the help we can get. You saved our asses in Eldareth. Besides, if anyone can manage what's down in those tunnels, it's you. Your night vision will come in handy."

"Not to mention the light of my Sacrificial Armor spell," he mused. Kargan stared at Justin for a long moment. "But I still have...reservations. Those men chasing you...you've kept that pretty close to your chest."

Justin nodded. "You deserve to know about that. It's a long story, but I'll try to be quick."

He proceeded to explain everything of importance: who he was, where he was really from, plus everything that had happened up to meeting Kargan. The orc watched with widened eyes for a good part of the story, not interrupting.

"So," Justin concluded, "that's why they're after me. At least, so we think. If you come with us, well, you'll be guilty by association. It's not a decision to make lightly, so there's no pressure."

Kargan seemed to consider this for a while. "This Earth place...it has to be real. I can tell you're not joking and that Lila and Eldrin believe you. It's just a bit crazy, that's all."

"I know," Justin said. "Every word is true. The point being, it would be great to have you with us, and if we find anything worth taking, well, we'll share the spoils. And if not, we'll make sure you're well compensated."

"And how long would this be for?" Kargan asked.

"At least through Drakendir. After that...it's your call."

Kargan thought it over, but he didn't think long, pushing his pint away. "All right. I'll come with you. Lila's right. It's better than sitting here feeling sorry for myself."

A small smile tugged at the corner of Justin's mouth. "Good to have you back, Kargan."

"Good thing you caught me before I'm too deep in my drinks. So, when do we leave? Thankfully, we orcs have a strong constitution. Do we still have that room in The Mountain's Rest?"

They shared a look, and then Eldrin quickly updated Kargan on everything that had happened because of the collectors coming after Lila. Kargan listened attentively.

"By Gor," he said. "That's tough luck, Lila. You all must be exhausted."

"We are," Justin said, stifling a yawn.

"I've already rented a cot here for the evening. Just twenty coppers a night. It's not much, but it beats sleeping on the street. You'll be safe enough here. The tunnel entrance will be closed for the night, anyway."

Eldrin nodded. "That may be what we have to do. We'll rest up for the night and get started tomorrow morning. We'll need all the rest we can get for the long march through the mountains."

"And just how long is this march?" Justin asked.

"It's about thirty miles to reach the Drakendir Gate, if those adventurers are to be believed," Eldrin said. "I'd like to make it by evening tomorrow. With luck, Gareth won't think we've gone that way, at least not immediately. And I suspect he won't know about the opening of the Tunnel as soon as he arrives. That should buy us more time."

"We should get some rest," Lila said. "It's been a long day."

[Kargan has joined the party. You now benefit from his Blood Pact, enhancing your natural healing.]

Eldrin, Lila, and Justin moved to the bar, where they asked the barkeeper, a burly man with a thick beard and a gruff demeanor, about a cot. Within minutes, all of them were heading back with Kargan to settle down for the night.

The space was shared with about a dozen other people in a single hall, a good half of them snoring, but Justin was far too tired to care. He set down his things, using his pack as a pillow while also ensuring it wouldn't be messed with.

Within minutes, he was fast asleep.

53

MASKS OF POWER

"The Autumn Festival in Aranthia is a weeklong celebration marking the height of the harvest and lifting spirits before winter's inevitable descent. The grandest of these festivals is held in Belmora, where travelers from every corner of the land are welcomed to join in the revelry. Even the smallest hamlets host their own vibrant variations, with feasts, dances, and games that draw entire villages together. Whether grand or humble, the festival reminds us that joy, like the harvest, must be gathered and shared while it lasts."

—Chronicler Dillon Roede
  Festivals of the Known World

THE AIR STUNG Justin's cheeks as he, Lila, Eldrin, and Kargan made their way through the winding streets of Windfall. The snow had stopped falling, but the remnants clung stubbornly to the cobblestones, making each step a cautious one.

But despite the frigid morning, the streets were humming with the Autumn Festival, the air filled with the aroma of roasting chestnuts, spiced wine, and freshly baked bread. Colorful banners hung from every building, fluttering in the crisp breeze, while laughter and music echoed through the streets. Jugglers and acrobats performed for delighted children, and vendors called out to passersby, offering their wares of handmade crafts and seasonal treats.

"It's the last day of the festival," Eldrin said, his voice barely audible over the din. "It should serve as decent cover."

They reached the main square, and Eldrin led them onto a narrow street that took them north, directly toward the main mountain looming over Windfall. The square was completely packed with revelers, and a stage had been set up in front of the clock tower. The crowd buzzed with anticipation for an upcoming announcement, while musicians played lively tunes to keep the energy high.

The entrance to Thalgar's Tunnel was impossible to miss. Its dark, imposing archway opened into the side of the mountain. Two heavily armed guards stood at attention in front of the gate. The gate itself was massive, resembling the heavy, fortified doors of a castle, with thick iron bars that ran vertically and horizontally.

"Closed," Kargan said, eyeing the gate warily.

"Perhaps it's still too early in the day," Eldrin said. "Let me handle this."

As Eldrin approached the watchmen, Justin noted the griffin emblazoned on their black surcoats, the emblem of the city of High-cliff. The Ranger offered the guards a friendly smile. "Happy Festival, friends! We need passage through Thalgar's Tunnel."

One guard, a broad-shouldered man with a clean-shaven face and rosy cheeks, shook his head. "The tunnel is closed."

Eldrin frowned. "Closed? On account of the festival?"

The guard exchanged a glance with his companion before answering, "There was an...incident. The gate's been ordered shut until further notice."

Eldrin remained unfazed. "Well, it's certainly nothing four seasoned adventurers can't manage." When the guards remained silent, he reached into his pouch, producing two five-silver coins. "I can make it worth your while."

The lead guard looked at the coins, then shook his head firmly.

"Can't do it. Five marks aren't worth my job. Orders are orders. Only the mayor himself can overrule them."

Eldrin's frustration was evident, but he kept his cool. He reached into his pouch as he produced twenty more silver marks, which made for fifteen for each guard. The second guard's eyes glazed over with greed.

"You need not open it all the way," the Ranger said quietly. "Just a hair. No one is watching with the festivities going on."

The first guard seemed to consider for a moment but shook his head. "The answer is still no. And if you attempt to bribe me again, I shall have to arrest you."

"That must be two weeks' pay for you," Eldrin said. "Imagine how much it could help."

The guard smirked. "Never let it be said that the Windfall Watch lacks honor."

"Honor or not, I'm determined to go through today. Where can we find the mayor?"

The guard shrugged. "Well, it's a big day for the city, so he could be anywhere. He's supposed to inaugurate the Autumn Games this morning, but after that, he'll be up at the Harrington House. There's some fancy event going on there today. A lot of the city's higher-ups are attending."

"The Harrington House," Lila said, a glimmer of hope in her voice. "We're in luck! We got an invitation to that just yesterday."

Eldrin arched an eyebrow, clearly surprised. There had been no chance to update Eldrin on everything.

"Lord Harrington himself extended it to me," Justin added. "Maybe we can ask for the mayor's help there."

The guard's skepticism was apparent as he looked them over—travel-worn and clearly not in the attire one might expect for such an event. But an official invitation carried weight, and after a moment's hesitation, the guard nodded. "You might have a shot. But don't expect much unless he has a reason to help you."

"We should head up there," Eldrin said. "If we leave now, we'll be there in time to intercept him."

The guard looked like he was holding back laughter. "You're not getting in looking like that."

"We'll have to try," Eldrin said, his tone unyielding. "You'll be getting those orders within a few hours; I promise you that. And then you'll wish you had taken my coin."

The guard smiled, clearly thinking this was all talk. It gave Justin the motivation to prove him wrong.

Eldrin turned to the others. "Let's move."

The Ranger led them up a side alley, which took them back to the main street where they had done their shopping the day before. The storefronts gave way to larger, more ornate dwellings as they climbed higher into the wealthier district of the city. The houses were larger, more elegant, with wrought iron fences and tall, snow-covered hedges. The roads were better maintained, the snow cleared to reveal pristine stone. Fancy carriages rolled by from time to time, sometimes carrying the laughter of nobles being transported within.

Lord Harrington's home was the largest of all, situated at the very end of the street. The manor was a sprawling estate, with towering columns and wide marble steps leading up to the entrance. The windows were tall and arched, and the roof was topped with elegant spires. Behind the dwelling lay the main mountain overlooking Windfall, covered in snow.

Justin set his thoughts upon the Ring of Hygiene, and within an instant, he was perfectly clean and groomed. While the others wouldn't get the same benefit, it was a necessary step for him. He straightened his new top hat. As a Socialite, this was his element, and he'd have to rise to the occasion.

A pair of black-liveried footmen stood beside a large iron gate through which they could see the manor's grand entrance. A line of carriages was already forming as guests arrived.

Justin, Eldrin, Lila, and Kargan walked up to the gate. The lead guard, a tall man with a sharp nose and an air of authority, seemed to be checking everyone's invitations as they entered. He eyed them first with confusion; while Justin was dressed the part, the rest were not dressed as richly. Then, the footman's expression became one of thinly veiled disdain. "The servants' entrance is on the side."

Justin activated his Dandy's Swagger skill, strutting forward and puffing out his chest. "The nerve! We're not servants, but honored guests. I'm Lord Talemaker, of the same house."

"Talemaker," the guard repeated skeptically. "I'm unaware of any noble house with that—"

Justin thrust the invitation right in his face, and he ensured his voice would drip with superiority. "Lord Harrington invited me himself. I will not suffer insolence from a lowly guard like you."

The guard's blue eyes widened as he took in Justin's friends, and he seemed to hesitate. "Sir, there is a certain code of dress for this event, and this code is strictly—"

"My carriage tumbled over outside the city, so my morning has already gone poorly. My companions are dressed for travel, and we meant to change once we're inside. Why am I explaining myself to a peon like you? You should know your place, sir!" Justin's haughty tone intensified, and he tilted his nose upward.

"All right, my lord! Forgive me," the guard stammered. "You have the invitation. Head to the front and ask for Mr. Willoughby, the butler."

"Good riddance!" Justin said, nodding at the others and twirling his cane. With his head held high, he strode toward the house, his nose in the air as they passed through the gate.

Once out of earshot, Lila smirked. "I'm starting to see your use, Justin."

"It's showtime, baby," Justin said, his voice laced with confidence, an affect of his Dandy's Swagger. As he surveyed the others, they looked far less assured. "Here's the thing: act like the most entitled, spoiled brat you've ever met, and then dial it up ten times further. Don't overthink what you're going to say—powerful people don't bother with that. They just say whatever comes to mind because they never have to deal with the consequences. They're so used to getting their way that it doesn't even occur to them that someone might question it."

Eldrin nodded, though his expression remained wary. "We've got it, Justin. But what about our clothing? We don't exactly look the part."

"Don't worry about that," Justin replied with a dismissive wave. "It's not about what you're wearing; it's about how you wear it. Confidence is everything. We can say we were trying to venture down into the tunnel to take out a dangerous Vault; that can explain our dress and weapons."

"That would create a trail," Eldrin pointed out. "People would remember we asked about the gate."

"The Mayor's going to find out anyway," Lila said. "What counts is making it all happen. We have to push through."

Eldrin sighed. "Seems we're all out of options. Now, Justin, I'm going to defer to you. This is your element."

Justin nodded as they reached the stone steps that led to the entrance of the manor. The prospect made him a little nervous, but this was what his class was made for.

They reached the front steps. The butler, who had to be Mr. Willoughby, was a tall, thin man with a narrow face and piercing gray eyes. His uniform was immaculate, the black coat and white gloves spotless, giving him an air of strict professionalism. His expression, however, was far from welcoming. It was a look of barely concealed scorn, as if he couldn't quite believe that these travel-worn adventurers were attempting to enter the Harrington House.

"Good morning," the butler said, his tone clipped and cold. "May I assist you?"

Justin didn't miss a beat. He stepped forward, brandishing the invitation with a flourish. "You must be Mr. Willoughby. You may indeed help us. We're here as guests of Lord Harrington, and I expect the proper treatment, unlike your footman at the gate. Vile man! It's already been a dreadful morning—our carriage overturned on the way here, and we're hardly in the mood for delays. Now, if you'll kindly stop wasting our time and show us inside."

The butler's eyes flicked over the invitation, then back to Justin and his companions, along with their weapons and packs. His lips pressed into a thin line. "Sir, there is a certain standard of dress expected at this event, and I'm afraid your servants—"

"Standards? Really?" Justin interrupted, his voice rising in mock outrage. "You think I don't know that? I'm Lord Talemaker, and I'll have you know I'm fully aware of your so-called 'standards.' Unfortunately, our situation doesn't exactly lend itself to your delicate sensibilities. Now, unless you want to explain to Lord Harrington why his esteemed guests were turned away, I suggest you reconsider your approach."

The butler's face tightened, but he knew he was cornered. The invitation was legitimate, and Justin's bluster left him little room to argue. "Of course, my lord," he said stiffly. "If you would follow me."

Without another word, the butler led them up the stone steps and into the manor. The warmth of the interior was a welcome relief from the cold outside. The entrance hall was vast, with lofty ceilings and walls adorned with tapestries depicting scenes of battles and grand hunts. A large crystal chandelier hung from the ceiling, casting a warm, golden light over everything. The murmur of voices from the adjoining rooms hinted at the number of guests already in attendance.

As they followed Mr. Willoughby deeper into the manor, Justin couldn't help but feel a surge of triumph. They were in. Now, all they had to do was find the mayor and secure his help. He glanced at Lila, who offered a small, encouraging smile. They were playing a dangerous game, but it was one they couldn't afford to lose.

The butler led them to a smaller room off to the side of the main hall, where a servant offered to take their coats and packs. Justin preferred to keep his gear close, but toting around heavy packs would just make them stick out even more, so he consented to let the servant take that, along with the rest of his companions. The weapons they elected to keep; from the surrounding nobles bearing canes, rapiers, and swords, they wouldn't be the only ones.

Once relieved of their packs, they were ushered into the main reception area—a grand ballroom filled with well-dressed guests. The men wore tailored suits, and the women were adorned in elegant gowns, the colorful fabrics shimmering in the chandelier's light.

Lord Harrington was easy to spot, standing near the center of the room, holding court with a group of other distinguished guests. His presence was commanding with his suit and new top hat, this one with a peacock feather. He moved with the confidence of someone who was used to being the center of attention.

Justin took a deep breath and led the way over to him. As they approached, Lord Harrington noticed them and raised an eyebrow in surprise. But then his expression softened into a welcoming smile.

"Ah, Mr. Talemaker, you've made it!" he exclaimed, his voice carrying a note of genuine pleasure. He turned to the other nobles with him. "This is the one I told you about, who bested me in the social duel yesterday. You wear my old hat well!"

There was an appreciative murmur from the surrounding guests, and Justin waved it away with a smile. "Lord Harrington, you flatter me. I was merely trying to keep up with a man of your caliber."

Lord Harrington chuckled, clearly enjoying the attention. "Well, I'm beyond delighted. I wasn't sure you'd be able to attend." He turned to Lila, bowing slightly. "And of course, the Lady Lila Fairwind, Bard of Beauty."

Justin gave a light-hearted grin, sliding his arm around Lila's waist. "Careful, Harrington, I've got a reputation to maintain here."

Harrington laughed, the sound more genuine this time. "Ah, no harm meant, Mr. Talemaker. Please, make yourselves at home! But my, it looks as though you're about to go off on an adventure!"

"Aye, so we were," Justin said, his voice filled with a touch of regret. "My lady and I hired these fine professionals to venture into Thalgar's Tunnel." He nodded toward Eldrin and Kargan. "This is strictly between us—and these esteemed gentlepeople here—but there are rumors of a Vault opening on the other side in the Everwood, and I plan to be the first to claim the prize while everyone else is preoccupied with the festivities."

A noble with a stern expression, blonde hair, and piercing blue eyes, with a longsword resting at his waist, gave Justin a cool look before offering a slight, formal bow. "Lord Bohemund Ashcroft, of the same county. Now, what's this about a Vault? I've heard nothing of the sort, and I usually keep an ear to the ground for these matters. I'm no stranger to the sword myself and wouldn't mind a sojourn into the Everwood at this time of year."

Justin met Bohemund's gaze with a confident smile. "Ah, a fellow adventurer, I see. But you know how it is with such information—it tends to flow through certain channels before reaching the broader crowd. A few of my sources, who owe me some favors, whispered of the Vault just yesterday. Timing, as you know, is everything, wouldn't you agree?"

He let the words linger for a moment, giving the impression that he was knowledgeable, someone with access to valuable, exclusive information. Then, with a slight shrug, he continued. "But alas, I found the gate to be closed this morning, and the city guards were most disagreeable. Usually, a few silvers are enough to get what you want, but this one was stubborn, saying that only the mayor could remedy the situation."

"Ah, aren't commoners just the worst?" Lord Harrington said, rolling his eyes. "They can be so uppity! Well, Mayor Carlisle himself will be in attendance soon if I understand things correctly. In fact, we have distinguished guests coming from all over Aranthia, even as far as Belmora. Tell me, from where does your noble house hail?"

"West of Mistwatch, in the Wildwood," Justin said smoothly.

"Ah! Those lands are ripe for development. The hunting is good, I hear! Are the Forest Goblins not a problem, though?"

"Nothing a good thwack of my cane can't manage!"

Justin mimed the action, and the nobles burst into amused, haughty laughter, their jeweled fingers covering smirking mouths and their eyes glinting with faux delight.

As the mirth cooled down, Justin indicated Eldrin with a nod. "This is my good friend, Eldrin Thornwood. A Ranger is a necessity for any adventuring party, wouldn't you agree?" He tittered and continued before awaiting an answer. "And this is Kargan Durzag, a mage of great renown. He might look young, but oh my, you should see him in action!"

Justin gave Kargan a sly wink, and the orc's lips turned downward in distaste. He hoped Kargan knew he was playing the game, and if anything, he might even get a job after this from this positive recommendation.

"A pleasure to meet you all, I'm sure," Harrington replied, taking in Justin's companions, though his tone had grown stiff. "Well, Mr. Talemaker, it was a pleasure to catch up. Make yourselves at home. There's food and drink aplenty, and there shall be dancing later. We also have some contests and games that might interest you—a chance to show off your skills, perhaps?"

"I thank you, Lord Harrington. You are a steadfast friend, though we have only just met."

"Likewise, my good man! Well, I must go to greet my new guests. But before I leave, a bit of advice: Mayor Carlisle, in case you haven't met him, is a cautious man of the Diplomat class. But he's also practical. I promise to introduce you and vouch for your need. I think there's a good chance he'll grant you the permission you seek."

A wave of relief washed over Justin, and he placed a hand over his heart, though inwardly, he worried about someone of the Diplomat class. He wasn't sure what to expect there, but like him, the man would likely have access to various social skills and boons. He would have to tread carefully. "Thank you, Lord Harrington. That would mean a great deal."

Harrington smiled, a glint of satisfaction in his eyes. "It's the least I can do for a friend. In fact, there's a small matter I could use some help with—a certain business venture I'm considering. We'll speak of it later. It's always good to have a friend who's into adventuring!"

"I would be delighted," Justin said, offering a respectful nod.

"Until later, Mr. Talemaker."

With that, Lord Harrington moved off to greet another group of guests, Justin's anxiety easing slightly. They had a plan, and it felt like they might actually have a chance.

As they wove through the gathering, Justin couldn't help but notice the curious glances they received from the other guests. Despite his smooth exterior, Justin felt a bit out of place. He observed other Socialites performing their skills, charming or delighting those around them with effortless grace. He even saw one guest deliver a scornful insult that had the surrounding crowd laughing heartily.

They grabbed hors d'oeuvres from passing servants—delicacies like smoked salmon canapés, stuffed mushrooms, and tiny tarts filled with rich custard—as well as glasses of champagne. They did their best to blend in, moving from group to group, making polite conversation, but really, they were just killing time until the mayor showed up. Justin got into a rhythm, spinning tales of their adventures, charming the ladies with exaggerated stories, and even indulging in a brief dance with a persistent guest. It was important for the crowd to be on his side—just in case.

At one point, a man commented on Justin's attire, admiring his Cane of Valoria and his Coat of Highcliff's Elegance. "I must say, Lord Talemaker, your fashion is quite unique. It reminds me of the portraits of my ancestors back home at Ravenwood Manor. Classic practicality and style—a rare combination!"

Justin smiled, twirling his cane. "I believe one should always be prepared for any occasion, my friend. Who knows when adventure lies around the corner?"

Finally, after what felt like an hour, Justin felt a light tug on his coat sleeve. He turned to see Lord Harrington standing there.

"Mayor Carlisle is here," Harrington said. "Allow me to introduce you."

Justin nodded as they threaded their way to a group where the mayor, a portly man with a neatly trimmed beard, was engaged in conversation with an elegantly dressed lady. Harrington approached him with the same calm confidence he had shown to Justin. He gracefully awaited a lull in the conversation and tacit acknowledgment from the mayor and the lady before approaching.

"Mayor Carlisle, a moment of your time," Harrington said.

The mayor smiled. "Lord Harrington! To what do I owe this pleasure?"

"I'd like to introduce you to Mr. Talemaker. He and his companions have run into a bit of trouble with Thalgar's Tunnel, and they need your help."

The mayor's expression became more serious as he turned to Justin. "Ah. What sort of trouble?"

Justin inclined his head respectfully, fully aware of the delicate situation. He had to tread carefully—Mayor Carlisle was a man who owed him nothing, and convincing him to grant access to the tunnel would require finesse.

"Mayor Carlisle, it's a pleasure to meet you," Justin began smoothly, his tone respectful but confident. "This morning, my companions and I discovered that Thalgar's Tunnel has been closed because of an incident. We were hoping to make use of the tunnel to reach the Everwood, as we've received word of a dangerous Vault that has recently opened."

The mayor's expression remained serious, his gaze sharp as he listened. Justin continued, carefully choosing his words. "I understand that the closure is for a good reason, but time is of the essence here. If left unchecked, this Vault could become a significant threat. My party and I are prepared to manage it before it becomes an issue, but we need access to the tunnel to get there quickly."

Mayor Carlisle's eyes narrowed slightly, and Justin could feel the weight of his scrutiny. The mayor was clearly assessing the situation, and Justin suspected that one of Carlisle's Diplomat abilities was at play, subtly probing for any signs of deceit or weakness.

Justin maintained steady eye contact, keeping his posture relaxed but purposeful. He couldn't afford to show any hesitation. He had to convince Carlisle that this was a legitimate concern and that his group was the best option to deal with it. Never mind that there was no Vault, at least as far as Justin knew.

After a moment, the mayor spoke, his tone measured. "Mr. Talemaker, I appreciate your concern. It's wonderful—and quite rare— that an outsider has taken such a keen interest in Windfall's safety. However, the closure of Thalgar's Tunnel was not a decision made lightly. There are risks involved in reopening it, especially given the circumstances. What assurances can you provide that your expedition will not only succeed but also prevent any further danger?"

"Mayor Carlisle, I understand your concerns," Justin replied, his voice steady. "But my team is well-equipped to handle this situation. Together, we've faced similar threats before and emerged successfully."

Mayor Carlisle considered Justin's words deeply, his silence stretching on, making Justin increasingly uneasy. The quiet scrutiny was unnerving. It was easier to navigate conversations filled with words, where he could play on nuances and manipulate the flow.

But this silence—it was hard to work with silence.

Justin cleared his throat, trying to maintain his composure. "Our goal is to neutralize the Vault and ensure that whatever dangers lie within do not spill over into the surrounding areas. By granting us access to the tunnel, you're not just opening a gate—you're ensuring that this potential threat is dealt with swiftly and effectively. We'll move quickly and discreetly, and we'll report back with our findings."

Carlisle's gaze didn't waver, his expression remaining inscrutable as if he were carefully weighing every word. The silence hung heavy in the air, and Justin could feel the pressure mounting.

Finally, Carlisle nodded slowly, breaking the tension. "Very well, Mr. Talemaker. I will arrange for the tunnel to be opened, but I would like to have a discussion with you first."

"With me?" Justin asked, a note of unease creeping into his voice. "What for?"

For the first time, the mayor betrayed a slight smile, which was quickly erased, leaving behind the same unreadable mask.

Something, at that very moment, told Justin to run as fast as the wind. This feeling was only reinforced when Eldrin tugged sharply on his sleeve.

"You know," Justin said, his tone light but hurried, "I just remembered something. I thank you for your help, but we really must be going."

He turned to leave, trusting the others to follow his lead without question. His heart pounded in his chest, and the sense of impending danger grew stronger with each passing second. But as they moved toward the ballroom's exit, Justin's worst fear materialized.

Standing at the entrance to the grand hall was the last person he wanted to see.

Baron Valdrik's tall, slender frame was accentuated by a tailored black velvet coat, and his pale, narrow face was framed by slicked-back hair that revealed a pronounced widow's peak. A thin beard traced his sharp jawline, and his piercing gray eyes, like those of a predator, seemed to see right through them, while his long fingers, adorned with silver rings, drummed a slow rhythm on the dark wood of his polished staff.

"What?" Valdrik asked, his voice smooth and dripping with barely disguised malice. "Leaving so early? The fun has only just begun!"

54

CONFRONTATION

"If the gods love us, why do they test us so harshly? Perhaps love for them is not what it is for us."

—Calira of Delonia,
Creator and Created

ELDRIN WAS the first to react, raising his bow and firing a swift arrow. The Baron, with a lazy smile, raised his staff and muttered a quick incantation that made the air go cold, instantly disintegrating the arrow in mid-air. Lila threw her knives, only for them to slow and pause just short of reaching the Baron. They clattered to the floor harmlessly. Kargan, who had no attacking moves, simply created a Blood Aegis, followed by a shield of sacrificial armor, standing between the party and further harm.

Justin, uselessly, just stared in shock.

The sudden eruption of conflict sent a ripple of shock through the crowd. Gasps and murmurs filled the grand hall as the guests recoiled, some stepping back in fear while others craned their necks to get a better view. The nobility, accustomed to polite conversations and subtle power plays, were unprepared for such violence. The musicians had abruptly stopped playing, their instruments still in hand, as they exchanged bewildered looks.

A few of the nobles instinctively activated their own defensive skills, casting quick glances at each other as if to confirm that what they were witnessing was indeed real. Servants, caught in the middle of their tasks, froze in place, unsure whether to flee or continue with their duties.

All eyes were now fixed on the Baron, whose calm demeanor only heightened the unease. The guests now found themselves on the edge of panic, uncertain of what would happen next.

That was when the Baron laughed heartily, the sound rich, as if he were genuinely amused by the whole spectacle. His laughter echoed through the hall, causing the tension in the room to falter, the fearful murmurs dying down as the guests tried to make sense of the situation.

"Oh, come now!" the Baron exclaimed, a playful glint in his eyes. "Is this how you treat an old friend? A bit of fun is all it is! You should know by now that arrows and daggers aren't enough to stop me!" He waved his hand dismissively, as if the whole incident were nothing more than a harmless prank.

The Baron turned to the crowd, his smile charming. "Ladies and gentlemen, I apologize for the little spectacle. Friendly banter among comrades-in-arms, you see. No need for alarm. We're all on the same side here." He winked at a nearby guest, who nervously returned a faint smile.

All Justin could feel was sick. He knew by now there was no chance of running, but from the Baron's reaction, the odds of dying immediately were remote. There was safety in a crowd, and using that cover was the only viable way to escape this situation.

Escape? Who was he kidding? The Baron had him. Like a cat who'd caught the mouse, he just wanted to torture the prey a bit before dining.

Valdrik spread his arms wide, as if to embrace the entire room with his jovial mood. "Mr. Talemaker, I know you have a penchant for pranks, but let's not ruin a perfectly good celebration, shall we?"

At that very moment, the Baron's gaze fell upon him, and without a word, Justin knew what he wanted. Join the act or regret it. The only saving grace was that the Baron had called him by his true name, Talemaker, rather than Caroway, the name Justin had used when introducing himself. Otherwise, all the work he had done so far in this ballroom would fall apart.

Justin forced a smile, his mind racing as he tried to find the right words to defuse the situation. He knew the Baron had him cornered, but he also knew that if he played his cards right, he might just buy time.

"Oh, you know me too well, Baron Valdrik," Justin said, his tone light and playful, masking the fear churning inside him. "Always up to some mischief, aren't I? But as you say, let's not spoil the fun for everyone else. I've been known to mix a bit of theatrics into my adventures—keeps things interesting! But I assure you, no harm was done here tonight. Just a little jest among friends."

He turned to the crowd, widening his smile as he spread his arms in a gesture of good-natured apology, even twirling his cane a bit. "I do apologize for the sudden excitement. You know how it is—old friends, old rivalries, and a touch of showmanship. We were just testing each other's reflexes, keeping our wits sharp! But let's not let that interrupt this wonderful celebration. I, for one, could use a drink after all that excitement. What do you say we all raise a glass to peace, good company, and the fine art of diplomacy?"

The tension in the room eased as murmurs of agreement rippled through the crowd. Some guests even chuckled, reassured by Justin's lighthearted explanation, especially as Baron Valdrik nodded gracefully, his expression so convincing that even Justin was tempted to believe this entire thing had been just an unfortunate misunderstanding.

He might believe that if it had not been for Alistair's death.

The musicians played again, and the festive atmosphere slowly returned, albeit with an undercurrent of unease.

Justin could feel the Baron's gaze on him, a silent warning that this was far from over. But for now, at least, he had bought them some time—and with Valdrik, every second counted.

"Justin..." Eldrin said. "What are you doing?"

"He's won, Eldrin," Justin said. "We've been outplayed. It's only me he wants. If you three slip out, there's a chance you can get out of this alive."

Justin's words were caught short as the Baron made his way toward Justin and his friends, taking his time about it with a few amiable greetings along the way. How could he be here, of all places? Obviously, all this was some elaborate trap, one so subtle that even Eldrin's Ranger's Intuition hadn't caught it in time. Had the Baron been responsible for closing the tunnel gate? Maybe Harrington's invitation hadn't been so random after all; perhaps Valdrik had put him up to it.

Justin had a million questions, and he wasn't sure if any of them would matter, since he was most likely dead soon.

At last, the Baron stood before him, a malevolent presence despite his plastered-on smile. "Come now," he said, clapping Justin on the back with a bit too much force to be entirely friendly. "Let's enjoy the festival together, as friends should." His tone was light, but there was a subtle edge to his words, a reminder of the power he held—and the danger that lurked just beneath his surface charm. "Let's grab a drink, shall we? Just you and me." He winked at his companions. "Don't worry. I'll return him in one piece."

He led Justin away. With a look, Justin warned the others not to follow. What chance did they have against whatever level Valdrik was at? Just like Valdrik, they could do nothing with so many eyes on them.

"I'm sure you have questions," Valdrik said, as they wove together through the crowd. "Many questions! Rest assured, Mr. Talemaker, every single one shall be answered to your full satisfaction."

Justin frowned in confusion. "Why answer questions when you intend to kill me?"

Valdrik laughed lightly, not seeming to care if they were overheard. "Kill you? No, my good man. This is the beginning of the rest of your days on Eyrth."

Justin threw a look over his shoulder, but his friends were lost in the crowd. Would Valdrik really let them escape so easily?

"I must apologize," Valdrik said. "It would seem we've gotten off on the wrong foot. This meeting is far more roundabout than I would have liked, but I will not be denied in the end! What I must tell you is far too important."

Valdrik paused before the banquet table, grabbing a haunch of meat from a strange creature reminiscent of an oversized bat. He ate with relish.

"Healthy appetite for not being alive," Justin observed.

Valdrik chuckled. "Oh, I'm very much alive. And my appetites are greater than most men. All of this has been an unfortunate misunderstanding, I'm afraid."

"Alistair is dead because of you. That's hardly a misunderstanding."

"Oh, him? Yes, sad business, that! I wish the Templars would keep their noses where they belong. I don't enjoy killing them, but he was a loose end, and the Templars could complicate my plans."

Justin looked around, but no one was paying attention to the conversation. For someone who operated from the shadows, the Baron was being forthright. Surprisingly so. It seemed the surrounding nobles were giving them plenty of space, while the din of conversation was enough to cover their words.

"He was a good man," Justin said. "And now, because of you, he's dead."

"Well, Alistair was never supposed to be part of this," Valdrik said. "I had hoped we could discuss these things more thoroughly in the safety of my Silverton Manse, but I suppose this frozen hellhole will have to suffice."

A beautiful woman walked by, with raven-black hair and near-perfect features, batting her eyes at the Baron while fanning herself. He gave her a genial smile.

"Now, where was I?" he asked. "Oh, yes. We never got to finish our conversation from last time. How would you feel about being employed by me? I see you have more experience under your belt now. The wage I offered before was low, but in keeping with one for your abilities. How does a salary of one gold crown a month sound? There is room for advancement in my organization, and I could use someone with your skills."

It was becoming increasingly difficult for Justin to keep his cool. Valdrik was acting as if nothing at all had happened.

"I'm...beyond confused," Justin said. "First, how did you track us here?"

"Track you?" He laughed lightly. "It wasn't difficult. Of course, you took the Umber Pass out of Silverton. Most don't go that way, owing to the difficulty, but with Mr. Thornwood at the helm, you had an advantage. Of course, it wasn't enough of an advantage. It took you two nights to reach Highcliff, where if you had taken the Silver Road, it would have taken just one. I was in constant communication with Lieutenant Gareth, of course. As my thrall, that's simple enough. When you got to the Guardian's Pass, there was nowhere else for you to go but Highcliff. I had Gareth surround the city and had his mages place wards on all the catacomb exits we could find. Luckily, the High Cleric at the cathedral was most accommodating."

"You killed him?"

Valdrik made a mask of affront. "Kill? Why would I do that? No, a simple Cant of Compulsion was enough for one of my wizards to get what he wanted, followed by a Cant of Amnesia to make sure he didn't remember the interaction. Memory magic can be quite tricky, but it can be well worth the risk in the right circumstances. I try not to mess with the Church, though, of course, sometimes death becomes unavoidable."

"Speaking of death, someone tried to kill me in the stairwell at the Silver Stag."

"That wasn't me; far too crude! My men did a bit of asking around while you and your companions were puttering about the Highcliff Catacombs. You'd crossed a Snow Goblin by the name of Gribble, and there was quite a tussle regarding a cane. Reading your reaction, it seems this story is true."

Justin could only stare in shock. Did the man know every step of their journey?

"Point being, that was Gribble's doing, not mine. You just mistakenly assumed I had a hand in that. Alistair, unfortunately, had to be dealt with. Too life-blinded, that one! However, depending on this conversation, I hope that you and your friends might be convinced to stand down. Furthermore, while we might not walk away as friends, we might at least walk away with something of a truce."

A truce? That did indeed sound appealing. The problem, of course, was one of trust.

"I still have questions," Justin said. "Those wards explain how you found us leaving Highcliff, but I still don't understand why you weren't at Highcliff yourself to intercept us. After all, you said it was easy to figure out that that was where we were going."

"I'm far too careful to have done that, Justin."

At first, Justin didn't understand what he meant. It could have ended the chase at once. But then, he thought about the Baron and his long-term goals. If Alistair was to be believed, the man was gathering an undead force right in Silverton. If the Baron got involved with a Paladin, things could get messy, and he might lose control of the narrative. In Aranthia, fighting Paladins and the Templars wasn't a good look, and at best, it would lead to investigation, and at worst, it would lead to the toppling of everything he'd worked so hard to build. Despite his level, the Baron's standing was precarious.

He remembered something Eldrin had said about Necromancers and getting caught too early. A weak point to exploit, perhaps?

"So, how did you know we were going to Windfall?" Justin asked.

"Ah. I suppose from your perspective, it might seem confusing. I'll explain, if only as a courtesy. I must admit, the Ranger gave us a bit more trouble than I initially thought. His abilities are obviously quite honed, even though his level is middling at best. Your Bard companion has proven herself quite plucky, too. As for the orc, I must admit I know little about him, but his involvement with your group seems circumstantial. Anyway, even if Eldrin was successful in leading Gareth astray, there were few options for you in the wilds west of the Marin. You did the smart thing, heading north into the Darkwood. A risky maneuver, to be sure, but one that paid off. When Gareth arrived at Darkstream, a bit of questioning was all it took to determine you hadn't been there. So, that only left one goal for you that made sense: Windfall. We considered that you might try to cross the Umbers west, but that would take you too far from your eventual goal of Mont Elea, and the orcish clans can be hostile to strangers. And coming east again, across the Marin while avoiding Darkstream, was far too risky. Those lands are open, and it wouldn't have been hard for us to sight you, either in the field or on the road itself. No. Windfall was your goal, and I had to assume you—or Eldrin—would correctly deduce that Gareth couldn't get there as fast as you. However, in all of Eldrin's careful plans, he forgot about one thing."

"You, right?"

"Very good! You see, I was the missing piece of the puzzle. With Alistair dispatched, I could at last get more involved. I came to Highcliff shortly after you began your escape north along the Marin. Once Lieutenant Gareth realized he'd been fooled, he returned to Highcliff. I ordered him to Darkstream Crossing, telling him not to purchase horses until he got there. Why, might you ask? Because of the Ranger's damnable bird! If it had noted Gareth on horseback too soon, it would have changed Eldrin's plans to turn west rather than go to Windfall. And I wanted you to go to Windfall. So, while Gareth walked to Darkstream Crossing, I traveled by carriage to Windfall with all speed. I arrived early this morning, in fact, well ahead of Gareth and his retinue. Well, I would say it all worked out, in the end. Thankfully, I'd noticed rumors that Thalgar's Tunnel was open, so I made all haste to the mayor's home. I have a good relationship with Mayor Carlisle. He ensured the gate was closed as a personal favor. You were just a few minutes too late, but even this would have done you no good; I would have simply followed you to have this meeting. It's better this way, anyway."

All Justin could feel was a mounting sickness. He felt like such a fool. Even Eldrin, the wise Ranger, had been completely played. And now he and all his friends were most likely going to die unless he could find some way to turn this around.

He hoped they were well on their way out of town. Not that it would matter. All three were loose ends, as they knew the Baron's plans, or at least part of them. That was not something the Baron could just leave alone, despite his words. Yet, he seemed completely certain that Justin's companions presented no danger to him.

"I suppose Lord Harrington is one of your contacts?" Justin asked. "It's only with his invitation that we could get inside this manor."

"I know him, but your chance meeting was just that: a chance, however unlikely it seems. Of course, once I was in town, I could sense you, and I was simply seeking the right opportunity to make contact. It's not like you had anywhere to go at this point. When you headed up to the manor, I knew your goal was to get the tunnel open. So, it was simply a matter of following you. I'd rather confront you here and allow you to see my side of things."

"Well, you have me," Justin said. "And you claim you don't want to kill me. If that's the case, then what do you really want, and, more importantly, why should I trust you?"

"I've already said what I want," the Baron said. "I would like you to work for me."

"I don't understand," Justin said. "Why go through all this trouble just to give me a job? What's so special about me?" He frowned. "How is it that *I'm* the one who grabbed that parcel to deliver to you, anyway? And what was in it? What does it have to do with me?"

"Ah! Now you're finally asking the important questions, Mr. Talemaker. September 21. Does the date ring a bell?"

"Of course. It's the day I came to Eyrth."

Justin figured there was no point in hiding that from him. Eldrin had mentioned one of the Baron's agents was almost certainly listening to him at the Moonlit Alehouse. And the Baron wouldn't have picked that date out of the air unless he already knew the truth.

"Yes," the Baron said. "I imagine you must have felt terrified. It's a feeling I know all too well."

Justin frowned. What was he getting at? How did he know the very day he arrived? "Could you just get to the point?"

The Baron extended his hand, and Justin blinked as he muttered a strange incantation, and a parcel appeared. But not just any parcel. It was the same one he had delivered to the Baron all those days ago.

"Why don't you open it and see for yourself?"

Justin looked at the parcel, unbelieving. "How...how did you do that?"

"A Cant of Repository. It can be bothersome having to carry things around! This handy spell makes it so you can store many things within the Aether itself." He offered the package. "Would you do the honors?"

Justin could not help his curiosity. His hands shaking, he opened the parcel and couldn't believe what he found inside.

55

REVELATIONS

"A leaf knows the wind, but a fool trusts the breeze."

—Elven proverb

JUSTIN STARED at the book and its title for a solid minute, struggling to make sense of it.

The tome was small and unassuming, yet its presence felt heavy in his hands, as though it carried the weight of another world within its pages. The cover was bound in rich, dark leather, with intricate gold embossing that glimmered faintly in the light.

Justin's fingers traced the smooth, cool surface of the cover, feeling the subtle ridges of the embossed design. He hesitated for a moment, almost afraid to open it.

Finally, he tilted the book just enough to reveal the title on the spine, elegantly scripted in the same golden lettering: *The Wonderful Wizard of Oz.*

The title shone up at him, and for a moment, the room seemed to spin.

"This can't be here," he murmured. He looked up at the Baron, his voice trembling. "Where did you get this?"

"It would seem you recognize the title. Where did this book come from, Mr. Talemaker?"

"My world: Earth."

Baron Valdrik nodded. "Yes. Earth. You aren't from here, Justin."

"Well, you know that much already. You had someone listening to us in the Moonlit Alehouse that night, didn't you?"

"Yes, but I wanted to hear it from you. The book you hold in your hands is an Earth artifact. Such things are priceless treasures, and I've gone to great lengths to acquire many of them over the years."

"I get that it's from Earth," Justin said. "I just don't understand how it ended up in the post office for me to deliver to you. It makes no sense."

"You were drawn to it, Justin, like a moth to a flame. You see, people from Earth are naturally drawn to objects from their home world. Something about the otherness of it reacts to the magic of this world. Like attracts like. That's why you, of all people, picked up the parcel to deliver it to me."

"Wait. People from Earth? I'm not alone here?"

The Baron smiled. "Is it so surprising? If it happened to you, why not to others?"

Justin's eyes widened in realization, and he felt something of a thrill. "Wait. You're from Earth too, aren't you?"

"Yes."

Justin's heart raced as he processed the revelation. The implications were staggering, and a flicker of hope sparked within him, despite his and the Baron's complicated history.

"How long have you been here?"

Valdrik hesitated before answering, "Twenty years."

Justin couldn't help but open his mouth in surprise.

"Yes, it's a long time. It's been quite a while since I've found one like you. Eight years, in fact. We're a rare breed. Navigating a dangerous world like this is not for the faint of heart. Most Earthers end up dying before they can find any sort of help. Once upon a time, I was President of the Terra Club. The organization is now defunct, at least in this part of the world. We were a bit careless, shall we say. But once, the Terra Club existed as a beacon of hope for all Earthers who believed they were suffering this fate alone."

"How noble of you," Justin said, his tone laced with skepticism. He wasn't a fool; he knew the Baron had ulterior motives. "So, let me get this straight. You collect Earth artifacts and then put them in random post offices all around Aranthia, hoping that it draws people from Earth to deliver them...right to you?"

It sounded far-fetched, and yet, the Baron nodded once again. "That's the gist of it. Of course, it usually doesn't work out that way. Most of the time, the courier who delivers the parcel is a native Erythian. I receive several such deliveries a month. As I said before, you're the first Earther to show up on my doorstep in eight years. I also set low bids that no normal courier would want to take. Sometimes, the parcels sit for months until the right person comes along."

"Why not just say you were from Earth from the beginning?" Justin asked. "I would have been on your side. It seems like all you did was make a mess of things and accomplish the opposite."

"In hindsight, you are right. But at the time of our first meeting, you were not alone, and I wasn't entirely sure you were from Earth. Admitting as much while Lila was with you would have been the height of foolishness. Earthers, you see, prefer to keep a low profile, especially these days."

"And yet, we're having this conversation in broad daylight in a crowded ballroom where anyone can overhear it."

Valdrik waved his hand dismissively. "Please. Do you really believe I would be so careless? A Cant of Silent Warding is protecting our conversation."

"How many Cants do you know?" Justin asked.

"Hundreds," Valdrik said. "However, we're not talking about my carefulness, but rather your carelessness."

Justin swallowed. "What do you mean?"

The Baron looked at him meaningfully. "Come on, now. Rap battles? 'Islands in the Stream'? Such exploits might seem harmless, but if even a whisper of Earth culture is heard by the wrong ears, you might wake up with a knife in your throat. Or worse."

"I don't understand," Justin said. "Are you trying to tell me that people from Earth are being hunted?"

The Baron nodded somberly. "We are, unfortunately, an endangered species."

"Why?"

The Baron's eyes darkened. "Because we don't belong here, Justin. More than natural-born Eyrthians, we have the potential to disrupt the balance of power. I came to this world, much like you, on the Autumn Equinox. September 21, 2004. Four times a year, a portal opens, though never in the same place. On Eyrth, they'll open in sites of powerful magical concentration. And on Earth, they seem to occur in spots where great natural energy coalesces, usually in the form of a natural disaster. Hurricanes, earthquakes...even tornadoes. Mine happened to be an earthquake. Trapped under the rubble of my office building, the blue portal appeared, and it was my only way out. But unlike you, my portal took me outside an extremely dangerous cave with a fire-breathing dragon guarding the entrance. Somehow, by sheer luck, I survived." He hesitated a moment, apparently remembering the trials of those early days. "I worked hard, but eventually, I acquired a class core, realizing classes were the only true way to advance in this world. We Earthers have something of an advantage. While the natives cannot change their Core Attributes, we have something of a choice. Earthers take on the Core Attribute of whatever class core they absorb first. I ended up becoming a Wizard."

"Not a Socialite?" Justin asked.

"No, that came later. While a Wizard's powers are indeed useful, I soon learned that even it can be limited, especially in the social sphere. Because it's not the command of magic, the power of the sword arm, or the accuracy of an arrow that determines success in this world. It is winning the hearts of others. You have made many mistakes since first coming to Eyrth, Justin, but choosing Socialite as your class was perhaps the best decision you could have made."

Justin thought of his own entry to this world. If portals opened to sites of powerful magical concentration, he supposed a Prismatic Core sitting out in the open would qualify. The tornado as the entry point on Earth was simple enough to understand. "How many of us Earthers are here, exactly?"

"Fewer than you would think," the Baron said. "So far as we can tell, only one person comes through each time, but not always. Of these four entries every year, most don't survive long. Half might survive their first year. And of course, if they aren't careful, or announce themselves through sheer ignorance, they get caught quickly."

With a chill, Justin realized that it could have been him. But that begged the question. Who was doing the catching?

Valdrik paused, considering. "This world—this reality, if it can be so called—is clearly an advanced simulation, a highly sophisticated technology that's far too advanced for our own era. I can only assume that someone, or something, from our future is having a bit of fun, marooning people here for unknown reasons. As such, whoever made this wretched game is certainly human, or even transhuman, given the insane level of technology on display, with the ability to create portals in the past. It's also possible the maker of this game is a super-intelligent AI performing experiments and seeing how we would act in its creation."

"Is it possible the creator of this game is literally that—the Creator everyone here keeps talking about?"

"It's a possibility, but the Creator seems to be more of an administrator of the 'System.' It responds, reacts, and adapts to everything we do, and as far as I can tell, it can't be exploited because it adjusts the parameters based on users' actions. It's possible that the Creator is quite literally the creator of this world, but this might be unknowable."

Justin felt like he was having vertigo discussing this. Could it really be true? This world was so real that, in recent days, he had hardly questioned it.

"You said we're being hunted. By whom?"

Valdrik simply smiled. "You haven't guessed?"

"I don't know."

"The Templars of Arion have long served the Creator and the Six

Gods, or at least they claim to. In other lands, there are similar orders. But the powers that control this world do not want us here. Of course, not everyone knows about us, but people in high places do, enough to be wary and have systems in place before we become a threat. And they know, just as we do, that four times a year a new Earther enters their world. We have too many unfair advantages. Imagine a Bard who recreates Bach or Mozart. Imagine a Craftsman who learns to create guns. Imagine a Scholar who uses his knowledge of history or warfare to revolutionize military tactics. Such things could tip the scales in unimaginable ways."

Justin saw his point. "Has that actually happened?"

"Yes. You can see Earth's influences here if you look closely, though the authorities do what they can to scrub it from history. The technology of this world is decidedly high medieval, or even Early Modern, with magical influences, of course. And yet, you also find fashions, architecture, and technology that are orders of magnitude ahead of where Eyrth should be. Did you see anything strange in Highcliff, for example? Something that might not be found in a late medieval or early modern setting?"

Justin thought it over. "There was that streetcar. Those didn't show up until the 19th century unless I miss my guess. I didn't really question it."

"The Highcliff streetcar was created by a man named Gavrik Iron-holm. Of the Artificer class. Why he focused his efforts on this, I can't say. Something to do with his previous occupation, I'm sure. He created the streetcar system for which Highcliff is famed about a hundred years ago. He figured out a way to not only create the cars but also the entire industrial and mechanical processes that allowed them to be built in the first place. Rather than use steam, though, he devised a way to recharge them with aether crystals. Quite ingenious, really, though these days, horses are usually used due to the cost. He had plans to revolutionize all of Aranthia with similar train tracks, only on a much larger scale, and even kick off a large-scale industrial revolution."

"He was killed?"

The Baron nodded somberly. "He was. Not for his invention, but for giving himself away."

"How did that happen?"

"Knowing things he shouldn't have known was a big clue. And of course, he probably told the wrong person the wrong thing, enough to fall under suspicion."

"That's all interesting, but you're suggesting that Alistair was trying to kill me. If he was, why didn't he do it on the spot?"

The Baron gave an understanding smile. "Your Paladin friend probably didn't know what he had, and if he did, he would not have known the significance. Alistair was Level 25 or thereabouts; probably not high enough in the Templar hierarchy to know about Earth. In short, it was me he was after, and you were caught in the crossfire. But had you reached Mont Elea, things would have gone badly for you, assuming High Priest Kaive discovered your origins."

"And what would he have done?"

"Well, he would have nipped Eyrth's newest stranger right in the bud, I can guarantee it. I doubt Alistair knew your secret, but if he did, he would have reported it for sure."

"So, I guess that makes you my rescuer. Only that's difficult to believe, given all the pain and hardship you've caused. I guess that would make Eldrin the bad guy, too."

"I can't speak to the Ranger's motives, but I'm sure he told you something about me being after your Prismatic Core. I won't lie. Getting my hands on that would be a tremendous advantage. But it would draw far too much attention to myself. Rarer than even a Prismatic Core is an ally—an ally from the same world who wants the same thing as I do."

Justin could guess what he meant. "You want to get back home."

"Yes," the Baron said. "I very much do. The humble life I led in Bulgaria might not mean much to you, but I had a job, a wife, and a family."

The Baron, a family man? Justin found that a bit difficult to imagine. Then again, he had had twenty years to spend here, and that was enough to change anyone.

The Baron continued. "My life back on Earth was humbler than this one, but it's real. I've worked hard to become powerful here, to learn as much as I can, all while staying off the radar." He leaned toward Justin conspiratorially. "Off the radar. Be careful when you use such idioms. Some don't exactly translate into Aranthian, and it could be enough to tip off the wrong person."

"Seriously? How do they know so much about people from Earth?"

"You'd be surprised. It's hard to say how long Earthers have been sent here, but it's been at least a few centuries, if not more. The Templars keep meticulous records going back hundreds of years. Who can say what they know and don't? People can get caught for extremely minor things. And of course, once caught, the Templars have no trouble extracting useful information and cataloging it. As for why they go after us, they tie us to Morvath and Death Magic. Of course, Earthers don't always align themselves with the God of Death. But the connection is there. It's a quick path to power, and people from Earth lack the same religious fear and piety that a native-born person is subjected to from birth."

"It seems you chose to go in that direction."

"I did, but it took me a while to arrive at that decision. But that's a story for another day."

"So, all this is to convince me that we're really on the same side?"

Valdrik watched him carefully. "Truth be told, I'm not sure we are. I would like us to be, but that requires trust."

"You placed a Death Mark on me without my consent," Justin said. "That does little to build trust."

"I did it to track you once you left my manor," he said. "Sending someone to follow you was far too crude, and too many things could have gone wrong. Having someone eavesdrop in a tavern is one thing, but requiring someone to tail you for days or weeks? Eldrin would have wised up at some point. Remember, I wanted to be certain of who and what you were. Given the dangers of this world, Earthers have a penchant for dying before they can really take root. The Death Mark is insurance, a guaranteed way I can reach you beyond the grave if it comes to that." He smiled. "Besides, being undead is not a terrible thing. There are many advantages."

"Like what?"

"In 'game' terms, yes, you would be undead, and yes, enthralled to me, the one who placed the mark. But you have a class, Justin. You wouldn't become some mindless zombie or ghoul. You'd be an undead Socialite, and as such, a wide number of paths would be open to you. I don't know if you noticed, but your class isn't exactly known for excelling on the battlefield; however, there are ways around this. Vampirism is the easiest path, and it would increase your survivability greatly. But assuming you can unlock an advanced class and gain access to magic, Necromancy, Dread Summoning, and even becoming a Lich aren't off the table. You'd also be immune to poison and disease and gain an extended lifespan."

"If being undead is so great, then why aren't you undead?"

"A fair question. Being undead is quite noticeable, and right now, I need to lie low. My intention was never to turn you undead. It was insurance in case you died before we could have this conversation."

"So, you would have no problem with removing the Mark?"

"That depends. I still have a few more things to say." The Baron leaned forward, his eyes intense. "First, you need to realize that this is a game. It's not reality. Of course, you can treat it as reality. Many Earthers have chosen to 'go native,' so to speak. But there's no proof that any of these people you've met—Eldrin, Lila, Alistair, and all the rest—are anything more than highly advanced AI agents. They act and behave as any sapient being would. They even respond to you as fully autonomous agents. But are they real?" The Baron gave a sharp smile. "Oh, I struggled with this for a long time. I didn't want to believe it was true, but as soon as you embrace this truth, how free you become! We already know this is a game, created in the distant future, sending actual humans into it four times a year for reasons unknown. You are one such human, of course, as am I. Everyone you've met so far, aside from me, is just part of the game, no matter how real they seem."

Of all the things the Baron had said so far, this was the most shocking. Justin's mind raced, and doubts crept in. Could all these people who had become his friends just be AI? Could their relationships, sacrifices, and help be nothing more than programmed responses? The thought made Justin's stomach turn. He couldn't believe it—or could he?

He felt as if he wanted to throw up.

"I know," the Baron said, sipping a glass of red wine. "It's a lot, isn't it? Of course, you could continue to resist the idea. Such an endeavor, of course, would be pointless."

"How can you really know they're AI? Maybe this is just an alternate universe that happens to have game-like mechanics, just as real as our own. And even if it is a simulation, what if their feelings and thoughts are so genuine that there's no practical difference?"

Valdrik smirked. "Wishful thinking, Justin. Magic? Skills? Classes? These are all the hallmarks of video games, not real life."

Justin clenched his fists. Valdrik had a point, but it was a point he didn't want to accept. "Unless you have some actual proof that everyone here, besides Earthers, is an AI, you have no way of knowing."

Valdrik sighed, his expression unreadable. "Perhaps. As a Lexicant, I use words to manipulate the reality of this game. I've seen the code behind the curtain, the cracks in the illusion. You'll see them too, in time. Whether you accept it or not is up to you. And if we want to survive, and more than that, to escape, we need to figure out how to use the System to our advantage. Yes, agents of the game will get hurt. Even die. But no matter how real they appear, no matter their pain, none of it is real."

Justin felt a chill at these words. "I just can't buy it."

"It's a pity that things happened the way they did. I'm extremely careful, but sometimes, that care can prove to be the greater risk than acting boldly. If I'd been able to reach you before you'd intermixed with the agents, your story would have turned out differently. If you can't learn to disassociate from them, your progress will be hampered. Perhaps even stunted entirely."

"Even if everything you're saying is true, you placed the Mark of

Death on me. You claim to have good reasons for it, but those reasons seem hollow to me. The only way you can even begin to prove yourself is by removing it entirely."

"If you agreed to work for me, then yes. I'd remove the Mark gladly and even let you keep your Prismatic Core. Any other person —or rather, I should say, agent—I would take it without question. But you are no mere character, Justin. You are a fellow Earther. True, you know little yet, but your potential is boundless. I've spent two decades here. While I've learned a lot, I'm bound by the System, the same as you. I need all the help I can get. As do you, if you are to progress to a point where we can start helping each other. Everyone else born into this world simply sees it as life. Only one in a hundred will ever get a class since it is so prohibitively expensive. The agents can be of no help to me, except in securing further power and resources. Progression, Justin, is the name of the game. Progression at all costs, except the extinguishing of sacred Earth life. That's the only way we can reach a high enough level to affect reality and survive our enemies."

Justin could see why the Templars wanted to kill Earthers. If most Earthers believed as Valdrik did, it would make them a huge threat. Even Earthers who disavowed such views might fall under suspicion by default.

"I have more questions. What about Earth objects? How exactly do they attract people like me?"

"Well, the magic is not understood, but the effect has long been observed by those in the know. In fact, the Templars also use the little trick I employed to catch Earthers. That's how I got the idea. They set up honey pots all around Aranthia, and a great many Earthers have been caught in this way." The Baron smiled. "You're lucky that it was I who found you first."

Justin wasn't so sure of that, but he had further questions. He didn't believe the Baron for a second, though much of what he'd said seemed disturbingly accurate.

He still had questions. Questions that could determine whether he and his friends walked out of this alive.

56

THE PRICE OF SURVIVAL

"In the Foundation Languages, a name is more than just a word. It's a key, a weapon, a blessing, and a curse—sometimes all at once."

—Althier Bander,
The Languages of Creation

THIS ENTIRE TIME, Justin had been holding the book, and he put it down on the table. It felt dangerous to even touch. "How did you find so many Earth artifacts, anyway?"

"Carefully. You gain a sense for them eventually, and my magic helps me extract them safely. As for how they come to be here, well, they have been brought by Earthers themselves."

"What made you think I was from Earth?"

"I'm good at reading people, both a product of my class and my charisma. It was why I offered you the job, so I could learn more. But a lie about your origins, as you did, wasn't enough proof. So, I placed the Mark upon you, while my agent reported your conversation, as you already mentioned."

"And that agent is dead, I assume?"

The Baron smiled. "The man I sent is completely loyal. I erased his memories to be on the safe side. But his intel confirmed my suspicions. Alistair was already meddling around, so I had to move quickly. Unfortunately, you ran before I could further explain myself."

"What about Gareth? If he weren't so hostile, it might have won my trust."

"He had orders to deal with Alistair only, as Paladins cannot be trusted. The intention was to bring you to my manor and then reveal myself. While Alistair was doing what he thought was right, you must remember he was bringing you to someone who would ultimately prove to be your demise."

Justin thought back to the conversation he'd overheard in the Silver Stag. Eldrin had mentioned Justin had an interesting story to the Paladin, but it wasn't his place to tell. As far as Justin could figure, Alistair's intentions were pure. Hell, Justin had even told him where he had come from in their very first conversation, a fact that had slipped his mind until now. Even then, the names "Earth" and "Oklahoma" hadn't rung any bells. The man clearly didn't understand the supposed implications of Justin's origins.

"And your goal is to leave Eyrth?" Justin asked. "Alistair thought you're after an Ascendant Class. Something only a Prismatic Core can give you." Justin paused. "It might even be worth murdering me for."

Justin did his best to read the Baron's face, but it remained unchanged, perfectly neutral. "I see you as a potential ally, Justin."

"Is that it? How can I possibly benefit you?"

"We come from the same world. Of all the people who occupy this game, you are the only one I can trust. I'm taking a significant risk in telling you all this. If I merely wanted power, I would wait to ambush you in Thalgar's Tunnel rather than reveal myself so openly. Wouldn't you rather work together?"

Justin supposed that was his strongest point. Why waste his time with explanations if he could have just killed him? Maybe the Baron wanted to work with him, but that didn't mean his intentions were good.

"Tell me about these other Earthers. The Terra Club, I guess. What happened there?"

"It was going well, at least for a while. But we became too bold in our aspirations. The Club, of course, has existed in some form or other over the centuries, though it is difficult to say just how far it goes back. It fades in and out of existence, depending on the needs of the time. At the time of my presidency, the Terra Club had a record ten members, but it all fell apart over some...disagreements. We felt it better to go our separate ways."

"What disagreements?"

"Some members wanted to act more boldly, that we had gained enough power to get more directly involved in the politics of this world. Others, like me, felt we needed to stay in the shadows. And others still concluded that there was no way back to Earth, that we had to find our own happiness here. Sadly, the differences could not be reconciled, and the Club was doing more harm than good. I ended up dissolving it, and that was that."

"Do you know where these other Earthers are?"

"Some, but I will not betray their identities or locations. It is a courtesy we have for each other. Some have sadly passed away. I haven't seen a fellow Earther in about five years, which was when I dissolved the Club."

"I thought you hadn't seen an Earther in eight years."

"You misunderstood. The last time I met a *new* Earther was eight years ago. The last time I *saw* an Earther was five years ago. Of course, your beloved Templars had a hand in it, as they always do. So, for now, as far as I know, all of us are in hiding." Valdrik eyed him closely. "That's why an alliance with you is valuable, even more so than a Prismatic Core. Perhaps you are weak now, but you won't always be. I can help you progress much faster than you would alone."

Justin still thought the Baron was full of shit, but he had to at least pretend he was buying it somewhat. "Maybe you have a point, Valdrik, but you put a Death Mark on me. So why should I listen?"

"If you agree to collaborate with me, I will happily remove the

Mark. What do you say? Do you want to find the way back home? Or keep living in Fantasy Land?"

Justin would believe that when it happened. "Okay, Morpheus."

"Yes, Justin. The analogy is very apt. The Matrix is one of my favorite films. Indeed, I chose Lexicant as my advanced class because, like Neo in that film, it allows me to manipulate reality—or more accurately, the *unreality*—of this world using words and Charisma. If there's a way into this world, then there must be a way out, and maybe we can even control that outcome." He paused, letting his words sink in. "We were brought here through no fault of our own, and if there's a higher purpose, I'm certain it doesn't serve us. We can either get lost in the illusion—some Earthers I've known have made that choice—or we can see it for what it is and use it to our advantage. I choose the latter, and I believe you should too."

Justin thought this over, but he still had trouble wrapping his mind around it. It was all too much, too soon. He wasn't ready to let go, and he knew he couldn't trust Valdrik.

And yet, he couldn't poke any holes in his logic. It was a way of seeing this world, even if he didn't agree with it.

"Tell me. If I say 'no,' do you plan to kill me? That's the only real question, isn't it?"

The Baron gave a chilling smile. "If you say no, Justin, then I will be disappointed, but I hope you will change your mind later. I would ask to have your word as a gentleman to reveal nothing of me or my ambitions and to give your assurance that your friends will say nothing either. There are greater stakes than even you know."

"And let me guess. You're not going to tell me about that."

"You've guessed correctly. But, as a sign of good faith, I will also remove the Mark to show that my intentions are pure, whether or not you choose to work with me."

"Okay. Would you do that now?"

"Think carefully, Justin. I'm offering you power, knowledge, and a way to survive—even a way home. If you say 'no,' you'll find out just how unforgiving this world can be for Earthers—without a powerful ally to save you."

"Is that a threat?"

"It's a warning. You must remember your friends are simply agents of this game. Though it might not feel like it, I'm the only real person you've spoken to ever since you set foot on Eyrth."

Justin forced himself to think about it. The mere thought of everyone being a sophisticated agent was beyond unsettling. Especially where it concerned Lila. It made every relationship he'd formed, every bond he'd built, feel fragile and meaningless.

When he looked Lila in the eyes, it didn't *feel* like he was talking to an AI. She couldn't just be a figment of a complex game, no more real than pixels on a screen. Could she?

Even if this was a game, there were compelling arguments that his own universe was just a simulation, too. Did that make it any less real?

The Baron watched him closely, his gaze sharp and calculating. Justin realized Valdrik might already know what he was going to decide. But that didn't mean he had to play into his hands.

"I can't make this choice lightly," Justin finally said, his voice steady. "I'm not ready to give up on the people I care about. Maybe they're real, maybe they're not, but they matter to me. If there's even a chance they're more than code, I can't walk away from that."

Valdrik's expression darkened slightly, but he didn't interrupt.

"So, here's my decision," Justin continued. "I won't go with you. Not yet. I need time to process all of this, to figure out what's real and what's not. After everything that's happened, I simply can't trust you. Removing this Death Mark would help, but I still need more time. If you're trying to find a way out of here, we'll cross paths again. I'm sure of it. But for now, I'm staying where I am. This isn't a yes or a no. I'm doing it my way, and you need to respect that."

Justin knew he was taking an enormous risk, but it was the only option that worked for him.

At last, the Baron broke his silence. "All of you know too much, Justin. How can you assure me you won't get in the way?"

"Because you have my word. And the others are worthy of trust. I wouldn't be with them if they weren't. If I ask them to keep their lips sealed, they will. I swear it. Remove the Mark. Live and let live."

The Baron smirked as he considered this. "You are bold, I'll give you that. And you have me believing you. Almost."

"Do we have a deal?"

Valdrik's eyes narrowed, but then he smiled—a tight, controlled expression. "Your words, Justin, have convinced me—at least for now. I'm going to agree to your terms on one condition. We will meet again on September 21 next year, a date of great importance for both of us. We will meet at my home in Silverton, and you will give me a more definitive answer. It gives you plenty of time to figure out how to make your way in this world, to become stronger. I would like us to check on each other's progress and share whatever information we've gained. It could be the key to getting back home."

Justin nodded. "I suppose that's fair."

Despite the information the skill had given him, the Baron's manner was so genuine that Justin had doubts. He didn't *believe* those doubts, but it was hard not to second-guess everything.

"But be warned," Valdrik continued. "The more you intertwine yourself in the false lives of these figments of a dream, the more you become like them, and the harder it will be to extricate yourself. The world you're choosing to stay in is filled with illusions. One day, you'll have to confront that reality, and when you do, I hope you're ready for it."

Justin nodded, his resolve firm. "Maybe. But for now, I'll take my chances."

Valdrik stood, his posture still relaxed but his eyes calculating. "Very well. I will honor our agreement."

"And I'll honor my side."

The Baron smiled. "If my instincts are right, you will rise high in this world. All Earthers whose ambitions are unchecked do. But you also must be extremely careful not to rise too high, too fast. And whatever you do, stay far from Mont Elea and the Templars. It's not just the Paladins who serve them. Their agents can be anywhere, and if one has already caught wind of you, it may already be too late.

Know that if you go your own way, there is nothing I can do to protect you."

Justin nodded. "I understand. Thanks for the advice."

"But let's be clear. I require that you and your companions speak no word about me or my ambitions to anyone, in exchange for removing the death mark, on pain of death. Look me in the eye as you swear it."

Justin met his gaze. At least at this moment, he had no intention of betraying the Baron's confidence unless the Baron proved himself unworthy of it. "I swear it, Valdrik."

Valdrik nodded, a glint of satisfaction in his eyes. Justin had the feeling he was using some sort of skill to determine his sincerity, and he had passed with flying colors. Justin did indeed intend to stick to his side of the bargain, but only if the Baron actually removed the Mark.

"Good," Valdrik said. "And now, I will fulfill my side of the bargain in good faith."

At that moment, the Baron muttered a few words in Vranthillis: *"Nethralis Orinthial Rethik."*

A cold sensation washed over Justin, and it felt as if an invisible shroud had been removed, a touch of warmth infusing into his bones. Justin closed his eyes.

Valdrik gave him a final, inscrutable look before turning away, his figure disappearing into the crowd.

Justin stood frozen, his eyes widening as the message flashed before him:

You have gained 1,000 experience points! Your experience stands at 1,319/940. Level-up available!

Justin nearly sputtered in disbelief. One thousand? That was more experience than he had ever gained in a single event.

His mind raced, trying to make sense of it. How could a conversation—if that's what you could call his tense exchange with the Baron

—be worth so much? It wasn't as if he had fought a powerful beast or cleared an entire Vault on his own.

Then it hit him. The experience wasn't just from talking. It was from surviving. From standing toe-to-toe with a much more powerful opponent and walking away with a sliver of control. It was about surviving the machinations of someone who could have easily crushed him.

His heart pounded as he stood there as the reality of his decision —and its consequences—sank in. He still had to test if the Mark of Death had actually been removed, but not until he had gotten some distance.

He hurried through the crowd to find the others.

57

HOW TO WIN FRIENDS AND AGGRAVATE BARONS

"Win the crowd, and your fiercest foes will bow down,
The ruse need only last 'til you get out of town."

—The Master of Masks,
Proverbs of the Swindler

JUSTIN APPROACHED the far corner of the hall, completely lightheaded as he wove through the revelers. Eldrin, Lila, and Kargan had taken refuge there, unnoticed by the rest of the crowd. Justin forced himself to move casually.

He waited until he was a suitable distance away from the Baron before he even set his thoughts on the Amulet of Equilibrium. Unlike Reginald Fairfax, who clearly had some sort of skill that allowed him to see the amulet's value, and Percival Harrington, who had learned about the amulet from his Gentleman's Gauntlet skill, it seemed that the Baron had no inherent ability that allowed him to detect the amulet.

That was a fact the Baron hadn't counted on. It was the ace up Justin's sleeve.

Justin focused his thoughts on the amulet, willing it to bind to his core.

[The Amulet of Equilibrium can only be bound to characters with a Life Affinity. Death Affinity detected.]

Justin smiled, though the reaction felt strange. Of course, he was disappointed. For a moment, he had almost believed the Baron had been genuine. His manner had been so persuasive that it had been enough to sow doubt.

Knowledge, however, was half the battle. There might still be a way to save the situation, as unlikely as it seemed. That required beating the Baron at his own game.

But how?

As Justin reached the others, they stood expectantly, their eyes full of questions. Even now, he could feel Valdrik's gaze on him from across the room, watching, calculating. The thought made his skin crawl.

"What did you talk about?" Lila asked, breaking the silence.

Eldrin watched him intently. "That was a long conversation, lad."

"It's too much to explain right now. What's important is getting out of here alive. He won't make a move in the middle of a party like this. Long story short, he faked friendship and pretended to remove the Death Mark. Only..."

Justin's fingers brushed the gold chain around his neck, a subtle gesture that conveyed everything they needed to know.

"It doesn't work," Eldrin muttered grimly.

Justin nodded. "We can save this still. He doesn't know that I know. It's the one advantage we have."

Eldrin leaned forward. "While you were talking, I scouted around and found a side entrance. It leads into a courtyard garden and a ledge. If we climb down, we can access the Undermarket. My suggestion is to lose ourselves there and figure out the next step."

Justin shook his head. "That won't work. No matter where we go, he'll be right on our tail. We need to get distance from him, but he'll never let us get that far. The Mark will lead him right to me."

Eldrin frowned. "What do you suggest? We can't stay here forever. Not with Gareth due to arrive in just hours. Then the Baron won't be operating solo."

"The mayor is working with him for sure," Lila said. "The whole thing with the Gate was clearly a setup."

"It was," Justin confirmed.

Justin glanced over his shoulder, catching sight of Valdrik mingling with the other guests. The Baron was the center of attention in a circle of laughing nobles, perfectly at ease. Justin turned back to the others, lowering his voice.

"We have to beat him at his own game," Justin said. "We're safer here than anywhere else right now. The Baron won't make a move with all these important nobles around. But he's underestimating us. He thinks we're going to run at the first opportunity. That gives us an opening."

"What are you thinking?" Lila asked.

Justin hesitated, glancing around the room. Now, more than ever, he was convinced this wasn't the time to run. This ballroom was a battlefield. His battlefield.

He wasn't without resources. He had himself, his wits, and the pieces on the board.

And, of course, he had an opponent who fully expected him to resign without a fight. An opponent who was up to no good and didn't want the world to know about it.

It was time to air some dirty laundry.

"Follow my lead," Justin said.

"What are we doing?" Eldrin asked.

"Spilling some tea, as they say in my world."

Straightening his posture, Justin activated his Dandy's Swagger and strolled toward the crowd with a confidence that belied the situation he was in. His heart pounded in his chest, but he forced a smile onto his face, masking his fear with an air of charm.

At first, no one noticed him, and Justin wondered if this was a huge mistake.

But then one noble, a man with salt-and-pepper hair and a velvet coat, touched his arm. "Mr. Talemaker, was it? Baron Marston of Greymoor. Please forgive the crude introduction, but you simply must tell me—are you and the Baron of Silverton old friends? That little display earlier was just what this party needed! These events can be so dreadfully dull without a bit of excitement."

Justin's smile stretched. This was already off to a rollicking start.

"Well, I do my best to entertain," Justin said with a wink. "Are you enjoying the festivities?"

"Quite! But everyone is dying to know how you and the Baron know each other. He's such an enigma! Rarely seen at events like these, and so far from Silverton!"

Justin chuckled, his voice loud enough to draw the attention of nearby guests. "Ah, yes, the Baron and I go way back. My estate is close to Silverton, nestled in the Wildwood Forest. We've hunted together a few times. A fascinating man, though often misunderstood."

More nobles drifted closer, their curiosity piqued. None seemed to call him out on his lie, so he could only assume they were taking it at face value. A necessary risk, given the stakes.

Justin could feel Valdrik's eyes on him from across the room, but the Baron made no move to approach. Perfect.

"Of course," he said in a conspiratorial tone, "I've heard some interesting rumors about him. But you didn't hear them from me."

A ripple of laughter passed through the group as they leaned in, eager for gossip.

"I once had a courier who delivered something to me after a stop at the Baron's manor," Justin said. "You know how hard it is to get in there. The people of Silverton have many theories about what goes on inside. A beautiful home, but with more empty rooms than full. So, after a generous tip, I pressed the courier for details. He was nervous, but you know what they say—money talks."

The nobles chuckled again, waiting eagerly for the story.

"Well," Justin went on, "the courier mentioned that the Baron's manor is filled with strange and rare artifacts, the likes of which you'd never believe. He's quite the collector of treasures, some of which are rather...unsettling. Makes you wonder what he keeps even deeper in those halls, doesn't it?"

"What kinds of treasures?" an older gentleman asked, his curiosity piqued.

"Oh, I couldn't say for certain," Justin replied, lowering his voice. "But the people of Silverton have long whispered about hidden passages beneath the Baron's manor. While some say it's filled with only artifacts, others tell darker tales. They say there's a constant stream of mysterious visitors going into his home, especially at night."

The nobles exchanged intrigued glances, some of them frowning in thought. Justin could almost see the wheels turning in their minds. Valdrik was always an enigma, but now he was something more— something dangerous.

"Of course," Justin added with a wink, "eccentricity isn't a crime. But it makes one wonder, doesn't it?"

The nobles murmured in agreement, casting furtive glances toward Valdrik, who remained across the room, apparently none the wiser. He was talking to the same raven-haired lady from earlier.

Justin made his rounds, weaving through the crowd, engaging in similar conversations, each one laced with subtle hints and insinuations. As the minutes ticked by, Justin started noticing a change in the Baron's demeanor. His laughter, once rich and confident, carried a frantic edge. Valdrik's eyes flicked toward Justin more frequently, as though trying to gauge just how much damage was being done.

Justin played his role perfectly. His words slid into the ears of curious nobles like honeyed poison.

"Oh, the Baron? Yes, he's still a bachelor, though I can't imagine why! Quite handsome, don't you think? And richer than a dragon on its hoard! Not to mention more dangerous than a dragon, too, especially during the hunt! Would you like me to introduce you? No? Oh, your loss, truly!"

The noblewoman blushed, laughing nervously, and Justin winked before moving on, leaving her to glance toward Valdrik with a mix of curiosity and caution.

At another cluster of guests, Justin lowered his voice just enough to add a touch of mystery. "Ah yes, the Baron. Quite the Lexicant, they say. Spends long hours in his manor, learning spells that haven't seen the light of day in centuries. It's impressive, of course—takes dedication. I'm sure he's up to something very important. I have to say, it's nice to see him stretching his social muscles tonight. It's so long since he's been seen in society! I always urge him to marry, you know. As they say, it is a truth universally acknowledged that a single man in possession of a good fortune must be in want of a wife."

The surrounding group hummed in agreement, nodding and exchanging impressed glances as if Justin had just crafted this brilliant observation on his own. One noble even offered a polite chuckle, while another lady murmured, "Well said, well said indeed."

"On that note, I'm collecting the names of a few eligible ladies for him to court. That's what friends are for. So, who's in?"

The guests chuckled, but Justin could see the unease in their eyes. He kept his tone light, but the implications were sinking in. Valdrik, the mysterious recluse, dabbling in ancient magic—what could he be up to?

Justin continued his campaign, all while mixing in other stories of his adventures, so he wasn't too obvious. His voice carried just enough weight to stoke the flames of gossip. "The Baron spends long days away from his manor in Silverton, always off on some grand adventure. They say every time he returns, his wealth doubles! Well, maybe not *quite*, but he's so secretive about his exploits that the rest of us lesser nobles are left to fill in the gaps. Even those of us who know him best...well, we don't really know him at all, do we? Some say he's cold, but I disagree. Once you've gotten past his aloofness, he's a steadfast friend—the best you could ask for!"

Justin could feel the whispers spreading through the room, little threads of doubt and suspicion weaving themselves into the fabric of the party. In a world where reputation was everything, those whispers would spread far beyond this one gathering.

As Justin continued to work the room, Valdrik's unease and annoyance grew more visible. His smile remained fixed, but there was a tightness to it lurking beneath his composed facade.

Eventually, he would be forced to make a move. And that was what Justin wanted.

Justin joined a group of young nobility about his age, including Lord Harrington and Lord Bohemond Ashcroft, the blond-haired, blue-eyed one with a stern demeanor.

"Making waves, I see," Lord Harrington said with a wink. "We've all learned a great deal about your good friend, Baron Valdrik, tonight!"

Justin smiled. "Well, you heard the Baron himself. He and I go way back, so it's only natural that people have questions. Consider this his grand reentrance into society!"

Of course, Justin hadn't known for a fact that the Baron shunned company, but given the state of his home and what he'd told him about staying off the radar, it was an easy guess. And that guess was paying dividends.

"Ah," Harrington said, a sly smile on his lips. "It's all about giving the people what they want, eh? I wonder if Duke Darrow has heard such rumors. I would have thought you and the Baron would be at his estate at Glendwoode rather than here. I'm honored, of course, but it makes a gentleman wonder!" He gave a small sigh. "Though I do not blame you. It would be hard not to be envious of Valdrik. A mere Baron, and yet the Crown afforded him all those special privileges concerning Silverton."

Justin chuckled. "Perhaps I have overplayed my hand. What are you putting in this champagne, anyway?"

Harrington laughed. "Oh, it's all in good fun, Mr. Talemaker."

Justin smiled, but at this point, he wished he had learned a bit more about these things. Of course, the title of "baron" was relatively low on the noble hierarchy, and he never questioned why a baron might have control of an important city like Silverton. More than that, it seemed Harrington had assumed Justin was spreading lies for a different reason, one of jealousy of Valdrik's special status. That worked for him, at least in this situation.

Thankfully, or perhaps unfortunately, Justin wouldn't have to explain further because Baron Valdrik himself was approaching, his figure casting a shadow over the group. The young noblemen fell silent, their previously easygoing demeanor replaced by tension. Valdrik's smile was as charming as ever, but his eyes glinted with something darker.

"Ah, Mr. Talemaker," the Baron said smoothly, his voice carrying the polished tones of a man who had mastered every room he entered. "I see you've been making quite an impression tonight. You always had a way of captivating a crowd."

Justin forced a smile. "Only following your lead, Baron. You've been the life of the party."

Valdrik's eyes flicked to the group of noblemen, who stood awkwardly, sensing the undercurrent of the conversation but unsure of how to proceed. "Yes, it's been quite a lively evening, hasn't it? So many stories being shared—old friends catching up, new connections being made. It's fascinating how quickly rumors can spread, don't you think?"

Justin met Valdrik's gaze. "Well, stories have a way of taking on a life of their own. But then again, there's always a bit of truth in every tale, wouldn't you say?"

Valdrik's smile didn't waver, but there was a dangerous gleam in his eyes. "Ah, yes. A slippery thing, truth is. Often dressed up in the most elaborate of costumes, making it hard to tell what's real and what's just a clever illusion."

Bohemond Ashcroft, oblivious to the tension, chuckled. "Well, if it's entertaining, who cares? It's all in good fun, and parties can always use a little intrigue."

The Baron's gaze remained locked on Justin. "Indeed. But one must always be careful not to let the game go too far. Some tales are best left untold, wouldn't you agree, Mr. Talemaker?"

Justin's heart pounded in his chest, but he didn't let it show. He smiled coolly. "Depends on the tale, Baron. Some stories are too important to keep hidden. How can one expect to make friends if they can't see the real you?" Justin leaned in slightly, as if sharing a secret in confidence, even adding a friendly chuckle. "We all have our little secrets, don't we? But a wise man knows when to let a friend in on a good one. After all, what's friendship without a little trust?"

For a moment, the air between them crackled with tension, an unspoken challenge hanging in the space between their words. The Baron's smile remained fixed, but Justin could see the calculation in his eyes.

He still wasn't making a move, calling Justin's bluff that he wouldn't take things any further. Of course, the point of all these rumors was to send a message. If the Baron didn't let him go, didn't remove the Mark, Justin would spill the metaphorical beans on just what he was up to in Silverton and what Alistair had died for.

"You know," Justin said, "speaking of rumors, I heard quite an interesting one while passing through Highcliff." The surrounding noblemen pretended not to be interested with Valdrik present, but Justin could tell he had them. "It concerns a certain Paladin of Mont Elea, a Templar: Alistair of Drakendale." Justin looked at Valdrik innocently. "Have you heard the name?"

Justin tried to communicate his thoughts with a look: I can stop anytime.

Valdrik smiled. "I haven't heard the name. He must be no one of true significance."

Bohemond's face flushed with indignation. "Not of significance? Paladins are the chosen warriors of Arion, trained in both body and soul to uphold justice. Every Templar of Arion deserves our respect!"

The young noble's outburst brought a ripple of discomfort through the group, and a few exchanged uneasy glances. Valdrik's smile tightened, but he didn't lose his composure.

"Well," the Baron said smoothly, "we all have our heroes, don't we? I'm sure this Alistair is especially important...to some." He looked right at Justin.

"A Paladin is always important, like good Bohemond said here,"

Justin responded. "And when one goes missing, well, can you fault the faithful for noticing, Baron?"

"If that's true, then it's most unfortunate," the Baron said. "That said, Paladins are not known for being in a safe line of work. The realm is grateful for their sacrifice. It lets the rest of us sleep, never fearful of the terrors of the night, of which there are many."

"Yes," Justin said. "They say he passed through Silverton before going missing. Of course, everyone is familiar with the horrible news surrounding Silverton. Murder. Wanton corruption. That's the type of thing a Paladin might want to investigate, no? As the Baron of Silverton, certainly you are close to such matters." Justin smiled. "I mean, I don't want to point the finger, but you mention the terrors of the night. You don't think it could be possible if, among all things, that a Nec—"

Before Justin could finish, he felt a curious pressure in his mind, like fingers trying to pry into his thoughts. The Baron had made his move. But from Valdrik's outward composure, it was as if nothing had happened.

[Mind Control attempt resisted by the Top Hat of Mental Clarity!]

Justin caught the slightest flicker of surprise in Valdrik's eyes. Justin's smile stretched even as he tipped his hat. "Now, as I was saying—"

All this was too much for the Baron. "Mr. Talemaker, a moment of your time, if you will. Some things are not meant for casual conversation."

Without drawing attention, Justin followed him through the crowd, keeping his expression calm. His heart pounded in his chest. With a simple thought, Valdrik could kill him. And indeed, from the Baron's seething expression, Justin could tell that part of him very much wanted to.

They reached a secluded corner, far from prying eyes and ears. Valdrik turned on him, his face a mask of barely repressed fury.

"Leave, Justin," he hissed through clenched teeth. "Now, before I end you!"

Justin held his ground. "What? And have you hunt me down once I'm isolated and alone? No, I won't be doing that. Did you truly think you'd fool me about the Mark? You played me, so I'm playing you right back." He leaned forward, narrowing his eyes. "All this rumor-mongering is just a taste of what I can do. So, unless you're willing to kill me in cold blood right here, with the eyes of the Aranthian nobility right on you, I suggest you do as I ask. It'll take me just ten minutes to drive the nail in the coffin of your reputation. You're a Necromancer, Valdrik. And you're still too early in the game. You've overplayed your hand and you know it. Just imagine: twenty years of work flushed down the toilet. Maybe I die, but I'll take you down with me. Just a few simple words, shouted at the top of my lungs. That's all it takes."

Valdrik's eyes narrowed dangerously, his entire demeanor radiating pure rage.

For a tense moment, Justin thought the Baron might lash out, throw it all away to get his revenge. Valdrik didn't even have to kill him outright. Maybe he could just force his mouth shut with magic.

But even that would be a risk, because it would only give weight to the rumors.

With a forced calm, Valdrik gave a wintry smile. "Very well, Justin. While you have spurned my friendship, I can at least get something else of value. Trust me, you will be sorry you rejected my alliance. Even without the Mark of Death, I will catch you and make you wish you had never been born. North, south, east, or west: wherever you flee, I will find you, and you will wish death had come swiftly." His smile stretched almost maniacally. "The Mark of Death is no matter. Whatever can be removed can be replaced. I only invite you to think about the wonderful things I will do when you are bound to me in undead thralldom. That reward will be almost as grand as that Prismatic Core you stumbled upon by blind, stupid luck." He leaned in closer. "Because that's the only reason you're still alive, Justin: blind, stupid luck. And that can only carry you so far in this world."

Before Justin could respond, the Baron raised his staff and muttered under his breath. Justin felt a strange sensation ripple through him. It was like a shackle breaking loose from his soul. The oppressive presence that had been lurking in the back of his mind vanished.

"It's done," Valdrik said icily. "Now leave. I have a lot of damage to undo."

With a final, tense glance, he melted back into the crowd.

Justin exhaled slowly, the tension lifting ever so slightly from his shoulders. He was far from safe, but for now, he had bought some time.

[You have gained 1,500 experience points. Your experience stands at 2,819/940. Level-up available!]

Justin blinked in surprise. He would almost certainly not have one but two level-ups to process. The reward was well-earned, given the stakes and solution Justin had found. It was enough to give him and his companions a chance.

He set his thoughts upon the amulet. Now came the moment of truth.

[Would you like to bind the Amulet of Equilibrium to your core?]

The mere question brought a flood of relief. Justin couldn't help but smile. He was free to go all in on his Charisma Attribute and be rewarded for it. With a base Charisma of 18, he would get +3 to all other attributes, the equivalent of 15 level-ups. The advantage could not be overstated, especially as he leveled up further.

As he accepted, the amulet's power flowed through him like a warm current, spreading from his chest to every corner of his body.

His Power surged first. He felt strength flood his muscles, his body feeling more solid and capable, as if he could take on the weight of the world and still stand tall.

Then came the boost to his Endurance. The fatigue and tension that had been gnawing at him for hours melted away, replaced by a deep, steady well of energy.

Coordination followed. He could almost feel the air shifting around him, and the knowledge of how to move through it instinctively filled his mind. He flexed his fingers and marveled at the grace and speed with which they responded.

His Intellect blossomed next, his mind buzzing with newfound energy, sharper and more focused, ready to tackle any challenge.

Finally, his Spirit sharpened. He felt more in touch with himself, a sense of calmness that pervaded all. These newfound sensations were minor, but still noticeable.

It had been a long journey, and he had finally made it. The Amulet of Equilibrium was fully his.

But it was far from over. The Baron was still a threat and could easily kill them all as soon as they left. He could no longer track Justin through the Mark of Death, but they were still stuck in Windfall with no easy way out. And with their escape routes limited, and Gareth just hours away, they had to move quickly.

Justin hurried back to the others and opened his interface.

Justin Talemaker
>   Class: Socialite
>   Level: 7
>   Experience to Level 8: 2,819/940 (Level-up available!)

Attributes:
>   Power: 14 (Base 10 + 3 + 1)
>   Coordination: 14 (Base 10 +3 + 1)
>   Endurance: 15 (Base 10 + 3 + 1 +1)
>   Intellect: 14 (Base 10 + 3 + 1)
>   Spirit: 13 (Base 10 + 3)
>   Charisma: 21 (Base 18 +2 + 1)

Attribute-boosting gear and buffs:
>   The Cane of Valoria: +1 Charisma and Intellect

The **Coat of Highcliff's Elegance:** +1 Endurance and Coordination

The Ilvari Ambassador Boots: +1 Endurance

Squire's Armlet: +1 Power

The Amulet of Equilibrium: +3 to all non-dominant attributes

Refined Aura: +1 Charisma

He smiled. Things were starting to look up.

That was, if they could get out of town in one piece.

58

THALGAR'S TUNNEL

"Power isn't taken. It's given—by the weak, to the clever."

—Daelorian proverb

QUICKLY, Justin made his way back to the group of young nobles. As much as he was ready to run, he had other plans to ensure everyone's safety and survival. The others quickly rejoined him.

"Quite the character, isn't he?" Harrington said as Justin approached, trying to diffuse the tension with a light-hearted tone. "You weren't kidding about the intrigue."

Justin forced a laugh, but inside, his mind was racing. "The Baron and I have come to a sort of understanding. You know how it can be between friends. I may have teased him a bit too hard. Unfortunately, my companions and I must beg our leave from your wonderful party." He gave a noble bow. "Thank you for the invitation, Lord Harrington. It's been...enchanting."

"Likewise, Mr. Talemaker. Come back anytime. But before you go, guess what? I received word from Mayor Carlisle that the gate to Thalgar's Tunnel has been opened again."

Justin blinked in surprise. "Wondrous news!"

"Yes," Harrington said. "The mayor left soon after you and the Baron first started talking. Within minutes, I had news that the traders from the north side were complaining that it was a safety issue to leave it closed."

"Gods be praised!" Bohemond said, his eyes lighting up. "So, are you still heading after that Vault in the Everwood?"

Justin smiled, seizing the opportunity. "Yes, that was the plan. Do you have a mind to team up? What is your class and level?"

Bohemond's chest swelled with pride. "I'd be honored! I'm a Level 10 Knight. If you need a stout defender, I'm your man!"

"We already have a tank," Kargan said. "Me."

Justin stepped in to smooth things over. The orc didn't seem to understand the point of involving Bohemond; if an important noble was with their party, Valdrik was far less likely to attack them. "We could always use another party member, Bohemond. After all, the Everwood is no place to venture lightly. Having a Knight of your caliber would be a great asset to our group." He smiled warmly, making sure Bohemond felt appreciated.

Bohemond's pride softened into a grin. "Then I'll gather my things and meet you at the gate. The sooner we leave, the better!"

"You're right," Justin said. "We plan to leave within minutes. Try to hurry. If you're not there, we're likely to go on without you."

"By Arion!" Bohemond exclaimed, his eyes wide. He gave a quick bow to Harrington. "I thank you for this wonderful party, Mr. Harrington." Then, to Justin: "I shall be waiting."

As Bohemond left, Harrington chuckled. "I'd join you myself were it not for this blasted party!"

Justin chuckled, giving Harrington a sympathetic smile. "Ah, the burdens of hosting! Someone must keep the festivities lively while the rest of us go gallivanting through dark tunnels. But don't worry, Lord Harrington—there will be plenty of tales to share when we return. Next time, you can join us."

Harrington laughed, shaking his head. "I'll hold you to that, Talemaker. Safe travels! I will have to call upon you next time I'm in the Wildwood."

"Please do," Justin said with a slight bow.

Justin glanced at his friends, and they all exchanged a knowing look. At least Lila and Eldrin understood that Bohemond's presence would be their insurance. Even a Cant of Amnesia wouldn't be enough to fully cover the Baron's tracks if he got his hands dirty.

But a single high-ranking Knight wasn't enough.

For good measure, Justin faced the crowd, adopting the air of a merry drunk. "Hear ye, hear ye!"

To Justin's surprise, a good half of the nobles turned, and he had their full attention. He capitalized immediately. "Our party here is going to raid a Vault in the Everwood! I propose a friendly wager. Fifty crowns to the first party that clears it! Who's in?"

A ripple of laughter and excitement spread through the room as several nobles voiced their interest. Some were already discussing their plans to join the hunt, while others laughed at the prospect of such an adventure.

Valdrik's eyes narrowed from across the room as he watched the growing enthusiasm. His control was further slipping. He'd have to wait until later to pursue them, hopefully giving enough time to lose him in the depths of Drakendir. With the Mark of Death removed, their options had opened significantly. No longer did they have to head for Mont Elea. Of course, Eldrin still might want to report Valdrik's activities, but Justin wasn't too sure about that anymore. For all the Baron's deceit, Justin was certain a lot of what he'd shared was true.

Justin would have time to figure all that out later.

"We should hurry," Eldrin said. "It would seem things have gotten a lot more...interesting."

They headed for the coatroom, retrieving their packs. They left by the front entrance, and when Justin looked over his shoulder, they were not followed.

From the sun high above them, they had already spent far too much time in the Harrington House. Eldrin set a fast pace across the front yard and through the gate.

Only when the street turned did they run.

When they reached the entrance of Thalgar's Tunnel, it was indeed open, and much to Justin's surprise and relief, Bohemond Ashcroft was already waiting. The tall, broad-shouldered Knight cut an imposing figure in his gleaming plate armor, complete with a visor with the face open. He stood out drastically from the revelers in Windfall's streets. A large, intricately engraved shield rested against his side, featuring what had to be the emblem of his house: a roaring sabretooth cat, its fangs bared and claws poised. His armor was adorned with small, engraved symbols of his faith—a sunburst representing Arion, the God of Power.

"Hope this turns out okay," Lila said quietly. They were still too far away to be heard.

"It'll be fine," Justin said. "So, what does the Knight class do, anyway?"

"It's a Power class, but more specialized in defense," Eldrin said. "They favor one-handed weapons like maces, swords, and hand axes, along with shields."

Indeed, Bohemond seemed to be the quintessential heavy armor and sword-and-shield type. A steadfast tank to hold the line against overwhelming odds could be useful, but Justin was mostly interested in using him as a shield against Valdrik rather than monsters. Hopefully, there was a way to gracefully boot him before they descended into Drakendir.

At last, they came within a few paces of the Knight. He gave a rigid nod. "Well met. I'm pleased you've made all haste."

"You as well," Justin said. He quickly introduced the others, not sure if Bohemond had caught their names at the party, as well as their class and general abilities. When he got to Kargan, he simply said he was a healer, knowing that Blood Wardens often faced preju-dice. Thankfully, Bohemond didn't question it.

Bohemond nodded impatiently. "Arion willing, we'll reach the Vault before any of our competition gets too far ahead. I've already spotted a few other partygoers nosing around down here. A few of them were even on horseback."

Justin nodded, pleased that his words were having the intended effect. "Well, where we're going, horses can't follow. I'm confident we can reach the Vault first. My information is good, as you will soon see."

"I'm glad for it," Bohemond replied, his eyes gleaming with fervor. "As the Faithful of Arion, and those gifted by the Creator with a class, it is our sacred duty to dispatch Vaults. Allow me to lead the prayer before we go into the Tunnel."

Without waiting for approval, Bohemond kneeled, resting his armored hands on the hilt of his sword as if it were a holy relic, closing his eyes. Justin exchanged worried glances with the others as the Knight's voice spoke, deep and resonant.

"O Arion, Lord of Power, guide our steps through the shadows of Thalgar's Tunnel. Protect our journey through the Everwood and beyond. Illuminate our path, that we may walk with righteousness and smite the darkness that festers in forgotten places. Strengthen our arms so that we may strike with righteous fury, and grant us the wisdom to discern the true evil that lurks in the depths. And let us not forget the battle of the soul, which every man and woman on Eyrth fights in the shadows of the heart. By your grace, may we emerge victorious, cleansed in the fire of your holy light. For we are your chosen, those who wield the gifts of the Creator, and because of this grace, we will not falter. In your name, we seek the glory that awaits."

The last word lingered in the air, and Bohemond remained on his knees for a moment longer, his eyes closed, as though awaiting a divine sign. For a man in a hurry, he certainly wasn't rushing through this ritual. Eldrin gave a subtle shrug, while Lila raised an eyebrow, clearly unsure what to make of the Knight's fervor. Kargan looked wide-eyed, caught between awe and confusion. It was the most surprise Justin had seen from the young orc, and by now, he had certainly seen some things.

When Bohemond finally rose, Justin couldn't help but wonder if the prayer had triggered some hidden skill or divine blessing. But there was no sudden burst of light, no aura of power surrounding the Knight. Just silence.

"Thank you, Lord Ashcroft," Justin said, trying to sound respectful. "Shall we proceed?"

Bohemond nodded, his blue eyes shining with fierce conviction. "We shall. In Arion's name, justice prevails!"

"Hear, hear," Justin added, casting a quick glance back toward the city, checking for any signs of pursuit. It was high time they got moving.

[Bohemond has joined the party. You are edified by his Steadfast Resolve, increasing your resistance to the Stagger effect.]

"Let's go," Eldrin said.

And just like that, the Ranger led them into the gaping maw of Thalgar's Tunnel.

The tunnel stretched before them, a seemingly endless corridor carved from the mountain's heart, its walls and ceiling meticulously hewn from dark stone. The craftsmanship was impressive, with smooth, uniform surfaces that could accommodate four carts traveling side by side. The path forged ahead, with only the faintest of inclines or curves, almost imperceptible.

Bohemond cleared his throat, his voice echoing slightly in the stillness. "So, Lord Talemaker. What has brought you so far from the Wildwood to the esteemed City of Windfall?"

Justin's story only needed to hold up long enough to keep Bohemond satisfied. The Knight was only a temporary ally—at least, that was the plan. But by now, Justin understood plans had a way of unraveling when faced with unexpected complications.

"We are seasoned adventurers," Justin finally said, keeping his tone casual. "Eldrin, Lila, and I have cleared three Vaults in the last two weeks, while Kargan joined us for the last one. We came to Windfall looking for something more challenging. Lord Harrington's party was a detour, but we thought it would be a good place to make contacts."

"Three Vaults in two weeks," Bohemond mused. "Impressive. Arion's favor must be upon you."

Justin continued. "That's why we're heading to the Everwood. We're after better gear and treasures. Given our skills, we thought Windfall was the perfect place to prepare."

Bohemond nodded thoughtfully. "Treasure and fortune, yes. Many adventurers are drawn here for the same reason, even more so because of the tunnel reopening. But surely there is more to your quest than gold and glory? It seems strange you'd advertise the Vault to so many, which reduces the chance of you claiming its rewards."

Justin smiled faintly. "There's always more to any quest, Lord Ashcroft. But some things are better discovered along the way, don't you think?"

The Knight looked at him strangely. "Are you saying all that was a ruse to distract others from the true direction of the Vault? If that's the case, why say anything at all?"

"Well, word was going to get out anyway. I've found that it's best to control the narrative in these sorts of situations."

The Knight hummed thoughtfully. "Perhaps, Mr. Talemaker. You're the Socialite, so you are more well-versed in these things than I am."

Thankfully, Bohemond left it at that. They just needed to keep this going a little longer. Bohemond's only purpose was to be a shield between the Baron's careful nature and their lives. At some point, Justin had to admit that the Baron might throw caution to the wind.

The monotonous journey through the tunnel continued. Every mile, they passed small alcoves where travelers could rest. Occasionally, they encountered traders and their carts heading toward Windfall or travelers making their way through the tunnel, usually in groups of four or more, most of whom were armed. Several groups on horseback passed them, one even calling out a challenge.

"You'll never make it in time on foot!" a rider jeered as they galloped by, laughter echoing in their wake.

Eldrin shook his head as Bohemond's face reddened in indignation.

"It won't matter in the end," Lila said brightly. "They still don't know where the Vault is."

Justin allowed himself a small smile. The tunnel had far more traffic than he had expected. It would be impossible for the Baron to ambush them here. At the same time, if nobles from the party were already passing them, the Baron could have easily caught up by now. It was an uncomfortable thought.

Justin absently touched the Amulet of Equilibrium, its steady power fortifying his body. He couldn't believe that it was finally his, that it was working as intended. And in the end, it hadn't been the High Priest of Arion who had removed it, but the Baron himself.

Hours passed in near silence, the monotony of the tunnel making it hard to tell how long they had been walking or how far they had to go. Finally, Bohemond yawned, breaking the quiet.

"I wouldn't be opposed to taking a rest."

"No rest," Eldrin replied curtly.

Bohemond frowned. "Well, we must rest at some point. It's another three days before we reach the end of the passage."

"We'll rest at the Drakendir Gate," Eldrin said firmly.

Bohemond's expression darkened. "The Drakendir Gate is dangerous. Creatures of darkness lurk in those depths. Goblins, trolls, and far worse. I'd rather rest at a proper inn."

"There are inns here?" Justin asked, surprised.

"Aye," Bohemond replied. "Five of them, spaced every twenty miles. The dwarves built them for travelers, though they've since been repurposed by humans. They were reopened as soon as the tunnel was unsealed."

As if on cue, the first inn appeared in the distance, built into the surrounding stone. Its name, Stonehearth Haven, was engraved in the stone archway above the entrance. The structure was impressive, blending seamlessly with the tunnel walls, its sturdy stonework and reinforced doors giving it the appearance of a fortified gate rather than a simple rest stop.

The sight of the inn was far from tempting, knowing who was behind them. Eldrin pressed on, his pace unwavering. They passed the inn without stopping, much to Bohemond's dismay.

At last, after what felt like an eternity, they reached a deviation in the tunnel—a side passage that branched off from the main path.

As they turned in, Bohemond waited a moment. "Hold on. Is this where the Vault is? I didn't sign up for this."

"The Everwood was a diversion," Eldrin said calmly. "The true Vault is down there."

Bohemond's expression darkened with anger. He turned to Justin, his voice trembling with fury. "You lied to me. Where is your honor, Mr. Talemaker?"

Justin met Bohemond's gaze, trying to keep his tone measured. "I must admit, honor is not always my strong suit."

Bohemond's jaw clenched. "Ah, so you intended to waste my time. A brilliant play, indeed!"

While Bohemond's presence in Drakendir wouldn't save them from the Baron, Justin realized they couldn't afford for him to turn back. If he left, he'd surely cross paths with the Baron and reveal they had gone down to Drakendir. Oversights tended to happen when plans were made hastily.

Then again, if Justin could convince Bohemond to hang on, a Level 10 Knight could be invaluable in the dangers that awaited them below. Of course, it wasn't fair to Bohemond not to know the extent of the danger he was in, but as he saw it, there was no other choice.

It was time to put those Charisma points to use.

"Listen," Justin said, "I did lie to you, but if I had told you we were going to Drakendir, well, it might have turned you back. The truth is, we need someone of your caliber to round out our party. The true prize is in these tunnels, and if we wait too long, other adventurers will clear them all out. Trust me, we are highly capable, even clearing a Level 15 Vault for the Church of Highcliff."

Bohemond's eyebrows raised in surprise. "Indeed? Well, perhaps I misjudged you." Bohemond stood there for a long moment, wrestling with his thoughts. Finally, he spoke, his voice firm but laced with disappointment. "The Church teaches that deception is a sin, but it also teaches forgiveness. I'll go with you, but know this—I do so not for you, but for Arion."

Thankfully, despite his piety, Bohemond was still motivated by greed. Justin felt bad for lying, but sometimes, certain choices had to be made. "Thank you, Bohemond. We'll need your strength in the trials ahead. I promise it will be worth it."

They followed this passage for about five minutes before a grand gate blocked the entrance, wrought-iron bars intricately carved with sturdy dwarven runes. The gate led down a set of stone stairs into darkness, the faint echo of dripping water hinting at the unseen depths below.

A lone guard with the griffin of Highcliff on his surcoat sat on a wooden chair by the gate, half-asleep. He rose as the party approached, his eyes narrowing in suspicion.

Eldrin stepped forward with confidence. "We seek passage into Drakendir," he said, producing fifteen silvers.

"It's five silvers a head," the guard grumbled.

Eldrin handed over the additional ten silvers, and the guard pocketed the coins without a word. Apparently, this guard had no qualms about his corruption. The vaunted honor of the Windfall Watch didn't apparently exist in the depths of this tunnel.

The guard stepped into a small alcove, where a lever was hidden behind reinforced metal plating. With a creak and a groan, the gate lifted about four feet, just high enough for someone to pass through while kneeling.

"You've got quite the business here," Justin said.

"Get a move on," the guard said from the window of the gatehouse. "You have half a minute before I close it."

Bohemond, surprisingly, was the first to duck beneath the gate and enter the passage.

The rest followed, and as soon as Justin brought up the rear, the gate shut behind them softly, probably so it didn't echo through the tunnel and alert others to the guard's operation.

Justin followed, casting one last glance over his shoulder.

With luck, they'd lose the Baron for good in the darkness of Drakendir.

EPILOGUE

"The Cultists of Morvath would have you believe their deity of choice isn't merely the God of Death, but the God of Endings. Without death, they say, there can be no endings, and without endings, nothing new can begin. They argue the curse of death is a mercy, not a cruelty—for without it, the world would drown in eternal stagnation. Throw in the promise of eternal life for his most faithful (a convenient arrangement involving increasingly dubious deals, a case of bad skin, worse hygiene, and, yes, no blood flow, even to the important bits), and you almost have to admire the logic. Almost. Of course, the hordes of undead shambling about cast another unpleasant pall over an otherwise tidy philosophy."

—Orvel the Apostate,
   A Racket of Religions: Why the Gods Don't Need Your Belief (But Take It Anyway)

Dragomir Valdrik sat astride his majestic black destrier, which snorted restlessly beneath him. The Baron's grip tightened on the reins as they descended further into the tunnel's depths, frustration simmering beneath his carefully maintained facade.

Behind him, Gareth and his retinue kept a cautious distance, sensing their master's foul mood. The undead members of the party, their faces concealed by dark hoods, moved with chilling silence.

A few paces behind rode Rothian Nightflame, his smooth, bald head gleaming in the torchlight. The Pyromancer's plump frame was draped in crimson robes, and his pudgy fingers gripped a black staff topped with an ever-burning flame.

His eyes, calculating despite his obsequious manner, darted constantly between the Baron and the path ahead.

"My lord," Rothian called out, perhaps a bit too eagerly, "shall I illuminate our path further? The darkness grows...oppressive." As if to emphasize his point, the flame atop his staff flared momentarily brighter.

Valdrik let out a sharp breath. "Silence, Rothian. Your light will only announce our presence from a mile away."

"Of course, my lord. Most wise," Rothian replied, immediately dimming his staff's flame and bowing his head. "I merely thought—"

"That's your problem, isn't it? You think too much about how to impress me and too little about what actually serves my needs."

Despite the rebuke, Valdrik made a mental note of the Pyromancer's usefulness. For all his irritating mannerisms, Rothian's flames had proven effective against enemies in the past. And unlike most of the others, he was at least not undead, which allowed him to move through society more easily.

He could hardly say that about the others following behind. Normally, Valdrik wouldn't risk being so close to his foul minions—though they served him well, their very presence was a constant reminder of the precarious balance he maintained.

Even here, in the relative safety of Thalgar's Tunnel, a Level 36 Lexicant could never be too careful. The odds of encountering a Paladin or Priest who could detect Death Magic were slim, but Valdrik's paranoia had served him well in the past, and he wasn't about to let his guard down now. His options were thinning.

He kept a steady pace—not too fast, not too slow. The last thing he wanted was to trip the damnable Ranger's class boon. If Eldrin sensed him coming, all his careful planning might be for nothing.

As they walked, all he could think was how it had come to this.

He, Dragomir Valdrik, a high-level Lexicant with two decades of experience manipulating the powerful and subduing the weak, had been bested by a low-level Socialite. The upstart had no business challenging him, yet somehow, he had outmaneuvered Valdrik at his own game, knowing full well he wouldn't throw everything away with everyone watching.

And worse, Justin had walked away alive and unscathed, mocking him with every step while damaging his reputation almost beyond repair. The rumors he had sown would escape Windfall; the Baron was sure of it.

Oh, it had been hard to let him go. Incredibly difficult. But every time he was tempted to snuff out a life, Valdrik had only to think about his journey, his past mistakes, to know that patience was the key.

It had been a mistake to reveal himself so soon, but the risk had been calculated. What he hadn't counted on was Justin becoming so intermeshed with the agents of this world. In hindsight, he should have expected it.

Valdrik had long since divorced his own feelings from these agents. They were nothing more than pieces in a game. But he had made the novice mistake of assuming others would see them the same way. While Justin had been lucky enough to experience kindness early on in his journey, Valdrik had the opposite experience.

That might have been the simple difference between the two of them, despite their similar Earth origins.

The memory of Justin's words still burned in his mind. The audacity of the young man to make demands of him, to call his bluff in front of the crowd of nobles. To even *suggest* he was some recluse, tapping into dark powers for personal gain! He'd been perilously close to losing everything. Valdrik had thought himself untouchable, the master of every situation.

Yet Justin had shown no fear. That was what rankled most—the fact that a young upstart with so little power had stood up to him with such quiet determination.

Valdrik knew not to underestimate that. After all, he had once been that young upstart.

And that blasted immunity to mind control! He wasn't certain what piece of gear afforded it, but it had to be the hat; typically, that's where those enchantments were placed. The gall to walk away from an offer of power, of protection, of knowledge—it grated on Valdrik's pride.

Recruiting Bohemond had been a clever move. The foolish noble was no real threat, but his father's influence could complicate things if he were killed openly. Keeping Bohemond alive, for now, was the best course of action.

The Baron allowed himself a small, tight smile. He had not risen to power by being easily thwarted. Justin had won this round, yes, but the game was far from over.

He could afford to keep chasing him a while longer. He had a system in place to keep things running smoothly in Silverton, at least for a few weeks.

Patience, he reminded himself. This setback was merely temporary. There would be another opportunity, and when it came, Justin would not be so lucky. The Mark of Death could be replaced.

That was another thing. How had Justin figured that part out? Had he merely bluffed?

No, Valdrik decided. He'd known the truth. But how? Some rare skill, perhaps, that could detect a lie. That was the most probable answer.

The answer would have to wait. For now, there were more immediate concerns.

The tunnel stretched on as they came to a stop at an inn built directly into the rock. Gareth quickly dismounted and went inside to check for any sign of their quarry. When he emerged, he shook his head, and they were on the move again.

Rothian edged his mount closer to the Baron, his voice lowered to a conspiratorial whisper. "My lord, if I may be so bold...my fire can do more than illuminate. I have been perfecting a tracking spell that traces the heat signatures left by footsteps. Perhaps—"

"If I wanted your counsel, Rothian, I would ask for it," Valdrik cut him off, his voice cold with disdain. "You forget yourself. You are of the Sorcerer class, one who has bargained for power rather than earned it through careful study. Your 'perfected' spells are mere parlor tricks compared to true mastery."

The Pyromancer immediately backed his mount away, head bowed in apology, though Valdrik noted the slight tremor in the man's pudgy hands—eagerness, not fear. Despite the rebuke, Rothian's ambition remained undimmed.

The next place Justin and his companions could have gone was Drakendir. Valdrik knew the risks of pursuing them down there; it was the main reason he'd waited for Gareth and his retinue. The ancient dwarven city was beyond perilous, filled with forgotten horrors and creatures that had survived centuries in the dark. It would be a desperate maneuver, but Valdrik wouldn't put it past the Ranger to take such a risk in order to lose him.

As the passage to Drakendir materialized in the distance, breaking off from the main tunnel, Valdrik's eyes narrowed. He kicked his destrier into a trot, and within a couple of minutes, the massive iron gate loomed. The Baron had never been here personally, but he had read enough about it to never want to delve into its depths.

A Highcliff Watchman stood outside the gate, his eyes weary as the Baron approached. Seeing the Baron's countenance and the retinue at his back caused him to straighten up quickly.

"Did anyone go through the gate recently?" Valdrik asked, his voice cold and commanding.

The man licked his lips nervously. "Might be I remember that."

"Might be? Did they or did they not? Speak, worm!"

Valdrik's words shattered whatever price the guard had been about to ask. "Yes, m'lord. Five people—three men, an orc, and a young woman—passed through a few hours ago."

Valdrik turned to Gareth, who had approached his side. "Can Wolfram track them?"

From the shadows behind Gareth, a figure emerged—a tall, gaunt man with pale skin, greasy hair, and gray eyes. Just as Justin had a Ranger, so did Valdrik. Once a feared hunter in life, Wolfram Gravesong was now a silent stalker of the night. A large black Blood Bat perched on his shoulder, its red eyes shining with intelligence. Valdrik tried to ignore the subtle, sickly-sweet scent emanating from the man. Even for an undead, he was particularly rank.

Wolfram inclined his head slightly, his voice carrying a characteristic undead rattle. "They will not escape us. Even if the Ranger leaves not a trace, Nighthollow need not see a speck of light to find his way in the darkness."

The bat gave a hideous screech, as if in confirmation.

"The darkness does not concern me," Rothian interjected as he moved forward to stand beside Wolfram. The contrast between the portly, clean-shaven Pyromancer and the gaunt, deathly Ranger could not have been greater. "My flames can reveal what hides in shadow and burn through any resistance we encounter."

He raised his staff, and the flame atop it shaped itself into a miniature dragon that coiled around the black wood, its ember eyes seeming to search the darkness beyond the gate. He gave a sick smile. "Fire finds everything, eventually."

Valdrik, without a word, raised his hand and snuffed out the dragon with a simple gesture. Rothian gasped, his confidence visibly deflating.

"Fire may find everything," Valdrik said, "but dies without fuel. Remember your place, Pyromancer. You are the torch I wield, not the hand that guides it."

As Rothian fell into silence, Valdrik's gaze turning toward the steps leading downward into darkness. "Let us proceed. I have no intention of letting them slip through my fingers again." He turned to the guard. "Open the gate."

The guard moved quickly to comply, the grinding of gears and chains echoing as the ancient iron gate slowly creaked open.

"The horses, my lord?" Gareth asked, glancing back at the steeds.

Valdrik considered for a moment. At first, he hadn't been sure if the Ranger intended to lead them to the Everwood or Drakendir. He'd brought the horses just in case it was the former.

The Baron answered, "Have a couple of men take them back to Silverton. Stable them there and wait for further orders. There is no need to waste perfectly good mounts."

Gareth gestured to two of the human soldiers, both among the living, who quickly stepped forward to take the reins of the horses. "Make haste."

The soldiers nodded and led the horses away, relief clear in their eyes. Unlike their comrades, they were getting off easy. They gathered the reins, expertly looping them through a thick lead rope. With practiced skill, one of them clicked his tongue, guiding the horses forward as they moved in a line, one after another, like obedient shadows trailing behind him.

Once this was done, Valdrik's eyes peered into the yawning darkness of the passage ahead. "Head in first," he ordered. "There's one last thing I need to take care of."

Without question, Gareth and the rest of the retinue moved forward, disappearing into the gloom of the tunnel. Wolfram whispered something to his bat companion. Nighthollow launched itself from the Ranger's shoulder, screeching and flapping into the darkness below.

Rothian lingered a moment longer than the others, the flame of his staff momentarily brightening as if in anticipation. "My lord—"

At a warning look, the words died on his lips. He scurried into the darkness after the others.

The Baron turned back to the guard, who stood frozen with fear in his wide eyes.

"Don't be afraid," Valdrik said smoothly, his voice laced with an unsettling calm as he raised his hand: *"Thalvesh Vorritha."*

The Cant of Amnesia settled over the guard like a veil, his eyes glazing over as his memories of the past hour unraveled and dissolved into nothingness. The fear drained from his face, replaced by a blank, passive expression. He blinked, as if waking from a dream, completely unaware of what had transpired.

Valdrik watched for a moment, satisfied, then turned and descended into the depths after his men. The darkness welcomed him, and a stiff smile played on his lips. He was certain of one thing: he was far more equipped to navigate Drakendir's dangers than his quarry.

With the resources at his disposal, it was absolutely inevitable that they would catch up. In the deep places of Eyrth, things were utterly silent—until they weren't. The Drakendir Cavern was the largest in Serenthel, and sounds echoed for miles.

If one of them so much as kicked a rock, the blood bat would pick it up. And if they faced any sort of interruption, it would just speed up their demise all the more.

Ahead, Rothian's flame cast just enough light without revealing their position too far ahead. For all his irritating eagerness, the man's mastery of fire would prove useful in the dangers to come.

Valdrik watched the bobbing flame with calculated appraisal. Rothian was a tool, like any other—valuable when wielded correctly, dangerous if given too much freedom. The Baron had seen many ambitious underlings rise and fall during his time on Eyrth. A tight leash of doubt and occasional praise kept them hungry, desperate to prove themselves, yet never confident enough to challenge their master. It was a delicate balance that Valdrik had perfected over time.

And if all went well, within days—perhaps even sooner—the Prismatic Core was as good as his. It was a fitting consolation prize since Justin was so set on being enemies.

And this time, nothing—not even the shadows of Drakendir—would stop him from claiming what was his.

THE END OF BOOK ONE

ALL IN CHARISMA CONTINUES IN BOOK 2:

THE FROZEN NORTH...

ABOUT THE AUTHOR

Kyle West is the author of a growing number of sci-fi and fantasy series, including *All in Charisma*, *The Starsea Cycle*, *The Wasteland Chronicles*, and *The Xenoworld Saga*. His goal is to write as many entertaining books as possible, with interesting worlds and characters that hopefully give his readers a break from the mundane.

Kyle's stories aren't just about surprising twists—they're thought starters, meant to spark curiosity and spread a bit of positivity despite bleak happenings. He lives with his wonderful wife, two sons, and outrageously spoiled cats.

To dive into Kyle's imaginative realms, visit kylewestbooks.com.

THE DRAGON AND THE SPARROW

www.ingramcontent.com/pod-product-compliance
Lightning Source LLC
Chambersburg PA
CBHW031433200726
48289CB00001BA/18